WEIRD & Wonderful
Holiday Romance Anthology

Copyright © 2019 RoseLark Publishing
All rights reserved.

ISBN-13: 978-0-9981684-2-5

All rights reserved. No part of this publication may be reproduced, distributed, or transmitted in any form or by any means, including photocopying, recording, or other electronic or mechanical methods, without the prior written permission of the publisher, except in the case of brief quotations embodied in critical reviews and certain other noncommercial uses permitted by copyright law.
This is a work of fiction. Names, characters, businesses, places, events and incidents are either the products of the author's imagination or used in a fictitious manner. Any resemblance to actual persons, living or dead, or actual events is purely coincidental.

Table of Contents

A Note from the Publisher	4
Heat Rating Guide	5
Taking the Plunge by Shoshana David	6
Phoebe and the Pea by Catherine Bilson	33
The Boy Next Door by Mei Edwards	75
A Holiday (or Two) to Remember by Christina Rose Andrews	107
The Editor by Siobhan Kearney	151
Easy as Pi by Leslie Bond	192
Lip-Locked Besties by Livvy Ward	223
Melting Hearts by Annika Steele	257
Naked Attraction by Liv Honeywell	291
Wrong Number by Krissy V	317
A Guide to Playing Rich by Ava Bar	350
Finding Pride by Diana Ferris	381
Dane's Redemption by Susannah Kade	413
Dear Dolly by M.T. Kearney	459
The Seadog's Wife by Katherine Moore	493
Feral Heart by Regina Griffiths	528
Crewel Intentions by Joy Demorra	563
Unlawfully Ugly by Caitlyn Lynch	603

Welcome to the *Weird & Wonderful Holiday Romance Anthology!*

Thank you for taking the time to read this. We've got some important information for you. Inside you'll find stories of all types and flavors, including everything ranging from squeaky clean to sensual and steamy.

This anthology is unique in that every story will list not only the heat rating, summary, and pairing type, but also what major triggers you might encounter. We want this anthology to be accessible for as many readers as possible. We have done our best to list the major triggers, but we know that there is no all-inclusive list. If you have a trigger and would like to know if any stories have it, please reach out to us at roselarkpublishing@gmail.com.

Enjoy!

*

RoseLark Publishing is a small publisher based in Grand Rapids, Michigan, which focuses on supporting authors transitioning from transformative to original works. They provide top tier editing services at an affordable price and offer basic author support to new and up-and-coming authors on a budget.

Founded in 2016, RoseLark Publishing is the brainchild of Rose Feuer and Andrea Konecki. Since that time, they've edited several successful anthologies and novels/novellas, as well as mentored several budding romance novelists, including helming their own Anthology— Weird & Wonderful Holiday Anthology.

However, romance is not the only genre in which they have interest. Both founders are long time readers in the fantasy, science fiction, young adult, speculative fiction, and other diverse genres. RoseLark Publishing has within its ranks cover artists, formatters, editors, and mentors. Their authors have presented at internationally recognized events and mentored several USAT and Amazon bestselling authors.

Visit their website at www.roselarkpublishing.com.

RoseLark Publishing's Heat Rating Guide

Every publisher has their own heat guide; it can be a little confusing to keep them all straight, which is why we are including our guide in this anthology for easy reference.

In order to keep things sex-positive and non-judgmental (in either direction) we've based our guide on the Scoville scale for judging peppers.

0 - No Heat - This is your meal sans peppers. Stories with this rating will feature no sex, no kissing, no violence, no cursing, and no innuendo.
1 - Mild Heat - This is your bell pepper. Stories with this rating will feature no sex, some kissing but without description, mild violence or mentions of violence, mild cursing, and vague hints of innuendo.
2 - Medium Heat - This is your banana pepper. Stories with this rating will feature no sex, kissing with description, some mild foreplay, some violence, non-sexual depictions of nudity, some cursing, and light innuendo.
3 - Medium High Heat - This is your jalapeno pepper. Stories with this rating will feature fade-to-black or literary sex, explicit kissing, heavy petting levels of foreplay, graphic descriptions of violence, mild sexual nudity, heavy cursing, and heavy innuendo.
4 - High Heat - This is your cayenne pepper. Stories with this rating will feature explicit sex including mild kinks (BDSM, roleplay, etc.), graphic descriptions of violence, and heavy cursing.
5 - Extreme Heat - This is your scotch bonnet pepper. Stories with this rating will feature explicit sex including heavy kinks, graphic descriptions of violence, and heavy cursing. (There are no stories in this anthology that have this rating.)

Taking the Plunge
♥
Shoshana David

Story Information

Holiday: Polar Bear Plunge Day
Holiday Date: January 1
Heat Rating: 4
Relationship Type: M/F
Major Trigger Warnings: None

January First is Neve's favorite holiday. Not because of the new year but because it's City Island's annual Polar Bear Plunge. She expected the usual day: an icy swim in Long Island Sound, a beach party, and a long hot shower. She definitely didn't expect her neighbor's visiting friend to be as hot as he is. But is that all there is?

Will Neve be able to act on her attraction?

Or will she be stuck out in the cold?

Taking the Plunge

The First of January was rocking. It was rolling. While the sanitation department labored cleaning up the mess left in Times Square, the cool cats knew that the place to be was City Island for the annual Polar Bear Plunge. And Neve Caldwell definitely considered herself a cool cat.

By the time she made it down to the beach, the place was already bustling. Adults chatted. Kids played. Teens ignored everyone else to stare at their phones. Just a normal morning at the beach.

In January.

On New Year's Day.

When the temperature was quite literally freezing.

It was perfect!

Making her way through the crowd carrying her beach chair and her bag, Neve looked for a good spot to set up. She'd participated in the Polar Bear Plunge every year since she'd started middle school; she knew exactly where she wanted to be.

Spotting one of her long-time neighbors, Justin, she headed in his direction. He made a good landmark, standing half a head taller than everyone else around him. More importantly his wife, Carmela, always brought warm drinks and blankets for those who took part in the plunge. Neve wasn't the only one with the same idea. It was definitely the most active spot on the beach. But she was able to find an opening to set up her beach chair a few feet away from Carmela's supplies.

Gazing out at the water, Neve drew in a purifying breath of ocean air. The surf was high, crashing into the sand, but not so high as to be dangerous. The white spray crashed, causing a teenager who was a little too close to squeal and sprint away from the water.

It was going to be cold. It always was. But that was half the fun.

She took off her jacket and folded it neatly, placing it in her bag. She wasn't quite ready to strip yet, but she wanted to get used to the cold air.

About three feet away, a man sitting in a beach chair with his knees pulled up to his chest turned to her. "Aren't you cold?"

"That's the point." Neve eyed him up and down; he was wearing a parka, sweatpants, and boots, along with a hat, scarf, and gloves. He was so bundled up that the only part of him she could see was his face, and even that was half-covered by his scarf and hat. In the beach chair, he appeared remarkably out of place. "Not joining in, I take it?"

He shook his head emphatically. "Hell no. I don't do cold."

Then why is he even here? Must be a tourist. She shrugged. "Your loss."

"And I'm happy losing it!" He grinned at her, his brown eyes gleaming in a way that made her think he was a bit of a trickster.

Biting her lip to stop herself from smiling in response, Neve nodded. "I hope you have fun watching."

He shrugged. "It looks like fun. Besides, Carmela promised there would be hot chocolate. And who can say no to hot chocolate?"

Neve couldn't. She wasn't sure what else to say, so instead she looked around at the crowd. Most of the faces were familiar, but there were a few new ones. She waved at a few of her neighbors and pulled her warm cable-knit sweater over her head, making sure her wispy pale blonde hair wouldn't come out of its braid when she jumped into the water. She wasn't the only one starting to strip. A glance at her phone told her the runners would be back soon; she wasn't a fan of doing a 5k first thing in the morning on New Year's—not after staying up late to watch the ball drop—but there was a group that did it every year. And once they got to the beach, it would be time for the plunge.

With only a bathing suit covering her top half, Neve was cold. Not surprising, given the weather. Goosebumps spread across her arms and—once she took her shoes, socks, and pants off—down her legs. She shivered and rubbed her arms, trying to get just a little bit warmer.

Amusingly, the bundled-up man inched his scarf up around his mouth and nose. *He really must not be used to cold*, she thought, hiding a grin.

There was a screech of laughter, and Neve barely had time to brace herself before a child barreled into her. Planting her feet in the sand, Neve managed to stop both herself and the kid—Justin and Carmela's eldest, Emilia—from falling over.

"Neve! Neve! Neve!" Emilia grinned up at her. "Mom said I get to do the plunge this year!"

"That's great, Emilia!" Neve enthused as she helped Emilia get back upright. "I like your bathing suit."

The little girl twirled, showing off the red ruffled suit. "Thanks!" She regarded Neve's sleek purple one-piece. "I like yours too!"

Justin shook his head as he came up behind his daughter. "Emilia, what did I say about running into people?"

Emilia blushed. "Not to?"

"Yeah. That." He sighed and gave Neve a rueful smile. "Sorry, Neve."

Neve shrugged. "No big deal. I hear Emilia's participating this year?"

Justin grinned. "Yeah. Carmela finally okayed it." He swung his daughter onto his shoulders where she clutched his hair and giggled. "We're going in together." He glanced over at the bundled-up man Neve had been talking to. "Still determined to sit it out, Jimenez?"

The man shook his head. "Dude, you may be used to freezing your ba—" he glanced at Emilia "—butt off, but I'm not. Florida, man. Flo-ri-da." He emphasized every syllable, drawing the word out.

Neve stifled a giggle at his tone.

Justin laughed. "What can I say? I'm a clam digger." He seemed to spot something. "What is Gabriela..." He sighed. "Kids. See you in the plunge, Neve." He held onto Emilia's legs and rushed to the ocean—where his four-year-old daughter was examining seashells just a little too close to the water.

Neve watched to make sure Justin got Gabriela away from the water. Once he did, she returned to getting ready for the plunge and folded her pants and sweater. She placed her shoes with the socks inside neatly in the bottom of her bag.

"Clam digger?" Jimenez—Neve wondered what his first name was—tugged at his scarf, loosening it just a touch. What she could see of his face looked adorably confused.

Not surprising he doesn't know the slang if he's not from around here. "City Island native. Someone who was born on the island. Strict definition is actually born on the island, as in at home, but no one cares about that anymore." She shoved her clothes into her bag and pulled out her towels. Carmela always had extra towels and blankets, but it never hurt to bring her own. Especially after that fiasco when they'd run out two years ago. She shivered at the thought. Or maybe at the cold. Or both. Definitely both. "Nowadays, we count people born in hospitals off the island who live here as soon as they're out of the hospital too."

He chuckled, seeming surprised at the sound. Looking her up and down, his eyes finally coming to a stop on her face after a short detour at her breasts, he said, "So that's... you too?"

She grinned as she tucked her phone in her bag. "Born and raised."

His brow furrowed. "What am I, then?"

Neve bit down a laugh. "A tourist."

He shook his head ruefully. "Should've guessed." He leaned forward and held out a hand, looking almost comically awkward in the chair that was clearly too small for him. "I'm Alex, by the way. Alex Jimenez."

"Neve Caldwell," she replied, shaking his hand.

"Good to meet you." Alex looked down the beach at where Justin and his daughters had rejoined his wife. "So if you and Justin are clam diggers and I'm a tourist, what about Carmela? She wasn't born here, but she lives here. That's... something, right?"

"Right. She's a mussel sucker."

"...Huh." His brow furrowed.

Shrugging, Neve zipped her bag shut and dropped it on the chair on top of the towels. She didn't really have anything to say. She was a clam digger and always would be. City Island was her home. Even though her parents had moved to Florida and her brothers now lived in Manhattan and New Orleans, Neve didn't want to join them. She liked it here. She was lucky her parents were willing to help her make it work.

Alex glanced back at Justin and Emilia, who were now helping Carmela lay out blankets and towels. More than their family would need, and if Neve was counting correctly, even more than the previous year. "She's only seven."

"Yeah." Honestly, Neve was a little surprised Carmela had okayed it, considering she wasn't a City Island native and didn't do the plunge herself. But then again, Justin had probably worn her down—with Emilia's help, no doubt. "Her dad'll watch out for her."

"I'm sure." Alex pulled off his gloves. "If a seven-year-old can do it, I can too."

"Wait, what?" Neve blinked at him. He'd seemed pretty determined to just watch.

"If a seven-year-old kid can jump in the icy waters of Long Island Sound in the middle of winter, so can I." He took off his coat and shoved his gloves, scarf, and hat into one of the sleeves. Rising and rising to what had to be almost six and a half feet, he stood to toe off his boots and pull off his socks to reveal that he was wearing a second pair.

That's a terrible idea. She didn't say it aloud. He was an adult, capable of making his own choices. But he'd learn. One way or another, he'd learn. And, well, she'd laugh. "Welcome to the club," she said instead. "I hope you enjoy your first Polar Bear Plunge."

"Thanks." He pulled off his shirt and pants, dumping them in a messy pile on his beach chair.

Neve's breath caught. Hiding under that parka was a body she couldn't help but notice. It was the body of a man who worked out. The body of a man who played sports because he enjoyed them. His skin was a dark bronze, like he spent a lot of time in the sun. Every line of his muscles stood out, the bronze glow highlighting the ripples. And now that his hat was off, she could see the lighter, sun-streaked highlights in his dark brown hair. Her tongue darted out to lick her lips before she managed to say, "Wearing a bathing suit even though you weren't planning to do it?"

He glanced down at his bathing suit. "Justin told me to." He gave her a half-smile. "Never thought I'd actually go in."

"Well, now you'll have the chance. Hey, how do you—" She was cut off by a loud whistle and the screams of the crowd as the runners came flying down the street toward the beach.

It was time.

The crowd descended, stripping out of their clothes and shoes. In the chaos, Neve lost track of Alex.

She joined the group, and they all rushed forward, plunging into the icy water. It was cold. Bracing. A fresh start to the new year. She wasn't shivering. Not yet. She would, but not yet. The water felt cleansing. Fresh. Cold, but good.

She dunked underneath the waves until she was completely covered. As she floated, she felt her cares drop away. It was going to be a good year.

When she came up for air, she turned in a slow circle, keeping an eye on as many people as she could. No one looked like they were drowning—not as far as she could see, at least.

Around her there were dozens of people, all of them as wet and cold as she was. Justin had Emilia in his arms. The two of them dunked then came up, Emilia giggling all the while. On Neve's other side she saw one of her high school exes along with the middle-aged woman who lived three houses down the street. Other faces were familiar—the couple who ran the toy store and their twins, one of the waitresses at the diner, the teen she paid to mow her lawn.

Someone had brought a beach ball, and it soared above the crowd as it was batted back and forth. Everyone was having fun, although some less hardy souls were already starting to make their way back to the shore and the people gathered there. Neve wasn't going to judge; her first time doing the plunge, she'd only stayed in the water for about thirty seconds. It was hard if you weren't ready.

There was the sound of feet slapping against wet wood; Neve turned to see Alex running down the dock. He jumped off, cannonballing into a gap in the crowd.

As soon as he hit the frigid water, he started shouting, "Cold cold cold cold cold!"

Neve laughed and shook her head. *Wait. Why am I so amused by this?* Usually she'd be rolling her eyes at the sheer idiocy of someone doing what Alex had just done. But for some reason with Alex, she found it funny. *Huh.*

Justin caught her eye and tilted his head at Alex. His arms were still full of his daughter; Neve knew what he was asking. She nodded as she began swimming toward Alex. Someone needed to rescue the poor tourist, and it might as well be her.

By the time she got to him, he'd started swimming for the shore, doing a fairly respectable breaststroke. At least he hadn't jumped in without being able to swim at all. Unfortunately, he was shivering too hard to get out of the water as fast as he probably needed to.

"That was silly," she said when she got near enough that he'd be able to hear her without straining.

Alex nodded but didn't stop. Neve joined him, swimming alongside him and making sure nothing happened. She was cold and starting to shiver, which meant it was time to get out. She wasn't the only one—she spotted a number of swimmers already wrapped up in blankets or towels while others waded toward the shore, many of them headed straight for friends or family members holding up towels or blankets. The water was emptying quickly as everyone bundled up and some of them walked up the street to their homes.

Fully shivering now, Alex climbed out of the water the instant he could. Neve followed. She'd brought two towels, but...

Oh good, she thought as Carmela approached holding two full-sized blankets.

Carmela passed her one before helping Alex situate the other around him. Shaking her head, Carmela said, "I can't believe you did that."

"I c-c-can't either." He huddled as far into the blanket as he could with only a little of his hair sticking out of the top. He looked almost like a burrito. It was strangely adorable.

Grinning, Carmela tugged on his blanket. "Come on. Let's get a hot drink into you. You too, Neve."

"W-What d-d-do you have this y-year?" Neve asked as she followed the others back to the warming station. Emilia was there, wrapped in a blanket that almost engulfed her, telling her younger sister all about the plunge as she watched her with adoring eyes. Justin wasn't; he was still in the water, chasing the last few stragglers out.

"Your choices are hot chocolate, hot chocolate, and—" Carmela picked up a carafe "—oh, looks like more hot chocolate!"

Neve gave a wry grin. "I g-guess I'll have a h-hot chocolate." Hot chocolate probably would have been her choice even if she'd actually had options. She happily accepted the disposable cup.

"You want mini-marshmallows?" Gabriela held up three bags in her mittened hands. They'd come prepared.

Neve ruffled her hair. "I always want m-marshmallows." Oh good, she was starting to warm up. She could hear it in her voice.

"Good. Mini-marshmallows are the best," Gabriela said definitively. She passed an entire handful to Neve. It was a good thing her hands were small, or they wouldn't have all fit in Neve's cup.

She savored the drink, enjoying the sweet smoothness, relishing the way it warmed her from the inside even as the blanket did the same on the outside. Her shivering lessened. It was still cold, but wrapped up like this with a hot drink… well, she felt almost toasty.

But only almost.

Pretty much everyone who hadn't already left the beach brought their chairs or towels over, forming a wide circle centered around Carmela's supplies. Hot chocolate was poured and passed around—often doctored with mini-marshmallows and even a bottle of rum. Carmela's cajoling finally lured her husband out of the water, and she made sure everyone still on the beach was properly bundled up for the cold air.

Neve dragged her beach chair to the circle, and after a moment, Alex followed, settling his chair in the sand next to hers. "So how was your first plunge?" she asked, taking a sip of her hot chocolate. It was almost halfway gone already; she'd have to get a refill soon. And maybe some food as well. She wondered if Carmela had brought soup this year.

"C-Cold." At least, she was pretty sure that was what he said. He'd unwrapped the blanket just enough to show some of his face—just enough for his cup to reach his lips.

She grinned. "We did warn you!"

He cradled the paper cup in what she assumed were his hands, which were completely wrapped in folds of the blanket and not at all visible. "You d-did." He slurped his drink and added, "You kn-know, I'm glad I did it, but I'm n-never doing it again!"

"Your choice," Neve agreed, biting down her laughter.

Alex sighed and shook his head. "It's okay; you can laugh."

She stopped holding it back. "I wasn't expecting you to run down the dock and just jump in like that!" she said through her giggles.

His answering grin was wry. "I figured in for a penny, in for a pound, right?" He shook his head again. "Man, was that stupid."

"A little, yeah."

They sat and drank their hot chocolate. After a little while, Carmela passed around lentil soup, which hit the spot even more than the hot chocolate had. The soup sent a ball of heat to Neve's stomach and through her entire body. Even though the wind was beginning to pick up, Neve didn't feel like she had to go back inside quite yet. The blanket and hot food were doing their job.

Someone got out an MP3 player and a set of speakers and turned music on. While there wasn't a bonfire, the gathering had that sort of feel. This was one of Neve's favorite parts of the plunge: the aftermath. When all of the locals sat and chatted and hung out before eventually drifting off to get warm. It was the sort of gathering that only happened a few times a year—and only once in the winter.

She accepted a refill of her hot chocolate—plus more mini-marshmallows—and let the sounds wash over her. She belonged here. This was home.

"So what do you do when you're not jumping into the icy waters of Long Island Sound?"

Neve startled from her thoughts. "What?"

"What do you do when you're not jumping into the icy waters of Long Island Sound?" Alex repeated.

"Well, sometimes I jump into the tepid waters of Long Island Sound."

He laughed. "Not what I meant, but sure."

Neve pulled her blanket closer. The chill in the air had grown from unnoticeable to just barely biting. "I work at the bank near the bridge, but that's just my job." It paid the bills, she didn't hate it, and she got along with her coworkers. Plus, it was only a twenty minute walk from her house—and a five minute drive when the weather was too disgusting to walk. It was enough. "I also like to bake, make pottery, sing, and… well, honestly, I do spend a lot of time swimming." Every weekend, once the weather was nice enough.

"Oh!" The blanket pointed vaguely in her direction. "You're the one who made Gabriela's birthday cake! She spent half of dinner Monday night showing me the photos."

Neve was extremely proud of that cake. It had been decorated to resemble a swimming pool with fondant people in and around it. It had taken hours and hours of work, but seeing the expression on Gabriela's face had made every moment worth it. The effusive thanks—and a decent chunk of change—from Justin and Carmela hadn't hurt either. "Yeah," she said. "Best one I've done so far, I think."

"I haven't seen your others, but that one would be hard to top!" Alex sighed. "I'm a decent cook, but I suck at baking. Cookies from one of those pre-made cookie dough rolls are about my limit."

"But cookies. Who doesn't love a good cookie?"

He laughed. "You have a point." He grinned at her. "Come over sometime, I'll bake you cookies."

"All the way to Florida? I mean, I like cookies, don't get me wrong. But that's a long plane flight just for a couple of cookies."

His head tilted. "Who said it would just be for a couple of cookies?"

…*Huh.* Was he actually inviting her to come visit? They'd only just met this morning. They hadn't even known each other for two hours yet.

But maybe he was enjoying her company as much as she was enjoying his. "Maybe," she said. "As long as it's not during hurricane season."

"…Fair."

They sat in silence for a little, but it was a comfortable silence. Neve was a little surprised at how easy it was to just be with Alex. She'd rarely felt that way with someone she'd just met. She was also surprised by just how much she liked him. He'd been brave enough to take the plunge, secure enough to admit it had been a mistake, and funny enough to keep her entertained. She was enjoying their conversation. She wasn't sure she wanted to visit him in Florida or anything, but if he was here for more than just the day… well, a date wouldn't be out of the question.

He nudged her elbow with his and held out his hot chocolate in a toast. "To City Island, Florida, and new friendships."

Neve touched her glass to his, slightly disappointed the paper cups wouldn't make anything remotely like a clinking sound. "To Polar Bear Plunge Day."

They drained their cups. This time when Carmela came around with more hot chocolate, Neve refused the refill. She was good. She tossed her cup in the trash bag Carmela had prepared while collecting a few others along the way including Alex's.

Justin got out his guitar. "Who's up for a sing-a-long?" There was a chorus of shouts and claps of agreement, and Gabriela crawled into her father's lap occupying the space between Justin and the instrument.

Carmela dug into a bag and pulled out a tambourine, which she tossed at Alex. "Do percussion, won't you?"

He held it up, awkward with the blanket still covering his hands. "Where did you even get this?"

Justin sniffed in a pseudo high-and-mighty way. "I kept all of our instruments, of course."

"Of course," Alex replied just as snootily.

As Justin started to strum, Neve leaned over to Alex and murmured, "Our instruments?"

"We had a band back in college." His smile was rueful. "Honestly, we kind of sucked."

That answered the question of how he knew Justin and Carmela. Not that Neve needed to know; it was none of her business. But it was always nice to have her curiosity satisfied.

Justin's voice rang out, starting one of the songs Neve associated with bonfires and camping trips. Alex finally pulled his hands out of the blanket to join in. The rest of the group began to sing along, but unusually for her, Neve's thoughts were distracting enough that she didn't join in.

And they were focused on one person: Alex. It had been a few months since she'd last had sex, and she was surprised to find herself wanting Alex. Yeah, he was hot. But he was also nice and fun and willing to take risks. Plus, he had a very nice voice, a velvety sort of baritone which spoke to her soul. And her, well, other parts.

Her body clamored for sex, but Neve wasn't sure if she should take that step. While she didn't mind a good one-night stand, she was torn. She liked Alex. Like really liked him. But she wasn't even sure she wanted to date Alex. He lived in Florida; she lived in New York. Long-distance relationships were complicated. But he was here right now. He was funny, he was sexy, and he seemed interested in her too. If he offered a one-night stand, she might say yes. If he offered a date... she might say yes to that too.

Her decision made, she joined in on the next song. She couldn't help but grin at Alex's expression when he heard her strong soprano. Neve would never be the next pop star, but she could carry a tune. And he was clearly enjoying it.

The hot chocolate, soup, and warm blanket weren't quite doing the trick anymore, and Neve knew she wasn't the only one shivering. Even as the singing continued, people began to pack up and head back to their homes, undoubtedly in search of warm showers and even warmer beds.

That sounded like a very good idea.

And she wasn't the only one who had it; Justin put down his guitar, shook out his hands, and said, "Time to go home, kids." He carefully picked up his now-sleeping daughter and glanced at Emilia, who was shivering despite being wrapped in at least three blankets. "No arguments."

Neve stood up, stretched, and pulled her shoes out of her bag. She didn't bother with the rest of her clothing. "I'm going to go get a nice hot shower."

"Sh—shoot," Justin said, obviously correcting himself. His eyes flicked to Emilia, then to Alex. "Alex, I don't want to make you wait, but..."

Even though he had to be freezing, Alex shook his head. "You guys go ahead, I can wait."

Oh. Right. It had been a few months since she'd been in Justin and Carmela's house, but if Neve remembered correctly, it only had one and a half bathrooms. Which meant there was only one shower. Which meant someone was going to have to wait.

"Come to my house," she blurted out.

Everyone stared at her.

To hide the blush starting to crawl up her cheeks, she avoided everyone's eyes by concentrating heavily on putting her shoes on and folding the beach chair. "I have two bathrooms."

"That's right, you do," Justin said. He would know; he'd been over often enough when they were all kids, and he'd been part of her brothers' group of friends. He tilted his head an interrogatory expression on his face.

Neve knew he was making sure she was really okay with Alex coming to her house. He was a good egg. It was why they were still friends. She caught his eyes and nodded.

"You sure?" Alex asked. Well, unlike Justin, he couldn't read her expressions. At least not yet.

And where did that thought come from?

"Yeah, of course."

Alex regarded Carmela assessingly, his fingers plucking at the blanket. "Can I return this to y-you later?" He was shivering again. He definitely would need that shower sooner rather than later.

Carmela grinned, her eyebrow quirking at Neve. "When you come back to our house, sure."

Neve rolled her eyes at her neighbor. This was about having two showers, not about sex.

...And she wasn't even fooling herself, was she?

"Th-Thanks," Alex said, seemingly oblivious to Neve and Carmela's unspoken conversation. He shoved his feet in his boots and tried to pick up his clothing, but without a bag to put it in, he kept dropping things.

After the third time he dropped a sock, Neve silently held her bag open.

Ruefully shaking his head, he obeyed the implicit command and dumped his clothing in her bag. He picked up his coat and chair and with a wave at their friends, they headed up the beach to the street.

Luckily, Neve lived in the first house on the left. Her fingers fumbled a little as she tried to insert the key into the lock—as much as Alex needed that hot shower, she did too.

Once she got the door open and they made it inside, Alex glanced around. "N-Nice h-house," he said, taking in the wall of family photos, the couch and TV in the living room, and the dining room table. His eyes lingered on a painting of Long Island Sound which she'd bought at an art fair up in Connecticut.

"Thanks." She pulled the door closed behind her and leaned her beach chair against the wall. "It's the house I grew up in. My parents moved to Sarasota, and I'm buying it from them." There was no way she'd have been able to afford the place otherwise, not on her salary.

"Makes s-sense." He nodded. "W-Where should I g-go?" Alex asked as he put his beach chair next to hers.

Neve's breath caught. She had two showers. They could shower separately.

Or they could not.

Licking her lips, she said, "Well, if you want to shower alone, there's a bathroom down the hall." She pointed in the general direction.

He seemed to get where she was going, since his eyebrows shot up and he just said, "Or?"

"Or you could join me. If you want." She wasn't going to blush. She absolutely refused to blush. Instead, she held his gaze and smiled slowly, invitingly, letting him know she meant it.

He smiled back. "I want." He caught her hand in his. "I most definitely want."

"Good." With that decided, Neve led him to the master bedroom and her recently redone bathroom. Letting go of his hand, she dropped the bag of clothes on the floor in the corner by the toilet, kicked off her shoes, and stripped off the blanket she'd been bundled in. She'd have to remember to wash it before giving it back to Carmela; the thing was completely soaked through. She didn't take off her bathing suit. Not yet.

Alex removed his boots and his blanket, shivering even harder once he was down to just his swim trunks. "Shower?" he asked.

"Shower," she agreed.

Without removing her bathing suit, she turned it on to the temperature she preferred—just short of boiling—and waited the minute it took for the water to warm up before climbing in and making space for Alex to join her. Luckily, her newly installed shower was big enough for two, so they fit easily. She silently thanked her past self for being indulgent and choosing the shower with multiple heads. With only one shower head, there was no way both of them would have fit completely under the spray.

Despite the space, they bumped into each other as they moved—little touches which sent electricity up her spine. Each touch felt heightened, like her skin was extra-sensitive. From Alex's reactions, she thought—hoped—he felt the same.

Finding the body wash, Neve passed it to Alex, her fingertips almost jolting when his hand met hers. She was sure he felt it too: his breathing came faster, his pupils blown wide. His tongue poked out to lick his lips. Hers echoed the motion.

"Wash first," Alex said, pulling his eyes away from hers. He held up the body wash. "I'd rather..." He seemed to be thinking of how to phrase what he was trying to say. "I'd rather get clean before getting messy again."

Neve laughed. "Sounds good to me." She took a moment more to warm up in the water, then pulled the straps of her bathing suit down her shoulders.

Alex choked. "You're going to strip now?"

"Well, how can I get clean if I'm still wearing clothing?" Yeah, it would be intimate. But they were already sharing a shower. And the longer she waited, the more time her nerves would have to overwhelm her. She wanted Alex. She wanted this. Her entire body tingled with anticipation and desire—it was in on the plan. "Besides," she said, watching him watch her slowly slip her bathing suit down her breasts, "you can just call this foreplay."

His small gasp as her breasts were revealed was incredibly rewarding, causing heat to pool between her thighs and her nipples to harden, as if they were seeking his touch. To be honest, they were.

His hand came up, but it paused just before it reached her breast. Passing it by—her nipple aching for his fingers the whole time—his hand slid up her shoulder to cup her cheek. "Can I?"

She knew what he wanted. She wanted it too. Leaning forward, Neve whispered, "Yes," before their lips met.

It felt like a beginning. Shivers ran through her, each one going straight to her core. The kiss was tender but full of want. She'd been kissed before but rarely with such desire. Every touch, every taste—Neve knew he wanted her... knew she wanted him.

Her eyes opened—when had they closed? Alex's eyes met hers as they pulled back from the kiss, his pupils so wide that the brown of his irises could barely be distinguished.

"Wow," she breathed.

He grinned and leaned forward to peck her on the lips. His hands slid down her shoulders to cup the air just over her breasts. "May I?"

"Please do."

In unison, his thumbs tweaked her nipples, drawing a gasp from her. Carefully, his hands caressed her breasts, tracing designs over her sensitive skin.

She wanted more. Reaching down, Neve continued pushing her bathing suit down her body, eager to get out of it as fast as possible.

Naturally, it couldn't go quite as smoothly as she wanted. The suit stuck to her skin, clinging from the wetness, and she had to step away from Alex to get it all the way off. Once she finally managed to disentangle herself, she stepped out of the purple garment and tossed it into the sink. She'd deal with it later. Now, she had other things on her mind.

Alex's frank appraisal—and the arousal in his eyes—ramped her own arousal up.

But at the same time, she felt just a little bit gross. Swimming was great and all, but Long Island Sound wasn't exactly the cleanest body of water. Holding out her hand, she said, "You're right, we should get clean first."

He passed her the body wash. "Definitely."

As Neve slathered body wash over herself, Alex watched and absently pulled at his bathing suit. Finally he pulled it off, revealing himself to her.

Her eyes were immediately drawn to his cock. It was about average length-wise, but definitely above-average in width. It was hard, standing proud. Neve's mouth watered at the knowledge it was all for her. She pulled her eyes up to meet his and smiled at his expression. He looked half-stunned, half-excited, like he couldn't believe this was happening but absolutely didn't want it to stop.

"Hand me the body wash?" he managed to say.

"I have a better idea," she responded. She poured more of the body wash into her hands before running them down his chest, leaving behind swirls of foamy white on his tanned skin.

The little gasp he let out was supremely gratifying.

Neve washed him all over, including his cock. Each touch of her fingers made him harder. It felt like he was straining for her touch. So she gave it to him... to a point. With the softest of pats, she left his cock and returned to the rest of him, outwardly ignoring the slight groan he let out when her hands moved to his shoulders. When she'd finished lathering him, she helped him back under the water to rinse himself off.

When he was done, he picked up the shampoo. "Let me do your hair?"

Quid pro quo, right? "Sure, but just let me remove this first." Carefully she unraveled the ponytail holder from the end of her braid. Getting it out of her hair after a swim was always a bit tricky. Better to just do it herself instead of letting him pull on her hair—as it was, the tugging of the hair trapped in the elastic was slightly painful. But once it was out and tossed in the direction of the bathroom sink, Neve turned around so Alex could reach her hair.

He gently unbraided her hair, detangling the strands. His touch was much more gentle than hers; she wondered if she should have let him remove the ponytail holder. *Oh well, too late. Maybe next time.*

Wait. Next time? Alex was visiting his friends; he lived in Florida. There wouldn't be a next time.

...But she wanted there to be.

Before she could fully accept her own thoughts, Alex poured shampoo into his hand and began to massage it through her hair. That felt surprisingly good. His fingers used just the right amount of pressure to leave her scalp tingling. To stoke her arousal—which had lowered to a simmer—back into a blazing fire. Each touch, each press of his fingers on her scalp sent little jolts straight to her clit. *Wow*, she thought, barely managing to hold back a moan. She hadn't known her head was an erogenous zone.

And then his hands were gone, and he was nudging her shoulder. "Time to rinse."

Damn it. But Neve knew he was right, so she washed the shampoo out of her hair even though she just wanted more of his hands on her. *Besides...*

She reached around him to pick up the conditioner. Alex's brow furrowed when she offered it to him. *Men*, Neve thought. Aloud, she said, "Conditioner. The longer the hair, the more you need it."

"Huh," he said as he took the bottle. "How much should I use?"

"A bit more than the shampoo." Neve's hair was straight enough that she didn't need the tons and tons of conditioner some of her friends used, but it was long enough that she needed some. "Focus more on the ends than the scalp." Yes, she wanted his hands on her head, but her hair was important.

Alex did as she asked, massaging the conditioner into her hair. Even though he focused on the ends, he still took a little time for her scalp.

Neve slowly sank toward the same state of bliss she'd reached before, but she never lost that edge of awareness. As Alex conditioned her hair, she reached behind herself and ran her hands up his sides, feeling his smooth skin against her own. His cock brushed against her lower back. It twitched—a slight movement, but one that was obvious in her hyper-awareness of everything that was Alex. She twisted her hand around to run her fingers up his cock, enjoying his responsive moans.

"Damn," he said, letting out a breathy sigh. His hands slid down to her shoulders and stroked them gently.

Carefully, Neve pulled away, making sure to keep her hair out of the water. She needed to let the conditioner sit for a moment. Her hip bumped into the shampoo, so she picked it up and held it out to Alex. "Do you want me to do your hair?"

His eyes opened and he frowned. "Can you reach?"

"...Good point." He was just enough taller than her own five foot one that holding her hands up to do his hair would be a hassle.

He grinned then gave her a light kiss on the nose, making her laugh. "Don't worry about it. You already got my body. And—" he took the shampoo out of her hand "—the faster I finish this, the faster we can get to the more interesting parts of our day."

And there went her core again.

Once Alex began to shampoo his hair, Neve decided to distract herself from her lecherous thoughts by dealing with the conditioner in her hair. She enjoyed the caress of the warm water as she rinsed her hair, the way it streamed down her body, running over every inch of her skin. It wasn't his touch, but for now it would do.

His side brushed hers, and she opened her eyes just wide enough to see him joining her in the water. The feel of his thigh pressing against hers as he dealt with the mundanity of getting the shampoo out of his hair just added to the want and the need already pooling inside her.

Carefully, she stayed against his side while she reached for her comb and ran it through her hair. She didn't want her hair to end up a mess of tangles, but she didn't want to lose his touch either.

When they finished, she put down the comb to catch his left hand and bring it to her mouth, carefully kissing the back—just the lightest press of her lips on his skin. His breath came a little harder in response.

"I think we're clean enough, don't you?" Neve asked, making her meaning very clear by wrapping her hand around his cock.

"Yeah. Yeah, I think we are," Alex agreed. He panted, his breath catching with each caress of her hand, each twist of her wrist. He cupped her breasts, pinching the nipples just the slightest amount. One of his hands snaked farther down to slide between her legs, a touch she'd been anticipating. "But if you keep going like that, I'm not going to last long."

"I think I'm okay with that." She wanted to climb him right now, be pressed against the wall of the shower while he pounded into her.

But something was stopping her—two things, actually. First, all of her condoms were in her bedroom, and she wasn't on birth control. Second, while she was still massively aroused, the shower had washed away all of her wetness. And taking him dry sounded like a very bad idea. So even though she wanted him like she wanted air, she refrained... at least for now.

Besides, there were other things they could do in the shower.

Neve made sure the bathmat was in the right position. When it was, she pushed Alex against the wall and knelt, bringing Alex's cock to exactly the right height, and leaned forward.

"What are y—" His words broke off with a moan.

Letting the head of his cock pull out of her mouth with a pop, Neve smirked up at him. "I would think it's obvious."

"Damn," he hissed, then threw his head back when she swallowed him again.

He tasted like clean skin and that masculine scent that didn't have a name. She swirled her tongue around his tip, enjoying the moans he made. Each moan seemed to go straight through her, keeping her arousal high even though her legs were spread and only air touched her center.

Bringing her hand up, she cupped his balls, gently rolling them between her fingers. Alex's groan told her exactly how much he was enjoying this. He kept babbling little things, most of them pleas for her to keep going. Well, she wasn't planning on stopping! Neve bobbed her head up and down, using her hand to circle the part of his cock she couldn't cover with her mouth. At least, not if she wanted to keep breathing.

His cock, already standing proud, grew even harder and began to twitch. The flavor changed, growing saltier. She knew he'd been telling the truth—he was close.

With a hoarse moan he came, his cock spurting almost as though it had a life of its own. Neve swallowed some before pulling off, using her hands to stroke him through his orgasm. When he was finished, she stood up, her knees protesting a little at having to move, and leaned against his chest.

Even though Alex was breathing heavily and definitely using the wall to hold himself up, his arms came up to wrap around her, holding her close. He tilted her chin up and said, "Thank you," before kissing her.

When they pulled apart, Neve rested her head on his shoulder. His cock was now quiescent. Her hip pressed against it, but it didn't so much as twitch. Of course, men had refractory periods. She couldn't expect anything else. But she was still aroused.

Once again, Alex's hands reached between her legs. This time, his thumb found her clit, drawing gasps from her as each pass of his thumb sent her higher. His fingers left her clit, and she groaned, pushing her hips toward him to try to get his hand back. "I'm not stopping, don't worry," he said with a reassuring pat to her hip. Before she could respond, he knelt.

Was he—

Okay, Neve definitely wasn't going to object to *that*.

His tongue slid between her legs, finding her center. "Fuck," she gasped.

She felt him smirk against her before his tongue returned to its task. One of his fingers brushed against her opening but didn't go in. It just danced across her opening, as though tracing each part of her. She wanted that finger inside her. She wanted more, really, but the finger would do for now. But Alex distracted her from that thought when his tongue flicked across her clit before his lips fastened around it. He sucked hard, and her hips thrust against his mouth, pushing as close to him as she could get.

She moaned. "More!"

Each suck, each lick, even the slight pressure of his teeth sent her spiraling higher and higher. She raced for that peak, wanting it, needing it.

His finger finally entered her, and there it was, that highest of heights, that peak she'd been aiming for. She shuddered and gasped through her orgasm, through the sensations of his lips and tongue and fingers stroking her through her bliss.

When she finally came down, he pulled his hand and mouth away. He peeked up at her with a smile. "Good?"

"Wow," was all she could manage.

Leaning on the wall, he stood up. She had a feeling his knees were creaking as much as hers had. "To the bedroom?" he asked, holding out a hand.

She took it. "Definitely." She leaned up and kissed him again, pulling him against her. She could feel his abs pressed against her stomach, his chest against her breasts. His cock wasn't quite hard. Not yet. Not so soon after he'd come. But it was beginning to swell.

Good. She wanted it inside her.

His mouth felt as good as the rest of him. It was hot and warm and perfect. His tongue flicked as he tasted her, testing and teasing each bit. She kissed him just as fervently. She wanted every inch of him, and this was a good start.

They had to separate to breathe. She rested her head against his chest while his heart beat into her ear.

"Wow," she said again.

"Uh huh."

Standing up on tiptoe, Neve wrapped her arms around his neck. "Think you can blow my mind with your cock as well as your mouth?"

He grinned. "I'll do my best."

Neve reached to the side to turn off the shower. The instant the shower stopped she was cold. But instead of having to climb out of the shower to get her towel, Alex reached out with one long arm and managed to snag one for each of them. She accepted hers, appreciating his thoughtfulness.

Neve wiped herself off and wrapped the towel around her hair to let it get at least a little dryer. Alex seemed to consider wrapping his towel around his waist, but eventually he hung it on the empty towel rack and stood gloriously naked in her bathroom. His bronze skin glistened with a few last drops of water, and she was reminded of Poseidon emerging from the sea.

This time he kissed her. His hands cupped her ass, pulling her closer. She had to lean back and he had to almost bend over, the height difference was so great. But the kiss was so good it almost made her forget the rapidly forming crick in her neck.

Pulling back, Alex straightened and said, "Bedroom."

"Definitely bedroom," Neve agreed. She pulled the towel off her hair, hanging it on the hook on the door, and kissed him again.

Tangled like that, still kissing, they stumbled their way out of her bathroom to her king-sized bed. She was suddenly glad she'd made the bed that morning; she didn't always bother on her days off. But her dark blue plaid comforter appeared a lot more inviting than a tangle of sheets would have.

With a bounce, Alex sat down on the edge of the bed, and Neve climbed up to straddle him. She kissed him, running her hands up and down his shoulders and sides. He responded with a pinch of her nipples and a caress of her ass. His cock poked her lightly—it stood proud and eager, ready for more. Ready for her.

"Condom?" Alex asked. "I didn't bring any."

Well, of course he didn't—he hadn't been expecting to get laid after the City Island Polar Bear Plunge. Neither had she, for that matter. Luckily, Neve believed in being prepared. She leaned over and pulled open the night table, revealing a few of the prophylactics. Grabbing the nearest one, she handed it to Alex. "Good?"

He glanced at the packaging. "Perfect."

Neve eagerly watched him roll the condom onto his cock, completely ready to finally have him inside of her. Once Alex finished, she shifted forward, brushing her clit against his cock. The electricity from earlier was still there. It shot straight from her clit up her spine, sensitizing every inch of her skin. She wanted him. She needed him.

And, judging by the now rock hard cock between them, he needed her too.

Neve lightly squeezed his cock, enjoying his gasp.

"You ready?" Alex asked, his breath coming out in a whoosh.

"One hundred percent."

"Good." Putting his hands on her hips, he slid her forward and helped her kneel until she hovered over his cock.

She took a moment to anticipate this moment—a surprising one-night stand, possibly the only sex she would ever have with him… something she didn't want to rush. Slowly, oh so slowly, she lowered herself onto him, her hands on his shoulders for support. She needed something to clutch onto as he filled her, the sheer fullness almost whiting out her vision. Neve moaned as she sank down until every inch of him was inside her. It was even better than she'd imagined.

Alex groaned in response and squeezed her hips. It was not quite on the edge of pain, just the right amount of pressure. Seated like this, Neve was the same height as Alex, so she leaned in to capture his lips, pushing every bit of what she was feeling into a kiss. He responded, and it was quite possibly the hottest kiss she'd ever had in her life. Between the sweet salty taste of his mouth, the hot wetness, the way he seemed to be about to devour her… what more could she ask for?

His hips thrust, pushing his cock and her up, and she knew. *This*. This was what she could ask for. This was what she wanted. This was what they wanted.

Neve knelt up, raising herself almost off of him, then thrust back down. Her hair fell around them, a not-quite tangled mess of wet blonde strands. She did her best to shove it behind her ears, but it didn't want to go. *Should have grabbed a scrunchie.*

"God, you're beautiful." Alex tweaked one of her nipples and leaned forward to lick the other. "I love your hair."

"It's a mess," Neve pointed out between moans as she gave up on getting her hair out of the way. Instead, she gave herself over to the sex. And what he was doing was good, but she wanted more. Nudging his hand away from her breast, she replaced Alex's fingers with her own, pushing him down to her clit instead. Her breasts were heavy, and she caressed the undersides, shivering slightly from the almost tickle of the motion.

"You look like... like Aphrodite." His fingers traced lines on her stomach as they drifted down her body. "Emerging from the waves. It suits you."

She laughed. "I thought you looked like Poseidon earlier."

Leaning up, Alex kissed her again. "Good."

For a moment there was quiet, the only noises the slaps of skin meeting skin and the grunts and moans of two people working toward their mutual pleasure. Alex's tongue darted around her mouth, tangling with hers, caressing it. When they pulled away, Neve struggled to breathe. She leaned against his shoulder as the pleasure spiraled through her. It pushed her higher, sky-high, not at the precipice but close to it.

His thumb found her clit, and without warning she was there.

Neve ground herself down on Alex's cock and his thumb. The waves crashed, then grew, then crashed again as her orgasm washed over and through her. She threw her head back, barely noticing Alex's mouth on her neck, her nipples, her everywhere.

When she finally came down, she still knelt astride Alex, his cock iron-hard within her. Squeezing his cock with her inner muscles she smirked. "Your turn."

"Our turn," he countered, his breath coming out in a gasp, as he pushed his thumb harder against her clit.

...Okay, I guess I'm not entirely done, Neve thought as even that single touch sent her back up the ramp. She'd had two orgasms before. Fairly often, actually. But three was unusual.

Caressing Alex's back, she licked a stripe up his right ear then back down, finally settling on his neck. It was one of her favorite spots on a man, so she licked and sucked and tasted as much of him as she could.

All the while, she maintained her rhythm, pushing herself up and down his cock. Alex met her, thrusting as much as he could from his seated position. His cock pulsed inside her as his fingers worked her clit.

He was close. She could tell from his panting, his moaning, the way his hands roamed her body... hell, the very feel of his cock. And she knew she wasn't far from the edge herself. Neve slid her clit along Alex's thumb and pushed down, clenching around his cock.

That was enough. With a cry, Alex came, throwing his head back as his cock thrust of its own volition, plunging into her and filling her with its hardness. Even so, he never stopped rubbing her clit.

Breathing harshly into Alex's ear, Neve pinched her nipples and peaked for the third time. "Alex," she moaned, the orgasm washing over her leaving her breathless and sated.

"That was amazing," he replied.

As Neve began to come down, she felt Alex lie back onto her bed, pulling her down on top of him. His cock was still inside her. He felt solid. Safe.

But also sexy.

They lay there for a moment before she leaned forward and licked his shoulder, pulling a chuckle from him. He brought his fingers to his mouth and licked them, a sight which would have sent Neve's arousal spiraling if she'd had any energy left. But she didn't. Instead, she rested as he sucked his fingers clean before carding his fingers through her hair. It was messy but not tangled—she was lucky it tended toward straight with just a hint of waves—and with all their vigorous activity, it was even starting to dry.

The sweat was beginning to get to her. Neve managed to roll over so she could lie next to Alex instead of on top of him. She let the cool air of her bedroom waft over her and seriously considered taking a nap. According to her bedside clock, it wasn't even mid-afternoon. But after staying up to see in the new year, plunging into the icy waters of Long Island Sound, the not-quite-bonfire afterward, and three orgasms, Neve was wiped.

Alex seemed just as tired, his eyes closing as they lay there. With a jerk, he grunted and pushed himself up, unrolling the condom and using a tissue to clean himself off.

"Pass me one?" Neve said lazily. When he handed her one, she wiped herself down. Both tissues and the condom ended up in the trash, and Alex lay down again, this time with his whole body on the bed.

Neve snuggled up to his shoulder. "That was good."

"Very."

"So... how long are you in town for?"

Alex rolled onto his side to regard her with visible curiosity. "Huh?"

"That was the best sex I've had in a while. And I think…" She took a breath. "I think there might be something. Between us. Or at least the possibility of something."

A slow sexy smirk spread across his lips. "I took the whole week off. I'm at Justin and Carmela's until Sunday." He cupped her face. "And I think you're right." His thumb stroked her cheek. "I wouldn't mind taking you out on a date. Something fancier than swimming and shower sex. Although I definitely wouldn't say no to repeating the sex."

Neve laughed. His thoughts were going in exactly the same direction as hers. "That sounds good to me. Tomorrow night? Say, six or seven?"

He grinned, his eyes bright. "I'll pick you up at seven."

Neve wasn't sure which of them moved first, but they met in a kiss—a slow, languid kiss, but just as sexy as all the ones before it.

When she pulled back, she smiled at him. "I'll see you then." She couldn't wait.

Yep…it was official. January First was definitely her favorite holiday.

About the Author

    A native New Yorker, Shoshana David adores celebrating the romance in and of the city. Unlike many authors, she didn't catch the writing bug until college, but since then she has filled up notebooks and thumb drives with her various writings. Her stories feature the kind of hero/heroine she wishes she'd seen in fiction, including characters who share her own Jewish Heritage.

    When she's not typing away at a computer, you can find Shoshana working as a librarian at a small library in one of New York's suburbs, exploring the city on the hunt for a CVS which doesn't print out receipts taller than her, or taking in a show. Shoshana lives for tea, chocolate, and latkes... probably in that order.

Website: www.roselarkpublishing.com/shoshana-david
Twitter: @authorshoshana

Phoebe and the Pea

Catherine Bilson

Story Information

Holiday: Three Kings Day
Holiday Date: January 6
Heat Rating: 0
Relationship Type: M/F
Major Trigger Warnings: None

Governess Phoebe Faraday is aghast when she finds the pea in her Twelfth Night cake and is crowned Queen for the day… only for not one, not two, but three beans to be found by eligible gentlemen! Three Kings is two too many, but which king will Phoebe choose?

Phoebe and the Pea

"Phoebe, Phoebe, look!"

Miss Phoebe Faraday turned, obedient to the childish demand of her charge, and smiled indulgently at the misshapen snowman. "That's lovely, Ellie!"

Miss Eleanor Holt, aged seven, planted mittened hands on tiny hips and tipped her head to one side consideringly. "He needs a hat," she declared. "Do you think Papa will have an old one we could use?"

Phoebe winced at the idea of asking the very fashionable Lord Edmund Holt for a hat for the snowman. "I think we should look in the garden shed first," she suggested as an alternative. "I'm certain I saw an old cap hanging on a peg there which nobody would miss."

The little girl agreed and soon the snowman was completed to Eleanor's satisfaction. With that done, Phoebe convinced the little girl to go indoors to warm up with the promise of hot milk and jam tarts in the kitchen. Just one day into the new year, the weather had turned quite bitterly cold and even the snow which had fallen in the last few days was frozen solid. Phoebe was shivering in her thin coat, even wearing all her petticoats beneath her warmest gown. *At least Eleanor is warm enough*, she consoled herself. Her charge was bundled up in a thick scarlet wool cloak, hat, mittens, and scarf, which had been among the little girl's many Christmas gifts from her doting parents.

Eleanor barely tolerated Phoebe disentangling her from her outerwear and exchanging her snow-covered boots for house slippers before she took off running for the kitchen. "Cookie, Cookie! Are there really jam tarts? Miss Phoebe says there are!"

"Bless my soul." Cook, a jolly, round-faced woman who doted on Eleanor and had a soft spot for Phoebe, smiled down at the little girl. "There might be once those hands have had a wash. Go on into the scullery with you, and Molly will help you wash up."

Sweet-natured, despite being surrounded by adults who did their best to spoil her rotten, Ellie danced off to the scullery without complaint and was soon back at the table where Cook worked, holding up freshly-scrubbed hands for inspection.

"Good girl, sit down there." Cook motioned to a stool under the central work table.

By the time Phoebe had washed her own hands, Ellie was already halfway through her cup of hot milk and starting on her second jam tart. Cook waved Phoebe to sit down too and poured her some tea, the drinking of which began to warm Phoebe up at last. She sighed with pleasure, accepting a jam tart from the plate Ellie generously pushed her way. "Thank you, I needed that," Phoebe said, warming her hands on the cup. "It's bitter out there!"

"That it is," Cook agreed. "Good thing all the guests for the master and mistress' house party are already here, or I think they'd be spending the night in roadside inns. Joseph said the roads are freezing hard."

Phoebe sighed soundlessly. Holt Manor was full almost to bursting; she'd even had to give up her own small room and sleep on a trundle beside Ellie's bed.

Lord Edmund and Lady Eugenia Holt loved nothing more than to entertain. Their parties were near-legendary among their friends; nobody turned down an invitation to a Holt party. Especially a week-long house party at a time of year when the nights were long and dark.

The Holts were an exception among their circle of friends in that they had a child. Eleanor had hoped for at least one other child to play with and had drooped when every arriving carriage had only disgorged fashionably dressed ladies and gentlemen who patted her on the head and then dismissed her from their thoughts entirely. Phoebe had even made a game out of staying out of the partygoers' sight. At least, Eleanor thought it was a game. For Phoebe, it was self-preservation. Phoebe had her work cut out for her keeping the disappointed child amused while her parents entertained their guests while at the same time avoiding some of the guests' unwanted attentions.

*

"What are you making, Cookie?" Ellie demanded, watching with interest as Cook measured out ingredients into a large bowl.

"Twelfth Night cake. For the big party tomorrow," Cook answered. "Had the dried fruit soaking in brandy for two days, and now it's all ready to mix in."

"Oh, oh!" Ellie bounced in her chair. "May I add the pea and the bean? May I? May I, please?"

Phoebe smiled and nodded encouragingly as Ellie remembered to say please and gathered up the dirty plates and cups to take to the scullery.

Cook chuckled. "Of course you may, Miss Eleanor. Just one of each, mind, while I grate this sugar to add in!"

Ellie scrambled down from her chair and around the other side of the table, watching as Cook turned away to fetch the sugar grater. Quick as a flash, a small hand dipped into the jar of dried peas set open on the table and snatched out a single pea, dropping it into the pocket of her dress. Just as fast, Ellie scooped three dried beans from the other jar, dropping them into the cake batter and taking up the big wooden spoon to mix them in.

"All done!" she sang out.

Cook beamed at her. "Good girl, Miss Eleanor. You'd better run along, now, let me get on, or this cake won't get baked and there won't be roast lamb for dinner, neither!"

Ellie's face fell.

"Come on, Ellie." Phoebe returned from the scullery and held out her hand. "Let's go up to the nursery."

"Lessons?" Ellie said in a piteous tone, making Phoebe smile.

"Not proper lessons while all the guests are here, I promised. But you did get those lovely new drawing pencils from your aunt for Christmas; I thought perhaps you'd like to do a drawing of our friend the snowman? You should be able to see him from the nursery window."

Happy enough with that proposal, Eleanor allowed herself to be lured away from the bright, busy kitchen. They used the servants' stairs, making a game out of staying hidden from the house guests.

The nursery, and Eleanor's bedroom beside it, was a sanctuary from the madness of the house party. So when the two opened the door to find a man sitting in the rocking chair beside the fire, Phoebe froze in shock.

Eleanor, however, strode confidently into the breach, entirely unafraid of the stranger. "Who are you?" she demanded.

"I do beg your pardon." The man stood, revealing himself to be quite tall with dark hair falling into his eyes in a tumble of untidy curls. "You must be Miss Eleanor Holt. I'm Major John Randwyck, a cousin of your father's." Going to one knee, he offered a hand gravely, and when Eleanor accepted it, placed a gallant kiss on the backs of her tiny fingers.

Eleanor giggled, charmed. "Why are you in my nursery, Major?"

"Well, when I was a little boy, I lived here with your grandparents for a while. My parents were away in India, you see. I hadn't been back here since, and I was just reminiscing a little. I do beg your pardon for intruding."

"I forgive you," Eleanor said magnanimously, and the major smiled, showing he had laugh lines around his eyes. Ellie revised her original age estimate at seeing them. Why, he had to be older than her father, who was five and thirty!

"And this must be your governess. Would you do me the honor of an introduction?" He rose up to his feet and waited politely, his eyes on Phoebe.

*

Phoebe blinked. This dashing man wanted to be introduced to her?

"This is Phoebe," Eleanor said.

"Miss Phoebe…?" he left it on a question as he offered his hand and bowed over Phoebe's.

"Faraday," Phoebe said.

"Ah, you're related to Eugenia, then? Faraday was her maiden name, was it not?"

"Distant cousins," Phoebe admitted. Something in the major's penetrating gaze made her add, "I'm a poor relation, I'm afraid. We shared a great-grandfather, but I'm the only one left of my branch of the family. I lived with Eugenia's grandmother, my great-aunt, until she died, and then my cousin the Earl, Eugenia's father, thought I could be of use to Eugenia while Eleanor was young."

And once she'd outlived her usefulness here, she'd be shuffled off to whatever family member wanted a companion or governess next for the price of her room, meals, and a few cast-off dresses. Her great-aunt and then the Earl had made it clear that she was merely a hanger-on of their illustrious family tree, and should be grateful for whatever meager scraps they deigned to toss in her direction.

Randwyck, she suspected, worked all of this out without her having to say so because he nodded, and the slightest tinge of pity entered his expression. "I'm honored to make your acquaintance, Miss Faraday, and I do apologize for intruding on your domain," he said with a respectful bow. "I shan't bother you again, though I do hope to make your further acquaintance… and yours, Miss Eleanor."

"You can call me Ellie," that young lady pronounced. "Shall I call you Major?"

"You can if you want, but Uncle John sounds better, does it not?" He had a pronounced twinkle in his eyes, which were an interesting shade somewhere between blue and gray.

"Uncle John!" Ellie practically danced on the spot. "I never had an uncle before—except Uncle Viscount Pabley, but he's boring!"

Randwyck was obviously biting back a laugh as he said, "Well, technically I'm not exactly an uncle, but it's close enough. I don't have any nieces either."

"Would you like to come and draw with me?" Ellie invited.

Much to Phoebe's surprise, Randwyck said he'd be delighted, though he did add the proviso that he was expected downstairs for dinner shortly so would not be able to stay above half an hour.

Half an hour was at least ten times as long as any guest at the house party had devoted to Eleanor thus far, so the little girl was visibly overjoyed when Randwyck crammed his long legs under a schoolroom desk to sit beside her and admire her drawings. He even took up a pencil at her command and colored in some green trees and blue sky in the background of her drawing. Relaxed, Phoebe let herself enjoy the Major's and Ellie's conversation. Ellie chattered away happily, though Phoebe had to wonder what made Ellie glance over at her so often. And why the little girl's hand kept stealing to her dress pocket.

*

Eleanor had begged her mother to be included in the Twelfth Night celebrations. Eugenia had conceded dotingly that she might come down to the special breakfast, at least, and see who would be crowned king and queen for the day when the Three Kings cake was cut.

"Even a servant could be king or queen, and everyone would have to do what they said all day!" Ellie told Phoebe excitedly as they entered the large dining-room.

Eugenia saw them enter and waved them over, patting the empty seat beside her and gesturing Ellie to sit there. Phoebe was a little surprised to see there was a seat available for her too, on Ellie's other side, as one of the footmen held her chair, giving her the ghost of a wink as he did so.

Major Randwyck was seated just across the table and smiled at Phoebe after bidding Ellie a good morning. Phoebe had the distinct feeling he was the only one who actually welcomed her presence.

Cook came in beaming, bearing the now magnificently iced cake to great applause. She placed it before Eugenia with great ceremony. A large knife lay ready at Eugenia's right hand and two maids waited to assist with plates.

"Now gentlemen," Eugenia said as she cut the first slice, "if any of you finds the pea, you must pass it secretly to the lady seated on your left. And ladies, if any of you finds the bean, you must pass it to the gentleman on *your* left! Whichever lady has the pea shall be queen for the day, and whichever gentleman has the bean will be her king!"

There was some rather raucous applause around the table as the maids began to carry plates around, serving all the seated guests first, of course. Phoebe had been startled last year to discover that the servants were included in this tradition at all. But seeing how thin the slices the servants received were compared to those the guests got, she cynically guessed that it was far less likely one of them should find either the pea or the bean.

"Thank you," she said automatically as a plate was set down in front of her, and Eugenia shot her a glance, brows drawing down in faint reproach. Phoebe looked away. She hoped she would never fall out of the habit of thanking servants, no matter what Eugenia might think of such middle-class manners.

"See if you have the pea, see if you have it, Phoebe!" Ellie nudged her excitedly, and Phoebe sighed and took up her fork. Undoubtedly one of the eager young ladies digging into her cake and mashing up the crumbs would find the prize. At least the cake should taste good; Cook made the most delicious fruit cakes.

Her teeth clicked on something hard. Discreetly, she spat the pea out into her napkin and stared at it in dismay. *Oh dear! Eugenia is not going to be pleased.*

"I have the bean," a deep voice said, and Phoebe looked up to see Major Randwyck holding up a bean just as two other voices proclaimed exactly the same thing.

"Phoebe's got the pea!" Ellie shrieked before Phoebe could say anything.

And then all devolved into confusion.

*

"How can there be three beans?" Lady Eugenia demanded, obviously bemused.

John eyed the small smirk on Miss Eleanor's face and thought he had a very good notion just how there happened to be three beans in the Three Kings cake. *The cook is eyeing the little miss with a suspicious frown too*, he noted.

Well, he did not mind giving up his bean to ameliorate the confusion and was about to say so when a squabble broke out behind him.

Frank Cobley and Joseph Davies were typical of his cousin's friends: young, boisterous, and well-off sons of the aristocracy. Cobley was second in line to a minor baronetcy, Davies an earl's grandson. Right now, they were waving beans clasped between finger and thumb in each other's faces, both loudly arguing that they were to be king for the day.

Looking around, John saw Miss Faraday's face, noted the near-panic in her expression as she watched the two young idiots, and immediately discarded his plan of giving up his bean. "I think it's a capital notion," he said loudly, rising to his feet. "Three kings for Three Kings Day, what could be more apropos? How clever of you, Lady Eugenia, to think of such a unique scheme!"

Eugenia's disgruntled expression faded away like snow melting in the sun, and she at once declared how clever John was to have discerned her plan. He bowed in her direction, thinking cynically that she was certainly quick-witted, before turning to Cobley and Davies and placing a heavy hand on one shoulder of each.

"Come, my fellow monarchs. Let us rule together in peace and harmony while ensuring our lovely queen has everything she might desire for the day!"

"Ah, yes," Cobley nodded jovially. "Miss, ah..." He looked at Phoebe with a frown.

"Miss Faraday," John supplied.

"Yes, indeed." Cobley gave him a helpless look. "Who is she?" he hissed under his breath.

"A distant cousin of Lady Eugenia, I believe," John said blandly.

The servants filed out of the room, one of the maids catching Eleanor by the hand and leading her away after exchanging a few whispers with Miss Faraday. No doubt making arrangements for Ellie to be kept amused in the absence of her governess. The child looked pleased as Punch, not at all distraught to be deprived of her boon companion, which only settled John's conviction Ellie had engineered the whole thing. Or at least, that Miss Faraday should get the pea and there should be three beans in the cake; he couldn't quite see how Ellie might have managed him getting a bean since she hadn't come near him or touched the plate before his cake was handed to him. That occurrence had to be nothing more than a coincidence.

Moving toward the end of the table, John overheard Lady Eugenia conversing with another lady, a close friend of hers, Mrs. Myles.

"It's rather a shame your cousin Phoebe got the pea. The little mouse wouldn't know what to do with one gentleman, much less three!" Mrs. Myles laughed loudly, almost a cackle, the sound grating on John's nerves. He would never understand why women felt the need to be so cruel about others of their sex; Miss Faraday was hardly a threat to either of them. Mr. Myles was one of the wealthiest men in Sussex, doting on his young wife, while Lord Edmund was quite devoted to Lady Eugenia, spoiling her with whatever she wanted. In her plain dun-colored gown several years out of fashion, poor relation Miss Faraday faded into the background beside the two ladies in their bright silks and satins.

"That's enough," Eugenia muttered to her friend, at least making John think a little more kindly of her for defending Phoebe.

"We must have some royal robes," John declared, finding he thoroughly disliked the way Miss Faraday was almost folding in on herself as though trying to disappear in plain sight. "Bright coats or capes for us kings, I think. Edmund, can we prevail upon you to provide? And Lady Eugenia, I'm sure you can supply Miss Faraday with something worthy of a queen from your extensive wardrobe."

His cousin Edmund was a good sort, if rather self-centered at times, and he immediately rose to his feet, declaring their kings and queen must indeed be suitably attired, and Eugenia at once agreed, telling Phoebe to go on up to her dressing-room and choose whatever she wished.

*

Phoebe stared at herself in the long mirror mounted on the door of Eugenia's dressing-room in silence as Eugenia's French lady's maid, Anais, tweaked the long ribbon sash of the gown she was wearing to fall in the most flattering way.

"You are a little taller than my lady but a little slimmer as well, so your ankles do not show," Anais said in her softly accented voice. "Please do not tell Lady Eugenia I said you were slimmer than she."

"Of course." Phoebe smiled at Anais, who was probably the person in the house closest to her own status—somewhere above most of the servants but below the family.

"You look very pretty in this gown," Anais said, standing up straight. "The color suits you."

"Do you think so?" Phoebe brushed her fingertips lightly over the heavy skirts. The gown was wool, not silk, but still easily the finest garment she had ever worn, the wool finely spun and soft, the color a rich emerald.

"The same color as your eyes," Anais pointed out, gesturing her to sit down and taking up a hairbrush and a handful of pins. "You look very much like m'lady wearing it."

Phoebe considered that, still looking at herself in the mirror as Anais began braiding and pinning her hair. Her hair was brown to Eugenia's gold, but otherwise, dressed in a fine gown for the first time in her life, she did look quite like her cousin, she supposed. Which was a very strange thought, for Eugenia was an acknowledged beauty, and Phoebe had never thought of herself even as pretty.

Sitting in silence as Anais arranged her hair, Phoebe wondered what she was even supposed to do that day. Nibbling on her lip, she debated if the older Frenchwoman would have an answer to the question and finally plucked up the courage to ask.

Carefully placing a last pin, Anais opened a drawer and took her time selecting something from within before returning. "Just enjoy yourself, *mademoiselle*," she advised. "I believe m'lady has a number of games planned; if you do not wish to play, you have the perfect excuse to set yourself up as judge, *oui?*"

That was an excellent point, and one which made Phoebe brighten a little. She was sure she wouldn't know how to play half the parlor games Eugenia might wish to play and had no wish to make a fool of herself.

"Oh," she protested as Anais drew a green silk ribbon around her neck, a cameo of carved jet hanging from it, "I couldn't possibly borrow any of Lady Eugenia's jewelry."

"It's only a trinket," Anais dismissed. "A gift from one of her sisters m'lady has never worn. She prefers the pearls m'lord gave her."

Since the cameo was already seated in the hollow of her throat, Phoebe gave in with grace, though she thought privately that if Eugenia so much as frowned at it, she would take it off at once. Instead, she thanked Anais for her help. "You have made me look like a true lady, Anais."

Anais' slightly severe face broke into a smile as Phoebe stood up. "It was a pleasure, *mademoiselle*. And do not worry for little Miss Eleanor; we shall all take care of her today so you may enjoy your time as Queen. Perhaps I shall go to dress her hair, too."

Ellie would like that, Phoebe knew. Impulsively, she seized Anais' hands in hers and squeezed them. "Thank you again. I'm sure Lady Eugenia does not say it enough, so I'm afraid you must tolerate me saying it too much," she persisted when Anais tried to wave off her gratitude.

"Go," Anais insisted. "No more time wasted talking to me, you have three handsome gentlemen who are waiting to pay court to you!"

Phoebe chuckled as she obeyed Anais' urging, enjoying the feel of the fine lawn petticoats swishing against her legs as she descended the stairs. The only thing of her own she still wore was her shoes; Eugenia's feet were a size smaller than Phoebe's, and the pretty shoes Anais had tried to press on her had pinched abominably. Hence, she still wore her practical black boots, knowing they would not be visible beneath her gown.

"There she is, Her Majesty appears!" Mr. Cobley cried as Phoebe descended. He strode gallantly to the foot of the stairs, extending his arm. "Miss Faraday."

"Queen Phoebe, you mean," Lord Edmund said jovially, "and you are King Frank, Cobley!"

"Quite right, quite right," Cobley nodded solemnly.

"King Frank, why, you must have brought the gift of frankincense," Phoebe said, trying to enter into the spirit of the day.

Cobley's round face lit up, and he beamed at her. "Why, that's capital! Brilliant, Miss Fara—Queen Phoebe, I mean. That means Davies, er, King Joseph must have brought the gold, for he's rich as Croesus, you know. And the major has brought the myrrh. What's your first name, Randwyck?"

"John," Major Randwyck answered with a small smile. "Not a particularly auspicious name for a king, I'm afraid."

"Oh, indeed, I should say not!" Cobley said, dismayed.

"In England's histories, perhaps," Phoebe put in quietly. "But there was a King John of Denmark as well, and in fact, he ruled all of Norway and Sweden too. His descendants still hold the thrones of all three countries, I believe. And while John of England may not have been the finest of men, it is an indisputable fact that he was the king who signed the Magna Carta—the document which forms the basis of England's laws to this day and enshrines many of the common man's rights. For that alone, King John deserves to be remembered with respect."

Mr. Cobley stared at her as though she had suddenly sprouted a second head. Mr. Davies looked no less befuddled. And Major Randwyck... started to chuckle, before applauding her.

"Very good, Queen Phoebe! If only England's King John had had a queen of your education and intelligence, no doubt England would still have dominion over Normandy and Brittany, at the very least."

Phoebe smiled back at him in relief, glad at least one of the gentlemen hadn't dismissed her knowledge. As she passed into the drawing-room, though, she heard Cobley say in an undertone to Lord Edmund, "Cleans up well enough, but you didn't say she was a damned bluestocking."

Ouch. Phoebe winced. On the other hand, what did she care for Mr. Cobley's opinion of her? Stiffening her spine, she kept walking, refusing to look back. *I'm queen for the day,* she told herself. *Just one day, and then I go back to my normal life, invisible to these people. My life where my education is the only thing I really have to make myself useful.*

"Where did you come by your knowledge of John of Denmark?" Major Randwyck murmured in her ear, startling her. For a large man, he moved very quietly indeed.

"My father was a professor at Trinity College, Cambridge," she said proudly. "My mother, though of course not permitted to study or qualify, was the daughter of an academic herself. She acted as my father's secretary and assistant, and they were both my tutors until..." She trailed off.

"Until they passed?" Randwyck said gently.

Phoebe nodded, suddenly unable to speak as she thought of her parents: her kindly, absent-minded father and her mother, quiet around strangers but coming to life around those who knew her and accepted her intelligence.

"How old were you?"

"Thirteen," she whispered through a choked throat.

"That's when you went to live with your great-aunt? So your education stopped at that point?"

She nodded.

"Then I'm all the more impressed you remember so much." Randwyck smiled down at her.

Phoebe tried to smile back but was sure she managed little more than a grimace.

Eugenia clapped her hands just then, however, and declared the festivities were to commence. "Every king—and the queen, of course—will nominate an activity for the day," she announced. "Though you must leave it to me, as the hostess, to decide what we shall all do first!"

"She's not very good at giving up control, is she?" Randwyck murmured, and Phoebe bit her lips to keep down a smile.

"King John?" Eugenia came to him first with a pretty smile. "What activity do you select?"

Randwyck paused, glanced about the company, all of whom were eyeing him with great interest, hanging on his choice. "Perhaps cards?" he said. "Depending on what the other choices are, we may welcome an hour or so to sit down quietly. Speculation, perhaps, or loo?"

"I daresay, people may divide up as they wish when the time comes and play the games of their choice; we have quite enough for several games," Eugenia said, giving him a nod. "One for the afternoon, I think, Major. King John, I mean!" She laughed her pretty, tinkling laugh, and Randwyck bowed to her.

Eugenia turned to Mr. Davies next, as Phoebe chewed on her lower lip and wondered what she should suggest. *Charades, perhaps?* But she was immediately thwarted in that idea when Davies promptly announced he loved a good game of charades and would settle for nothing else.

"You are all very dull," Mr. Cobley declared. "The sun is shining, though it is cold, and it is a perfect day for ice skating! We had such fun on the pond three days ago; we must do it again!"

"We shall do that this morning," Eugenia decided, "and then we can play the other parlor games after we return. I shall have Cook prepare a nuncheon for us, for skating will surely make us all hungry!"

There was a general chorus of agreement. Phoebe felt a certain relief that none of her 'kings' had suggested an activity in which she did not know how to participate; she had skated many times when younger and indeed had been out just a few days earlier on the pond herself while skating with Eleanor.

"What about you, Queen Phoebe?" Eugenia asked, and before Phoebe could reply with her new idea that they should have a game of riddles, Eugenia turned around and declared, "No doubt Phoebe will have thought of something very *clever* for all of us to do!"

Horrified, Phoebe listened as several gentlemen groaned and ladies sighed, looking at each other with pursed lips. Quickly, she changed her mind. "Indeed not, Lady Eugenia. I was going to suggest a musicale evening after dinner, and request you and Lord Edmund sing together at the climax of it. I have only heard you duet once, yet the beauty of it has stayed with me ever since."

Obviously startled, Eugenia looked back at Phoebe. Then she smiled. "That is a capital suggestion, Phoebe! Everyone shall have a chance to shine."

"And if you permit, I know Miss Eleanor has been practicing her music most diligently," Phoebe suggested timidly. "She might sing a song for you to begin the musicale."

Both Edmund and Eugenia looked delighted at the idea, and Phoebe gave a little hidden sigh of relief. Having satisfied Eugenia with her suggestion, hopefully she could avoid her cousin sniping at her the way Great-Aunt Susan used to whenever Phoebe displeased her.

"A born diplomat," Major Randwyck murmured at her side with a thread of laughter in his voice, and she looked up at him.

"I beg your pardon, sir?"

"You're a born diplomat, Miss, ah, Queen Phoebe. That was nicely done."

"I haven't the slightest idea to what you might be referring, King John," she said with the most saccharine of smiles. "Now if you'll excuse me, I must go find my skates."

*

John watched Phoebe walk away, amused by her denial. She'd obviously chosen her activity deliberately to please Eugenia. A very intelligent young woman and one who was wasted as governess to a little girl, in his opinion, even a child as precocious as Miss Eleanor.

She would make a fine wife for a diplomat, he thought before banishing the thought. He hadn't even decided whether he should accept the position he had lately been offered by the government: that of senior aide to the ambassador to the royal court of Denmark. In essence, being the man who would manage England's affairs in that country since the ambassador was a duke's second son—long on noble connections but short on brains.

"Have you skates, John?" Edmund asked him then.

He shook himself from his reverie. "Not with me. Do you have some spares I might borrow?"

"You can use mine; I bought a new pair this year, but my old ones are still perfectly serviceable, to tell the truth." Edmund gestured for John to follow him, and the pair left the room to go in search of skates.

"Then the old ones will do me well enough," John insisted, making his cousin smile. "'Tis more important by far for you to cut a dash for your lovely wife in your new ones!"

"It's not I who should be seeking to impress the ladies, cousin. You should look to taking a wife yourself now that you are home for good. I can vouch for the joy marriage has brought me, at least!"

"You are fortunate in your family, Edmund. Perhaps I will indeed follow your example. Perpetual bachelorhood is a lonely business." John thought wistfully of his house, Randwyck Abbey, an enormous stone pile in Shropshire. He and his mother were the only ones left of the family, rattling around the huge place even when they were both there. Which wasn't often; Mrs. Randwyck preferred to spend her time in Bath or Cheltenham with friends unless he was at home. And John wasn't home much.

"Hear, hear!" Edmund nodded vigorously. "There are some lovely, eligible ladies at the party, you know. Miss Cottesloe is one," he lowered his voice to a whisper, even though they were outside now walking toward the pond and nobody was close enough to overhear, "quite a dowry there, thirty thousand pounds, though I know you've no need of the money."

"Indeed not and I am glad for it." John had seen too many of his fellow officers marry for money—since most of them were younger sons not destined to inherit their family fortunes, such as they were. Very few of them seemed to have found happiness with their heiresses. "Miss Cottesloe is pretty enough to please the eye," he made sure to keep his voice low too, "but I fear her continuous stream of inane chatter would have me avoiding her in defense of my ears within a few weeks at best. I pray you and Eugenia will not try to make a match for me, cousin."

"We should not think of it," Edmund disclaimed, but he had ever been a terrible liar. His gaze slid away, and he pursed his lips.

"I hope you do not play cards for money with that face, cousin," John chuckled. "You lie very ill!"

Edmund had the good grace to laugh. "I do not gamble; indeed, Eugenia has forbidden it!"

"A good thing, or you should no doubt lose the entire Holt fortune at the gaming tables within weeks," John said dryly. "I forgive your interference because I know you wish only to see me content, but please, tell your lady wife not to throw any young ladies at my head? I have some very particular requirements for a wife, which will not be easily filled. I should hate for any expectations to be raised which I could not fulfill."

"Well enough," Edmund said good-naturedly, "but pray, what are these particular requirements of yours? Eugenia is acquainted with everyone in society, you know. She might be able to think of a few ladies who fit the bill without your having to take the time to conduct a search yourself."

"Intelligence," John said promptly, "first and foremost."

"Well, as you're such a damnably clever fellow yourself, your wife will need to be sharp in order to understand you!" Edmund laughed.

John smiled at his cousin. They had finally come to the pond, and his eye was caught by Miss Faraday. She was already on the ice and skimming about, a graceful figure in a long green cloak which matched her dress.

"Truth is, Edmund, I've been offered a diplomatic post. I haven't said anything yet because it may not come to fruition, but I'll need a wife with a good education who can hold her own in gatherings of all social levels. Preferably one with a good knowledge of languages and an ability to learn more."

"That's exciting, John! But are you sure?" Edmund looked at him seriously as they sat down on a fallen tree trunk to attach their skates. "Have you not served long enough?"

"I've a good steward taking care of the Randwyck estates," John disclaimed, "and I'm in the habit of working for His Majesty now. Besides, there's still a few cities around the world I haven't explored yet."

Edmund laughed loudly, and John saw Miss Faraday turn toward them, her attention caught by the sound. "I wouldn't have your itchy feet for quids, cousin! I'm quite content in my own little corner of England; I leave the traveling to you!"

Others were joining them now, sitting down to put on their skates, and John decided he should get on the pond before it became too crowded. Additionally, someone of greater weight than Miss Faraday should probably test the ice before it became too stressed.

It had been a few years since he had skated. With his first step on the ice, his left foot tried to go in the opposite direction he intended, leaving him wobbling briefly.

Miss Faraday, close by, skated up and caught his arm with a laugh. "Major Randwyck, are you all right?"

"Yes, thank you," he said, a little embarrassed. "It's been some years since I've skated, that's all."

"Would you like to hold my hand a moment until you have your balance?"

Emerald eyes glinted with mirth as she spoke, but he sensed the offer was sincere.

"Just for a moment, yes, if you wouldn't mind. I'd like to skate over the center of the pond, ensure it's up to a man's weight before any of the others venture on, actually." Her small hand in his felt alarmingly pleasant, and he resolved not to get too used to the situation.

*

Major Randwyck was a thoroughly decent man, Phoebe decided, and he was really quite a good skater once he got his feet under him. By the time they reached the center of the pond, he was skimming along smoothly. He released her arm with a remark that if he fell through the ice, he certainly should not wish to drag her in with him.

"The ice does seem quite thick," she ventured to say. "I was out here a few days ago with Miss Eleanor having a lovely time, and the weather has barely ventured above freezing since." Indeed, she had been a lot colder last time she was out here, but then again she was wearing one of Eugenia's beautiful thick cloaks instead of her own threadbare one.

The major stood on one skate and stamped the other experimentally a time or two. "I do believe you're correct, Queen Phoebe."

He has a very nice smile. Of course, she shouldn't be noticing it. Even if she was queen for the day, Phoebe knew her place. Recalling herself even in the middle of smiling back at him, she cast her eyes down.

"Come now, what's this?" the major said jovially, and to her surprise, he reached out to take her hand again, this time tucking it into the crook of his arm. "Come skate with me, Your Majesty. Show me some of your moves. Where did you learn?"

"There was a pond directly opposite my parents' house in Cambridge," Phoebe said. "I spent many happy hours skating there while my father met with students or worked on his lectures. Mama would only call me in when she said I had turned the same blue as my coat."

He laughed, a rich sound, carrying in the chill air. There were other skaters on the pond now, though, talking and laughing, and nobody looked across at them, no one seemed to care that Phoebe was overstepping her place.

"I had little opportunity to skate for some years until I came here," she said. "Then, last Christmas, Ellie asked for some skates, and Lady Eugenia said I might teach her."

"You're very fond of Eleanor, aren't you?"

Surprised, she turned her head to look at him directly. "Of course I am. She's a very dear child."

"Intelligent, too, I think?"

"Oh, very! But then, my father always said young children are like sponges, soaking up every droplet of knowledge which comes their way. Especially with languages. The earlier one begins their education, the better. Ellie had only a few words in French that Lady Eugenia's maid Anais had taught her when I arrived a little more than a year ago. Today, she converses with me almost as well in both French and Italian as she does in English."

"Impressive," the major said with a nod.

"Thank you. This year, she has asked to begin German as well, but I have yet to ask Lord Edmund and Lady Eugenia's permission." Phoebe's lips twisted a little as she thought once again of how she might approach the topic. "Lady Eugenia... she doesn't want her daughter to become, well, a bluestocking."

"An educated woman is a blessing any educated man should recognize," Randwyck said seriously. "I most certainly do, and I hope it will not be many more years until women are permitted to attend university and study whatever they wish."

"A progressive! Though some would probably call you a heretic, sir." Phoebe smiled at him. "My mother would have liked you very much, I should think."

"I do not doubt I should have liked her as much as I do her daughter," he said gallantly.

Blushing, Phoebe looked away. While years as a companion and governess had taught her how to handle importunate gentlemen who might try to catch her alone in an isolated spot, she had not the slightest idea how to deal with genuine compliments.

"I will speak to Edmund about allowing Eleanor to learn German," Randwyck said after a few moments in which they skated in silence, and she looked back up at him in surprise.

"That would be very kind of you, sir. Thank you."

"You need not thank me; it's something which will clearly be of benefit to Eleanor, in my opinion. Edmund will recognize that and override any objections Eugenia may have. While he may defer to her on social matters, I suggest you should consult with him about Eleanor's academic education."

She had no opportunity to reply as some other skaters caught up with them at that moment.

"Why, King John, you're monopolizing our queen!" Joseph Davies declared, and he tucked his arm through Phoebe's free one with a proprietorial air.

"Do come and skate with me, Your Majesty!" A pretty girl several years younger than Phoebe batted her eyelashes at Major Randwyck. "You're such a good skater, and I'm ever so wobbly on my own!"

Randwyck released Phoebe's arm with an apologetic smile. "As you like, Miss Cottesloe," he said gallantly, and Phoebe heard Miss Cottesloe giggle as she took Randwyck's arm and skated away with him.

She was fairly sure Mr. Davies had no real interest in spending time with her and had been brought over solely to separate her from Randwyck, probably at the urging of Miss Cottesloe. He took her promptly over to a large group doing more socializing than skating and immediately abandoned her to fend for herself as he jumped back into the conversation.

I will not be jealous, Phoebe told herself silently as she watched the major skate around the pond with the pretty, golden-haired debutante on his arm. Miss Cottesloe's laughter rang out again, and she smiled up at Randwyck constantly.

No wonder she's a poor skater; she isn't watching where she's going. At once, Phoebe felt guilty for the mean thought. She didn't even know the girl.

"It's far too cold out here," a lady nearby announced. "I'm going back to the house before I freeze!"

Seizing gratefully on the excuse, Phoebe declared she'd had enough of skating as well. She was unwilling to dwell on her feelings of jealousy over how Major Randwyck's head inclined to listen to Miss Cottesloe's breathy giggles. She needed an escape from her own emotions.

Upon returning to the house, Phoebe took the opportunity to slip up to the schoolroom. There she found Eleanor happily ensconced with Anais, reading a French storybook together.

"Phoebe!" Ellie jumped up, her face wreathed in smiles. "You look beautiful!"

Anais stood too, glancing a silent query at Phoebe.

"Lady Eugenia isn't back yet," Phoebe answered Anais' unspoken question first before stopping to embrace Ellie. "Thank you, my darling! It's a dress your mama has very kindly loaned me for the day, and it's quite the prettiest gown I've ever worn."

"I like it," Ellie declared and then added with a very mischievous glint in her eye, "but you'll have to borrow another one for tonight. That's not an evening gown."

"I believe you and I will be having a conversation quite soon about today, Miss Holt," Phoebe said warningly. Eleanor looked innocent until Phoebe leaned close to whisper, "I know you hid the pea in my cake."

A little giggle sounded, but by the time Phoebe had straightened to look back at her charge, Ellie's face was smooth again.

"I don't know what you mean, Phoebe," Ellie claimed, her eyes wide.

"*Three* beans?" Phoebe responded, not believing Ellie for a moment.

"My hand might have slipped," Ellie allowed. "Though I also think three kings for Three Kings Day is an *excellent* idea. Aren't you having a nice day, Phoebe? Are your kings nice? I'm so glad my Uncle John is one of them. You must like him, at least!"

"Major Randwyck is everything gentlemanly," Phoebe admitted, and that praise seemed to satisfy Ellie.

A maid came hurrying into the room just then advising Anais that Lady Eugenia had returned. Anais excused herself quickly. Phoebe thought she should probably remain with Ellie, but the maid, Molly, told her she was to take Ellie down to the kitchen for something to eat. "You go back to the party and enjoy yourself, Miss Faraday! We're all hoping you have a lovely day and will tell us all about it at supper tomorrow," Molly said with a wide smile, seizing Ellie's hand.

"I shall," Phoebe promised. She was touched by the maid's enthusiasm and vowed to memorize every detail of the day so she could tell all the stories the maids might wish.

*

Downstairs, she found the rest of the party reassembling in the drawing room where servants were bringing in trays of tea, dainty sandwiches, and cakes. This, Phoebe supposed, was Eugenia's idea of a light nuncheon with enough food on the trays to fill the bellies of everyone present three times over.

"Ah, the queen rejoins us!" Mr. Davies announced to the company at large, and to Phoebe's surprise a number of faces turned to her with welcoming smiles. Eugenia even waved her over to where she was holding court on a couch and pressed a dish of tea upon her, remarking that it was most pleasant to come in to hot drinks after the bitter cold outside.

The room felt rather too warm to Phoebe, what with a roaring fire in the fireplace and a score of warm bodies surrounding her. She accepted the tea with profuse thanks, however, grateful for Eugenia's kindness.

"You must allow me to serve you some nuncheon, Queen Phoebe," an older lady said with a warm chuckle. "What would you like? I can highly recommend the lemon tarts."

"Have you met Mrs. Hamersby yet, Phoebe?" Eugenia asked.

"I haven't had the pleasure, ma'am. Thank you kindly, a lemon tart sounds delicious." Mrs. Hamersby had a nice smile and dancing blue eyes. Phoebe decided she liked the older lady a good deal, especially when Mrs. Hamersby insisted she was hopeless at charades and should like Phoebe for a partner.

"Undoubtedly you're a clever creature, and we shall have an excellent chance at winning!" Mrs. Hamersby declared, eyes twinkling.

"I hope you'll forgive me when you discover you have vastly overestimated me, ma'am," Phoebe said apologetically.

Mrs. Hamersby chuckled. "We'll see, we'll see."

Miss Cottesloe had already claimed Major Randwyck for a partner, Phoebe saw from the corner of her eye. She chastised herself sternly for feeling jealous. She had no reason to be, after all; he was a guest, and she merely the poor relation.

Newly focused, she turned her attention to the game. Phoebe gained a little satisfaction on discovering Mrs. Hamersby to be quite an astute partner, contrary to her claims, while Major Randwyck was obviously frustrated with Miss Cottesloe's failure to actually try at the game. *She might do quite well if she put some effort into it*, Phoebe thought, but the debutante was more interested in batting her eyelashes at her partner and giggling every time he spoke. Randwyck looked across at Phoebe just then; caught her eye; and much to her astonishment, smiled while tipping his head to her.

"What do you think to this one, Phoebe?" Mrs. Hamersby asked.

Phoebe started, blushing. *Why, I am just as guilty of inattention as Miss Cottesloe*, she thought, furious with herself, and she begged Mrs. Hamersby's pardon.

"I should be quite distracted too, if I were your age," Mrs. Hamersby murmured in Phoebe's ear a little while later. "And if a fine figure of a man were paying me such attention."

Bemused, Phoebe stared at her companion. Mrs. Hamersby tilted her head, and Phoebe followed the motion to find Major Randwyck's eyes on her again.

This time, when he caught her eye, he winked. Phoebe felt a scalding blush beginning to rise up her cheeks. Wrenching her gaze away, she said quietly, "I'm afraid no good can come of a gentleman's attentions to a governess, ma'am."

"Goodness, let me set your mind at rest on that score, my dear! I've known John Randwyck since he was a babe, and he'd never show such disrespect to a lady as you imply." Mrs. Hamersby kept her voice low so that none of the chattering throng around them could overhear. She leaned closer and laid her hand on Phoebe's wrist for emphasis. "Besides which, you're Eugenia's cousin, aren't you?"

"The connection is distant," Phoebe insisted.

Mrs. Hamersby shook her head. "You value yourself too poorly, Phoebe, and if you do not hold yourself to be of value, why should anyone else?"

Eugenia clapped her hands just then and declared it was time to end the game and set up to play cards, leaving Phoebe with something else to ponder. *Perhaps Mrs. Hamersby was right*, she thought. It wasn't as though she was officially Eleanor's governess. She'd just been sent to stay with Edmund and Eugenia, had realized how lonely Eleanor was, and fallen naturally into the role of nurturing the little girl. She'd even asked to have her things moved from the pleasant guest chamber she'd been allotted to the simpler room beside Eleanor's.

Had a desire to make herself useful relegated her to the position she now occupied? It was certainly something to ponder as Mrs. Hamersby abandoned her to seek a whist partner among the gentlemen.

"What would you care to play, Queen Phoebe?"

She looked up to find Major Randwyck standing before her, a smile on his handsome face.

"Oh, I don't know. Aren't you going to play with Miss Cottesloe?"

"She declared a passion for the game of lottery tickets, which I'm afraid I despise."

Phoebe hummed in agreement. She found the game boring as well. No skill or strategy was needed, the winner being entirely down to chance.

"Do you play piquet?" Randwyck asked. "We can play for tokens; Eugenia has baskets of them ready."

Piquet was her favorite card game, but she hesitated. "It's only a two-player game, should we not..." She gestured toward the tables filling up with players.

"Why? Remember, you're Queen for the day, and I'm one of your kings. Let us please ourselves by enjoying a game of piquet, if you should enjoy that?"

"I should, very much indeed." Making up her mind, Phoebe accepted his offered hand and let him lead her over to a small, unoccupied table. "I must confess, however, that it's been some time since I played against an opponent over the age of eight."

Randwyck threw back his head and laughed, displaying even white teeth. "Considering Eleanor's precocious tendencies, I consider myself duly warned!" Picking up the deck of cards waiting on the table, he quickly rifled through and discarded the low cards, shuffling the remainder and offering the pack to Phoebe to cut.

She cut to find a nine and made a face. "Not a wonderful start; that bodes ill for my luck."

Randwyck put the pack down and made his own cut, chuckling when he found the seven of clubs: one of the lowest cards remaining. "If your luck is poor, it seems mine shall be worse! Will you deal?"

Phoebe couldn't recall the last time she'd enjoyed herself so much. The major was a skilled opponent, and he did not hold back in his play. They were, she thought, evenly matched, or they would have been if she were not quite so rusty. As their first partie came to an end, she was behind but only by a few points. Phoebe felt she had acquitted herself well. She had gotten over the Rubicon, at any rate, but felt glad they weren't playing for money when she had to slide a large handful of Eugenia's tokens over to the major's side of the table.

"What wonderful fun this is," Randwyck said, rising to his feet.

Phoebe looked up in sudden disappointment. Everyone else was still playing, and she'd thought they might have time for another partie. "Oh. Yes, thank you for the game, Major." She began to rise from her chair.

His voice stopped her. "Well, I'd hoped we might play another, if you're agreeable? I thought I might fetch a drink. Would you care for a glass of sherry?"

"Oh, I... yes. Yes, please, that would be very pleasant." Surprised yet oddly buoyed, Phoebe busied herself shuffling the cards until he returned, placing a glass at her elbow.

"You're a worthy opponent," Randwyck said, taking his seat again. "I don't know when I last enjoyed a game so much."

"You played a great deal while on the Continent, did you?" Phoebe tried for a light tone.

"More than you'd think. In war, there is a great deal of time spent sitting around waiting in sheer boredom, punctuated by short periods of intense, terrifying action. A pack of cards was always a good way to pass the boring times." For a moment he sat, chin on his hand, eyes distant.

"I know nothing of war," Phoebe said quietly, "save that I think you would be the kind of leader soldiers would follow into the very fires of Hell itself if need be."

"Waterloo was not dissimilar to Hell, in truth, at least how I have always imagined Hell to be." Randwyck's smile was weary. "I thank you for the compliment, though. England's common soldiers are not always the most couth of men, but their courage under fire was humbling to see. I considered it an honor to lead them."

She lifted her glass to him. "The honor was England's, sir. We all owe you a great debt of thanks."

Phoebe was surprised to see he looked a little embarrassed and quickly changed the subject. *A humble man at heart*, she thought, glad he was not puffed up with his own consequence.

They had just enough time to finish a second partie, which Phoebe won handily, much to her delight. Major Randwyck insisted she had won overall since her total of points exceeded his over the two games, and she accepted his concession with grace.

At the next table over, Eugenia rose to her feet and announced her intention to retire to dress for dinner. "Do come with me, Phoebe," she lowered her voice and stepped closer to their table. "I have a gown in mind I think would suit you well."

Eugenia has changed her tune since this morning, Phoebe thought as she trailed her cousin up the stairs. Earlier, Eugenia had seemed displeased Phoebe had been crowned queen for the day, but now she was being very friendly. Phoebe had to wonder why.

No sooner were they closeted within Eugenia's rooms than Anais came bustling up. "I've laid out the sapphire gown for you as you requested, my lady, and I have wash water ready."

"Very good, Anais. Now, Phoebe will require your help as well; do you think you can manage both of us?"

"Of course, my lady."

"Since Phoebe looks so well in green, I thought perhaps the jade gown with the jet beading might suit her this evening. Don't you agree?"

Anais looked quite startled for a moment, but she nodded quickly. "*Mais oui,* Miss Faraday shares your green eyes, my lady. The jade will become her very well."

"I thought so." Eugenia hummed happily to herself, crossing to her dressing table and busying herself with plucking pins from her hair. "Maybe a little rouge for your cheeks and lips too," she remarked.

Anais traded quizzical looks with Phoebe before going through to the dressing room, presumably to collect the requested jade gown.

Deciding to make herself useful, Phoebe crossed to Eugenia and picked up a hairbrush. "May I brush your hair, my lady?"

"And when did you start calling me that? It's Eugenia, Phoebe. We played together as girls, and I asked for you to come and live with me when Grandmama passed because I recalled our friendship fondly." Eugenia's eyes met hers in the dressing mirror, and Phoebe thought her cousin looked a little shamefaced. "You've been acting as Eleanor's governess, but I swear, it was never my intention to press you into service."

"I'm delighted to spend time with Eleanor." Phoebe drew the brush gently over Eugenia's shining golden locks. "And the truth is, if you hadn't taken me in, I probably would be working as a governess somewhere. Somewhere with a great deal less security in my position and a great deal more fear. Fear of the male servants or men of the house potentially seeking to take advantage of me. I'm grateful to you, Eugenia."

"You are too good, Phoebe. It is I who should be grateful to you!" Eugenia shook her head. "I have been lax in giving you your due courtesy as a member of my family, and I vow it shall not continue."

"You are my dear cousin," Phoebe said, "and I am glad to be here with you and Eleanor and Lord Edmund."

"Should you not like your own home and family, though?" Eugenia's green eyes, so like her own, caught her gaze in the mirror again.

"Fate has not seen fit to send me a partner as well-suited to me as Lord Edmund is to you," Phoebe deftly evaded the question, and then followed the evasion with a truth. "My parents loved each other dearly, and I should not care to marry just for the sake of not being alone. I'm quite content with my lot."

"Quite understandable," Eugenia nodded in agreement. "Why, I turned down a marquis and two earls who sought my hand; because even though Edmund is only a baronet, I knew he was the only one for me. You *would* like to marry though, wouldn't you? If you met a man for whom you cared?"

"If I met such a man—who would take me with no dowry and only my distant familial connection with you to recommend me—I would indeed," Phoebe said with a laugh, "but since I think such a man would be as rare as the mythical unicorn, I shan't hold my breath waiting for him!"

Eugenia laughed too, and Anais returned then bearing in her arms the most beautiful gown Phoebe had ever seen, so the subject was allowed to drop.

"I hardly feel like myself," Phoebe whispered to Eugenia as they descended the stairs together an hour later. The silk skirts of her gown—beaded with jet in Greek key patterns around the hem—swished heavily around her legs. Her hair was pinned up in an elaborate arrangement of curls, a strand of crystal beads woven into it shimmering whenever she turned her head.

"You look beautiful," Eugenia replied, threading her arm through Phoebe's, "and I have no doubt Major Randwyck will think so too."

"Wait, what?" Phoebe stopped walking, but Eugenia's arm through hers propelled her on into the grand parlor where the rest of the party awaited their arrival.

Major Randwyck stood close by the door. After Eugenia's comment, Phoebe couldn't help but look straight at him to see how he reacted and was both gratified and astonished by the way his mouth fell open, his gray-blue eyes widening as he gaped at her.

*

Could this be the same woman who'd laughed as she skated around the pond with him earlier, her cheeks and nose pink with cold? The same woman who'd beat him at cards, her quick mind always one step ahead? She looked every inch the elegant Society lady.

John wasted precious time staring agape at the vision before him and learned anew a lesson he should have recalled: he who hesitates is lost. Cobley almost leapt past him and seized Phoebe's hand to kiss.

"Queen Phoebe, you are radiant this evening," Cobley gushed. Phoebe's brow furrowed as she stared at the man in apparent confusion.

No wonder, John thought. Cobley hadn't shown any indication all day that he'd even noticed her existence, and here he was now fawning over her like a lovestruck dandy. Two more men approached, their eyes fixed on the creamy swells of flesh over the fashionably low-cut bodice of her silk gown. John saw red, his fists clenched at his sides as he watched the three young bucks with Phoebe, standing close to look down her bodice. Worse, Cobley pressed a glass of sherry into her hand, his eyes fixed to her bosom.

"You should go and rescue her," a light voice remarked beside him.

He glanced down to see Lady Eugenia, sipping on her own glass of sherry, her amused green gaze fixed on his. "Miss Faraday is hardly a city under siege," John said dryly. "I'm sure she is safe from harm in your drawing room, Lady Eugenia."

"From harm, certainly, but my cousin is an educated and intelligent woman; the conversation of those three will bore her to tears before we even go into dinner. If you are at all a gentleman, you will rescue her from such a fate."

John was pretty sure Eugenia was laughing at him, but he was also quite sure Phoebe's eyes were already glazing over.

"I am at your service, my lady," he said gallantly to Eugenia and was sure he heard her laugh softly behind him as he determinedly set off across the room.

Phoebe definitely brightened as she saw him coming, a smile curving her soft lips. He used a broad shoulder to nudge his way into the circle of admirers and offered a respectful bow. "Good even, Miss Faraday."

"Queen Phoebe, sir!" Cobley laughed, and John eyed him askance. *Is the man already in his cups?*

"I beg Her Majesty's pardon," he said anyway and was rewarded with a full smile from Phoebe.

"You are quite forgiven, King John."

He cast about for a topic to discuss with her, though her smile threatened to drive the wits right out of his head. "Is Miss Eleanor ready for her performance after dinner?" he asked at last.

"I regret that I did not see her, but Lady Eugenia's maid Anais has spent the afternoon with Ellie and assures me she is very excited to be allowed to entertain the company."

"The child is how old?" Cobley inquired.

"Seven, sir."

"Seven, eh, and confident enough to perform before strangers?" Cobley chuckled. "Best rein in those tendencies now; else she'll put off every suitor by appearing too pushy and forward when she comes of age!"

John was quite sure he and Phoebe were both staring at Cobley in mutual dislike, and the man seemed to sense it despite his inebriation, flushing and mumbling something under his breath before retreating with unseemly haste. His two friends followed.

Phoebe let out an audible sigh. "Pushy and forward indeed," she muttered.

John nodded. "I hope nobody will ever seek to rein in Eleanor's natural high spirits," he said, "or tell her to appear less than she is merely to appease others."

"Should you ever have daughters, Major Randwyck," Phoebe said, surprising him, "I hope they will understand how lucky they are to have a father such as you."

John floundered helplessly for a response to that remarkable sentiment, sure his ears were turning red. All he could envision when he tried to imagine daughters of his own was Phoebe surrounded by darling little girls with her wide green eyes.

Thankfully, he was saved by the butler entering the room to announce that dinner was served. Nothing could be more natural than for him to offer his arm to Phoebe and invite her to accompany him in. She accepted with a shy glance sideways at him, and an unfamiliar feeling of tenderness coiled in the pit of his belly as he looked at her slender, delicate hand placed on his sleeve.

Eugenia had the happy habit of not insisting everyone be placed at table according to her satisfaction, reserving only her own place at one end and Edmund's at the other. Everyone else sat wherever they wished, so there was nothing to keep John from holding a chair for Phoebe and then taking the one beside her.

"I normally take my meals with Ellie in her rooms," Phoebe leaned close to confide, "so I pray you will forgive me if I fail to be a scintillating conversationalist. I am not in the habit of making polite adult conversation any more, I'm afraid."

"Miss Faraday, you have never been less than delightfully interesting in our every conversation to date," John said with perfect truth, "including the conversations of which Eleanor was a part. Failing all else, you might tutor me in languages; my French and Spanish are well-practiced of late, but my German is sadly rusty."

She let out a soft peal of laughter and turned eyes brimming with mirth up to his. "If you wish it, sir! Though all of my languages are of the schoolroom quality. I fear I never have had the chance to travel and consult with native speakers."

"Should you like to?" he asked curiously.

"Very much." She looked briefly wistful before shaking her head. "Though I could not wish for a more comfortable situation than residing in this household, I admit the opportunity to travel would be wonderful. I did suggest once—now the war is over—it might perhaps be of educational benefit to Eleanor to travel to the Continent with her parents, if they were so inclined. But Lord Edmund looked so aghast at the idea I never mentioned it again."

"Edmund is a landsman, I'm afraid." John chuckled reminiscently. "He would likely be open to touring England and

Scotland, but if you suggest a sea crossing, he will find any excuse to avoid it. I distinctly recall him becoming decidedly nauseous even when sailing on the lake near our mutual uncle's seat at Chawley."

"That explains a good deal," Phoebe agreed. "Well, I have seen little of Great Britain save for Cambridge, here, and my uncle's house at Hatfield where I lived with my great-aunt for a time. Perhaps I should suggest a tour of the Lake District as an alternative."

John nodded in agreement. By now everyone was seated, and the servants were bringing in the soup course. Conversation quieted as the diners applied themselves to their meal.

"Should you care to travel again, Major?" Phoebe asked when he laid his spoon down. "For pleasure, I mean, now that the war is over?"

"I should, indeed." He debated with himself briefly before confiding in her. "I have been offered a post as an aide to our Ambassador at the Danish royal court."

Phoebe's eyes flew very wide. "Oh, how exciting!" she gasped. "Shall you accept?"

"I am seriously considering it."

"Of course, you have been out of England a long time. It would be quite understandable if you wished to settle down," Phoebe said thoughtfully.

"That's not the reason for my hesitation," John admitted. "My former commanding officer, who has recommended me for the post, advised me that it would be beneficial for me to be married before taking up the position."

"Oh." Phoebe was in the process of taking a sip from her barely-touched wineglass, but she set it down again abruptly. "Of course, a diplomat's wife is his right hand, is she not?"

"She is." He chose his next words carefully. "A lady with a knowledge of, and talent for, languages would be a superior choice."

"Oh," Phoebe said again. "Well. Young ladies entering the Marriage Mart are very well educated, you'll find. I'm sure Miss Cottesloe, for example, would have an excellent working knowledge of French and Italian at the very least." She inclined her head toward the pretty child who'd been hanging around him for the last two days.

John sighed. "Without disrespect to Miss Cottesloe," he said, "she is neither more nor less than every other milk-and-water miss who has been presented to me as a potential bride since I expressed my intention of seeking one. A very pleasant young lady with the emphasis on *young*."

"Time will fix that soon enough," Phoebe answered.

He barked a short laugh. "Quite correct, as always, Miss Faraday, but throwing such an innocent into the intrigues of a royal court would be as kind as introducing a sheep to a wolf pack."

She giggled behind a gloved hand, eyes sparkling. "What a sorry image that evokes!"

"I could not be so cruel, you see. Therefore, I'd be inclined to a wife with a little more knowledge of the world. One who has seen more than the very upper echelons of high society, who has an understanding of the way the common man lives—the common man of whose existence a debutante like Miss Cottesloe is probably barely aware even exists."

"Not only young ladies," Phoebe agreed dryly, glancing across the table as Mr. Cobley roared with laughter at some feeble jest by his dinner partner. "There are plenty of gentlemen who do not notice the existence of those not clothed in silks and satins."

"You understand, then," John said gratefully.

"Oh, indeed." She tapped a finger against her lips thoughtfully, drawing his attention once again to their softness. "Hm. Would you consider a young lady many would consider a bluestocking? I have another cousin, Miss Arabella Flyte…"

John suppressed the urge to place his head on the pristine tablecloth and groan. He was making a dreadful mess of this. "Miss Faraday, I have already met a most admirable young lady. One who fits every criteria I could possibly want fulfilled in a wife and would make any diplomat a partner to be proud of. I appear to be making the most appalling mull of expressing my admiration for her, however."

He stared at her intently, willing her to take his meaning. After a moment, her lips parted on a soundless gasp, her eyes widening until he could see white all around the bright green of her irises.

*

Phoebe was saved from having to respond to the major's stunning declaration—for declaration it clearly was—by the arrival of the next course. Convention dictated that she must turn to the person seated on her other side to engage in conversation. She was intensely aware of Randwyck beside her, though, his shoulder in his red dress coat not quite touching hers as he cut his meat.

The man on her other side was a gentleman to whom she had been introduced but nothing more. He seemed to have little time for conversation between applying himself to his food and wine. The gentleman instead whiled his time listening to Edmund holding forth as he regaled his end of the table with an account of the Boxing Day fox hunt, which left Phoebe alone with her thoughts.

Could Randwyck really be serious about considering her as a suitable wife? She had the facility for and knowledge of languages he said he required, and at six and twenty, she was no debutante and had indeed seen something of the world. However, she was quite untraveled and had no connections which could be advantageous to an ambitious man looking to make a career in the diplomatic service.

Though Randwyck hadn't actually said that was his intention, had he? He'd said only that he'd been offered the post.

He had not mentioned love, of course, but then, why should he? They scarcely knew each other, and marrying for love was considered a mawkishly sentimental idea in this age. Still, she both liked and respected him, and that was a far better beginning than so many couples who married only for advantage ever had.

When the lamb was cleared away and a fish course set out, she turned back to Randwyck with so many questions burning her tongue that she hardly knew which to ask first. "What comes after Denmark?" she asked baldly and rather awkwardly, but he seemed to understand her.

"That rather depends on how things go in Copenhagen, I dare say. If I make a mull of things, the Foreign Office will thank me politely for my service and not offer me another post." He shrugged. "I have an estate of my own, which has been left in the hands of capable stewards these last years. It could comfortably support a family and is not entailed, incidentally. Should I father no sons, a daughter might inherit."

It would be impolite to ask about the income from his estate, so she bit back the urge. Surely Eugenia would be able to supply that information anyway, likely without being asked. "Would you *like* to advance in the diplomatic service?" she hesitantly asked instead.

"Perhaps," he replied. Phoebe thought she respected him all the more for his honesty and the way he paused to consider the matter. "I don't honestly know the answer to your question because I don't yet know whether I will enjoy the work!" His smile invited her to join him in his amusement, and he continued, "However, I do think I should enjoy an opportunity to travel more, and if His Majesty's government sees fit to compensate me for it, then that's all well and good."

"Understandable." Phoebe nodded in agreement. "Essentially, then, your future plans are subject to change?"

"Yes, but I assure you that my wife would always have a say in any decisions I made." He gave her a very earnest look. "I should wish for her wise counsel on all matters, and from what I have learned of you thus far, I think you would not hesitate to tell me if I was making a serious error of judgment."

She hesitated before voicing her next remark because to her, at least, it was a significant mark against her. "A wife with more noble connections would be of more use to you in the advancement of a diplomatic career."

Again, he gave her point due consideration before answering. "Only, I think, if I aspired to an ambassadorship, and I don't believe I do. A little too much bowing and scraping would be required for a plain-spoken military man like myself to comfortably stomach."

Phoebe couldn't imagine the major abasing himself to anyone. Eating a few bites of fish, she tried to think of another question, but she was in a state of shock at the mere fact of his suggesting an interest in her. Or had he actually proposed to her? How were these things supposed to go? She was above the age of majority and therefore had no legal guardian, but she supposed that Lord Edmund should be applied to for his approval.

"Should I accept the post in Copenhagen, I would be expected to depart in March." Randwyck's low-voiced remark brought her attention back to him. "Thus, there would be plenty of time to call the banns, or if you should require more time to make up your mind, I could obtain a special license and we could marry in London immediately before departure."

The fish tasted of nothing. Placing her fork down, Phoebe took a deep breath. "I will consider your offer, sir. You do me a very great honor, but one I confess to being caught unprepared for." Willing him to understand, she looked at him pleadingly.

"I am honored you will even take the time to consider it, Miss Faraday," he replied, his expression reassuringly calm. "I am at your disposal if you think of any further questions you would like answered, or you can apply to my cousin Edmund for confirmation of my character."

That, at least, she was sure she did not need. Major John Randwyck was as honest and straightforward a man as she had ever met, and she thought one of the most noble despite his lack of a title. "When do you depart Holt Manor?" she asked.

"Four days hence, though I can easily delay my departure if need be."

"I will have an answer for you before that." It wouldn't take four days for her to make up her mind. Every instinct shouted at her to accept him now before he had second thoughts and withdrew the offer, but she would not leap blindly into something which would have such far reaching effects on her future. Nor would it be fair to make such a decision without at least consulting with Edmund and Eugenia. Though considering the way Eugenia was watching her and the major with a little smirk on her face, Phoebe thought Eugenia was rather pleased with her matchmaking efforts.

For the rest of the meal, they discussed innocuous topics, safe topics. For the life of her, Phoebe could not have recalled afterward what was said. At last Eugenia announced it was time for the ladies to retire to the music-room.

"We shall permit you gentlemen twenty minutes to enjoy your port and blow a cloud for those of you who wish to," Eugenia advised, "and then your presence is *required* to applaud my daughter's performance. Am I making myself clear, Edmund?" She sent her husband an admonishing glance.

"I would not miss Eleanor's performance for the world, my dear," Edmund promised dutifully.

Phoebe slipped away to go and collect Eleanor, delighted to see her charge beautifully dressed in her best gown with her hair prettily braided and pinned up. "My, don't you look lovely!" Phoebe admired.

"Am I really to perform for all the grown-up guests?" Ellie asked, her eyes huge with excitement.

"You are, my darling, and I know you'll be brilliant because I've heard you practice. It'll be just like our practices, in fact, because I'll be playing along with you as I always do."

"Everyone will be looking at me." Ellie was showing nerves, which was rather unlike the normally precocious child, but then doing anything for the first time could be nerve-wracking, Phoebe thought.

"You can close your eyes if that helps," Phoebe suggested. "Pretend it's just the two of us. Or look at your mama or papa, I know how proud and happy they are that you're coming down to sing for their friends."

Entering the music-room clinging tightly to Phoebe's hand, it wasn't long before Ellie's customary confidence reasserted itself, and the little girl was soon sitting beside her mother being made much of by Eugenia's friends.

Phoebe busied herself sorting the sheet music at the pianoforte, though she knew the music she would play to accompany Ellie's song by heart. She was seated there alone when the gentlemen entered the room and found herself more than slightly flustered when Major Randwyck came immediately to her side.

"Do you need someone to turn the pages for you while you play for Eleanor?" the major offered.

"I thank you for such a kind offer, but I have the song memorized." Phoebe smiled her thanks. "When you play only the same piece of music several times every day for a month or two, it becomes very familiar. I could probably play it with my eyes closed."

"Well, I will not challenge you to do so, but I do believe you could if you set your mind to it." His smile was warm, admiring. It made her feel butterflies of excitement in her stomach. Shyly, Phoebe looked away, shuffling sheets of music to give her trembling hands something to do.

Fortunately, Eugenia brought Ellie over a moment later and clapped her hands to demand everyone's attention. "My daughter Eleanor has graciously consented to open this evening's entertainment for us with a song. She will be accompanied on the pianoforte by my cousin Miss Faraday—excuse me, I mean Queen Phoebe." She cast a laughing look at Phoebe who smiled in return.

Ellie's song began quietly, but within moments the child had gained confidence and raised up her sweet little voice to give a performance which met with universal acclaim. Flushed with pleasure at the applause, Ellie reached for Phoebe's hand and urged her to rise to take a bow too before giving her a tight hug.

"You were wonderful, darling," Phoebe murmured proudly. "Go and give your mama a kiss and say goodnight, now. And Papa too. Then I'll take you upstairs."

"Oh! But Mama promised she and Papa would sing next and I could stay to listen to them!" Ellie gave her an appealing look.

Phoebe smiled. "I would not deny you that pleasure, darling."

"Uncle John has saved seats for us, look!" Ellie towed her over to Major Randwyck who was sitting alone at one end of a small settee. "Did you like my song, Uncle John?" she demanded at once.

"You sang beautifully," Randwyck assured her. "I cannot recall when last I was treated to such a professional musical performance."

Phoebe appreciated that he didn't wink at her over Eleanor's head or allow even a hint of amusement to enter his tone as he spoke. She was sure he couldn't be entirely in earnest, but nothing about his demeanor would have given that away to Ellie who settled down with a happy smile as Eugenia took her seat at the pianoforte. Edmund stood beside his wife with one loving hand on her shoulder.

"Well, we are about to be thoroughly eclipsed, I'm afraid," Phoebe said quietly, leaning toward Randwyck. "Have you heard these two perform?"

"I have not, but by your words, I sense we are all in for a treat?"

Phoebe smiled but said nothing. She kept her eyes on Randwyck as Eugenia began to play, and the room quieted. She wondered how he would react and what he would think of the performance.

Eugenia was no virtuoso at the pianoforte. While she and Edmund both had pleasant enough voices, nobody would ever have called them great singers when they performed alone. Together, though, something magical and wondrous seemed to happen. The love and happiness in their marriage shone through somehow in the harmony they achieved in their duet. Phoebe could have listened to them perform all night.

"Ahh," Randwyck gave a soft sigh of pleasure as the last notes died away; he rose to his feet, along with everyone else, to applaud. "You were quite correct, Miss Faraday," he turned to Phoebe, nodding. "That was truly something wondrous."

Eleanor ran to her parents to congratulate them and to receive her due in embraces and goodnight wishes. Smiling fondly at the lovely picture the little family made, Phoebe glanced up at the major and said, "My parents were as well-suited and as happy together as Edmund and Eugenia are."

Randwyck nodded, his expression serious. "You desire such a partnership for yourself, of course."

"I do." She chose her next words carefully, hoping he would take her meaning. "I also believe strong marriages require work… from both parties. Such harmony as you see with these two does not happen overnight but takes years to grow from a foundation of mutual admiration and respect."

*

She seemed to be looking for reassurance, for a reason to accept his proposal, and he was more than happy to give it to her. Nobody was looking in their direction, so John took Phoebe's hand in his, giving it a gentle press. "I am willing to make the effort, Phoebe, and please let me assure you that I already respect and admire you greatly. I expect those sentiments to increase immeasurably as I come to know you better."

For a long moment, she met his eyes fearlessly, searching his expression. She was looking for proof of his sincerity, he supposed. He held her gaze and waited.

"Thank you," Phoebe murmured at last. "If you will excuse me, Major, I must see Eleanor to bed." Her small hand slipped from his, and John was suddenly overwhelmed with a feeling of loss.

"Will you return to join us afterward?" he asked, more out of hope than expectation.

She was already shaking her head, confirming his suspicions. "Ellie's excited and will take some settling, and I'm afraid I'm feeling very tired. I'll seek my own bed once she's asleep."

"Will you walk with me tomorrow?" he pleaded, not caring that he was showing perhaps too much of just how badly he wanted to spend more time with her. He had a few days, at best, to convince Phoebe to accept his suit, and he didn't want to waste any time. 'He who hesitates is lost' as he'd so often heard.

His boldness brought a reward in the form of a joyous smile, which lit up Phoebe's whole face. "I shall try to make time," she said, "but if you wouldn't mind a little extra company…"

John took her meaning immediately. "Of course I should be delighted to accompany you and my niece on a walk," he said. "Eleanor can act as our chaperone." He kept his tone deliberately light and teasing, accompanying the words with a wink.

Phoebe laughed, bright and clear, and John saw heads turn toward them. People were starting to take notice of the way they stood close together. Decorously, he stepped back to create space between them, allowing her to move away to collect Eleanor and remove her from the party.

With Phoebe gone, all the light seemed to have left the room. John found he could take no more enjoyment from the evening's proceedings. Quietly making excuses to Eugenia, who looked at him with a knowing eye but waved him away, he slipped out of the room and made his way to his rooms. He had the feeling he would not find restful sleep until Phoebe had given him her answer.

*

The morning, thankfully, brought a note from Phoebe delivered by one of the footmen as John ate his breakfast, advising that she and Ellie would be delighted to have his company on a morning walk around ten o'clock. John didn't bother trying to restrain his obvious pleasure as he read the note. Edmund, sitting alongside him, immediately asked what he was grinning about.

"I am anticipating a pleasant walk with two lovely ladies," John answered, folding the note back up and tucking it into his pocket. "Your daughter and Miss Faraday."

Well, I daresay Miss Faraday will be a suitable enough chaperone for you and Eleanor," Edmund quipped with a chuckle.

"We'll see how sanguine you are about the prospect of Eleanor going walking with unmarried gentlemen when she's a bit older," John answered dryly, making Edmund chortle and nod.

"Fair point, cuz! Enjoy your walk. Rather you than me, though; it's cold out there today."

"I understand Copenhagen's a deal colder, so I'd best get used to it." Even as he spoke, John wondered how much Phoebe knew about Denmark beyond the history of its royal lineage. Perhaps he would offer to loan her one of the books he'd brought with him to read: accounts by Englishmen who'd traveled in the Scandinavian countries. He'd be happy to give her the book, in truth, but was quite certain she'd refuse to accept such a gift.

Returning to his rooms to fetch his greatcoat, he chose one of the books and put it in his pocket. He'd ask Phoebe if she would like to read it, at least. He would not have her make any decisions without being fully informed.

Eleanor made him a cheerful greeting and promptly skipped off down the carriageway, so John and Phoebe set off at a brisk pace after the skipping child. After a few steps, John pulled the book from his pocket and offered it to Phoebe.

"What's this, Major Randwyck?" she asked, accepting it and turning it in her hands to read the title. "*A Year in the North?*"

"Something I thought you might find of interest. Call it research, if you will. You might even wish to read it with Eleanor as a topic of education."

Phoebe tucked one hand into his arm to steady herself, thumbing through a few pages of the small book with her other hand as she walked. "How interesting. And how very thoughtful of you." She flicked a glance up at him and smiled. "Were you thinking this might help me make my decision?"

"Indeed, whether you ultimately decide in favor of my offer or otherwise, I would not have you do so without being as fully informed as it is in my power to make you. Having not yet visited Denmark myself, this second-hand account is, unfortunately, the best I have to offer on that topic. If there is anything else you would know of me, be it my circumstances or my plans, you need only ask. I will answer to the best of my abilities."

"Every word out of your mouth, sir, makes me more inclined to accept you, I must say," Phoebe said, startling him.

"I beg your pardon?"

"Your every word and action shows a consideration for my feelings and sensibilities. Something I had never expected to be shown by any man, much less a potential suitor. It does you great credit."

"Oh." Feeling a little embarrassed, John looked away but then back down at her, puzzlement creasing his brow. "I'm but a soldier, Miss Faraday. Plain speaking and honesty are all I have to offer instead of pretty words. If you don't mind the lack, I think we might do well together."

Her lips twitched, her eyes dancing with what he thought was amusement. "Well, with a career in the diplomatic service ahead of you, perhaps we should work on that."

"We?" he queried, feeling suddenly hopeful.

"I have decided to accept your offer, Major." Her smile was shy, but bright. "John."

"But you haven't read the book yet," he said stupidly, unable to comprehend why she should have made the decision without doing so.

"The very fact that you thought to give it to me is enough." Phoebe squeezed his arm.

Shaking his head, John tried to comprehend, before realizing he was trying to understand the unknowable: the mind of a woman. "I am more honored than I know how to express. I will do my best to continue as you seem to think I have begun."

Phoebe's laugh was joyous, carrying in the cold, clear air. Ahead of them on the path, Eleanor paused in her skipping to glance back.

Her eyes shot to her uncle and Phoebe walking close together, John's hand placed protectively over Phoebe's where it was tucked into the crook of his arm. Eleanor grinned and let out a happy giggle.

"Not too far ahead, Ellie," Phoebe called after her as Eleanor resumed her skipping.

"I suspect we owe Miss Eleanor a great debt of gratitude," John said. "For without her contrivance to ensure you received the pea from the Twelfth Night cake, you likely would never have allowed me to spend enough time in your company to persuade you to consider me."

"You realized she did that?" Phoebe turned laughing eyes up to him. "Three beans was doing it up a touch too brown, though."

"She just wanted to make sure you'd have the best chance of finding at least one suitor you would like, I think." He squeezed her fingers gently. "I'm very glad I found one of the beans."

"So am I," Phoebe agreed. "Oh, John… so am I!"

About the Author

Growing up in North Wales in a house for which the foundations were originally laid in the 14th century, Catherine Bilson's interest in history was probably inevitable, but she despised the 20th century geopolitics which passed for history at school. Instead, she devoured every historical novel she could lay her hands on and found her greatest joy in the clever social commentary and witty repartee of Jane Austen.

When she moved to Stevenage in Hertfordshire for work in the late 1990s, she could not help but imagine Old Town Stevenage as Meryton and the nearby Knebworth House as Netherfield.

She married an Australian and moved to Queensland in 2001, far from the history she had grown up with, and it was then she started to write historical romance herself.

Website: www.catherinebilson.com
Facebook: www.facebook.com/catherinebilsonauthor

The Boy Next Door
♥
Mei Edwards

Story Information

Holiday: Wave All Your Fingers at Your Neighbors Day
Holiday Date: February 7
Heat Rating: 0
Relationship Type: M/F
Major Trigger Warnings: None

Jane is supposed to be on vacation. One whole week to relax and unwind, if only she can tear herself away from her work. Fortunately, there's a distraction over the fence. She hasn't seen Toby in years, and the connection is immediate. But when push comes to shove, is she willing to take a chance on a holiday romance?

The Boy Next Door

"Put your phone down, Jane, you're not at work anymore. You've barely touched your breakfast."

Jane Spencer frowned at her mom but complied, spearing a dainty slice of her pancake with her fork and dousing it in the puddle of syrup on her plate. "Just because I'm on vacation doesn't mean I can ignore my emails. I didn't slave through five years of law school to get fired for missing an important announcement."

"You've barely been there a year. Surely nothing is that important?"

Mouth full of pancake, Jane shrugged, glancing over at her upturned screen as if to reassure herself that nothing had come through during the last two minutes. Just in case, she checked her notifications to be sure.

Her mom noticed and sighed. "I have a meeting with the church board and am having lunch with the ladies in town afterward. Will you be all right on your own?"

"I'm twenty-four, not ten," Jane reminded her mom. "I think I'll be okay on my own. I can take advantage of the sun, maybe get some reading done. I need to decide where I'm meeting Maddie for dinner tomorrow."

"You could always have her over, she hasn't been around in years—no, I have the admin committee meeting here this month. Well, I'm sure you'll work something out. As long as you're not glued to your phone the entire day, dear."

"Be glad I left my work laptop at home," Jane muttered.

"Oh, I am." With a quick kiss to the forehead and a flurried search for her keys, her mom was gone.

Jane took a little longer over breakfast, waiting until her mom was well out of the house before sneaking another look at her phone. A new email had arrived in her personal inbox, one of those fun facts of the day that made her co-workers roll their eyes.

Holiday of the day! the email announced. *Today is 'Wave All Your Fingers at Your Neighbors Day!'*

Stuffing another bite of pancake into her mouth, Jane clicked through to the website and read the blurb. She didn't even know her parents' current neighbors. A young family had moved in on one side in her first year away from home, and old Mr. Dale on the other side had passed away six months ago, leaving the house to be sold by his out-of-town heirs. From the view from her second-story bedroom window, the new owners were using the summer to put in a new deck.

With breakfast done, Jane grabbed a hat and her book, pulled her straight brown hair into a ponytail, slathered sunscreen on her pale skin, and headed outside. Even though it was still early in the day, the temperature was ticking ever higher. She was grateful that she'd thought to pack her loose capris and old band shirts—the ones she'd loved so much that the logos had faded into obscurity. Thankfully, the hammock her dad had put up during her high school years hung half in the shade. Opting to keep her head uncovered, she dropped her hat by the door and settled in to read with one of her long, thin legs resting idly on the ground to keep up a steady swaying motion.

During her studies, reading had been a chore. Now that she was accredited, it was taking longer than she'd expected for it to become a joy again. The mountain of reading she had to do for work probably didn't help. Bored with the modern classic she'd picked up from the airport bookstore, she'd grabbed a tattered paperback from her mom's collection instead.

Surprisingly, Jane became so engrossed in the book, it took her awhile to realize the sun had shifted overhead, bathing the entire hammock in light and reflecting off the page. She put the book down, blinking hard to dispel the black spots floating in front of her eyes. From the sounds over the fence, the new neighbors were working on their deck.

Jane disentangled herself from the hammock to grab her discarded hat, using the opportunity to study the guy on the other side of the slatted wooden fence. With messy black hair, deep brown skin that spoke of Māori ancestry, and facing away from her, he was industriously sawing away at a piece of wood in a way that highlighted his rather nice biceps.

Something about him seemed familiar. Jane tried to recall if her mom had mentioned the name of the family who had moved in. Of course, he could have been a hired builder, but she could see the empty driveway from her spot and hadn't heard a van pull onto their sleepy street.

With a mental shrug, she returned to the hammock, settling in again as the rhythmic sounds from next door switched from sawing to hammering. Now facing the other way, she had an excellent view of their neighbor, one she carefully ignored in favor of her book. It wouldn't do to get caught staring.

After another few chapters, the noises next door halted with a crash and a curse, causing her to look up from her book to meet the gaze of the boy next door. He was waving his left hand in a way that indicated the hammer in his right had found his thumb rather than a nail, but when their eyes met, he stilled.

Her cheeks flushed. Jane went to look away but remembered the email from earlier. One hand held her place in her book and the other rose to give him a wave, a wave he returned with his injured hand an amused tilt to his lips that brought the familiarity from before into sharp recognition.

"Toby?"

Warm brown eyes widened before settling on her own face. "Jane? Jane Spencer?"

She nodded, hopping out of the hammock to approach the fence. "Yeah. I haven't seen you since… huh, since middle school. That was twelve years ago, can you believe it?"

"Can't be. Twelve years?" He shook his head and put the hammer down; Jane did the same with her book. "We were in a band together," Toby said. "For like a month, remember?"

Jane's jaw dropped. "I'd forgotten that! For the inter-school rock quest! What was our band name again? Star Power?"

"Lost Stars, I think." He walked across the yard to lean over the fence.

"Of course." Jane nodded, shading her eyes with her hand so she could look up at him. "That was Carrie's idea, wasn't it?"

"Yeah. You two still friends?"

"Actually, we are! We catch up every Friday over lunch." Jane smiled wistfully, her fingers picking at her faded shirt. "Remember that original song we played for the rock quest? Egg something?"

A grin split Toby's face. "*Chicken or the Egg?*"

"Yes, that was it! Man, you're really good at remembering this stuff. We were so proud of that song."

"Did you know I wrote it?"

"No! Really?"

"Well, we, me and Henry Maclean. He played the guitar as well, remember? We were good mates back then. Didn't go to the same high school, so we kinda lost touch." Toby shrugged lightly.

Jane screwed up her face in memory. "I think he went to mine, might've been in my chem class. But how have you been? What are you doing next door?"

"My folks moved in a few months ago, and Dad has me putting in a deck. Says it's time for me to pay for room and board now I'm living with them again. What about you? I haven't seen you out here before, and I've been working on this thing for weeks." Toby gestured in the general direction of the house.

"Oh, I'm on holiday. I've got some vacation time, so I'm back here staying with my parents for a week. They've lived here all my life."

"I didn't realize. I've seen them around a few times but didn't know they were your parents. Hey, I need to get back to working on the deck, the weather forecast says it's going to pack up and rain tomorrow, and I want to get this bit done before that." He flashed her a shy smile. "You want to catch up sometime? Like over coffee?"

Jane hesitated, before remembering the entire reason she was back in town was to catch up with people. She had no meetings, no agenda other than the one she wanted to set. "Sure! Tomorrow afternoon, okay?"

"Absolutely. Do you have a favorite place in mind? I don't know the cafes on this side of town."

Jane cast her mind back to after-school hot chocolates. "Do you know Sierra, outside the mall?"

Toby nodded. "By the Warehouse? Yeah. Shall I meet you there at three?"

"Sounds like a plan."

Grinning, he turned back to his building, and Jane returned to the hammock—but not before scooping up her phone to text her friend Carrie, nestling the phone between the pages of her book to hide her actions.

Hey remember Toby Kahui from the band in middle school? Turns out he lives next door. Moved in with his parents who bought the house after our neighbor died

Carrie's reply was swift. *What? That's hilarious! He still tall and gawky?*

Jane cast her eyes across the fence and took her time in replying. *No. Well, he's still tall. What are you up to today?*

Instead of a message, her phone lit up with an incoming call. Peeking over at Toby, Jane decided to risk answering it from her place in the hammock. "Hey, Carrie!"

Carrie launched straight into it, not bothering with a greeting. "You changed the subject. Does that mean he's hot now?"

"No comment."

She could her friend's peals of laughter through the phone. "I'll take that as a yes. Can you set us up?"

"C, you have a boyfriend."

"Fine, you date him."

"Um..."

"No way! When are you going on the date? You're only in town for a week!"

"It's not a date," Jane hissed, risking another look over the fence. "It's more of a catch up, okay? I haven't seen the guy in years."

"Yeah, but you sound interested."

"Well, I'm not. Okay, maybe a little, but you know I'm not interested in dating."

"Sweetie, please. That was months ago."

"Can we not talk about that? That was on me, I'm too busy for a relationship right now."

Carrie snorted. "You are so full of—"

Jane cut her off. "Bye, Carrie! See you at Friday lunch next week."

"But I didn't even tell you about my day!" Carrie protested, still laughing as Jane ended the call.

*

The little cafe was bustling as Jane arrived. Small tables spilled from the open front onto the sidewalk, full of kids in familiar uniforms huddling close to avoid the rain. She came to a halt under the awning, pulling back the hood of her old blue raincoat as she looked around. Maybe she should have borrowed her mother's gumboots to go with her jeans and blouse instead of the simple, and now soaked, ballet flats she was sporting. Unfortunately there was no sign of Toby. Reaching into her back pocket, she pulled out her phone.

"Jane!"

She turned as Toby approached, one arm raised in a wave and the other shielding his face from the downpour. He took in the crowd with a raised eyebrow. "I didn't think it would be so busy. Lot of kids here."

"Yeah, it was hangout of choice when I was at St. Catherine's. We used to come here after school, seems like it's pretty popular still. You went to Whangarei High, didn't you?"

"I did. It's closer to our end of town." Toby grimaced. "Or where we used to live, I guess. You want to fight the crowds here?"

Jane considered their options. "As nice as it would be to revisit puberty, you know, I'd rather not. Everyone here is so small. Mum mentioned a cafe that took over the garage on the corner. You want to check it out instead?"

Toby grinned, the crooked smile creasing his face. "Sure."

The cafe on the corner was a bit more pricey but not nearly as crowded. They ordered at the counter—a trim flat white for her and a long black for him—and there was a brief struggle over who got to pay. The cashier, her name tag reading *Allie*, watched with an amused smile.

"I haven't seen you in years, it's my treat," Toby insisted.

"That argument works just as well for me as it does for you," Jane countered, sliding her credit card to the cashier. "Besides, Allie was in my class." She gave Toby a sunny smile as the machine beeped in acknowledgment, and Allie passed her card back. "See?"

Toby groaned. "Foiled by nepotism."

She laughed. "It's not what you know; it's who you know. You can pay next time."

"I'll hold you to that," Toby promised. "Allie stands as witness. Right, Allie?"

"Sure." Allie passed them a number to take to a table. "You can sit anywhere, we're not too busy. Good to see you, Jane."

"You too, Allie." Jane led the way to one of the tables by the window. "So what have you been up to these last few years?"

"Not much, really. Went to college, changed up my major a few times, and ended up with a degree in teaching."

"Teaching? What level?"

"High school, teaching music. I did what everyone said and picked music because I wanted to share some of that around. Sure didn't help me get a job, so I'm crashing with my parents while I work out what I'm gonna do with my life. What about you?"

"Studied law on top of a BA in history. I'm clerking at a firm in Wellington while I study for the bar." Toby let out a low whistle, and Jane fought not to cringe. "It sounds like I'm boasting, doesn't it?"

"What? No! Damn, I'm impressed. Who would've thought the girl who set the curtains on fire during science would grow up to be a lawyer?"

"I'm not there yet, and it's not my fault the Bunsen burner was too close to the curtains!" She narrowed her eyes. "How did you hear about that, anyway? That was during high school!"

Toby smiled. "I have my sources." At her look, he threw up his hands defensively. "One of my mates, who was in your class, mentioned it. I always thought it sounded hilarious." He settled back. "How come they had curtains in the science labs? Isn't that a health and safety hazard?"

"Yeah, probably. They didn't even get rid of them after that, though. They just replaced the one that got a bit singed."

The waiter arrived with their coffees. Though Jane thought he looked familiar, she couldn't remember his name. Meanwhile, once he'd put down the drinks, Toby greeted him with that clasped hand and back slap all guys seemed to use. Jane took the opportunity to sneak a look at her phone, but her only email was a workmate complaining about the constant construction on their road.

"Ouch!"

She looked up to see Toby clapping a hand to his heart. "I'm that boring, huh?"

"No, I—I'm sorry. Couldn't resist."

"The firm falling apart without you?"

"Absolutely. No one there knows how to set the curtains on fire." Jane slid the phone into her bag. "Okay, out of sight, out of mind, right?"

"Only as long as you're not talking about spiders."

Jane laughed. "Lots of those at your parents' place?"

"No, thank goodness. Except for under the house, so you won't catch me crawling under there to do the insulation installation. Dad can get a contractor in for that."

"So if you're not doing the insulation, what are you doing?"

"Oh, this and that. Dad wants an office, Mum wants a deck—like you saw—and they want to convert the sleepout to a granny flat, but they'll have to get a qualified plumber and electrician for that. I'm just the cheap labor."

"You looked pretty handy with that saw."

"You were watching?"

Jane fought the blush rising in her cheeks. "I may have happened to see, yes. You might have noticed that the fence isn't particularly high."

"Of course." He smiled ruefully. "Probably means you saw me get my thumb with the hammer. I managed to go weeks without injuring myself, then the first time a pretty girl is watching, bang."

"If it helps, I wasn't watching at that exact moment." She tried not to dwell on the compliment, though it felt like her cheeks were on fire.

He considered her answer. "I'll take the win."

"So how did you get so experienced at the whole building a deck thing? Surely you didn't learn it off a YouTube tutorial."

"That's not a bad idea, but really my mate Brandon's dad was a carpenter, and I used to do some work for him. It was a pretty good time, if I'm being honest, and I learned enough to help my parents with some of the renovation."

"I'm sure they are very grateful for the help."

"Absolutely, and I'm glad I can do something for them. Least I can do after they helped me get a degree and put me up after said degree failed to help in the job stakes."

"It can't be that bad, can it?"

Toby made a face. "Most of the jobs going were unpaid teacher aide positions, and I needed to pay rent. Anything that paid also required experience, which I have exactly zero of." He cocked his head. "What about you? How'd you get your foot in the door?"

"I did a summer internship at this firm before my last year of law school, and they offered me a job after graduation."

"They must really have liked you; I'm impressed."

She shook her head. "Don't be. They wanted cheap labor over summer and hired most of us back because it's easier than hiring graduates fresh."

Toby narrowed his eyes. "Why are you being so down on yourself? You're doing great; it's nothing to be ashamed of."

"I—I guess I feel like I'm being up myself, you know? And I don't want you to think I'm like this super lawyer like in *Suits* or something. I can't even call myself a lawyer yet."

"You can't?"

"No, not until I pass the bar later this year. If I pass."

"What happens if you don't?"

"I'll probably be fired and be homeless for a while." She grinned. "Might have to live with my parents again."

"Can confirm: always an option."

Jane took a long drink from her coffee, savoring the taste. The coffees at work were never this good, but she needed at least two to make it through the day so she tended to gulp those down as fast as possible.

Toby looked up from his own drink and paused. "You—uh—you have a little…" He gestured to her face.

"What?" Mortified, Jane pulled out a mirror to see the coffee mustache adorning her upper lip. She grabbed a napkin to wipe it off, also smearing off the lipstick she'd tried on this morning. She sighed. "Congratulations, me. I knew the lippie was a mistake." She wasn't big into makeup; she never had the time these days. But she'd wanted to look nice for Toby, even if she didn't want her appearance to scream that she wanted to look nice for Toby.

"I thought it looked nice," Toby offered as if reading her mind.

Jane flapped a hand at him. "I've already managed to get most of it on the napkin, no need to compliment me now."

"Then, at least, you have a pretty good-looking napkin."

"Flatterer."

"Me? Flat? I'm perfectly three-dimensional, thank you very much."

Groaning, Jane balled up the offending napkin and threw it at his head. "That was terrible."

"I know." Toby ducked his head and tried to look contrite. "Can you ever forgive me? Or am I forever—" he gestured at the blackboard behind him, "—off the menu?"

Jane snickered before she could help herself. "You're a dork."

"Yeah, but you love it."

"Do I though?" At Toby's alarmed look, she laughed. "I kinda do, to be honest. I'd forgotten how funny you were."

Toby clasped his hands beneath his chin and batted his eyelashes. "You think I'm funny?"

"Not if it gives you a swollen head, I don't! But if you can keep your towering ego under control, I reckon we could get along."

"I'll have to try and keep it in check, then."

The conversation fell into a lull and Jane took another sip of her coffee but found it empty. She caught sight of the time on her watch. "Oh! I have to go. I didn't realize it was so close to five o'clock."

"Dinner plans?"

"Yeah, with Maddie. Maddie Krugler, remember her?"

"Of course, you two were joined at the hip during middle school. Nice to hear you two are still friends."

Jane stood, gathering her things and fighting the urge to peek at her phone in the process. "Yeah, we both studied together, but she moved afterward, so we don't get to see each other as much as I'd like. She's back in town for a bit as well, so we finally get to catch up again."

"Sure, sure." Toby glanced down then back up at her. "Are you doing much tomorrow?"

"Was going to the beach with a couple of girls from high school, but otherwise, not really."

"Would you like to have dinner tomorrow? I know it's fast, but if you're only in town for a week—you don't have to if you don't want to or if you're busy, or—"

She could feel the smile breaking across her face. "No, I'd like that."

"You would? Great! What time?"

"We're going to the beach out past the Kamo Wildlife Sanctuary and will probably be back about five, so how about six o'clock?"

Toby grinned. The expression lit up his entire face. "Awesome. I'll pick you up at six."

*

At exactly two minutes to six the next day, the sound of a door had Jane flying down the stairs, stuffing her arms into her cardigan.

"Where are you going?" her mom called from the kitchen, giving her the strongest sense of déjà vu.

"Out!" she hollered back as she had so many times before. She paused at the kitchen to stick her head in. "I told you, I'm meeting a friend for dinner." She pulled open the front door to find Toby outside, one hand ready to knock. "Hey."

"Hey yourself." Toby cocked an eyebrow. "Were you waiting behind the door?"

Jane stepped outside, shutting the door behind her, and pointed at the open window above them. "Heard you coming."

"It could've been anyone. A lot of people live around here."

She scoffed. "Please, I've lived here all my life, I know what Mr. Dale's front door sounds like. Well, you know, your front door now."

"I don't know whether to be impressed or weirded out."

"Go with impressed, it'll make dinner less awkward. Speaking of dinner, where are we going?"

"It's a surprise. When was the last time you were here?"

"Last Christmas, why?"

"Just checking. The place I'm thinking of is new, only opened a few months ago."

On the drive there, Jane filled Toby in on her day at the beach, and he updated her on the progress of the deck now that the rain had stopped (slow, but steady). She tried to get more details about the dinner place, but on this topic, he stayed resolutely tight-lipped. He parked in town, near the waterfront, and they made their way along the boardwalk.

Jane squinted up at the restaurant they stopped in front of. "Was this Fisherman's Plate?"

"Yeah, but it shut down when we were in high school, remember? It's cycled through a few places since then, but apparently, this one is pretty good."

The maître d' led them through the restaurant and out to tables on the terrace. Despite the waterfront views, the vibe was refreshingly casual. Jane inspected the menu and looked up at the waiter. He looked vaguely familiar, in that 'I think I went to elementary school with your older sibling' way. "What do you recommend?"

"The fish of the day is very good," Jane tried to hide her grimace but the waiter must've noticed, "but tonight I would recommend the fettuccine."

"I'll have that then." She passed the waiter her menu.

"I'll have the surf n' turf," Toby said, doing the same. He looked over at her. "You don't like fish?"

"Never really liked it, or really any seafood." He looked slightly alarmed at that, and she waved a hand in dismissal. "It's not a big deal. Do you come here often?"

"Naw, only once. We came here for my mom's birthday just after it opened, and I've wanted an excuse to come back here since."

"Do you like living with your parents?"

Toby shrugged. "It's okay. I love Mum's cooking, and it's nice to see my cat, but it's weird, you know, being accountable to someone again. I got used to eating when I felt like it and cleaning when something was dirty, but my parents get upset if I don't let them know if I won't be home for dinner, and they keep a pretty strict chore schedule still." He made a face. "I love them, but I don't want to live with them forever. I just, I just don't know what else to do right now, and they don't make me pay rent, which is pretty sweet." He cocked his head at her. "What about you? What's it like being back?"

"Similar, yeah. Mom doesn't make me do chores, but she can't help but comment if I don't make the bed in the morning when she walks past, and Dad still worries if I'm out late and don't call. It's a bit different than you. I'm only home for a short time, so it's a bit like a holiday, except it's the house I grew up in."

"Do you like living down south? You live alone down there?"

Jane smiles. "Yeah, I used to live with flatmates but got myself a studio apartment when I got this job. Thought it'd be a nice change."

"And is it?"

"Uh-huh. I can come home and eat dinner whenever I want, and I know the only mess will be what I make. It gets a bit lonely sometimes, though, and I miss being able to split the cleaning."

"Bathrooms not your thing?"

"Bathrooms aren't that bad, to be honest. It's the kitchen that gets filthy in three seconds flat."

"Do you think you'll go back to living with other people?"

She had to think about it. "Maybe? I've just gotten used to living on my own. My lease finishes next year, so I've got a while to think about whether I want to renew it or not. I probably will; I don't imagine my life will look too different next year. There are some nice apartments across the road that are always looking for tenants if I want a change."

Their food arrived and conversation dwindled as they tucked in.

"This is really good," Jane mumbled around a mouthful of pasta. "I'd eat here again."

"I'm glad you like it. I think this probably makes it my favorite place in town at the moment."

"How long do you think you'll be in town for?"

"I dunno. Depends if I can get a job or not, and where."

"Well, what are you wanting to do?"

"See, that's the problem. I have no idea. I originally went to study design, but the workload was killing me, so I switched to teaching. I know there must be jobs here and there if I keep looking, but it feels like I'm selling out."

"Selling out… by getting a job?" Jane didn't try to hide her skepticism.

"I want to create stuff. I've always enjoyed working with my hands, but my parents pushed me to get a degree. They said it would be safer, especially when I switched from design to teaching, because teachers are always in demand." He grimaced. "It only sort of helps that they are very apologetic about it now given how all of that has turned out. Dad has tried to help with the whole job hunting thing, but every time I look at the jobs actually available around here, I imagine myself getting sucked into the system, and I—I can't do it."

"Sucked into the system, huh? Gee, thanks." She tried to keep her voice light but it came out sharper than she intended.

"I didn't mean it—OK, yeah I deserved that. Sorry. How do you cope?"

"With being sucked into the system?"

Toby winced.

"No, I get it. Lawyers are about as hierarchical as you get—all the partners have their own offices with little nameplates on the doors. But honestly, it's not that bad. The work is pretty interesting, most of the time, and the people I work with are great. Even when the hours get bad, I know I'm in good company."

"It's just funny, you know? You were great at the keys, I kinda figured you'd grow up to be a musician."

"Who, me?" Jane laughed. "I thought about it in high school, but it never really clicked. I still play the piano, I just play it for myself." She twirled a strand of pasta on her fork, trying to trap as much of the sauce as she could. "What about you? Still playing the guitar?"

"Kinda?" Toby popped a fry into his mouth and chewed thoughtfully. "I still have my guitar, but I haven't picked it up in months. Teachers' college was more about how to follow the curriculum than about playing. Maybe I should give it a go."

"You should, you were really good."

"Good for a twelve-year-old, maybe. I don't think you'd be too impressed if you saw me now."

"Don't sell yourself short."

Toby snorted. "It's the truth! Have you seen some of the guys on YouTube?"

"Who, the guys who practice regularly and do this for a living?"

"Yeah, compared to them I'm—"

Jane leveled her fork at him. "Don't do that. Don't compare yourself to them. Be you."

"Easier said than done."

"Most things are."

He considered this. "True."

The waiter arrived to remove their plates and offer them a dessert menu. Jane was about to turn it down but changed her mind at Toby's hopeful look. Once they'd ordered, he settled back into his seat with a sigh. "Enough about my mediocre guitar-playing skills. Why a lawyer? What's the big plan for you?"

She frowned and held up a finger when he went to ask again. "Gimme a minute, I'm trying to put this together in my head. Um. So law was something I tried because I didn't know what else to do and Dad thought I might be good at it. And I was. I like the challenge of working out a client's problems and finding the best solution that fits within the law, or of interpreting a particular judgment in the light of another resolution. I might like to be a partner someday, maybe at this firm, but probably not. Right now, I'm just trying to get admitted and rise up the ranks a bit. Doesn't leave a lot of time for a social life, but I make it work."

"Sounds a bit bleak."

Jane made a face. "I s'pose so. I don't think I'm going to stay there forever. I look at the partners at the firm—even the senior solicitors, the ones who have been there for ten years or more—and I'm not sure being partner at a big firm is worth it. We had this team dinner at a partner's house, and sure, it was a great house, but one of the other partners never turned up, and when we got back to the office to drop off some stuff, he was still there working. I just don't know if that life is for me."

"Are you looking for another job, then?"

"Nah. Being in the firm is great experience, and I'm still learning heaps. Maybe in a few years I'll look at other positions. Until then, this is my life right now."

Toby sat back to allow his dessert to be placed in front of him, and she leaned forward to inspect it. "What did you order?"

"I think it said it was a pumpkin and pecan pie. What did you get?"

"Just some sorbet." She tapped one of the scoops with her spoon, unreasonably pleased that it was already beginning to soften in the warm night air. "This is really nice."

He swallowed his mouthful of pie and nodded. "Yeah, everyone who's been here has said it's been good."

"No, not the food—though I am enjoying it. Sitting here and talking over a nice dinner. I haven't had a lot of time to do that for a while."

They ate in companionable silence until the pie was all gone and Jane found herself chasing a fragment of sorbet around the bottom of the dish.

"I think I'm stuffed."

"Me too," Toby agreed. He looked around. "I think it might be time to go. I'll just run to the restroom first."

He disappeared into the restaurant proper, and Jane sneaked a look at her phone. There were a couple of queries she needed to redirect to colleagues and one she had to answer herself, so she didn't notice how long he was away. When he exited onto the patio again, she dropped her phone back into her purse and went for her wallet.

Toby gave Jane a very unimpressed look when she pulled it out. "We agreed this time would be my treat."

Jane held up her hands in capitulation. "Okay, okay."

"Good."

"We could go Dutch," she suggested as they made their way to the front.

"Nice try, but no." He grinned and made no attempt to stop at the till. The maître d' there politely wished them good night as they passed.

Jane narrowed her eyes at him as he held the door for her. "Have you paid already?"

"Of course. Why do you think I took so long? Maybe we can go Dutch next time."

"Now you're just trying to get a next time."

"Can't blame a guy for trying, can you?"

"Not if he sneaks off to pay the bill for dinner," she grumped, but there was a warm feeling in her chest as she considered the possibility of a next time.

In her bag, her phone buzzed. "You don't mind, do you?" she asked, already pulling it out. It was a reply to one of the emails she'd sent from a workmate a scarce two years above her who was still at his desk.

"I kinda do," Toby said seriously. "If you really want to work, I can drop you home."

Jane looked up at him, startled. "Oh! Um, in that case..." She put her phone on silent and replaced it in her bag. "Sorry."

"Thanks." Toby motioned to the beach beside them. "You want to go for a walk? It's a nice night, seems a shame to cut it short. Unless you need to, of course."

"No, it wasn't urgent. It can wait." Feeling obscurely guilty, she stepped over the side of the boardwalk and onto the sand, where the pebbles shifted beneath her feet. The beach she'd visited earlier that day had been sandy, the perfect place to chat with friends and watch families build sandcastles. This was more of a beach for kitesurfing and dramatic wedding photos.

"Thank you for dinner," she said, trying to dispel the awkwardness she'd brought out with her phone. "I really enjoyed it."

"Does that mean there will be a next time?"

"I—I don't know. I am going home in two days, remember?"

"So home is down south now?"

She didn't even have to think about it. "Yes. I've spent so long studying there, my work is there, most of my friends are there too, and the rest are all over the place."

"Your family is here, though."

"They are, and a part of me wants to stay so I can keep an eye on them, especially as my parents are getting older. I do love it here, but I don't think I could stay. I don't know how you do it."

"Yeah, me neither." He paused, bent to pick up a pebble, and tossed it from hand to hand. "I went to college to find myself and when that didn't work, came home to find my parents had put our house on the market. What with packing up and the move, even home doesn't feel like home anymore. Like you said, most of my mates moved away from here, and the few who didn't are married. Some even have kids already."

"Nothing wrong with that."

"No, but they're in a different stage of life from me, and it's like we have nothing in common now." He fiddled with the pebble in his hand, then lobbed it into the ocean where it landed with a quiet splash. "I wish I knew what I wanted. All I know is it isn't this."

"Then why are you here? Why not try something new? It doesn't have to be forever."

In the moonlight, his face was unreadable. "That's a good point."

"Thank you. It's kind of my job. That, and a metric ton of research and proofreading."

Toby laughed. "I am honestly impressed. That doesn't sound easy."

"Eh. Sometimes it is, and sometimes it isn't. Sometimes I think I prefer it complicated because the easy stuff gets boring quickly, but as the newest hire at the firm with the lowest charge out rates, the easy monotonous jobs come to me first." She shrugged. "It keeps me busy, and I get enough new stuff to keep it interesting."

They walked a little further in silence. Jane stumbled slightly as the pebbles shifted under her feet, and Toby slipped a hand under her elbow to steady her. They found themselves at the edge of what used to be a pier before time and weather reduced it to a few planks and posts sticking out of the sand. Two of the planks made a makeshift bench; without speaking, they angled their way over to it. Sweeping the sand off the plank with her hand, Jane smoothed out her skirt and sat down, Toby beside her. She swung her bag into her lap, resisting the urge to look inside.

"So coming back here long-term isn't on the cards for you?" Toby asked.

She took her time in answering. "Not at this stage. Maybe in the future, but not for a long time yet. That's not what you're asking, though, is it?"

"See, I knew you were smart." He paused. "I like you, Jane, and I like hanging out with you, even if you do seem surgically attached to that phone of yours sometimes."

Jane laughed and looked at her feet. "I like you too. I didn't know what to expect after seeing you over the fence, but this has been fun. Maybe if I was living here…" she let her sentence trail off, unwilling to admit to what might have been.

"I don't suppose long distance is a possibility?" Toby asked, his tone hopeful.

Jane hated to dash that hope, but dash it she must. "Yeah, nah. I don't think that's a good idea. I'm bad at keeping in touch, even with my phone on me at all times. I don't want to start anything I couldn't see through, and long distance won't be giving it—us—a fair chance. Sorry."

"I get that." He angled his head at her, the moonlight casting shadows across his face. "So where does that leave us?"

"Friends?" she suggested, holding her hand out to shake.

He took it, his palm warm against hers, and shook. "Friends it is."

*

Feeling rather melancholy that her time with her parents was almost over, Jane was getting ready for a quiet night in when her phone buzzed.

Barbecue at Nick's. Time for a band reunion? As friends, of course.

Jane grinned. Nick had been the bassist in their short-lived band and, from memory, had gone to the same high school as Toby.

Sounds great, she replied. *who else will be there?*

Toby messaged a list of names, only some of whom she knew from school, and finished with, *feel free to invite anyone along*

Do I need to bring anything?

A delay, likely as he asked Nick, then, *Maybe a salad, if you're into that, and it's BYO drinks. Nick's dad's a butcher so we have a truckload of meat. And I can give you a lift, neighbor.*

I'll be there, she told him, then went to message Maddie.

*

Nick cheered as they came in the gate. "Look who it is! Jane, I didn't realize you were in town! Who's your friend?"

Jane paused, startled, but Maddie stepped in to introduce herself. "I'm Maddie—we were in Mrs. T's class together?"

Nick did a double take. "Seriously? Maddie, wow, I didn't recognize you."

"Clearly," Maddie replied dryly, before holding up a six-pack of ciders. "You got somewhere to put these?"

"What? Oh, yeah, yeah, follow me. Good to see you, man," he added to Toby almost as an afterthought.

"Okay," Toby said, closing the gate behind him. "What was that?"

Jane shrugged. "I guess Maddie's changed a bit since middle school—but then, I thought we all had."

"Oh for sure. For one thing, you've got—" Toby paused and grinned at the skeptical look Jane sent his way "—longer hair. Your hair used to be in this cute bob."

"Oh, yeah." Jane made a face. "That was annoying. Too short to tie up, but it was long enough to sit on the back of my neck and annoy me."

"Sounds like a hard life."

"Oh absolutely. It was the worst." Jane laughed. "I'd forgotten how much I hated having short hair right until you brought it up."

"Oops?"

"No, it's a good thing. Means I won't be forgetting and going out to get a haircut like that any time soon. Or ever." She scowled. "Not that I have time for that anyway."

"No time for a haircut? Really?"

"Most hairdressers are only open during work hours. Perhaps on the weekend, but that's when I do laundry." Jane shook her head. "And listen to me, complaining about hair. You must think I'm so vain."

"The worst," Toby deadpanned, shaking his head in mock solemnity. "If it helps, I like your hair."

"Thanks, I grew it myself."

This time, it was Toby who groaned.

*

After dinner, Jane slumped back on a beanbag. "I'm so full."

Maddie eyed Jane's plate critically. "Aren't you going to finish that?"

"I literally don't have space." She threw one hand over her forehead. "I flew too close to the sun, and my hubris has been my downfall. Anyone want half a sausage?"

"I'll take it," Toby volunteered, and she pushed her plate toward him.

Conversation rose and fell around them as people who Jane hadn't seen in years chatted over paper plates and glasses of punch. Her gaze fell on the guitar in the corner. "Nick, you play guitar?"

He looked up from where he'd been fiddling with the sound system and shook his head. "Nah, that's my brother's old one that he gave me to learn on, but I never got around to it." He glanced over at Toby, who had already inhaled another sausage. "Toby's the guitar player, remember?"

"That was years ago," Toby protested.

"Come on," Jane said. "For old times' sake?"

Her pleas were echoed by the others around them, and Toby got up and grabbed the guitar from its stand. "Fine," he said. "I succumb to the peer pressure."

"Yay peer pressure!" Maddie chirped, giving Jane a high five.

Toby sat down and settled the guitar against his knee. He ran his hands over the strings and winced. "I think this needs a bit of a tune."

"Hold on, I have an app for that." Jane pulled out her phone and opened an app she'd gotten for free once. "Okay, go."

Toby tuned the guitar, frowning in concentration as he fiddled with the tuning pegs. Finally, he strummed a few times and smiled. "I think we're good to go."

"What are you going to play?"

He picked out a few chords, a strand of hair falling across his brow as he focused on the strings. The chords resolved themselves into a pop song, one Jane recognized from their high school years. "Oh, that's a classic," she laughed as someone whooped.

She sang along to the first verse, and Toby, along with the rest of the room, joined her on the chorus. Once they got to the second verse, however, they all faltered.

"Is this the part where we admit that none of us know the words?" Jane asked the room as Toby continued to play the accompaniment.

"Yeah, but here comes the chorus again!"

Everyone launched in again, clapping and bobbing their heads in time to the music. The bridge was a bit of a struggle, but they got through to the end, and Jane laughed as Toby finished with a dramatic flourish.

"That was really good," she said. "Nice to see you haven't lost it."

"I think everyone who learned guitar knows that one," he said. "It's only got like four chords." He looked up. "Any requests?"

"I'll look them up," Jane suggested, pulling her phone out again. A notification flashed up, and she tapped into it without thinking. It switched over to her email app, and she read it quickly.

"You got the chords?" Toby asked.

"What? Oh, yeah, it's loading now," she lied, going back to her browser and searching them up. Toby looked at her skeptically when she presented her phone but bent his head to study the tabs on the screen.

The next song was one he already knew, and he picked another old favorite after that. Jane sang along, enjoying the feeling of hanging out with a large group of friends without having to worry about work. From the email she'd seen, there was plenty of that waiting for her when she got back.

"Weren't you guys in a band together?" Maddie asked when the song wound down. "How about you play something from that?"

"I'd love to, but that was years ago," Jane said. "I don't even remember what we sang."

Nick gestured for Toby to move off the seat he was on and opened it up, revealing a stack of paper. "Jane, you're in luck. My mom never let us throw away any music, so if I'm right—" he rummaged around and came up with a folder, "—I have our entire setlist right here. She was especially proud of our original song." He pulled out a few sheets and passed them to her and Toby. "We'll have to do without Max on the drums, but we have a piano over there, and I can get my bass?"

Toby looked over at Jane and raised an eyebrow.

Jane shrugged in reply. "Let's do this, then," she said, picking up the sheet music and going over to the piano. It was the seat Toby had been sitting on, closed once more. He looked around for somewhere else to sit, and she patted the seat beside her. "There's room over here, if you turn around and promise not to stab me with the guitar."

"No promises."

It took a few flubs and false starts, but along with Nick, they ran through their entire setlist and a few extras until Toby begged off, citing sore fingers from playing so long. He passed the guitar over to another girl who returned to the pop songs they could sing along to. Relieved of piano-playing duties, Jane closed the piano lid and swung herself around on the seat to sit next to Toby.

"That was fun," she murmured to him.

"It was," he agreed. "We should do it more often."

They stayed like that as the night outside grew darker and the guitar was swapped out for the sound system once more. Jane found herself yawning; Toby shifted his weight to look down at her. "You ready to head off?"

Jane nodded. "Let me grab my stuff."

"You guys are together?" one of the boys nearby asked.

Jane hesitated, but Toby shook his head. "Nah, but we're neighbors, so I offered her a lift tonight."

"You sure? You two look awfully cozy on that seat."

Toby flipped the bird at him cheerfully and looked around. "Will Maddie want a ride?"

"I think so. She was going to crash at my place tonight. Is that okay?"

"Of course."

Unable to see her friend, Jane flicked her a text. After a short delay, her screen lit up with a reply.

"She'll meet us at the car," Jane reported. "Where's Nick? I'd like to thank him for hosting and say goodbye."

"I'll pass it on when I next see him," Toby told her. "You can barely keep your eyes open."

"Thank you."

They made their way to the car where Toby unlocked the car and opened the passenger side for her. She was reaching for her phone to message Maddie again when her friend appeared at the gate. Spotting them at the car, she jogged over and got in, only swaying slightly.

"You all right there, Mads?" Jane asked, turning around to where her friend lolled in the back seat.

"I'm fine," Maddie said, before yawning hugely, setting Jane off again, and precluding any further conversation.

"Looks like I better get you two ladies home," Toby said, starting the engine.

Jane shifted her focus to him as he navigated them out of the cul-de-sac where Nick lived. "Thanks for inviting us tonight. It was really fun."

"I'm glad you were able to make it. It wouldn't have been as much fun without you."

"Just kiss already," Maddie interrupted, earning herself a glare from Jane as Toby spluttered.

"Mads, it's not like that!"

"Only because you won't commit to anything that isn't your nine-to-five—or is that five-to-nine?" At Jane's look, she waved her hand in defeat. "Don't mind me, I'm not even here. Just ignore the drunk girl in the back seat."

"Thanks very much, we will," Jane said primly.

The rest of the drive home was made in awkward silence, punctuated by Maddie humming tunelessly in the back seat. Toby pulled into his own driveway and pulled the handbrake as Jane released her seatbelt. She paused, one hand on the door handle. "Thanks for the lift."

He tipped his head in acknowledgment. She must have been imagining the way his gaze lingered on her lips. "Anytime, neighbor."

*

"How was the date?"

Jane stared at the woman who dropped into the chair across the table from her. "Nice to see you too, Carrie. Thanks for asking, I had a wonderful time away. How was your week?"

"Yeah, yeah, yadda yadda yadda. I was at work all week and a fair amount of the weekend thanks to a big project in the pipeline. I didn't even go out for lunch on Friday because my usual date—" she raised her eyebrows at Jane for a second "—stood me up. I want to hear about what you did. So. How was the date?"

Jane held up finger. "First off, it wasn't a date, and second," she raised another finger, "it was fine. We caught up."

"Oh yeah?" Carrie leaned across the table in her excitement, nearly knocking over the water jug. "Come on, Janie, spill! You like never go on dates these days. What'd you talk about?"

Jane fought the urge to hunch her shoulders. "I don't know. Stuff. What he was doing, what I'm doing."

"Okay, I know what you're doing, you're taking over the corporate world one deal at a time. What is he doing?" Carrie pretended to peruse the menu. It didn't matter, she would always get one of two things, and Jane was willing to bet today was an eggs benny day.

"Renovations on his parents' new house, which happens to be the one next door to my parents. You remember the old guy next door, the one who mowed his lawn every Saturday like clockwork? He died, and Toby's parents bought the house. Toby's putting in a deck out the back."

Carrie winced. "DIY, huh? Must've been riveting. Did you at least go somewhere nice?" She turned to the waiter who had already taken Jane's order. "I'll have the eggs Benedict, please."

Silently, Jane cheered, before remembering Carrie's question. "I suppose so. It was a fancy place by the waterfront where Fisherman's Plate used to be."

"Isn't that a restaurant? I thought you were having coffee."

Too late, she realized her mistake. "We did," she corrected weakly. "But we also had dinner."

Carrie's eyebrows practically leapt off her face. "Sounds like your boy moves fast."

"Not my boy," Jane corrected. "I don't want to talk about it."

"Oh, hun." Carrie schooled her face into an appropriately sympathetic expression and patted her hand. "These things happen. I'm sorry it didn't work out."

Jane made a face and changed the subject. "So tell me about this big project you've got going. What are you allowed to say?"

"It's a museum exhibition, not state secrets," Carrie laughed. "But we're trying to organize the Terracotta Warriors."

"No way!"

Conversation about her non-existent love life averted, Jane let herself relax. It was good to be home, good to be back. Even if a small part of her wondered what she'd left up north.

*

She messaged him late that evening, after she got home from work drinks that had gone longer than expected. *How's it going?*

Her screen lit up almost immediately. *Not too bad, how has your week been?*

Oh you know, work. She'd had a ton of emails to get through, updates on projects she'd been on, and the second she'd sat down at her desk, three people had given her work that had to be completed by the end of the day.

Tbh, I don't :P

How's unemployment? she fired back.

Ouch. Getting kinda old at this point, but at least I have something to do with my time. I'd be super bored if I wasn't doing anything.

Cool

There wasn't much more to say, after that. He asked a bit more after her job, but due to confidentiality, she could only give him the broadest of outlines—and after a week of it, talking about her work only reminded her how much of it she had waiting for her on Monday. Not the best way to spend her Friday night.

She refreshed her Facebook timeline once more, and a photo of Toby popped up. He was pictured with a gorgeous blonde girl, and the timestamp marked it as being posted less than an hour ago.

A wave of jealousy flashed through her, quickly followed by one of self-recrimination. He'd answered her messages, hadn't he? Even after she'd asked to stay as friends. It was no business of hers who he was tagged in photos with.

Jane enlarged the photo find the girl's name—to see that she was in a long term relationship with Toby's cousin, at whose party the photo was taken. Disgusted with herself, she closed the app and tossed her phone onto the sofa.

Boys aren't worth it, she decided. She had work to do.

*

Over the next few months after she returned to work, they stayed in touch, texting on and off. It was more off than on, if she was honest, and it wasn't all her fault when they went long stretches without messaging.

It was after a couple of weeks of no contact that Carrie called her out over blueberry waffles. "Okay, this stopped being entertaining a few weeks ago. J, what's up?"

Jane looked up from the salad she was pushing around her plate. "What do you mean?"

"You've been down since you got back from visiting your parents. I didn't want to say anything, but you've been a bit of a grump. I get the post-holiday blues and all, but you should've bounced back by now. This isn't like you." Carrie leaned forward. "Are you okay?"

"I'm fine," Jane said. She made a face. "I haven't been that bad, have I?"

"You've come out with us exactly once and that was Amy's birthday, and you disappeared before we even got to cake. You never miss dessert."

"I haven't been feeling like going out, okay?"

"If I didn't know better, I'd say you were going through a breakup again, but you haven't been seeing anyone recently, have you?" Carrie's manner grew exaggeratedly casual, and she propped one hand under her chin. "Have you heard from Toby lately, hmm?"

"What? Why do you ask?"

"You saw him when you were visiting your parents, you've been a downer since then—it's not hard to do the math. What happened on that date?"

"Nothing much," Jane mumbled. "We decided to stay friends."

"We? Or you?"

"It doesn't matter, I—"

"Don't have time for a relationship, I know. And yet over half my workmates, and likely most of yours, are in steady, long-term relationships, many with far larger workloads than you. You were away for a week. Did the office fall apart without you? Did your career come to a screeching halt?"

"No, but—"

"Then what's your real excuse?"

"I can't be bothered, okay? I need to focus on work. I don't have the time or energy to waste on something that won't work out."

"Who's to say it won't?"

Jane prodded at her meal instead of responding. As the food in question was a cherry tomato, it was rather less satisfying than she had hoped. The tomato eluded her fork and shot across the table and onto the floor.

"Ugh, this is perfect," she exclaimed, dropping her cutlery onto her plate.

Carrie eyed her carefully. "Why are you being so cranky? You don't even like tomato that much." Her eyes widened. "No way! You actually like him."

"No, I don't." Jane chased a caper around her plate with her fork, refusing to meet her friend's gaze.

"Yes, you do. Otherwise you wouldn't be glaring daggers at a very nice garden salad. You are cranky because you met a guy you actually want to pursue a relationship with but have no idea how to go about it because you already turned him down because you were scared."

"Gee, thanks."

Carrie popped a dainty bite of her own meal into her mouth. "You're welcome."

"Now that you've finished psychoanalyzing me, do you have any advice?"

Carrie smirked. "You have to be seriously desperate to be asking me for advice."

"Stop teasing and answer the question, C."

"Well, you said you were friends, right? Start from there. Actually ask him out! Get to know each other—no, I know you went to school together, I was there, and you've been on a couple of dates, like, three months ago. Doesn't mean you know him. Spend some time together."

"You may have forgotten one teeny tiny problem there."

"What's that?"

"He lives up north. Spending time together is a little difficult when two people live in different cities."

"Fair point. But hypothetically, if you were to live in the same city, you would actually want to date this guy?"

"Maybe," Jane muttered into her coffee.

"What was that?"

"Yes, okay? I like him. And he lives next door to my parents in a different city. Happy now?"

"Blissfully," Carrie said, draining her coffee. "Watch my bag, will you? I need to visit the restroom."

Jane took the opportunity to finish off her salad. She had popped the last piece of avocado into her mouth when a definitely-not-Carrie figure dropped into the seat opposite her. She was about to tell him off when she recognized the face framed by messy black hair. He'd grown some stubble, a part of her noted. It was a good look on him.

"I look that bad, huh?" Toby asked when she didn't say anything.

"What are you doing here? I mean, hi, Toby, no, you look great. I—" Jane scrambled for something to say. "Um, how's your deck? It must be done by now."

"Yeah, all done and dusted. All that's left to do at my parents' is the insulation and to redo the main bathroom, and they can get the professionals in to do all of that."

"Fair enough," Jane agreed. "But what are you doing here?"

He scratched the back of his neck, ducking his head so he wouldn't meet her eyes. "Heard you come here every week and wanted to see you."

"You heard I come here every week? Who told you that?"

"Oh please, we went to school together," Carrie said, swinging by to pick up her handbag. "We have some thirty mutual friends in common on Facebook. See you next week, Jane."

"So what, are you here on holiday?" Jane asked, giving her friend a distracted wave goodbye.

"Nah, I've got a new job here. See, someone told me to give something a try, so I got an apprenticeship with this guitar maker in town."

"Huh." Jane sat back as she tried to process this. "Where are you living?"

Toby shrugged. "I'm crashing at a mate's place, but I'm looking for a flat for the long term. Would you happen to know a place that's going?"

Numbly, she nodded. "There's an apartment across the road that's advertising an empty room." She shook her head. "I still can't believe you're here."

"If it makes you uncomfortable, I can go," he offered. "Well, not back north, not when I already have a new job down here, but I'm sure there's plenty of places to stay in the city. I don't need to live near you if that makes you feel weird."

"No, you should go for it, I took a look at those apartments when searching for a place last year and they are really nice." *This could go terribly*, she reasoned to herself. But he wouldn't be in her building, he'd be across the road.

Jane's phone buzzed.

"Aren't you going to get that?" Toby asked when she made no move to do so.

"No, it's my lunch break," she said. "I've decided to not answer calls at lunch time. I can call them back when I'm back at the office."

"Wow, setting boundaries," he said, sitting back. "I'm impressed. Not that you need my approval, of course," he added hastily.

Jane snorted. "No, I don't, but it's nice to have it all the same." A thought struck her. "You didn't just come here for me, did you?" she asked, an uneasy feeling in her stomach.

Toby shook his head. "Turns out this guy was looking for an apprentice, and he's based down here. There's a few specialized instrument makers around the country, but none anywhere else who specialize in guitars and who are looking for a newbie on board. I'd be lying if I said you weren't part of the decision, but you're not all of it. Even if Carrie hadn't reached out, even if she told me you weren't keen on seeing me again, I reckon I would've been okay."

"Wait, C contacted you? When was this?"

"About three days after I moved down." Toby grinned, and Jane felt her heart do an odd double thump at the sight. "I figured it was a sign I had made the right decision—I told her we were just friends, she asked if I wanted more, I said yes, she said she'd check with you, and here I am."

"Here you are," Jane echoed. "What would you have done if I'd said I wasn't interested?"

"Probably booked it out the back."

Jane screwed up her face. "It's very middle school, isn't it? Getting a friend to ask someone out for you?"

"It is," Toby agreed. "Though she wasn't the most clear on what you said."

"Well, technically I didn't say yes," Jane said, drawing the moment out. She leaned back and folded her arms across her chest. "Or I did, but I said yes to a hypothetical. No one has asked me anything concrete."

"Oops." Toby leaned forward, bracing his forearms on the table between them. "In which case: Jane Spencer, would you like to go on a date with me, and not just as friends?"

She pretended to think about it. "I'd love to. What are you doing this weekend?"

"I was going to go flat hunting, but if I don't have to—I'm not sure, to be honest. I don't really know my way around. You'll be busy, you wouldn't have time to show me the sights, would you?"

"I'm sure I can make time."

He grinned, and she had to take a sip of water to hide the answering smile on her own face and to calm the sudden swarm of butterflies in her stomach.

*

Jane's phone buzzed with an incoming email as she collected her house keys from their bowl, and she glanced down at the lit screen. *Today is Wave All Your Fingers at Your Neighbor Day* the email proudly proclaimed. Jane screwed up her face, trying to remember why that sounded familiar. She opened her front door, and as was her habit these days, glanced at the guy exiting the building across the road at the same time. *Oh.*

Phone in one hand, she waved. One whole year since she'd done the same over their shared fence.

Toby waved back. "We still on for dinner tonight?" he called.

"Only if I don't get a better offer," she called back. "I'll let you know."

He mimed being struck, staggering dramatically and garnering a few odd looks from the people walking past.

Jane laughed at his antics and crossed the road to him. "Are you going to tell me where we're going?"

"That would ruin the surprise," he said, as they fell into step. "You'll have to wait until after work."

"Surprises are overrated."

"I don't know, I was pretty surprised to hit my thumb and find my old bandmate hanging out next door. I almost didn't recognize you."

"Same," she admitted. "I almost didn't say anything."

"What, and leave it as awkward eye contact?"

"Yeah." She tucked herself into his side as he slung one arm around her shoulders. "I'm glad I waved."

He pressed a kiss to the top of her head. "So am I, neighbor."

About the Author

Born and raised in New Zealand, also known as the best middle of nowhere, Mei Edwards grew up a voracious reader. She could often be found leaving the library with a stack of books as tall as her, ready to read her way to a happy ending. Creating her own worlds for others to enjoy has been a long standing dream. When not writing, Mei can be found at her nine-to-five job or planning her next overseas adventure.

Tumblr: backwardsandinhighheels.tumblr.com
Twitter: @themeiedwards

A Holiday (or Two) to Remember
♥
Christina Rose Andrews

Story Information

Holiday: Do a Grouch a Favor Day
Holiday Date: February 16
Heat Rating: 4
Relationship Type: M/F
Major Trigger Warnings: None

In order to climb Mauna Kea, Grace needs to work on her endurance. What better place to do that than her neighborhood gym? Unfortunately there's a not-so-small problem. A problem in the shape of one of the hottest guys Grace has ever seen. He's got abs, arms, and the scariest resting murder face this side of the Terminator. Is Grace woman enough to overcome her trepidations? And is her new gym partner secretly an assassin in disguise?

A Holiday (Or Two) to Remember

January 2

    What the heck had she been thinking when she'd decided to start her 'Climb Mauna Kea without passing out' workout routine right after New Year's?

    It was dumb. It was stupid.

    It's freaking inconvenient, Grace thought, staring at the not quite literal wall of sweaty humanity grunting and groaning at her nearby gym, Hawk's.

    She wanted a treadmill. Ideally one that wasn't occupied, which was looking less and less likely. She wanted to avoid walking in the snow and ice of Brooklyn in January. She wanted to be able to climb five flights of stairs without becoming winded. She wanted to know why she couldn't just say no to her sister Hope when she floated her plans for her post-graduation trip.

    "What are you looking for?" a literal mountain of a Black man who looked remarkably like the Old Spice Guy asked her from behind the front desk. Yay, customer service! He'd obviously noticed her looking around the gym desperately.

    "Sanity?" she responded while flashing her brand new membership card.

    Chuckling, the man gave it a cursory look. "You won't find that here."

    "I didn't think so," She gave a half-shrug. "But it was worth a check. I don't suppose you have a treadmill," she said, even as she counted three, all occupied. Unlike most of the larger gyms she'd seen, Hawk's didn't have a row of cardio machines in one spot and the weight machines in another. Instead, everything was scattered around the gym with little rhyme or reason.

Old Spice Man looked at her, then back at the full gym, then back at her. "I got one."

"Great. One's all I need! I'll take it."

"You aren't gonna want it." While the tone was flat, there was a twinkle of amusement in the guy's eye.

He was testing her! The bastard. Well, she'd show him. Grace Anne O'Leary never backed down from a fight. Even when she probably should... like now. "Bold of you to assume so."

"Okay." He held up his hands in surrender. "You're right. I'm out of line. It's just, the last three people who used that treadmill left after less than fifteen minutes, and I haven't seen them since."

She pushed the little voice in her head screaming at her to ask why to the side. She had a point to make. She wasn't going to let a little thing like common sense get in her way. "I'm wearing my big girl panties. I'll be fine." She was too! Cute pink panties that didn't show off a panty line under her black leggings and oversized gray t-shirt. Along with two sports bras—a necessity with her huge tracts of land—a pair of socks with purple pom-poms on them, and white sneakers with purple accents that matched the scrunchy holding her light red hair up in a messy bun.

Plus, according to her days of the year calendar, it was Motivation and Inspiration Day. She wasn't going to just give up.

"Right. It's in the back corner next to the seated leg press." Old Spice Man pointed behind himself and to the left. "Don't say I didn't warn you." With that ominous yet cheerful farewell, the man turned back to flipping through the barrage of early morning talk shows searching for who knows what.

Grace didn't take the brush off to heart. She was used to it. Besides, she'd won the argument; it was hard to be angry at anyone who had the sense to let her win. Following the vague instructions, she wove her way through the throngs of sweat and clunks until she reached the corner. She wasn't quite sure which machine was the seated leg press, but the empty treadmill called to her like a beacon. With a little skip in her step, she made a beeline for the machine.

Then stopped.

Between her and the promised treadmill was a man. A sexy man. His chin-length sandy blond hair highlighted cheekbones that would make a model gush. His body reminded her of the kind she saw headless and shirtless on the covers of her many beloved romance novels. Add to it a square jaw, a straight nose that looked like it might have been broken once, and piercing blue eyes, and you had a mixture made in wet dream heaven.

That's assuming your wet dreams featured a guy with resting murder face. Which, much to her surprise, hers now would. Who knew? Here she thought she was the Daniel Radcliffe, Mayim Bialik, or Henry Cavill type of girl. Would wonders never cease?

The man glanced over at her from his place on the nearby cable machine then looked away. It was like she didn't even matter, like she was a bug not even worthy of his interest.

Well, screw that!

If he was the reason nobody was willing to use that treadmill, then by gum she was going to take advantage of their cowardice! She popped her earbuds into her ears, screwed up her courage, and climbed on. If she was going to die today, she was going to do it on her terms.

*

January 3 – 6

She didn't die that day. Or the next.

On Friday, she even flashed Mr. Murder Man—and she really needed to find a better name for him—a 'please don't kill me' half-smile. It seemed to work. She wasn't dead yet, anyway. For all she knew, the smile was the only thing keeping her from certain death.

He wasn't there on Saturday when she rolled in at 1:30. Apparently he was an early morning kind of guy. Which meant, unfortunately, without her murder-faced treadmill protector someone else had absconded with what she was already coming to think of as her treadmill. So regretfully, she was forced to find another one.

It might have been her imagination but the machine at the front of the gym sucked. Not like vacuum cleaners suck. But suck in that whole 'I'm going to speed up and slow down on you randomly, and it's going to throw your pace off and make you look even more uncoordinated than you are' kind of suck. Because despite the chubby girl stereotypes, Grace wasn't uncoordinated. She managed to stay upright on a regular basis. And that included while being leaned against, jumped up on, and plowed into by her many clients. Or, technically, her clients' dogs. But really, she thought of the dogs as her clients and the humans attached to them as the animals' accessories.

Whatever. It worked.

Unlike the crappy treadmill at the front of the gym. No way in hell was she going to use that death trap again.

She decided to skip the gym on Sunday. After all, she deserved a day off. And according to her days of the year calendar, it was Whipped Cream Day. She liked whipped cream. Especially on things like hot chocolate and apple pie. Plus, on Sundays her parents and sister tended to leave the apartment, so she could turn up her music and do her laundry to her heart's content.

Unfortunately, when Monday rolled around, she realized taking a day off was a Bad Idea™. She didn't want to wake up early. Worse, she didn't want to go to the gym. It was cold outside. She hadn't had her coffee yet. Her bed was warm. And her dreams of Mr. Murder Man were even warmer.

That, ultimately, was what got her out of bed. Even though today was Cuddle Up Day, it felt wrong somehow to have dreams of cuddling with a guy she hadn't even said two words to whose real name she didn't even know. Dang it, if she was going to have R-rated dreams about the man, she should at least get his name first!

It was only polite.

So once again she found herself at Hawk's. The Old Spice Guy lookalike greeted her with a bright smile. And today, unlike the previous times she'd visited the gym, he was actually wearing a name tag, so she could stop calling him Old Spice Man. Apparently his name was John. John was a much better name than Old Spice Man. Now if Mr. Murder Man would be so polite as to have a 'Hello my name is ___' sticker that was not filled in with 'Inigo Montoya. Prepare to die.' that would be awesome.

Plus it would save her the trouble of actually having to talk to the man. Win-win.

Grace wove her way through the machines to her preferred treadmill. Mr. Murder Man was on the cable machine next to it, much as she'd expected. Today his hair was pulled back into a messy bun, and he was wearing thick horn-rimmed glasses. *Oh be still, my ovaries.* All thoughts of asking for his name flew out of her mind as she was presented with this Oh-My-God epitome of masculine perfection. Or at least, her version of it.

How dare Mr. Murder Man wear glasses and destroy her ability to talk? Didn't he know she was planning to attempt polite conversation? Now it took all of her effort not to drool when she happened to look at him! Heart pounding in her chest for non-exercise related reasons, she fired up the treadmill and slipped her earbuds in. Maybe listening to her favorite podcast would take her mind off her screaming ovaries.

Maybe.

But probably not.

Somehow she managed to make it through her workout without melting into a pile of goo. As she stepped off the treadmill, she hazarded a glance over at Mr. Murder Man. He was still working out. Still sexy as heck.

Okay. Time to do something dangerous.

She smiled at him. Not a big smile or even a flirtatious smile. Just a little quirking uptilt to the corners of her mouth that she hoped reached her eyes.

And it might've been her imagination, but Mr. Murder Man's rhythm seemed to falter for a split second, and the left corner of his mouth might have tilted upward.

Success!

*

January 7

When Grace awoke on the 7th, she did what she did every day: automatically checked to see what weird holiday it was. What she saw printed on her calendar made her frown. Today, January 7th, was I'm Not Going to Take it Anymore Day.

If that wasn't a sign, she didn't know what was.

To psych herself up, Grace took care getting ready. Normally she didn't care about wearing makeup or doing anything cute with her hair. For goodness' sake, she was going to the gym, and she worked with dogs. The only kind of makeup the dogs cared about was the kind they could lick off her face. But today was different. While it didn't make sense to put on the full foundation with contouring effect, a little bit of lip gloss and a hint of mascara… that should be okay, right? Make her brown eyes pop. Make her mouth—that her last boyfriend had called her best feature—stand out. That was fine, right?

She didn't want to give Mr. Murder Man the impression she was trying to look good on his account… even if she was trying to look good on his account.

The gym was the same as it had been the last four times she'd been there. Still full, John still at the front desk, and Mr. Murder Man still working on his leg presses. The glasses were gone, much to her ovaries' disappointment, but he was as homicidal-looking as ever.

She didn't let herself obsess about it. One deep breath and she said the first word they'd shared since she'd started coming here. "Hey."

He tilted his head, his hair falling over his cheek as he looked at her. But he didn't say anything.

Maybe he hadn't heard her. "So, um... hello. I figured since you seem to be my workout buddy I should probably introduce myself." She took a half-step forward and stuck her hand out. "I'm Grace."

He grunted and shook her hand. If she was looking for a spark or a sizzle, she didn't get it. Probably because of the thin leather gloves protecting his palms. Besides, she wasn't really looking to hook up with her sexy murder face gym partner, now was she?

"So... it's nice to meet you?"

He grunted again.

This wasn't going anywhere. Fine. She'd respect his unspoken boundaries and leave him alone. "You know, I should probably start exercising since this is a gym and all. Sorry to bother you." She turned away, her heart sinking. *Well, that didn't go well.* She fished her earbuds out and unlocked her phone, searching for something light to lift her mood.

"You're not bothering me." The words were so soft—husky—she almost didn't hear them.

She pulled her left earbud out. "Excuse me?"

"You're not bothering me."

"Oh! Well, good!"

She waited for him to say something for several long agonizing moments. Nothing.

"So... thanks!" She put her earbud back in and hopped on the treadmill.

For the rest of her time at the gym, she studiously tried to ignore him. But every time she happened to glance in his direction, her eyes would meet his, and she'd have to turn away to hide the blush which stole up her cheeks. Damned stereotypical Irish complexion. Couldn't tan in the sun, couldn't cry gracefully, couldn't hide embarrassment. Her skin was like a lie detector. Or a mood ring. It sucked.

When she finished, she decided to throw caution to the wind and waved at Mr. Murder Man. To Grace's complete and utter surprise, he waved back.

*

January 10

By the time Friday rolled around, Grace had settled into a routine. Get up, look at her weird holidays calendar, eat her usual breakfast of a bagel and coffee, and then head to the gym. She felt accomplished. She felt successful. She even felt like she might be able to up the difficulty on the treadmill. Maybe. On Monday. *Let's not get too optimistic.*

When she got to the gym, she flashed her membership card, waved at John, and beelined for her favorite treadmill. She liked it here. Any gym that didn't have a steady stream of judgmental people nagging her with advice on what to eat or what to wear was a good one in her books. She knew what she looked like: curvy, really curvy, like Rubens's models had nothing on her curvy. And if it wasn't for Hope's graduation wish to climb the tallest mountain in the world—if you measured from the sea floor—she wouldn't even be here.

But here she was. And she was darn well going to enjoy it.

She didn't try to interrupt Mr. Murder Man. She still hadn't learned his name. As far as she knew, he had no name. Like Clint Eastwood in those Westerns her father insisted on trotting out every Christmas. She felt horrible that she couldn't seem to stop calling him Mr. Murder Man in her head. But it fit! In addition to his resting murder face, he was possibly the most taciturn man she'd ever met. He'd literally only said four words to her. Four! It was like he was shooting for the Academy Award for leading man with fewest lines of dialogue. His performance, if it was a performance, was a masterpiece. A triumph. Five stars! Mr. Murder Man could put Jason Statham or Sylvester Stallone to shame.

But his grumpy nature did have an upside. Because nobody wanted to risk finding out if his resting murder face led to actual murder, that meant the exercise machines, including her treadmill, next to his preferred area were often—thankfully—empty.

As on the previous days, she did her workout in silence.

But unlike the previous days, when she finished, in addition to her little half-wave, she said, "Hey. So it's been nice working out with you. I'll see you on Monday. Make sure to save the treadmill for me." She didn't really know why she added that last part. It just seemed to sort of flow.

He didn't say anything. She didn't expect him to.

And that was okay by her.

*

January 13

When she got to the gym Monday, there was a little three-by-five index card folded in half with the word 'Reserved' on it in blocky print on her treadmill's control panel.

It was sweet. Unexpected. Yeah, she'd asked Mr. Murder Man to save her treadmill for her, but it was more of an off-the-cuff joke than an actual honest-to-God request. The fact that he went to the trouble to do just that filled her with all sorts of warm fuzzies. No one else could have done it. No one else had been close enough to hear her request.

As she climbed onto the treadmill, she met his piercing blue eyes. "Hey." She wiggled the little placard. "Thanks."

He grunted.

"Oh!" She hopped off the treadmill and rummaged around in her purse. "This is for you." She pulled out a scratch-and-sniff sticker with a picture of a skunk on it and held it out to him.

He looked at it like it was toxic. Which, to be fair, it probably was.

"It's Sticker Day." She peeled off the backing and without waiting for him to accept or protest stuck it on his shirt right over his heart. "I figured you could use a sticker."

He looked down at his shirt and back up at her and grunted again. This time the sound was filled with amusement.

Progress!

*

January 14 – 17

For the rest of the week, the index card 'Reserved' placard was there every time she showed up. It even gained some embellishment. First the skunk. Then after each successive day, a little gold star appeared. She didn't know why Mr. Murder Man was doing it, but she appreciated the thoughtfulness all the same. And on the plus side, she figured if he was giving her a gold star, he wasn't planning on murdering her!

By the time Friday rolled around, she had increased the incline of her treadmill and was feeling pretty good about her ultimate goal. She could walk forty-five minutes on a fifteen percent incline without becoming winded. Not too shabby. Especially since she was one of those people who used to get winded climbing three flights of stairs. She wondered how many flights she could climb now. There were plenty of walk-ups in New York; she'd have ample opportunity to find out.

When she'd started, she hadn't been sure she'd actually be able to make it to the finish line. She hadn't known if she'd be able to build up the endurance and fitness needed to climb Mauna Kea. Now? It wasn't looking completely out of the question.

To celebrate, she stopped at one of her favorite bagel shops and indulged herself in an everything bagel slathered with cream cheese, lox, onions, and capers. She didn't normally get it—not just because it was expensive although it totally was—but because, for whatever reason, every time she ate an everything bagel the smell lingered on her for the rest of the day no matter what she did to wash it off. But today she decided 'screw it!' A milestone was a milestone. If a girl couldn't celebrate a milestone with an everything bagel, then why was life even worth living?

But because she stopped, she arrived at Hawk's later than usual. About twenty minutes later. There'd been a line at the bagel place. There was always a line.

John greeted her with the same polite yet uninterested nod that he reserved for every person who came through the door. And she expected Mr. Murder Man to do the same.

He didn't.

When she got to her treadmill with its little 'Reserved' index card, Mr. Murder Man actually stopped his reps and said in a soft baritone, "I was afraid you weren't coming."

Holy crap!

Six words! What had she done to deserve six words?

Tamping down the urge to apologize, she said, "Why did you think I wouldn't be here?"

"Look around." He pointed at the rest of the gym, which was decidedly less full than usual. "It's Ditch New Year's Resolutions Day. A lot of people stop coming today."

Her heart did a little flip. He knew what weird holiday it was! She'd never met anybody who kept track of the days of the year like she did. And now Mr. Built, Brawny, and Blond had to go out of his way once more to surprise her.

"I'm not here for a New Year's resolution," she said. "I think they're just a recipe for setting yourself up for failure. I haven't met anyone who's managed to succeed at keeping their New Year's resolution."

"I have." His tone was smug. Self-satisfied.

"Oh?" *He must mean himself. No one uses that tone about anyone else.* "And what was your resolution?"

"To not make resolutions." Mr. Murder Man followed up the statement with a saucy wink.

She couldn't help it; she laughed. "Well, that's one way to game the system!"

"I'm glad you liked it," he told her with a smile. A smile which transformed his face from 'You're going to die painfully' to 'You're going to die of thirst but that's okay—at least you were looking at something pretty.'

And she really needed to stop objectifying him. Like yesterday.

She held her hand out to him. "So thanks for saving my place, gym buddy. I'm Grace. And...you are?" She knew she was introducing herself for the second time, but this time she wasn't letting him go until he gave her something.

And he did. "I'm Rick. Nice to meet you, Grace."

Hal-le-lu-jah.

*

January 18 – 20

While Grace now had a name to attach the man firmly ensconced in her dreams, she was still no closer to holding a meaningful conversation with him. Oh, her dream!self held all sorts of conversations with him about every possible topic ranging from the weather to whether he was wearing underwear. It was a dream. Dream!Grace didn't have to follow societal norms.

However, she should probably consider giving them passing courtesy in real life. Unfortunately, real life was not like her dreams. All of her dresses did not have pockets. Chocolate was not dispensed on every street corner in case of emergency. And she and Rick had never truly talked.

The last was really starting to become a problem.

Armed with fifty or so conversation starters, Grace womanfully got out of bed at oh-dark-thirty on Saturday morning and dragged herself to Hawk's.

Only to find that both Rick and John weren't there.

They weren't there Sunday either.

That was unusual. That was weird.

Weirder still, Rick wasn't there when she stumbled into the gym at seven Monday morning. The little placard reading 'reserved' wasn't there. Although John was. She wanted to ask him about where he'd been. About Rick. But she held off. She wasn't Rick's girlfriend. And even if she was, jealousy and possessiveness like that weren't cool. Trust, now that was cool. Besides, how Rick and John had spent their weekend wasn't any of her business.

Telling herself that over and over like a scratched CD, Grace managed to power through her workout. It wasn't like Rick was her friend.

Never mind that she'd started to think of him as one. You couldn't be friends with a person you never talked to. Even if that person made sure your favorite treadmill was reserved for you and gave you little gold stars.

*

January 21

Grace had no expectations that Tuesday. After all, she was going to the gym to get in shape for her sister's graduation trip. Not because there was some good-looking grouch who happened to occupy the same space as her. Nope. Not at all. No-siree-bob.

When she got to the gym she nodded to John, who—for the first time—actually nodded back.

Wow. That's a change.

It was almost as if she'd done something to earn a place in his good graces. She wondered just what that might be. Buoyed by the unexpected show of acceptance, she practically floated to her usual treadmill. It didn't matter that Mr. Murder Man—Rick—wasn't there. It was going to be a good day.

It didn't take her long to get into the zone. Planting foot after foot to the sound of the soothing voices of her favorite podcast.

She was so engrossed in her workout that she almost didn't notice the guy setting down his stuff next to Rick's usual workout machine.

Almost.

She turned her head, and before she could stop herself, she jumped off the still-moving treadmill and threw her arms around a surprised Rick's neck. "You're not dead!"

"What?"

She realized what she'd done and jumped back. "Oh shit! I'm sorry! No permission. I'm sorry! Bad touch. Bad touch!" Her cheeks were no doubt candy-apple red. "But yay, you're not dead!" The words sounded lame to her ears.

"Was I supposed to be?"

As if her mouth was a faucet and those five words a twist of the wrist, pure unadulterated babble started spilling from her lips. "Well, you weren't here on Saturday, and then you weren't here on Sunday, and then you weren't here on Monday, and you've always been here, except for when I've come late, and then you weren't here, but that was my fault, and there wasn't the reserved sign and there were no gold stars, and I missed your silences, and I was afraid I'd scared you off because I asked for your name, and maybe I shouldn't have asked for your name, and—"

He held up his hand just shy of touching her lips. "It's okay. It's okay. As you can see, I'm not dead. I'm not upset with you asking my name. I will admit I've forgotten yours, but that's because I'm crap with names. Isn't that right, John?" He raised his voice for the last.

"Yup!" came John's shouted reply.

"See?"

"It's Grace. Like Grace Kelly if you like old movies and stuff, or like the virtue if you're channeling Puritanical times like my parents were when they were naming us." The faucet was still on. Yay. "Or like what you say before meals if you can't think of anything else."

He held up his hand again. "Okay, I think I'm going to remember that. Thanks, Grace."

"I'm... I'm sorry about the hug." The faucet stuttered to a stop. In its place was a giant brick of guilt.

Rick took one step forward, then another. Silently he lifted his arms and wrapped them around her. The hug was brief, achingly brief. "There," he rumbled into her hair. "We're even." He pulled away, a wry little grin on his lips. "Besides, it's Hugging Day."

She felt a little better. Not totally, because touching people without permission was bad, and she held herself to a higher standard. But still, hearing Rick joke about a weird holiday really helped lessen her anxiety. "You're right. It is."

"Of course I'm right. I'm always right. Isn't that right, John?"

"Nope!"

"How is he listening to us? That's creepy! Tell me that's not creepy! You're creepy!" The last was shouted at John.

"Yup!" he shouted back. "My gym! Don't care!"

"It's cameras, isn't it?" She looked around the gym with narrowed eyes, peering at the corners. "It's got to be cameras. Is this like a super secret spy safe house? Are you guys secret agents masquerading as hunky bodybuilders while saving the world from death and destruction in your spare time?"

Rick tilted his head. "You've got an interesting imagination."

"That's not a denial. You know, I promised myself I wouldn't ask where you were this weekend because, you know, prying and privacy and all that, but now I know you were off killing people. You're a hitman. And now you're going to silence me for figuring you out, aren't you." Apparently she'd traded the brick for the faucet again. *Great...*

"Is..." His brow furrowed. "Is that supposed to be a question?"

"No, not a question. Just a statement of fact. You're going to kill me now. It's okay. I should've known better. After all, you can never trust a guy with resting murder face even if he is, you know, really good-looking and does really sweet things like give you gold stars and reserve your favorite treadmill." She spread her arms out wide. "Go ahead. Do it now. I'm ready."

"You seriously think I'm going to kill you in front of an entire gym of people?" he asked deadpan.

"Oh, right, that would be stupid. So later, when I least expect it?"

"You're really into this whole 'I'm a murderer' thing, aren't you?"

"It's your face. And those abs. But mostly the face."

Rick collapsed against the weight machine, his shoulders shaking as he desperately attempted not to laugh. His mouth twitched, one corner quirking ever so slightly upward and upward and upward with each jolt. "I'm a model."

"Sure you are."

"No, really, I am. You ever heard of the series *Wanton Warriors*? The one that was on the bestseller list for weeks and that they're turning into a series for Cinemax."

She nodded. She had three of the books downloaded on her e-reader; the first was one of her favorites. "You're saying you've been cast in that?"

"No. I'm on the cover."

"...Of the books?" She blinked.

"Yeah."

"...All of them?"

"Yeah."

"Then how come I don't recognize you?" She had the books! She loved the books! She'd masturbated to the covers of the books!

He lifted the hem of his t-shirt and pulled it up over his head. "You recognize me now?" he asked, muffled by the fabric.

Sad to say, she did. And she recognized the abs that graced several other bestselling novels. Novels that she owned. Novels that she drooled over. Novels that apparently featured the abs of Mr. Murder Man. And now she understood why they only showed the torso and chest region. Grace was fairly certain nobody would buy the books if the hero had resting murder face. Even if said face featured a charming dimple in the one cheek that had now managed to quirk up fully into a smile. "You can put your shirt down now."

He did. "What, you didn't like the view?"

"I didn't say that." She liked the view very much, but she also felt super embarrassed about it. Like she'd failed How Not to Objectify Your Workout Partner 101. "So... I'm glad you're not dead. I'm also slightly disappointed that you're not a secret agent, but I think we should both move past that and forget I ever said it."

He shook his head with a grin. "Consider it forgotten."

She was biting her tongue, she was biting her tongue... nope. She was not biting her tongue. "So are both you and John models?"

"Yup. I also coach Little League in the spring, but... snow. Until then, I gotta do something to pay the bills."

"Hey, I get it. I play with dogs for a living." Fair was fair, right? Plus if she told him about herself, she'd feel less creepy asking him about himself.

"That sounds like an awesome job."

"It's not completely horrible. I mean, like all jobs it's got its good days and its bad days. But what job doesn't suck sometimes?"

"Tell me about it. Standing shirtless in Central Park on a Saturday in January is not my idea of a good time." He felt the bridge of his nose. "Nor is getting beaned in the schnoz by a six-year-old."

That explained the nose. "I don't think that sounds like anybody's idea of a good time." Grace was thoroughly enjoying this conversation with every fiber of her being. It wasn't necessarily one of her pre-prepared conversation topics, but if Rick was willing to bitch about the annoyances of having to pose shirtless and old head injuries, who was she to stop him? Yes, she had assumed Rick had great abs, and the little tank tops and t-shirts he always wore left almost nothing to the imagination, but seeing that taut tummy with a little tan trail of teasingly… and could she think of any more T words to describe the awesomeness of Rick whatever-his-last-name-was's abs? What was his last name? She should probably find that out sometime.

Rick asking her a question brought her back from her momentary journey into abs heaven. "I'm sorry, could you repeat yourself?" She pulled the earbuds out of her ears. It wasn't the reason she'd missed his question, but she wasn't about to tell him that.

"So you really thought I was a murderer."

She was able to catch the hint of sort of sadness tinged with disappointment in his tone. "Not really. I mean, you can't help the way you look. You know, some people have resting bitch face; you've got resting murder face."

"Is that code for you telling me to smile more?"

She'd suspected the abs show earlier was a test, and now she was certain of it. And this was another one. "I wouldn't object, but it wasn't a request. I'm not big into the whole hypocrisy thing. Guys don't get to ask girls to smile; we don't get to ask guys to smile."

"Sounds fair." He paused for a moment, seeming to debate something. "So I've been wondering something."

"Okay."

"About you."

"Oh! Okay."

Was he about to ask her for her number? Was he about to ask if she was single? Was he about to ask her out? That type of thing never happened to her! It barely even happened in romance novels about women like her. In novels as in real life, people like Grace—the plucky comic relief type—never got the guy. She needed to lower her expectations immediately.

"What made you start coming to the gym?"

And low expectations sign is a go.

Tamping down her disappointment, she answered, "I'm training to climb Mauna Kea."

To his credit, he didn't immediately scoff and say 'You?!' in an incredulous tone of voice. "Oh, cool. You do a lot of mountain climbing?"

She gestured at herself. "Do I look like I do a lot of mountain climbing?"

"I try not to judge books by their covers." The tone was deadpan, but the eyes were twinkling.

Two can play this game. "Well, considering you're a cover model and all, I'd imagine that's a good idea." She glanced at the clock on the nearby wall, possibly one of the hiding places for John's security cameras. "Hey, as much as I love this conversation—and let me tell you, I'm absolutely loving this conversation—I should probably finish my workout and go. People get kind of pissy when the person they hired to play with their dogs doesn't show up."

"Oh."

Was that her imagination or did he sound disappointed?

Deciding to throw caution to the wind, she forged on like Lewis and Clark. Or Hephaestus. Depending on what kind of forge you were talking about. "But... if you're not doing anything tomorrow afternoon, I know a great way we can celebrate Answer Your Cat's Questions Day."

He tilted his head in what looked like interest. "Go on."

"I know this really cute cat cafe that's not too far from here. If you're up for it, I can make us a reservation. My boss is friends with the owner. I've always wanted to go and now seems like a good time."

A low slow panty-dropping smile spread across Rick's lips until his entire face transformed from relentless killer to sexy boy next door. "That sounds like fun." He reached into his bag and pulled out his phone. "Let me text you my number."

The internal fist pump she made probably set off tremors in California.

*

January 22

It took a little finagling; it always did in New York. But after a few phone calls to the cafe, numerous text messages to Rick—she'd finally found out his last name: Falcon!—and one very impassioned pleading with her boss to let her leave work early, Grace had a time, place, and location for her date.

At least she assumed it was a date. It felt like a date. She hoped it was a date. She'd changed into her 'my ass looks amazing in these' jeans and a simple navy blue sweater. Grace had considered and ultimately rejected wearing one of her silk accent scarves. They were meeting at a cat cafe. The chances of her getting cat hair on everything: high. Her desire to go to the dry cleaner: low.

Laziness for the win!

So one of her polyester ones would have to do. At least she wasn't wearing pajamas or scrubs. Or her workout clothes. And she did look awesome. Rick wouldn't know what hit him.

And… that's sort of what happened.

Oh, Rick totally knew what hit him—her hair. Her cute high ponytail turned into a cat o' nine tails in the blustery January wind. Anyone who came within reach of the auburn strands risked losing an eye or getting a mouthful of hair. Including Rick. Not the way she wanted to start their date. But how was she supposed to know they'd be kept waiting outside the shop until their reserved time?

"Sorry! Sorry, sorry!" she kept repeating over and over as she fished around in her corduroy backpack purse for a scrunchie.

"Hey, it's okay. I'm just glad I wore protection." He motioned to his horn-rimmed glasses.

She'd definitely noticed the glasses. Glasses, man-bun, bomber jacket. Rick was ticking every single one of her turn-ons, as well as a few she hadn't known she had.

With a little bit of disappointment, she twisted her hair up, securing it with the scrunchie. But now they had matching buns. Although society had yet to embrace the messy bun on women as much as it had with men. At least her makeup was still on-point. "So now you see why I always wear my hair in a bun for workouts. It's a lethal weapon if not contained."

"Be careful; the DoD might want a piece of that action."

"Are you sure you're not a secret agent?"

Rick chuckled but evaded her question. "I think they're opening the door." He fished his wallet out.

She stopped him. "I'm the one who asked you out. I pay."

After a moment, he put the wallet away. "Sounds fair. But only if I get to buy you a drink."

She squinted at the various notices in the windows. "I'm not sure if they serve drinks here."

"We can always get one later." There was more than a hint of suggestion in his voice.

Wait. Is he asking me out on a second date? We haven't even technically started our first one! Her inner teenager was clutching a Rick-shaped pillow and squeeing for all she was worth. This was amazing! Exciting! She hadn't felt this ecstatic since that time in high school when she'd gone to see One Direction at Madison Square Garden. It was that level of awesome. *Play it cool. Play it cool, Grace.* "That—that sounds good." She winced internally at the stutter but hoped he'd pass it off as cold not nerves.

Thankfully the door opened, and a stream of people exited the shop saving her from any further foot-in-mouth problems… at least for now. She was sure she was going to eat her shoe later. It was as inevitable as the sun rising in the east and setting in the west.

It wasn't long before Rick and Grace were ensconced in a little booth, a tuxedo cat lazily batting at the feather at the end of a string Rick was holding.

"He likes you," Grace observed.

"How can you tell?" Rick asked, bouncing the string.

"He's letting you play with him. Cats don't stick around people they don't like." She paused for a bit thinking. "Neither do most animals. Humans are the only ones that hang around people or things they hate."

Rick's head swirled toward her, a confused expression plastered on his face.

Ah. It's time to eat rubber. "Not that I'm saying I don't like you, I mean, I do like you! I mean, I asked you out, on a date—clearly that means I like you!"

"Grace." Rick's voice was calm. "I'm not upset with you. You don't need to worry. I like you too."

"You do? I mean, of course you do. I'm awesome."

"Yes, yes you are." He reached out to bop her on the tip of her nose. "I'm glad you see it."

"So… since I'm so awesome, do you mind if I share a secret with you?" Grace leaned closer to him.

Rick echoed the motion. "I live for secrets."

"I have no idea what to talk about. I'm not an ace at this whole dating thing."

"Who is?" Rick shrugged. "Dating's hard. Flirting's hard. I think half the time that's the reason why people stay in bad relationships longer than they should. Putting yourself back out there? Having to go through the whole first date rigmarole and get-to-know-you phase?" He shuddered. "I bet it sometimes feels easier to just try to stick it through."

There was something in the way he said it that made Grace think he was speaking from personal experience. But she knew better than to ask. Past relationships were definitely off the first date menu. "So, you like cats?" It wasn't the most graceful subject change. But dang it, she gave herself props for not going down the landmine-filled highway Rick had hinted at.

Rick seemed relieved at the subject change. "Yeah. I like cats. And dogs. My roommate Eli has a dog."

"What kind of dog?" She couldn't help herself; it was a pitfall of the trade.

"Big, fluffy, tan."

"Golden retriever?"

"Maybe part of her." He shrugged again. "She's a mutt. And before you can ask, Eli has adamantly proclaimed he is not going to do a doggy DNA test. He wants Sadie to know he loves her just the way she is."

Grace didn't even bother to make a comment about the fact that Sadie would have no idea Eli was doing a DNA test, nor would she care. She'd long since learned pet owners were weird about their fuzzy children. Because she had yet to meet a pet owner who didn't regard their pet as something akin to a child. "Is Eli your only roommate? Other than Sadie, I mean."

"Well, technically Eli and I are both subletting from John. He's the one with the credit and the stable job." Rick sounded sort of dejected.

Throwing caution to the wind, Grace gently stroked her fingers over his hand, just a brief touch. "If it makes you feel any better, I still live with my parents."

"See, now you're smart. If I'd had any brains, I would've stayed with my parents back in Maine. Instead, I followed my dreams and even played for a minute for the Mets. And look where that got me."

"Yes. On a date with me."

He let out a guffaw that devolved into gut-wrenching laughter, startling the cat. The animal gave him an offended look with his yellow-green eyes before sauntering away, tail held high.

"I think we've lost our cat," Grace mock-whispered.

Rick nudged her shoulder with his before leaning his head against hers. "That's okay. I came here to spend time with you, not the cats."

She didn't know why, but those few words made her feel all warm and gooshy inside. "Well, that's a good thing since we are currently catless."

Rick's fingers slid along her arm to capture her hand in his. "I really don't mind."

"Okay." What else could she say to that without sounding horribly insecure or massively overconfident?

"I'm a little surprised you wanted to come play with kittens considering you said your job is playing with dogs. What kind of a job is playing with dogs anyway?" His thumb stroked the edge of hers. "And how can I get in on that action?"

She barely heard his questions over the pounding of her heart. *Damn it, self! Get it together!* "Have you heard of doggy day care?"

"Yeah, Eli brings Sadie to one when he's got a job."

"So, that's what I do. People drop off their dogs before they go to work or wherever, and we play with them, we watch them, we break up fights before they start, and…" she paused for a second, "we pick up lots and lots of poop."

Rick made a face. "Sounds decidedly less glamorous than what I was picturing."

"Well, considering you work in the super glamorous job of modeling, yeah. How'd you get into that anyways?"

"Eli."

"That tells me absolutely nothing."

He grinned at her. "All right. I see your game."

"Game? What game? I have no game." …*Wait.* "That didn't come out right."

He just shook his head as he laughed. "I love that your mouth has no filter. It's like being on an adventure. You never know what's going to happen next."

"Yes. But on adventures you also end up, you know, attacked by kobolds. Or eaten by a grue." She shrugged at his expression. "What? I played D&D in high school. It's fun."

"It is. I just… you know, I'm going to stop right there before I put my foot in my mouth and say something really sexist."

"Good plan." She squeezed his hand. "And A+ deflection, but I totally made my perception roll. So spill. How does Eli equal you becoming a cover model?"

"Eli's a photographer. Freelance. Which is just a nice way of saying unemployed a lot of the time. Considering playing in the minor leagues doesn't really pay the bills, and coaching Little League can only get you so far…" Rick's lips quirked up. "He needed money, I needed money, his then-girlfriend needed money. Which equaled take a lot of photos and upload them to various stock photo sites to get royalties. Twenty pictures turned into two hundred, and before I knew it, Eli and I had a decent client base."

"Huh. Cool. I totally want to say something much more intelligent right now, and I'm completely failing. Sorry."

"Kind of how I feel about your dog thing." He squeezed her hand again. "Let's call it even."

"We can do that." She dropped his hand to point at something. "Besides, I think a new cat has decided to come check us out."

A lovely tortoiseshell, who'd snuck up behind him, butted her head against Rick's forearm. Grinning, he obeyed the implicit command and stroked her head. The stately cat let out a little chirrup that sounded surprisingly interrogatory.

Grace clapped her hands. "I think she just asked us a question!" She looked at the cat. "Did you just ask us a question?"

The cat just blinked.

Skimming his hand along the feline's back, Rick leaned over and whispered in Grace's ear, "Happy Answer Your Cat's Questions Day."

Yes. She was very happy indeed.

*

January 29

A week later, Grace was still happy. Happy because she was able to walk for sixty minutes on a twenty percent incline without getting winded and happy because she was pretty darn sure she had managed to find herself a sexy, sweet, and silly boyfriend.

Rick embraced her weird holiday fetish with an enthusiasm that rivaled her own. The Friday after their first date, he gave her a little jar of peanut butter. The following Monday he gave her a slice of chocolate cake. And yesterday a kazoo. She didn't even know they still made kazoos! Now she was debating what she should do for him, considering it was Curmudgeons Day—a day that had Rick written all over it, or at least his resting murder face. Because Rick still managed to frighten away potential workout partners simply by looking at them. Now she understood why John had prophesied that she wouldn't like the treadmill she had now grown to love.

Ha! I sure showed him.

Grace got to the gym early, a handmade card carefully stuffed into her gym bag. Hallmark hadn't quite gotten around to acknowledging the holiday yet; besides, the nearest Hallmark store was two subway stops and a bus ride away from her house. And there was no way her local CVS was going to carry a card for an underappreciated holiday like this. They didn't even carry stepfamily birthday cards! Homemade would have to do.

Carefully, oh so carefully, she prepared her gift. Not just the card, but a USB thumb drive with all of the best songs guaranteed to defeat any grouch or curmudgeon. She'd spent hours on her computer picking songs by people like Pharrell Williams and The Lonely Island. Leaving the gift on the weight machine Rick used most often, she grabbed her earbuds and put on her favorite playlist.

Grace was hoping to convince Rick to go out with her this week. Their schedules hadn't meshed since the cat cafe. Maybe they could graduate from one coffee date with a dinner nightcap to two coffee dates and a dessert nightcap.

She'd just climbed onto her treadmill when she felt someone slip up behind her. She turned her head to see Rick standing there holding the card in his hand as if it were made of gold. The expression on his face was halfway between awe and adoration. For her. Her: Grace Anne O'Leary. *Huh. Apparently homemade weird holiday cards are the way to this man's heart. Who knew?*

"Is... what you wrote here true?"

She pulled out an earbud and nodded, a smile slipping across her lips.

"You're asking me to be your boyfriend."

Another nod.

"Like you really and truly want to be my girlfriend?" It was like he couldn't believe it.

"I'm pretty sure I didn't stutter in the card."

That seemed to shake his mood out of the low self-esteem sinkhole he'd fallen into. "How would you stutter in a card?"

"Trust me, if hundreds upon thousands of novelists can figure out how to write stutters in text, I could've figured out a way to write a stutter in a card. So you can take what I wrote there as truth. I want to date you. I want you to be my boyfriend. For reals."

His smile was breathtaking. "Okay."

"'Okay' you understand what I mean? Or 'okay' you're willing to be my boyfriend?"

"Both."

Success! Keep it together, Grace. I'm pretty sure John doesn't want me bouncing all over his gym like a ball of Flubber. "Cool! In celebration I declare that my first act as your official girlfriend is to kiss you. Do I hear any objections?"

Rick's eyes widened but not a peep came out of his mouth.

Taking his pointed silence as permission, she hopped off the treadmill and into Rick's arms, wrapping her legs around his oh-so-trim waist. The kiss was by necessity short. She could only hold herself up like that for so long. And she didn't want to overwhelm the guy. After all, if a card could render him ready to worship at her feet, what would a kiss do?

Oh, but what a kiss. Her lips on his, him responding. Everything tingled from her head to her toes. Her tongue darted out to tease along the seam of his lips, then darted back in again. She kept her mouth on his, tasting him. Taunting him. Being with him.

She knew she couldn't keep this up forever. People were probably watching. John was probably watching. Exhibitionism was not one of her kinks. Regretfully, she let herself slide down his frame. Her legs dropped until she could stand again, but she stayed with him, chasing every last bit of his flavor.

When they separated, Grace let her hand rest over Rick's rapidly beating heart. "Thanks for letting me be a little silly with you. I know it wasn't the kind of kiss you were expecting."

Rick brought a finger up to place it over her lips. "I liked it. It wasn't traditional, but I'm coming to find—especially around you—that I don't really care that much about tradition."

"Oh. So would it be a good thing or a bad thing if I were to ask you out on a date tonight? We could maybe go play on the swings in the park, and then I know this place that makes a killer cheesecake. Like I swear the thing is eight inches tall. There's no way one person could eat a whole slice all by themselves, but for you I'm willing to chance it."

Rick laughed and pulled her close. "That sounds absolutely perfect. See you at six?"

Heedless of the watching gym, Grace leaned up to press another kiss to his lips and murmured, "I wouldn't miss it."

*

January 31

There was something to be said for dating a person who had the same weird aesthetic that you did. With Rick, Grace didn't feel the need to justify her life choices. She played with dogs for a living. Liked celebrating the odder days of life. And reveled in the brainless joy that were things like *Face Off*, *Project Runway*, and *Chopped*.

Sure, Rick was way more into baseball than she would ever be. But that was okay. So long as she could read her Courtney Milan without getting a smug side-eye, she was happy.

She was coming to find that what made a good relationship wasn't an overabundance of common interests and beliefs, but a comfortable acceptance of the little quirks that made the other person unique. Maybe she was finally growing up.

She looked up from her place in Rick's lap and saw her boyfriend of two whole days staring at the TV, a rope of red licorice dangling from his mouth in a mirror of her own.

Nah. Growing up is definitely overrated.

After all, their definition of Netflix and chill didn't involve sexy bedroom times—they weren't quite ready for that, although she could see that coming eventually and would welcome it when it did. Instead, their version of Netflix and chill featured the two of them lying on Rick's sheet-covered couch in the apartment he shared with John and Eli above the gym watching *The Joy of Painting* with her feet propped up on top of his roommate's incredibly patient golden retriever mix, Sadie. Whatever. It worked.

"You know, we should do this sometime," Rick said, not even looking down at her.

Her eyes flicked to the screen to see Bob painting a happy little cloud. "I don't know. I'm not really all that artistic. I mean, I like looking at art. I like watching art being done. I just can't make what I have in my head come out on the canvas."

"Neither can I. But it'd be fun." He gestured to the screen. "And as Bob says, we don't make mistakes. We just have happy accidents."

"I guarantee every dog owner in the world will disagree with that statement."

"You got that right!" Eli's voice filtered in from the other room.

At the sound of her owner's voice, Sadie slid off the couch, her back legs stretching out to their fullest as she hauled her body upright. With a little shake to set herself to rights, she trotted off to receive pets from her person.

"Yo, dude, can you not eavesdrop on my date?" Rick's voice was simultaneously annoyed and amused.

"Nope! This is an 800 square foot apartment. The walls are thinner than cardboard. The doors are paper. I can hear Mrs. Moretti cooing over her grandchildren; what makes you think I can't hear you?"

Rick ran his fingers through her hair. "We should've gone to your house."

Grace shook her head. "My house is worse. At least Eli isn't deliberately trying to listen in. My sister and parents on the other hand? You can be damn well sure they'd be pressed up to the door with glasses held up to their ears."

"What makes you think I'm not doing that?" Eli called.

"Because if you did, my foot would meet your ass with alarming regularity," Grace called back.

Eli laughed. "Okay. Point made. Privacy is needed, and I'm the third wheel. I'm going to take Sadie for a walk so you two can have a good old snogfest. I'll be back in an hour. If you haven't boinked by then, it's not my fault."

After Eli left, Grace sat up and looked at Rick. "Eli's from Brooklyn, right?"

"Well, originally from Staten Island, but his parents moved to Brooklyn when he was three. Why'd you ask?"

"Oh, I don't know. He just keeps using terms that I've only ever heard from people in Britain."

"Ah. No, no, he's just a huge Shakespeare fan. He's been to Stratford-upon-Avon three times. Gets six yearly tickets for Shakespeare in the Park and uses them all himself. I think that's why his last boyfriend and girlfriend left. Two shows, six tickets, and he used them all himself." Rick shook his head and made a disapproving noise.

"Eli's poly?"

"Like an octopus."

"What does that even mean?"

Rick opened his mouth to explain then stopped. "You know, I'm not even sure. It just sounded good."

That brought up another question. "Not that I mean to pry, but have you and Eli and/or John ever…"

"Nope." His head shake looked long-suffering. "But you're not the first person to ask that. I swear my mother still doesn't believe me. The number of scarves she's knit for John and Eli is a little insane. Assuming you'll stick with me, I'm really looking forward to introducing you to my mother."

Grace liked scarves. She had a larger than was healthy collection of them. But she couldn't quite bring herself to Marie Kondo them. They all sparked joy. "Think she'll make me a scarf?"

"Schmoopy, she'll make you a hundred."

She frowned. "Schmoopy?"

"Yeah. Kind of like sweety and Snoopy put together. Schmoopy. I like it better than 'sweetheart' or 'darling' or 'babe.'" He grabbed her hand. "It fits you. You're funny and smart and not what you'd expect, like Snoopy. But you're also sweet and loving, and I just want to eat you all up."

The word still sounded strange. Weird. But she had to admit she liked it. "I hope you don't mind that I don't have a funny and unique nickname for you." Rick didn't need to know that, until she'd actually known his name, she'd called him 'Mr. Murder Man.' He really really did not need to know that. It'd be her secret… forever and ever and ever.

"Yet," Rick told her, stroking the back of her hand with his thumb. "Give it time." He paused. "Just so long as whatever name you come up with for me isn't along the line of 'Numbnuts.' Or 'That Bastard.'"

"So you're saying you have veto power."

Rick struggled for a long time, clearly searching for a good comeback. His mouth opened and closed as she was sure he was coming up with, and then promptly discarding, idea after idea.

Grace watched his discomfiture with amusement. "Did I get your tongue?"

"Are you saying you're a cat?" Rick countered, visibly relieved by the change of subject.

She tilted her head back and forth considering. "Well, on one hand, I really like laying in sunbeams. But on the other hand… fish? Ugh. Not even deep-fried and smothered in tartar sauce." She nuzzled closer to Rick, rubbing her body and face against him. "Then again, I like cuddling and stroking and sliding my body against my human's."

"But…" Rick's voice was strangled.

"Just go with it. Do you want me to stop?"

He shook his head.

"You know, I think we should take your roommate's advice and have ourselves a little snogfest."

"Okay, but what about Bob?" He pointed at the TV screen. "Aren't we supposed to be inspiring our hearts with art today?"

"Oh, I think Bob won't mind." She paused the stream and gazed deep into Rick's eyes. "And I'm plenty inspired right now. Just so you know, I am going to straddle you. Then I'm going to wrap my arms around your neck and give you quite possibly one of the deepest kisses ever known to man. From there, there may be progressively less and less clothing. There will not, however, be any sexytimes. Please let me know now if you have any problems with the above. Revision and editing is possible if feedback is given in a timely enough manner."

"A man would have to be out of his mind if he had a problem with you doing that to him, Schmoopy."

Taking that as the yes it was, Grace did exactly what she'd promised. She turned around in Rick's lap until she faced him, settling one knee on each side of his. If she positioned herself just right, she could grind her center into him. But that was for another day.

Her hands glided up Rick's arms, over his long-sleeved Henley, to loop around his neck. There, she went slightly off-script. Her fingers found the base of his neck and the silky smooth strands of hair curled there. She ran her fingers through his hair and along his scalp. As she watched, his eyes slid shut, an expression of utter contentment and trust settling over his slightly less murderous features. If that wasn't a cue, she didn't know what was.

She bent down to cover his mouth with hers. The kiss started off soft, just the way she planned. Just the gentle press of skin against skin. An act of trust. And an invitation for more. Rick's chin tilted up slightly, asking, pleading for her to deepen the kiss.

She did.

Her tongue slipped out to glide along the fullness of his lips. It was a request, not a demand. But Rick answered yes anyway, his mouth opening underneath hers, his tongue coming out to trace spine-tingling lines over hers.

Grace took time with the kiss, breathing through her nose to prolong it. There was no need to rush. They had time. Plenty of time. And as much as part of her wanted to do more, she knew kissing was all they were going to do today.

She pulled back. "Pick an item of clothing."

He stared at her. "Huh?"

"For me to remove."

"Um... uh... socks?"

She blinked. "I'm wearing a sweater, a shirt, a bra, a pair of jeans, and panties. And the clothing item you pick is socks?"

"It's the first thing that came to my head! I don't do well under pressure!"

She lifted an eyebrow at that. "If that's the case, then I definitely know who's taking charge in the bedroom."

"Oh! You!" One of his fingers curled around a strand of her hair. "Definitely you. Absolutely you. Never a doubt in my mind."

That was oddly heartening to hear. So many guys felt they had to be the leader when it came to sex. The fact that Rick was willing to let her call the shots? It was incredibly empowering. Empowering and more than a little hot. "Well, since you asked." She leaned backward to tug her socks off.

"Are those sheep?" he asked, peering at the pattern.

"Hedgehogs. You lose."

His arms slipped up to her waist to pull her closer. "You're here. I'm definitely winning."

A rush of warmth flowed at his words. "You are one funny boyfriend."

"But I'm your boyfriend. What does that say about you?"

"Point. So since tomorrow's February, I was thinking. There's this big Hallmark holiday in February and..." She trailed off as she noticed his expression change from contentment to guilt. "Did I say something wrong?"

"Yes. No. Kind of? So... I've got a gig. Nothing sexual, not really. But the publisher I do a lot of work for throws a huge party every Valentine's Day and invites all of the cover models to dress up as the characters from the covers that they've graced. And romance fans from literally all around the world come to this thing. We're auctioned off—it's 'spend Valentine's Day with your book boyfriend.' I can't get out of it. The gig pays enough to cover rent and bills for more than a month. Even John's going, and he only models part-time when Eli begs because Black cover models are hard to find."

"Oh." She thought about it. "So is it completely weird that I think that sounds like fun and I kind of want to go?"

Rick winced. "Oh please don't. I have a hard enough time trying to stay in character when I'm there. Having you there… I don't think I could do it!"

"Are you saying I'm distracting?"

"Yes! That is exactly what I'm saying. You distract the heck out of me. It's why I couldn't even say hi to you until, I don't know, two weeks after we met."

That explained the grunting. "Huh. Okay, no one's ever said that to me before."

"Yeah, well, it's true. As much as you were distracted by my abs, I was distracted by," his hands drifted lower to rest at the very top of her buttocks, "something round and curvy that I just wanted to put my hands all over but really, really couldn't."

She reached back and moved them all the way down. "Is this what you're talking about?"

"Oh yeah," he breathed just letting his hands rest there. "That's it. Day's made, can't get any better than this."

She bent down to kiss him again. "Sure it can." She glanced over at the clock. "We've still got forty more minutes before Eli gets back. How about we make the most of them?"

"More Bob Ross?"

She unpaused the stream. "It's like you read my mind."

*

February 16

February passed in a blink.

Between her job and his gigs, Grace and Rick managed to set aside at least a couple of days a week when they got to just hang out, have fun, and bask in each other's presence.

Because Rick was tied up on both Friday and Saturday of Valentine's Day weekend, Grace was able to trade with one of her coworkers to get off Presidents Day. But more importantly, she was able to snap up a suite at the St. Regis for a song. She was going to give Rick the best Do a Grouch a Favor Day ever.

As she walked up the steps from the N train, she went over her to-do-list one more time. They were scheduled to meet at the gym at 6:00 p.m. It was 3:00 p.m. now. Three hours to check in, decorate the room appropriately, arrange the Tim Tams she'd ordered online artistically, and make it back across town to her parents' to get all dolled up.

...Plenty of time.

It was, but only if you squinted and tilted your head. Ten minutes late wasn't late, right? Besides, she had a good excuse... that she couldn't use if she didn't want to spoil the surprise.

As it was, she ended up having to half-jog down the slippery sidewalk dodging trash bags and pedestrians in her haste to be on time. *Whatever male invented high heels needs to be stabbed with a stiletto... repeatedly!*

Rick's Dorito-shaped form materialized ahead of her, and she skittered to a stop. *Blue is definitely his color,* she thought inanely. His shirt matched his eyes almost exactly, and the black pants he had on fit him like a glove.

She had to stop herself from panting from desire. On the plus side, all of her workouts were paying off. She wasn't anywhere near winded... that definitely boded well for later.

"Hey," he greeted, taking her hand as soon as she got close enough. He gently tugged her toward him.

She went willingly, leaning up to kiss him lightly on the lips. That was a plus for heels: she didn't have to stand on tiptoe to reach his mouth. "Hey."

When he pulled back, he looked down at her. "You have something planned."

He knew her too well. Not that that was a bad thing. "I do. And it's a surprise. Are you okay with that?"

Kissing her again, he said, "Yeah."

"Okay, then... our Lyft is on the way. Put on this blindfold and these headphones—" she took them out of her bag "—and you'll find out the surprise when we get there."

He put the headphones on as the car pulled up. The driver rolled down her window. "Grace?"

Grace glanced at the license plate to make sure it matched the app and led Rick to the car. Once inside, she helped him tie the blindfold. "Late Valentine's Day surprise," she said to the driver who nodded and headed toward Manhattan.

Sitting in a car in headphones and a blindfold seemed like it would be pretty boring. Which meant it was up to Grace to keep Rick occupied. She held his hand, drawing little shapes and letters in the palm of his hand. *The Miracle Worker* she was not, but it passed the time.

The driver pulled up in front of the hotel, and she helped Rick out, making sure to guide him so he wouldn't fall. The doorman ushered them into the elevator leading into the lobby; thank you, ADA compliance. Trying to manage stairs and a revolving door while blindfolded and wearing headphones was nigh impossible.

She led him across the marble floors toward the elevators, ignoring the painted ceiling, gilt-covered walls, and chairs that wouldn't have looked out of place in Buckingham Palace. The elevators were as fancy as the rest of the place, all smooth wood and mirrors, but it didn't take long to reach their floor and then their suite.

Once inside, Grace leaned up to kiss Rick again and untied the blindfold.

He blinked as the light hit his eyes. Pulling the headphones off, he looked around.

Grace tried to see it through his eyes. They were in a beautifully decorated sitting room with a couple of couches and a flatscreen TV. On the coffee table, she'd put out a plate of Tim Tams, arranged as artistically as she could manage in about three minutes. AKA they were in a circle around the strawberries she'd also brought. A bucket of ice stood next to two empty glasses. On one of the window ledges there were three boxes, labeled 'Box 1,' 'Box 2,' and 'Box 3.' Through the door to the bedroom she could see the stuffed Oscar the Grouch sitting on the bed, a pink envelope in his arms. In it she knew there were condoms of varying sizes—she believed in being prepared.

"Wow," Rick said. "You really went all out. Tim Tams, Oscar the Grouch…" His eyes flicked to the boxes. "If there's whales or pangolins or almonds in those, I think you've hit every holiday."

Grace grinned. "I absolutely nailed Innovation Day."

"Yeah, Schmoopy, you did." He kissed her nose. "So which box has the stuff for Almond Day?"

"None of the above."

"Oh. So we're skipping—"

A knock on the door interrupted whatever Rick was saying, but Grace had already caught the gist. "You were saying?" she tossed over her shoulder as she sauntered to the door.

The delivery man smiled and handed her a large bag which smelled absolutely heavenly. With a five and a thanks, she shut the door again and motioned for Rick to join her at the small table and chairs in the corner.

She lifted the plastic takeout containers out of the paper bag. "I present to you your almonds."

Rick lifted the top of one container to reveal an order of almond chicken. "Huh. Chinese. I would've gone with mandelbrot. Or biscotti."

She reached into the bag and pulled out a foil-wrapped container which she opened to reveal a few slices of mandelbrot. "What makes you think I didn't? There's amaretto in the fridge. And I may or may not have gotten a few Almond Joys. So we're covered with almonds."

He blinked. "That didn't come out quite right, did it?"

"Well, it depends on if you choose between Boxes 1, 2, or 3," she said in her best game show host voice.

"Do I need to decide now or can we have dinner?"

"I'm down for dinner if you are." Her stomach echoed the sentiment. "See?"

As they ate, they talked, mostly about what had happened at the party Rick had attended the night before. But when they reached an acceptable pause in the conversation, Grace seized the moment. "So I have a question for you."

Rick's eyes widened.

"No no, not that kind of question. But related... kind of, maybe, sort of. Well, technically I have two questions that are definitely related. But I'll stop babbling now and ask them. Question number one, which you will answer first: is there anything about me that you want to ask but haven't really felt comfortable doing so? Bring it on. Tonight I am an open book."

Rick blinked, then blinked again. "Why do you want to climb Mauna Kea?"

She stared at him. "Out of everything you could possibly ask, you want to know why I want to climb Mauna Kea."

"I thought we'd already established that I am not good under pressure when it comes to these kind of questions. Or do I need to remind you of 'socks' one more time?"

"Okay, so to answer your question, I don't really want to climb Mauna Kea. But my sister does. And I want to be there for her while she does it. She's not expecting me to; Hope would be totally fine with me hanging back at the Airbnb, but I'm not."

"Huh. Okay. So if I want to ask if I can come along..."

"Oh! Oh, well, okay then. Well no, not okay. I mean, I'd love to have you come along, but it's a family trip, but maybe someday we can climb the highest mountains... and I'm going to stop now before I head too far into copyright infringement."

"You know that's not the line."

"Yes, I do know that's not the line, but how do you know that's not the line?"

"It plays every year at Christmas. My mom is the biggest Julie Andrews fan. I even know all the lines from *Victor/Victoria* if that tells you anything."

It didn't, but she wasn't about to say that. "Okay, so you answered my first question. The second, which I will also give you time to answer since it's going to put you on the spot, is: is there anything about you that you want me to know? That you wish you could sort of put out there to anybody who dates you?" She let him mull through the question, watching his expressive murder face as he tried to put the thoughts into words.

"That's a hard question," he said after a time. "If you haven't figured it out by now, I should probably let you know that I don't like being in charge. I don't like making tons and tons of decisions. I am the complete opposite of an alpha male. I may be built like one but I like being told what to do. It's... comforting."

"You like being told what to do in like a BDSM kind of way?" She hadn't considered that, but she was game. It would require some research on her part, but if Rick needed a domme, she'd be willing to try.

"No, not really. I mean, I like it when my partner takes control sexually, but being ordered around for being ordered around's sake isn't what I mean. Like, I really really liked it that you asked me out first. That you initiated our first kiss. That you initiated our touching. It let me know where the boundaries were, and I didn't have to sit there and guess." He paused for a moment. "I'm also not really into pain or humiliation. My last girlfriend was and I discovered I don't make a good sub."

"Is it because the sub's ultimately the one who's in control?" She'd read enough romance novels to know that.

He seemed to think about that for a moment, light dawning in his eyes. "Yeah, I think it is."

"I hope you don't expect me to make all of your decisions for you, like... when to do your laundry, or when and what to eat."

"Oh, no! I have no problems doing chores, especially if I make a list."

She noted that he said 'I' make a list, not his girlfriend or somebody else. "So what you're saying is that I'm probably going to have to be the one to decide if and when this relationship is over or if it's going to the next step."

He shifted around uncomfortably. "If by the next step you mean sex, I was ready for that two weeks ago. But if you mean like marriage and kids, then… probably yeah. I get comfortable with the status quo, and I'm sort of scared to change it."

"I think I can work with that. It may take some hard heart-to-heart talks like this, but so long as you're able to communicate with me, I don't see why that's a deal breaker."

A tension she hadn't realized he'd been carrying since they'd started dating flowed out of him. It really was a big deal in his book. *Huh.* For all that society said men had to be the ones in charge, she'd never really considered that not all men would want to be. She tilted her head at him. "Do you think you could play big alpha male if I asked you to?"

"Did you have something in mind? One of Eli's girlfriends had me go to the restaurant she worked at to stare down the manager who was harassing her. Do I need to do that to your boss?"

"Oh, no, Carol's awesome. And while I occasionally end up with touches in uncomfortable places, they're always canine. It's a hazard of the job. No, I was thinking more for fun. Roleplaying. Fun stuff like that."

"Oh, well, yeah. I do already for my job, so… sure?"

"So moving backwards while also moving forwards, I seem to recall hearing that you were up for sex. Is that on the menu for tonight?"

"It is if it's being offered. I don't want you to do anything overly special for my sake. I want you to want it too."

He was so adorably concerned as he said it. Like he didn't want to scare her off, but at the same time didn't want to talk her out of it. It was refreshing. She liked being able to do things at her own pace. Yeah, she'd have to check in with Rick to make sure that he was good with it, but she'd have to do that in any relationship. It wasn't a hardship.

"Moving on to more fun stuff, it does however require you to make a decision."

"I can make decisions about fun things. They might not be great decisions, but they'll be decisions. What kind of decisions will I need to make?"

"Pick a box. One box is sexy, one box is silly, and one is a combination of the two. Whatever box you pick, you can either keep or you can decide if you want to trade."

"You're doing a Monty Hall problem?"

"I do like *Let's Make a Deal*. They play the Game Show Network in the background at my job. It's a little hard to pay attention to the pups when Wayne Brady's on the screen. You're just lucky that setting up a *Press Your Luck* kind of board would take too much work."

Rick just stared at her.

She realized she was referencing a game show from the 1980s that had had a minor resurgence in the summer... and probably not one he'd watched. "You know, 'big money, big money, no whammies?'"

He shook his head.

"Never mind. It's not important. Pick a box."

"Uh... number three."

She lifted it up to reveal a frilly white negligee and a deck of cards. "If you choose this, Rick Falcon, you will get one evening of intense strip poker where you could possibly have your girlfriend end up wearing this or less. Or," she went to Box 1, "do you want to trade?"

"I'm not sure. Is this the sexy option, the little bit of both... the silly?"

"I'm not telling you. But how 'bout I show you something that you didn't pick?" She went to Box 1. "Last chance to trade for this box."

"No, I'm going to keep what I have."

"Okay." She lifted the box to reveal a smorgasbord of sex toys. Everything from multiple kinds of vibrators to a cock ring and even a pair of nipple clamps. Grace watched his face closely, trying to gauge how he felt about this revelation. As she'd hoped, there was a hint of excitement followed by disappointment that he hadn't picked this box. She wanted to tell him it was okay, they could play with the toys later, but that would break the whole *Let's Make a Deal* shtick. "So now you've got the hard choice, Rick. Are you going to go with Box 2 or stick with Box 3?"

"Where's a studio audience when you need one?"

"Are you really into exhibitionism?"

"Uh, not really."

"Then I think it's probably a good thing that there isn't a studio audience."

"Point." He paused for a beat. "I'm staying with Box 3."

"Are you sure?"

"I'm confident."

"Okay." She shimmied over to him. "Let's take your winnings and head into the bedroom."

He picked up the negligee and the deck of cards and followed her, pausing in the doorway to break out into laughter when he spotted the Oscar the Grouch plush on the bed again. "I forgot about that," he muttered.

"Go on, open the card."

He did as she said to reveal a belated Valentine's Day note and the condoms she'd placed in the envelope. "You really did plan ahead."

"Uh huh."

"That's, like, super duper sexy. I mean, I can't believe how lucky I am having you as a girlfriend. It's like I don't have to be something I'm not around you."

Grace crossed to him and cupped his handsome murder face between her hands. She stared into his eyes deeply before pressing a very serious kiss to his lips. The kind of kiss that said "thank you" with the added benefit of a promise of more. She took a half-step back, dragging her lips from his with some reluctance. "That goes double for me." She took a step back and tossed the deck of cards at him. "Shuffle up and deal. We're playing five-card draw, jokers wild." She held the negligee up. "I'll be right back."

After some frantic clothes gymnastics and a quick toothbrushing, Grace returned to the bedroom to find Rick propped up on the bed, the deck of cards placed neatly in front of him. She looked at it, picked it up, and shuffled it once, all the while watching Rick's face.

There it was: the tiniest hint of disappointment.

She smirked. "Stacked the deck, did you?"

"Can't blame a guy for trying."

She motioned to her outfit—an emerald green blouse and a knee-length, Slytherin patterned skirt with thigh-high stockings and a few surprises. "You want to see what's under this? You gotta play fair."

"Fine."

What she didn't tell him was that she had absolutely no intention of letting him lose.

She won the first hand. Not because she really wanted to, but because when you're dealt four aces, you really can't throw them away.

Besides, a girl had needs too. She pointed to Rick's chest. "Lose the shirt." She was pleased to see how fast he was willing to comply.

She pouted at the lack of bare chest—he was wearing an undershirt. *Damn.*

But Lady Luck was on her side, and the next two hands relieved him of said undershirt and his shoes.

Another three hands saw her lose her skirt, blouse, and shoes. Currently, the only things she had on were her slip, thigh-high stockings, and the negligee.

Rick dealt the next hand, and Grace couldn't resist a smirk at what she saw: a pair of eights and a pair of queens. She wasn't going to throw away a good hand again. It was time for Rick to lose his pants.

She threw down the odd three. "One."

His eyebrows went up. "That good, huh?"

She just smiled.

He drew two.

Her new card was an ace. It didn't really help her much, but then again it didn't really need to.

"All right, let's see what has you smiling."

She showed her hand.

"Ooh, very nice. But not quite as nice as this." He flipped his hand to reveal a pair of aces and a pair of nines with a spare jack.

Pouting, she said, "All right, what do you want me to take off?"

"The stockings. But… I want to take them off you."

She leaned back against the headboard and motioned for him to proceed.

With an expression like a cat who'd just gotten into the cream, Rick knelt between her feet and brought one stockinged foot up to his chest. He stroked his fingers up and down her calf, sliding higher and higher with each stroke.

Each stroke sent jolts of arousal up her spine. Her clit throbbed in anticipation, her core growing wetter as she watched his progress up her leg. Unable to stop herself, she leaned her head back against the headboard and sighed, "You can stop that any time after the earth stops spinning."

"I take it you like it."

She let out a small moan as his fingers caressed the back of her knee. "Mm, that would be a yes."

"Noted." He continued his soft sensual massage for a few more wonderful blissful moments before he found the edge of her stocking and slowly, ever so slowly, rolled it down her leg. Then he picked up her other foot and propped it up on his shoulder. Instead of his fingers, he kissed his way up her stocking-covered calf to her knee and her thigh, then finally the bare skin beyond.

When Rick's hot wet mouth met her sensitive flesh, Grace couldn't stop the shiver of anticipation that ran through her. Her eyes flew open, and she looked down at Rick's pleased expression from under hooded eyes. "You don't have to ask. I liked it. And I'd like you to do more."

He pressed another kiss to her thigh. "Maybe later. There's a game I need to win."

"Fuck the game." She wanted him inside her now. She wanted to feel his tongue, his fingers, something, rub against her core. She wanted to be filled by him, clench her body around him, devour and be devoured by him. But in that sexy fun way.

"Nuh uh. This was your idea. You need to see this through."

"Bastard."

He grasped the edge of her stocking with his teeth and ripped it down her leg with a smug expression.

"I repeat: bastard."

"And you love it."

She couldn't really deny that, so she just picked up the cards and dealt out the next hand. Which she won.

Rick had to forfeit his pants for his pair of twos, leaving him in only his socks and boxer briefs. The long line of his erection was clearly visible through the black material.

Her mouth watered; she was ready. And she could tell he was too. But now she was back to wanting to win, so she accepted her cards and tried to concentrate on the game. It was hard, and not in that Rick's cock kind of way although that was definitely hard too.

The thought of Rick's length took her head out of the game, and she lost her slip. Which meant that he had two pieces of clothing remaining while she had only the one. With that in mind, she shuffled up the deck of cards and dealt.

When she picked up her hand, she stifled a frown.

Unless there was a miracle, there was no way she was going to win this one.

No pairs, nothing really resembling a straight, all four suits… about the best thing she could really do was throw down all five cards and pray.

Which was what she did.

"That bad, huh?" he asked as he put down two cards.

"You have no idea," she said, giving him his two while counting out five cards for herself. A pair of sevens. Not great—she was probably going to be naked after this. Not that she minded. After all, getting naked was the goal. But she just hated losing like this. To luck, rather than on her terms. "All right, show me."

He laid down trip threes, and Grace knew she had lost.

Or, rather, won.

She locked eyes with Rick and slowly, ever so slowly, skimmed her hands up her body to cup her lace and satin covered breasts. She pinched her nipples, urging them to come to rock-hard points. With Rick's attention now firmly focused on her breasts, she slipped the thin spaghetti straps from her shoulders and down her arms, the tug of the fabric revealing first her breasts, then her rounded belly, and then finally, as she pushed the negligee over her full hips, her trimmed mound.

When she was fully nude, she tossed the negligee onto the pile of clothing and pulled Rick to her. The kiss she placed on his lips was the fulfillment of the promise from earlier. Her arms slid around his neck as she deepened the kiss, her tongue slipping in to caress his. As she kissed him, his arms skimmed up her body coming to rest at the small of her back. She knew he wanted to touch her, but Rick—being Rick—was waiting for her permission.

Reaching down, she placed his hands on her ass while lifting her leg to grind her core against his underwear-clad length. It wasn't enough. The additional movements of Rick's hands over her ass and up her sides to cup her breasts weren't enough. She wanted him. All of him. Inside her… now!

She pulled her lips away from his to whisper in his ear, "Fuck the foreplay; I just want you inside me."

The effect of her words on him was electric. Before she even had time to do anything, her lips were torn from his. His underwear disappeared as he grabbed one of the condoms from the card and rolled it onto his length. "Are you sure?"

"Are you?"

"Fuck yes."

"Then lay down on the bed."

He scrambled back to follow her command, still wearing his socks. His erection jutted upward, just waiting for her to impale herself on.

But she held back. She wanted to take him in her mouth, in her core, run her fingers over and around him. She wanted to do everything to him all at once. But patience. She needed patience. One thing at a time—and the thing Grace wanted most was his cock inside her.

She climbed up his body, her eyes never leaving her target. Slowly she positioned her center over him and then inch by glorious long inch, she eased herself down onto him.

"Oh God, yes." The words slipped from Rick's mouth as she squeezed her muscles around him.

"You ready for this?"

He nodded.

"I don't think I can do slow." Her whole body was aching with need.

"Do me however you want to do me, just do me."

She pulled him up to capture his lips and then set an absolutely heart-pounding pace. Her weeks of working out on the treadmill had given her the endurance necessary to see this through. Harder and faster, his hips rising up to meet hers, they came together.

Sweat cooled at the back of her neck and at the base of her spine, but still she rode him, chasing her orgasm that was growing ever and ever closer. She tore her lips away from his to lean back, finding better purchase, changing the angle just slightly, just enough. The scrape of his length along her clit was what she needed.

And he gave it to her. One. Two. Three thrusts. That was all it took to send her spinning off into space with a hoarse cry, her hips losing their rhythm to buck and jerk against him.

His hands came up to steady her, soothe her, to keep the rhythm going so he too could follow her into bliss. He took over control. And without changing positions, he used his strength to help her ride him to completion. It wasn't long before he came inside her, his cock twitching and jerking as it filled the condom.

They lay together, hearts pounding, for she didn't know how long. All she knew was that she didn't want to move—didn't want to speak. Rick seemed to feel the same because he simply held her close, peppering tiny kisses to her face and neck.

With a sigh of regret, Grace rolled off of him and helped remove the prophylactic from his softening length. A quick trip to the bathroom to take care of business and she was curled up beside him, her fingers tracing little designs on his chest.

He bent down to kiss her gently on the lips. "That was incredible, Schmoopy."

"So what are you doing for Random Acts of Kindness Day?"

"I don't know. I don't really have any plans for tomorrow."

"I do. I plan on spending it doing you."

With a smile on his face, he pulled her down for a soul-searing kiss and said, "I like those plans. And I love you."

"Happy Do a Grouch a Favor Day," she murmured.

"Same to you. I can't wait for March Twentieth."

"International Day of Happiness?"

Rick kissed one eyelid and then the other. "Sure, that and possibly a couple other holidays."

"I look forward to celebrating them with you." She turned in his arms, snuggled against him, and glanced at the clock on the bedside table. It was after midnight. "But for now, I want to celebrate My Way Day with my boyfriend by falling asleep together."

"I think that can be arranged."

As she drifted off to sleep, Grace couldn't help the stupid grin that stole over her features. She knew what other holidays were on March 20th including Kiss Your Fiance Day and Proposal Day. Either way, it was going to be a holiday to remember.

About the Author

Christina Rose Andrews is actually two friends, Lark and Rose, writing underneath one penname.

A native of Colorado, Lark currently lives in Grand Rapids, Michigan. She is the mother to four fur babies and several neglected plants. She initially studied Education and even made it to student teaching before realizing the career wasn't for her. She graduated with a degree in "Do you want fries with that?" otherwise known as History and Earth Science. She's a bit of Jack of all Trades, which is oddly useful when it comes to writing and gives her several real life analogues for characters and plots. In her spare time, she likes to help put on large fandom conventions and hang out with family and friends.

Rose is a New Yorker through and through. She is the proud parent of a well-mannered potted plant and the aunt to several adorable niblings. Instead of going to Harvard, she bucked tradition and went to Haverford, where she received a degree in "How to be a Cult Leader" aka Religion and Psychology. After graduating, she pursued a master's degree in Library Science. Currently, she works as a librarian in the suburbs of New York City. When she's not on the train to work, she likes to read, play video games, and have tea.

Lark and Rose met in an online writing community in 2009 and promptly had an argument. After that, it was a slippery slope into co-authorship. They chose to write cross-cultural romance since it was close to their hearts, and it was damn near impossible to find stories featuring characters they wanted to see. Both Lark and Rose are proponents for destigmatizing mental health, solving problems through conversation and listening, and creating real characters—not caricatures.

They have presented at internationally recognized events.

Website: www.roselarkpublishing.com/christina-rose-andrews
Twitter: @croseandrews

The Editor

♥

Siobhan Kearney

Story Information

Holiday: Organize Your Home Office Day
Holiday Date: March 10 (Second Tuesday in March)
Heat Rating: 1
Relationship Type: M/F
Major Trigger Warnings: Mild sexism, mild ageism.

    Being a published author isn't what Sophie expected. The pay isn't great. The hours are long. And the deadlines are impossible. At least her publisher-approved editor is decent. More than decent, dreamy. Too bad she can't graft her editor's personality onto her sexy downstairs neighbor. Except fate's got a funny way of throwing them together… in more ways than one.

The Editor

 The clouds hung low in the early March sky as Sophie Zychowski hurried home from the 'L' station. Cold, searing winds whipped through the streets rustling bare branches and causing her to shiver in her sensible black interview skirt. Another day, another job that she had no chance of getting. The wind tugged at her hair—blonde with faded pink strands, which whipped into her eyes, making her wish she'd remembered her scrunchie. Long hair and the Windy City were like oil and water: they didn't mix.

 Quickening her pace, she turned off of 59th onto Kilbourn. The one-way street was quiet. A few brave kids played in the yards across the street from her, but most of the neighborhood was inside, their brightly lit windows illuminating her evening walk home. Sophie wrapped her arms around her body both to shield herself from the cold and to soothe her wounded pride.

 What had she been thinking getting an M.A. in English? She'd been interviewing for over a year with only a few temp jobs to show for her troubles. Employers wanted concrete skills and looked at her askance. It didn't matter if the job was working at one of the few remaining brick and mortar bookshops or as a receptionist; she didn't fit. One potential employer even went so far as to tell her that as much as they liked her, they wouldn't hire her because she was too educated and would likely only be there until something better came along.

 It was a soul-sucking gut punch.

 At least she still had her fall-back plan. Sure, taking care of her ornery, particular, and stubborn grandmother meant that she didn't have to pay for any living expenses and even got a small stipend from her grateful aunts and uncles, but it wasn't something she wanted to do for the rest of her life.

Heck! She still wasn't sure what she wanted to do with the rest of her life. She'd thought college would solve that problem. It didn't. Aside from realizing she was bisexual, it just solidified her feelings of confusion. She just hoped she'd be able to identify it if she happened to run across it.

She thought she might have found her purpose. Well, kinda. Sure, most people who got M.A.s in English wanted to become successful authors one day. The kind who got feted with praise and canapés. The kind who agents clamored to represent. The kind who had multiple publishing houses vying to publish their novel. Who didn't want that?

What no one had told her was that after the bidding wars and the begging that she would have to spend over a year revising and rewriting her debut novel, *Waterhouse's Muse*, in order to meet the publisher's expectations. It sucked. She'd had to scrap whole scenes, characters, plot lines, and even her ending. She'd cut enough that she probably had a whole other novel of just the pieces that had been axed. Worse, they'd made her choose a pen name. Apparently 'Sophie Marie Zychowski' didn't test well with whatever focus group they used for trying out author pen names, but 'Sarah M. Zurich' did.

Thankfully she'd made it through the developmental editing phase. Now she just had to send her baby to the publisher-approved line editor. Unlike the large publishing houses in New York and London, which had editors in-house, this publisher was smaller, preferring to outsource editing to whichever freelance editor Sophie assumed was cheapest.

As if an editor called The Bloody Britpicker wasn't bad enough, just last week the Chicago Art Institute had announced that they'd received a large bequest of John Williams Waterhouse's artwork, and her publisher had moved her release date to coincide with the opening of the exhibit. If she'd known she'd have to go through all of these steps, she might have given up. She likely would have if the advance she'd gotten weren't so big.

In fact, it was big enough that her grandmother had insisted she turn the small guest room with its sturdy bunk beds and stuck closet door into a home office. Sophie had initially balked at actually setting up an office; the kitchen table and her laptop worked just fine. She didn't need to move.

But her grandmother had insisted. "I want a place to make kolacky and watch my stories in peace. I can't do that with you acting out that dialogue of yours. No peace. No kolacky."

Who could say no to Grandma Dorothy's kolacky? The cream cheese fruit-filled pastries were the closest thing to heaven she'd ever experienced. No one else in the family had managed to duplicate the recipe, and her mother had tried.

The closer Sophie got to the two-flat building she shared with her grandmother the more excited she got. There was a stack of large boxes piled by the mailboxes out front. Those had to be the furniture she'd ordered for her soon-to-be home office.

When she reached the three-story building, she made an inspection of the boxes. She'd ordered a lot and didn't want to start assembling things until she had all of the pieces. Wouldn't it just suck if she got her cute, glass-top desk all assembled but couldn't actually use the thing because the desk chair got waylaid in Poughkeepsie?

Comfy desk chair? Check.

Cute desk? Check.

Box of random desk accoutrements? Check.

Styrofoam container? Check.

Wait? Styrofoam container? Nothing she was expecting needed to be shipped in a large styrofoam box that looked like it could hold a medium-sized dog or a small toddler. The address was right, but the name was smudged. The only thing she could make out was a Z. Maybe it was a pick-me-up from her agent. Julia had been known to send her everything from chocolate to cute pencils to edible arrangements to keep her motivated.

God knew she needed the motivation after the day she'd had.

Sophie picked the package up, narrowing her eyes at the shipping label, when a baritone voice interrupted her, "I believe that is for me."

She stopped and turned to regard the basement resident, current owner of the building, and massive pain in her behind leaning heavily against the exterior door frame. "Huh?" It wasn't the most eloquent response, but it would do.

Xavier Robinson motioned to the box with one elegantly manicured hand. "The box. It's mine." His voice was soft, accented, possibly British; she couldn't quite pin it down in her previous encounters with the persnickety man.

Sophie turned the box, trying once again to decipher the address label. "Are you sure? I'm expecting a lot of stuff today."

An expression of annoyance flitted across Mr. Robinson's face, causing his full lips to curve into a frown. "Quite sure. Now if you would kindly stop manhandling my package, I would most appreciate it."

Sophie couldn't help it; she snorted at the double entendre. "Simmer down. It's not like your steak-of-the-month is going to suffer if I happen to accidentally drop it. No need for questionable requests."

"Questionable requests?" he asked, his refined accent making her think of candlelit drawing rooms and PBS specials. "What are you going on about?"

"That whole 'package' comment? Sounds like someone needs to bone up on their Yank slang," she said, referring to his accent and ignoring her own double entendre.

He stiffened and, if possible, drew himself up even taller to look down that long straight nose of his at her. "And I suppose you're some kind of language expert?"

"Yup!" She grinned showing a few more teeth than was necessary; there was something about Mr. Robinson that made her inner gremlin come out and play. "Even got the initials to go with it. I am a master of the English language!"

"You? A master? Hardly. With your nose ring and colorfully streaked hair, I'd be surprised if you were a master of anything, let alone the language of Shelley and Byron."

The muscle in her jaw twitched at the slight. Yeah, she didn't look like the stereotypical librarian or schoolmarm, but why did that matter? English was more than just long-dead stuffy old white dudes. It was a vibrant, ever evolving language with a whole lot of literature that didn't come from the British Isles. Yeah, a lot of guys assumed that's all English was, at least those who weren't gatekeeping her and grilling her about her reading preferences. She hated men like that. Men who thought that just because they possessed a penis it automatically made them smarter and gave them permission to be assholes. No wonder all of her previous encounters with Mr. Robinson ended badly. The guy couldn't see past his own prejudices. "You know what?" She thrust the package into his arms. "Here. Even if it's mine, you obviously need the pick-me-up more than I do. I'm done with you."

He took the box from her, cradling it to his lean body like it was something precious. He didn't even seem to care that it was getting his obviously freshly-pressed khakis and shirt dirty.

She tilted her head, letting her lips curl into a mocking smile. "Aren't you supposed to say something?"

His dark eyes narrowed. "I suppose you're looking for an expression of gratitude."

"It's generally considered polite."

He seemed to consider it for a moment before inclining his head while saying, "Thank you, then, for not absconding with my property."

"You're most welcome," she said, bobbing a little curtsy.

One elegant eyebrow lifted. "That was abominable."

She froze, slowly straightening to meet his gaze. It was difficult considering their height difference. Why oh why couldn't she have inherited her Polish father's height? Stupid genetics lottery! Instead, she gathered all sixty of her inches and said, "What are you, some kind of etiquette expert?"

His nostrils flared, his shoulders going back although he still held the box to him. "As a matter of fact, I am."

That took the wind out of her sails. She didn't have a comeback for that. Time to exit the conversation as gracefully as she could. "Well... um... cool. So, I gotta go. Gotta get this stuff inside. Have fun with your... package," she managed to say without dissolving into giggles. It was a near thing.

"Yes, well, have fun with your... stuff." There was a world of disdain in that single word.

"Oh, I will!" she chirped and deliberately turned her back on him. She knew it was rude. Grandma Dorothy would have a fit if she'd seen Sophie behave like that, but there was something about Xavier Robinson that just rubbed her the wrong way.

Maybe it was the way he always seemed to regard her as if she was a child and not a twenty-five-year-old adult. Maybe it was the British accent that grew posher and posher with each word he spoke until it even put the Queen of England to shame. All she knew was every time she ran into him he'd say something that would raise her hackles and she'd counter by being a little brat. She just couldn't seem to stop their never-ending snipe war. It had been that way since she'd moved in. Sure he was handsome, if on the old side, with his dark brown wavy hair and carefully trimmed beard with just a hint of gray in both. But just because someone had been blessed by the Goddess of Good Genetics didn't mean that they were also blessed by the Demi-God of Good Manners.

Worse, her grandmother seemed to dote on him. It was always 'Mr. Robinson is such a gentleman, just like his father!' and 'Mr. Robinson said the dearest thing today!' It drove Sophie mad. Why did the current bane of her existence have to be on best buddies terms with her grandmother? It didn't help that he was also the owner-slash-landlord of the building—along with the two neighboring two-flats—so she couldn't avoid him completely. Not if she wanted someone to come fix the ever-finicky kitchen light yet again.

No, she'd have to be polite-ish, grit her teeth, and hope that she had to interact with him as little as possible.

*

As soon as the door closed behind Miss Zychowski, Xavier ran his fingers over the styrofoam package. The tape was undisturbed, the label smudged but still affixed. Nothing appeared amiss.

But Xavier had been alive long enough to know that appearances could be deceiving. After all, he appeared to be hale and alive. When he most decidedly was not either hale or alive.

Xavier scurried down the half-flight of stairs and into his apartment. The room was dark, lit only by several unobtrusive picture lamps. Hidden by thick blue velvet curtains, not one ray of outdoor light filtered into his abode. The living room was divided by a lovely rosewood screen. One side held an overstuffed leather chair, a love seat that matched the curtains, a small coffee table, and a wall-mounted television with an array of entertainment electronics nestled into alcoves underneath it. The other side was arranged to be a small office with an ornate oak desk, high-end computer with multiple screens, bookcase, and file cabinet. Over the desk hung a richly-colored painting of a woman draped in gray and covering her head while being buffeted by the wind. More art from a variety of time periods and styles filled every square inch of wall leading to and down the hallway.

He immediately headed toward the office side and the desk. Xavier pushed aside the keyboard and mouse to set the package down onto the blotter. Carefully, he sliced through the packing tape with one fingernail and lifted the lid to reveal the contents. Several pint-sized plastic bags lay stacked one on top of the other in the bottom of the cooler. Blood bags. Taped to the top of the centermost bag was a letter-sized envelope. He detached it and set it to one side; he had other more important things to do.

Carrying the cooler down the hallway to the back of his two-bedroom basement flat, he entered his small, sparsely appointed kitchen. The only furniture in the room was a rickety round table and two chairs that looked like they'd seen better days. A kettle rested on the gas stove, and a tree of teacups stood next to the kitchen sink. Most of the appliances and fixtures were old, original to the building in shades of faded bright orange and avocado green. Everything screamed of disregard—except the shiny stainless steel refrigerator, which stood against the interior wall.

He set the cooler on the nearest counter and opened the fridge. The inside was mostly empty with only a few bottles of white wine, a pint of cream, and a single blood bag lining the shelves. Xavier emptied the cooler into the refrigerator, counting the bags as he did so. Twenty one. Not quite enough to get him through the next month even if he rationed. He'd have to hit up secondary sources.

Dispirited, he trudged back to the office to read the letter. He hoped that this was simply the first shipment and that another would be arriving later.

As soon as he opened the letter, he knew it was a false hope.

My Dear Xavier,

I hope you're doing well and have been weathering the early spring. March came in like a lion here bringing with it a blizzard which caused a twenty-five car pileup on the interstate. It was bad. So bad, in fact, that Paulo got called in on his day off.

Speaking of Paulo, he sends his apologies. He wasn't able to acquire as many expired or nearly expired blood bags for you. He'll see if he can cover a shift or two at another hospital to check out their stocks, but it's still uncertain at this time. I volunteered to contribute a pint or two for the cause, but Paulo refused. Something about me being too old. Pish-tosh!

What can you do? I argued for days about it, but he wouldn't give in, the silly old fool. Paulo worries about me, and I suppose he's right, I'm not as young as I used to be. But who is? I might be old, but I'm surrounded by people I love and who love me. And I wouldn't have it any other way.

Speaking of... Need I remind you that you need to be a bit more neighborly? I know you're a bit of a curmudgeon, my dear vampire, but if you don't curb your grouchy impulses you'll miss out on a whole lot of happiness.

You'll have to tell me about the novel you're editing in your next letter. I've been hearing all sorts of buzz about it at the River City Art Museum.

Ian and Rachel send their love. Paulo wants to remind you that you still owe him 10 drachmas plus 127 years interest. I'm just laughing that he still remembers.

Hugs and kisses,
Lottie

Well, the letter explained the smaller than usual shipment. And he chastised himself to be more grateful; Paulo didn't have to raid the hospital he worked at's blood supply. Xavier also wasn't surprised at the admonition to be more neighborly. Lottie had been on his case to be nicer ever since she'd met him over twenty years ago. He couldn't help it if he was a grouch. After all, he'd been alive for over two hundred years. He simply was an old man—in a not-so-old body—who wanted the kids to get off his lawn.

Especially one kid/decidedly-not-kid in particular.

Unwittingly his eyes drifted upward. He didn't know why Miss Zychowski irritated him so. All he knew was that there was something about her which made his very being tremble and roil. She stirred desires within him that had long been damped. He was better off avoiding her.

Something easily achieved since, as Lottie had so presciently intimated, he did have a new editing job. One *Waterhouse's Muse*. A job which, amusingly, was right up his alley. The artist had long been a favorite of his.

Settling down under Waterhouse's *Boreas*, he fired up his state-of-the-art computer and got to work.

*

"No, dear, the directions say you need to put tab A into slot B."

Sophie sat cross-legged on the floor, a whirlwind of desk parts arrayed in front of her. "I'm telling you, Grandma, there is no slot B. I have a slot I, I have a slot G, and I think that's a slot K." She picked up what she thought was each edge of the desk. "But there is no slot B."

"Well, I'm just telling you what the instructions say."

Letting the pieces fall to the floor with a thump, Sophie threw herself back onto the carpet and stared up at the ceiling grateful that she'd sent the manuscript to her line editor before she attempted to put her office together. "This is impossible! Why didn't I just order a desk from IKEA?"

Her grandmother wandered into her field of vision and stared down at her through her wire-rimmed glasses. "You said it was cute. Now I don't know why you didn't just take Mr. McGillicuddy up on his offer for his old desk." Mr. McGillicuddy was the upstairs neighbor. He and his wife were nice people, and their teenage son was sweet if a little tongue-tied around her. But the last thing she wanted was a formica computer desk which had the corners gnawed off of it by either a toddler or a terrier, she wasn't sure which.

"Because I didn't want to try to figure out how to move it without breaking it." It was the white lie she was comfortable telling her grandmother.

"You could've asked Mr. Robinson to help you. I'm sure that lovely young man would be happy to assist you. So tragic about his father."

Sophie blinked at the non sequitur. "What has that got to do with anything?"

"Well, it's tragic!" her grandmother said as if it explained everything, which it most certainly didn't. She shook her head. "That poor, poor man."

Deciding not to go down that road, Sophie returned to the main topic of conversation, "Yes, but it has absolutely nothing to do with him lugging D-grade furniture around." Maybe she could call Emma... her ex-girlfriend always knew her way around tools. Frowning from her place on the floor, Sophie glanced around for her cell phone. "Besides, I don't care how tragic his past is; it doesn't mean he gets to be an asshole."

Her grandmother's mouth thinned, her carefully drawn on eyebrows arching over her glasses' frames. "Don't you take that lip with me, young miss."

"Sorry, Grandma." Sophie sighed, giving up on calling her ex. Emma was probably at work, and their breakup hadn't been the most amicable. "It just doesn't feel right asking your landlord for help." Not to mention, he'd probably give her grief about it. Maybe make a snide comment about how she marred his perfect khaki crease or something.

"I've never had a problem talking to him. Nor his father. Nor his grandfather." She bopped Sophie on the nose with one liver-spotted knuckle. "Why, ever since I moved here in 1970, the Robinsons have been the absolute most wonderful dreams of neighbors. Always so kind. So considerate." She shook her head and sighed gustily. "If only the menfolk would stop dying so young."

"Sure, Grandma." Ignoring her grandmother's gossipy comment, Sophie pulled herself upright and picked up a flathead screwdriver. "Hand me that hammer over there. If there isn't a slot B, I can make one."

Before she got any further and potentially ruined her brand-new desk, someone knocked on the door.

"I wonder who that is," her grandmother said as she shuffled out of the room. "It must be one of the neighbors; otherwise, they would've rung the bell."

Her grandmother's prediction was right: it was one of the neighbors. Specifically, their downstairs neighbor and landlord, Mr. Robinson.

Great. Just great. Sophie stifled a groan.

"Is all well?" he asked, peering around the apartment with a decidedly disapproving frown on his lips. "I keep hearing this infernal clanking and banging."

"Just fine," she said with a tight grin-slash-grimace. "As you can see, we're just doing some mild home-office assembly."

The man peered at his watch. "At ten o'clock at night?"

"Well, you know..." Sophie glanced around the room searching for something, anything, that would give her a good excuse. She hadn't realized it had gotten so late! Her eyes landed on something. "It's Organize Your Home Office Day, and we wouldn't want to miss out on the celebration."

Once again the elegant eyebrow slid upward. "You're joking."

"No, really." Sophie stretched out, grabbed the desk calendar that she'd gotten as a gift, and held it out to the man. "See? Organize Your Home Office Day. Right there."

The man blinked once. Twice. Before letting out a long-suffering sigh. "Far be it for me to interfere with a legitimate holiday. Since I shan't be able to work while you're caterwauling up here, is there anything I could do to help you?"

"No, really, I think Grandma and I have got it," Sophie said, eager to have him gone.

At the same time her grandmother cooed, "Oh, that would be lovely! Let me get some coffee and kolacky going, and I'll leave you two to it!"

The infernal bastard's lips twitched while Sophie prayed to every god that she'd ever heard of to grant her the patience not to throttle her grandmother or her landlord.

"So... where are we?" he asked once her grandmother left.

She considered being a smartass and answering 'Chicago' before deciding that it really wouldn't get her anywhere. "According to the instructions, we're supposed to put tab A into slot B."

Mr. Robinson picked up the instructions, glanced at them, glanced at the unassembled desk, and then promptly tossed the instructions over his shoulder. "These are for the wrong desk. Hand me that piece over there." He pointed to one of the flatboards. "This shouldn't be too hard."

Annoyingly, agonizingly, the man was right. It was as if the arrogant asshole had an aptitude for assembly. Go alliteration. And as much as she wanted to stay angry at him for his attitude, having his help did make the chore pass quicker. They managed to get the top with its attached shelf put together in no time, but when they went to work on the legs, they hit a snag.

"Did the kit come with an Allen wrench?" he asked, eyeing the disassembled desk leg.

"Ummm..." Sophie rummaged through what was left of the box. "No? Maybe? What's an Allen wrench?"

"A hexagonal tool shaped like this..." he made an 'L' in midair. "Many do-it-yourself furniture kits include them."

She looked again. Definitely nothing L-shaped. "I don't think this kit did."

"Do either you or Mrs. Zychowski have one?"

Sophie shook her head. "Grandma is sort of a Blanche DuBois—she always relies on the kindness of strangers—and hasn't owned a toolkit since Grandpa died. I've just got the basics. You know: hammer, two types of screwdriver, pliers; I haven't needed anything more until now."

"Ah. The basics will do in a pinch, but unless you want to strip the screw and be unable to take this apart at a later date, I'd best get my tools from downstairs." His eyes met hers, and she was struck by the happiness there. "I'll be right back."

While he was gone, she grabbed her phone from where she'd stashed it on the windowsill and pulled up the online retailer's site. She might not be able to put together a desk without help, but she could write an eloquent one-star review about missing tools and wrong instructions without any assistance at all.

By the time she'd proofread her review to make sure no profanity had slipped through, Mr. Robinson had returned toolbox in hand. And what a toolbox it was! Dark burnished wood with slightly tarnished brass fixtures, it looked old. Like really old. Not the patina that could be achieved on Etsy, but the kind of old that only time could manage. This was a toolbox that had been loved and used for years. Decades.

"Was that your father's?" Sophie asked, nodding at it.

Mr. Robinson looked down at the toolbox. "It's a good deal older than that."

"Grandfather's?"

"I'm not sure how old it is, frankly. Nor do I think it matters. It too is a tool, and it serves its purpose well." He seemed oddly on edge, angry, and she wasn't sure why.

"Hey, I'm sorry I asked. I'm not trying to bring up bad memories or anything like that. I was just admiring it. It might not look like it, but I've got a thing for antiques. There's something sort of wonderful about things from bygone days. Things that have been used and loved and cared for." She motioned to the box. "Things like that." She glanced up from her place on the floor to see an expression of stunned disbelief flitter across his features.

Setting the box down, he ran one hand through his hair. "I owe you an apology, Miss Zychowski. I was rude."

"You were. Thank you for acknowledging that."

He blinked. "Yes, well, I suppose it's no excuse, but it's been a long day, and I'm under a good deal of pressure."

"Hey, I get it. We all are. Thank you for helping, but let's knock this puppy out so we can get to snarfing down Grandma's kolacky."

The look he gave her was odd, assessing. "Indeed. Let's."

And that's what they did.

*

Xavier had fully intended on lecturing Young Miss Zychowski for her poor attempt at carpentry when Lottie's often repeated words came back to him.

"You need to be a bit more neighborly. Your kindness will pay out in the end."

He didn't want to be neighborly. He wanted to be the curmudgeon Lottie had called him in her letter. But he also knew better; Lottie had visions like the Oracle at Delphi, and he'd have to be a poor scholar of the classics to fail to heed her pointed advice. So with a grudging sigh, he offered to help.

The experience wasn't as bad as he'd feared. Miss Zychowski made an admirable assistant and her compliment on his brother Fritz's toolbox was surprising. It made him reevaluate her.

He'd always seen Dorothy's granddaughter as feckless. Aimless. Without grounding or respect for what had come before. The comment had thrown him, given him pause. Instead of the little girl who'd used to ride her scooter up and down the sidewalk was a young woman who'd come to appreciate that just because something was old didn't mean it was useless. Yes, her hair was an abomination. Why she'd chosen to bleach her lovely dark blonde hair and then streak it with varying shades of pink, he'd never know. But her blue eyes were intelligent and her lips full. If he didn't know her ancestry was Polish and pure American hodgepodge, she'd be the embodiment of a pure English rose. And despite his Swiss heritage, he'd always had an appreciation for the country. He'd even gone to school there after the Napoleonic Wars.

Working together as a team, the task was completed with ease, leaving him enough time to partake in a cup of coffee and conversation. He hoped the convivial atmosphere would continue, and if nothing else, Dorothy was always a pleasure to converse with.

"I don't see any blood! I take it that you kids were able to play nicely," the still-stunning elderly woman greeted.

Xavier's mouth twitched. If only Dorothy knew.

"Grandma, we're not that bad."

Dorothy poured a cup of the decaf that she always had brewing and slid it across to him. She did the same with Sophie before refilling her own. "I don't know. I swear that you guys are like cats and dogs around each other."

"Which one of us is the cat?" Xavier wanted to know.

"Oh, you. Absolutely you," Sophie said before Dorothy could say anything.

Xavier's hackles raised. Despite his youthful exuberance for tigers, he'd always considered himself more of a dog person. He missed being able to have a dog. It was an unfortunate side effect of living alone while being a vampire; the temptation when starving would be too great.

He opened his mouth to speak, but Sophie cut him off. "See, Grandma? His hair even stands on end like a cat's. I bet if I poke him enough, he'll hiss at me."

Dorothy tapped the back of her granddaughter's hand. "Now, Sophie. Play nice."

"Sorry, Grandma," Sophie said obviously contrite. She peeked up at him through her eyelashes. "See? This right here. Totally dog."

"So you're telling me that if I throw a stick, you'll play fetch."

"Depends on the stick."

He couldn't help but smile at that.

"So, Xavier," Dorothy said pulling out the plate of kolacky and setting it on the table before taking her seat, "what's new with you? Is anything exciting happening in your life?" She waggled her eyebrows at him knowingly.

He took a sip of Dorothy's coffee to be polite before answering. "Now, Mrs. Zychowski—"

"Dorothy! How many times have I asked you to call me Dorothy?"

He inclined his head but continued without calling her by name, "You know that I am a severely introverted introvert—"

"Don't you mean misanthrope?" Sophie said around a mouthful of kolacky.

Before Dorothy could chastise her for her manners, he responded, "I suppose you could call it that. But introvert is more accurate. I don't hate people." And he didn't. He actually liked being social and missed the companionship of a large family. But vampires, like most predators, were by their very nature solitary beings. A few traveled in packs, but for the most part in a city like Chicago there were maybe ten of his ilk. And he didn't like any of them for a variety of reasons. "I merely find that the effort is not always worth the reward."

"Well, I guess we should be grateful that we're worth your while," Sophie said with a completely straight face.

He couldn't tell if she was being sarcastic or not, but somehow he suspected it was the former not the latter.

Her grandmother seemed to think so too because she poked Sophie with one immaculately manicured nail. "Now, stop it. You would think someone with your education and upbringing would have better manners. Why, your father never talked to anybody like that."

"Not around you."

"Sophie Marie Zychowski!" Her tone was scandalized, but Dorothy's eyes told a different tale, the corners crinkling to belie her annoyance.

"I know, I know, Grandma. But I come by my smartass tendencies naturally. My father was a smartass, my grandfather was a smartass—I was doomed to be a smartass."

Dorothy shook her head and just sighed. "Can't argue with you there. My Norbert was a smartass. It's why I loved him. Bless his soul." She blinked rapidly for a few moments, obviously remembering her husband who had died so long ago. Picking up a kolacky, she changed the subject. "Did I tell you that Sophie has a book coming out?"

"I think so," he said politely. The reality was that she had. Multiple times. But Xavier didn't think much of it; so many people nowadays were self-publishing into obscurity. He hadn't heard anything in his circles about a Sophie Zychowski novel. Granted, he wasn't everywhere… Post-Apocalyptic and Paranormal genres held no interest for him for a variety of reasons. But if she'd been picked up by one of the Big Five, he was certain Dorothy would have told him that.

Sophie, for her part, seemed embarrassed by her grandmother's gloating. "Grandma, I'm sure Mr. Robinson's not interested in that."

"Oh, but I am," he said even though he wasn't just to needle her. "What's the book about?"

She shot him a glance that promised more snide comments in the future, but said, "A love affair between an artist and his muse."

Xavier had read several novels with that premise and barely resisted rolling his eyes; the last thing the world needed was another one. "If you give me a copy, I'll read it." He knew that while the words sounded nice, it was actually a deadly insult. It was basically akin to asking the author to give away their work for free with no reward. All of the authors he interacted with hated it when people said that to them.

But Sophie had to either be a better actress than he gave her credit or was too green to recognize the insult because she didn't even blink. She just shrugged. "I'm sure Grandma will lend it to you when it's published."

"Oh I will!" Dorothy said, reentering the conversation. "I'm going to get my book club to read it." She turned to Sophie. "Do you think the gals at the library will order it if I ask them to?"

"It wouldn't hurt to ask."

"I'll do that then."

The conversation turned from the book to other things. Dorothy's volunteer work at St. Turibius. Sophie's job hunt. Xavier's movie collection. By the time he looked at the clock it was near midnight. He hated to leave, but he had to. He had work to do, and Dorothy's yawns were becoming more pointed.

When he returned to his flat, he immersed himself in Sarah M. Zurich's manuscript. Coincidentally, the plot was similar to the one Sophie had mentioned, but to say this was only a love story was selling it short. He flew through his initial skim-through. The prose was, for the most part, promising. There were some stilted bits here and there—there always were in the manuscripts he received—but it wasn't as bad as it could have been. The woman clearly had talent.

He could pinpoint which sections she'd been forced to rewrite because they didn't flow as smoothly as the sections which had had more time to be polished. But while Sarah excelled in her turns of phrase, her use of anachronisms, however, left much to be desired. For example: people could not be 'thrown for a loop' until around 1930. A good forty to fifty years after when the novel took place.

Xavier had his work cut out for him.

He worked through the night, his Oxford English Dictionary from 1889 at his fingertips. He'd managed to complete three chapters when he felt the unerring twinge between his eyebrows signaling that the sun was about to rise. While he was grateful he wasn't the kind of vampire who 'died' with the sun and was limited to only doing things at night, he also wasn't able to go out into daylight either. The sun burned. It wasn't the UV light (he could visit tanning salons all he wanted), but something else which caused what he now called his sunlight allergy. It was simply safer to sleep during the day.

However, his sleep this day was not to be sound. He received a call from the publisher. Or, rather, one of the random people who worked for the publisher.

"Have you gotten it yet?" the man on the other side asked without even bothering to say hello.

"Who is this?"

"Lance."

Xavier stifled a groan. He'd worked with Lance before. The man was the Merriam-Webster definition of impatient. "Assuming you mean the *Waterhouse's Muse* manuscript, yes." He was contracted with them for two other projects, but they weren't set to begin until after this one was finished.

"Yeah, what else would I mean? So you got it. How far are you?"

"I've started it," he said evasively. He'd learned long ago never to give exact numbers. Publishers and, now, authors always pushed to have things done faster and faster. If they knew just how fast he could do things, they'd push him for even more. As it was, his contracts were constructed to give him a comfortable cushion in case anything unexpected came up.

"Well, I hope you haven't gotten too far. There's been a change of plans."

"Oh?" That was unusual.

"Yeah. The publisher wants you to do it on their document sharing server."

"That's not in the contract." He'd learned long ago to spell his working conditions out in the contract.

"Well, you gotta do it." Lance's voice was even more impatient. Impatient and annoyed.

Xavier felt much the same. "I don't have to do anything that's not spelled out in the contract."

"Why are you being such a pain about this?"

As if name calling was going to make Xavier more likely to do what he wanted. "Because I dislike working with companies that fail to follow their obligations."

"Look. You don't gotta be so stuck up about it," Lance said in an offended tone, as if he'd had something to be offended about—which he didn't. Xavier wanted to introduce him to some less moralistic vampires of his acquaintance. "I know it's a change. The next two projects aren't going to be like this. My boss is under a crunch."

"Then your boss should have planned for this. I will continue working as outlined in our contract. Otherwise, the Changes and Conditions portions of the contract will be brought into force." Xavier didn't mind standing his ground on this. He didn't need this job. Or any job. As Albert Einstein said: compound interest is the strongest force in the universe.

He could almost hear Lance wince. "Yeah, about that... don't you think it's a little harsh?"

"No."

"You know, we could always find another editor."

"Then I invite you to do so. I wish you the best in finding a qualified editor willing to work under these conditions in the time period specified."

Xavier's willingness to lose this job seemed to throw Lance. The publisher's lackey probably wasn't used to dealing with a freelancer who wasn't desperate for income. "All right, all right, all right, all right. What will make this work? I've got to have you and the author in the same document at the same time. The proofreader's got to come in after the author finishes to clean things up. The whole shebang has to be out the door in two weeks."

Xavier's eyebrow went up. "An additional fifty percent in addition to the already agreed-upon rate for me to clear my calendar and work under less than optimum conditions."

"Done."

The fact that Lance didn't even bother trying to haggle drove home just how desperate the publishing house was.

There was an awkward pause, and then Lance cleared his throat. "Do you by any chance know of a good copy editor? One that can work fast? The one we had for this job… dropped."

Xavier wasn't surprised. And he did know of a good copy editor. Another vampire, much like himself. After all, finding jobs to keep you entertained and up-to-date on the current lingo was hard to do. He knew of several supernatural beings that freelanced in the publishing world, some of whom were friends. Maybe he should ask Lottie if her son-in-law was looking for work.

*

A few days after her office building fiasco, Sophie received a call from her agent. An actual phone call. Julia Montoya wasn't the kind of person to call if an email or text message would do. This had to be urgent.

So despite having her hair full of conditioner, Sophie picked up the phone. "Hello," she said, putting it on speaker.

"Are you in the shower?"

"Yes."

"You don't have time to shower." Julia's Brooklyn accent became stronger and more pronounced, a sure sign that she was stressed. "You need to get into the manuscript and start looking over the changes."

Sophie frowned. This wasn't how things were usually done. Usually she got back the fully edited manuscript and then was given a deadline to turn it around. The last time she'd had two months. It had barely been two days.

"How?" Sophie asked. She'd sent a Word document to The Bloody Britpicker; she was expecting to get it back as a marked up document.

"Shared doc." Julia's voice was tinged with disgust. "I've sent you the link. I swear, I've never had a publisher as problematic as this one."

"What's their reason for the hurry?"

"Something about special ARC printings for the exhibit and an Art Institute exclusive run. They're even doing a different cover for the thing." Julia sighed and muttered something in Spanish. "I'm sorry, but they want you to work on the changes while the line editor is going through. If it makes you feel any better, the publisher is going to be paying through the nose for the whole thing."

"It does make me feel better." Then she had a thought. "At least as long as it's not coming out of my royalties or payments."

"Oh, it's not. I made damned sure of that. This is their steaming pile of a mess, and we're not sanitation workers. Next book we go somewhere else."

There was a reason that she'd decided to go with Julia as her agent. As thrilled as Sophie was that her debut novel was getting this much support from the publisher, it was still a giant pain. She worried about quality. She worried she'd make bad decisions. She worried the editors would make poor decisions. There was a whole lot of worry and not a lot she could do to mitigate it.

Her scalp started to itch. "Thanks, Jules. I'll get on it in the hour."

"That's my author. I'll order one of those abominations you call a pizza for you tonight, publisher's treat."

Rolling her eyes at the never-ending pizza war between New York and Chicago, Sophie said her goodbyes and stuck her head back under the shower head. She hoped someone had informed the editor that she was coming. Otherwise it could get real awkward real fast in that document.

As promised, less than an hour later Sophie pulled out her brand new ergonomically configured Steelcase chair and opened the shared document link she'd gotten from Julia. Her laptop stuttered and whirred as it struggled to open all ninety thousand words of her manuscript. Why couldn't they just do the tried and true method? Why did her publisher have to make things difficult?

When the document finally finished loading, Sophie blinked and blinked again. Gone was her simple Arial font at a neat and legible 10-point. In its place was a thin, almost Roman, serif font in huge letters. At least 14-point. It felt like she was reading a billboard.

So she changed it.

And someone else immediately changed it back.

Sophie frowned. How was she supposed to get any work done if she couldn't read the text?

Her computer dinged.

On the right hand side of the screen a little pop-up appeared. *Please do not change the text; I need it to work.*

She pulled her laptop closer to her. *Well, I need to change it in order to work.* She sat back, crossing her arms over her chest to emphasize her point. Not that the person could see her.

And what, pray tell, is wrong with this text? The tone was so snide, she couldn't help but read it in Mr. Robinson's voice.

Which, unfortunately, set her immediately on edge. *It's too large,* she typed, her fingers punching the keyboard angrily.

Three dots appeared in the chat box for several long moments as the person she was sharing the document with formulated a response. Sophie watched, waited, her fingers tapping impatiently against the plastic of her laptop. Finally, the person on the other side of the screen hit enter, and four words appeared. *What's your screen resolution?*

It took them that long to type those three words? Sophie shook her head. She could call them out on it, or since they were supposed to work together, she could look past it and answer the question. So she did. It took her a little while to find the answer; computer-literate she was not. Oh, she could make a Word document or set up a spreadsheet like pretty much any recent college graduate could, but troubleshooting tech stuff? That's what other people were for. She finally found it after a round of Googling. *800 by 600.*

Bloody hell! How can you get any work done?!

I don't know? It's what my laptop's set at.

The three dots appeared again. Sophie couldn't help but feel as if the person on the other end of the computer was judging her and finding her wanting. Yeah, she wasn't the most tech-savvy user on the planet, but she didn't have to be to put words on a page. People had been doing it for thousands of years.

The chat popped up with, *Would you mind if I gave you a suggestion?*

At least the person was asking, unlike the person she was using as her mental voice for them. *Sure, so long as you understand I might not accept it.*

Immediately, detailed step-by-step instructions on how to change her resolution popped up on the screen followed by a long explanation as to why it would be better.

She shrugged as she started following the steps. *I mean, it couldn't hurt to try it and see what it looks like. If I don't like it, I can always change it back, right?*

The screen flickered and changed, and she almost hit 'Revert' without thinking. Everything looked so weird. Different.

But then she clicked into the manuscript and saw that the font wasn't so large, and in fact was readable. Maybe if she restarted, reopened everything, she could get used to the new setting. After all, that's what her older sister always told her to do: when in doubt, turn it off and turn it back on again.

brb, she typed. Then, without waiting for a response, she closed all the windows and restarted.

She hated how long it took for her computer to load. She probably should see about buying a new one. But she couldn't quite bring herself to do so. After all, it still worked, she still could write on it, and it backed up to the cloud server Kathleen had set up for her without her having to think about it. If she got a new computer, she'd have to do all sorts of techie things in order to make it work as good as her old one. Nope. No need to change.

While she waited, Sophie went and got herself a cup of coffee from the pot her grandmother always kept going until she switched to decaf around seven o'clock at night. Sophie had a feeling that she had several late nights ahead. Thankfully, she hadn't turned in her grad school credentials yet and could pull off an all-nighter with the best of them. A power nap or two and she'd be good.

She finally was back and into the document ten minutes later to find a long screed of messages waiting for her:

How does it look?
Wait a moment!
Where did you go?
Are you quite all right?
Hello?
It was not my intention to cause harm to your computer.
Please answer me.

Sophie pulled the laptop closer to herself while still getting used to the now-smaller resolution. *Hey, I'm not dead. Neither is the computer. The screen looks weird but it's okay. I'm still not fond of the text. What's wrong with Arial? Sorry to worry you.*

What's wrong with Bodoni?

Other than sans serif fonts are easier to read on a computer and serif fonts are easier to read in print, and last I checked this was a computer?

I did not know that. I find that looking at something as if it was meant to be in print aids the editing process. It's easier to tell a lowercase L from a capital I, for instance. There was a pause. *I would prefer to keep a serif font, but perhaps there is another serif that you would be more willing to use. Times New Roman? Garamond?*

The fact that the editor—who had the screen name of BloodyBrit—was willing to compromise made Sophie instantly more congenial. *Nah, I'll try to work in this one for a little bit. If it's really a problem, then we'll talk.* She thought about it for a moment, feeling like she needed to offer an olive branch of sorts. *You know, I'm not really used to working this way. Thanks for being a gentleman/lady/nice person about it.*

Man. And I'm not used to it either. This is a new experience for me.

I know, right? she enthused. *I've never been in a document at the same time as an editor."

Same, I prefer to print out the manuscript I'm editing and mark it up. But that method appears to have gone out of style.

Sophie shook her head. *Yeah it has... has anyone ever told you that you're really old-fashioned?*

You are not the first. The mental voice she'd assigned in her head for him was dry... like a good martini.

LOL. I should probably get to work. If I've got questions, I'll poke you.
Please do.

With that, she minimized the chat window and got to work. She hoped this BloodyBrit was as good of an editor as he was old-fashioned. She'd just have to wait and find out.

*

Xavier tried to stay ahead of Sarah, truly he did. However, it took a lot more time to line edit and fact check a document than it did to go through and either accept or reject the changes. Which meant that he had a bored and inquisitive author watching his every move, and rather than scampering off to work on her next bestseller she chatted at him.

He made a change to a dinner scene, drawing on his own memories of the time. He knew that most authors drew upon Queen Victoria's limited and bland diet to create their feasts when the reality was that Britain consumed imported foods like it was their God-given right, which at the time they'd believed it was.

The chat bubble popped up. *Isn't fish and chips anachronistic?*

No.

He tried to move on to fixing one of Sarah's overused sentence structures when the chat bubble popped up again. *Wouldn't meat pies be better?*

Not if you actually wanted to eat real food, he couldn't help typing back snarkily.

???

He took that to mean 'Why?' although it wouldn't have taken that much more effort to type the actual word out. *Because most meat pie sellers, especially those on the street, used things like sawdust, gypsum, and other non-edible ingredients to make the pies seem filling. Fish and chips was harder to fake. The fish might not be cod, but it was always some kind of fish.*

Huh. Cool. How'd you learn all this stuff?

Because I'm a vampire, and I was alive then. He knew she'd never accept that answer as the truth, but oftentimes the seeming absurdity of the statement would derail the line of questioning.

For a few blessed moments, the chat box remained silent, and he was able to get a page ahead in the story. Which, if he was honest with himself he was enjoying—even if the author kept spelling 'colour' as 'color.' Americans!

Ha ha. Good one. But seriously. Sources?

Anger burbled up inside Xavier like Mount Etna. He hated being questioned like this. Like he was just another hack hanging their shingle out on the internet proclaiming to be an 'Expert on Britain' when their only credentials were a stack of *Harry Potter* books and DVDs of *Little Dorrit*. He had been a scholar at Queen's College, Oxford. He had lived in Britain until midway through the Great War. While he might not be up-to-date on the modern slang, he was an expert on the Georgian, Victorian, and Edwardian time periods.

But he couldn't say that to Sarah. Not only would it be impolitic, it wouldn't assuage her concerns. Additionally, he needed to acknowledge that part of the anger he felt stemmed from Sarah being a woman. If he took a step back, he could see that *Waterhouse's Muse* had been carefully researched far beyond the artist's Wikipedia article. This was a test. And as much as he hated having his abilities questioned, Sarah was protecting her manuscript from the same pseudo-experts Xavier so despised.

He had to respect that.

So he quickly Googled a few books on food in England and dug out his copy of *Oliver Twist* which mentioned fish and chip makers in the text. Hopefully the sources would lead her down a rabbit hole and he'd get some time to work in peace.

And it worked... for all of about twenty minutes, and then Sarah was back again. *Well, that was an interesting distraction. I'm glad you know your stuff.*

I'm glad too.

My last editor, he was approved by the publisher too, and well...

Yes? He scratched at his full beard, wishing he could shave it off. But he couldn't. Not if he eventually wanted to stage yet another 'accident' and have a long lost 'son' come out of the woodwork.

He didn't know a thing about late Victorian England and kept trying to tell me that things like electricity and running water didn't exist then. So sorry if I seem on edge, but whoever SirLancelot was put me on my guard.

He saw the statement for what it was, an olive branch. *I understand. I take it chivalrous he was not?*

More like Monty Python's version of chivalrous.

Xavier chuckled, imagining an editor swooping through the manuscript with a sword trailed by his coconut-clapping squire. *Did you ask him his favorite color?*

Damn! I didn't think of that. Do you think it would have worked? It didn't in the movie.

True. We shall have to come up with a different test.

Like the airspeed velocity of an unladen swallow?

So long as you specify African or European, you should be fine, he typed back with a grin on his face. It had been a long time since he'd joked and teased like this with someone. He'd missed it. And if Sarah knew and liked Monty Python, it was all the better.

I'll keep that in mind.

Xavier could positively hear the dry amusement in that reply. Even though they hadn't met in person—although they would eventually if he remembered his contract right—he was beginning to get a sense of Sarah, and he liked who that person was.

Rest assured, I am no Sir Lancelot. For one, I have never slept with my best friend's wife.

I'm sure your best friend appreciates that.

He thought back to the last person he could call a 'best friend' and smirked. *Possibly not. Had he caught us together, William likely would have asked to join in.*

Touche.

You're missing an accent.

THE EDITOR

I'm not hunting for the right keystroke combination for a casual chat. I save my nitpickiness for when it counts... which is definitely not now.

And if that wasn't a reminder of what he needed to do, then nothing was. He, regrettably, needed to get back to work. Which meant, that as much as he didn't want to, he had to stop chatting with Sarah. *Alas, nitpickiness is a foible of the trade. A trade which I should be resuming now as much as I would rather chat with you.*

Oof. Your rigt, sry.

He winced at the message. *Did you do that on purpose?*

Maybe... ;-)

LOL Just because he'd lived for over two centuries didn't mean he was completely behind on modern slang. It just didn't come as easily to him as he would like, but he still learned it.

But you're right. I should let you work. I'll come back later so I'm not tempted to bug you.

Before he even had time to bid Sarah farewell, she was gone. And it had to be a trick of the imagination, but the room seemed oddly dimmer for her absence.

*

When Sophie sat down at her laptop late one afternoon over a week later, it was with a heavy heart. The Bloody Britpicker had sent her an email telling her he'd finished with her manuscript. She should be excited; her novel was about to be published! But she wasn't. Instead she felt like she did when she'd said goodbye to her high school sweetheart before both of them went off to college.

Her editor wasn't her significant other, yet somehow over the last week she'd formed a connection with him. Maybe she should ask him out. After all, she hadn't dated anyone since Emma and hadn't had the inclination to throw herself back into the dating pool. Until now. Until The Bloody Britpicker. But there was a part of her that balked. He was her editor. She was his author. While she wasn't his boss, she still felt a little weirded out about the thought of asking him out. Like, were they co-workers? Peers? Friends? What? The definitions and boundaries weren't clear, and because they weren't, Sophie wasn't sure how to go about navigating them.

No, the best thing to do was nothing. Finish the edits, turn everything over to the copy editor, and maybe, if she felt adventurous, broach the subject of chatting outside of a professional setting.

Yeah, that sounds like a plan.

With that in mind, she went through the document accepting most of the suggested changes, rejecting some, but mostly keeping an eye out for the flash that told her that someone had entered the manuscript. It didn't come.

So she kept working, pausing only to refill her coffee and heat up some leftovers. When she reached the end, she saw a note that wasn't a suggestion to reword a sentence or an anachronism notification. It was a short thing that simply read, *I don't like this ending.*

To be completely honest, Sophie didn't either. It was one of the major changes she'd been forced to make by her content editor, SirLancelot. Instead of the main character settling down with Waterhouse and his wife in the artists' commune they lived in, she'd been forced to kill her off to tragically inspire Waterhouse for the rest of his life. She'd hated it. Hated having to write it.

And she was relieved that someone else hated it too.

Taking a deep breath, she typed, *Me either. The other editor forced me to change it. What should I do?*

She waited. Got some more coffee and waited some more. She waited until after the sun set and the streetlights flickered on bathing the street in their warm orange-y glow.

Finally the screen flickered and BloodyBrit entered the document. The chat box popped up and the words *What was your previous ending?* appeared.

She detailed her plan of a happy open marriage and a long-lasting friendship between Esther, Waterhouse's wife and an artist in her own right, and Lucretia, the muse first seen in Waterhouse's *Lady of Shalott* painting. Her ending was happy. Emotionally satisfying. It made sense! It explained why Waterhouse essentially only had two model types after 1882 until his death. One was his wife. The other was Lucretia.

But SirLancelot had been insistent. Only a 'Lost Lenore,' as he put it, could inspire an artist for so long. So the character she'd spent years building, cultivating, loving was unceremoniously killed in a riding accident.

Your previous ending was better. The words solidified something she'd thought herself.

I know.
You should change it back.
I can't. The publisher had already approved the changes.
You can.

But the publisher...

I'll send them an email. Tell them that what they have is historically inaccurate.

But that's a lie.

Not necessarily. There was a long moment while she waited for the editor to respond. *Your version is likely closer to the truth. While I don't think the relationship ended in a menage à trois or an open marriage, there are too many depictions of her to be solely done from memory. Take it from me, the faces of those you love fade after a time. And he wouldn't be painting the same woman with such clarity over twenty years after her death.*

There was something about the way he said it that made her think he had a personal understanding of such a loss. *I'm sorry you lost someone.*

Thank you. It was a long time ago.

I'm still sorry. She sensed he didn't want to continue with this conversation. *So... I'll put the old ending back in. Can you edit it for me?*

Why do you think I'm still here? :-)

The smiley face was new but welcome. It made him feel more like a friend than a colleague. She liked that. Opening up her deleted scenes folder, she fished her excised ending out and pasted it back in. She didn't even save the rewritten ending that fridged her character. She hated it that much.

There. Thanks for being willing to go to bat for me.

Of course. I can already tell this is much better. I'm not always a fan of happily ever afters, but this one works.

While he worked, she debated trying to change the tone of their relationship. She typed and deleted several things. Nothing seemed right. Finally she settled on, *I was worried you weren't going to be on today.*

I had to wait until the sun went down.

Really?

I told you, I'm a vampire.

He was back to that old joke. While she'd noticed that he'd only really worked on the manuscript during her nighttime hours, she figured he was just in a different time zone. Or a night owl. She decided to play along. *Well cool, Mr. Vampire. What made you decide to take up editing?*

I was bored.

Don't you have to hunt down the blood of the innocent?

I'm not that kind of vampire.

So what kind are you?

Isn't that a little personal?

That was an odd response. One that didn't really go with their joke. *Sorry. Just making conversation. But seriously, you're not really a vampire.*

I told you I was.

Yeah, but vampires don't exist.

How do you know that?

Because they're a myth. Like the Greek Gods or ghosts or single payer healthcare. The whole thing is a metaphor for the loss of innocence and a medieval idea of virginity. She felt pretty secure in that interpretation. *You're probably one of those people who have to work two jobs to make ends meet.*

It didn't take long for him to reply. *I don't. I'm what you might call independently wealthy.*

While she was annoyed that he didn't take the bait and strike up a philosophical discussion with her, she was also pleased he didn't shut down the conversation entirely. *Lucky! I have a heap of student loans, and while my advance was nice, it's not enough to make a dent in the loans and have any left to live on.* The thirty thousand she'd gotten wasn't nothing, but there were agent fees and taxes that had been taken out of it. Worse, the way the system worked, there was no guarantee that she'd ever see any royalties. And while it was better than most debut novelists got, it was still barely enough to live on in Chicago. Without being able to share her grandmother's apartment, she wouldn't even be here.

What are you going to do about them?

Other than hopefully find a job?

Yes, other than that.

I haven't quite gotten to the 'offer up sacrifices to the gods phase' yet, but I'm getting there, she joked.

Are you going to write another book?

There was something about the way he asked it that she couldn't put a finger on. *Probably. I've got a few ideas floating around.*

Good. I'd hate for this to be your only outing.

The words warmed her more than any fire. *So you liked it?* She hated that she had to ask. Hated that she cared what this man thought of her writing.

I did. I like it better now that you've put back your original ending.

She twirled her hair around her finger and bit her lower lip. She desperately wanted to change the tenor of the conversation, but she didn't. Something stopped her: the realization that her conversation with BloodyBrit wasn't private. Up in the corner was another icon showing that there was a third person in the manuscript. Someone who could essentially eavesdrop on their entire conversation. So instead of the flirting she desired, she simply typed, *Thanks. I've really enjoyed working with you.*

I have as well. I'll notify the publisher that I've advised you to change your ending back to the original for historical accuracy. While this is a work of fiction, you've hewn very close to the reality, and the story should end as such.

The words were so formal that Sophie knew he'd seen the interloper too. Saddened that this was her last conversation with him, she said goodbye. While she had his business email, there was no guarantee that it wasn't a shared account.

She'd have to hope that another opportunity would come up for her to meet him again.

*

The acoustics in the Chicago Art Institute's restaurant were horrible. Like all too many restaurants these days, the place had followed the trend of raised ceilings, hard floors, and hard chairs, leaving nothing soft to absorb the sound. A live band attempted and failed to do justice to what probably was a lovely jazz piece. Voices echoed and bounced, creating a cacophonous din which had already sent Xavier pawing for an aspirin. Thank God, that was one thing that becoming a vampire hadn't taken from him. The headache that threatened was promising to be a doozy, and no amount of Jameson was going to make it better.

Xavier retreated to the far side of the restaurant. Close enough to the main doors to make his escape as soon as his part in this ungodly charade was over, but far enough away from the steadily increasing drunken crowd of museum patrons and literary wannabes. If it hadn't been demanded as part of his contract, he wouldn't be here. He preferred to work from the shadows, gaining clientele through word of mouth rather than notoriety.

Which was probably why he'd found the most shadowed place he could in this overly bright restaurant.

He gave the ceramics in their display case a cursory glance before turning his attention to the architecture illuminated by the street lamps. Chicago's eclectic architecture was what had drawn him here when he'd first moved to this country in 1915. That and the sewer system. How they'd managed to reverse the Chicago River he still couldn't quite wrap his head around, but he appreciated the result.

He let himself drift back into his memories keeping only half an ear open for his part.

The din of the crowd changed, became more anticipatory. Apparently Sarah M. Zurich was here. *Glorious. They can get this bloody thing over with.*

Thanks to his height he was able to see over the tops of most of the crowd to the small dais up by the brightly-lit bar. The lead editor at the publishing house stood there, shifting from foot to foot, obviously unused to wearing heels. She kept glancing at her assistant, a weedy young man wearing thick black glasses, a tweed jacket with elbow patches, and what looked to be a faded yellow-and-black striped scarf around his neck. The assistant was making frantic come-hither motions with his hand toward somebody Xavier couldn't quite see due to their diminutive stature. The person was short, Queen Victoria short, so the only thing he could make out was the flash of her light blonde hair.

The assistant ran out and forcibly hauled the woman up onto the dais. Xavier took a step forward. The 19th century gentleman in him wanted to smack this young twit's hand for manhandling one of the fairer sex like that. He didn't care who the woman was, no one deserved to be treated that way. Thankfully, he didn't have to step in. The woman smacked the assistant's hand away with an audible *thwack* that carried over the din then turned to regard the crowd assembled there.

Time stopped—morphed—as he stared at the woman… at Sophie Zychowski. Her mess of colorfully unkempt hair had been tamed into an elegant chignon at the base of her neck. Gone was her usual heavy eyeliner and brightly colored lips; in their place was something softer, gentler, reminding him of Waterhouse's models. Even her dress was reminiscent of the idealized medieval style Waterhouse had favored in a deep greenish blue with hand-painted peacock feathers decorating the skirt and hem. The bodice was plain, unadorned, of an off-the-shoulder long-sleeved design that Xavier had never understood the practicality of, but on Miss Zychowski Xavier found that he had to revise his earlier opinion. She was lovely. A vision.

But why was she here?

He got his answer soon enough when the publisher took a step forward and started to speak. Once again he missed her name, but it didn't matter. Only the name she uttered as she introduced Miss Zychowski mattered.

"And it's with my great pleasure," the woman said, stumbling over the lines, "to introduce you to the star of the evening: Sarah M. Zurich."

He didn't hear any of her speech that followed. He couldn't believe that Sarah, the woman he'd been communicating with for several weeks, was his annoying neighbor upstairs. Yes, he and Sarah had had their differences when they'd first started chatting. They were both strong personalities. But that was what ultimately drew him to her. She was intelligent, opinionated, and... he couldn't believe it was Sophie. He wracked his brain trying to dredge up any memory of Dorothy telling him about her granddaughter. He vaguely remembered her telling him that Sophie was publishing her novel while helping her around the house. But never in a million years would he have connected 'publishing her novel' with 'penning a likely bestseller.' *How did I miss this? Oh dear God.* He'd come to this thing with the half-formed notion to ask permission to court Sarah. The only reason he hadn't asked via their now-long chat was that it wasn't private. Personal. Matters of the heart were not spectacles for others' eyes. What was he going to do now?

"...And I'd like to extend a special thank you to my editing team." The woman whose name he still didn't know had taken over from Sophie. "Without whom *Waterhouse's Muse* would not be the brilliant piece of prose we're delighted to share with you today. We have two of our three here with us tonight. Would you like to meet them?"

Oh God. Here it comes. He couldn't take his eyes off of Sophie. He had to see her reaction.

"My dearest assistant, Lance Peachtree, you really showed your strength as a brilliant developmental editor. I'm so excited to see you blossom and thrive..."

Xavier winced at the effusive praise heaped upon the less than stellar Lance. No wonder Sarah—no, Sophie, dammit it was Sophie—had questioned his credentials if she'd had to suffer through Lance. The man was a poseur of the worst sort, a talentless hack who dreamed of making it big. Lance was a bully. A con-man. He'd had to deal with the man more times than he cared to, and he'd lived long enough to recognize the type.

Tuning out the rest of her gushing, he focused on Sophie. The smile on her face was brittle. The kind that was only accomplished by a clenched jaw. She clearly hated the effusive praise as much as he did. He wished he was next to her so they could whisper snarky commentary to each other. That would be heaploads more entertaining than whatever drivel was coming out of Ms. I-Can't-Recall-Your-Name-Because-Sophie-Is-Sarah's mouth.

Eventually, the woman wound down. Her eyes scanned the audience searching for someone, brightening visibly when she spotted him. She pointed in his direction and said, "And of course, our go-to man for all things historical, Xavier Robinson, the bloody best Britpicker in the biz!"

He didn't move. Couldn't move. His eyes were riveted to Sophie's face. He saw the widening of her eyes at his name. Saw her scan the crowd looking for him. Saw her find him. Her mouth formed a little 'o' as the shock of his identity radiated through her entire body. He couldn't tell if her reaction was pleased or angry. He wasn't sure he wanted to know.

"Well come on, Xavier! Don't keep us waiting," the woman called, motioning for him to join her onstage.

Slowly, oh so slowly, he dragged his body up onto the dais.

He wasn't sure how he made it through the next several minutes. Just that he did. As soon as his part was over, he beelined for the bar. He needed a drink—alcoholic rather than bloody. He signaled the bartender and ordered another tumbler of Jameson. How was he going to deal with this?

He didn't think he'd been imagining Sarah's—Sophie's—interest in him when they'd chatted online. An interest that seemed to signal more than just friendship. The social mores had changed so much over the years. While he preferred not to rush into things, he'd known many a happily married couple who'd only danced a few times before becoming engaged.

And why was he thinking about marriage! She hated him. He only marginally tolerated her. She was a mortal. He was a vampire. It would never work! Even as much as a part of him wanted it.

Blasted hell! Where was that drink?!

The bartender set the glass down in front of him but before he could pick it up, a pale hand snaked out and grabbed it. Turning to confront the whiskey thief, he froze. Standing there, pilfered drink in hand, was Sophie.

"We need to talk." The words were flat. Unyielding. And were there four more hated words in the English lexicon?

She motioned for him to follow her out onto the terrace outside of the restaurant. He did, incredibly grateful it was April, and a cold April at that. The sun had set long ago, and it was still too early in the year for it to be pleasant out-of-doors.

As soon as Sophie seemed to decide they were alone, she whirled. "When were you going to tell me that you were BloodyBrit?"

He opened his mouth to correct her then decided against it. Being pedantic wasn't going to win him any points in Sophie's book, and for once, being right didn't matter as much as someone else's feelings. "I didn't know it was you. The author's name was Sarah, not Sophie. And I've never seen your writing, only heard you speak. The difference is..." he struggled for the right word "...incomparable."

She seemed surprised by that admission. Her eyes widened, and the pulse under her jaw fluttered for an instant.

Xavier quashed the urge to reach out to run his fingers over the spot, feel her warmth, her life. Still, the desire simmered just under the surface, waiting. "Why'd you change your name?"

"Lance told me no one would buy from an author with an 'ethnic' name like mine." Her voice was filled with bitterness.

And rightfully so. If a man named Umberto Eco didn't have to change his name to be a bestselling author, then there was no good reason why Sophie had to change hers. Lance lowered even further in his estimation, something he hadn't thought possible. "Lance is an idiot."

She giggled. "Yes, but..." she waved her hands in the vague direction of the restaurant, "Melissa likes him. I have no idea why."

Melissa. That was the woman's name. Not like it mattered. "Not everyone is a good judge of character." He took an unneeded breath. "I admit, I haven't judged you in the best light."

"Same."

He let the subject drop to return to the previous one. "So Lance was your content editor?"

"Apparently. I also found that out tonight." She went to take a sip from the glass before seeming to think better of it. "It's been one hell of a night when it comes to editor surprises."

"Not all bad, I hope?"

Holding the tumbler out to him, she said, "No, not all bad."

Xavier had lived long enough to recognize that tone. It was light, flirtatious. There was a lyrical lilt to it. A question. An opening.

He took it and the proffered glass. His fingers slid along hers as he grasped the drink and downed it in one go. The amber liquid flowed through him, not quite warming him, but stirring the blood in his veins to flow more swiftly. Or that's what he told himself. It wasn't that fleeting touch which caused his heart to race, because despite legend deeming otherwise, his heart did beat; it just didn't usually beat so fast.

Clearing his throat, Xavier took a chance. "Might I have the presumption that I was a less bad surprise?"

In the warm glow of the streetlights, Sophie's eyes glittered like the light-hidden stars. "Less bad, yes. But still a surprise. I didn't know you were an editor."

"It's something to do to pass the time." He didn't really want to go down this path with her, the safe path where they only talked of jobs and projects always dancing around the subject but never quite landing on it. "You look lovely."

"Tonight."

He took a half-step toward her. "No, not just tonight. Always."

"Even with my streaked hair and nose ring?" she quoted his insults from what felt like ages ago at him. Her tone was arch, challenging. He'd stepped off of the safe path into a minefield.

Still, she had the right to call him out on his unkind comments. They were cruel. He had no excuse he could give her that she'd believe. Yet, he couldn't lie to her. Not if he wanted to court her, and to his surprise, he did. "I'm a bit of a throwback to a different time." If that wasn't the truth! "I'm not a fan of most fashion trends that change with the seasons if not more frequently. I like simple things. And that is one thing you are not. You are complex, brilliant, and—even with your embellishments—lovely."

And she was; in this light—out of the harsh fluorescent lights of the restaurant—she reminded him of the women of his youth. He wanted to take her into his arms and lead her around the terrace in a dance.

"And yet, you like me."

"I liked the person I got to know while editing your manuscript. I'd like to get to know her more. Possibly over coffee?" And there it was, the final, treacherous step. The one that placed him oh so firmly on dangerous ground. The ball was in her court, and he could only hope she'd pick it up.

"Wait. Wait. Wait. This is not happening." She tilted her head. "Are you asking me on a date?"

"Yes."

The simple confirmation seemed to stun her. She blinked at him once, twice, and then once more. "How old are you?"

The question was loaded. More loaded than she knew. Again, he didn't want to lie to her, but the truth was well and truly out of the question. "I'm older than I look." Without the dye and other aging effects he used, he appeared to be in his late twenties... the age when he'd died.

"And how old is that?" She wouldn't be dissuaded.

"Guess." It was a gambit he'd used in the past.

"Forty."

It wasn't a bad guess considering he was shooting for that age. "I'm not forty." That was true, at least.

She screwed up her face. "Forty-five?"

"What makes you think I'm older?" Yes, he intended for people to guess he was in his forties, but for her to guess older... He'd have to check himself out in his webcam again. Maybe he'd overdone the beard.

Motioning to his artistically applied dye, she said, "It's the gray."

"Ah. But it could be premature gray; after all, I do have a stressful life dealing with both unruly tenants and fractious authors." He kept his tone light, teasing. He hoped his words would distract her.

They didn't. A little smile fluttered on her lips, and she guessed, "One hundred and fifty two."

The number was absurd. Ludicrous. And dangerously close to the truth. He gaped at her. "Whyever would you guess that?"

"You said you were a vampire." She shrugged. "I figured I'd throw it out there."

"And?"

"I'm pretty sure I'm wrong, but go big or go home, right?"

He shook his head with a laugh. "Right. I mean, you're wrong about the age. I am not one hundred and fifty two." He'd been born in 1782 which meant that he was two hundred and thirty eight years old. "But you're right about the sentiment. No risk, no reward."

"Yeah. But back to my point, you're a lot older than me. You're my grandmother's landlord. I just don't know."

His heart sunk. "I understand." The age difference and the power differential were too great. He hadn't even thought about the latter, but it was there. He'd never do anything to harm Dorothy, but Sophie didn't know that and couldn't trust that he wouldn't strike against her grandmother if she upset him. He had to respect her wishes even if it pained him to do so. He moved to leave.

Her voice stopped him. "That wasn't a no."

Turning, he asked, "Then what was it?"

"It was an 'I don't know.' I don't know if I want to date you." She took a deep breath. "But I'm willing to see if I'm open to the proposition."

"Coffee?"

She stepped forward. "I was thinking something a little more proactive."

"Dinner?" He didn't usually eat because, unlike his heart, his digestive system did not work on anything non-liquid. Still, he was willing to deal with the repercussions if it meant having the opportunity to court Sophie.

She moved forward again until she was breathtakingly close. Her head tilted, causing her face to be illuminated by the streetlights overhead. There was a question there. A question he wasn't quite sure he believed was possible.

"What do you suggest?" His tone was playful, hopeful. He wasn't sure what the social conventions were for dating in this time period, but he guessed that whatever came out of Sophie's mouth next would not be within the proscribed.

He was right.

"I want to kiss you."

"I beg your pardon?"

"I want to kiss you," she repeated in the same matter-of-fact tone.

"I understand the words," he said, his whole body itching to draw itself upward into an imperious stance. He quashed the urge; sliding back behind his armor wasn't going to do him any good. "What I don't understand is why."

"So, it may sound corny, but I'm a big believer in sparks. Like the whole fireworks, leg popping, ferris-wheel-spinning shebang. There's got to be a connection on top of the attraction or things are a no-go."

Xavier was still confused and said so.

Sophie sighed. "I could give all sorts of examples like from *Buffy* or *The Princess Diaries*, but something tells me you still wouldn't get it."

Oddly enough, it did help him understand, but only because he collected vampire fiction of all varieties. It was always useful to know what information was out there. And like most of his brethren, he cursed both Bram Stoker and that asshole, Dracula. "You're thinking of Wesley and Cordelia."

Her face brightened. "You know it!"

"I do."

"Cool, even if we aren't date-compatible, we should totally get together and binge the show." She didn't wait for him to agree but just plowed on, "But yes. Like Wesley and Cordelia. Age difference? Check! Stuffy Brit and hip and stylish babe? Check! What if we start dating and there's the same negative chemistry? *No es bueno.* So I want to head that off at the pass."

"So you want me to kiss you?"

She shook her head. "Reverse that. I want to kiss you." Her eyes lowered and a warm blush stole up her cheeks. "Assuming you let me."

Understanding that this was the test that had the potential to shape his future but also realizing that she was giving him the choice, Xavier let his heart guide him. "I'm horribly out of practice."

"Is that a yes?"

"Yes. Oh dear God, it's a yes."

Sophie reached up and tugged him down to her. He thanked every deity he knew, which was more than one might imagine, that she was wearing heels and willing to stand on tiptoe to kiss him. She started slow, the soft brush of her lips over his. A breeze signaling the main storm.

And what a storm it was!

Cradling his head in her hands, she captured his lips with hers. It was like no kiss he'd had before. If he'd had breath to steal, it would be stolen. As her mouth slanted over his, he felt the cyclone overtake him. Desire flooded through every inch of him, and with the hand not holding the glass, he pulled her closer to him. She was his anchor. His refuge. His destroyer. With her, he felt a wholeness that he'd never even realized was missing, yet he knew that she held in her very mortal grasp the power to unmake him.

He couldn't let this go on. So aching in more ways than one, he regretfully ended the kiss.

As she settled back on her heels, Sophie blinked as if to get her own bearings. "That was... Wow."

"That's an eloquent way of putting it," he couldn't resist quipping. "So, what is your verdict?"

"I'm willing to consider dating you."

"Consider?"

"I might need more persuasion."

He laughed. "If you're ready to leave this godforsaken party, I know a wonderful old bar that plays the best jazz in the city."

"Consider me persuaded." She smiled up at him and brought his free hand up to her lips. "You're freezing."

"Really? I hadn't noticed."

"Come on," she held his hand in hers, "let's go grab our coats, and we can both warm up."

"Sounds like a brilliant plan. And perhaps later, you will allow *me* the pleasure of kissing *you*."

Sophie peeked up at him through her lashes. "You know, I think I'd like that."

Taking that for the invitation it was, he bent to press a quick kiss to her mouth. They had a long way to go and one heck of a secret to overcome, but Xavier was confident they'd make it through.

Once we manage to escape this infernal party, that is!

About the Author

Siobhan Kearney has always believed in fairy tales, spirits, and kissing underneath the mistletoe. She wrote her first story when she was eight—a harrowing tale about a brave Amtrak who saved a slow moving freight train in the mountains of Colorado and had a romance with an equally heroic commuter train. She was eight; it wasn't that complex.

A practicing Green Witch, Siobhan is often frustrated by inaccurate depictions of her religion in the media. Her stories will often incorporate aspects of various forms of Wicca or Paganism. And some point she'll write that series on Paganism in Writing her publisher wants.

When she isn't beating her head against the keyboard creating paranormal love stories, she works as a research assistant for a world-class structural engineer. One day she hopes to join her boss in being Wiki-worthy, but for now she'll settle for relative obscurity. She enjoys spending time with her family, exploring nature, reading, gardening, and talking about herself in the third person.

Website: www.roselarkpublishing.com/siobhan-kearney
Twitter: @siobhan_writes

Easy as Pi
♥
Leslie Bond

Story Information

Holiday: Pi Day
Holiday Date: March 14
Heat Rating: 4
Relationship Type: M/M
Major Trigger Warnings: Depictions of a panic attack, discussion of parental illness & death, mentions of alcoholism, mentions of surgery, mentions of past abusive relationships.

It's Pi Day, and someone's got to make all those pies. That someone is Cassidy, working at his boyfriend Bobby's family bakery. The pressure of being an outsider is bad enough, but having to make dozens of perfect pies is enough to turn Cassidy's body into one big knot. It's a good thing Bobby's there to help relieve all that tension…

Easy as Pi

The alarm on Bobby's phone went off earlier than normal—and since he and Cassidy were in charge of getting the day's treats ready at the bakery, that was very early indeed. With a yawn, Bobby swiped the alarm off and stretched.

"Why?" Cass asked when he saw what time it was. He rolled over and put his arm around Bobby, skin against skin.

"If I tell you, are you awake enough to remember?"

"You know that I am not." Cass attempted to snuggle in, but Bobby slipped out from under his arm.

"Fifteen minutes," Bobby said as he walked to the bathroom.

Cass made a noise halfway between annoyance and acceptance, pulled the blanket up to his chin, and dozed off. Fifteen minutes later, he made the same noise when Bobby roused him again.

"Come on," said Bobby. "I'll make coffee, but you gotta get up."

Levering himself into a sitting position, Cass said, "You know, it wasn't so long ago that being awake in bed at this hour would have been an early *night* and not an early *morning*."

"You said you wanted to help me at the bakery," Bobby reminded him. "Sometimes that makes for really early days." He nudged Cass with his elbow. "Up and at 'em. You know I'm not leaving here until you're vertical."

"Fool you once?" Cass said as he swung his legs over the side of the bed. As Cass dragged himself to the bathroom, Bobby headed downstairs to the kitchen.

They'd been living in the little detached condo for just over three months. Upstairs, the master bath, guest bath, linen closet, and guest bedroom closet fitted together like a jigsaw puzzle made of lumber and drywall. The third, smallest bedroom had a closet that overhung the stairs; that was technically Bobby's home office, but he mostly used it to video chat with his sister in the Army in Texas. Most of their furniture was secondhand, except for the bed and dressers in the master bedroom. Bobby had taken those from his old bedroom, but without a spare bed, the guest room contained a single cardboard box that represented Cassidy's only non-wearable worldly possessions, tucked away in a corner out of sight of the door.

Downstairs was the kitchen with a breakfast nook, a half-bath, the living room, and the garage with Bobby's car. Cass had found good deals on a TV, couch, and XBox One, so he was set, and Bobby had gone to a restaurant supply store to get wholesale prices on stuff for the kitchen. Bobby had plans for how to decorate when they had the money; Cassidy was happy to let him take the lead. It was all just stuff to him. He preferred things that couldn't be lost, like, well, Bobby. To everyone else, Roberto Miguel Santiago Perez was "Beto," but not to Cass; to Cass he was "Bobby," always, something precious that couldn't be taken.

In the bathroom, Cass winced as the bright-as-the-sun LED lights stung his eyes. He caught a glimpse of himself in the mirror; the dark circles beneath his dark eyes weren't a good look. Was Raccoon Chic a thing? He didn't see it catching on. After he'd brushed his teeth and showered, he slid into a pair of faded jeans and a long-sleeved green Henley. Despite being cut for someone slender, the clothes were still a little baggy on his so-thin-it-was-almost-fragile frame. He laced up an ancient pair of Converse and grabbed his wallet and phone before lumbering downstairs.

Somehow, his boyfriend managed to be cheerful at o'dark thirty, bustling around the small kitchen with an unfair amount of energy. Running a hand through his still-damp brown hair, Bobby said, "You want eggs, Cass?" He handed over a steaming mug of coffee with a little splash of milk.

Cass grunted in the negative. There was leftover pizza in the fridge: the breakfast of champions. He didn't even bother to heat it up, grabbing a couple of slices and tucking in.

"You know, I have asbestos fingers from spending so much time baking, but I think you have an asbestos throat," Bobby said, watching Cass chug the cup of hot coffee. "One of these mornings, you'll have to try my *chilaquiles*. Or *huevos rancheros*. A steady diet of cold pizza is probably not sustainable in the long-term."

"Try feeding me sometime after dawn," Cass suggested. "I am more adventurous in the daylight hours. If you slapped down a plate of sausage and home fries, I'd be down. I never say no to a good sausage."

"I noticed," Bobby said with a chuckle.

"I'm gonna remember you said that." He held out his empty mug, and Bobby refilled it with the rest of the coffee. "Seriously, do you ever get a day off?"

"Thanksgiving, Mexican Christmas, and New Year's Day," Bobby said promptly. "When my dad gets back from Mexico, it won't be so bad. He likes the morning shift. And believe me, I wish I knew when that was going to be."

"Your poor grandparents have had a rough couple of years." Cass was sympathetic. Somehow, his grandparents were still healthy, but then, Bobby's were older.

"I talked to my dad yesterday. Grandma only has two more rounds of chemo, but now it's looking like Grandpa needs his other hip replaced. And then, maybe, Papá gets to come back here, and my parents can work the wee hours again."

Cass tossed back his coffee. "I don't understand morning people."

"I might make one of you yet. There's still time."

"Many have tried." Cass set his empty mug in the sink. "Is your brother coming in today?"

"That's sort of the 'family' part of 'family business.' I'd be more surprised if he didn't show." He reached up and stroked Cassidy's cheek with his thumb. "Hey. It's not about you. Change happened while he was gone, and he's not happy about it. He doesn't even know you."

"He doesn't want to."

"His loss. I can handle my brother. Just let it stay between me and him."

"Yeah, okay."

Bobby grabbed a jacket on the way to the car; Cass didn't bother. He liked the cold. Besides, when they left the bakery, it would be a mild spring day. They were barely out of the driveway before Cass dozed off again, despite the pot of coffee working its way through his veins. This time of night, it was a quick drive, no traffic on the streets. Beto parked behind Te Amo Bakery and shook Cass awake.

"So why are we here so early?" Cass said around a yawn.

"You haven't seen the orders for today, have you? I do actually set a cap on special orders, but we were just shy of it last night. Thanksgiving's a different story, we'll max out on orders starting on Tuesday and have to deal with shouting people on Wednesday because they can't have a last-minute pumpkin pie." He shrugged. "I think those are the same people who go shopping Christmas Eve and complain that they can't get what they want. That probably won't be a problem today, though; just make sure to make some extras."

"That sounds ominous." Cassidy unlocked the back door and walked in, squinting as he turned the lights on in the kitchen. When he opened the walk-in cooler, he was greeted by a veritable mountain of wrapped, chilled pie dough, neatly labeled in Bobby's mother's handwriting. "Why?"

Bobby handed him a clipboard full of special orders, the white and yellow duplicates of each order still attached to each other, ready to be processed. "Today's Pi Day."

"Pie Day? There's a holiday for pie?" Cass riffled through the forms: apple, cherry, blueberry, peach, over and over and over.

"P-i, not p-i-e. Like the number."

"The circle thing? Pi-r-squared." Math hadn't been his strong suit to begin with, and there had been a cute boy sitting a row over and two seats up in Geometry: the perfect recipe for distraction.

"Yeah, exactly right." Bobby smiled at him. "It starts 3.14, and today's March 14th. And since number-pi sounds like food-pie, people started buying food-pie on March 14th because of the date, which wasn't a huge deal here until those tech companies moved in downtown, and now…" With a sweep of his arm, he indicated the heaps of pie dough in the cooler. "This is kind of like second Thanksgiving. Except people want pies with a top crust so they can have a number-pi on top, either latticed in or cut as the vents. Do you remember what it looks like?"

Cass sketched it in the air. "Two lines and a squiggle across the top, right?"

"Uh-huh. The squiggly part goes up, then down, like a tilde, otherwise there will be some angry nerds at the gates."

As he closed the cooler door, Cass had a sudden thought. "Wait, so do they do this in Europe? Because, like, they do the day first, then the month, so 3-1-4 would either be 3-14 or 31-4, and neither of those work, because there's no fourteenth month and April only has thirty days."

Bobby gave him a look that was equal parts affection and amusement.

"Am I doing that thing where I overthink things again?"

"I think it's kinda cute, *mi corazón*," Bobby said. "Anyway, if you deal with all the pies, I'll deal with all the… everything else."

The weight of the clipboard in his hand felt overwhelming. Cass took a deep breath. One thing at a time. "I got this."

"Hell yeah, you do." Bobby gave Cassidy's free hand a squeeze and rocked up on his toes to plant a kiss on his cheek. Cass turned slightly and caught Bobby's lips with his own, wrapping his arms around him and holding him close. After a moment, Bobby pulled away. "We'll have to pick that up later, or we're going to be behind. Definitely a rain check, though." He retreated to his own corner of the kitchen, ready to do battle with their normal assortment of bread and sweets.

Cass pulled on an apron and scraped his shoulder-length blond hair back into a short ponytail, then flopped a ballcap onto his head—had to keep the health inspectors happy. Plugging his phone in to charge, he cued up some '90s rock, synced his noise-canceling headphones, and started sorting through the order sheets. He separated them into two piles, one for the before-work pickups, and one for later in the day, then sorted each of those piles by type of pie. The smaller piles felt more manageable, and he felt like he could breathe again as he set the oven to preheat, washed his hands, and started prepping.

Cass was thankful that the previous day's afternoon crew—Bobby's mom and brother and whatever random cousins had decided to show up—had planned ahead by making the pie filling and the mountain of dough in the cooler. He grabbed a package of dough and a tub of apple pie filling, taking them over to his bench and pulling out a stack of pie tins. Pies were one of the first things Bobby had taught him to make when he'd hired Cass on as help in the bakery.

He'd taught Cass to make pie in the kitchen at his mother's house, a far more cozy setting than the industrial kitchen at the bakery. When he'd put his hands on Cass's to show him how to roll out the dough, it had brought back a memory Cass had forgotten: he couldn't have been more than six, and he'd been making sugar cookies with his mother. She had put her hands over his on the rolling pin to help him flatten the cookie dough, then handed him a stack of cookie cutters. A stray curl of hair had fallen across her face, and she'd blown it out of the way, but it had bounced right back into place. They'd laughed at the little curl that had a mind of its own and spent the next few minutes cutting out cookies and blowing hair out of their faces. Cass and his sister Dee had inherited their mother's curly hair, but Cass's was surfer-dude blond instead of rich chestnut brown.

The memory of his mother had been overwhelming. Blood pounding in his ears, breath catching in his throat, Cass had started to lose his balance. Bobby had hooked a chair with his foot and yanked it over in time for Cass to sit heavily, everything feeling a million miles away. Cass had focused on Bobby's voice, repeating, "What's my name, Cass?" until he'd been able to gasp out "Bobby" and pull himself out of the episode.

He knew now she'd already been diagnosed, that day in the kitchen with the cookies—amyotrophic lateral sclerosis, Lou Gehrig's Disease. There were so many holes in his memories, things he'd chosen to forget or simply not been mentally present for in the first place, but he was glad that he didn't remember her decline. In his mind, she was healthy and happy forever. Cass had been ten when she'd died, Dee six. He'd never asked his sister if she remembered their mother being healthy. He didn't want to know the answer.

Cass and Bobby had continued the pie-making session another day, and Cass was a practiced hand at it now. The dough had to be kept as cold as possible. If the butter got too warm, the pastry wouldn't be as flaky, so Cass had to work in small batches with the dough, minimizing the time it spent between the cooler and the oven. Flour, too, was the enemy of flaky pie crust, so he barely dusted the counter before unwrapping a batch of dough and grabbing his rolling pin. Plain wood, tapered at the ends, it was unremarkable and efficient; Cass thought there were worse things to be. One pass across the dough, then a quarter-turn, repeated until the dough was an eighth of an inch thick.

He set a round thirteen-inch template on the dough and slid a knife around the edge, cutting out the bottom crusts for several pies out of one package of dough. Bobby could cut dough freehand, but Cass wasn't quite there yet, and he didn't want to get it wrong. Working quickly so the heat from his hands didn't melt the butter, he picked up each round and set it into a disposable pie tin, using a balled-up scrap of leftover dough to press it into the bottom edge of the tin.

The pie filling came next: peeled, sliced Granny Smith apples cooked in cinnamon, nutmeg, and brown sugar. Cass wasn't above taking the leftovers home, throwing them in a blender, and making applesauce, but there wouldn't be any of that today—not with the stack of orders staring him in the face. He spooned the apple mixture into the waiting crusts and used the back of the spoon to smooth out the top of the layer of fruit. Apples, they could always get fresh, but in March, the blueberries, cherries, and peaches came frozen. Fresh peach pie in the summer, though, that was the best, especially Bobby's—his secret ingredient was a pinch of cayenne pepper, which Cass hadn't been entirely sold on until he'd tried it. But once he'd taken his first bite, he understood why they flew off the shelves of the bakery.

Fruit pies were generally double-crust, so Cass had to roll out a second layer of dough, same as the first, but cutting smaller rounds, since it didn't have to go up the sides of the pie tin. He laid each round on top of the filling, trimming the edges with his knife, pinching the crusts together with his thumb and forefingers. Normally, he'd cut the vents in an apple pie as five quick slashes in a star shape, like the seeds in an apple core viewed from above, but today, it was all pis: two parallel vertical lines topped with a tilde. Later, he'd get to do some lattice tops, which were more tedious, but he liked doing them. His slender, nimble fingers always made quick work of weaving dough.

Cracking a few eggs into a blender, Cass whizzed it for a few seconds to make an egg wash. Once brushed onto the tops of the pies, it would brown in the oven and give the pastries their characteristic golden color. When he finished the batch, he double-checked the order forms to make sure he hadn't missed anything, then put the pies onto a baking sheet and slid it into the oven, setting a timer for halfway through the cooking so he could flip the sheet around and give everything an even bake.

He glanced over at Bobby across the room, kneading bread dough, shaking his cute little butt to whatever pop music was running through his headphones. Bobby's musical tastes could best be described as "teenage girl," but since occasionally listening to Katy Perry was the worst Cass had to deal with while dating him, he'd consider it a win. Besides, Ariana Grande was starting to grow on him, and who didn't love Beyoncé?

Chris Cornell and Eddie Vedder growling in his ears, Cass lost track of time, a human assembly line of pies. When a banana suddenly appeared in front of him, he was so startled that he nearly dropped the lid to a cherry pie onto the counter. He pulled his headphones off.

"Eat something, Cassidy." His sister held out a banana and a sandwich.

"Hey, Dee. Is it that time already?" As he reached up to pause his phone, he realized that the sky was beginning to lighten.

"Uh-huh. And I'm sure you haven't had more than a cup of coffee and a slice of cold pizza today."

"Hey, I'll have you know it was *two* slices of cold pizza." He looked at the oven timer. "Anyway, can't eat now, pies are almost ready."

"I'll get Beto to take care of it." Dee sighed. "Cass, your stomach's grumbling, and you don't even know it." She pressed the food into his hands and gave him a gentle shove toward the tiny room that served as an office and break room.

He took a bite out of the sandwich as he went. "Strawberry?" he asked.

"Eat your pb&j with lesser jelly, you choosy beggar!" she joked. "Nate used the last of the blueberry on his toast this morning. Now shut up and eat your free food!"

Once he stepped away from the counter, Cass became aware that he was, in fact, hungry, and his shoulders were starting to ache from the constant rolling of dough. He plopped down on the ancient, sagging loveseat and ate the rest of the sandwich. The banana was almost gone when Dee and Bobby came in.

"How's it going?" Bobby asked.

"Done with the morning pies. Just started on the afternoon pies. Made some extra… extras. Half with a pi-shaped vent for the techies who forgot to preorder, half with regular vents for the normies."

"You may want to make extra… extra extras," Dee said. "I remembered what day it was and did a social media push. Get us in on some of that sweet hashtag-Pi-Day action." She glanced over at the phone, whose message light was blinking.

"No more pie," Cass groaned. "If I never see another pie, it'll… be tomorrow."

Bobby sat down next to Cassidy. "That's the spirit!" He took the banana peel from Cass and tossed it at the trash can across the room, missing by a mile.

Rolling her eyes, Dee picked it up and dropped it into the trash. "Clearly, I was right to set you two up, match made in heaven right here."

Cass looked down at the splotch of strawberry jelly on his shirt, just above his apron. "I have no idea what you're talking about."

"The *gallinas* are ready, if you want to add some powdered sugar to the stain," Bobby said. "Could be artistic."

"I will settle for nothing less than a *concha*."

"Still warm. You want chocolate?"

Cass nodded.

"Strawberry for me!" Dee called as Bobby went back into the kitchen. "Free *conchas* are the best part of this job," she said to Cassidy as she perched on the edge of Bobby's desk.

"You're not the one getting up at two in the morning and making a zillion pies. Free *conchas* are the least of it." Cass laced his fingers and raised his arms above his head, leaning to one side, then the other, stretching his torso. His back cracked with an audible pop.

"That sounded like it hurt," Bobby said, coming back with his hands full of pastries.

"Feels so much better now. I think I need new shoes if I'm gonna be standing all day." He winced as he took his *concha*. "Although, that won't do much for my shoulders."

Bobby waited until Cass was finished chewing, then leaned over and kissed him. "I'm sure you could talk your roommate into giving you a back rub later."

"I don't know, that dude's a pretty tough taskmaster. Got me chained to a counter making pies all day."

Dee grabbed a stack of order forms and picked up the phone, hitting the button to listen to the messages. "I have reason to believe you're not entirely chained to the counter—see Exhibit A, where you're currently not chained to the counter—but you may want to pretend like you are. I have a feeling we're going to need to cut off pie orders, and it'll have to be first-come, first-served on whatever's not claimed."

Walking over to the desk, Bobby jiggled the mouse to wake up the computer. "I'll make a note for next year. Mention it a few days early, suggest getting the pies a day before, like Thanksgiving. Or making extras the day before, people who order ahead get a fresh one, poor planners get a day-old, it's not like they won't keep overnight in the cooler." He typed out some notes.

"How is it not exhausting to think about next year already?" Cass asked.

Bobby shrugged. "The whole point is to turn a profit. Something my idiot brother has trouble comprehending. Selling a lot of what people want to buy is better business than making what you want and hoping people want to buy it." He checked the time. "Have you started boxing things up yet and attaching the order forms?"

"No," Cass said. He'd been so focused on making new pies that he hadn't even thought about finishing up the ones that were cool and ready for sale.

"I'll do it," Dee said, waving Cass off. She tightened her ponytail and tucked it through the hole at the back of her ballcap. "And I'll see how many new orders I can get out of the extra pies you've already made, try and cut you a break before I hit you with more paperwork."

"I'll stock up the bake cases, then," said Bobby.

The three of them split up, Dee with the stack of finished orders and a stack of new forms fresh off the voicemail, Bobby for the pastries and bread, and Cass back to the counter for more pie. He got back just as the timer dinged—was he turning into Bobby, with his unerring sense of timing? Either way, he pulled the pies out and set them on a rack to cool, stopping by the walk-in on his way back to the bench for another package of dough.

He was vaguely aware that the front doors had opened for customers, but that didn't affect him much in the back. Bobby kept the bread and pastries refreshed out front, and Dee ran the register and answered the phone. While technically Bobby had hired her for marketing, working at the bakery in the mornings got her out of the house and socializing with people instead of becoming a work-from-home hermit. She was the one who'd introduced Cass and Bobby, and although Bobby was easily the best person Cass had ever dated, he still vaguely suspected that Dee had set them up just to reclaim the spare bedroom Cass had been living in for a year. She never would have kicked him out—too much history for a dose of tough love—but he'd chosen to move in with Bobby on his own, and now Cass was getting the idea that his little sister and Nate, the Good Doctor Stone, were talking about having kids. If the Stones had a kid, did that make it a Pebble? He filed that away for a possible niece or nephew nickname. Dee would hate it, Nate would roll with it because the Good Doctor took everything in stride, and the kid would probably think it was great, because Cass fully intended to be the best uncle ever.

The chime of the back door was loud enough to be heard over his music. Bobby was up front, so Cass put his pie making on hold long enough to let the delivery driver in. It was Joe, the usual guy, who knew where everything went, so after the obligatory exchange of pleasantries, Cass went back to his pies and left Joe to it. Bobby returned before Joe was done, so he signed for the delivery, leaving

Cass uninterrupted in his assembly line of pies. The stack of orders was dwindling, and Dee hadn't given him any more, so either she'd covered the new orders with already-made pies or assumed he'd make enough to get them through the day.

On his next trip into the cooler, he saw it packed with pies ready to sell. It took him a moment to realize that the weird thing he was feeling was pride. He'd done all that. He went to grab another batch of dough and was greeted with the odd sight of beer: Guinness and Harp in neat cases stacked up on the floor, tucked away alongside the bakery stalwarts of butter, eggs, and milk. Closing the door, he went over to Bobby and pulled off his headphones. "What's up with the beer in the cooler?"

"St. Patrick's Day," Bobby replied. His face fell. "Shit. I wasn't thinking. Are you okay? I mean, can you help, or should I get my brother to come in early?"

"It's fine." Cass saw the look of doubt on Bobby's face. "I promise, it's okay."

"Don't say that if it's not. Javier can come in early for once." Bobby made a face. "Got up at all hours in Afghanistan, can't be bothered to crawl out of bed before dawn for the family business."

"Really, I'll be fine." Cass pulled Bobby in close. At 5'10", he was only three inches taller than Bobby—not quite tall enough to rest his chin on the top of Bobby's head—so he settled for leaning his cheek against Bobby's forehead. "Beer was never my poison. But thanks for being worried about me. So what do you make with the beer, anyway?"

"Cupcakes," Bobby said. "We sold out last year. Half-and-Half, that's dark chocolate Guinness cakes with Harp buttercream. Irish Boilermakers, that's the dark chocolate Guinness cake filled with Jameson caramel and topped with Bailey's buttercream. Irish Coffee, that's espresso cake with the Jameson caramel and whipped cream frosting." He leaned into Cassidy. "I wanna do some kid-friendly ones this year too. I'm thinking Shamrock Cupcakes, vanilla mint cake with whipped cream frosting and a cherry on top, and maybe a Pot of Gold? Chocolate, with rainbow buttercream and gold sprinkles."

"I legit want a Shamrock Cupcake right now," Cass said, smiling.

"I might make some later," Bobby said. "I need to make sure it's the right shade of green and the right amount of minty before the seventeenth."

"Well, I will happily be your cupcake guinea pig."

Bobby poked him in the ribs. "Where was that exploratory spirit when I had *chilaquiles* this morning?"

"Did I not say to try me after the sun came up?" Cass said with a shrug. "It's daylight now."

"And not at all because cupcakes are a known quantity and *chilaquiles* are weird breakfast food?"

"Speaking of cupcakes and not at all changing the subject from weird breakfast food, on a scale of one to ten, how much is your brother going to hate us making a mess of cupcakes for St. Patrick's Day?"

"On a scale of one to ten? Like, infinity." Bobby sighed. "On one hand, the fact that he came back means that I got to move out and get a place with you. On the other hand, I promise he was not this much of a pain in the ass when we were growing up." He booped the end of Cassidy's long, narrow, upturned ski jump of a nose. "It looks like you're almost done with the pies."

Cass nodded. "I'm gonna use up whatever filling and dough is left and call it good, unless Dee suddenly appears with a pile of order forms."

"I already told her not to take any more. They can put their names on one that's already made, or they can show up and hope there's one available when they get here. Your Pi Day torment is almost over!"

"Hooray," Cass said with a decided lack of enthusiasm. He'd still be on pie duty tomorrow, and the day after that, and apparently every day after that, except for Thanksgiving, Mexican Christmas, and New Year's Day.

"I'll get you making other things soon enough," Bobby said, correctly reading the room. "But you haven't spent decades here making all this stuff, and there's a lot to learn." He looked up at Cass. "You don't have to stay here if you don't want. I get it, it's a lot of early mornings and hard work and sore feet and singed-off arm hair."

"There's worse places to be." Cass winced. "And I think the sore shoulders are worse than the sore feet. Although my feet are not in great shape either."

Bobby looked down. "I'm pretty sure those shoes came over on the Mayflower. We'll get you something better, and I'll work the knots out of your shoulders later."

"I will happily let you." Cass returned to the counter, to the small pile of order forms that were left. He'd saved the lattice-top afternoon pies for last. He was prepping a batch of cherry pies when

Bobby's mother and brother came in with a pair of random cousins. Cass offered up a cheerful "*Hola*" to Mamá Santiago, whose English was better than his Spanish, which was admittedly improving, mostly because the little green Duolingo owl kept nagging him to do his daily practice.

Mamá Santiago, like Bobby, had an average build, with warm hazel eyes and a kind smile. Her long, dark hair, shot through with gray, was braided and coiled into a low bun to appease the health inspectors. Cass had seen plenty of pictures of the whole family; the patriarch was somehow gawky, like a teenager made of knees and elbows, and Cass had no idea where the Incredible Hulk proportions of Bobby's older brother had come from. Bobby had mentioned once that his grandfather had been a *luchador*, one of those masked Mexican wrestlers, so maybe the man-mountain genes had skipped ahead.

Cass deliberately avoided Javier, who could pack an impressive amount of contempt into the two syllables of *gringo*. As a person who was terrible with conflict, Cass did what he could to limit contact with Bobby's brother, which wasn't easy when they worked together. Dee didn't seem to engender the same hostility, but then, she was Bobby's employee, not his boyfriend. Bobby had cautioned Cass not to try mediating the frequent family arguments, but he needn't have bothered. Cassidy's instinctive response to someone shouting at him was to mentally check out and come around some time later when the storm had passed, so he could clean up the blood and ice the bruises. He was the last person who'd be of any use in a tense situation, unless curling up in a ball was helpful.

Still, Cass knew the fight between the brothers was coming. Out of the corner of his eye, he saw Javier open up the walk-in, then stomp over to Bobby, invading his personal space. Cass nudged one of his headphones partway off his ear with his shoulder. At 6'4", Javier towered over Bobby, an imposing presence even before he leaned in aggressively. Bobby somehow stood his ground, arms crossed, glaring back up at his brother. Just watching it made Cassidy's heart race. He didn't understand how Bobby could stand there, the immovable object in the path of the unstoppable force.

Cass's head started to spin and he remembered to breathe.

"*¿Estás bien?*" Mamá Santiago asked, a gentle hand on his arm.

"Yeah, *está bien*, uh, *estoy bien*. I'm fine." He was okay, he *was* okay, the fight was on the other side of the kitchen and didn't involve him, *he was okay.*

The arguments between Javier and Bobby always happened in rapid-fire Spanish, so he could only pick out bits and pieces. Still, focusing on trying to understand a language he was learning gave him something to ground himself with and stave off the panic attack that was very much lurking at the edges of his vision. It helped that the fights between Bobby and Javier had a certain rhythm to them; even if he didn't understand all of it, he knew where the argument was headed next. His brain racing out of control, Cass heard something that sounded like "pie" but didn't know whether it was food-pie or math-pi, and as far as he could tell, there wasn't a consensus on what an American-style pie was called in Spanish, but then he heard "*cerveza*," which he'd known was "beer" from back in his bartending days, so at least the fight had turned to the beer in the cooler, which meant that it was reaching the point where Javier was mostly pissed about the fact that things had changed since he'd gone into and come out of the Marines, like Bobby being in charge and not doing things the way his dad did them, and then Bobby would snap that their father was in Mexico, and—

"*¡Está en México!*"

There it was. Cass wondered if Javier got tired of having the same fight nearly every day, then realized there was probably comfort in the familiarity. After a little more angry Spanish, Javier stormed away. Cass jerked his head to settle his headphones back on his ears and shrank against the counter to avoid contact as Javier passed by. The heavily muscled vet put a lot of force behind a shoulder-check and had rocked Cass off-balance more than once, which usually led to a second, smaller fight and Bobby, dwarfed by his older brother, refusing to back down. On no occasion had Javier ever offered up an apology to Cass, who'd never expected one. Bullies of any stripe were consistent, at least.

Cass finished the lattice over the last pie. They had a tool that cut multiple ribbons of dough at once, like a little pizza cutter with several round blades next to each other. Cass put two ribbons horizontally over the top of the cherry pie, then laid a vertical ribbon over them. The last two horizontal ribbons went over that, then the first two were bent back over the vertical ribbon and a second vertical ribbon was laid down. He repeated the folding until the last ribbon was in place, then took his knife, freehanded a pi out of the remaining dough, and placed it gently on the top, trimmed up and fluted the edges, used the last of the egg wash on the top crust, and slid the tray of pies into the oven.

He wiped his hands clean, tossed the towel onto the counter, and walked over to where Bobby was kneading a lump of dough with extreme prejudice. "Do you need to take it out on the brioche?" Cass asked, the rolled metal edge of the counter cool against his back.

Bobby dug into the dough with the heels of his hands, leaning into it, then lifting it and slapping it back down onto the counter with a splat.

"This is usually the part where you tell me it's clearly not brioche," Cass prompted.

"It actually is brioche," said Bobby. He lifted the dough one last time, dropped it into a tub, and draped a towel over the top.

"It's not like you didn't know the fight was coming," Cass said.

"He had the chance to come back and run the bakery! He stayed in the Marines instead, so Dad left it to me when he went back to Mexico! I'm in charge! The decisions are mine to make! I've seen the monthly expense sheets, I know that my dad ran this place in the red sometimes, and you know what?"

"You haven't," Cass said, knowing perfectly well that Bobby just needed to rant.

"I haven't! Dad wanted to run a traditional *panadería*, and he did, and he even turned a little profit, but he wasn't going to keep up with expenses, and I still serve all the Mexican pastries people wanted to buy back when he was here, we still have all the same regulars, but what my idiot brother doesn't seem to understand is that *gringo* money spends the same, and there's a lot more of them! And if that means doing things differently from my father, then I will happily make Corona with Lime cupcakes for Cinco de Mayo, and I don't care if Javier likes it or not!"

"He is really, *really* gonna hate that." Cass was pretty sure Cinco de Mayo was just May 5th in Mexico and not an excuse to get wasted on Dos Equis and Cuervo while wearing a poncho and a hat that was also a bowl of salsa.

"Well then, he's really gonna hate the margarita and churro cupcakes I'm doing this year too!"

"To clarify, those are two separate things, right?" Cass joked. "I can't see margarita-and-churro cupcakes being a big seller."

To his relief, Bobby laughed, and the residual anger seemed to drain out of him. "Yeah. Two separate things." He slid the tub of brioche dough to the edge of the bench. "Pies done?"

"The last of them are in the oven," Cass said. He craned his torso around, his sore back protesting, and gave Bobby a kiss. Bobby tipped up the brim of Cass's ballcap and leaned in, kissing him back, tasting faintly of cinnamon and sugar.

Bobby, perhaps more than Cass, was aware of their audience, and didn't allow things to get even PG-13. "Kill an hour or so? I want to fiddle with some recipes before we leave."

Cass nodded. He'd learned there was always something to do in the bakery. First, he checked in with Dee and did some refreshing of the bakery cases out front, then he pulled the last of the pies from the oven and set them on the racks to cool. The cooled pies were boxed up in pristine white cardboard bakery boxes, and the special orders had the order forms taped to them, ready for pickup. For the extra pies, he took a Sharpie and wrote what kind of pie it was on the outside of the box before stashing them in the cooler. Once he'd finished with the pies, he cleaned up his workspace and restocked the items he'd need for the next day.

Bobby pulled a tray of cupcakes out of the oven and waved Cass over. "What do you think?"

It was clearly a trial run of Shamrock Cupcakes, a half-dozen cupcakes ranging from pastel to emerald green. "I like the middle row best," Cass said. "That dark green is sort of off-putting. If I had to pick between the two, I'd say the one on the right."

Nodding, Bobby said, "I like that one too. For color, anyway. I thought the dark green was too dark, but it never hurts to try." With his asbestos fingers, he popped the properly green cupcake out of the tin and split it in half, handing a piece to Cassidy. "How's the taste?"

Cass juggled the hot cake from hand to hand, giving it a chance to cool down. His morning coffee wasn't nearly as hot as something that had just come out of a bakery oven, and that was a mistake he didn't care to repeat. He tore off a smaller piece and popped it in his mouth, reminding himself that he needed to assess the flavor, not just devour the mouthful of cake. "It's a little toothpaste-y." He swallowed. "Maybe a lot toothpaste-y. Definitely getting a Colgate vibe. Ten out of ten for color, four out of ten for taste."

Bobby grabbed another cupcake out of the tin and gave half to Cass. "Ignoring the color, is the flavor better?"

Looking at the aggressively green lump of cake in his hand, Cass said, "Give me a second to get past the 'ignore the color' stage."

With a casual wave, Bobby indicated that Cass should get on with it, then made a few notes on the piece of paper on his counter. "The quicker we decide, the sooner we can go home."

It was a compelling argument. Cass meditated on the flavor of the cupcake. "Maybe still a little too minty. What's the next one down?"

The third cupcake turned out to be the winner in the taste category, even if the color was anemic. Cass leaned over and looked at Bobby's notes. "Looks math-y."

"Yeah. I'll need to scale up the recipe for color and taste." He glanced over at Cassidy. "Do you want to be in charge of these and the chocolate cupcakes on St. Patrick's Day?"

"You mean it? You'll let me do something other than assemble pies?" Sudden panic bubbled up. What if he made a mistake? What if he did something to make Bobby disappointed in him? "I've gotten good at pies. I don't want to mess anything up."

Bobby ran his thumb over the back of Cass's hand. "Cupcakes are easy. That's why I do them for special occasions. I can teach you how tomorrow, and I promise you'll be a pro by the end of the day."

"Okay," Cass said. "Are you ready to go?"

"Just gotta clean this up." He suited action to word, and a few minutes later, he and Cass were out the door.

The air in the car was stuffy, and Cass rolled the window down. Pollen Season wasn't quite nigh, and he'd take the fresh air as long as he could. "Permission to suspend Winchester Rules for the duration?"

"Play whatever you'd like," Bobby replied, and Cass found the classic rock station, humming along to Led Zeppelin. Bobby reached over and gave Cass's hand a squeeze. "You did good today."

"Yeah?"

"Your pies looked really good. I'm sure all the nerds will be very impressed."

Cass winced as he rested his arm in the window. "I'll tell you what's impressive; these knots in my shoulders are impressive."

"After dinner, I'll see what I can do about it." He turned the radio up. "Is this song about hobbits?"

"Bobby, were you today years old when you realized that Zeppelin is sometimes deeply weird?" Cass said with a shake of his head. He pulled the hair elastic loose and let the wind toss his curls around his face.

Once they arrived home, Cass plopped down at the kitchen table with a big glass of ice water. Aside from forgetting to eat—which seemed weird at a place where he was surrounded by food—he generally forgot to pop into the office area to hit up the water cooler too, and he was usually parched by the time they got home. On slow days, Dee reminded him to hydrate, but today had been busy with all the Pi Day pickups.

"You could just set an alert on your phone," Bobby said after observing Cass chug his third straight glass of water. "I do."

"I thought about getting a Fitbit or something, but then I remembered I'm broke."

Bobby opened the fridge, contemplating meal choices. "You know what? Let's do this. How do you want your eggs?"

"Huh?"

"Breakfast for dinner. You're gonna try my *huevos rancheros* and you're gonna like 'em. So how do you want your eggs?" Bobby began setting pots and pans on the stove and pulling ingredients from the fridge and cupboards.

"Scrambled, I guess. Or over easy. Whichever." Cass rolled the water glass between his hands. "Fair warning, I come from a far more *schnitzel*-based people. I have serious and deeply-held opinions on the best side for potato pancakes."

Setting a container of black beans on the counter, Bobby said, "I didn't know there were options for that."

"Applesauce is *far* superior to sour cream, even though sour cream is a more obvious choice. Oma made a batch of *kartoffelpuffer* every Sunday, with fresh applesauce. Probably the closest thing I've got to comfort food." Those memories, at least, were clear: Dee, his grandparents, and him, sitting at the breakfast table, digging into mountains of sausage, potato pancakes, toast, eggs, and homemade jam and applesauce, Opa drinking coffee so strong Cass was always surprised he couldn't stand a spoon in it, Oma with a mug of herbal tea sweetened with just a hint of clover honey. He didn't think he'd ever eaten so well as when Oma was trying to put meat on his bones, but somehow, even after he'd grown out of the awkward teenager phase, he'd never been anything but painfully thin. In the afternoon, after the food coma had worn off, Opa would ask Cass if he wanted to listen to records with him, and they'd retreat to the den. When Opa sat in his recliner, it would puff out the faint odor of pipe smoke and shoe polish. He'd always choose first from his collection of vinyl, leaning toward jazz, blues, and classic rock, but he'd set aside a shelf for Cassidy, who'd filled it with his mother's favorite albums: *Purple, Nevermind, Vitalogy, Superunknown, Achtung Baby*. Always a professor, Opa would talk about the music, interjecting stories about seeing B.B. King or Aretha Franklin in concert, going off on the occasional tangent about teaching little Jane to swim in Lake Michigan or watching her in a school play. It hadn't taken Cass long to realize that to his grandfather, she was always the little girl who'd turned brown and freckled in the summer sun; to Cass, she was forever the thirty-something who'd kissed his skinned knees and tucked him in at night. When it was his turn to choose the music, he'd play one he remembered listening to with his mother. At first, he'd been silent, but gradually he'd tell his own stories or quietly sing along in his pleasant tenor. Even if, at fifteen, he wasn't supposed to admit it, he'd come to enjoy the quiet afternoons with his grandfather.

Bobby's voice cut through his reverie. "Are you okay? You look like you're a million miles away right now."

His eyes snapping back into focus on Bobby's face, Cass replied, "Yeah, sorry. I was just thinking I should call my grandparents and say hi."

The concern faded from Bobby's eyes. He gave Cass an affectionate poke in the shoulder. "You know, your phone can do more than check your email and play amusing cat videos. It can remind you to drink water during the day and even call your family once a week."

Cass watched Bobby bustle around the small kitchen, cracking eggs, retrieving the omnipresent Mason jar of fresh salsa from the fridge. There was something almost poetic about Bobby's economy of motion and the ease with which he did something he'd done a million times before. Cass had always loved being in the zone like that: a dark bar, thumping bass, the coldness of a cocktail shaker in his hands, showing off for bigger tips by flipping bottles in the air, the perfect three-second pour while flirting shamelessly with a hottie. "I don't know how you do it," he said. "Spend all day at the bakery, busy in the kitchen, and then come home so you can be busy in the kitchen."

Bobby set the jar of salsa on the table. "Cass, the bakery is home too. I grew up there. I remember Javier reading to me when *he* could barely read. That's where I learned two languages, where I learned math by sitting down with my dad and helping balance the books, there was always family in and out…" He scooped out an avocado and added it to a bowl of onions, tomatoes, cilantro, and lime juice, mashing it for a quick guacamole. "It's not *going to work* for me. It's just a different version of home."

Cass drew a squiggle with his finger in the condensation on the outside of his water glass. "I guess that makes sense. I just don't think of *home* that way. Mostly, *home* is where I sleep." Louis Armstrong and the faint smell of tobacco felt like a lifetime ago.

Leaning over, Bobby wrapped his arms around Cass from behind. "This can be a proper home if you let it."

"I'm trying." He chuckled. "Hey, I've even got a picture of me and Dee and the Good Doctor from their wedding on the mantle."

"Dee put that there," Bobby reminded him.

"Still counts?" Cass smelled something vaguely acrid. "Is something burning?"

"Tortillas!" Bobby yelped as he leaped for the oven, yanking two very brown tortillas onto a plate. He slid one onto a separate plate, then topped the tortillas with beans and over easy eggs, careful not to break the runny yolks. "Enjoy!" he said as he set a plate in front of Cassidy.

Cass spooned salsa, guacamole, and sour cream on top. "I have to say, my German-Irish ass is looking for the potatoes here. It's like a missing food group."

"My Mexican ass is happy to let you cook," Bobby shot back.

"Kidding!" Cass took a bite. "Okay, this is pretty good." The egg yolk, finally broken, ran out over the beans, and he caught a hot-and-cold mouthful of egg, beans, and sour cream.

"See? You could have been eating this all the time, instead of cold pizza or toast for breakfast." Bobby shook a half-dozen drops of hot sauce onto his next few bites of dinner.

"I like cold pizza," Cass said, but he had to admit that a plate of something hot and filling did sound awfully good first thing in the morning. "But the next time you want to make something weird for breakfast, I promise I'll try it."

After they'd eaten, Cass took care of the dishes, loading up the dishwasher and wiping down the counter and stove. If nothing else, working in the bakery had made cleaning up after himself in the kitchen almost automatic, though he'd never truly been a slob. He linked his fingers and stretched his arms over his head, wincing as the tight muscles in his shoulders protested.

"Want me to take care of that?" Bobby asked.

"I absolutely do," Cass replied. He popped into the laundry room to pull off his shirt—a little blob of salsa had joined the splotch from the strawberry jam—and rubbed some stain remover into the fabric before tossing his shirt into the washer. Heading for the stairs, he saw Bobby smiling. "What's got you so happy?"

"If that's all it takes to get you to take your shirt off, I'll make you drippy foods more often." He licked his finger and swiped it on Cass's jeans. "Does this work too?"

"I don't think I need to take off my wet pants," Cass said with a shake of his head.

Bobby shrugged. "It was worth a try."

As Cass headed up the stairs to the bedroom, he could feel the soreness in his legs and feet. At the top of the stairs, he stepped out of his shoes and flung them in the general direction of the guest bathroom. "If I try to put those on again tomorrow, you have my permission to physically restrain me until I see reason."

"Noted."

Cass flopped onto the middle of the bed face-down. The sheets were cool against his bare skin. "This is good. I'm just gonna lay here for a while. You don't need to sleep tonight, right?" His voice was muffled by his pillow.

There was a faint noise as Bobby opened the nightstand drawer and pulled out a bottle of massage oil. When he uncapped it, the scent of eucalyptus and mint filled the room. The creaky bed frame protested Bobby clambering astride Cass, warming the oil in his hands. "This is probably going to be a little cold," he said, running his hands over Cassidy's back.

"Don't care," Cass mumbled. It was, in fact, a little cold, but it also felt pretty damn good.

Bobby started at Cass's lower back, just above his hip bones. He ran his thumbs up a few inches along Cass's spine, then back down. He put some pressure on his palms as he moved his hands to Cass's sides, then lifted his hands up so his fingertips trailed over Cass's skin as he returned to his starting position.

Cass had been so focused on the tightness in his shoulders that he hadn't even realized his lower back was achy too. Under Bobby's hands, the stiffness melted away. He grunted as Bobby leaned in more firmly, getting at the deeper muscles.

"You okay?" Bobby asked.

"Yeah. I'll let you know if it gets to be too much." He meant it, mostly. Suffering through popping a knot in a muscle felt a whole lot better than having to deal with the knot for the next few days until it went away on its own. Besides, if he protested too soon, Bobby would stop touching him; perish the thought.

Bobby slowly moved up Cass's back, along the spine and out over his ribcage, using barely any pressure where the muscles weren't tight. For Cass, it was almost meditative, the slip of skin against skin, and he found himself dozing off until Bobby got close to his shoulders where the first knot made its presence known. Cass's whole body twitched involuntarily.

"Do it," Cass said, forestalling Bobby's question.

He started gently at first, light pressure from his thumbs along the edge of Cassidy's shoulder blade, but even that was enough to let the small knots go *pop pop pop* like bubble wrap in Cass's left shoulder.

"Ouch," said Bobby. "Still okay?"

Cass nodded against his pillow. He didn't trust himself to speak. As Bobby continued, a few more knots let go, but Cass could feel the big ones lurking deeper. Bobby rolled his thumb over a large knot deep in Cass's right shoulder, just above a quarter-sized strawberry birthmark; Cass couldn't help but grunt at the sudden stab of pain.

"That's a good one. Want me to go after it?"

Mumbling in the affirmative, Cass braced himself for what was coming. Bobby slid his hands along Cass's shoulder. He was able to massage loose a smaller knot, but Cass knew the big one hadn't gone anywhere. Although he tried to relax, his body tensed automatically when Bobby's thumbs put pressure on the big knot.

"Just—just do it," Cass said.

"It's gonna hurt."

"Lean into it. Hard."

He did. It hurt. Cass breathed into it, his hands grabbing fistfuls of the sheets.

"Cass, I'm stopping."

"No, a little harder," Cass gasped. He had to focus on that little bright spot of pain in his shoulder; concentrating on the discomfort kept him in the moment. It was clear that Bobby wasn't happy, and when Cass couldn't take it any longer, he said, "Enough!"

Bobby immediately jerked his hands away. As the pressure released, so did the knot. Cass was almost disappointed that it didn't make a satisfying cracking noise as it loosened. With a conscious effort, Cass let go of the sheets and took a few deep breaths.

"Please tell me it's gone," Bobby said, his voice strained.

"Yeah." Cass moved his right arm as much as he could from his position flat on the bed. "That actually feels a million times better. It might be a little tender tomorrow, but at least I'll be able to move."

"Good." Bobby ran his hands over Cass's shoulder, gently, whispering over the aching muscles.

If Cass had been a cat, he would have been purring. "I hate to make you stop doing that, but I think there are a couple knots left in my other shoulder too."

"I'll give you a minute to catch your breath first." Bobby traced lazy circles on Cassidy's back.

"Your terms are acceptable." Cass almost fell asleep, just letting Bobby touch him.

The last two knots popped easily as Bobby rolled over them with his thumbs. He didn't stop, though, instead moving on to Cassidy's arms, massaging the tiredness out of his biceps and triceps. Much like his lower back, it hadn't occurred to Cass that they were aching, but somehow Bobby had known.

When Bobby reached Cass's left forearm, he took care around the long-healed surgical scar. Even though it was nearly as pale as Cass himself, the shine of the scarred skin betrayed it, and the titanium plate and screws it covered were easily felt with even a little pressure in the right place. For Cass, the sensation of metal rubbing against flesh from the inside was oddly electric, like biting into aluminum foil with a metal filling, only in his arm, and it almost had the same ozone smell as a true electric shock. As careless as he could sometimes be, he'd learned to protect that spot on his arm to avoid the unpleasantness that came with hard contact between muscle and metal.

Cass turned his head and glanced back at Bobby.

"I didn't get your arm, did I?" Bobby asked.

"No. I was just wondering if there's anything you're actually bad at, because I feel amazing right now."

Chuckling, Bobby replied, "Clearly, you've never seen me play sports. Javier and Carmen both played *fútbol*—soccer—and Javier was on the wrestling team too. My cousin Anamaria was even the head cheerleader. I sat on a lot of bleachers in high school."

"That's a relief. I'd hate to think you were perfect or something."

"Hey, dragging you out of bed first thing in the morning in violation of your innate sleep schedule and my 'banana-peel-in-the-trash-can' basketball skills aside, I'm hardly perfect. My brother knows how to instantly get under my skin, and I'm not exactly thrilled about that particular short fuse. I think I have a lot of *machismo* bullshit to unlearn." Bobby slid his hands over Cassidy's back one last time. "Let's be honest here, I'm an average guy, but your sense of what's normal is pretty out of whack. Giving someone you love a back rub because they busted their ass for you all day isn't exactly 'above-and-beyond'-level consideration. I'm not saying it's your fault, but you've set your 'decent human being' bar fairly low."

Before Bobby shifted his weight off Cass's butt, he leaned forward and kissed the little birthmark near his shoulder. Cass immediately felt his skin break out in gooseflesh. "You always do that when you see that stupid little thing," he said, shivering.

"That's because it always gives you goosebumps," Bobby teased.

Cass sat up and moved his shoulders, which felt tired, but no longer stiff and sore. "Thanks for that. I think I can function again."

"Anything for the hero of Pi Day in the bakery."

"I am definitely not a hero," Cass said, shaking his head.

"No way! You made a lot of really great pies today." Bobby reached up and twisted a strand of hair in the middle of Cassidy's forehead around his finger, letting it spring up into a Superman curl. "There. Now you even have the proper superhero hair."

"I feel like Pie Man is a cheesy '60s Batman villain who speaks entirely in pastry-related puns." Cass huffed the curl out of his face, but it bounced right back where it had been.

Bobby laughed. Cass stifled it with a kiss. He cupped Bobby's face in his hands, Bobby's two-day stubble prickling his palms. Hands skimmed along his ribcage, drawing him closer. Teasing the hem of Bobby's shirt up, Cass reveled in the warmth of his skin against his fingertips.

Leaning back so that Cass could pull his shirt off, Bobby asked, "Are you sure? It's been a long, busy day."

It definitely had been. "Yeah, but then you fed me a tasty meal and put your hands all over me." Cass ran his hand down Bobby's arm, interlacing their fingers. "I know I don't owe you anything, okay? But I'm totally down for getting down."

"I should have guessed," Bobby said. He traced the scar on Cassidy's forearm with his thumb. Grinning, he said, "Usually it takes more to get you half-naked."

He wasn't wrong. Cass wasn't overly fond of being vulnerable; even the protection of a threadbare flannel was better than none at all. "You know it's not you, right?"

Bobby kissed his forehead. "You're getting better, Cassidy." He tugged at a stray curl. "Give me a minute to go wash my hands?"

Like he'd say no. "I hate to see you leave, but, you know. Love to watch you go." Cass was appreciative of the extra wiggle Bobby gave to his ass as he walked to the bathroom. The way Bobby filled out a pair of broken-in Levis was a thing of beauty. He was one of the least self-conscious people Cass had ever met, and there was something deeply sexy about the fact that Bobby wasn't constantly checking his hair in the mirror or asking about the definition of his six-pack—if he'd had one in the first place. Cass hadn't realized how much his ex's obsession with appearances had affected him until the relationship was in his rearview mirror; while he'd always been hyper aware of his thinness and the scar on his arm, he hadn't always felt guilty about them.

He was getting better, though. He ditched his jeans and his boxer briefs and yanked off his socks. When he lobbed his socks and underwear at the laundry basket, he managed to make two of three.

"Not bad," said Bobby from the bathroom doorway, toweling his hands dry.

"My aim or the view?"

"Yes."

Cass gestured to his burgeoning erection. "Solid D on both counts?"

"Does that count as a pun? Either way it was pretty bad."

"I always considered it one of my better features."

"Your dick or your dad jokes?"

"Yes." Cass stuck his tongue out. "Get over here, will ya?"

"I see you've made me an offer I can't refuse." Bobby yanked his jeans and underwear off together and left them in a pile on the floor. He tossed the towel onto the bed.

Cass slid over to make room. "You got me. I'm the Godfather. Except for the parts involving money and power."

"What else does that leave?"

"I like a good cannoli?"

"I can't tell if that's another dick reference." Bobby tucked Cass's hair behind his ear and messily kissed up the side of his neck, nipping gently at his earlobe. When he let Cass's ear slip from his mouth, he blew softly on the trail he'd left up Cass's neck, the saliva cooling as it dried.

The frisson went directly from Cassidy's neck to his cock. "Fuck me, Bobby."

"If that's what you want."

"Pretty much always."

As Bobby dug around in his nightstand drawer for condoms and lube, Cass reached out and touched him, running his hands over everything he could reach. Bobby leaned back into him, and Cass obliged, sliding a hand down Bobby's chest, peppered with rough curls of chest hair, until he was able to trace the line of Bobby's cock with a finger. He felt Bobby stiffen against him. "I think you might wanna fuck me too." With his thumb, he smeared precum over the tip of Bobby's erection, chuckling at Bobby's gasp.

Bobby turned around and nudged Cass over onto his back. A few seconds later, he propped himself up on one arm, kissing Cassidy while slipping a lubed finger into his ass. Cass held Bobby close; he couldn't get enough of touching him. Bobby added another finger, and Cass finally started to feel the stretch. Bobby's breathing grew ragged as Cass gently massaged his balls, ever so softly rolling them in his palm. A third finger slid in as Bobby worked the lube up and around, carefully stretching the sensitive flesh.

Cass couldn't take the wanting any longer. "Come on," he said.

It seemed Bobby was more than ready too. "It might be easier on your poor shoulders if you lean up against the headboard."

As Cass assumed the position, he heard the foil crinkle of a condom packet. When he felt Bobby's cock against him, he leaned in, feeling the stretch and friction that he so desperately craved.

"You okay?" Bobby asked.

"Goddamn, you feel amazing," Cass replied. His hips inadvertently twitched forward then back, moving himself along Bobby's erection.

Bobby's hands clenched on Cass's narrow hips. "I think you might be a little worked up." He settled into thrusting at the rhythm Cass had set, the slapping of his pelvis against Cass's cheeks keeping time.

"Just a little." Cass arched his back slightly, changing the angle of Bobby's motion, creating more of that delicious friction.

Bobby reached around, his hand still slick with lube, and gave Cass's cock a firm tug. It was a shock. Cass's chest felt tight, and the tunnel-vision started to flood in. "Wait," he gasped with the rest of his air.

Freezing in place, Bobby said, "Are you okay?"

The reduction in stimuli gave Cass a chance to breathe. "I need a minute."

Bobby wrapped his arms around Cass's chest, leaned his cheek against Cass's back. "Do you need me off?"

"No. No! I didn't expect that." Now that he could breathe, he could pull himself together. "I'm okay."

"Who am I, Cass?"

"You're Bobby." The comforting weight on him, the scratch of stubble on his back. "Sorry. Sometimes I forget I'm with someone who gives a shit about me now. As you were."

"Crisis averted?" At Cass's nod, Bobby kissed the side of his neck and sat back up. "Do you need me to not do both?"

"I'll be okay now. I was kind of focused on how good you felt, and you surprised me with that." He sighed. "Just more fuckin' baggage."

Bobby thrust deeply, once, twice, and Cass fell into the rhythm. "Better?" Bobby asked.

Cass didn't try to think too hard about why sex seemed to fix the problems caused by sex. "Better." This time, he was ready when Bobby reached around and took hold. As Bobby thrust forward, he slid his hand up Cass's erection, running his thumb across the tip with each stroke. He changed his timing when Cassidy's hips rocked into the motion of his hand so that Cass was moving back as Bobby was moving forward, creating a deep penetration that finished with the slip of Bobby's thumb across his head.

With his free hand, Bobby caught up the towel he'd tossed onto the bed and tucked it under Cass's cock. Cass hadn't realized how close he was to orgasm, but he was nearly there. So was Bobby, who thrust a few more times, hard and fast with his gasping moans. His hand clamped down tighter—not painful, but firm—and Cass had just enough brainpower left to yank the towel up to come in, the amazing full-body tingle that left him breathless in the good way.

Bobby leaned forward and kissed the birthmark on Cass's shoulder.

Even though he was sweaty, he felt the goosebumps ripple across his skin. "Dammit," he said affectionately, shaking his head.

Bobby laughed. He slipped out of Cass's ass with a grunt and used a clean corner of the towel to wipe Cass clean. Cass sank onto the bed and flopped over as Bobby tied off the condom and dropped it into the wastebasket.

Pulling Bobby in for another long kiss, Cass said, "You know I love you, right?"

"I love you too, Cass. Baggage and all."

Cass checked the time. "Damn. It's still too early to go to bed after we shower even for us. We're gonna have to find a way to kill some time, and we've already done the sex thing."

"I can teach you to make cupcakes, if you want. Do a couple of little batches from scratch in the kitchen."

Cass lobbed the dirty towel at the laundry basket and made it. "Yeah? You promise they're easy?" As soon as the words were out, he cursed himself for setting it up.

Bobby twisted a strand of Cass's hair into that superhero curl in the middle of his forehead. "Easy as pie," he replied.

About the Author

Leslie Bond lives in North Carolina with one husband, two house panthers, and way too many books. And yes, that really is the secret to the best peach pie you'll ever have!

Facebook: www.facebook.com/LeslieBWrites
Tumblr: lesliebwrites.tumblr.com

Lip-Locked Besties
♥
Livvy Ward

Story Information

Holiday: Lips Appreciation Day
Holiday Date: March 16
Heat Rating: 4
Relationship Type: M/F
Major Trigger Warnings: Mentions of depression, mentions of mild BDSM, mentions of infidelity, minor slut-shaming, minor misogyny.

Ally always was a fun-loving, confident woman… right up until the supposed love of her life broke her heart. Chris is charming, handsome, and sometimes an over-confident flirt with a history of not seeing what's right in front of him. When fate turns these besties into roomies, can they see what's right in front of them? Will they finally find the piece they didn't know was missing? Maybe with the help of an odd holiday, they'll find out!

Lip-Locked Besties

Ally Jones was many things, but a procrastinator wasn't one of them. In college, she'd always been the first among her group of friends to get essays and tasks done. Yet, lately it seemed there was one aspect of her life in which she was sorely lacking, and she couldn't for the life of her figure out why.

It had been said, when you fall off a horse, you get right back in the saddle. So why was she not getting back in the saddle? Back in the dating scene? It wasn't as though she was short of chances or had a lack of options for a wingman/woman.

Her friends went out every night after work, especially her best friend/roommate, Chris Walker. It was something they'd done since they had all met in college, but somewhere down the line Ally had begun withdrawing from their nights out. When she thought about it, it was around the same time she'd started dating her ex, Nate.

Ally shook herself out of the memory, tearing her gaze from the Netflix search bar. She grabbed her smartphone off the coffee table. Her eyes dropped to the lock screen—there were no missed calls, messages or emails.

5:55 p.m., Saturday, March 16th.

Staring at the time and day on the screen, Ally sighed dejectedly as her brain inwardly screamed at her. *Where the hell is he? I haven't seen him all day. Did he even come home last night? Did he forget what day it is? Is he okay?*

It wasn't like Chris to miss their weekly Netflix session, at least not without good reason. When he'd asked her to move in after her nightmare of a breakup, they'd established a rule that Saturday was their Zen Day. A day to relax after the long work week. No one else allowed, phones stayed on silent, the doorbell was ignored unless they'd ordered takeout. Just them and the series they planned to binge.

Unlocking her phone with deft fingers, Ally opened her messages and pulled up Chris's conversation. She tapped idly on the back of her phone, her creamy skin and pale pink polish a stark contrast to the black case as she considered what to type. Before she could stop herself, her fingers flew automatically over the keys and hit send.
You'd better be dead… or dying mister and not chained to some woman's bed! >.< You know what day it is right?

Ally shoved her phone in her pocket and pushed herself off the couch as she looked over the floor and the coffee table. As much as she wanted to leave behind a mess to show Chris she'd carried on without him, at the same time she knew she'd have to clean it up anyway.

She switched off the PS4 and TV. From there she picked up the trash bag on the coffee table and set about collecting the empty lollipop wrappers, chip packets, and soda cans. She winced at the sheer number. Her diet had definitely gone out the window today, and she made a mental note to spend extra time in the gym this week. Pushing her shoulder-length, ebony hair back out of her face Ally straightened, her warm brown eyes doing another sweep of the room for any trash she'd missed.

As she stowed the full bag in the utility closet beside the fridge for later disposal, Ally felt her phone vibrate against her leg. Pulling the phone from her pocket, she set it on the counter, turned to the fridge, and pulled the door open.

Her hand drifted past the soda cans, juice bottles, and water before, eventually, she snagged one of Chris's beers. Just as she was nudging the door closed with her hip, there was a buzzing sound. Ally twisted the cap off the beer bottle as her phone vibrated against the counter. She took a quick gulp of the cold alcohol before pressing the power button.

When her lock screen illuminated, showing two new messages from Chris, she lifted the bottle back to her lips and took a drink. Liquid courage, her dad used to call it, and she definitely felt like she needed it right now. Ally set the beer on the counter and reached for her phone to open the messages.

^o^? How did you know Harmony tied me up? Although technically it was handcuffs.

Ally's phone slipped from shaking hands, clattering against the granite countertop. That definitely fell into her TMI file. Trying to get her fingers to work, Ally's hand slipped over the granite. She grappled for her phone, finally getting a solid grip on the offending device. She returned her gaze to the screen to read his second message.

The day? I know what day it is. Why it is Lips Appreciation Day, see here look!

Clicking the link in Chris's message sent her to a page on the website daysoftheyear.com. Quickly reading the page, she rolled her eyes toward the ceiling with a huff. She closed the web browser and returned to the messages, propping a hip against the counter as she tried to work out her response. It was obvious she needed to start with his overshare. There were just some details she didn't want to know about his sex life, after all, especially when hers had been the equivalent of the Sahara over the past five months.

First, Christopher, TMI! I don't need to know about your kinky sex games with your latest booty call. Second, while your humor is oddly accurate with the date that didn't answer the question. Which FYI, it's Saturday. -_- If I'd known you had other plans today I'd have gone shopping with Jess and Mel.

She watched the dots in the message's corner switch between flashing and vanishing, a clear sign that Chris was typing and then stopping to reread or rethink whatever he was preparing to send. Her fingers tapped rapidly against her screen before hitting send again. *You bailed on Zen Day for a booty call? You are in sooo much trouble, mister. ~.~ *

As she set her phone down, waiting for Chris to gather his thoughts into words, Ally reached for the beer bottle. She took a long swig before scowling against the neck of the bottle. Why exactly was she so worked up over one missed hang out day? And why exactly did her stomach wrench and her temper flare when she thought about him with the latest in a long line of conquests?

She didn't think her friendship with Chris had changed at all in the months since her breakup, yet as she reconsidered now, she noticed more and more things had been getting on her nerves. Namely, the revolving door of girlfriends. While she'd known of Chris's proclivities prior to moving in, having to face the aftermath wasn't something that she'd been ready for honestly.

Holy shit, I'm jealous! The thought struck Ally like a bolt of lightning. It wasn't her friendship with Chris that'd been changing, but her feelings toward him. But what exactly was she feeling toward Chris? That question wasn't as easy to answer as it really should have been, she soon realized.

Their friendship was still as strong as ever, but now when she thought about it, she couldn't help realizing she felt the need for more. Was it a result of her extended dry spell? Did she need to take a page out of Chris's playbook to just go out and get laid?

No, it can't just be because I'm horny. Ally considered the idea more closely before realizing that even when she'd been with Nate intimately, it had still felt like that special spark of passion was missing. Sex had felt more like a chore or a duty than something she craved. It probably hadn't helped matters with Nate being her first and only lover. One who was always more focused on getting himself off than in her pleasure.

Her phone buzzing and rattling against the counter pulled Ally out of her head and away from thoughts potentially dangerous to one of her closest friendships. Opening the message, she released the breath she hadn't realized she was holding as her eyes flicked down to her screen.

OMWH, detouring for food. ETA twenty minutes.

Ally arched one brow as she shook her head with a chuckle. A traditional Chris Walker apology. She knew he'd arrive home with way too much Chinese, Thai, or Italian food, depending on what he was craving. An impish smile curved her lips as she teased him, and her fingers moved quickly on the screen her grin getting bigger as she typed. *Who says I will be home? Might get all dressed up & hit the town 2nite with the girls.*

NO! You sit that little ass of yours down and stay put.

The rapid response surprised her. Chris and rapid never seemed to go hand in hand, and this wasn't just rapid but also seemed more authoritarian, as though he was adamant she not go anywhere.

"Weird," Ally mumbled to herself. She left the half-drunk beer on the counter as she left the kitchen heading to her room. Her phone was almost dead, so she plugged it in to charge. Peeling off her shirt and sweatpants, she tossed them into her hamper before rifling through her drawers to find something comfy.

If Chris would order her to stay in, then he could put up with her eating takeout while lounging around in her favorite shorts and the hockey jersey she'd 'borrowed' from her sister.

"Allyson Sarah Jones, you'd better still be here!"

Startled by the sudden echo of Chris's voice in the silent apartment, Ally quickly pulled on the shorts and her sister's jersey. She was just about to leave her room when Chris's larger frame filled the doorway. With a yelp, she leaped backward, only to lose her footing as one bare foot landed on a sock on the floor.

Her butt hit the hardwood floor with a thud as her eyes swung up and over the six foot two, broad shouldered masculine figure that eclipsed her doorway. Startlement gave way to embarrassment as she quickly tried to get back up on her feet—not that she had much success in doing so as Chris's rumble of amused laughter made her more flustered. "Damn it, Chris, you can't just come barging into my room. What if I'd just gotten out of the shower and was getting dressed?" Ally swatted at the large hand that appeared in front of her face as she scowled up at her too-handsome best friend's face.

"Then it would have been a hell of a view?"

"Wrong answer," she grumbled in a mixture of irritation and embarrassment.

"Sorry," he mumbled repentantly as a concerned expression appeared, his brown eyes roving over her sprawled form as though looking for visible injuries. Crouching down Chris hooked one arm around her waist and hauled her up over his shoulder, the move so unexpected Ally hadn't even been able to stop the squeak that slipped free.

"You ass," Ally huffed as she swatted at Chris's lower back with the hand not pinned between their bodies.

From her prone position over his shoulder Ally stared down at his denim-clad ass and the floor. While ordinarily she wouldn't ogle her best friend, at the current point in time she had nowhere else to look. If she lifted her head or struggled to get down, she had a suspicion it'd end up with her getting a firm spanking.

No, bad Ally. We should not be getting ideas about that, she inwardly chastised herself while listening to the heavy thuds of Chris's boots on the hardwood floors; he was likely either heading toward the kitchen or the lounge, she guessed. She broke the silence by asking what had just popped into her mind. "What happened to twenty minutes?"

"Chang's was busy, so I didn't bother putting in an order, came home instead. I got the impression we needed to have a discussion, and if need be, we can try ordering in later."

Ally felt the shoulder she was slung over shrug upward, and suddenly she lay flat on her back on the couch, blinking dazedly up at Chris who leaned over the back of said couch with a smirk.

"Ass," she muttered while considering the benefits versus the risks of attempting to roll off the couch.

Instead, she pushed herself up into a seated position, pulling her knees up to her chest beneath the large hockey jersey just as Chris launched himself over the back of the couch and landed with a bounce on the empty cushion.

"So, I'm sorry? It totally slipped my mind it was Saturday," Chris blurted out to which Ally just blinked.

That seemed like a half-assed apology and excuse. Wrapping her arms around her concealed legs she snorted, "Funny, Saturday has always come after Friday. Maybe you were just too busy appreciating Harmony's lips?"

Shit. Ally cursed inwardly as she realized how she had just sounded. If she was lucky maybe Chris would have missed it or mistaken it for sarcasm. Her head dropped forward to rest on her arms. She would not look at him. Nope, no way was she going to look for any sign of a reaction.

"Now if I didn't know better, I'd think someone was jealous?"

The low murmur of Chris's voice was far too close for her liking. In fact, she could still feel his breath against her ear. Which could only mean he'd shifted his position on the couch and was leaning over with his head either above or to the side of her own. Both were rather intimately within her personal space.

Knowing Chris as she did, Ally had an inkling of what was coming. She had, after all, opened the door to that barn, and it was far too late to shut it as the horses were galloping toward the exit.

"But, you are partly right. Harmony's lips distracted me, and what she was doing with them. She has this wonderful little talent of pursing her lips just the right way. It feels…"

"Stop! Not another word." Ally's head jerked upward, only to have the back of her head collide with something solid. If Chris's sudden grunt was anything to go by, it was his forehead or jaw. Lifting one hand to her head, she grunted, "Ow, why are you so hard-headed?"

"Me? I could ask you the same thing, it was your head hitting mine," Chris shot back instantly with a chuckle.

"Look, I really don't want to know what you got up to with your latest fake floozy, okay?" She wasn't proud of her name calling and slut-shaming, but she couldn't seem to stop herself. Argh! Why did she have to develop feelings for her best friend?

Without lifting her eyes, Ally forced herself off the couch and padded toward the kitchen. Grabbing two dish towels off the rack, she laid them out on the counter. She crossed to the fridge on autopilot and pulled open the freezer door, grabbed the ice container, elbowed the door shut, and moved back to the counter.

Placing some ice onto each of the towels, Ally returned the container to the fridge as she tried her best to ignore the soft thud of boots getting closer. She twisted both towels closed into makeshift ice packs. Turning, she lifted one to the back of her head as she leaned back against the counter, holding the other out to one side and waiting.

It wasn't long until she felt the brush of his fingers against her own as Chris took the ice pack from her. With her eyes still shut, Ally felt the familiar nudge of their elbows bumping as he mimicked her stance at the counter.

"What's going on, Ally? You seem a little… off today?"

"Nothing, I've just been reminiscing."

"Uh huh. You've been thinking about Nate."

What is that tone? Ally wondered, her head turned toward Chris as she opened her eyes to look at him. She was sure there was a hint of disgust in his tone along with something else she couldn't quite identify.

"Well, yes, and no. I was thinking about lots of things; that asshole was one." Her admission came out a lot quieter than she'd intended, her cheeks heating slightly with embarrassment. She sighed, bare feet shuffling against the sleek and shiny hardwood floor before attempting to redirect their conversation. "Thought about college mostly and our friendship."

Chris turned his head toward her then, his mouth opening as though preparing to speak which had Ally shaking her head as she lifted her free hand. She placed it over his mouth as her brain whirled a million miles a minute to plan her next words.

"Wait, let me finish okay? Remembering our college days, I wondered about something. I mean you flirted with virtually every girl you met back then, even our friends, and yet it just occurred to me never once did you flirt with me like that. I was just automatically slapped into the friendzone. Why? Was I not enough? Not good enough for anything more than a study buddy and friend?"

Strong, warm fingers curled around Ally's wrist and gently tugged her hand down from over his mouth. Her eyes locked with Chris's briefly before he averted them to stare over her head as he rasped, "You were with him."

His voice was little more than a guttural growl, even as his thumb stroked lazily against the back of her hand. Dropping her gaze to his boots, she scowled at his answer. If it could really be called an answer.

Ally lowered the ice pack from the back of her head, her fingers clenching tightly around it before she threw it across the kitchen at the sink and growled back, "No, I wasn't. Not at first. We both know Nate didn't come into the picture until six months after we met, Chris. So you don't get to use that ungrateful ass as an answer. After we met on orientation day and started to get to know each other... I really liked you." Ally felt as though she were on a roller coaster, her emotions going up, down, and all around. Her voice had started off angry but then had detoured rather unexpectedly to regretful as her heart wrenched in recollection.

"I really liked you too, Ally. It's why we became such great friends and why our friendship has still lasted."

Even years later, Chris was still occasionally dense. Unless she walked right up and slapped him in the face with what she was feeling, he would be utterly clueless. She sighed with bone-deep exhaustion and shook her head. "No, Chris, you're not getting it. I really liked you, in that I spent those first six months of our friendship hoping and wishing you'd notice me like you noticed every other girl on campus. So when Nate showed interest... I guess I played it safe and figured I should take what I could get."

His fingers started to twitch against her wrist before tightening firmly, and Ally chanced a glance up from his boots to Chris's face. He was still staring off into space over her head, his jaw clenched so tightly she wondered why she couldn't hear his teeth grinding.

Shit, now I've done it. Wincing at her own thoughts, Ally frantically tried to figure out how to get her foot out of her mouth before she ran her best friend off. Her brain backpedaled over the conversation, trying desperately to come up with a save and failing spectacularly as she mumbled, "I cherish our friendship. I don't know where I'd be if you weren't in my life, but a small part of me has always hoped, I guess, that you might see me differently someday."

Chris let go of her wrist, as though it were an open flame that had just burned him. Ally did her best not to react to his action even though it felt as though someone had stabbed her with a thousand tiny knives. Taking it to be a sign they were done talking for now, Ally exhaled, her head drooping slightly to stare at the floor as she moved past Chris to head out of the kitchen.

"Ally..."

It was the tone of Chris's voice which stopped her dead in her tracks; it was not a tone she'd heard from him before. He sounded pained. Maybe nearly as pained as she felt? Ally started to turn back to him, her voice quiet and cautious. "Yeah…"

"Ally, I… I didn't—" His words cutting off prompted Ally to lift her head enough to peer through her bangs. Chris moved slowly toward her and she found herself moving toward him. Like they were two minute particles that had been circling each other for eons and had both finally been dragged into each other's gravitational pull, his large hands settling on her cheeks to tilt her head up slightly as his own lowered. He paused for a moment, a question in his eyes, and when she nodded he leaned forward again. Ally sucked in a sharp breath mere moments before Chris slanted his mouth over hers. Her brain shorted out at the contact, one sole thought zinging around her head: *Chris is kissing me.*

Lack of participation on her part had a growl rumbling in Chris's chest. His teeth tugged at her lower lip before he pulled away and leaned against the counter. Ally licked at her lower lip in puzzlement as Chris lifted his hands to rake through his hair in frustration and grunted to himself. "You idiot."

Ally pushed herself off the fridge. Her mind made up, she closed the distance between them and stepped up onto Chris's booted feet. One of her hands gripped at his leather jacket as the other slipped up around the back of his neck and tugged gently.

Chris had a deer in the headlights look on his face. Despite his surprise, his head lowered at her non-verbal command. Ally pressed a feather-light kiss against the curve of his jaw, her lips making their way down to his chin before jumping up to nip sharply at his lower lip in retaliation.

When Chris hissed, Ally felt her lips curl into a satisfied grin. She felt like the cat who got the cream. She sucked gently at his lower lip, pulling it between her own lips to brush her tongue over the abused flesh. Easing herself back from the kiss, Ally let her forehead rest against Chris's, her fingers slipping up from his neck into his hair as she murmured. "Well, that was… different."

"Good different or bad different?"

While his tone and grin were teasing, Ally couldn't help but notice his eyes didn't light up the way they normally did when he teased her. Was he uncertain of her answer? Even after what she'd said and when she'd just kissed him back?

Her fingers stroked idly through the back of Chris's hair for a moment before giving a gentle tug. She pressed a chaste kiss to his lips before responding, in an almost purr, "Fantastic. You caught me off guard with the first kiss."

"That was the point, I wanted to see your reaction. So when you didn't kiss me back I figured... I may have overstepped?"

"Well, you got a reaction, just not a clear one, apparently. My brain kinda shorted out, I'd been wanting you for so long," she admitted sheepishly. Ally shifted slightly, rubbing against Chris. "I still want you."

Firm hands roamed down her back, over the curve of her ass, and pulled her in tighter. "I want you too." His hands dipped lower, grabbing hold just before the top of her thighs. Chris lifted her off the ground, dragging her up along his body.

Ally readjusted her grip and gasped against his lips, her hand letting go of his jacket to slip beneath it and glide around his side to rest on his back. Her knees tightened against his hips. "God," she breathed.

"So what you're telling me is I kissed you senseless?" Chris's amusement was written across his face; his eyes glinted with a mixture of mirth and hunger as his mouth curved into a rakish grin. His hands flexed, giving her ass a squeeze as he laughed joyously.

"Hmm, I guess you could phrase it like that."

"Technically, Ally, you phrased it like that, I was just clarifying I understood you correctly."

Needing to shut him up before his ego grew too large, Ally rolled her hips, grinding herself against Chris's groin. As he groaned at the move, she reclaimed his lips in a heated kiss, her tongue sweeping along his lower lip before delving exploratively into his mouth.

She had to admit to herself that kissing Chris was an entirely different experience than kissing her ex had ever been. It was easy to just lose herself in the pure sensation, the bliss that jolted through her.

Before she realized what was happening, Ally found her back pressed down against the granite counter. Instinctively, her legs wrapped around his waist. His hands wandered up from her ass beneath her jersey to settle on her sides.

It was Chris who pulled back from the kiss first, his head moving to one side so he could nuzzle against her neck. She was just as breathless as he was, but she relished the delicious sensation of his weight as it settled her against the counter.

"You know, I can't say I approve of you wearing another man's shirt, Ally."

Chris's growled words vibrated against her neck. Ally didn't miss the underlying tone of possessiveness in his voice. With a quiet chuckle, she stretched languidly beneath him, her head turning until her lips brushed his ear so she could purr teasingly, "My, my. Are you jealous? Of Sam, of all people?"

"Sam? This is your sister's jersey? How was I supposed to know that?"

With a hum of acknowledgment, Ally nibbled and sucked at Chris's earlobe, a thrill spreading through her as he shuddered in response. She traced the outer shell of his ear with her tongue, her path precise and speed just slow enough to tease before she pressed a kiss to his cheek.

"Maybe because I've only dated one guy in my life, and I don't recall him being a hockey player or fan."

She felt Chris shift his hands from her sides to brace against the counter moments before the pressure of his upper body lifted from hers.

"Ally, are you telling me when we met you were a… and when you and the asshole dated, he was your…"

Blinking at the unfinished sentences and the flashes of surprise and rage on his face, Ally nibbled on her lower lip in thought for a minute. Her hand in his hair slid down to curve around the nape of his neck again. She assumed her cheeks were beet red by how hot they felt as she whispered, "Virgin? Yes. And he was my first? Unfortunately."

"Unfortunately? Please tell me he at least took his time and made it pleasurable for you?"

Her eyes flicked away from Chris's face to stare beyond his ear at the ceiling. Her teeth once again found her lower lip and worried it as she contemplated her answer. She huffed, "Not exactly."

If she'd thought it was embarrassing discussing sex with Jess and Mel back in college as a virgin, it was by far even more embarrassing now discussing it with her best friend and potential lover.

"Hell, maybe it was why he cheated in the first place?" Ally mumbled uncertainly.

A low, fierce growl rumbled through Chris's chest as his face came back into her line of sight, his forehead resting against hers as he all but snarled. "No, Ally. That's his fault, not yours. He slept around just like he used you like his personal toy. I'm thinking I need to call your sister, Mom, and your two favorite aunts to come and help me teach his ass a lesson in manners and how to treat a lady."

"Don't forget to include Jess and Mel in this 'lesson' or they'll never forgive you." Chris had always been as protective of her as her own sister was, but there was something different about his current protective streak. What that something was Ally wasn't certain, but it was rather hot and had an unexpected jolt of arousal coursing through her.

With a subtle arch of her back, Ally rolled her hips against Chris's. Releasing her hold on his side and neck, she dropped her hands to the counter and pushed herself up enough that her lips brushed his ear as she spoke, "How about you call them to plot your ass-kicking later. Right now you need to go shower. Then, maybe, you can show me how things should have gone?"

He buried his face against her neck with a groan, his hands shifting from the counter as one arm slid around her waist while the other slipped beneath one of her arms. With his hand splayed between her shoulder blades, Ally felt her backside leave the counter as Chris pulled her tightly against him. "And why, pray tell, do I have to shower?"

Wrapping her arms around his neck, Ally giggled at the tickling sensation of his lips moving against her throat as he spoke. Leaning her upper body back slightly to meet his eyes, she arched one eyebrow her tone sarcastic as she retorted, "Well, who knows where Harmony has been or who she's been with."

Pausing for a moment of thought, Ally mentally slapped and chastised herself for that comment. She sent a silent apology to Harmony for judging her and mumbled, "I'm sorry, neither you nor Harmony deserved that comment."

"Well, apology accepted, but I have something I need to confess. You remember my friend from work, John? Well, Harmony is his sister, and he asked me to give him a hand moving her into his apartment today. Nothing happened. I was just teasing you."

Ally blinked slowly, whether because of the confession or the sheepish expression on Chris's face she wasn't sure. She moved one hand to swat lightly at the back of his head as she feigned a scowl. "You know, just for that I'm inclined to make you go have a cold shower and wait."

Wedged between the fridge door and Chris's muscular body, Ally watched as his lips curved into a smirk, his face moving closer to hers as he hummed, "No, I don't think you would."

Chris punctuated each word with a subtle rock of his hips, the growing bulge in the front of his jeans pressing firmly against her and causing a low whimper to slip free of her throat. Leaving one arm around Chris's shoulders, her fingers clutching tightly against the soft leather of his jacket, her other shifted allowing her fingers to tangle into his hair as she murmured, "No, but there are a few things I'd like to try out."

"Oh, are we a curious kitten? You remember what they say about curiosity and the cat."

"This coming from the man voted as the biggest player on campus during college? But yes, I'll own up to being curious, not so much a kitten. There's only so much you can learn from magazine articles."

"A title which I am still trying and failing to live down. But don't you worry, honey, you're in the hands of a master and I'll teach you anything you want to know. Plus, it's Lips Appreciation Day, surely we can come up with something to make us both appreciate the other's lips more."

Ally physically cringed at the nickname, her grip on Chris tightening as she buried her face against his neck and muttered, "The asshole used to call me that. Call me anything else, please?"

"Kitten it is, then, at least in private."

She felt Chris's arms tighten as the fridge door disappeared from behind her back, the thud of his boots on the hardwood floor the only sign she had that they were moving. Her body felt as though it was floating adrift, so to ground herself, Ally started to press feather-light kisses against his neck.

The slight shudder she felt roll through Chris made Ally feel intoxicated. The knowledge she could provoke such a reaction from him with mere kisses was a heady experience. Her fingers disentangled from his hair and dropped to the collar of his leather jacket, slipping just between the leather and his skin guiding it away to expose more of his neck to her questing lips.

Kissing along his neck, Ally worked her way around toward his throat. She dropped lower, her teeth nipping firmly at the skin of his exposed collarbone. Chris jerked with a hiss at the unexpected bite. She released the abused skin from between her teeth and laved at it gently with her tongue.

Chris groaned at the sensation which only prompted Ally to suck the tender skin between her lips as her tongue continued its languid strokes. There was a sudden jolt and swooping sensation as Ally felt the world tilt. Pain flared red hot in her elbow as it collided with something hard.

Chris grunted, and she assumed they'd both just hit the hallway wall. Her mouth lifted from his skin with a pained laugh as she yelped, "Oh my God, Chris! Put me down before you kill us both."

"Well, if someone hadn't been distracting me with their wicked mouth, I wouldn't have lost my balance."

"Well, maybe if I was walking, I wouldn't be distracting you with my wicked mouth." Ally tossed back with a wry grin.

"No, you'd be distracting me in other ways, kitten."

"You know that I can still distract you in other ways from my current position too, right?" To prove her point, Ally rocked her hips forward and added a slight twist, her lips curving upward into a grin as he muttered softly.

Her toes touched the hardwood first. Chris purposely made her descent along his body torturous, the slow drag of her body over his sending sparks of heat flying through her nerves. Once her feet rested flat on the floor, Ally stared up into Chris's eyes. He rested his forehead against hers. The usual whiskey brown color of his eyes had darkened substantially with his arousal.

"And here I thought you wouldn't put me down." Making sure her tone was light and teasing, Ally slipped one hand beneath his leather jacket to tickle at Chris's side with a grin. Chris chuckled and reached to still her tickling hand. Ally had other plans, however, and sprung backward out of his reach.

"Ally, you're making me regret putting you down," Chris growled warningly as he took a step forward.

Ally matched his pace with a step back for every one Chris moved forward. Something in the warning made her stomach flutter. She knew it wasn't a threat, more Chris trying to assert his dominance. With her next step backward, an idea struck. Sliding her hands up her thighs, Ally raised the hem of the hockey jersey enough to grab the elastic waistband of her gym shorts.

With a gentle sway of her hips, Ally turned her back to Chris, her head turning enough to watch him over her shoulder as she performed a little dance to music within her own head. The sway of her hips slowly changed, her body now undulating to an unknown tune as she inched the slinky material down over her hips.

Once the garment passed over the curve of her ass and moved along toward her knee, Ally dropped herself down into a squat to guide the shorts the rest of the way to the floor. Her lips curved into a shy smile as Chris growled while drifting toward her much like a tiger stalking its prey.

The moment his knees pressed lightly against her, Ally leaned back, her head coming to rest against his groin as she tilted her chin up slightly to peer up at him. His large, strong hands brushed over her hair before heading down along her neck as far as he could reach.

She reached back to wrap her left arm around Chris's leg, her other lifting so she could catch hold of his right wrist to guide his fingers over her throat. The move had his thumb coming to rest against her lips; nibbling lightly at the pad first Ally eventually pulled his thumb between her lips to the first knuckle.

Hollowing her cheeks, she sucked firmly before her tongue started to stroke and swirl around his thumb, her teasing ministration drawing a guttural groan from Chris's throat. She felt the light tug of the fingers of his free hand twining their way into her hair; she released his thumb from her mouth with a wet pop as she pushed herself teasingly slowly back up to her full height her body rubbing intimately against his.

"You're killing me here, kitten."

As his breath brushed against her ear, Ally shivered, her entire body vibrating against Chris's before she pulled together the strength to twist around and face him. His hand had at some point disentangled itself from her hair and both were now fisting the fabric of the jersey at her sides.

"Kinda the point," Ally murmured slightly breathless. Her gaze raked over Chris from head to toe before returning to meet his eyes as she added, "Hot stuff."

One slight tug was all it took for Ally to find herself firmly against Chris. It was near to impossible for her to ignore his burgeoning arousal as it pressed against her stomach. She heard a low keen echo in the hallway's silence; it took a good minute, maybe two, for her addled brain to realize that the sound had slipped from her own lips.

Dragging her fingers up along Chris's thighs, Ally worked her hands between them to grab hold of his belt then started to move backward along the hall, pulling him along with her. She didn't need to look to see where she was going. She could walk the apartment in the dead of night with no lights on.

As she crossed the threshold into her room, pulling him in after, she heard his booted foot connect with the door before it banged shut. Ally took this opportunity to let go of his belt, hands moving up over the shirt covering his abs. She kept moving higher, her hands sliding beneath the soft leather of his jacket and up to push it off his broad shoulders.

Before it could slip entirely from his arms, Ally stepped forward, backing Chris into the door as her mouth settled over the faint mark she'd left on his skin earlier, where she alternated between smattering the abused skin with feather light kisses and teasing caresses of her tongue.

Chris didn't release his hold on her jersey. Ally used this to her advantage; she pushed his jacket down to his elbows, temporarily restraining him. Her hands roamed back up over his biceps toward his shoulders before sliding down his chest and coming together to meet at the strip of buttons down the center of his shirt.

Her deft fingers made their way along his shirt, unfastening each button they came across until she hit the waistband of his jeans. Ally gripped the edges of his shirt and parted the cloth, her mouth lifting from the mark she'd left on his collarbone as her eyes swept down over his chest.

An appreciative hum rolled from her throat as Ally started to kiss her way down along Chris's chest, lowering herself as she went. She soon found herself in trouble when she was midway down his sternum. Between his makeshift restraint and grip on her jersey, Ally now found herself entangled and restrained. A wicked idea came to mind. Ally's hands glided their way back up his chest until her arms were straight above her head.

Ally dropped herself into a crouch, squirming and wriggling as she went to work herself free of the restraining jersey. Once free of her predicament, she pressed her palms flat against Chris's hips. Her lips roamed teasingly over his abs before she nuzzled against his navel, her teeth nipping gently at the beginning of the fine trail of hair that disappeared beneath the waistband of his jeans.

From the corner of her eye, Ally saw movement. Turning her head so her cheek pressed against the tanned skin of Chris's stomach, she caught sight of his jacket and shirt dropping to the floor. As her hands started to slide down from his hips toward his muscular thighs, Ally sat back on her heels, her gaze falling to Chris's boots.

Her head dipped as she made quick work of unfastening the laces, tugging his boot and sock from each foot as Chris lifted it. Ally was about to stand when Chris moved. His fingers dragged gently through her hair before sweeping it aside and over her right shoulder.

Strong hands gripped beneath her arms and hauled Ally to her feet. Feeling Chris's hands stroke along her arms, a breathy sigh slipped from her lips. The press of his bare chest against her back moved Ally forward a step as Chris's hands guided her arms up to brace against the door.

The tickle of his breath as his lips brushed against her shoulder, combined with the languid stroke of his fingers along her spine, sent a delicious shiver coursing through Ally's body. Her eyes fluttered closed as his lips moved to follow the path his fingers had taken.

Thick, yet apparently nimble, fingers made easy work of the fastening of her bra, the straps sliding loosely off her shoulders as his fingers trailed around her sides following the contour of the elastic band. With one deft move, Chris not only pushed her bra up but molded his hands perfectly over her breasts and gave a firm squeeze.

Ally shuddered as Chris's hands shifted. He caught her peaked nipples between his fingers. The addition of his tongue stroking a hot, moist stripe up along her spine had her stifling a moan as her legs clenched together.

When he blew against the damp skin over her spine, the shift in temperature had Ally's restraint flying right out the window as a shaky gasp slipped free. Her back arched up toward Chris's mouth as her breasts pressed more firmly into his palms, her body wantonly seeking more.

"Hmm, I didn't take you for a cotton briefs girl."

Chris's husky voice vibrated against her lower back, sending another delicious shiver coursing through Ally's body. She licked at her suddenly dry lips. When she finally found her voice, it came out as a low, breathy murmur. "Well, no one is comfortable wearing g-strings or thongs for extended periods. And while cute underwear can be comfortable, the fact that some guys think we need to wear dental floss between our butt cheeks to look sexy is demeaning. I'd like to see any guy wear one of those items for the time they expect us to."

The rumble of his laughter started against her back before his mouth left her skin. She felt his chin come to rest against her left shoulder, where he pressed a kiss behind her ear before whispering, "I'm not complaining; it's a nice surprise."

One of his hands slid down off her breast. His palm dragging over her sensitive nipple had Ally emitting a soft whine at the loss of pressure from his hand. When Chris's fingers tickled a teasing path along her rib to her sternum before starting southward, Ally sucked in a sharp breath as the surge of sensation washed over her.

As his hand roamed down over her stomach, Ally squirmed restlessly beneath his questing fingers. The path he made ended beneath her navel as his fingers traced over her skin at the waistband of her briefs. His open mouth settled against the delicate skin of her neck.

When Chris's fingers finally slipped beneath the waistband of her briefs to cup her mons, Ally's thighs clenched tighter. She knew that would prevent his exploration, but she found herself unable to relax her muscles. A tickling feeling at her ankle had Ally dropping her head between her arms to look at her feet; she caught sight of Chris's bare toes stroking along the skin of her inner ankle.

After a minute, his toes tapped lightly against her inner ankle, a non-verbal request her body apparently understood as her foot shifted out enough to spread her legs. Chris's approving growl rumbled against the skin of her neck as his hand slipped lower into her briefs. The first brush of his fingers along her slick folds had Ally sinking her teeth into her lower lip to prevent herself from crying out.

Not that she held back for too long. She lost it the moment his fingers delved between her folds and dragged slowly upward to circle her clit. His name fell from her lips in a strangled cry.

Her vision blurred as Chris's deft fingers worked against her clit. Some small part of her brain that was still capable of logical thought knew he was experimenting, finding out what she liked. The subtle strokes of Chris's thumb over her clit reminded Ally's hazy brain of a musician strumming their guitar. The sensation, while pleasant enough on its own, was only winding her body tighter. She needed something more. To get her point across, Ally rocked against his hand and ground herself against it.

He rewarded her by two of his thick fingers seeking her entrance, probing gently before sinking inside. Ally's breath hitched as his fingers moved, back and forth, sliding deeper each time.

When his fingers crooked and found her g-spot, Ally's body spasmed, rocking harder against his probing fingers. Her voice was shaky and hoarse as she cried out, "Oh, yes! There, right there."

Chris's teeth bit down firmly against the patch of skin he'd been sucking methodically at the same moment he crooked his fingers and hit that pleasurable little spot again. The dual sensation of pleasure and pain sent Ally careening right over the precipice and headlong into bliss.

Her inner muscles clenched around his fingers as her orgasm washed over her unexpectedly; her first orgasm she hadn't brought herself to using her own fingers or her toys. Ally jackknifed away from the door, her bra falling to the floor as one arm swung up and behind to grasp blindly at Chris's hair, her other dropping so her hand landed over Chris's still stuck down her underwear and holding it in place.

Ally could swear she was seeing fireworks even though her eyes had fluttered shut. Her body still swam with aftershocks of the strongest orgasm she'd ever felt. It wasn't helping matters that Chris's fingers were still teasing her through the aftershocks and starting to wind her up all over again.

She fell lax against him, her head lolling back against his right shoulder as she tried to get her body back under control. It'd be rather embarrassing, after all, to collapse to the floor because her own legs wouldn't keep her upright.

His hand still squeezing her breast released its hold; the arm it belonged to shifted to wrap around her ribs. Chris's teeth and lips released the patch of abused skin on her neck, a warm and gentle kiss pressing against the raw skin as he murmured, "Jesus, Ally. I've never had someone come like that from just my fingers before."

Feeling her cheeks grow red hot, Ally turned her head slightly toward his. Her eyes were bright and wide as she admitted sheepishly, "I've never come like that, period."

In her slightly dazed state, Ally noticed she was being gently guided backward, Chris's arm around her ribs about the only thing keeping her upright as her feet fumbled along the floor. His warm breath tickled against her ear before his voice broke the silence. "Hard to believe. I mean, I can understand the asshole not getting you off like—"

"He never got me off." Ally interrupted Chris mid-sentence, her eyes locking with his glinting ones. Nibbling her bottom lip, she continued, "He'd come and go to sleep. I've always then dealt with myself... but it's never been like that."

Their backward motion stopped, and Ally felt his confined arousal press firmly against her ass. She tried her best not to squirm as Chris growled, "Definitely calling your sister, mom and aunts tomorrow."

Ally curled her fingers around Chris's wrist, tugging it down gently to guide his fingers out of her core and helping his hand out of her briefs. She untangled her fingers from his hair, both her hands coming to hook into the waistband of her briefs. Taking a slight step forward, she inched the material down over her hips and bent at the waist to push them the rest of the way down.

Her now bare ass pressed back firmly against his arousal, the move coaxing a guttural growl from Chris's throat as his hands gripped her hips tightly to hold her in place. Looking back over her shoulder with a coy smile, she purred, "We seem to have two issues here, handsome. For starters, you are still wearing entirely too many clothes."

"That's easily rectified, kitten. What's the next issue?"

Kicking her feet free from her briefs, Ally once again straightened, her hands dropping to slap Chris's knuckles sharply. When his grip loosened, she turned to face him, her hands falling to grasp his belt buckle and work at unfastening it as she rose on her tiptoes to press her lips to his ear. "Next issue, you need to move this gorgeous ass and get a condom."

With her fingers now gripping the unfastened ends of his belt, Ally used it to pull their bodies flush, her lips moving to close around his earlobe and sucking gently before releasing. "Move it!"

Honestly, Ally couldn't remember the last time she'd seen Chris move so fast. He turned and bolted for the door, throwing it open so fast in his haste she half-expected it to fly off its hinges. With a barely withheld chuckle, she turned to draw her bedding down, folding the quilt and sheets neatly at the foot of her mattress.

Her stomach fluttering with nerves, Ally moved to situate herself on the bed. She tried settling into different positions but wasn't sure which appeared more seductive. She ended up opting for just sitting on the side of the bed, her upper body reclined slightly with her hands braced on the mattress.

It wasn't long at all before Chris came careening back through her door, a thump and his sudden hiss clear evidence he'd taken the turn just a fraction too sharp and had hit the door jamb. His jeans had been discarded somewhere during his trip. He tried to saunter across the room to the bed in his boxer briefs, one hand triumphantly holding the foil packet while the other rubbed at his hip.

Despite her lips twitching in amusement at the scene, Ally didn't dare laugh. Instead, she straightened herself on the edge of her bed and crooked her finger at him in a 'come hither' gesture. Her legs parted invitingly as he approached. When he settled between them, Ally gently batted his hand away from his hip and leaned forward to press a kiss to the red mark marring the skin over his hip bone.

"Poor baby, took the corner too sharp did we?" Ally teased gently against his skin before she sat up again. One hand shot out to snatch the packet from his grasp. She looked at it and frowned. "Not gonna work. Allergies." She leaned slightly to the side, her hand closing on the handle of the drawer in her nightstand and pulling it open. She rifled blindly in the drawer before emerging with her own box of condoms. Shoving the drawer shut, Ally dropped the box by her leg.

Her gaze never left Chris's face, even when his head turned slightly to see what she was doing. It allowed her to watch his whiskey-colored eyes darken and his pupils dilate further. Her fingers ghosted their way up along his thighs, the unexpected move causing a sudden hitch in Chris's breath.

As her fingers reached the waistband of the boxer briefs he still wore, Ally arched one brow. Whether he'd forgotten he still wore them or had purposefully left them on she wasn't sure. Hooking her thumbs beneath the band at his hips, Ally slowly dragged the material down just enough to release his erection, her hands settling against Chris's hips as she leaned in to flick her tongue over the engorged head.

"Fuck..." Chris hissed from above her, the raspy tone of his voice making her lips curl wickedly moments before they closed around the tip of his arousal, her tongue swirling around the head as she sucked gently. It was the same thing she'd done to his thumb earlier that had driven him wild. This time, it seemed to push him further as one of his hands curled around the back of her head.

Ally teased him for one or two moments longer before easing her head back; pressing a kiss to the tip she hooked one finger in the elastic of his briefs and snapped it against his skin. "Lose them."

While he hastily shed the shorts, Ally pulled out a condom.

As she started to tear it open, Chris snagged the package out of her hand to look at it. "Do I want to know why you have—" he looked at the label, "—extra-large ribbed for her pleasure condoms? What it is you are planning to do, exactly?"

"Single girl's gotta have protection for her toys, so I figured why not treat myself to ribbed ones?" Ally retorted with a grin and a slight shrug as she grabbed the condom and tore open the packet. "And you'll soon see what I'm planning. This is one of my research tidbits I wanted to try."

Easing the condom out of the foil she tossed the wrapper on the floor. Parting her lips, Ally positioned the condom so the tip rested against her tongue. The rim of the condom rested against her lips as Ally guided one of Chris's hands to the base of his erect shaft.

Settling her hands once again on his hips she leaned into his arousal and guided her lips over the head.

Slowly working her mouth down along his length Ally rolled the condom into place using her lips. She stopped every so often to give a gentle hum, suck, or to stroke her tongue along the underside of his erection. Another strangled groan, leaving Chris's throat as his free hand slipped into her hair his fingers twining loosely in the ebony waves, rewarded her efforts.

Ally eased her hand on the sore hip away, sliding it across to follow the V down to his balls. Her fingers stroked softly over his sack, exploring and experimenting with different amounts of pressure as she cupped them in her hand.

"Ally?"

The husky tone of Chris's voice had Ally's eyes peering up at him. She hummed against his erection even as she started to slide the condom down the last section of his length. She felt his fingers tighten in her hair and tug gently before he grated out a warning, "You keep that up, kitten, and I will come far too soon for either of our likings."

Her mouth slid teasingly slow back along his length; she paused at the head and hummed before sliding off with a pop. Ally looked up and shuffled back further on the bed just as Chris released a low, rumbling growl and crawled after her.

She brought her right foot up and pressed it against his chest, briefly halting his chase. A wicked grin formed on Chris's face as his fingers curled around her ankle. Lifting her foot from his chest, Chris pressed a kiss against the sole before guiding her ankle up to rest on his shoulder. When he continued forward and braced his hands against the mattress at her sides, Ally couldn't prevent the moan that slipped free.

A delicious burn spread through the muscles of her leg as they stretched to accommodate its current position on Chris's shoulder. His head lowered toward hers, lips brushing against her cheek before finally claiming her mouth in a sizzling kiss.

As Chris pulled back from the kiss, Ally felt his weight shift on the mattress. His fingers moved along the inside of her right thigh, and he gently guided her leg from his shoulder to wrap around his left hip.

His sheathed erection rubbed teasingly against her clit. Chris purposefully rocked against her. Ally whimpered needily, part of her knowing he was trying to buy himself some time. Her eyes fluttered open to find him hovering over her with his weight braced on his right hand; a slight shift of her head allowed her to see his left forearm snaked between their bodies.

It was at that moment she felt his erection probing gently as he sought her entrance. Ally wriggled and braced her left foot against the mattress to lift her hips to readjust her angle, feeling the tip of his arousal dip into her core. Her leg around his hip shifted enough that her heel dug into his ass.

With a tug of her leg, Ally caught Chris off-guard. His balance was thrown off with his surprise; she pulled him into her. Her lips parted with a soft moan as she felt Chris's erection slowly sliding into her. Chris's sigh soon joined it as, with a thrust of his hips, he bottomed out inside her.

Lowering his head, Chris rested his forehead against hers. They both lay still for a moment, adjusting to each other's body. Ally slipped her arms around Chris's ribs, her hands settling against his back as her fingers idly stroked along his spine. While he was bigger than she was used to, it didn't hurt. In fact, it felt oddly right, like she'd been made to accommodate him.

"Oh," Ally gasped as Chris subtly rocked his hips.

"Did I hurt you?" his concerned voice murmured as he stared down into her eyes.

Ally shook her head in response as one of her hands slid up along his spine, the light drag of her fingers causing Chris to shudder as she curled her fingers around his neck. She pressed a light kiss to his lips, her hips rocking into his as she purred, "No, you didn't. But… I think I need you to move?"

Chris eased back, almost entirely withdrawing from her before returning. His movements were deliciously slow and tender, yet pure teasing torture. He shifted slightly, his movement subtle, but Ally felt the right side of the bed dip beneath her as his weight shifted.

His left hand gripped tightly at her hip, a wicked grin curving his delectable lips mere moments before he pulled out of her and flipped their positions. Ally yelped at the surprising move as she found herself sprawled over Chris's chest. His now free hand came to join the other at her hips, his arousal standing at attention between her thighs and rubbing against her labia as Chris used his hold to rock her hips gently back and forth.

Burying his face against her neck, Chris nuzzled against the skin of her throat, nipping gently before the vibration of his chuckle hummed through her nerves. "You should see the look on your face, kitten."

"Well, when I asked you to move, I wasn't expecting that!" Ally huffed as she swatted half-heartedly at Chris's bicep.

"To be fair, you didn't tell me which way to move."

She had to admit he had a point there. Bracing her hands on either side of his torso, Ally pulled her knees up to rest against Chris's hips. Using her arms and core muscles, she pushed herself up into a sitting position.

Her core rested against the skin just below Chris's navel as his erection now nestled between her ass cheeks. Arching one brow as she looked down at him, Ally giggled at the boyish grin forming on Chris's face.

His eyes roamed over her adoringly, his hands skimming lightly up and down her sides. Ally's head swam with the sudden surge of her own arousal. Her hips rocked gently as her fingers stroked teasingly along his ribs.

It was a heady feeling: this sudden rush of power she felt coursing through her as her body rubbed against his. Chris's large hands stroked along her skin, sending sparks flying along her nerves as his thumbs dragged over her pert nipples.

Pushing up onto her knees, Ally shuffled backward, one hand gliding teasingly over Chris's ribs and down his stomach between them to curl around his erection. Ally guided Chris's thick, throbbing length back between her lips, her body lowering to rub over the sheathed sensitive head before she started slowly sinking down.

"Fuck, Ally," Chris hissed, his hands dropping from her breasts to her hips, his fingers digging tightly into her flesh and pulling her down even as his hips bucked up to meet her body.

Ally's head fell backward with a gasp, her nails biting into Chris's forearms when he thrust up and buried himself back inside her. Her hips stilled while she allowed herself a moment to adjust. It felt different in this position; she felt fuller. An experimental rock had her eyes flying wide as she looked down to where they joined. In their current position, his thick arousal pressed and rubbed over that hidden patch of nerves his fingers had found earlier.

"You gonna ride me, kitten? 'Cause I have to admit, I'm enjoying the view," Chris rumbled, his voice rolling over her like thick, rich honey.

Her response to the question was non-verbal, a slow roll and a grind of her hips against him as she tore her gaze away from where their bodies joined. Ally leaned forward slightly, altering the angle of her hips as her hands settled on Chris's abs, her nails raking lightly over the taut, toned skin.

She experimented with her pace and movements, trying to find the perfect blend that would drive them both wild. Ally not only watched but felt Chris's reactions—it was his body that told her what it wanted. She started by alternating between rolling her hips forward, rolling them backward, and flat out grinding against him.

Without warning, Chris jackknifed off the mattress into a seated position, his hands pulling her hips flush with his own as he captured her lips. Ally wrapped her arms around Chris's shoulders, her hands locking behind his neck as he started to nip and tease at her lower lip with his teeth.

His fingers flexed against her hips before disappearing. A low whine slipped from her throat in protest at the loss of his hands. They didn't stay gone for long, however, as one arm wrapped around her waist the other went under her arm and up her back so his hand could curl around her nape.

Ally leaned back against Chris's arm, her head dropping back slightly and to one side, exposing her throat to his questing mouth as it roamed over and down her cheek. The move altered the angle of her hips slightly so each rock and grind of her hips allowed Chris's thrusts to move just that fraction deeper.

The sharp sting of teeth where her neck met her shoulder made Ally gasp. Her body jerked forward into Chris's chest, sending them both tumbling back onto the mattress as her inner muscles began to flutter in that familiar way.

She was so close and was guessing Chris wasn't too far behind if his heavy breathing was anything to go by. With a sudden jerk and a twist of his hips, Chris had her pinned back against the mattress beneath him. Sliding her hands free from his neck, Ally lifted her arms to brace her hands against the headboard.

Bracing her feet flat, Ally pushed her ass up off the mattress slightly. Pressing her hips up to meet his thrusts she whimpered against his throat, "Harder, please."

Whether Chris was a diligent lover or just exceptionally talented, Ally was glad she didn't have to plead with him twice for what she wanted. Almost as soon as the 'please' left her lips, his hands repositioned on the mattress to brace his upper body as his thrusts picked up speed and force. Ally shuddered beneath him, the opening crescendo of her orgasm flowing through her.

"Yes, God, yes. Chris…" His name fell from her lips on a blissful cry, her inner muscles clamped tightly around him in spasmodic intervals as she came. The orgasmic waves crashed through her stronger than ever as Chris kept on, his thrusts driving her welcoming body back into the softness of the mattress.

One of his hands left the mattress at some point, her bliss-addled senses only registering the change when it gripped tightly at her hip as he pistoned in and out. His head lowered, mouth coming to rest against her ear, and when he finally spoke the husky growl of his voice pushed her over the precipice. "Shit, Ally. You feel so good around me. Come for me, kitten, take me with you over that edge."

Three sudden, sharp jerks of his hips later and Chris's own hoarse cry filled her ears, her thighs tightening against his hips to hold him close as she felt him spasming with his own release, buried deep inside her.

Ally's hands came away from the headboard, her arms wrapping around his sides and pulling his quaking body down on top of her. Her fingers stroked soothingly along Chris's back, his body still shuddering occasionally with the faint tremors of his orgasm as he nuzzled against her throat. Holding him close, her eyes fluttered shut, a content sigh slipping from her lips at just how right this moment felt.

*

When she'd awoken, nestled snugly against Chris's toned body, Ally had barely had time to reflect on what had happened between them before her phone had sprung to life. Jess's ringtone filled the silence, echoed soon by Chris's phone ringing from somewhere out in the hall.

Ally nuzzled back into Chris's chest with an annoyed grumble, she was warm, comfortable and content. Chris's arms tightened around her moments before he rumbled sleepily into her hair, "Sounds like our friends are looking for us."

They'd both known if one of them hadn't answered their phone that their friends would soon pound on the front door. It'd been with that in mind that she'd reluctantly reached over to her nightstand for her phone.

That decision had led to her current predicament, namely being stuck in the middle of a crowded dance floor with Jess and Mel. While normally that wouldn't be such a problem, right now Ally would honestly much rather still be back in the apartment curled up in her bed with Chris.

By the time she and Chris had reached the club their group of friends normally frequented, it had been clear their friends had been there a while. Which meant that Jess and Mel were three sheets to the wind and their inhibitions were non-existent at this point.

She was at least partly grateful for that as it meant the two women she considered sisters weren't quite as eagle-eyed as they usually were. In their haste to meet up with their friends, she hadn't had a lot of time to get ready, which meant the only way she could hide the rather clear bite mark Chris had left on her neck had been with a red silk scarf she'd tied around her neck to accessorize her black backless skater dress.

"So what's up with you and Chris?"

Mel's out of the blue question startled Ally. *Maybe my friends aren't drunk enough after all*, she mused. "What do you mean? There's nothing up."

Hoping the pair of women were at least drunk enough not to notice how rapidly she'd answered, she spared a brief glance back to the booth where Chris appeared to be in animated discussion with James and Colt.

"Something's up," Jess declared. Her arms wrapped around Ally's waist as she glanced over to the guys. "He's broodier than usual and scowls whenever he notices guys getting too close to us."

"It's as though he's in overprotective caveman mode," Mel agreed with an uncharacteristic giggle before looking pointedly at Ally. "And you, you seem more…" Mel trailed off with a wave of her hand to encompass Ally's body.

The move had Ally frowning slightly. Was it obvious to her best friends she'd gotten laid? Jess's nodding head in response to Mel's silent assessment wasn't all that encouraging, and Ally sighed before quietly admitting, "Okay, something may have happened."

Before she could even take a breath to elaborate, Ally was met with two smug grins and her friends' simultaneous responses: "It's about damn time you two got your shit together."

Her cheeks heated with mild embarrassment as she groused, "Would you two keep your voices down a little, please?"

Allowing them to pull her into a group hug, Ally dropped her forehead against their shoulders with a groan. She'd swear they were trying to embarrass her to death, or they were preparing to wheedle her incessantly.

Personally, Ally didn't like the thought of either option. She was pulled out of her thoughts by a gentle tug at her neck followed by Mel's crowing, "Ahuh! Looks like it was a big something."

She jerked her head up and took a step back as her hand flew up to cover the telling mark at the join of her neck and shoulder. Ally winced at the sudden attention of the surrounding people, their attention having been gained by Mel's loud exclamation.

"Seriously? Do you have absolutely no filter or sense of volume when you are halfway smashed?" Ally growled lowly as she reached to snatch her scarf back from Jess's dancing fingers.

As she finished tying the scarf back in place around her neck, Ally felt a sudden chill run down her spine. Before she could even attempt to figure out what had caused it, she noticed Jess and Mel's eyes widen a split second before an unwelcome voice hissed, "Well, well, if it isn't my runaway girlfriend."

No, no, no, no, her brain screamed at her. Of all the times and places she could run into him, it had to be now? Just when she was finally starting to feel fully content with her life, fate threw her cheating ex in her face... almost literally.

Her skin crawled as Nate's knuckles stroked up the side of her thigh. As they inched higher toward the hem of her dress, she felt anger bloom within her. He had no right to touch her like that anymore, let alone a right to even talk to her, and it was time he knew it.

Ally twisted away from her ex's wandering hand, one of her own hands flying out as she did so to collide with his cheek with a resounding crack. The sting in her hand felt oddly satisfying. Ally poked Nate firmly in the chest as she snarled, "You don't get to touch me anymore... or talk to me. We were done the moment I found you screwing your assistant in our bed."

"Honey, come on. It was a one-time thing when I thought you were out of town."

The fake pleading tone to Nate's voice rang in her ears like nails on a chalkboard and Ally soon found her hands clenching with her growing irritation. She'd wasted so many years of her life on this ass when something better had literally been standing right next to her the whole time.

"Don't you 'honey' me, Nate. You can take your lameass excuses and your lackluster lovemaking and get the hell out of my sight," Ally snapped before turning back to her girlfriends only to find Mel gone and Jess grinning like a Cheshire cat.

Oh, that was not good. Knowing Jess and Mel like sisters, she had absolutely no doubt that Mel had gone to the guys for backup the moment she'd turned to slap her unwelcome ex. That Cheshire cat grin Jess was sporting was just as bad, and she had a sinking suspicion that her remaining friend was about to weigh in on the encounter.

"You heard her, asshole. Get lost."

Ally envied Jess's icy, take-no-shit tone and wished she was capable of a take-charge attitude. With a small smile of gratitude, she was about ready to leave with Jess when fingers locked firmly about her wrist.

Nate's voice broke the moment. "Shut it, slut. No one asked for your opinion on the matter. Allyson is coming home with me."

Hell no, he did not just slut-shame one of the closest people in her life. Ally's free hand balled into a fist. As Nate's firm grip tugged her toward him, she used the momentum of her body's turn to power the punch she threw at his nose.

The crunch she heard, moments before Nate growled a curse as he released her wrist to clutch at his bloody nose, was oddly satisfying. Shaking out her slightly stinging hand, Ally took one step forward and shoved Nate's chest. Sending him falling backward onto his ass in the middle of the dance floor, she snarled, "You do not get to slut-shame my family for enjoying sex! They, at least, don't cheat on their significant others to enjoy themselves. Unlike someone writhing on the ground like a spineless worm in front of me. And for the record, I prefer Ally, and I'm not going anywhere with you."

Nate was scowling up at her, and Ally suspected he was about to argue the matter with her. Bracing herself for the argument that seemed inevitable, she found herself surprised when his expression shifted to something she'd never seen before. Was that fear?

She considered that possibility for a moment before her body suddenly realized the presence looming behind her. The soft huff of breath that tickled the sensitive skin just behind her ear and firm large hands that gripped her hips possessively set her nerve endings aflame.

Chris was here. Not just here but right behind her and blatantly making his claim on her in front of not only her idiot ex but also all their friends and the curious onlookers in the club. The tension seemed to ebb from her body as she leaned back against Chris's muscular chest. She'd never realized until now how safe she felt when Chris was around. He felt like home.

"Think your next words over carefully, Nate. Or you'll have a broken jaw to go along with that potentially broken nose you have there."

The normal low, husky rumble of Chris's voice was now laced heavily with menace, his fingers flexing against her hips. She noticed just how tense he was behind her, all six foot two of him wound tight like a tiger ready to pounce upon its prey.

Lifting her arm, Ally curled her throbbing hand around the nape of Chris's neck. She turned her head and rose slightly to press a kiss to the curve of his jaw, murmuring gently, "Easy, tiger, he's not worth it."

Chris turned his head slightly, their eyes locked. Ally could read the confusion in those dark whiskey eyes along with his barely restrained anger as he quietly muttered, "You're protecting him now, kitten?"

Ally sighed quietly at the subtle mixture of anger and hurt in his tone. She turned her body slightly and gave a gentle tug with the hand at the nape of Chris's neck, followed by another, until he took the hint and lowered his head so their foreheads were touching.

"No, fuck him. I'm protecting you, Chris. I only just got you and would rather not have you ending up in jail over breaking an entitled jerk's jaw."

His breath rushed out in a relieved exhale against her cheek. She skimmed her aching hand around his neck to cup his jaw as she pressed a chaste kiss to his lips before murmuring quietly for his ears alone, "Besides, if you are really that dead set on beating the shit out of him, you need to at least include Dad and Sammy, or Mom. Nate's too scared of my family to risk attempting to have them brought up on charges."

Chris's familiar rumble of laughter rolled through his chest. He appeared to consider those words before admitting, "The Colonel is very scary, especially when he gets that look, and you know which one I'm referring to."

"Ah yes, 'the murder face' as Mom likes to call it. You know, he only does that outside of work with people we bring home the first time to see how they react?" Ally grinned. Turning her head to brush her lips against his ear she whispered, "Wormface over there made up an excuse why he suddenly had to leave upon seeing that face."

"You know, not to interrupt your oh-so-cute PDA happening here, but I think our current nuisance is about to become an even bigger problem," Colt chimed in just a little too brightly for Ally's liking.

The sharp sound of a slap had Ally reluctantly pulling her head back from Chris's with a quiet laugh. If she didn't miss her guess, either Mel or Jess had just slapped Colt upside the head in warning.

"As much fun as a full on club brawl sounds, Colt, I think I'll pass. I'd much rather spend the rest of my Saturday night celebrating Lips Appreciation Day."

Ally gave Chris a pointed look as her hand slid along his jaw and down his chest until her fingers curled around his belt and tugged. She turned and looked down at Nate, an annoyed huff escaping her lips at his scowling features. "Goodbye, Nathan. Be warned, if I see you again or if you cause me trouble again, my family will hear about everything."

Moving toward the club's exit, Chris easily fell into step with her. His arm draping around her shoulders prompted Ally to nestle into his side and slip her arm around his waist. For the first time in a long time, her world felt complete.

"I'm proud of you, kitten." Chris whispered against her temple, his lips brushing against her skin. His arm tightened around Ally's shoulder as she shivered, gently pulling her to a stop. With an easy motion Chris shrugged out of his leather jacket and draped it around her shoulders as he looked into her eyes, a charming grin curled his lips. "What's say we stop and get some food on the way home. I can make up for bailing on Zen day with some Netflix and chill?"

♥

About the Author

Livvy Ward was born and raised in Australia. She's been a fan and avid reader of paranormal romances for the past twenty years and has worked numerous mundane jobs. If asked she'd tell you her absolute favorite aside from writing was her time as a professional dog trainer.

Website: livvyward.com
Twitter: @livvywardauthor

Melting Hearts
♥
Annika Steele

Story Information

Holiday: Snowman Burning Day
Holiday Date: March 20
Heat Rating: 4
Relationship Type: M/F
Major Trigger Warnings: Mention of medical procedures.

April moved to Pittsburgh. She misses her sunny Texas skies. Snow on her birthday? The worst. If burning a snowman on the spring equinox will guarantee the snow will go away, yep, she's all in. So what if her neighbor happily scoops heaps of snow out of his driveway--and whistles while he's shoveling!

Melting Hearts

April Garza jammed the shovel into the pile of drippy ice at her front door. "Why," she muttered, "did I think this was a good idea? I hate snow. And ice. And what's the deal with *wet* snow? Snow is supposed to be fluffy and fun and disappear about five minutes after the sun comes out."

Shoveling snow definitely wasn't at the top of her things-she-liked-to-do list, especially when she had to clear enough of the cold stuff to keep it from falling through the back door and onto the old wooden floor in desperate need of refinishing. (After, of course, she peeled off the green and gold wallpaper gracing all four walls of her kitchen.)

Moving from Austin to Pittsburgh had seemed like a *great* idea when she'd visited on Memorial Day weekend two years ago. The job offer had been fantastic, housing was reasonable, and Pittsburgh had been stunning then—green with flowers and real, honest spring weather (the kind that only happened in Texas for about five days before everything turned into a hot, sticky mess). In Austin, she could barely afford a tiny downtown apartment, even with the decent salary and benefits she'd had at Breckenridge Hospital.

Here, the Swissvale house she'd found was affordable and had good bones, never mind the work it needed to make it pretty again. Frick Park was only a few blocks away, and April liked walking through it on sunny days. She loved her job at West Penn. She'd made fast friends with a few of her coworkers, and they had a standing Thursday night date at either the movies or the bar, depending on their mood.

But snow. Seriously. This was her second winter, and she wasn't any more a fan of this one than she was of the first.

Who would have thought she would miss ninety-and-humid when it meant year-round patio weather and margaritas? Well, the margaritas weren't a problem since she owned a blender, and any version of humidity Pittsburgh could come up with didn't faze April one itty bit. She'd definitely missed sunny spring days when she'd spent her last birthday scraping snow off the flight of steps leading from her street to her front door so her friends could get inside for the fajita bash she threw that weekend.

April grumbled under her breath as she shoveled a path down all those same steps, then started in on the driveway to the garage under her house.

Her neighbor, Nina Larsen, waved from her own patio where she was sweeping off her own little pile of snow, albeit without the same vigor April attacked hers. Nina and her husband, Steiner, lived in the same house Nina's parents had built in 1925. Her parents had immigrated from Norway, started a bakery in Wilkinsburg, and built a house in Swissvale. Steiner and Nina had moved in with her mother after her dad passed over forty years ago, had two children of their own, and never left. Between them, they knew all the gossip in the neighborhood for three generations and were happy to share it with April.

Walkway cleared, April shuffled back into the house and shoved the door closed. She had to lean on the wood to get the lock to catch. She wrinkled her nose, knowing it was one more thing on a long, long list of refurbishments the house needed.

She loved this house, with its squeaky floors and layers of paint on the door frames. Though her family back home frequently urged her to hire out the work to be done, April had been content to live in the house and learn its secrets before she embarked on the changes she wanted to make. She'd peeled back corners of wallpaper (four layers), chipped away at linoleum floors in the bathroom (two layers over hardwood she hoped to save), and knocked a hole in the covered-over fireplace to see what might be hiding there (brick! yay!). For certain, the kitchen needed to be stripped down to the wall studs and rebuilt entirely. (Next summer, she promised.)

Steiner and Nina were a godsend—they knew every contractor on this side of Pittsburgh and had been invaluable when it came to deciding which repairs were best made right away and which ones could wait. (The roof was still in good shape, so pretty much *anything* to do with the basement, wiring, and heating systems had been done first. She tried not to look too hard at all the holes in her walls.)

They'd laughed at April's grouching about the snow on her birthday last year. April 3rd should be plenty late enough for snow to be done, right? Nina had brought her butter cookies in sympathy on the first week of May last year. With an all-knowing smile in her bright green eyes, she'd sworn by a Swedish tradition of burning a fake snowman on the first day of Spring to ward off any more snow.

With one eyeball on the new calendar hanging on the pantry door that sported a sunny beach for the month of January, April was all in.

*

A week into the new year, April climbed out of the employee shuttle to slog through the cold rain and mess left from last week's snowstorm to her job as an MRI tech. Halfway through her shift, she was startled to discover her neighbors in the waiting room. "Mr. Larsen. Mrs. Larsen!"

"Told ya t' call me Steiner," the older man grumbled, leaning hard on the "ah" sounds in his Pittsburgh accent.

"Mr. Larsen, my mama would have fits." April flashed him a grin, then glanced at her tablet. "Your knee is giving you trouble again?"

"More than fits," Nina answered for him. "He's been a cranky old man all week."

"All right," April said with a chuckle—both to keep the mood light and because Steiner was *always* cranky. The elderly couple fidgeted, nervous as they waited. She hastened to calm them. "You know you're in good hands with me. I'll talk you through this."

Steiner grunted with a vague nod.

"I do feel better knowing you're the one doing all this," Nina said, waving her hand toward the MRI room.

"So am I," April admitted. "I know my coworkers are great, but you're important to me."

"Do I have to go in a tube?" Steiner asked, worry making his forehead wrinkle.

"Nope. We've got an MRI just for knees. You'll see. It's not so bad."

The hour-long procedure passed quickly as April walked the Larsens through the whole process, got Nina settled in the waiting room, and then chatted to Steiner during the procedure about her latest idea for taking out part of a wall between the kitchen and living room to give her place a more open floor plan. Steiner had a few good ideas and promised to sketch them out for her.

Two days later, Nina invited April over for coffee to tell her the results from the doctor. Steiner wasn't happy as he limped with a knee brace around the kitchen, but he stubbornly puttered around to make thick sandwiches with the fresh bread Nina liked to buy from Wood Street. April studied Steiner's sketches for her kitchen as Nina filled her in on the surgery Steiner would be having in a few days.

April frowned as she glanced around the house. "How are you going to manage?" Like most four-square houses in this area, the only bathroom and all the bedrooms were upstairs. (She refused to count the Pittsburgh toilet in the middle of the basement.)

"Do you remember our grandson, Jan?"

"Hanne's son. Graduated from Penn State with a degree in IT, right?" April offered. "I don't think we've met."

Nina gave her a broad smile. "Good memory. He's working for the big steel company on the river."

April sipped her coffee to cover a burble of laughter. "On the river" described half the city, and Pittsburgh wasn't called "Steel City" for nothing.

Steiner limped to the table with a plate of fat sandwiches made with a healthy layer of ham in between the crusty slices of sourdough. "Eat up," he ordered. "Jan's gonna schlep me around the house 'til I'm back on m' feet. He's sold his place and wants to move on this side of the river."

"It's closer to his work," Nina agreed.

"That's sweet of him to help." April squashed the automatic pang of guilt over moving so far from home. Her mom was just fine living with her sister, and April didn't mind spending some of her vacation time in Austin to give her sister a break. Still, she missed her family. Her brother had promised to help her with the kitchen when the time came.

A rattle of wind slapped the screen against the window, bringing her attention back to the here and now.

"Gonna snow again," Steiner muttered as he dropped into a chair. He bit into his sandwich as he eyed the clouds.

April groaned. "I'm demanding sunny skies and clear sidewalks for my birthday."

Nina patted her on the wrist. "She needs a snowman," she told Steiner.

The old man's eyes lit up. "Yeah, you do," he said to April. "Make it a good one." Then, with a sly glance, he offered, "Maybe Jan can help you build one."

Oh no. April was all too familiar with that gleam. She didn't need any more matchmaking, thank you. She had a house to renovate. She reached for her sandwich, not saying a word.

*

Jan wedged his arm under his granddad's shoulder, giving support as the two of them crabbed sideways up the stairs.

"I'm about done with this business," Pop grouched. "Can't take a piss without making a to-do about it."

"It's just a few weeks," Jan soothed. "And you're doing me a favor, letting me stay here while I find a house. Crosstown traffic is terrible."

"Makes your grandma happy, you being here."

Jan squashed a smile. He adored his grandparents, and his Pop's crankiness was legendary—as was his generosity.

The timing couldn't have been better, though he didn't wish for Pop's bum knee. With the new job, Jan was ready to find a place on this side of town. He'd already received an offer on his condo when he'd called his grandparents to beg for a place to stay. Any guilt he'd had over taking advantage of their guest room had vanished when Nana had told him about Pop's surgery. They'd been looking into a home health aide, but were nervous about having someone coming by only a couple of times a day. As it was, the home nurse was scheduled to come by at lunch for a professional checkup, and Jan could handle the mornings and evenings with Pop.

At the top of the stairs, Pop patted Jan on the shoulder and limped off toward the bathroom. "I'm gonna nap," he told Jan. "Go keep your Nana company. It'll keep her from fussin' over me."

Jan laughed at that. "Sure thing, Pop."

The stairs squeaked in a familiar pattern as Jan descended. Nana was still in the kitchen, wiping down the counters from the remains of their lunch. She gave him a broad smile as she opened her arms for a hug. Jan loved the way she smelled—baby powder and springtime—and her crunchy curls brushed the bottom of his chin.

"Thank you, love," Nana said. She gave him one last squeeze and shooed him off. "Go get settled. I'm gonna nap in front of the TV, then get to the grocery store before it snows tonight."

"Want me to go?"

She mock-scowled at him. "I'm old, but I can drive."

"Yes, ma'am." He saluted her, making her laugh.

"Be nice, and I'll introduce you to April."

"Your neighbor who did the MRI?"

"April Garza. She's a good one. Got a lot on her hands with that house. You know the Mastersons never did a thing with it. It's still got the wallpaper they put up in '75. Good bones, though, on that place. Just needs some love. April's good for it."

Careful not to show his dismay at the prospect of matchmaking grandparents, Jan deflected, "Maybe I'll get my stuff set up first."

"You do that," Nana chided. "But we'll have her for dinner when Steiner's less of a grump."

Jan bit his lip as he turned away, not wanting his Nana to catch him rolling his eyes.

"I saw that!"

*

Jan hung his clothes in the small closet of the second of the three bedrooms upstairs—the same room his mom had lived in when she was growing up. She'd been the one to suggest he stay with Nana and Pop. He missed her. She'd flown in from Chicago at Christmas, and he'd make an excuse to go see her before the summer was out. It was hard to believe Dad had been gone five years now, but Mom was happier now that she had a fresh start and a good job to distract her. That last year of Dad battling cancer had been a hard one.

Shaking off the melancholy, Jan finished stuffing his clothes into the dresser and shoved his luggage in the bottom of the closet. The door stuck when he tried to close it. A good look at the hinges proved one of them needed to be replaced, and he added it to his mental list of honey-do's he'd take care of this weekend. Pop liked to putter and generally kept the house in tip-top shape, but Jan had learned first-hand even in his condo how fast chores added up when one couldn't get to them.

He liked this old house. At nearly a century old, a little care would see it stand for another hundred years. Jan had grown up in the suburbs in a modern house with big rooms and carpet everywhere. Here, the wood floors squeaked, the concrete sidewalks were laced with cracks from the big maple tree out front, and the whole backyard needed the overgrowth cleared. There was history in the marks on the door casings and the nicks in the plaster. His grandparents appreciated all that, modernizing where it made sense in the kitchen and bathroom while leaving the old millwork alone.

Jan sat on the bed and pulled out his laptop. He'd taken the next two days off, but it couldn't hurt to check in to work and make sure nothing catastrophic had happened with the computer systems. A quick glance at his emails turned into an hour's worth of work, but Jan felt better when he closed out of the company website.

The floor in the hallway squeaked. Jan found Pop making his way down the stairs.

"I'm fine," his grandad scolded. "Getting up is the hard part. Down, not so much."

"Sure thing, Pop." Still, Jan followed, much to Pop's obvious annoyance.

Nana had her purse out and was busy making a list for the grocery store. Jan slipped a couple of twenties out of his wallet and passed them over. She nodded, tucking them in her bag. "Thank you, love."

Pop eyed Jan. "Go for a walk, son. I'm fine getting dinner on. Takes me a little longer, that's all. You go on and get some air."

Jan snickered at the dismissal. His grandparents were firm believers in good food, fresh air and long walks to stretch the legs. He retrieved his coat from the hall closet and sauntered out into the cold evening. The front porch still had ice packed into the shadowy corners. There was a bite to the wind, promising more snow tomorrow, but he had four-wheel-drive on his SUV and wasn't afraid of a few inches.

He strolled down to Frick Park, dodging the evening dog walkers as he did. He'd explore the park another time, but he had fond memories of sledding on the hills as a kid. On the walk back, he caught a glimpse of the neighbor on her front porch, caulk gun in hand as she sealed up a window. She was bundled up in gloves, scarf, hat, boots, and a heavy coat, with thick ropes of brown hair lying across her shoulders.

"Nana? Where's your neighbor from?" he asked later over dinner.

"April? She's from Texas. Austin, I think. Did you talk to her?"

Jan shook his head. "No. Just saw her working. Nobody around here wears gloves until it's freezing."

Pop chuckled. "Ain't that the truth. But she'll get used to it."

*

April scrambled out of bed, annoyed at herself for hitting the snooze button one more time. Even after rushing through her morning routine, she barely had time for coffee. Slapping the machine on, she listened to it percolate while she inserted herself into the pile of winter clothing. Two of her coworkers, Maria and Phillip, made fun of her sometimes because April got cold when it was sixty outside. But she snickered right back at them when they complained about the summer heat. Today, though, not even Maria would give her an ounce of grief about bundling up.

She peeked out the front door into the predawn darkness and sighed while grabbing the broom to knock the snow off the first few steps. It didn't seem too icy, at least.

Coffee in hand, she picked her way down the steps to get to the garage. It and the basement made up the first floor of her house. There *was* a staircase inside the house leading down to the basement and garage, hidden behind a china hutch built into a door in the dining room. But with a rickety railing and several rotting steps, the stairs were the next item on her renovation list. For now, it meant she had to use the front door and the steps outside to get down to the garage level.

Each step had at least two inches of snow. She sidled down sideways, her heavy boots crunching as she crabbed down the stairs with a firm grip on the railing. April eased down on the walk path, then shuffled down the driveway, glad that at least it wasn't fully detached and forty feet away, as in so many houses she'd looked at before she found this one. Now *that* was weird. Who decided that design was a great idea in a city of snow and ice? Then again, she mused, cars didn't exactly have emissions standards in 1920, so maybe having an attached garage in the basement was the stranger idea back then. (Just like the Pittsburgh toilet, and April refused to think about that.)

April huddled down in her coat as the bitter air slapped her in the face in spite of the heavy scarf she'd used to cover it. Fat snowflakes dancing on the wind currents didn't bode well for the weather today. She studied the sky for a moment, and then the dark bulk of the house next door reminded her that Steiner was having his surgery today.

She'd promised to bring cookies tonight as a treat. The anticipation of making something yummy later brightened her mood as she jammed the garage door key in the lock.

The lock refused to move. Three attempts later, April bumped up a garage door opener a lot higher on her mental list of priority repairs. She leaned on the lock to get the old latch to turn. It released with a pop, startling her as the overhead door sprang open at her feet. She jerked backward, stepping on a slippery bit of ice.

With flailing arms, she lost her balance, keys, coffee, and dignity when she landed on her ass on the snow.

A low chuckle, deep and male, echoed from across the chain link fence. "You good?"

Mortified by her clumsiness and mourning the loss of her coffee, April snapped, "I'm fine." She rolled over to her hands and knees, brushing through the snow. Under her breath she added, "Irritated, embarrassed, annoyed, and it's dark and I can't find my keys." She couldn't see a thing. Digging for the phone she'd stuffed in her pocket proved futile at this angle, and she got stuck on her own coat as she tried to stand up, stumbling again and falling on her butt once more. "Damn it!"

That came out louder that she intended, and the bark of laughter from next door did *not* help her mood. She muttered under her breath as she rolled to her knees again. She could feel the water soaking all the way through her scrubs and thermal underwear.

A light popped up over her shoulder, darting around before landing on her keys and the tumbler of coffee lying beside them. April snatched both of them up and scrambled to her feet. She turned around, shading her eyes against the brightness. "I'd thank you, but you laughed at me, and I sort of think those cancel each other out."

There was another chuckle from the dark as the flashlight clicked off. "You got me there."

April blinked. "Are you Mr. and Mrs. Larsen's grandson?"

"Jan, yeah." The Pittsburgh accent came through loud and clear on that simple phrase, and April would *not* admit that it made her want to grin.

"Take care of them today," she said instead.

"I will."

The fervent promise in that husky voice alleviated some of April's irritation. She turned away to shove the garage door the rest of the way into the air—successfully and without incident this time. She backed the car out of the garage, then climbed out again to shuffle her way to the garage door to close it.

A spritely whistle to the tune of *Frosty the Snowman* accompanied by the scrape of a shovel brought back every ounce of irritation. Who *liked* shoveling snow at five in the morning?

She grumbled as she climbed back into her car to ease it backward, tires crunching through the snow. With careful effort, she pulled out into the street and made slow, if steady, progress to work on the snowy roads. April muttered all the way to the hospital, making plans to install an automatic garage door opener with her next paycheck. *After* she got another cup of coffee.

*

A fresh cup landed on April's workstation. Her coworker, Maria Santos, had a sympathetic wry smile as she leaned against the wall with her own mug in hand. "Still hate snow?"

"With a vengeance," April grumbled. "And I don't like an audience when I'm fighting Mother Nature."

"Ah, gimme deets, girlfriend."

"You know my neighbors, the Larsens?" April asked as she sipped her coffee, reveling in the smell as she drank.

"The one having surgery today?"

"Their grandson watched me make an idiot of myself getting down to the garage." Even now, April flushed with mortification. She hated looking less than competent, especially since she'd fought so hard this past year to make good decisions on her house and job. Relocating to another part of the country wasn't easy, and she didn't want to look like she'd done it rashly.

"Are you okay?"

April sighed. "The good part about five layers of clothing is the only thing that got hurt is my pride."

"True." Maria chuckled, then leaned over with a squeeze to April's shoulder. "Look at it this way: since the snow is keeping everyone home today, just let me know when you want to take your break and check on your neighbor. Phillip's coming in at ten, and we're not going to be terribly busy."

"Think I can sneak in without running into the grandson?"

"Probably not."

"Damn."

Maria's snort echoed as she crossed the floor to her own workstation.

*

Unlike this morning, April got lucky. She peeked in on Mr. Larsen near the end of her shift. He was ready to go home, and Jan was out getting the car. Nina fussed at Steiner when he chided the nurse for making him use a wheelchair. April bit her lip against a smile when he apologized in his usual gruff voice. The nurse, Shonda Carter, just patted him on the shoulder. Shonda was one of the Thursday night crew, and she shot April a wry smile over her shoulder.

"You bringing cookies?" Steiner swallowed, then tilted his chin up with a cranky-but-hopeful jerk.

"I promised." April kissed him on his cheek.

"You did, honey, you did."

She gave Nina a quick hug, then skedaddled back to her end of the hospital before what little luck she had ran out.

*

The heavy morning snow slackened into a light dusting that eased Jan's worries about the trip home. His grandparents were exhausted by the long day, and Jan's drive was quiet when they both fell asleep in the car.

Getting Pop up the stairs and settled in his own bed with an enormous brace on his leg was a real trick, but they managed. Nana fluttered around the bed, getting Pop comfortable.

Relieved to have his granddad home, the stress and worry of the day settled into Jan's bones. "Nana, I'm gonna shovel the driveway before the snow gets too deep."

Nana flashed an understanding smile in his direction. "You do that."

Jan shrugged on his heavy coat and pulled on his gloves. The snow wasn't too bad yet, just an inch or so deep. After a long day in hard waiting room chairs, Jan appreciated the physical work. He rolled his neck to relieve the tension there and swept the snow out of the way. He worked his way up one side and down the other, first humming, then whistling under his breath.

"Seriously?"

He whirled around at the voice, familiar only from this morning, his heart pounding at being startled. "Huh?"

The woman shook her head. In the twilight, he could see her dark hair dancing over her shoulders, but not much more. Given the hair, the voice, and the fact she only wore a heavy sweater and a scarf, instead of a coat, and was carrying a plastic container, Jan figured this was the neighbor.

"Nobody should be that happy shoveling snow," she scolded, coming closer.

Jan frowned, giving the shovel in his hand a quick glance. "I… like it?"

The woman humphed. "Sure." She shuffled closer, the scent of peanut butter and chocolate chips wafting between them. "April Garza," she offered with a smile, holding out one gloved hand.

The professional confidence laced with a Texas drawl hit a button Jan didn't know he had, sending a shimmer of interest straight through his spine.

"Jan Larsen." He straightened, shifting the shovel to rest against his middle so he could shake. He hadn't bothered to cover his hands, and the soft fleece tickled a little, making him smile. She had a nice grip, not too firm, not too soft. He couldn't really see her face in the low light. "Pop's upstairs," he offered. "Might check with Nana to see if he's still awake."

"I'll do that." There was that drawl again.

From the delicate way April picked her way up the steps, Jan didn't figure she was too familiar with snow. He'd be lying through his teeth if he said he didn't notice her backside, though. The jeans she wore hugged her curves—and there were plenty of those to admire as she climbed.

He ambled after her, following closely enough to keep appreciating.

April gave the door a double-knock and breezed through without waiting for an invitation. She handed over the cookies, hugging Nana and Pop with an easy familiarity that warmed Jan. He liked knowing his grandparents had someone so close who cared about them.

His eyes drifted over her once more as she dropped her gloves and scarf over the sofa, and then he was totally busted: first by Pop with a wink and then by April when she spun around, holding out a cookie.

If her backside was pretty, the front damned near bowled him over. Dark eyes, dark hair, and a smile lighting up her whole face, flushed a deep rose from the cold. She licked her lips as she handed over the cookie. "Hope you like peanut butter."

Jan grinned as he took it. "Sure thing." Their fingers brushed at the tips. He jerked at the spark of energy where skin touched skin. April's eyes widened, and she flexed her hand as she tucked it in her pocket. Jan stuffed the cookie in his mouth so as not to say anything stupid.

The cookie tasted pretty good: better than store bought, for sure. Pop surely loved them, as Nana had to peel the container out of his hands.

April darted the occasional look at Jan while she got a quick rundown of the day from Nana. She, in turn, confessed to her driveway mishap this morning—and told on Jan for laughing at her.

Nana leveled a dark look at him. "Jan Larsen, you apologize to April. She's a good neighbor, and your lack of manners will not be the reason she moves away."

Said neighbor giggled, and Jan promptly made his amends. "I'm sorry, ma'am." He bit his lip at any explanation. He seriously doubted April wanted to know how funny the whole incident had appeared as she and the garage door went in opposite directions, her things flying in every which way. But nobody liked to be humiliated, and for that he *was* sorry. "Can I fix your garage door lock?"

April arched an eyebrow in surprise. "Ah——no. Uh, thank you though," she stammered. "I've got someone coming to install a new garage door opener."

Nana piped up, "What she needs is a hand fixing those basement stairs in her house."

"Not yet," April countered. "I've got to do the siding first."

"Those stairs are dangerous," Pop agreed. "It's why she goes out the front door even when those stairs are covered in ice."

"And I wear snow boots and cleats and keep a shovel by my front door," April reminded them. "I'll get to it when I don't have to have four blankets on my bed from all the drafts. But it will be soon, I promise."

Jan had to admire April's resolve. Nana and Pop had a fair amount of wisdom and worry in their bones, but April had a way of letting them know she appreciated both without letting them dictate her next move.

She didn't stay long after that, reminding Pop that he'd had a long day and needed rest to heal. She bustled right back out the door with a wave goodbye. Nana kept an eye on her through the window to make sure she made it home, nodding to herself when April did.

Nana positively smirked when she turned around. "You like her."

Jan liked what he saw today, for sure. But past experience taught him to be patient, in any case. "I'm not here to date, Nana."

She shrugged. "Nobody's stopping you. Now help me with your Pop. He's all but asleep in his chair."

After his grandad was settled in bed with Nana close by, Jan sat at the kitchen table to catch up on his emails. When the wind blew hard, hissing as it slapped against the glass, he wondered how April was managing. The weather was turning colder yet again. But the snow would end after midnight, and cold was just part of Pittsburgh this time of year. He decided April probably had a plan for that too and went back to his computer, though those deep brown eyes and darker lashes kept pulling his attention time and again.

*

April spread another quilt on her bed and crawled under the covers, covered neck to ankle with fleece pajamas and a thick pair of socks that she would undoubtedly kick off in the middle of the night. She'd tried sleeping in little more than a comfortable t-shirt when she first got to Pittsburgh, but the first cold snap in the old house had put a stop to that.

The new double-paned windows she'd had installed last summer had gone a long way to fixing the worst of the drafts. Now, she just had to suffer through a few more weeks of freezing temperatures before the new siding and insulation would be installed, then she could get serious about making over the inside.

April tugged the soft cotton sheets up to her neck, then twitched the layers of electric blanket, comforter, and quilt in place. The blanket warmed up the bed quick enough, but she didn't like to sleep with it on. She clicked it off and rested her head against the cold pillow.

Here, in the quiet of her room, she unpacked the myriad of emotions of the day, from the embarrassment of the morning to the unexpected shock of attraction for Jan Larsen this evening. She'd been startled to discover the voice this morning belonged to a reddish-blond lumberjack with a cheeky grin and sharp eyes that didn't miss much. Given the way he shoveled snow, April could hardly believe he was an IT kind of guy with a laptop and not a steelworker.

But *that* would be judging, right? And April hated when people sized her up on her looks rather than her skills. If April knew anything, it was that she was "cute." Cute butt, cute in jeans, oh-your-face-is-cute, isn't-she-dressed-cute. She'd learned to live with it, but having to prove again and again that a cute face didn't mean she was forever fifteen and couldn't negotiate a salary contract was a constant annoyance.

She had to admit it was flattering to know she was being checked out (several times, ha!). But she got that at work often enough to not take it seriously, especially when *some* patients didn't understand that being nice was part of her job, not an indication of interest.

Jan didn't act weird. He was polite to her and sweet with his grandparents, both big pluses in her book. And he'd apologized with a flush of pink staining his pale cheeks, which was an even bigger check. April had learned *that* lesson on boyfriend number one in high school.

April wasn't the kind to fantasize over a guy she'd just met. At the moment, her sheets were more interesting, and she snuggled into her pillow for a good night's sleep. But Jan sneaked into her dreams with a low chuckle and soft singing that kept her company through the night.

*

"So, how's the neighbor?" Maria asked. Phillip poured himself a cup, listening with interest.

April huddled around her coffee as she leaned against the door of the break room, holding it like the most precious object she owned. (At the moment, it was.) "Mr. Larsen is gonna be fine. I went by this morning, and he was reading the paper. Had his knee all propped up and everything. Mrs. Larsen seemed pretty chill, so I'd guess he had a good night."

"And the grandson?"

"Was in the backyard clearing out those old bushes."

Maria laughed. "I guess he likes the cold. It's not supposed to get above thirty-three today."

"He was singing again."

"Seriously? What was he singing?"

"*A Hazy Shade of Winter*," April grumbled. "Talk about an earworm that won't go away."

"Could be worse."

April plugged her ears. "Do *not* start singing *Gilligan's Island*."

Maria and Phillip both groaned. "Now *I've* got an earworm. Thanks a lot."

Phillip waggled his finger at her. "I liked *A Hazy Shade of Winter* better."

"Happy to help." April headed back down the hallway to pick up the chart for her next scan. A young girl this time who'd torn a ligament while sledding with her friends. "Solange Walters?" she called out.

The girl in a bright pink puffy jacket stood up, along with both parents who were pretending not to hover too protectively. April smiled at all of them. "Hi, I'm April."

*

Two days later, she had *Cold as Ice* stuck in her head after shoveling the whole driveway. Jan cheerfully belted out the tune as he squirted the windows of his SUV with some concoction that instantly melted the frozen water. April absolutely did not notice the way his jeans cupped his butt or the cheeky grin he sent her as he got in his car and drove away.

The following week was a rousing baritone rendition of *Let it Snow* while she scraped ice off her front steps in a futile effort to get it off before the predicted two inches of snow finished falling. Fat flakes swirled around her head as she scraped. Her fingers were frozen, and she couldn't feel her cheeks under the heavy scarf she'd wrapped around her head. As the notes wafted across the yard, April had to stifle the urge to stuff the whole scarf in Jan's mouth.

Honestly, it was enough to make April want to crawl into bed until spring. Bears absolutely had the right idea.

There was *Winter Wonderland* the day after that when they got another inch of freezing wet snow that needed the miracle snow melt stuff to make her steps walkable again. She'd found a whole bucket of it just outside her front door with a recipe card in neat printing and signed, "J." She looked up to find Jan pouring a similar bucket on his grandparents' driveway, whistling the cheery tune as he sloshed it about.

April dropped off enchiladas for their dinner that night, along with a whole container of lemon cookies. She wasn't sure who was happier, Jan or Steiner. But the slow smile Jan gave her did melty things to her insides, and she shuffled back off to her house a little warmer than she was before.

She got a reprieve once the sun came out. At the same time, Steiner got a checkup and was cleared for physical rehabilitation. Mr. and Mrs. Larsen celebrated by having April over for dinner: a nice broiled salmon with roasted yellow squash and zucchini.

"What are you doing for your birthday this year?" Nina asked.

April poked at a piece of squash. "A taco bar, I think. I got a new grill when they went on sale last fall, and I want to try it out. My mom, my sister, and my brother want to come too. It should be a good time."

"And if it snows?" Steiner scooted the bread rolls closer to her. "Take one."

She sighed as she plucked one out of the basket. "Do it all in the oven and it won't taste half as good." She shrugged. "I'll still make margaritas, though. Maria liked them." She stuffed the bite in her mouth.

"Maria?" That was from Jan as he reached for his water glass.

"Friend at work. One of my Thursday night crew."

"We all liked them," Nina agreed. "Jan, you'll come, even if you have your own place by then."

Jan ducked his head in agreement. "Sure. Who's the Thursday night crew?"

Swallowing, April said, "Me, Maria, Phillip, Shonda, and any tagalongs. We like to hang on Thursday nights. Sometimes a movie, sometimes we make dinner. Sometimes we hit a bar after work. You found a place?"

"Put a bid in yesterday over in Wilkinsburg." He quirked his mouth, betraying his excitement. "Thursdays sound like fun."

"You should go sometime." Nina got a bright smile. "The house is just two streets from where my parents had their bakery."

April was familiar with the location of the old bakery, as Nina had shown it to her last year. There was a deli in the space now that Nina had insisted April try. "It's a pretty neighborhood," she agreed.

"Place will need some work," Jan replied. April tried not to laugh, because it was such a Steiner answer. Nina caught her eye and winked even as Jan continued, "When's your siding going up?"

"It's supposed to snow again on Friday, but the weatherman says we'll get a good warm up after that. The company swears I'm first on the list and they'll get it up and painted before the next round of freezing temperatures." April speared her last bite of salmon and ate it.

"Good," Jan rumbled. "What kind of siding are you putting up?"

As April explained her pick, she discovered she liked the way Jan genuinely listened. He even pulled out his phone and noted the brand she chose and the contracting company.

"Did you get a bid from the Carleton kid?" Steiner asked.

"I did. I liked the package Sideworks put together better, plus they have their own crews, not subs. That's important to me after all those storms in Texas."

"Carleton does good work."

"Pop," Jan chided. "I know you're loyal to the neighborhood, but it's not like April's getting someone from Jersey."

Nina laughed at that. "Don't get grumpy, love. She's got a good sense about these things."

And that, April decided, was about the nicest thing anyone had said about her.

When dinner was done, April and Nina cleaned up the kitchen while Jan helped Steiner up the stairs. It didn't take him long, and then they could hear the periodic *thunk* against the floorboards as Steiner moved about with his walker.

The two women had just wrapped up when Jan strolled in. April wiped her hands on a dishtowel, noting how tired Nina seemed. "I'm going home, Mrs. Larsen. I've got a few things to do before work tomorrow."

Accepting the polite excuse, Nina gave her a quick hug. "You do that. Now, be careful, the steps are still damp."

"Yes, ma'am."

"Can I walk you home, April?" Jan asked in that quiet, warm voice that sent a thrill (Really? When did that become a thing?) through April.

Her mouth fell open a little. She shot Nina a confused smile—and the old woman beamed right back at her. Jan licked his lips. Nervous, April realized, as he waited for her answer. "Uh, Yeah. Yes. Yes. I'd like that."

Jan held out his hand. April took it.

If fifty-year-old courting rituals seemed odd in this time and place, right now it was perfect. The heat and sizzle where their fingers touched only grew as they wound their way through the living room and out the front door. Hand-in-hand, they descended the stairs, and then Jan tucked her hand in his elbow as they meandered toward her house.

"I like you, April Garza," Jan said. "I like the way you think."

April's heart stuttered at his blunt declaration. "I like you too." (Holy cow, was this really happening?) She fumbled for words as they reached her house. "You're nice. *Really* nice," she emphasized as they took the stairs arm in arm.

"Thought the ladies didn't go for nice," he teased, green eyes dancing.

"This lady does," she insisted. "A 'bad boy' is just another way of saying he's an immature idiot demanding all the attention."

He laughed outright at that as they reached her front porch. "I think I've met a few of those."

April let go of Jan's arm so she could face him. "So have I," she agreed, as her heart thumped in double-time.

With a long breath that betrayed a few nerves, Jan told her, "It didn't seem right to say anything until Pop was getting back on his feet. I didn't want to make things weird. But it seems right now." He lifted his hand to brush the backs of his fingers along her cheek. "Can I kiss you?" He tucked a lock of hair over her ear, his first finger sliding down one long strand.

A shiver of pure need ran through her. Happiness bloomed, and her cheeks felt hot. "I'd like that." She took one step closer, setting her hands on his shoulders. They moved at the same time, meeting in the middle with a brush of lips in a tentative exploration.

First, they had to figure out how to fit together. April tilted her head and shuffled a little closer. Jan leaned in, one hand sliding into her hair. And then it was heat and need as she tasted his lips, claiming them for hers alone.

Jan moaned into her mouth, pulling back just long enough for her to see his eyes glitter with need. He dove back in, this time with parted lips and a tongue that coaxed hers into dancing with his.

Hoo boy, yeah, she was on board.

She was five seconds from climbing him like a tree when he broke the kiss, panting hard. His mouth widened into a delighted smile as she leaned in to steal one more quick kiss. With a satisfied smirk, she jerked a thumb toward her front door. "Do we take this inside?"

Jan made an unhappy noise, darting a look back at his grandparents' house. "Maybe not."

"Maybe not," she agreed. But she leaned in to peck his cheek as she opened her door. "I like you, Jan Larsen. You can darken my doorstep just any ol' time."

She darted inside, closing the door with a wink to him. Then leaned against the door so she could listen to him clomp down the stairway.

Then she fumbled for her phone to call her sister. "Gracie? I think I like a guy." April winced at her sister's squeal of happiness.

*

Pittsburgh flirted with freezing temperatures for two solid weeks, giving Jan and April ample time before her next house renovation to flirt too. They'd gone on a handful of evening walks to Frick Park after Pop was settled and slipped off to the movies last Saturday afternoon. April told him about her family back in Texas. He'd noted how her accent became more pronounced when talking about home, finding it sweet when it happened. He told her about his parents and losing his dad and how his mom was coping.

The speed at which Jan developed serious kinds of feelings for April scared him a bit. The stolen kisses on her doorstep weren't nearly enough to slake his thirst for her.

He couldn't wait until he had his own place again. He'd like to cook her dinner.

Nana and Pop had stayed remarkably quiet on the subject. They were happy at the development, that was clear, but mostly they stayed out of his business.

When Jan pulled into their driveway after a long day at work, he darted a look at April's house out of habit.

"Oh fuck," he breathed.

Like a good many houses in the borough, the exposed parts of the basement floor, the first floor, and the front of April's house were all brick, but the second floor had siding on the other three walls. Or should have siding. The wall facing Jan was nothing more than insulation with *Tyvek* stamped in ink on the outside. It looked like the contractors had taken measures to cover up any exposed gaps to protect the house from rain and ice, but those efforts wouldn't do much for the cold. Pittsburgh would have freezing temperatures by noon tomorrow, and this storm promised to be a bad one.

April paced on her front porch, phone to her ear as the first raindrops from this round of storms began to fall.

Jan parked his car and darted up the stairs. "Nana? Pop?"

Pop puttered around the kitchen making dinner. He beetled his brows at Jan. "Stop yelling, boy. Ain't deaf. Yet."

Catching himself, Jan lowered his voice. "I thought the contractor was going to finish April's siding today?"

"They didn't?" Now Pop looked worried. He poked at the sauce he was stirring up. "Got enough here for an extra plate. Would you let her know dinner will be ready in an hour? And she can stay here if she wants."

Since that was exactly was Jan was hoping, he zipped over to April's place just as she finished her call.

She looked miserable huddled up in her jacket, with a red nose and tears that she did her best to blink back. He opened his arms, unsure if she wanted a hug or not. She leaned in, wrapping both arms around his middle. She was tall enough to be cheek to cheek with him, and he brushed a kiss on her temple. "What happened?" he murmured.

"Somehow my order got shorted and nobody noticed until late yesterday." She waved at the house. "It was supposed to be delivered by noon so they could finish. They got everything that's up caulked and painted, but the truck bringing in the materials got stuck in Chicago." April wiped her face with one hand as she stepped back, the other hand sliding down to catch his. "Come on. It's too cold already."

Jan followed her into the living room. The house was definitely on the cool side, but that could just be because April hadn't turned the furnace on with the work being done today.

She shivered, darting to the wall to crank up the heat. As she turned the dial, she told him, "I'm almost afraid to go upstairs."

"Your bedroom is on that side?"

"And the bathroom. Even though the plumbing isn't on the outside walls, I'm worried the pipes are going to freeze tomorrow."

Frozen pipes could mean broken plumbing when the water warmed up. Jan wasn't sure how many tricks April knew. One, at least, when she promptly turned all the faucets on to let a thin, steady stream of water through. But given the raw temperatures coming, even he wasn't sure that would be enough. "Need any help keeping them warm? Pop's got a couple of space heaters we can set up."

"I've got one for my bedroom."

"Then I'll get the other for the bathroom."

April hesitated, and Jan wasn't sure if she didn't want to accept his help or if she was thinking it through. In the end, she decided, "I'll take it. Got any other good ideas?"

"Nana and Pop offered their extra room."

But she shook her head. "I'll worry if I'm not here."

"Extra blankets and a warm dinner? Pop's making spaghetti."

She gave him a weary smile as she rubbed her hands together. "Okay."

At dinner, Nana and Pop asked April no less than three times if she wanted to stay the night. April declined each time, but accepted the loan of blankets and spare heaters.

Afterward, Jan retrieved the space heaters from his grandparents' garage and carried them upstairs to April's bathroom. Like the rest of the house, it was in sore need of an update. But it was neat and clean, and April talked through her plans for the remodel with pride as she plugged in the heater. She squinted at the window. "I could nail one of my old blankets over that."

"That's a good idea," Jan blurted in relief.

April barked out a surprised laugh. "How long have you been trying not to mention that one?"

"Pop tends to tell everyone everything they need to do for anything. Been getting the laundry list since I put the offer in on that house."

"Did you get it?"

"Yeah, paperwork is going through tomorrow," he said with pride. "The sellers wanted to lease it back for a few weeks until they can move into their new place. Since I'm here through March with Pop anyway, I don't mind the extra cash."

April threw her arms around him with a big squeeze. "I'm so happy for you!"

He caught her in a hard hug. "Not like it's my first house," he deflected—though, yeah, he was excited. She smelled good too.

"But it's what you want now," she insisted with one more squeeze before she let go. "And it's close to your work like you wanted."

"Close to Nana and Pop too." The sparkle in her eyes egged him on a bit, and he caught her fingers to drop a kiss in her palm.

April smiled. "You worry about them."

"They don't need a babysitter, just a helping hand now and again."

"Told you, you're nice." April captured his face in her hands to brush a kiss on his lips.

He growled. "Not that nice." With that, he kissed her thoroughly enough to leave her flushed. His body awakened, his cock hardening uncomfortably in his jeans.

To his surprise, she slid her hands under his jacket and tugged at his shirt so that she could dip her fingers under the fabric. Skin against skin, he burned where she touched.

She grinned against his mouth. "How far do you want to take this, Jan?"

"I'm not stupid, April. I'll take anything you'll give me."

*

Sex with Jan turned out to be surprisingly easy. Maybe it leaned more into hookup territory, considering they didn't make it past the bathroom counter, but Jan was sweet and thorough as they fumbled through buttons and zippers together, then did the same with a condom from her bathroom drawer moments later.

April had both hands braced on the countertop to keep from falling in the sink as Jan stroked inside her with increasing urgency, his hands firmly clamped on her hips. She was getting close to her own release, but not fast enough to keep pace with him. Frustrated, she demanded, "Jan, I need—" she gasped as he slowed his stroke to a slow drag. "Not that, damn it."

He chuckled. "More?"

"Need your hand on my clit," she blurted.

Jan stopped only long enough to free a hand, then he created a rhythm of deep strokes and flickering taps that had April flying in no time at all. He followed, coming with a great growl of her name.

April panted in the aftermath, sure that was the best sex she'd had in months. "More please, and in a bed next time?"

"All right." Jan gently slid out of her, handily disposing of the condom. He glanced down, looking his pants. They lay on the floor, discarded with hers on top of a pile of shoes, socks, and thermal underwear. "And I'd like to see all of you too." He drew a hand down the vee of her scrub top, layered as it was over a thermal tee, then brushed fingertips across a nipple.

She shivered at the light touch. "Yeah, okay. I'm in." She blew out her breath as she reached for the pants he handed to her. "So sex is a yes. What about dating? I'm off Sunday, or if dating isn't a thing, the Thursday night crew is doing darts at the tavern nearest the hospital this week." She blurted all that out in a rush, nervous now that the sex ice was broken. She'd thought they were dating and moving toward this, but maybe she'd misread his intentions?

But when Jan leaned in for a gentle kiss that turned into a thorough exploration of her mouth, her heart fluttered into place.

"Dating is good," he told her. "Sunday works. We can catch a matinee and an early dinner."

April grinned with relief, pressing another kiss to his lips. "I'll put it on the calendar."

*

They got their date, April got her siding, then Jan's schedule became a tangled mess with Pop's rehab schedule and a new server upgrade that turned Jan's days and nights upside down.

Still, he surprised her with coffee one morning on her patio on her off day, and she took him out for a late night trip for drinks on his. She held his hand under the table while they listened to the band play.

Jan's closing date was set for the last week of March. The previous owners promised to move out by mid-April, giving Pop plenty of time to finish rehab before Jan moved out.

Another series of snowy days meant shoveling the stuff at odd hours. He pulled out a little Mick Jagger, singing *Winter* loud enough for April to plug her ears as she scraped her own staircase.

The first morning Jan got back on day shift, he grinned as April happily pressed a button on a new remote and her garage door lifted overhead without a squeak. He pumped his fist in victory. She blew him a kiss as she shuffled through the slush.

*

From the dining room doorway, April looked over the worn staircase and loose railing leading to the basement and garage one last time. She'd studied it from every angle and watched a dozen YouTube videos to see if she could make the repairs herself. Years of traffic had taken their toll on the treads and risers. Half a century back, someone had decided that outdoor carpeting them was a good idea. Sometime in the last decade, somebody else had decided to try to pull all that up, didn't do a very good job of it, and coated the treads with a varnish that turned into a Slip 'n Slide the moment something wet touched it.

April was left with a fabulous trip hazard that she avoided at all costs. Every bit of the mess would all have to come up. There was good news, though. The stair structure itself seemed to be in good shape, though the handrails needed a whole new set of anchors. (She'd bet money somebody had slipped on the stairs and grabbed at the railing so hard that it had pulled out of the plaster.)

If she was lucky, really lucky, she'd get it all done in three weekends, and April's days of shuffling down slick and icy steps outside in the mornings would be a thing of the past. With that in mind, she pulled out her sander, hammer, chisels, scrapers, and a thick pair of gloves. She cranked up her music and got to work, starting with a big container of chemical stripper.

On Monday, she happily reported to Maria that the steps were free of carpet and adhesive, even if her shoulders were sore from all the scraping.

The following weekend was spent sanding every last bit of wood on the treads, risers, and stringers. Jan helped her with that, and she filled him in about her plans for her party while they worked. She'd hold the party the first weekend in April, which gave her just one more weekend to finish the stairs, and one to clean the house and make preparations for the party.

If lunch was spent making out on one of the newly sanded steps, nobody tattled. If they ended up in the shower together to wash off the dust at the end of the day, well, it was just convenient and they were saving water, right?

Jan slept over that night for the first time, and April decided it was nice waking up warm and toasty with her back cushioned by his furred chest. It had snowed overnight, though, and while April sanded down the handrail, Jan scooped the slush out of both of their driveways. She had the garage door open and listened while he cranked out Sia's cover of *California Dreaming*.

April had it stuck in her head for the rest of the day.

It wasn't that she minded Jan singing. He had a nice voice, for sure, but did he have to be so *cheerful* about the whole shoveling snow thing?

Monday brought another round of snow, and another round of scraping her front stairs so she could get to her car. She couldn't *wait* until the basement stairs were finished. The drive to work was slow and slippery, but not the worst she'd driven in. Parking in the employee lot was yet another chore: putting snow mats on the windows to keep any more ice from sticking and covering the mirrors with plastic bags. Her car looked rather silly, but so did all the other cars.

She danced in place while waiting for the bus to arrive in a futile attempt to keep warm in the icy breeze.

Maria and Phillip appeared, both of them eyeing her "heat dance" with amusement.

"How are you cold wearing all that?" Maria asked, glaring at April's boots and heavy coat. "Are you naked under there or something?"

"Ha ha." April rubbed her gloved hands together. "It's the wind, I think."

Phillip shook his head. He had nothing more than a sweater on over his scrubs. "Or you're from Texas, and it shows."

"I'll remember that when we're drinking margaritas on my patio and you're bitching about the heat in July."

Maria flashed her a grin, and the three of them complained about the weather all the way to the hospital.

That night and the next, April ran a fine grit sandpaper over every last inch of the staircase, treads, and railing, then cleaned it all up so the wood was silky soft to touch. It was safe to walk on now, though she'd go barefoot until the wood was stained and sealed over the weekend. She practically danced down the basement stairs on Wednesday. One push of a button in the garage, and the garage door opened.

The day geared up to be bright and cheerful, without a snow cloud in sight. April only had to clear out a tiny patch of ice off the driveway before backing out into the morning sun. Coming home made her giddy. She only had to touch the button in her car to get the garage door open. She drove right inside and the brand new steps were right there waiting, even if she did pull her boots off before climbing the bare wood staircase.

April called her sister to crow about the victory.

Wednesday turned out to be nearly perfect, with highs in the 50s that made April positively gleeful—that is until she caught the weather forecast on the evening news. "Seriously?" she yelled at the TV.

A knock on the door interrupted her disgruntled complaining. She yanked the door open.

Jan still had his hand in the air, and those bright green eyes widened. "Hi?"

"I can't stain the stairs this weekend. It's gonna be too cold," she complained. "It's March, for heaven's sake. Snow tomorrow. Snow Friday. Highs in the 20s until Tuesday. And there's another round of snow forecast for the weekend after that."

Jan opened his arms, and April went right in. Here, at least, she could be warm and cozy.

"It's the way it is, sweetheart. Can't do anything but learn to live with it," he told her.

"I want my stairs done, and I don't want it to snow on my birthday," she whined. Then she shook her head. "Ugh. I'm annoying myself. Dinner?" she said brightly.

Jan laughed, kissing her firmly on the lips. "What kind?"

"Are you staying?"

"I can stay. Pop's slow, but he can do the stairs now. Nana will call if they need help. She promised."

April still didn't know how she felt about the Larsens knowing she was sleeping with their grandson, but their attitude hadn't changed a whit, so she assumed all was well. It probably helped that she delivered peanut butter cookies at least once a week.

"Food first, then," she decided, then dove in for another kiss that ended with April scraping her nails under Jan's shirt and flicking at his nipple.

His swift inhalation told her how much he liked that. "If we order pizza," he cajoled as he dropped kisses along her neck, "we can do this while we wait."

April pulled up the app on her phone, thumbed a new order, and hit send before tossing the phone on the couch. "Thirty minutes."

"I can work with that."

April shivered at Jan's words, but with that kind of invitation, she wasn't going to let it go unanswered. While Jan sucked kisses along her collarbone, April toyed with his nipple until he groaned. Jan countered with an arm around her waist while he traced a line along her neck. One hand cupped her hip, pulling her close. But it wasn't enough.

"Keep me warm?" she said, admiring the way his shoulders stretched out his button-down shirt.

"Anytime, honey." Jan shed his shirt and undershirt, leaving his upper half bare. It wasn't fair. He didn't even get goosebumps from the cold, though that might have been because his chest and stomach had a fine layer of reddish-brown hair dipping down into the waistband of his jeans. She skimmed her fingers through the soft curls, smiling at the way it tickled.

Jan *mmmm'd* his pleasure, even as he managed the button and zipper one-handed, unfastening them so that April could see the hard bulge peeking out.

She licked her lips, darting in to drop a kiss on his jaw. Jan tugged at her shirt. She glanced down, forgetting for a moment what she was wearing and how to get out of it. April wrinkled her nose at her outfit. Her blue scrub top was covered in tiny yellow suns just because it made her feel cheerful on cold days. "This is probably the least sexy outfit in my closet," she said ruefully, "and that's not saying much because all my work clothes are scrubs." She reached for the bottom edge to pull it over her head. Jan helped her shove it off, letting out a pleased hum at the blue lace bra she wore.

"I'm in IT," he countered as he stepped out of his boots, hopping a little as he did. "Jeans plus polo or button-down shirt every day. It's not much better." He rubbed a thumb over the top edge of the bra fabric. "But knowing now what's underneath?" he said with a smile. "You've got my attention."

April ditched her shoes and socks, then did her best to wiggle out of her thermal underwear and scrub pants at the same time. It wasn't sexy, especially when she instantly got goosebumps from the cold. But she forgot all that when Jan rubbed his hands along her arms, pressing trailing kisses from her mouth to her jaw with little nips. Somewhere in there, he ditched his jeans, and she could see the same dusting of dark hair scattering down his thighs. (Maybe now wasn't the time to admit she wanted to run her fingers through all that too. Later, she promised herself.)

She pulled him down on the couch, appreciating his warmth as he settled between her legs. They were hip to hip, with a scrap of cloth and another of lace barely separating them. When his cock brushed her clit, she gasped. "Do that again."

Jan didn't do that. Instead, he thumbed across the lace of her bra just over her nipple, making it peak. "You like this?"

"I do. A lot. You?" She did the same to him, liking the way he pebbled under the tips of her fingers. Just for good measure, she drew her nails around his areola.

He let out a happy sigh. "Yeah."

She leaned in to lick at his nipple, shoving him upward so she could reach it. He hovered over her while she played, and she could feel him twitch against her folds when she nipped.

Abruptly, Jan rose up on his knees. He pressed a hand to his bulge, breathing out hard. "I'm gonna embarrass myself in a minute if I'm not careful."

April laughed. "Strip and you don't have to wait." She reached for his underwear to drag it downward, tossing it to the side. Jan tugged her thong off, dropping it to the floor as he stretched out on the couch. He fumbled for his jeans to dig a condom out. With one in hand, April slung a leg over his body to sit astride his hips.

Once she rolled the condom on his cock, Jan laced his fingers with hers. He drew their joined hands to his lips to kiss her knuckles. "I love a woman who knows what she wants."

The thrill of energy that shot from April's hands to her brain wasn't entirely unexpected, but the sudden ache in her heart was. Jan had sneaked right in and taken hold with his quiet determination and cheerful demeanor. "There's a lot to want here." She shifted, taking his length inside.

"Damn." Jan sucked in his breath, fingers clutching her hips as he bucked up into her. His green eyes fogged over. "April, sweetheart, I want—"

April rose and fell, looking for the angle that worked best. She found it just as Jan circled, then tapped her clit with his thumb.

"Jan—" Her voice came out needy.

Words were lost to the rhythm of two bodies connecting. Jan's thumb slipped along her folds as she leaned back to take him deeper. She got lost in the sensations, and her orgasm caught her by surprise. She shivered as she came. Jan followed with a soft grunt as he emptied himself into her.

He tugged her down to hold her against his chest. It was nice here, breathing in tandem as their heartbeats slowed. They dozed there, tangled together, until April's phone chirped with a notification.

A one-eyed glance at her phone told her the pizza was on its way. "Ten minutes or the pizza delivery guy gets an eyeful."

That got a laugh, and they danced around getting dressed as they traded kisses between layers.

April didn't mind the cold so much that night, not with Jan keeping her warm as they snuggled in bed and watched a movie until they fell asleep.

*

When April woke, she wasn't happy about the empty bed, but there was a note from Jan.

Not sure how all the covers ended up on your side of the bed. Would like to return soon to investigate. XOX—J

Sure enough, she'd burritoed in the sheets and blankets. Oh well. Jan was warm enough to fend for himself.

April dressed for work and headed downstairs for her first cup of coffee.

As she sipped, she couldn't miss the big arrow drawn on the bright pink sticky note stuck to her back door, complete with a smiley face and signed, "XOX—J."

It really shouldn't have surprised her when she found a three foot tall snowman built on a little wooden frame over the firepit in her backyard that morning. Complete with a carrot for a nose, twigs for arms, and acorns for eyes and mouth, it was pretty cute. It was the first day of spring, after all.

"Snowman Burning Day?" called out Nina from next door, entirely too cheerful to be innocent.

"Looks like it," April yelled back. "Want to help me light it tonight?"

"We'd love to. I'll bring cake."

Phillip, Maria, her girlfriend Angel, and Shonda got texts from Jan to come by after work to help with the impromptu celebration. They brought Thai for their dinner, to April's glee. Steiner took careful steps across the two backyards, but his newly repaired knee didn't give him any trouble. Nina handed over a scrumptious lemon cake with thick, creamy icing on top.

Jan was last to arrive, still wearing a tie and button down from work. He was smug, for sure, as he handed over a bottle of wine, but April rewarded him anyway with a kiss that made the Thursday night crew whistle and cheer.

Over dessert, they lit the snowman. As it melted, April had to keep piling up new wood as the old stuff got wet. It made for a smoky mess in her firepit, but the laughter was worth it as they watched it burn.

Nina raised her glass for a toast, "Happy Snowman Burning Day, April. Here's hoping for an early spring and no snow on your birthday!"

"Here, here!" Jan echoed before he drank.

As Jan kept an eye on his grandparents, April decided then and there that it could snow on her birthday all it wanted. Winter, it seemed, hadn't been bad at all.

About the Author

Annika Steele began writing in third grade: an illustrated fanfic of the Atari game "Defender." After filling notebooks, utterly unaware that she was a writer at heart, she abandoned her stories somewhere around her third year of college, probably when the typewriter/word processor died and was replaced by the roommate's new 386. A ridiculous number of years later, she stumbled across a fanfic site, put fingers to keyboard, and hasn't stopped writing since.

Website: annikasteele.com
Twitter: @annikasteelewr

Naked Attraction
♥
Liv Honeywell

Story Information

Holiday: World Naked Gardening Day
Holiday Date: May 2 (First Saturday in May)
Heat Rating: 4
Relationship Type: M/F
Major Trigger Warnings: Minor character death, very mild BDSM—some holding down and teasing, voyeurism.

Juliet is enjoying relaxing in her recently inherited roof garden on an unusually hot day for May in the UK when she decides to take part in World Naked Gardening Day. It's freeing and extremely pleasurable to bare all outdoors, and she finds that dancing naked is great fun too. Except she's not as alone as she thinks.

Naked Attraction

"So, do tell what's got you all ruffled. You're practically red in the face." Helen's eyes narrowed, and she paused in kneading her cinnamon and raisin loaf. "Is it a man? It is, isn't it?"

"How could you possibly know that?" Juliet gaped at her.

Helen regarded her niece fondly over the top of her glasses. "I have known you since you were born. I remember when you first started noticing boys. Like that—What was his name? Dozy? You could barely string a sentence together around him."

Juliet laughed. "It was Dawson, as you well know. Though to be fair, Dozy was a better description for him."

"Indeed. Anyway, out with it. Make an old woman very happy and tell me you've found someone wonderful." Helen finished kneading the loaf and popped it back into its bowl to rise then washed and dried her hands. She picked up her walking stick and made her way into the lounge.

"Oh please. You're not old." Juliet picked up the used dishes and dropped them carefully into hot, soapy water. She wiped her hands on a tea towel and then followed her aunt through with the tea tray.

"Well, I am ninety-four, so I might just qualify, dear." Helen lowered herself into her favorite chair near the bank of windows.

Juliet dropped onto the sofa opposite her aunt and poured them both a cup of tea. "You are the least old person I know. You've got more energy than I have."

"Thank you. But if you think you can distract me, you're mistaken, missy. Tell me about this man that has you all aflutter."

Juliet laughed. "Okay, okay. Though there's not a lot to tell really."

"But you'd like there to be," Helen said shrewdly.

"I think I would. I don't really know him, but every time I see him, he makes me—" Juliet searched for the right word. "He makes me fizz. I feel like I'm a teenager all over again," she said, her eyes sparkling.

Helen smiled. "That's exactly how it was with me and your Uncle George. Oh, that man. I do miss him. You know, I never so much as looked at anyone else after I met him, and neither did he. And that's what I want for you. So tell me everything. How did you two meet?"

"I can't say we have met exactly. I almost ran into him a few weeks ago when I was on my way from the office to see you. I was looking down at my phone and didn't see him until it was almost too late. I managed to stop just before I walked right into him and knocked his drink all over his nice white shirt. Can you imagine?" Juliet blushed at the memory, absent-mindedly stirring milk into her tea.

"Nooo," said Helen, leaning forward as she listened. "Good thing you stopped in time. What did he say?"

"Well, I apologized, and he was really nice about it. He just smiled and told me not to worry, cracked a joke about saving his coffee from disaster, and that was it, really. But did he ever look good in a suit! I couldn't stop thinking about him afterwards, though I didn't think I'd see him again."

"But you did."

"Yes, we've bumped into each other—not literally this time—quite a bit over the last few weeks. I think he might have an office in one of those buildings near mine."

Helen leaned forward even more. "Really? What makes you think that?"

"It's always around there that I see him, so I just thought that must be it. Why?"

"Oh, no reason," Helen said, airily. "Just curious. As ever. You know me."

Juliet frowned but let it go. She took a sip of her tea, "Anyway, we've said 'hello' each time we've seen each other, but we both always seem to be in a hurry, so there hasn't been time for much else. Well, until today at least."

"Do tell. What happened today?"

"Oh, you really couldn't make this up." Juliet laughed. "It couldn't have been coordinated that perfectly if we'd tried."

"Go on."

"I was going into the big post office, and he was coming out. And you know they have those old-fashioned revolving doors?"

"I do. Well?" Helen said impatiently.

"I was in a rush, and I thought I could slip into one of the door sections just behind him as he was coming out so I could get inside faster, but it didn't work out too well as I had a lot of shopping bags, and he was carrying a bunch of balloons."

"What kind of balloons?"

Juliet looked puzzled. "Is that important?"

Helen waved her hand. "Oh no. Just—"

"Curious. Yes, you said. Is there something you're not telling me?"

Helen looked the picture of innocence. "Of course not, dear. Carry on with your tale."

"Okay. I didn't take much notice of the balloons, to be honest. There was a lot of pink, though I did notice the present he was carrying was covered in fire engine paper which didn't really go with all the pink."

Helen coughed sharply.

"Are you all right, Aunt Helen?"

"Oh yes, perfectly, dear." Helen picked up her cup and took a sip of her own tea. "What happened then?"

"Honestly, I've no idea what happened exactly, but somehow we ended up all tangled together. We had to step back onto the street and sort everything out. It didn't help that he was laughing, and so was I, so it took us a while to get free."

Helen laughed. "Oh priceless. This is just like one of those romantic comedies I like. And then?"

"Well, nothing, unfortunately. I did think for a moment that he was going to ask me out, and I know I thought about asking him, but then he looked at his watch and said he was sorry, but he had to go. And that was it."

"Dear me. So you don't even know his name?"

"No, I don't know a thing about him. Except that he's very tall, dark, and gorgeous. Oh, and he has what looks like the top of a really intriguing tattoo on his neck that I'd like to see in full. From what I could see above his collar, it looks like the tip of a bird's wing." Juliet smiled. "And I may have mentioned, he looks spectacular in a suit. But none of that tells me who he is." She sighed, heavily. "Fingers crossed I bump into him again."

Helen patted her hand. "Oh I'm sure you will, dear. I have a feeling about these things."

*

Three Months Later

Shrugging out of his jacket, Josh Carter undid his tie and opened the top button of his shirt. Today of all days, when the temperature was through the roof, he'd had to put on a suit and spend a couple of hours in a stuffy office for a client meeting instead of being outdoors at one of his building sites where he belonged, enjoying such an unexpectedly warm day for early May.

Finally, he stepped into the cool, air-conditioned lobby of his building and headed for the elevator. He pushed in his keycard and leaned back against the wall. He still couldn't get used to the fact that this elegant building he'd visited for years but had never been able to afford was now his new home.

The elevator pinged open on the top floor, and Josh stepped out and opened his door.

He dropped his briefcase, jacket, and keys on the table near the door then rolled his sleeves up and opened another couple of buttons on his shirt before looking around. He headed for the kitchen and grabbed an ice-cold beer from the fridge, rolling the cold glass of the bottle across the back of his neck, before popping the top open and taking a long swig.

He wandered through the large open-plan seating and dining area, opening the windows onto the balcony and mentally planning where he could put his own furniture, what he would keep of what was already there, and how he would make the place feel like his own. He went back into the lounge and dropped into a chair, taking another drink from his beer and staring out across the incredible view of Manchester and the surrounding countryside below. He didn't think he'd ever get tired of seeing it.

His mind went back to the day when he'd found out the place was his. He smiled as he remembered his friend, Helen. He'd been shocked when he'd realized she'd left him this amazing apartment. Though he'd still much rather have her around to chat to.

She'd been an older lady, one of his dad's friends, but when his dad had passed on, he'd kept in touch with her and helped her out with jobs around the place. He'd been there for her when he could just to keep her company, and he'd grown fond of her himself. She'd been one of those people who was endlessly positive and warm, no matter what was going on for her, and she'd loved to laugh. Just spending time with her could make anybody's day better, and he did miss her.

He'd known she'd owned property across the city, but he'd had no idea she'd been planning to leave him anything in her will, never mind this place. But he was beyond grateful both for having known her and, thanks to her, for now having somewhere permanent to live where he could really begin to feel like he was home instead of moving endlessly from one faceless hotel to another depending on where his projects took him. Now he could really put down roots and build the company up the way he'd been wanting to do for a while.

He stared out of the floor-to-ceiling windows again, his eyes not really taking in the view as his thoughts turned to the stunning woman who'd been occupying his attention these last couple of months. What he wouldn't give to have a proper conversation with her and get to know her.

He kept seeing her coming and going near his office building, and they'd exchanged smiles and pleasantries on a few occasions. He could tell from her expression and the way she blushed whenever he spoke to her that she was as attracted to him as he was to her, but there never seemed to be the chance to talk to her properly and ask her out. Either he was dashing to a meeting, or she was hurrying to whatever she did, and they always seemed to be going in opposite directions.

That hadn't stopped his imagination from going wild, though. He couldn't forget the first time he'd seen her. He'd been on his way to another client meeting, and she'd almost run into him as she'd turned the corner onto the main road in front of his building. She'd apologized and continued on her way, but he'd been left staring at her retreating back like he'd been thunderstruck, taking in soft, gray eyes, dark hair almost to her waist, the shape of her legs and her stunning figure in a green shift dress that showed off every luscious curve. Since then his brain and his cock had gone on what had become a well-worn track wondering what it would be like to kiss her, to slowly peel that dress off her tanned shoulders, explore every last inch of her skin, and taste her.

He took another swig of his beer. This wasn't like him at all. Any of it. It wasn't like he'd never been attracted to a woman before, but he just couldn't seem to get this one out of his head. He found himself hoping to see her whenever he was in that part of town.

Not that it was at all helpful to his concentration when he did see her. Too often, he found himself having to walk into his office with his briefcase covering his erection, and he spent time when he should have been working staring sightlessly at his laptop or out of the window, remembering the way she moved and her expressive face and wondering what she would look like when she came.

*

Juliet relaxed on her lounger and idly turned the page of her book. After a few minutes, she lowered her book and glanced out across the roof garden. It might belong to a beautiful penthouse, but it really did need an awful lot of work. Drooping plants and far too many weeds decorated the flower beds, and her fingers itched to get to work and neaten everything up.

This was supposed to be her day off. She'd only come up here to see what the garden was like and get an idea of how much work was needed, but it was so warm for May that she'd decided to stay and relax with a good book, some music, and a glass of wine or two. It was no use, though. She couldn't keep her eyes on her book with so many ideas running through her mind. She couldn't wait to plant fresh vegetables and herbs, and to have fruit trees loaded with blossoms, trickling water features, trailing roses and jasmine, and gorgeous blooms in a variety of colors bringing their rich fragrance back to the garden.

She dropped her book onto the table next to her and picked up her tablet, looking at the rough sketch she'd made of the garden. There was so much potential here, and she still couldn't believe that it was all hers. Well, almost. Her letter had said there was another beneficiary who had the other penthouse and shared the roof garden, but from what little Helen had said about him, he lived abroad so there was zero chance he'd be interfering with her plans.

Smiling, she stretched and reached for her glass of prosecco, toasting in memory of her aunt. She'd loved visiting her and playing on the roof garden when she was little.

It was odd, living in the penthouse. She'd moved her things in a week ago, but it still didn't feel quite real, as if at any moment she'd wake up and realize that she was back in school, staying in her old bedroom, with the mouthwatering aroma of fresh cakes and baking bread drifting through from the kitchen.

Raising her glass again, she blinked away the sudden tears that came all too easily at the moment. "Cheers to you, Aunt Helen, wherever you are. I miss you."

She thought for a moment about picking up her book again, but she was too excited to concentrate on it. She decided to look at her calendar to see when she'd be able to start work on her very own rooftop garden. She picked up her tablet and paged through the calendar, marking out possible days and checking her appointments for the following week. Then she clicked back to the current date, almost as if to double check she really did have the entire weekend off.

She was just about to close the calendar and shut down the tablet when an entry at the top of the page caught her eye: *World Naked Gardening Day*. She blinked and read it again. *Seriously? That couldn't be a real day. Could it?* She clicked on the link and read the first paragraph.

Get ready for the Annual World Naked Gardening Day (WNGD)! People across the globe are encouraged, on the first Saturday of May, to tend their portion of the world's garden unclothed as nature intended.

She shook her head. *Wow. That was a new one.* She didn't think any of her clients would be thrilled if her team turned up butt naked. That might raise a few eyebrows with the neighbors. She laughed out loud, imagining old Mrs. Gaffney's face if the team turned up to her rather proper home with more than just the plants blowing in the breeze. Just as well it was today rather than a day she had to work.

She scrolled farther down the page, reading more about the day and how people felt when they got involved. One lady talked about feeling completely connected with nature, and Juliet smiled. She knew that feeling. There was nothing like when she was in the zone, just her in the peace of a garden and the chance to transform it into something beautiful. She'd never tried it naked, but she was curious. What would that be like?

Should she? Enjoying the garden with the sun warming her and the cooling breeze drifting right across her bare skin did sound wonderful. She looked around the roof garden again and smiled. Well, why not? There was no one to see.

Juliet took off her sandals and wriggled her toes in the short grass. Heaven! She slipped her skirt down and took her top off, leaving her in just her bra and panties.

As she went to undo her bra, she glanced around, suddenly feeling a little vulnerable, and then she laughed at herself. She was completely alone and the building was too high for anyone to see her.

Unhooking her bra, she dropped it onto the pile of her clothes, following it with her panties. She stretched her arms over her head and looked up at the sky, smiling and enjoying the warmth of the sun and the caress of the breeze on her body.

As if she'd planned it, *Walking On Sunshine* began playing on the radio, and she let out a completely uninhibited whoop, turned it up to top volume, and began dancing on the small patch of lawn. She boogied her way down the full length of the roof garden and then all the way back, still not quite able to believe she was actually doing this but enjoying every second, nevertheless. It was like dancing on the roof of the world with the open sky above her, the grass at her feet, and the sun beaming down and heating her skin. It felt like no one was around for miles.

Singing along, a little off-key, she skipped across the patio near the steps leading down to her penthouse, waving her arms in the air. Then she built up for the big finish with a rather lopsided splits jump. "Oh yeah, oh yeah, oh yeah, oh d—"

She jumped again, only this time almost out of her skin, as an enthusiastic round of applause broke out behind her. She froze on the spot. *Oh fuck*. Her heart raced at a million miles an hour, and her skin went from pleasantly warm to cold and clammy. There was someone behind her. There was someone here! And she had no idea who it was or what they wanted. Or what they would do. *Oh shit, oh shit, oh shit!*

And she was naked! She quickly covered her bottom with both hands, looking around frantically for something she could use to cover herself properly. Her face flushed almost red enough to match the aptly named Adrenalin rose that flourished in pots on the patio. Adrenaline was certainly coursing through her right now.

Cover herself. Cover herself, and then, somehow, find the nerve to turn around and see who it was. What with? What on earth could she use? There was nothing here. Her clothes were over there, and whoever it was had to be between her and them.

The only thing on hand was a very small plant pot with a less than concealing baby cheese plant drooping over the side. *Well shit.* She could at least use it to throw at whoever it was if she had to. Her face flaming, she drew herself up proudly, picked up the pot, and covered between her legs as best she could, stretching her other arm across her breasts and turning side on to look over her shoulder at whoever it was who had dared to invade her space.

*

Josh pushed himself up out of his chair, downing the last of his beer. Extremely pleasant though it was, he needed to stop thinking about that stunning woman's curves and start moving in properly and getting his furniture transferred across. First things first, he had to check out the bedrooms and think about where he was going to put his home office.

He jogged up the stairs, heading into the master bedroom first. There really was very little to do in there. The whole place was immaculate, and it was just a case of changing things to his tastes. The remaining two bedrooms were a decent size, and either one would make a great home office. He settled on the one with the best view over the city and called his team to help with moving his furniture from his old apartment over the next day or so.

As he came out onto the landing, he stopped to listen, sure he could hear music coming from somewhere. He did have the windows open, so it must be one of the neighbors from the floor below. As his foot touched the top step to head back downstairs, the music suddenly went up in volume to the point that he could make out what the song was. *Walking On Sunshine*. Wow, he hadn't heard that in a while. Where was it coming from, though? It must be really loud if it was coming from downstairs.

He went back down the steps, but the music was much quieter in the lounge.

Josh frowned, realizing that it could only be coming from one place—the roof garden. And who could possibly be up there when Helen had left it to him? Well, he hadn't planned to look at the garden until the following day, but he was definitely going up there now.

He climbed the stairs again and walked down the corridor to the end, where a door opened onto a short flight of steps leading up to the roof garden. He reached into his pocket for his keys and found the right one for the door. As soon as he opened it, the volume of the music increased. And he could hear something else too. A woman was singing along very enthusiastically, and he couldn't help but smile.

He stepped up onto the roof garden as the song reached its climax.

Coming out into the full sun after the dimly lit staircase, he thought his eyes must be mistaken at first, either that or he'd developed very sudden sunstroke or had a bang on the head. It was a naked woman. On his roof. Dancing and skipping about to *Walking On Sunshine*. *What the actual fuck?*

He averted his eyes and shouted across to her, "Excuse me. What are you doing here?"

Well that was a bloody stupid question. It was obvious exactly what she was doing here. He was trying not to look because he didn't want to embarrass her, but she was dancing back and forth in front of his eye line. She clearly hadn't heard him.

He shaded his eyes with his hand so he couldn't see her, moved a little closer, and tried again. "Hello? Lady? Can you hear me?"

No response. Just more, if his brief glimpse had been anything to go by, enthusiastic dancing and butt wiggling.

Dear God. Okay. This wasn't working. He walked the length of the garden, keeping his eyes fixed firmly on the ground in front of him. He stopped just near the far patio and opened his mouth to try again to attract her attention, but just then his eye was drawn as she did a quite spectacular jump, right into the splits in the air while singing at the top of her voice.

He couldn't help himself. He burst into a spontaneous round of applause then wished he hadn't. *Shit.*

He looked away again quickly, but just out of the corner of his eye as he turned away, he caught a glimpse of her face and realized it was the woman he'd been flirting with for the last few months.

*

Juliet drew in a breath as she turned, preparing to confront whoever was behind her. "Just what exac—" She stopped short, her voice dying away and her eyes widening as she realized who it was. "It's you," she blurted in surprise.

She didn't know his name, and thankfully, he was looking away, but it was definitely the man who'd been occupying her thoughts over and over for the last few months. Tall, dark haired, gorgeous, and built as if he spent every waking minute in the gym. He was the stuff of fantasies. Well, certainly hers anyway.

Oh God. Why, oh why, did it have to be him? Why couldn't just about anybody else in the world have found her naked and dancing with complete abandon on the roof garden? There really was no justice. She might as well pack up right now and move because she couldn't possibly stay here and keep running into him after this. The only way this could have been worse was if he'd also been a client.

And why had she just gaped at him and blurted out, "It's you!" Like he didn't know that! And she'd just given away the fact that she'd noticed him when they'd bumped into each other a few times. There was no possible way her face could get any redder than it was right now. That had to be it. Maximum blush achieved. Any hotter and she'd be able to cook eggs on her cheeks.

He picked up her clothes and came toward her slowly, eyes averted, almost as if he was worried that she might bolt. "Yes, it's me. I know it's quite the surprise. For me too." He handed over her clothes. "Here. Look, I'm sorry I scared you. I'm going to wait over there."

She grabbed her clothes from him, covering herself with her T-shirt while she watched him walk away, and then she put the thrice-blasted cheese plant down. He kept his back turned, giving her time to get dressed, and she dressed quickly, hurriedly putting her underwear back on, dragging her T-shirt over her head, and pulling up her skirt.

Even with her clothes safely back on, she was still squirming at the idea that he'd found her in the state he had. Oh God, he pretty much knew what she looked like naked, and they hadn't even so much as gone on a date.

For a moment, her mind ran back to the point when she'd realized he was there. She'd been completely naked but for that ridiculous potted plant, and he was wearing formal trousers and a shirt that was open at the neck. The contrast couldn't have been more marked. She felt her nipples harden again and the familiar electric surge of arousal between her legs. Okay, apparently there really was another level of blush red that she'd surely never managed before in her entire life. She was turned on at the idea of being naked when he was clothed. On some level, she'd liked how it felt, and she knew that moment would become one of those well-worn, scorching hot scenes that she fantasized about when she touched herself.

She gulped, trying to calm down, sure it was totally obvious what she was thinking—all he had to do was turn around, and he'd know how turned on she was.

She glanced over at him. He hadn't moved as far as she could tell and hadn't peeked at all while she was dressing. That was... nice, reassuring. And kind of disappointing!

She cleared her throat. "Excuse me, I'm... you can turn around now." She'd been about to say 'I'm dressed now,' but she didn't want to give him a reminder—as if he could forget—that she'd been naked not two minutes earlier.

He turned to face her and smiled. "How about we start again? Hi, I'm Josh Carter. And you are?"

"J—" she started, but nothing else came out. She cleared her throat and tried again. "Juliet. Juliet Adams."

"So, not that this was an unpleasant surprise or anything, Juliet, but what exactly are you doing here?"

Juliet's eyebrows almost reached her hairline, "Me? What am I doing here? What the hell are you doing here?"

They glared at each other, neither giving an inch.

Finally, Juliet spoke, "Look, this is my roof garden. And I'd really like to know why you thought it was okay to come up here. How did you even get up here anyway? The other penthouse is closed up."

Josh shook his head. "It was. It's now mine, and that means so is the roof garden, which is why I came up here when I heard your music."

"No. My aunt left it to me in her will. And I don't have to justify why I might choose to be naked in my own garden."

The look in Josh's eyes could have scorched the grass right off the roof. She'd reminded him of the naked thing. She glanced down quickly and then gulped and looked away. Yes, he was definitely thinking about the naked thing.

She backpedaled hurriedly. "I… didn't mean to say that. You didn't ask me to justify it."

"No, I didn't. Though by all means, please do go on if you want to."

Juliet opened her mouth to speak and shut it again, not sure how to respond to him. She swallowed hard, feeling her nipples hardening into tight buds and moisture pooling between her legs again. She crossed her arms over her chest to try to conceal her peaked nipples. *Don't think about how amazing he looks in those trousers, how closely they hug his well-muscled thighs and the curve of his incredible arse. And definitely don't look at that… oh God, that extremely impressive and noticeable bulge in his trousers.*

She tore her eyes away, completely unable to think of a thing to say.

"Wait a minute, you said your aunt left it to you?" Josh said. "You have to be Helen's niece."

"I am." Juliet frowned. "How did you know that, and how did you know Helen?" This conversation was not going the way she had planned.

"She was a friend of my dad's, and I got to know her through him. I used to do a lot of jobs for her after he passed on, and I spent quite a bit of time with her." His eyes softened. "She was an amazing lady. I'm very sorry for your loss."

Juliet swallowed. "Thank you." She took a deep breath. "Look, I still don't understand. How are you here? She definitely didn't mention you when she talked about the other penthouse."

"She didn't tell you?"

"Tell me what?"

"She left me the other penthouse, and she said the roof garden came with it."

"Why would she do that?"

"Well, you'd have to ask her, but I suspect it was in part because of my dad, and because I helped her out a lot with all those jobs. I really was very fond of her."

"But she told me the roof garden was mine. Oh, apart from an old man who'd inherited the other penthouse but lived in Europe and didn't want to live here."

Josh thought for a moment. "This is beginning to make a little more sense now. I think you'll find that I'm the man who got the other penthouse, though less of the 'old,' if you don't mind."

"But... but she said you lived abroad. And you're supposed to be ninety at least."

Josh laughed. "Ninety? Really? Is that what she said? Well, not just yet. I did live abroad, though. I spent about six months in Spain on one of my building projects and only came back a few months ago. But your aunt always knew it was temporary and I'd be coming home."

Juliet shook her head. "Unbelievable. Did she say anything to you about me?"

"Oh yes, she did." Josh smiled wryly. "She mentioned she had a niece that she was close to, and she talked about you very fondly, but she didn't tell me that you would be inheriting her penthouse. And she certainly didn't say we'd be sharing the roof garden."

Juliet swallowed. It was a lovely thing to hear that Aunt Helen had talked about her with such warmth, and for a moment it was hard to think about anything else but how much she missed her. But then her thoughts turned back to their current situation. "But what on earth was she thinking? Why didn't she tell us? You know, I even had a lovely note from her to say she hoped I'd enjoy spending time in the garden and making it my own space as much as she'd enjoyed having me here. I don't understand it at all."

Josh frowned. "No, me neither. I really don't know. Though I suppose there is one good outcome: we did get to finally meet properly."

Juliet's eyes widened. "That's it. That's exactly it. She set us up."

Josh stared at her. "She wouldn't."

"Oh yes, she would! She was a huge romantic, and she said she'd give anything to have me happy with someone I loved. And I told her about you, and—" Her voice trailed off, and she blushed all over again.

"You talked about me?"

Juliet looked away, unable to meet his eyes, "Well, yes. I came to see her one day after I'd just seen you. It was when you had all those balloons, and we got all caught up. Do you remember?"

Josh grinned. "I do. I don't think we could have managed to get any more tangled up if we'd actually planned it."

Juliet smiled. "No; balloons, shopping bags, and revolving doors definitely don't mix."

"They don't. My niece was very happy I managed to get everything to her in one piece, though. It was a very good sixth birthday, apparently."

"Six years old? So cute."

"Yep. And as mischievous as a bag full of monkeys." Josh smiled fondly. "Anyway, back to your aunt."

"Oh yes. Well, I was on my way here when we ran into each other. And I was still a little flustered when I arrived after bumping into you like that. She spotted that straight away and asked me what had made me look like that, or rather who, so I told her what had just happened and that we kept running into each other. I can't think how she knew who you were, though."

Josh thought for a moment. "I can. I'd gone to see her that same morning, and I had the balloons and present with me because I was seeing my niece right after work. Helen must have realized it was me from your description."

Juliet nodded. "That's it then. She did. She set us up."

"It's a bit convoluted, though, isn't it? She could have just arranged for us to both visit her at the same time."

"Who knows? Maybe she did, but one or the other of us couldn't make it. And she can't have left us the apartments just because she wanted us to meet. That would be a bit extreme, wouldn't it? I knew years ago that she was going to leave me her penthouse, so I'm thinking she perhaps just made a plan to leave a few pretty important details out of what she told us."

"True. Though I doubt very much that in all her matchmaking she planned for *Walking On Sunshine* and your er... performance earlier, much though she would have thought that was hilarious. Nice moves, by the way. Especially the splits."

Josh smiled and then began to laugh, and Juliet couldn't help but join in, until her laughter turned to tears for missing her aunt.

Josh held out his arms, and Juliet stepped into his embrace. He hugged her to him as she cried, stroking his hand through her hair. "I know, sweetheart. I miss her, too." He fished in his pocket, took out a handkerchief, and passed it to her. She took it, grasping onto his shirt as if she didn't think she could safely let go without floating off into space.

Finally the tears dried up, and she looked down at his shirt, realizing she was still gripping it in her fist. She let go of him and stepped back a little, embarrassed that she'd been so emotional in front of someone she didn't know all that well. "I'm so sorry. I... didn't mean to do that to your shirt." She wiped her eyes. "Wow, I must look like such a mess."

Josh smiled. "Not at all. In fact, I think you're beautiful."

Juliet looked up at him, her eyes wide, a blush dusting her cheeks. "Oh." She put her arms around him and hugged him, hiding her face in his shoulder, and then looked up, meeting his eyes. "I think... I think you're pretty damned awesome yourself." Her gaze dropped from his lust-filled eyes to his mouth, and she leaned in closer.

Josh closed the gap between them further, their lips less than an inch away from meeting for the very first time.

Juliet swallowed, her eyes still firmly fixed on his mouth. "I—" She cleared her throat nervously, "I really want to kiss you," she whispered.

"Well, that's good news," Josh said, hoarsely. "Because I really want to kiss you too."

Juliet could hear the smile in his voice. She stood on tiptoe to trace a series of tiny kisses across his lips. "You taste good."

Josh wrapped his arms tighter around her shoulders. "Do I?" he growled. "I think I need to find out just how good you taste." He pressed his lips firmly against hers, taking his time, savoring every second. "Hmm, absolutely delicious." He grinned down at her. "But on further consideration, I think I need to do that again just to be completely sure."

Juliet's eyes sparkled. "Oh you do, do you? Well, I think it's always good to be sure. And I really am comple—" She didn't get any further as Josh swept her up in his arms and pressed his lips firmly to hers, his tongue teasing hers and scattering her senses.

He released her mouth. "You really are completely what?"

Juliet tried to focus but she was still thinking about the touch of his lips on hers and his tongue teasing her own. "What?"

"Before I kissed you again, you were going to say, 'I really am completely' and then you stopped. Actually, I may have had something to do with that." Josh grinned unabashedly.

"I have absolutely no idea what I was going to say. I got distracted somehow. Actually, you may have had something to do with that." Juliet playfully walked her fingers up his chest. "And I think I'd like you to distract me again."

Josh nipped lightly at her mouth. "You would? You want me to do this again?" He tipped up her chin and held her still while he thoroughly explored her mouth. "Like that?"

"Definitely like that."

"Good to know." He carried Juliet over to the lounger and sat down carefully, putting her down next to him. "So," he idly traced his fingers down her neck and across her collarbone, "I wonder what else you'd like me to do?"

"Oh, I think you should keep exploring and see what er… comes up." Juliet grinned cheekily.

Josh let out a surprised bark of laughter. "I see."

Juliet blushed bright red and buried her face in his shoulder. "I'm sorry. I don't usually do this, you know. Not so quickly."

Josh sat up slightly. "Don't be sorry. Are you sure you're okay? We don't have to do anything you don't want to do. We can just sit, have a drink, and get to know each other if you'd rather."

Juliet shook her head and then looked him in the eye. "I'm fine. Honestly. And… and I really want you. I don't want to wait."

Josh cupped her face gently. "Are you really sure?"

She drew him toward her and kissed him thoroughly, tangling her fingers in his hair. "I am absolutely sure."

"In that case, come here." Josh shifted Juliet onto his lap. He reached for the jug of iced water, glancing at the bottle of prosecco and the variety of snacks on the table. "Well, you do seem to have the er… bare necessities on hand for such a hot day."

Juliet let out an unladylike snort. "Really? That's what you want to go with? Are you sure your name's not Bond?"

"The name's Carter. Josh Carter," Josh said in a passable take on Sean Connery's accent. He held up his middle and index fingers like a gun and blew on them. "License to thrill."

"Oh please." Juliet laughed.

Josh smiled and then gave her another thorough, demanding kiss that made her toes curl. Then he picked up an ice cube and trailed it gently across the back of her neck and down across the tops of her breasts, following the cool path of the ice with the warmth of his mouth on her skin.

Juliet took in a shaky breath as her nipples pebbled and heat began to blaze between her thighs.

Josh dropped a kiss on her lips and then stood. He took her hands and pulled her to her feet, then picked up the jug of iced water. "Come with me." He led her to the small patch of lawn and sat down, pulling her down to sit beside him.

He lifted her top over her head and gently stroked across the swell of her breasts. His mouth followed his fingers, trailing kisses across the tops of her breasts that felt like fireworks under her skin everywhere his lips touched. He kissed her again hard as he slipped her skirt down over her legs, leaving her in just her underwear.

Juliet kissed him back just as hard and started to unbutton his shirt, wanting to touch the warm skin of his chest. She pushed his shirt off his shoulders and trailed kisses over his neck. Then she finally got to look at that mysterious tattoo of the bird that had tantalized her for so long. It was a swooping peregrine falcon with incredible detail that swept over his shoulder and part way down his back, so beautifully done that she could swear it was about to fly away. She traced her tongue around the outline of the falcon, as she explored the muscles on his back and chest lightly with her fingertips.

Josh groaned aloud, and Juliet smiled against his skin, encouraged by how aroused he obviously was. Her hand slipped lower following the trail of hairs that disappeared under his trousers, but she didn't get any further as he sat up, slipped off his shoes, unzipped his trousers, and took them off, pulling down his boxer shorts with them. Then, he returned his attention to her and swept her panties down her legs before unhooking her bra and removing that too.

He took his time looking over her body from head to toe. "Hmm, I recognize this view."

Juliet gasped. "Oh! You shouldn't. You shouldn't have been looking."

"Believe me, I tried. I looked away as soon as I realized what I was seeing. But I've got to say I'm finding it very hard to take my eyes off you right now."

Juliet felt as if his gaze was scorching her body, heating her skin and arousing her beyond anything she'd ever felt before. "Please. Please touch me."

Josh's eyes darkened. "Oh I'm going to. I plan to explore every last inch of you. Slowly. And then I may have to do it again just to be sure I've covered everything."

"Yes. Oh God, yes!"

Emboldened, Josh cupped her cheek then moved his hand down to her neck, trailing his fingers over her collarbone and down between her breasts. He stopped for a moment to drop a kiss on her nipples and then continued his slow deliberate exploration of her body.

Juliet's hip was pressed against him, and she could feel how aroused he was. Her last coherent thought was that she couldn't believe his self-control and his total focus on touching her and bringing her pleasure.

After that, she could barely think at all as he swept his hand down her stomach and lightly trailed his fingers between her legs. He moved his hand away, and Juliet groaned aloud. Then he took his time, gently massaging her thighs and her calves before playfully tweaking her toes.

Juliet giggled and squirmed under his hands as his touch grew lighter, tickling her ribs and her waist, before he moved back up to massage her breasts firmly and circle her nipples to hard peaks. She was overwhelmed. It felt as if his hands were everywhere. No sooner had he finished pleasuring one part of her than he started again somewhere else, and the sensations quickly brought her to the edge.

But no matter how much she wanted him to touch her there, he carefully skirted the area between her legs every time.

He stopped for a moment, watching her face, and then blew gently across her nipples.

Juliet almost screamed in frustration. "I need... I need... Please."

"I know what you need, sweetheart." He stroked his thumb over her lips. "I'm just taking my time in giving it to you. I want to drive you wild and then hear you scream my name as you come on my tongue."

Josh dipped his hand in the jug and took out another ice cube. He circled her left nipple with the ice, watching it peak even harder and listening to her breathing change. He moved his hand and circled her other nipple with the ice while sucking her left nipple into his mouth.

Juliet bucked, her body almost arching off the ground. The contrast of ice cold and warm heat left her breathless, and she could feel the electric rush of arousal between her legs. She was close. She was so close, and he hadn't even touched her clit yet.

As if he'd heard her, Josh dropped the ice onto the grass and stroked his damp fingers down the curve of her stomach and then finally, blessedly, between her legs.

Juliet relaxed, expecting him to touch her and bring her to orgasm, but he stroked her inner thighs, teasing her and still avoiding the soft, damp curls that she was desperate for him to touch. "Josh, please."

"Shhh, sweetheart. I'll get you there." He grinned. "In my own good time."

Juliet moaned and covered her face with her arm.

"Oh no. Don't do that. I want to see you. I want to know what you look like when you come." He pressed his finger against her clit and held it still, promising everything but not giving her enough to go over the edge.

Juliet dropped her arm to her side, her eyes pleading with him, hoping that he would finish what he'd started.

Josh smiled. "There you are. Look at me, gorgeous, and don't look away. Let me see you." He started to circle her clit very slowly, then dipped his finger into the moisture gathering between her legs and tasted her. "I just knew you'd taste as good as you look."

Juliet blushed a deep red. No one had ever done anything like that before, and she didn't quite know how to react, but she did know it was turning her on, and she wanted more. She lifted her hips up, hoping Josh would take the hint, and he did.

"You are so wet," he growled. "I can't wait until I'm buried deep inside you, but first I want to make you come."

"Oh yes, please. I really need to."

"I can see that." He dipped his finger inside her and then went back to lightly circling her clit. "I can feel it too."

Juliet lay back, her breathing ragged. Her mind focused only on that one spot, her body building up to orgasm as Josh continued to tease her clit.

Then just as she was almost there, he moved his hand away and made her wait a little longer.

Juliet let out a groan of frustration, and he swallowed the sound with a hard kiss that rocked her to her toes. Then he kissed slowly down her stomach, taking his time and drawing out the moment until she could feel his hot breath between her legs.

Josh slowly ran his tongue up her seam and then licked slowly all the way around her clit without touching it.

Juliet was beyond thought. She had no idea what to do. All she could concentrate on were the sensations between her legs and her desperate need to come.

Finally, Josh began to flick his tongue lightly over her clit, increasing the speed and the pressure until she writhed helplessly against him, her hips bucking with every stroke and her orgasm so close she could taste it. And this time he didn't stop. He grabbed her hips and held her still, controlling every sensation that she experienced, until at last she really did scream out his name as she soared over the edge.

She collapsed back onto the grass, absolutely spent, and Josh drew her close and cuddled her, stroking her face. "So beautiful," he said quietly.

He laid her back down on the grass for a moment and patted his trouser pockets. "Ah. I, er, don't suppose you have any condoms hidden in your notebook, do you?"

Juliet could barely focus on his face, still trying to recover from the most earth-shattering orgasm she'd ever had. "What?"

"Small problem. I don't have any condoms on me. Any chance you do?"

Juliet shook her head, her whole body still trembling with aftershocks. "In the apartment maybe. I'm not sure."

Josh rested his forehead against hers. "I am going to be right back, I promise. Just relax and rest up." He grinned wickedly. "You're going to need all of your energy shortly."

He jumped to his feet and hurried across the roof garden to his apartment, just as naked as Juliet had been earlier. The thought made her smile as she lay back and relaxed on the soft grass, completely sated and spent.

She must have closed her eyes and drifted off for a few moments, because she awoke to Josh gently saying her name. Juliet stretched like a cat, feeling the delicious ache of her previous orgasm. Smiling, she patted the ground next to her.

"Are you still up for this?" he asked while holding up the condom in one hand.

"Oh yes!" She couldn't wait to feel him inside her.

But wait he seemed determined to make her. Getting to his knees next to her, he stroked her breasts and lightly tweaked each nipple in turn. When she arched her back, he leaned down and took her nipple in his mouth, sucking hard and circling his tongue over the hard nub.

Juliet's breathing quickened, and she cried out at the sensation as he pinched her other nipple between his thumb and forefinger. To her surprise, the pain added to her quickly building arousal, and she squirmed, already needing to orgasm again.

"You like that," Josh said. It wasn't a question.

"I… I do. It feels so good." She put her hand on his chest, feeling the solid muscle underneath her palm. "I need you inside me," she whispered.

Josh dropped a kiss on her lips. "Oh, I think we can do that." He unwrapped the condom and rolled it into place then positioned himself between her legs, teasing her with his cock. "Is this what you want?"

Juliet's eyes widened as she felt him nudging her entrance. "Yes, oh yes. Definitely."

Josh pushed himself just inside her, holding himself still to make sure she was okay, and when she lifted her hips toward him, he thrust all the way inside.

Juliet held her breath for a second, getting used to how he felt, and then she gasped as he began to move. She moved her hips, following his rhythm, and wrapped her legs around his back, wanting him deeper.

Josh responded, increasing his speed, pushing as deep as he could and thrusting hard into her.

Juliet could feel her orgasm building again, and she pressed herself against him, needing the pressure to take her over the edge. She'd never come just from sex before, but she was sure it was going to happen this time. She rocked against him, wanting to enjoy every last second. He felt amazing inside her, and she didn't want this to end.

Josh lifted her legs above her head, holding her still, while he fucked her hard. All Juliet could do was hold onto his shoulders and feel every last sensation. She closed her eyes, concentrating on how incredible he felt and feeling her orgasm get ever closer.

Josh released her legs, and Juliet began to move with him again, both of them drawing near to the edge. As Josh drove into her, Juliet's hips met his, and she cried out as her orgasm overtook her. As Juliet's center clenched around his cock, Josh came hard too.

For a moment, they both lay spent before Josh pulled her onto his lap and hugged her close. "That was amazing. Though I really think we need to do that again just so I can confirm that."

Juliet curled up against him, her eyes closed and a happy smile on her face. "I'll get right on that, just as soon as my muscles stop feeling like jelly."

Josh grinned, "Oh by the way, just to satisfy my curiosity, why exactly were you in your birthday suit earlier?"

Juliet laughed and opened her eyes, starting to recover. "Didn't you know it's World Naked Gardening Day? I thought everyone knew that."

Josh stared at her. "Seriously? Is that a real thing?"

Juliet nodded, still smiling, and wriggled on his lap, feeling his growing erection against her hip. "I find it very freeing."

"Do you indeed? Well, that's not a gardening technique I've ever seen before." Josh stroked his hands down her still-naked back. "I can't say I disapprove, though."

He kissed her again and cupped her breasts, his thumbs lightly flicking her nipples. "Hmm, maybe we could try that together next year."

Juliet wrapped her arms around his neck and pressed a kiss to his jaw. "Oh, I was really hoping we could try a lot of things together, and definitely before next year."

Josh grinned. "I'm sure that can be arranged. Now come here and kiss me, woman."

*

One Year Later

The doors of the church burst open to the sound of *Walking On Sunshine* at full volume. Josh and Juliet ran down the steps hand-in-hand, Josh in a perfectly fitted new suit and Juliet in a stunning off-the-shoulder ivory wedding gown.

Josh lifted Juliet off her feet and swung her around, the train of her gown just long enough to sweep the ground, and then he kissed her until she was breathless. "We did it, Mrs. Adams-Carter. We really did it. Happy?"

Juliet's smile could have lit the entire city. "Absolutely ecstatic."

After posing for photographs, Josh helped Juliet into the wedding car that was taking them back to the now beautifully finished roof garden for their reception and joined her in the back seat.

Juliet popped the cork on the champagne provided and passed a glass to Josh before pouring one for herself. "I think we need to have a toast. To Aunt Helen, bless her. Thank you for everything."

Josh raised his glass. "To Helen. And to my gorgeous wife." He clinked his glass against hers then wrapped his arm around her shoulders and whispered into her ear, "I can't wait to have you all to myself so I can get you naked."

Juliet snuggled into his shoulder and smiled. "You first this time."

As the wedding car purred away, it was followed by a rattling trail of cans and a sign that read, *'Gardeners Do It Naked.'*

About the Author

Liv Honeywell is a BDSM erotic romance writer and, when not writing about delicious, hot male dominants and the female subs who love them, she's usually doing something craft-like, reading, or baking and trying to decide which of her many other book ideas to work on next.

In her books, she includes a lot of humor, with realistic characters who aren't perfect and scenes where sometimes things go wrong. D/s is often portrayed as terribly serious, with constantly subby subs, and frowning Doms who never crack a smile. That hasn't been Liv's experience at all, and she likes to bring some of that fun and laughter into her books, as well as some really hot kink!

Website: liv-honeywell.com
Twitter: @livhoneywell

Wrong Number

♥

Krissy V

Story Information

Holiday: Two Different Colored Shoes Day
Holiday Date: May 3
Heat Rating: 2
Relationship Type: M/F
Major Trigger Warnings: Detailed description of attempted sexual assault, physical assault, binge drinking, vomit, internalized ableism, PTSD flashbacks, mention of medical procedures.

Two very different people are brought together by a misunderstanding. Sometimes love blossoms in the most unusual of places.

Daisy has a secret she doesn't want anyone to know.

Eoin gets stood up and decides to give his blind date a piece of his mind, except he has the wrong number. It turns out his mistake was the best thing that happened to both of them.

Daisy needs to overcome a lot of issues to meet Eoin. Can she get past her insecurities and compulsive tendencies to meet him?

No one knew how significant two different colored shoes would be.

Wrong Number

Five Years Previously

"This party is banging," I shout over to Gracie, my best friend. It's hard to be heard over the loud music. "There are some really hot guys here. Look at that guy over there." I point over at a man across the room. He's tall, rugged looking with tattoos showing through his T-shirt. He looks over at me and smiles. Then, just as quickly, he turns back to his friends.

"Phew, Daisy, he is smoking hot." Gracie giggles as she waves her hand in front of her face like a fan. "There are a lot of guys here; we will definitely not be going home alone tonight." We hug each other, laugh, and then we both walk to the kitchen to get another drink.

After another hour, Gracie is hooked up with a guy in the corner of the room, I sashay over to her, bumping into the furniture as I go. "Gracie, I'm going home," I slur. "I'm a little bit pished." I giggle and lean forward to kiss Gracie, even though she is in the middle of a very heavy petting session. Gracie opens her eyes and winks at me. I roll my eyes and turn around, grabbing hold of the sofa as I go. Anyone watching me can see how drunk I am. I keep reaching out to grab ahold of the furniture to get to the front door. I giggle and look around me. I can't wait to get home and get into bed, I really need to sleep. I just know that I'm going to be asleep for a long time.

Walking down the steps from the house and down the drive, I grab ahold of the gate as a wave of nausea washes over me. Holding onto the iron fence, I retch and eventually I vomit. Repeatedly. God, I really need to go home.

When I feel a little bit better I wipe my mouth, stand up really slowly, and start walking down the road to see if I can grab a taxi. The need to lie down is a priority.

As I'm walking down the road, I can see five guys standing up against the railings and I say, "Hi," to them as I walk past. They all nod their heads in acknowledgment, and I keep walking. They could've been at the same party as me, I don't know. To be honest, I don't take much notice of them, they're a bit blurry. It's very dark, but I can feel the hairs standing up on my neck. Gracie and I never let the other walk home on their own, we always go home together. Why did I walk home alone tonight? I can feel myself starting to sober up, but I keep my head down and keep on walking.

I can see the end of the street where there's a lot of lights and activity. It's only a few minutes, I'll be there soon. Something is making me feel uneasy. I'm not sure what it is, but I don't like it. I'm still dragging my feet, walking from side to side and banging off the railings at every opportunity. Walking a bit quicker to get away from whoever is behind me, I hear the steps getting closer. I hear another noise, it's strange. It's there with every step I take. It takes me a minute, but then I realize it's the sound of my heart beating. It's so loud I can't hear anything else. Thud... thud... thud.

There's a cab pulling up at the end of the road, I smile to myself; it won't be long now before I'm home in my bed sleeping off this bad trip I'm having.

As I get closer to the end of the road, I suddenly felt my body being pushed to the ground. I hear a loud scream and then realize it's me. Then, I feel a hand go over my mouth, muffling my screams. I vomit almost immediately, but the hand doesn't move. I feel myself gagging on my own vomit. This is the moment when I think I might die. I might choke.

But I'm wrong! It only gets worse. I'm face down on the floor, lying in my vomit with a man's hand over my mouth. I know what you're thinking—how can this get any worse?

I just keep on vomiting, and whatever the guy wanted to do to me, he obviously decides it's not worth it. I can feel his body starting to lift off me, yet his hand doesn't move; it's still in front of my mouth. All I want to do is take a breath of fresh air, but it's impossible. There's only a small gap between his fingers where I can breathe. I thought he would have taken his hand away when I vomited, but no, he's persistent.

When I feel his body leaving mine, I release a breath I didn't realize I was holding. Then just as I start to take another desperate breath he grabs hold of my hair and smashes my head down on the ground. Repeatedly.

It hurts so much. I can feel sticky stuff running down my face. I start to cry. I'm going to die tonight. Why didn't I stay at the party? Why did I drink so much? These are the thoughts that are going through my mind. The last thing I see are five pairs of shoes neatly in a row as they stand next to my head. Then, one of them kicks my face, and suddenly everything goes black.

It goes quiet.
It just ends.

*

I hope everyone is enjoying the party tonight, Gracie. Have one for me! ;-)
I see I have another notification.
***Gracie Nugent** commented on your status*
Wish you were here, honey. Miss you loads. The girls are coming round tomorrow—see you later xxx

Laughing, I wipe away the silent tears forming in my eyes. I love Gracie, we've been friends since preschool, and she has always been there for me. She lives with me, but she's gone out to a party tonight. I wish I could have gone, but I didn't feel like it. If I'm honest, I don't feel like much these days.

Hearing a ping on my computer, I see I have another chat message. I chat for a bit; it's my main source of communication with the outside world. There's something safe, secure, about the anonymity online.

I glance at the clock, noting the time. Another night spent in front of the screen. I turn the computer off, turn around, and slide into bed. I take my phone and send a quick text to Gracie.

I'm off to bed; enjoy yourself, tart, and try not to bring the party back here lol.

I turn the phone off, take my pills, and slip into oblivion.

*

Five Years Previously

"Daisy, please wake up. We love you. We miss you. I'm so sorry."
I can hear someone who sounds like Gracie, but her voice sounds so strange. I try to turn to see where the voice is coming from, but I can't. I can feel her voice getting more distant. I feel like I'm slipping away from it, not getting any closer.

"Daisy, please." It sounds like Mom, but now they just sound jumbled up. I'm confused.

*

I wake up to some giggling and music being played. I know, then, that Gracie must have brought someone home with her. She brings home someone new every week. She says she isn't ready to settle down. I wish I could meet someone, but I know that isn't going to happen any day soon. No one would want me now that I'm broken.

Getting out of bed, I make my way to the kitchen. We live in a loft-style apartment, so it doesn't take me long to get there. I flick the switch on the kettle and sit back, watching it boil. When it does, I take a cup off the mug tree and put a tea bag into it. After I have made my tea, I go and sit down at the table looking out onto the roof garden. I love my garden; it's big and beautiful. We have a deck area which spills out onto a pathway snaking its way through all the flowers. We have barbecues out here in the summer; they're always such good fun.

As I sit there, staring out into the garden, I can feel someone coming up behind me. I start to shake; I can feel the sweat starting to form on my hands.

"It's okay. It's me," Gracie says, gently reaching out and touching my shoulder.

I feel the tension in my shoulders releasing. Turning to face her, I smile. "Morning, Gracie, or is it still goodnight?" I laugh.

She smiles at me and makes herself a cup of tea. She comes over to the table and sits down with me. "It's goodnight, but I wanted to have a cup of tea with you first. Ben has gone home. I didn't want him to stay." She smiles and takes a sip of her tea.

"Ben, huh? At least this one has a name." I laugh again.

She smiles. "I like him, actually. I definitely want to see him again," she says looking really coy. Gracie doesn't do relationships, she does one night stands. She doesn't want to get involved. I know why—because she doesn't want to leave me.

"Really?!? That's great, Gracie; you should have introduced him."

"I wanted to, but I wanted to tell you first. If he still wants to see me again after he's slept all the alcohol off, then I'll definitely see him again, and I promise I'll introduce you." She comes over to my side of the table and kisses me on the head. "I love you, Daisy."

I reach up and put my hand over hers. "I know you do, Gracie, I love you too."

She turns and walks out of the room to go to bed. I'm happy that she has met someone she likes, and I hope he feels the same; she needs to find some happiness.

She feels guilty about what happened, but I don't blame her. She just blames herself.

We've lived together for the last three and a half years. Mom wanted me to move home after everything that went on, but I'm too independent to be looked after by someone else. I don't want anyone to feel pity for me. I don't, so why should someone else?

My life changed completely that night. Not only do I have the physical scars, but I also have emotional and psychological ones that run deeper. My therapist thinks she can help me, and she's trying some new radical techniques. So far, it seems to be working, but I don't hold out much hope. She's coming over this morning to try something new.

After looking out into the garden, I go back into my room to get showered and dressed. After Anne-Marie comes I'm going over to Mom and Dad's. They still don't think that I should live with Gracie, but I'm old enough to make my own decisions.

An hour later, Anne-Marie rings the buzzer. I let her in and wait for the elevator to trundle up. We live in an old warehouse-type building with one of those big elevators that you could fit anything in. When it comes to our floor, it makes a noise, and then the door opens and Anne-Marie walks out, smiling. She's such a lovely woman; she puts me at ease just by looking at her.

"Hey, Daisy. How are you?"

"I'm good, I'm off to see Mom and Dad after we've finished."

"Great. I'm glad you're getting out. Have you been anywhere other than your parents' and the hospital?" Straight down to business, Anne-Marie doesn't waste any time.

Pouring water into her cup of instant coffee, I put it down before thinking about my answer. I don't go anywhere other than my parents', the hospital, and sometimes my doctors. All my food shopping is done online and my clothes shopping too. "No, not this week."

She smiles. "Then we need to change that." Taking her coffee cup, she walks over to the sitting room. My apartment is all open plan making it quick to move from room to room. After sitting she asks, "How've you been this week, Daisy? Have you painted any more pictures?"

"I have. You know how we talked about my compulsive tendencies and my obsession with shoes? Well, after thinking about what you said, I know that I need to break the cycle. So, I painted two odd shoes. Not just odd, but two totally different colors, shapes, and sizes." I get the painting from my studio area and bring it over to her. "My friend Gemma has said she's going to put it in her gallery along with some of my other paintings."

Handing the painting to her, I watch her face for a clue as to what she thinks. I paint as part of my therapy. I never thought that art therapy would help as much as it has. It gives me something else to focus on rather than *The Incident*.

"This is amazing, Daisy. You have a real talent. It would be great if you could go and see it in the gallery. Think how proud your parents would be to be there with you."

"I'll think about it," I say, knowing that I won't go. "Apparently, it's Two Different Colored Shoes Day next month, and she thinks it will be perfect for the featured painting."

"Perfect indeed. Now, tell me how you've been. I think this week we need to push you a little more. Small changes. If it's Two Different Colored Shoes Day, how about you wear odd shoes on that day?"

I shudder at the thought of it. Since I was attacked, I've had an issue with shoes. It was the last thing I saw before I passed out. "I'll try," I whisper. Just the thought of it makes my body coil up tight. My muscles tense up, and the pain reverberates through my body. Anyone who suffers from chronic pain knows what I'm describing.

"That's all I ever ask of you, Daisy." She sips her coffee, watching me. "So, how do you feel about wearing your cardigan inside out for a day?"

Again my heart rate increases. My compulsive tendencies rush to the surface. I have this thing in my head about being fully dressed, perfectly matched, and presented, just in case I end up in the hospital. I think, because I was drunk, my hair was a mess, and my clothes were disheveled when I ended up in the hospital the last time, I just have this deep need to be perfectly dressed. Anne-Marie knows it, and she's pushing me.

"Ern..." My mouth opens, but I can't seem to make any words come out.

"Let's do it now, then you can change it back after our session. If anything happens to you, then I promise to change it back before we call anyone." She stands and comes over to me, not really waiting for an answer. She knows I'll do it. I don't want to be a recluse and beholden to my insecurities, but damn, it freaks me out to think about my cardigan being inside out.

I nod and lean forward as she takes my cardigan off, turns it inside out, and puts it back on me again. My heart is beating erratically. Anne-Marie sits back down and talks about the weather, what's going on in the world, and just anything to take my mind off it.

After about ten minutes, I can breathe normally, and we chat about my late night chats.

Before she leaves, she turns my cardigan back the right way and puts it back on me. It wasn't that bad. I just need to be pushed.

*

Five Years Previously

I'm so tired, but I know that I want to open my eyes; I can hear Gracie and Mom are there. They are talking to each other: "Gracie, she will come round soon, I just know she will."

"I'm sorry, Mrs. Michaels, I can't tell you how sorry I am. I shouldn't have stayed at the party and let her go home on her own." Gracie is sobbing.

"It's not your fault, Gracie, stop blaming yourself. When Daisy makes her mind up about something, she does what she wants."

I try to make a noise, but nothing comes out of my mouth. I open my eyes and try to turn my head, but it won't move. I try again. It feels like there is something in my throat, it hurts to swallow. Actually, it feels like I'm choking. I try to say something, and all of a sudden, I hear a noise. It's a strange noise. What is it?

Beep…beep…beepity beep… it's getting faster. Suddenly, I see a nurse come over quickly to the bed. She puts her hand on my hand. "Hey, Daisy, welcome back."

I hear a sob, and my Mom and Gracie come into my vision. They are both sobbing, and they take a hand each. My hands feel wet, and when I look at them both, I can see they are crying and their tears are falling onto my hands. I try to move to get closer to them, but I can't.

Two doctors come into the room. "Please, can you leave, we need to assess Daisy now that she has woken up. You can stay just outside, but we need to check for neurological damage."

Mom starts to argue with them, but they just look at her, and then I hear, "Baby, me and Gracie are just outside. I'm going to call Daddy, and he'll be here before you know it. Please stay with us. We love you." Then I see them disappear from my line of vision.

*

My taxi arrives and takes me to Mom's. The driver, Sarah, is my usual driver. I like to make sure I know who is picking me up and taking me places. I don't like surprises and don't want someone I don't know coming to collect me. I always have a lady driver too because I don't feel comfortable sharing a small space with a guy.

"Morning, sweetheart," Sarah says as she helps me into her car. "Off to your mom's for dinner today, are you?"

"Yeah, you know how I like my homemade dinner."

"Ask her to save me some, it's always a nice treat when she gives me a plate for me to have for my dinner." She laughs as she climbs back into the car and pulls away from the curb. "So any news this week, Daisy?"

"Same old, same old, Sarah. Nothing much happens in my world, you know that." I sigh. I'd love to be able to tell her that something really exciting happened this week, but it didn't. It never does.

"One day you're going to surprise me, Daisy, you're going to tell me something so exciting you won't even wait for me to ask you about it." She turns and smiles at me, and I smile back.

After about fifteen minutes, we pull up outside Mom's house, and Sarah helps me out of the taxi. She is such a nice woman, and I love her driving me around. Mom is waiting for me, and she waves at her. "Hi, Sarah, thanks for bringing her over."

"No problem, Mrs. Michaels, it's always a pleasure." She waves back at her. "Call me when you want collecting," she says, looking at me.

"I will. Thanks, Sarah, have a good afternoon."

She smiles and waves at me as she climbs back into her taxi and then drives off.

I turn when I see her get to the end of the street then I go into the house. Dad comes over and gives me a hug. "How's my angel today?"

"I'm good, Dad," I say when he releases me. I follow him into the lounge, and he hands me a glass of wine.

I take it from him and take a sip. It's lovely and cold. Savoring it in my mouth before I swallow it, I go over to the patio doors and look out at the garden; it's beautiful. I remember playing in it as a child. Seeing the swings makes me remember Gracie and me playing on it; we used to love standing on them and swinging as high as we dared to go. Shaking my head to get rid of the memories before the tears flow as I recall our innocence, I turn back to Dad.

Taking a sip of my wine, I go out to the kitchen to see if I can help Mom. I'm not sure what I can do, but I'll offer anyway; it makes me feel better.

"Hey, Mom," I say, and she turns and smiles at me. "Can I do something to help?"

"No, angel, it's all done. Just go and sit at the table and I'll bring the meat over." She turns back to pick up the meat tray, and I make my way over to the dining table.

Dad sits down next to me, and as always, he takes my hand and kisses it. He smiles at me and then places my hand back down on the table. Mom and Dad have been so good since *The Incident,* but I can see how it affects them.

Dinner is so tasty, as always, and I tell Mom that.

"Thanks, Daisy, I'm glad you liked it. I made your favorite: roast beef."

I know she did; she always makes my favorites when I go over for dinner. I stay for a couple of hours, and we play cards, and then Dad makes hot chocolate for me while I wait for Sarah to come pick me up to take me home.

Once I get home, Gracie is there waiting for me. "Hey, did you have a good day, Daisy?"

"Yeah, it was nice, we had dinner, talked about nothing, and then Sarah came and collected me. The usual!" I laugh. "What did you get up to today? Did you talk to Ben?"

"Yeah, he messaged me, and he's taking me out this week. Come and sit over here. Do you want a drink?"

"Yeah, why not, then you can tell me all about Ben and how wonderful he is." I smile. I love hearing her stories about her men, but sometimes I get a bit jealous. I'd love to have someone who likes me, but no one is ever going to look at me long enough to give me a chance.

We sit in the lounge for a couple of hours while she tells me all about Ben and the party last night. It sounds like great fun, and I wish I hadn't stayed at home, but she wouldn't have been able to have so much fun if I was there—she would have been looking after me. That's why I never go. She feels guilty enough without having to look after me when she should be having fun.

She tells me about who was there, who got together with who, and about the antics of the people who got drunk. It sounds like a wild party. "I wish you were there, Daisy, I miss you when I'm out."

"I know, we need to have a party here soon, and then we can show everyone how to party," I say smiling.

"That sounds like a good idea. It's my birthday in two weeks; we can organize something for then."

"Game on," I say, high fiving her. "Right, I'm off to bed."

"Yeah, I've got work tomorrow," she says, giving me a hug. "Night, night."

"Night, I love you," I say, going to my room.

*

Five Years Previously

The doctors are all talking to me at once. "Can you feel this?" "Can you feel that?" "Move this!" "Move that!"

"I'm tired, please let me sleep. I want to go to sleep." I start slurring my words.

"Stay with us, Daisy. Come on, your mom and your friend want to talk to you. Don't close your eyes."

The doctor stands up, and I can see him waving Mom and Gracie back into the room. I hear them both run to the bed. They grab a hand each and pull them up to their mouths, and they keep kissing them.

"Oh my God, Daisy, I'm so happy you're okay. We were so worried about you, angel," Mom says. I try to smile at her, but I can't.

"I'm so sorry, Daisy," Gracie says.

I can't talk. I try, but the tube has made my throat so painful. I just close my eyes and blink a few times. They are both talking at the same time, and then I hear, "Where's my angel?" I can hear Dad walking toward the bed. He comes over to Mom's side and takes my hand and lifts it to his mouth to kiss it. Then he looks at me and says, "I love you, Daisy. Don't leave us again."

I blink twice; I hope they understand me

*

Getting into bed, I notice I have a message. Who is texting me at this time of night?

When I look at my messages and see it's from a number I don't recognize, my heart starts beating really fast; I don't get texts from anyone except Mom, Dad, Gracie, and a few other friends. Even my closest online friends don't know my number.

I open the text and close my eyes. I don't know what I think will happen, but just in case it explodes. Laughing at myself, I open my eyes.

Thanks for nothing. I waited for an hour at the bar and you either didn't turn up or you walked on by without acknowledging me. What a waste of time that was!

WRONG NUMBER

I don't know who this is or what they're talking about. I'm curious though, so I reply. *I'm sorry, I think you might have the wrong number, but just so you know, I'd have made myself known.* I press send before I can change my mind. A little bit of banter never hurt anyone, and it's been a while since I chatted with someone new. Anyway, who says they'll text me back?

It takes about five minutes before I get a reply, but when I do, I open it straight away.

I'm sorry if I have the wrong number, that just finishes off my evening. Thank you for trying to make me feel better. I hate blind dates, but my friends set me up on one and she didn't show. God, I sound so sad.

I know how he feels; I hate blind dates too. I can just imagine standing there waiting for someone to show up and introduce themselves. It's no wonder he's annoyed.

No you don't at all. Well actually maybe a little bit lol.

Thanks lol. Now I feel so much better.

I like his sarcasm, it's just like mine. *It's okay, I'm quite lonely and I don't get out much—that's sad. Not having a blind date turn up is unfortunate, but not sad.*

Why are you lonely?

That's a good question. I guess I don't put myself out there too much. That's one of the things that I need to get over and do something about. Hopefully my counseling will help with that. *I don't get out much and I'm shy.*

You can't be that shy if you replied to my text. Most people would have ignored it.

I think about what he just said. He's probably right. It's not too bad when I can hide behind a computer or a phone—then I'm actually not that shy. It's just in person. *Yeah I suppose, but I just wanted you to know it was the wrong number, instead of ignoring you.*

Well thank you. My name's Eoin by the way.

Hi, Eoin, my name's Daisy.

What a lovely name, daisies were my mom's favorite flower. She always used to wear them as daisy chains. She died two years ago and I leave them on her grave whenever I can.

Sorry to hear about your mom. That's sad. I bet she loves you leaving them though. Very considerate. That shows he has a soft side to his personality. I don't know why that pleases me, but it does.

Yeah I'm sure she does. I'm glad you messaged me back, I feel better now.

Well I was just getting into bed when you texted, ten minutes later and I would have been asleep.

Timing is everything, my mom always said that. Well if you are in bed then I don't want to keep you awake.
I don't mind, I'm not sleepy now anyway.
Good because I'm enjoying talking to you.

I lie in my bed for another two hours texting back and forth with Eoin. He tells me about his mom and how she died from cancer. He helped to nurse her toward the end, and it meant that he had to put his relationships on the back burner. Since she died, he has retrained as a palliative care nurse and helps other people and their relatives to cope with imminent death.

Wow, just wow, he sounds like such an amazing and wonderful person.

Daisy, Daisy did you fall asleep on me?
Daisy, thank you for tonight; I really enjoyed myself and for a blind date it was absolutely perfect. Goodnight. Sleep tight.

*

Five Years Previously

I'm just so tired, I can't talk, and everyone is asking me questions. I blink my eyes, and the time in between is getting longer. I close them, and I know I'm going to sleep again.

"Daisy, wake up." I can hear Dad.

Then I hear another voice. "She's worn out, her body needs to rest again. Let her sleep. She will wake again. I promise."

"Thanks, Doctor. Can we wait here?"

"You know you can, or we will ring you when we she wakes up if you want to go home."

I hear Mom say, "We'll wait, if that's okay."

Then I don't hear anything more.

*

Waking up, the first thing I do is check my phone. I smile when I see my messages from Eoin. I didn't dream it, then; it really did happen.

I get dressed and go into the kitchen to make my morning tea; I always like my tea before I do any painting.

After sipping my drink and taking the few minutes to wake up, I think about Eoin. It was so nice to talk to him, and I felt normal and not like someone who was scared of being outside. Going over to my studio, I grab my paints and work on a portrait. I don't know who it is, but they're wearing a daisy chain for a necklace. Something about my conversation with Eoin last night spoke to me.

Gemma is coming over today to take some of my paintings for her gallery. She is using my paintings for a feature in a couple of weeks. I'm nervous—what if no one likes them—but excited at the same time that she feels they are good enough to be viewed.

Gracie finally rolls out of bed and comes over to me with another cup of coffee. "Wow, that's really good, Daisy. I love the daisy chains."

"Thanks, I just got inspired." I turn to face her with a big smile on my face.

Gracie looks at me and asks, "Hey what's up with the stupid grin? What have you been up to while I was in bed?"

"I'm good. I slept really well. You'll never guess what happened to me when I went to bed."

"What?!? Did you go to a party and not tell me?" She laughs.

"No, I had a message from a random number who thought I was his blind date and I hadn't turned up."

"No way! What did you do? Did you text him and tell him to fuck off?"

"Actually no! I texted him and told him that I wasn't his date, but that I would have made myself known."

"Shut up! You did not! Oh my God, that's fantastic, Daisy."

"Oh yes, I did," I say laughing. It is so out of character for me.

"Okay, well, I have to go to work, Daisy, but I want to see these messages tonight."

"Well, you'd better get a bottle of wine or two on your way home, because I was up 'til about two-ish, so there are a few of them."

"You're on—we are having a girlie night tonight. Love you."

"Love you more," I say as she leaves for work.

I go back to painting and don't notice the hours pass me by. Before I know it, Gemma is buzzing to get let in. After letting her into the elevator, I wait for her to come up to my floor.

She chats about how her gallery is going and that she can't wait to see the new pictures that I've painted. Bringing her to the studio, she stops, staring at the two shoes painting and the portrait with the daisy chain. "Daisy, this work is amazing. I'm so happy you are going to let me show your paintings. What's the chances of you coming down, and we can do a night where we feature your work?"

I recoil, and my mood changes. She knows I don't like to go out unless it's to Mom's or the doctors. "I don't know, Gemma. I'm not sure I could be around that many people."

"What about if we limit the number of tickets to, say, fifty of our best customers? Do you think you'd be able to manage that?"

"I'm not sure. Let me think about it. I'd have to do a lot of work with my therapist before then. When are you thinking?"

"Maybe next month because it's Two Different Colored Shoes Day, and it would tie in nicely with this picture, which is phenomenal by the way."

"Thanks. Okay, let me think about it and see if my therapist can work extra with me to achieve it. I'd love to see your gallery."

"Why don't we get you down one night on your own and show you around; that way it wouldn't be new on the night of the showing?"

"That sounds great. Let me know when you can do that, and I will definitely try to do that."

We talk for about an hour about my paintings and what ones I have in the pipeline. Then it's time for her to leave.

As I'm getting some lunch, my phone pings with a text.

It's Eoin. *Hey, hope you weren't too tired this morning. It was a late night.*

My heart is beating really fast reading his text. I wasn't sure if he would contact me again, even though I really wanted him to. *I was inspired to paint this morning.*

Really, what did you paint? Can I see it?

Promise you won't be angry or laugh at me?

I promise.

I painted a portrait of a lady who was wearing a daisy chain around her neck. It was after listening to your story of your mom.

Why would that make me angry? Can I see it?

I send him a photo I took just before Gemma left.

Eoin doesn't come back to me immediately, and I panic that he won't like it.

Daisy, it's amazing. You are so talented. Look at this. He sends a photo back to me.

Oh my God, it's a picture of his mom. My painting looks so much like her. He must have told me what she looked like last night, and it was in my subconscious.

I want to buy that painting.

My friend is taking it to her gallery but we're going to have an open night if you want to come along. It's going to be one of the featured paintings. I'll make sure you get a discount.

I'd love to come; let me know the date when you have it. Wow, you are amazing. What else do you do or are you a full-time artist?

I think about what I want to say in reply. I enjoy talking to him and don't want to frighten him off. *I paint full time. I have a studio at home and then I sell some of my smaller works on Etsy. I love it. I can picture anything in my mind, which is strange as I don't leave home often.* Shit, why did I tell him that? He's going to think I'm odd.

Why not? Maybe that's why you paint so well, you take in every detail when you do leave home.

I had an accident five years ago and it's made me very nervous leaving home. I only go to my mom's and the doctor. Everything else I do online.

So this gallery night would be a really big thing for you then?

Yes, I haven't decided if I am going yet.

Can I take you? I'd love to meet you and get to know you more.

Shit. I didn't think he would progress so quickly. I can't meet him. What happens when he sees me and is disappointed? How can I cope with the rejection? *I'd love that, but I'm not sure I'm going. When I decide then I'll let you know. Is that okay? There's a lot about me you don't know.*

You didn't say no immediately so that's a win for me. There's a lot you don't know about me either. That's why people meet up and chat, to get to know each other. I want to get to know you. What I've seen so far I like. You're my type of woman, Daisy.

You don't know what you're talking about. I'm no one's type of woman. I'm different to everyone else. I'm not normal.

Why? Because you don't like to leave the house? Then let me come over to you. You can have a friend there too if you want. Don't push me away before you've given me a chance. You gave me a chance last night and I'm so glad you did.

But there's something you need to know first...

I don't want to know anything else. You are who you are. I am who I am. We all have our insecurities. Let me find out in my own time, let me work these things out. They shouldn't define you or us.

I cry. He's so in tune with how I feel. He knows I have a secret, and he knows it's hard for me to tell him, but really he should know before he decides he wants to meet me. *I'm in a wheelchair. I can't walk.* I wonder if he will message me back, or will he just walk away?

And? Why would that change the way I would feel about you? I like you, your personality, the way you make me laugh. That won't change when I meet you. Unless you're really three dogs stacked on top of each other wearing a trench coat. Are you?

I laugh out loud. The one thing I don't like to tell anyone who doesn't know me has just been brushed over, and he made a joke. I am so glad I texted him back last night; I have a feeling this man is going to change my life. *I am definitely not three dogs. Just don't expect me to run after you, because I can't lol.*

I am serious that I want to meet you. When can I come over?

I am having some wine with my flatmate tonight, but maybe in a couple of days we can arrange something. I would love to meet you too. Now I need to get back to painting. You are an inspiration, Eoin.

Glad I can help, and make sure you text me when you've had a few drinks. I love drunk texts; it shows your real personality lol.

I put my phone in my pocket and roll back over to the studio. I reflect on how much my life has changed in the last five years. I can honestly say I am a better person. Perhaps not so optimistic or positive, but I am a better person.

Picking up my paintbrush and a brand new blank canvas, I drift into my artist mode and paint.

*

Five Years Previously

I've been drifting in and out of sleep for the last few days. I've heard my parents and Gracie come and go. I can hear what they are saying, but I can't communicate with them. It's so frustrating that I keep crying. When they see my tears, they think I am in pain. I'm not because I'm drugged up, but my heart is breaking for them. Gracie thinks this is her fault. It's not; it's mine for leaving and walking home alone.

My parents think that they should have been there to collect me. We can all go on blaming ourselves, but what about the monsters that did this to me? What happens to them—nothing?

They finally take the tube out of my throat so that I can try and talk. My throat is scratchy and sore, but I want to tell these three people that I love them. "I love you all," I croak out in between sips of water. We all start crying, and they hug me.

The doctor comes in and says he wants to talk to me. "Daisy, I'm sorry to tell you that you suffered some spinal damage in the attack. You may never be able to walk again. We haven't been able to do too many neurological tests while you were asleep, but now that you're awake, we want to perform some tests to see what you can and cannot do."

I cry. One party. One mistake, and I may never walk again.

*

Gracie comes in with the wine after work. I've made spaghetti Bolognese, and we sit at the table. After a couple of glasses and talking about our day, she says, "So, tell me about these texts."

"Well, I've been talking to him today as well. He's really nice. Funny and friendly. He started off sending a message to his blind date moaning because she didn't turn up but got me instead. I told him he had the wrong number but that I would have introduced myself if he was my blind date. We chatted back and forth for a couple of hours. He made me laugh, and I felt normal again."

"You are normal, you know that, Daisy."

"I know, but sometimes I don't feel it. Anyway, listen, today he asked to meet me. Gemma was over earlier and took one of my paintings, and I was inspired by something Eoin said last night and painted this." I roll over to the studio and pick up the picture of the lady with the daisy chain. When I show Gracie, she takes it from me.

"You were painting this this morning when I left for work. It's beautiful. Who is it?"

"Well, that's the funny thing. Eoin was telling me about his mom last night—she died a few years ago. He used to give her daisies, and told me that she used to wear the daisy chains he used to give her. When I started painting today, I just painted, and this was the result. I showed it to Eoin, and he told me that it looks like his mom, and he wants to buy it."

I show her the picture that Eoin sent me last night.

"Wow, it looks like his mom; that's a bit spooky, isn't it?"

"Yeah that's what I thought, but he thought it was lovely. I asked if he wanted to go to the night at the gallery, but he said only if I was there."

"Oh my God, are you going?"

I shake my head. "No, I don't think I can. Even though Gemma says she's only going to invite fifty people max. It's too much for me. But Eoin wants to come over here and meet me first."

"How do you feel about that?"

"I don't know. I want to meet him. I really do. I just don't know."

"Well, I can be here with you, then you won't be on your own if you freak out or want him to leave."

"Would you do that?"

She smiles. "Of course I would." She reaches out and takes my hand. "We could have a double date, and I could invite Ben."

My breathing gets a bit erratic thinking of two new people in the room with me, but I've realized over the last couple of days that I have to step outside my comfort zone, or those five men who attacked me will have won. They will have succeeded in destroying my life. I don't want that. "I'd like that. But this thing with Eoin is only a friendship. He wouldn't want someone like me."

"Why, what's wrong with you, Daisy?"

"I mean my wheelchair. It's a lot for someone to take in and look past."

"Did you tell him about the wheelchair?"

"Yes, I did."

She smiles. "That's the first time you've done that. You never tell people about the chair, you just let them think you don't want to meet them. This is your first step. How about we invite the two of them over tomorrow? Let's strike while you feel like doing it." She takes a sip of her wine.

I take a sip of mine. Neither of us talk. She knows that I need these few minutes to clear my mind and make a decision. Taking a deep breath, I say, "Okay."

I don't know if Eoin will come over or not. He might have just said that to be nice to me. I send him a text to find out. *Hey, would you like to come over tomorrow? I want to meet you. I don't want to just text you.*

He takes a few minutes to come back. *I'm working tonight and will be sleeping during the day, but I can come over tomorrow night.*

Can I panic before you come over? I might send you texts telling you not to come, so just ignore those, right?

Noted. And that's fine. I get the impression this is a big step for you and I'm delighted you're going to take that step with me.

"Gracie, he said he will come over tomorrow, and he will ignore any of my panic texts that I know I'll send him. You need to give me a makeover."

Gracie laughs. "Maybe we'll start with wearing your cardigan the right way round."

Looking down, I laugh. "I turned it inside out today after talking to Anne-Marie about my compulsive tendencies yesterday. I guess I was so busy that I forgot I had it on back to front."

"That's the key thing, Daisy. Keep busy, and you won't think about everything so much."

"Maybe." We move into the sitting area and bring the wine with us. Turning on a movie, we laugh and chat our way through it.

I get a couple of messages from Eoin, but I know he's working, so I don't expect to hear too much from him.

When I'm in bed, he sends me a text. *I'm guessing you're in bed already. I'm on my lunch break—funny at this time of night, right? I just wanted to say how proud I am of you. I don't know you very well but you amazed me today. I am looking forward to tomorrow night. I'm so glad I messaged you by mistake.*

Me too. Night x

I fall asleep, and for the first time, I don't have any nightmares.

*

Five Years Previously

After telling me I might not walk again, the doctors do every test imaginable. But I can't feel my legs. The rest of my body is normal. I can feel it and move it around exactly the same as before. They think one of the attackers stamped on my back when I was face down and did some damage.

I have to learn how to do everything from a chair. My muscles in my arms are weakened and need to be built up, so they give me exercises every day. I go to a gym that is specially designed for wheelchair users. It helps tremendously and it builds me up.

I'm not going to let anything stop me from living a normal life.

*

When I wake up, the nerves hit me. *I can't do this. What if he hates me? What if I hate him? What if Ben is horrible to me?* I don't get out of bed—I stay there, staring at the ceiling. Gracie comes in an hour later. She knows exactly what the problem is. She gets me out of bed and pushes me into the apartment and over to the door out to the rooftop garden. Opening the door, she rolls me outside.

"What do you see, Daisy?" she asks, sweeping her hands in front of her. "Is the world coming to an end?" I shake my head. "Did anything happen in the world after you went to bed last night?" I shake my head again. "Are you still alive? Living in an apartment with your friend? Living life as you want? An amazing artist? A beautiful woman? And are you having a blind date tonight?"

"Yes," I whisper.

"Then we need to get this show on the road. We need to find something nice for both of us to wear. We need to get some food organized. We need to tidy up and make sure it's nice for both of our men. We've got this. Not me. Not you. Us. Both of us. I'll be here all the time. If you feel uncomfortable, then they can leave. No problems."

"Gracie, thank you." I hug her to me. She grounds me when she knows that I'm about to freak out.

"Enough talk; let's eat breakfast and get cleaning."

So that's what we do.

Having a shower and getting dressed isn't an easy task, but it's something that I do every single day, and I have it down to a fine art. Except tonight I want to look nice and pretty. Gracie sits on the bed while I slip into my specially designed wardrobe. I reach for clothes, and she shakes her head until my hand falls onto a dress I had forgotten I had. I don't wear dresses very often; I don't like looking at my legs. Because I don't use them every day, they've become thin and weak, but I decide that I want to be pretty, and I want to wear a dress.

"That's perfect," Gracie says, clapping her hands. The dress is black, fitted at the top and flared at the bottom. It comes down below my knees, but it has daisies all over it.

"Yes, it is perfect," I say, smiling.

After getting dressed, I head out to the sitting room. Gracie has put out some nibbles and passes me a drink while we wait for the boys. The buzzer sounds, and Gracie lets Ben in. My butterflies are going mad in my stomach; I feel sick. The elevator rattles up to our floor, and Gracie is waiting when the door opens. I hear Ben kissing her and talking to her as they move closer behind me. I can't turn around yet. I feel sick.

Gracie rests her hand on my shoulder and squeezes.

This centers me, and I spin around with a smile on my face. "Hey." I hold out my hand for him to shake.

He's gorgeous; I can see what she sees in him. He smiles and clasps my hand warmly. "So pleased to meet you, Daisy. I've heard so much about you and both your antics."

I laugh. I can only imagine what she's told him about us. He sits, and she hands him a drink, and then the buzzer goes again. Shit, I'm nervous. Gracie looks at me and nods her head toward the buzzer.

I shake my head; I want to be the one to welcome Eoin to my home. Rolling over to the intercom, I say, "Hello?"

"Hey, Daisy, it's Eoin. Are you going to let me in?"

I laugh. "Yeah. When you get in the elevator, it will bring you straight to our floor."

"Thanks, see you in a few." I hear him open the elevator door, and then I hear the elevator trundling upward.

If I thought my nerves were bad when Ben arrived, they were only a starter compared to how I feel right now. My hands are sweaty; my heart is beating so hard I can hear it pumping in my ears.

The elevator never takes this long; surely it's been a few hours since he pressed the button. Everything moves slowly as the anticipation builds.

Then I hear the elevator stop and the door rattle as he opens it. When he steps out of the elevator, my heart stops beating. He's gorgeous. His brown hair is slightly longer on top than on the sides. It looks like he's just run his hands through it in the elevator. He's so handsome in his blue jeans and light blue shirt. He has a bottle of wine and a bunch of flowers in his hands. After looking around, when his sparkling green eyes land on me, he smiles and shows off his bright white teeth. "Hey, Daisy. You're so beautiful." He smiles at me as he steps closer to me.

I can feel the blush rising from my chin up to my forehead. "Hey, Eoin. So good to meet you."

"I was nervous," he whispers in my ear. "I thought you were three dogs in a trench coat, and you lured me here under false pretenses."

He grins at me, and I remember our chat when I told him I had to tell him something. And just like that, I feel relaxed. He knew what he was doing when he said that.

"Do I look like three dogs?" I whisper in return.

He smiles. "No, so much better."

I smile and make my way into the sitting room, where I introduce him to Gracie and Ben.

We have a few drinks and order some food. The laughs are loud, and none are forced. When we've finished our food and the boys have cleaned up after us, Eoin and I move to the rooftop garden.

Gracie and Ben are sitting on the couch, staring at each other, so I guess they want some privacy.

When we get outside, I lift myself onto the couch that's there. Eoin sits next to me and holds my hand. "I really enjoyed myself tonight. Thank you for meeting me. Gracie is a great girl, and Ben is really funny. I've had so much fun."

"I have too." I take a deep breath. I am so far out of my comfort zone that it's not funny. "I never do this. I don't think anyone has been up to visit the apartment except family and really close friends. I've never even met Ben until tonight."

"Why do you hide away, Daisy? You've got nothing to hide from. You're beautiful and funny, and I'm very happy to be here with you tonight."

"Thanks. But if I tell you my story, you'll understand why I don't socialize very well. It changed my life. Drastically. In many ways, not just having the wheels. But it made me fear everything and everyone for a couple of years. I'm just starting to get over some of those issues, and meeting you tonight has been a big step in getting back on my feet, so to speak."

"I won't push you to tell me your story, Daisy. You should only tell that story when you feel comfortable enough to do so. But I don't want tonight to be a one-time thing. I want to see you again." He stands up and walks to the edge of the garden. Holding onto the railing and looking out over the city, he says, "I want to take you down there and show you some of my favorite views. I want to go to the gallery with you and see your paintings. I want that. What do you want, Daisy?"

Wow, he's upfront. I guess he's learned in the last couple of days that I can procrastinate, and he's putting himself out there for me to know how he feels before I do. He wants me to feel comfortable with him.

What do I want? I've never asked myself that question. "I just want to get through each day in one piece. I want to live every day and not just survive every day." I haven't thought about what I want for so long. I just survive—yes, that's what I've done up to now.

I hate that he's over there and I'm still on the couch. I move so that I can get into my chair when, all of a sudden, he's standing in front of me. He holds out his arms as though he's going to pick me up but hesitates for a moment.

"I don't need help getting into my chair," I say, wriggling. I don't want him to feel that he has to help me. I've done this for years.

"Trust me?"

After a moment, I nod, and he picks me up by putting one arm under my legs and the other behind my back. He doesn't put me down in my chair; he walks right past it and moves to the edge again. This time he puts me down on the edge, facing him. He still has hold of my waist. I'm not scared. I'm not upset.

He opens my legs, and then he stands in between them. My heart is racing. I want him to kiss me, but I'm not sure if that's what he wants to do.

He reaches out, and his hand grazes my cheek. "I want to kiss you, but I don't want to push you into anything."

Looking up into his eyes, I want to kiss him too, more than anything I've ever wanted. "Kiss me," I whisper as I stare into his eyes.

He slowly leans in, and his lips caress mine. Then he moves his head away from mine to look in my eyes. He smiles and moves back down again—this time taking my lips in his.

I've never been kissed like this before. It's soul consuming. Every part of my body comes alive. It's like all my nerves are standing on end, and I melt into him.

His hands cup my face, and he kisses me like he needs me to breathe.

When he stops and pulls away, I lean into him, wanting more of him.

He chuckles. "Wow," he says. "That was..."

"Yes, it was," I say before laughing. I have no words. It was amazing and so special.

He sits next to me on the edge. "Who knew my blind date would turn out like this?"

"I know. I'm just glad I answered your message."

"Me too, Daisy."

I shiver as the coolness in the air wraps itself around me.

"Come on, let's go back inside, I don't want you getting sick from a cold or something." He leaves me and gets my chair, bringing it over to me. Then he watches me climb into it. I'm glad because I don't want him to think he has to do everything for me. That's not how I operate. I never want anyone to feel sorry for me; that's not me either.

We go back inside, and Ben and Gracie have disappeared. I feel slightly awkward because I wonder if he thinks we should disappear to my room. I'm not ready for that yet. "Do you want a cup of coffee?" I ask, going into the kitchen.

"I'd love one, and then I'll be off. I'm tired what with working last night," he says following me into the kitchen. As I put the kettle on he finds the cups. We work together silently.

When I hand him his cup, he leans against the counter. "Do you think you'll be able to go to the gallery with me? I'd love to go with you." He takes a sip of his coffee.

"I'd love you to go with you as well, but I'm not sure I can cope in crowds."

He moves closer to me, takes my coffee, and takes my hand. "I'll be there with you, Daisy, and if you need to leave, then we can leave. At the first sign of discomfort, we can just leave and come here."

When he puts it like that, I think I could do it. "I'll talk to Gemma; she wants me to go down there a night or two before the exhibition to have a look around so that I'm more comfortable."

"That's a great idea. I can go with you if you want. Or not. Whichever you'd prefer." He leans closer and kisses me on the cheek. "I'm going to go home now. I've had a great evening, Daisy. Hopefully we can do it again soon."

"I hope so too," I whisper before smiling at him.

We move over to the elevator, and he kisses me once more before he gets in. He waves as he goes down, and then it's quiet. He's gone.

I listen to the elevator as it stops on the ground floor. Then I go into my bedroom, undress, and get into bed.

I have the biggest smile on my face when I get a message.

Thank you for tonight. I know how hard it was, but you were amazing. I'm glad you gave me a chance.

I had a great night. Thank you so much.

Sleep tight, talk tomorrow.

I smile as I feel myself drifting off to sleep. Today was a good day. A really good day.

*

Four Years Previously

I've been out of the hospital for a few months, staying with my parents until I'm strong enough to decide what I want to do. Gracie and I have been talking about moving in together, but it has to be the right place. I don't want somewhere that will be difficult where I have to live downstairs in a house. No, I don't want that.

I've always been an independent person, I've never relied on anyone and I don't intend on starting now. It doesn't matter that I can't move my legs; I can still move around and do things for myself.

At breakfast when I'm drinking my coffee, I say, "Mom, Dad, I want to go and look at apartments today. Will you come with me? I want something that is wheelchair accessible. I don't want to compromise my independence."

Mom cries. "I knew this day would come, and I'm so proud of you, Daisy. Of course, we will go with you."

Hours later we walk into the warehouse apartment with the trundling elevator and open plan area, and I know it's perfect. Gracie loves it too, and we decide there and then that's where we are going to live.

Today is the day I take my independence back and stop letting my attackers define who I am.

*

It's been a month since Eoin came around for dinner, and I've seen him every day since. I talk to him all day, and everything is so easy. I haven't left the apartment, though, but today I am changing that. After dinner at Mom and Dad's, I am going to surprise Eoin at work. I know when his shift ends, and I want him to come with me to Gemma's gallery. My paintings are going on display next week, and I want to be able to attend. This is the first step.

Dinner is good, as always, and Sarah, my driver, is waiting for me outside. When I tell her where I want to stop on the way home, she's surprised. "Wow, Daisy. I'm impressed. This boy is bringing out a different side of you. I love it."

I laugh. She drives me to the hospital where Eoin works, and I take a few deep breaths before I leave the taxi and head inside. My heart is racing, and I can feel everything closing in on me as I have to maneuver through a crowd of young guys. I need to concentrate on what I'm doing, not those around me.

Finding his department, I go to the nurses' station and ask for Eoin. The nurse looks at me and smiles. "You must be Daisy; he is going to be so happy to see you. He's told us all about you."

I'm surprised she knows about me, but I smile. "Thanks, all good I hope."

She nods her head. "Oh definitely. He's smitten, honey." She gets up and walks over to a room, and I hear mumbles before I see Eoin come out. When he sees me, his face lightens up.

"Daisy, you came here. Is everything okay?" He leans down and kisses me gently on my lips then he takes my hands.

"Everything is perfect. I have a surprise for you. I know you finish your shift soon. How do you feel about going to Gemma's gallery... with me?"

"Really? Are you serious? I'd love to go with you. I'll see if I can get off a few minutes early, and then I'll get changed before you change your mind."

"I won't," I say, smiling. I'm not afraid when I'm with him. I've realized that over the last few weeks. He makes me feel invincible.

He disappears to go and get changed, and I sit by the nurses' station. All of the nurses take turns to say hi. It's not long before he comes back out, and we make our way to the elevator.

When we get into her car, Sarah says, "Hey, Eoin. I've heard lots about you."

He laughs, "Same."

She drives us to the gallery, and I can feel my hands getting clammy, but if I managed to go to the hospital, then I'll manage an empty gallery, right?

When I'm out of the car, we walk to the front door, and Gemma is there waiting for us. She's met Eoin, and she really likes him; she thinks he does wonders for me. When I get inside, I gasp. My paintings are all over the walls.

It's the one that's like his mom that Eoin goes over to first. He stands in front of it taking everything in, and I'm sure I see tears in his eyes.

"This is so beautiful. It looks just like my mom."

We stare at it for a few minutes until we move through the rest of the gallery. When we get to the back, there is a blank wall and slap bang in the middle is my picture of the two different shoes. It looks stunning. "Wow, Gemma, it looks great there."

"It sure does, but I've written something next to it—go have a look."

When I get over to it, I see some writing. It's small, and you have to be close to read it.

Two Different Colored Shoes Day is a special day where people wear different shoes. This has helped the artist to overcome some of her daily struggles. It's funny how people become hung up on looking perfect to feel perfect. Sometimes you need something out of the ordinary to really push your boundaries and reassess them. This picture is the artist's rendition of how she wants to feel. She doesn't want to feel that she has to conform, but that it's okay to be different. She doesn't want to be hidden from society because she's different, and this is the beginning of that metamorphosis. Like the life cycle of a butterfly, this is the artist's moment of breaking out of her cocoon of safety and flying away as a butterfly. Beautiful and free.

"Oh my God, Gemma, it's beautiful. Thank you so much." She comes closer to me, and I hug her.

"I'm just so proud of you, Daisy. So proud."

We spend another hour going from painting to painting, talking about my inspiration. Eoin rests his hand on my shoulder every time we stop to remind me that he's there and that he's always going to be there.

When we leave and go back to my place, he stays the night. I'm falling in love with this guy, and it doesn't frighten me.

*

A week later is the gallery night. Gemma invited fifty influential people. Of course, my family and friends are going to be there to support me, but I still have a panic attack before we leave. As always, Eoin just rests his hand on my shoulder, and it grounds me. We've come such a long way in a remarkably short time, and my outlook on life has changed.

The gallery night is a success; most of my paintings have sold, and I've been asked to do a few commissions. The picture with the daisy chain wasn't up for sale. I asked Gemma to not sell that one—I'm going to give it Eoin.

As it's Two Different Colored Shoes Day, everyone attending was asked to wear two different shoes. It's funny to see people dressed up and then have mis-matched shoes. All of them are walking funny.

The night is nearly finished when Eoin comes over to me. "Daisy, will you dance with me?"

"I can't dance, Eoin, it's too difficult with the chair."

"I don't need the chair. Do you trust me, Daisy?" He stares at me, and I know that I trust him with anything.

I nod.

He reaches down and pulls me up, holding me at the waist so that my weight isn't on my legs. Then he lifts me gently and places me close to this body so that my shoes are resting on top of his.

Looking into his eyes, I whisper, "I used to dance with my dad like this when I was younger."

He looks at me. "Me too with my mom."

As he holds my waist with one arm and his other hand is in mine, he moves us gracefully around a small piece of the floor in front of one of my paintings. Soon there is a small crowd of my family and friends, and I can see tears in my mom's eyes. She dances with Dad, Gracie with Ben, and a few others join in.

I lean my head on his chest and quietly say, "Thank you." He kisses the top of my head, and I feel content for the first time in a long time. "I love you, Eoin." I know I shouldn't say the words yet, but I can't help myself.

"I love you too, Daisy," he replies, and my smile is huge.

I can feel that my life is going to change drastically from now on, and Eoin is going to be with me every step of the way.

*

Two Years Previously

Anne-Marie is coming today; she told me last week that she wants me to try art therapy. I can't paint to save my life. I was really bad at art at school, but if she thinks it will help, then I'll try it. I'm the only one who can put obstacles in the way of my recovery.

When she arrives, we move to the area in the apartment that I have assigned as a studio, and she talks to me about what she wants. She wants me to paint whatever comes into my mind. Think about how I feel, think about what I miss the most.

An hour later, I realize I've painted a picture of the beach. I haven't been to the beach since The Incident. *But what surprises me is my raw talent. Anne-Marie is clapping her hands. "Daisy, that's amazing. You are so good at this."*

That's how I start my love affair with painting. Sometimes she gets me to paint things from The Incident. *I paint five pairs of identical shoes. That's the last thing that I remember.*

She tells me that this is where my tendency for compulsiveness started. Which is why she likes to try and push my boundaries.

*

One Year Later

"Come on, Daisy," Eoin shouts from the sitting room. "We're going to be late. You only have to pick two different shoes. It's not that hard."

I laugh. My compulsiveness is being pushed by wearing two different colored shoes, but I know that we will be celebrating this day for years to come.

Rolling out into the sitting room, I see that he has a sneaker on one foot and a dress shoe on the other. He looks funny, but he doesn't seem to mind at all.

Gracie moved out two months ago and has moved in with Ben. They are having a barbecue today to celebrate Two Different Colored Shoes Day. I think all my family and friends have embraced the holiday.

When Gracie moved out, Eoin moved in. Not because I didn't want to be alone. No, he moved in because we are madly in love with each other. He brings out the best of me, and he never does stuff for me. He lets me try, and when I need help, he doesn't hesitate. He gets me.

At Gracie's house, there are already a few people there. Crowds don't bother me as much these days. Eoin has taken me to a lot of things that have crowds, and we always have an escape route planned if we need one.

We have so much fun, and it's late before I even realize that I haven't seen Eoin for a while. I've been chatting and laughing with some friends. It feels like I'm at a party and everything is back the way it used to be, except I'm a totally different person. But tonight I don't feel different; I feel like Daisy.

I see Eoin coming over to me, and I can't help but laugh at his shoes.

He smiles, and then he bends down to do up his laces. As he raises his head, he looks at me and stays on the floor; reaching out, he takes one of my hands. "Daisy, you've made my life so much better by being in it. I was coasting along in life, never knowing the direction in which I was headed, until I sent you that text by mistake. It was the best thing I ever did. You came into my life, and you've been a ray of sunshine ever since. You make me see the best of everything. I want to spend the rest of my life with you. Will you marry me?"

I can't believe what he's saying. The tears are streaming down my face before he asks me. I nod; it's all I can do.

"I need to hear you say it, Daisy," he says, smiling.

"Yes, yes, yes, odd shoes and all."

Everyone claps as he stands up and leans down to kiss me.

Then he pulls me up for a dance. I feel like I'm floating around with Eoin. I know life is going to send us some big challenges, but I feel better knowing that Eoin will be there with me every step of the way.

♥

About the Author

Krissy V is a mother to two young children, who in turn keep her young. She lives in Dublin, Ireland, but she's originally from South Devon in the UK. She works full time in a pharmacy and writes in all her spare time, in her lunch hour, when watching TV at night and anywhere the urge takes her.

She is always thinking of situations that can be turned into a story and has started a few stories, which in turn will be completed and released to her readers.

Facebook: www.facebook.com/authorkrissyv
Twitter: @authorkrissyv

A Guide to Playing Rich

Ava Bari

Story Information

Holiday: Be a Millionaire Day
Holiday Date: May 20
Heat Rating: 1
Relationship Type: M/F
Major Trigger Warnings: None

Stef and Eli haven't led glamorous lives. They're simple. Normal. Nobody. The same cannot be said for Viv and Terrance, America's hottest new power couple and Stef and Eli's respective best friends. At their friends' engagement party, the pair find themselves inexorably drawn to each other. There's just one problem: they each think the other is a stuck-up celeb. Can their budding attraction overcome one whale of a misunderstanding?

A Guide to Playing Rich

Stef had lived in New York for all twenty-five years of her life, but she'd never once been to the Hamptons.

It was pretty much what she expected from the brochures and Viv's photos of her father's property. To the right was a stretch of beach. In the distance was a picturesque farm village. Mansions bigger than all three of her childhood homes dotted the coast. They had a perfect view of the ocean, and the bright orange sky was made for a painter's brush.

That last part might've been just Viv, who drew inspiration for her watercolor paintings from pretty much everything and could create a masterpiece out of a pile of toothpicks. Stef, whose idea of art was doodling in the margins of inventory sheets while working drive-thru, couldn't relate.

The party was already in full swing, putting to bed the old idea of being 'fashionably late.' If anything, Stef was early. Anticipating a long train ride from Smithtown to the Hamptons, she'd taken the earliest train out and even skipped lunch to make her travel time. That had to be the first time in months.

'Three meals a day,' she repeated the mantra, *'three meals a day, regular exercise, eight hours of sleep, not overworking yourself at a minimum wage fast food job while living with three loud roommates who make so much as reading the back of a cereal box impossible is how you make yourself the ideal candidate for any prestigious graduate program.'*

Just like Mom always said.

Excluding that last part, though her mother definitely would have added it if she'd met Stef's roommates.

"Name please?" A man in a waiter's getup stopped her at the gate, tapping his fingers on an iPad.

"Stef," she said, blinking. "Er—Bianchi. Stefania Bianchi for Vivian Walker's engagement party—"

"Thank you," the man said, his eyes firmly on the screen. "You may enter."

"You may enter," Stef muttered under her breath as she wandered through the tables to the bar. "What is this, a mountain full of forbidden treasure? Who talks like that? All he needs is a fake accent and he'll be ready for Broadway."

She found Viv chatting with a group of glamorous women in skintight dresses and silver jewelry. A few had gone for dark blue or purple eyeshadow, which didn't seem right for an engagement party, but most of them shined with perfect pink lips, blemish-free skin, and styled hair. Not a strand nor a string was out of place. They had to be famous. Up and coming actors or online influencers. That girl with the white polished nails probably had her own makeup line. The one with the throaty laugh would have a bunch of hit singles on the charts.

Her hundred dollar Macy's dress suddenly felt like a pile of rags.

"Stef!" Viv broke away from the group, charging with her arms outstretched. A passing waiter had to duck so as not to get slapped in the face. "Hey girl, you finally made it!"

"Sorry I'm late," Stef gasped as Viv hit her square in the stomach and hugged her insides out. Maybe because the top of Viv's head barely reached her chin, but Stef never seemed to remember how strong she could be. "Am I late? I hope not."

"You kidding? The party don't start until I say so."

Viv looked amazing. Like a million bucks, pun semi-intended. Her hair was curled into tight coils, forming a cloud around her heart-shaped face. Her hazel eyes glowed with warmth, her eyeshadow making them pop more than usual. She wore a powder blue sundress, simple yet elegant, hugging her curves and showing off just enough blemish-free dark brown skin to maintain respectability and get Terrance's blood pumping.

Stef glanced down at herself, tall and weedy, her floral print pink and white dress barely scraped her knee caps. She wished she'd gone with flats instead of heels. As if she didn't stick out enough.

"What's that face?" Viv put her hands on her hips and leaned forward even though she already had to crane her neck up to meet Stef's eye. "Don't tell me you're *sad* at my party."

"I thought the party hadn't started yet," Stef grinned. "And I'm not sad, just tired. The train was way too crowded, and I'm pretty sure we derailed twice and they just didn't tell us."

Viv rolled her eyes. "This is why you should've let me send a car for you."

"I live over an hour away."

"Well, if a train can do it, my driver can do it ten times better." Viv took Stef's hand and dragged her to the refreshments table. "Now, you look parched. Let's get some alcohol in you, and then you have to try these nachos!"

Stef's stomach rumbled like a chainsaw backfiring. That's what she got for not eating all day. She wobbled on her heels but managed to keep up and not trip. By the time all the limousines and Bugattis and Rolls Royces had crowded the driveway, they were munching on tortilla chips and giggling about the petty dramas of life like high school never ended.

*

This was the biggest house Eli had ever seen.

Not the biggest building, obviously. Growing up in Queens one car ride away from Manhattan, he felt more overwhelmed by the comparative smallness of Long Island suburbia than a sprawling mansion the size of three apartment buildings.

But knowing just one family lived there, and not even the whole year round… that was making his head feel funny. He prayed to God they had drinks ready to go. He would need several to get through this in one piece.

He found Terrance on the front porch straightening his tie. There was no drink next to him, not even a light beer. Eli wouldn't be surprised if he'd been completely sober since his last match for the Olympics.

"You made it," Terrance grinned. His tie still wasn't right, but he left it for now. "What's up, man?"

"What's up?" They high fived, and Terrance pulled him into a hug. "You ready for this?"

Terrance blew out a puff of air. "Ask me again at the wedding."

"If you make it that far," Eli teased.

Terrance threw a playful jab at him, miming a hit to his jaw. Years ago, when they first started training together, Eli nearly lost his front teeth to one of Terrance's Super Mega Punches (as his then twelve-year-old self so eloquently put it). His mother yelled at him for an hour and grounded him for a week. She forbade him from roughhousing with Terrance ever again.

That last one did not stick.

A chorus of bells in Eli's pocket made him freeze. A full three seconds passed before his brain kicked into gear, and he fumbled for his phone, nearly dropping it in a mud puddle.

"Hello!" he shouted, before realizing he hadn't accepted the call. First, he took a breath and straightened his shirt, as if that would help him with a phone call. "This is Elijah Johnson speaking."

"Hello, we're calling because the warranty on your vehicle has just expired—"

"Goddammit!" Eli reared back his arm, then remembered the phone had cost him five hundred dollars and stopped. "Every day with this robocall shit…"

"Woah, relax, bro," Terrance said as if Eli needed that more than something hard and heavy to break. "You still waiting on that callback?"

"It's been two weeks since my interview, T. *Two weeks*. How long are they going to make me wait?"

"I don't know," Terrance shrugged. "I've heard it can take up to a month for some people."

The great thing about Terrance was how good he was at saying just the right thing at just the right time. Since he neither felt like causing a scene at his best friend's engagement party nor getting his head knocked off, Eli did not kick Terrance in the shins and instead sunk into the nearest deck chair.

"Maybe I should've stayed at the gas station," he moaned.

"Didn't you get fired?"

"For stopping a robbery, which is bullshit anyway." Eli still couldn't drive past the old place without 'discreetly' flipping the colorful sign off.

"Let's be real, it was because Mr. Franks thought his daughter was into you."

Eli scoffed. "Shows how much he knows."

"What's that mean?" Terrance clapped him on the shoulder. "You can get a girl if you want. You ain't that ugly."

Eli shoved him off. "Could say the same to you. How'd you get Viv to go out with you once?"

"You know how," Terrance said, brushing non-existent hair back from his face. "I used my sweet moves and charisma to knock her off her feet."

"Got it. You begged until she took pity on you."

"Man—"

They pushed each other back and forth, laughing and cursing each other out. It was like they were kids again, except now they didn't have to worry about getting put in timeout if they wander off.

As more and more people Eli recognized from ESPN and major blockbuster films stopped to greet Terrance by name and congratulate him on his engagement, he couldn't help but miss those simpler times.

*

Stef checked her email, refreshing the page three times before she was satisfied that nothing other than spam and a JCPenney coupon had been delivered. She put the phone away and ate another shrimp off her cocktail. Then, she took her phone back out.

"Hey," a hand appeared from the air to rip the phone away from her, "how long have you been looking at this thing?"

"Just once or twice." Stef made a grab for the phone, but though Viv was smaller, she was also faster.

"Once or twice an hour? Or a minute? There's a difference."

Stef sighed. She would've tried again to retrieve her property, but Viv slipped it into her purse and, with dexterous hands a magician would envy, had the strap off Stef's shoulder and into a waiter's hands before Stef registered the lack of weight.

"Hey! What are you—"

The waiter avoided her with even less trouble than Viv had. Either both of them had ninja training, or Stef was just that uncoordinated.

"Stefania Bianchi," Viv declared, her hands on Stef's shoulders forcing her to hunch over slightly, "are you my best friend?"

"Viv, come on—"

"Are you my best friend?"

Stef rolled her eyes. "*Yes*, okay? Give me my purse back!"

"And is this my engagement party?"

"Yes."

"And are you my maid of honor who will stand by my side when I take my vows?"

"No, your sister is."

"And are…" Viv stopped and blinked a few times. "Okay yeah, but if I hadn't made a childhood pact with my sister that we'd be each other's maids of honor, would you be the one standing by my side when I take my vows?"

"Uh... maybe?"

"No, *yes*." Viv shook her. "The answer is yes. So do you understand that, as my best friend at my engagement party, I want you to have fun and not be worrying all night about some grad school application?"

Stef wanted to balk. This was not just some grad school program. This was *the* program which would send her down the path to her dream career and a long life of respect and fulfillment. No longer would she just be Stef, middle child of Don and Anna, fast food worker and proud holder of the record for most soda spilled on her shirt by unruly children while trying to mop the floor. Soon, she'd be Professor Bianchi, doctor of English and head of the department at... well, whatever school hired her when she graduated. She hadn't gotten quite that far yet.

Explaining all that to Viv, when she was already set on getting her way and certain she was acting in her friend's best interests, would be like breaking down a brick wall with a pool float, so Stef put on her best smile and gave Viv the hug she was waiting for. "You're right. I need to relax and enjoy myself."

"That's my girl!" Viv squeezed until most of Stef's ribs were cracked. "Gotta get ready for the big show tonight. Atlas-K is performing."

"Atlas-K the rapper?" Stef straightened up and smoothed her dress out. "How'd you get him?"

"My dad plays golf with his PR guy. Plus, Kanye and Drake both had scheduling conflicts."

Viv kept talking, but Stef found it hard to listen. Another limousine had just pulled up. Out came a woman in a fur coat with tinted shades and perfectly coiffed hair. Diamonds the size of cherry tomatoes adorned her fingers. She took off the shades, and Stef had definitely seen her somewhere. Probably YouTube or Netflix. Maybe she was an A-list movie star, and Stef was about to make a complete fool out of herself by not remembering her name.

She checked her dress one more time. It felt thinner and scratchier with each inspection. Viv stepped away to greet her new guests while Stef wandered in search of another shrimp cocktail. And maybe an actual cocktail to go with it.

The party was just getting started. She didn't see Atlas-K, and until he arrived, the DJ spun heavy beats for the growing number of guests on the dance floor. Music pulsed in Stef's ears and chest. Looking around, she spotted more familiar faces from the covers of magazines and movie posters. Nobody she would've fangirled over, but just the mere presence of so many 'elites' made her whole body itch. A woman in a silk-chiffon gown walked over with a half-full wine glass in hand.

"Excuse me, can I get a refill?"

Stef tried not to turn red but knew she was failing. "I'm not a waitress, sorry."

"Oh, okay." The woman turned on her designer heels and disappeared into the crowd.

Well, at least she didn't start yelling, Stef thought. Last week at work, a woman had literally thrown a drink at her head because the soda machine was out of ice.

"Stef!" Viv came running to her side, having apparently given every single guest enough attention. "Are you still over here playing wallflower?"

"I'm hungry. Not my fault these hors d'oeuvres are so good." She grabbed a piece of gouda off the cheese tray. "Plus, didn't we just talk three minutes ago?"

Viv rolled her eyes. "Look, why don't I introduce you to some friends of mine. See that guy over there? He's a Russian model and a competitive swimmer. Interested?"

The man in question had to be at least seven feet tall and had arms the size of an average adult's head. That alone would've made Stef shrink, but the way he made eyes at a woman in a tight red dress and seemed not to notice anything else sent her right back into the depths of the cheese tray.

"I think that might be a bit much." She picked up a slice of provolone and crammed it in her mouth.

She couldn't see Viv's face but could imagine the wheels in her head turning. "Okay fine, how about that one? He's a dancer with the Paris Opera Ballet. Think how flexible he must be."

"Think how ridiculous I'd look doing the hustle with him to a hip-hop song."

"The hustle?"

"It's the only dance I know."

Viv facepalmed. "See? This is why I wanted you to take dance classes with me when we were nine."

When they were nine, Stef had already been five feet tall and threw every school photo off balance. One supremely uncreative child had dubbed her 'Stef the staff.' Going to an after school class three times a week and learning to jump around on her giant feet had never appealed to her younger self. To her older self, who knew the lengths professional dancers went to for their craft, it was practically torture.

"Why don't I just go find someone myself?" She turned away from the cheese tray so she wouldn't be tempted again. "If I dance with one guy to one song, will that make you happy?"

"It will make me marginally less disappointed in you, but I'll take it," Viv grinned. "Besides, it's Be a Millionaire Day. Go out and be a millionaire!"

Stef tried to put some heat behind her glare, but it just wasn't possible. Viv had her patented 'cute' face on. The one she used in her Springtime Fashion Instagram posts. Those pics always got a tidal wave of likes and comments, and now Stef knew why.

She moved away from the refreshments, smoothing her dress one more time and almost reaching for her phone before remembering it was lost in the coatroom. There could be a dozen messages right now from the school, accepting her into the program, congratulating her on her hours of hard work, letting her know she needed to respond in the next five minutes or they would rescind the offer, telling her that the five minutes were up and she'd missed her golden opportunity and would spend the rest of her life regretting this day and all that she could've once had—

Three meals a day! She internally smacked herself. *Exercise. Hard work. Stop freaking out. Stop. Freaking. Out.*

Viv's squeal was both loud and unmistakable. She had rushed into the arms of a tall, handsome man in a fitted blue suit which outlined his sculpted torso with the perfection of an artist. The man himself was a work of art according to the many star-struck cover articles in teeny bopper magazines. Terrance Kirby, superstar boxing champion and promising candidate for the summer Olympics. Son of a legendary major league ballplayer, Terrance had more than carved out his own identity in the sports world. It wouldn't be a surprise if a random child found one of Mr. Kirby's old baseball cards and thought, *Oh yeah, that's Terrance Kirby's dad!*

In a few weeks, Terrance would marry the love of his life. Vivian Walker, painter, online influencer, fashion designer, and part-time model, and undoubtedly his perfect match. Though he dwarfed her considerably, she was larger than life. An inescapable presence wherever she went. Some might say it came from years of being spoiled by her millionaire parents, but Stef did not agree. Viv knew exactly what kind of privilege she'd been born into. She knew her audience, how many people looked up to her, and she worked hard to be a role model. One magazine listed her as the second most influential Black woman in the past year. Number one was Beyoncé. Again, Stef did not agree. As far as she was concerned, Beyoncé had nothing on Viv.

They posed for a few photos. Terrance's suit shined in the flashing light like it was made of sapphires. He glanced at Viv, and she nodded. He smiled back and thanked the photographers for their time, but they were needed elsewhere. Viv gestured to the right, and they disappeared behind some trees. They veered towards the mansion, and the cameras followed. Multiple landscape photos, which they could not sell to TMZ, were all they got as the happy couple snuck through the back gate.

What was it like to be so in-sync with another person? Stef hoped she'd find out someday.

In the meantime, she had a party to enjoy and a dance partner to find before her best friend got tired of waiting and tried to hook her up with a professional hockey player.

A man sat alone away from the dance floor. Dark skinned, handsome, and far less intimidating than a Russian gymnast. He stared at his phone for a long time, then put it away. Then he took it back out again. Probably waiting for a call from a business partner or something, but Stef could relate.

Her feet moved independent of her body, making their own decisions about what they should do and when. Stef hunched her shoulders like it would make her less of a beanpole. She stood before the man who needed a moment to realize he wasn't alone anymore. *Be a millionaire,* she reminded herself.

"Hi, I'm Stef. Want to dance?"

*

Eli would not check his phone again.

Seriously, he wouldn't.

He would stop. He would put it away. He would have a nice time tonight and then go home to his basement apartment and pray the family next door wasn't cooking beef stew again. (Dear God that stench...)

He checked his phone one more time for a missed call. The screen was blank. Not even a text alert. That was it. No more. Time to stop obsessing and start tearing up the dance floor. First, he needed a partner.

Or maybe he could check one more time, just in case—

"Hi, I'm Stef. Want to dance?"

The woman standing in front of him seemed to have come out of nowhere. As a professionally trained amateur punching bag, Eli knew how to spot a sneak attack. He might've been the only person on earth who could tank a Super Mega Punch, and yet this random woman had gotten right in his face, and he never saw her coming.

At least she was pretty. Really pretty actually. Her dark brown hair was clean and styled, her brown eyes round and bright. She had fair skin and a round face. Meeting her eyes made his neck hurt, and he couldn't say for sure he'd be taller than her on his feet.

She said nothing else, so Eli assumed she was serious. This party was full of people he regularly saw on TV, but he couldn't place her. Going by her tall, slender build, he'd guess she was some kind of runway model.

A runway model was asking him to dance, and he hadn't even started drinking yet.

"Uh… sure," he said, which was obviously the smoothest way he could've put it. "I'm Eli."

He went to shake her hand. It occurred to him that might be too formal, but by then she'd already taken it. They shook for one too many seconds, and then Eli found the strength to let go and get off his ass. At full height, they were almost perfectly level. The top of her head reached the tiniest bit higher than his.

"Woah," he said before he could stop himself.

She blushed. "It's just the heels. Without them, I'm only 5'10'."

"Great," Eli said, wiping fake sweat off his brow, "my masculinity is saved."

Stef giggled, which eased the tightness in Eli's chest. He made a note to not say a single word while they were dancing. Next time, he might put his foot so far into his mouth, he'd choke.

They walked into the crowd which had grown since the DJ switched to a big Top 40 hit, which was tearing up the charts. Eli had heard bits of it on the radio while driving to work, but he always switched it off. Speaking of, maybe he should've turned his phone off. Then he wouldn't be staring at his pocket every few seconds waiting for it to vibrate.

"So…" Stef rolled her shoulders, fiddling with her dress to create creases. He didn't know why. If it weren't for her posture and uncertain expression, she'd be ready for the catwalk.

"So…" Eli repeated.

"You know this song?" she asked.

"Kind of." He listened again to see if it sounded more familiar. It didn't. "You know it?"

She thought for a second. "Kind of."

They found a clear spot in the corner, just out of the strobe light's reach. None of the glamorous celebrities and influencers noticed the pair quietly swaying to a groove they weren't feeling. Eli stared at Stef's face as she stared at her feet. Her heels were silver and strappy. Looked like they cost a pretty penny, not that Eli was an expert on footwear. He was stuck in Wal-Mart brand loafers.

"So…" he said, too low to hear over the music. *Man, why do I suck at conversation?*

*

I really suck at conversation. Stef moved carefully on unsteady feet. This was what she got for buying heels from the bargain bin. *Why did I ask him to dance again?*

"So…" she repeated, "are you a friend of Terrance?"

"Yeah, T and I go way back. Used to whup his ass every day when we trained together."

"You're a boxer?" Stef wobbled as her foot came down wrong. She wanted to say it was the cheap shoes, but it might've just been her. *Great job, Stef, now you get to embarrass yourself in front of a pro-athlete.*

"Nah, not really," he said. "I've had a few fights, but mostly just for fun. I always win, though."

He added the last part quickly as if trying to impress her. She certainly believed he could beat someone in a fight. His broad shoulders and tight sleeves straining to contain his arms told her all she needed to know. Speaking of which, maybe she shouldn't stare.

"You play any other sports?" she asked while looking intently at his face like a normal person.

"Just some football in high school. I've been getting more into investments lately."

"Wow," Stef said. Not an athlete then, but a big businessman. Even better. "That sounds… interesting."

Eli laughed. "You can say boring, it's okay. Not doing it because it's my lifelong dream to sit at a desk all day, but that's what makes you money, so that's what I do."

*

Technically, he wasn't an investment banker yet, but as long as this job went through (and it would go through, it *would*) then he wasn't lying or making an ass of himself in front of a gorgeous supermodel.

The DJ switched to a new song, this one even more up-tempo and less familiar. This was why he needed to listen to the radio more and not just play his mom's same old Run-DMC mix tapes from the Eighties. He tried not to think of his beat-up yellow Toyota in the parking garage at home. At least Stef would never have to see it.

"No, I totally get that," she said. "Sometimes the best you can hope for is getting a good paycheck every month. My job is sort of like that, too."

"Really?" Eli furrowed his brow. He'd never thought to compare sitting at a cubicle with getting your picture taken a hundred times a day. Granted, he could be completely off on his model theory, but even if he was, that just meant she had to be an actress or something. Right?

"Let's just say I have a lot of eyes on me."

Oh yeah, definitely right.

"That's cool," he smiled. "We don't have to talk about it."

"Thanks," she said, sounding genuinely relieved. "I mean, I don't *hate* my job, I just… don't expect to still be doing this ten years from now."

*

Oh dear God, I hope not. Stef did her best to suppress shudders at the thought of cooking fries and getting shake mix sprayed down her front by a defective machine all the way into her thirties. Serving the same pushy customers who thought going through the drive-thru made them royalty.

Must be nice having a cushy desk job in an office and not going home every night smelling like burger grease.

"I bet you're the best they got," Eli said.

Stef didn't want to laugh, but her mouth didn't get the memo. The sound she made before swallowing her tongue was sort of like an animal mating call, but that was all his fault. Him and his stupidly pretty face distracting her.

"I don't know about that," she said. She played with her dress. She really needed to stop doing that. "If my manager is to be believed they can replace me with a trained monkey, and he'd lose nothing."

His look of shock and mild horror seemed over the top. Then again, he probably thought she was talking about office work or something. "Well... managers suck."

"Now you're speaking my language."

The music faded, bringing the party to a pause as the DJ took the mic.

"Hey hey, ladies and gentlemen. Everyone having a good time tonight?"

A few people cheered. Others clapped politely. Stef looked around, but there was no sign of Viv or Terrance anywhere.

"We're here to celebrate our favorite couple, Terrance Kirby and Vivian Walker." Even louder applause. "Before we begin the love fest, who's up for some Atlas-K?"

The response reminded Stef of the time she blew out an eardrum when she was six. The pain was rough, but this was on a whole other level. The DJ went on hyping the crowd. He seemed to know exactly what to say to push all the right buttons with them.

"You like Atlas-K?" Eli asked.

Stef chewed on her lip. "Kind of. You like him?"

"Kind of." He rolled his shoulders. She thought he might make an excuse and head back into the party without her. "You want a drink?"

Now that he mentioned it... "Some champagne would be nice. I hear they have the good stuff out tonight."

What that 'good stuff' was, she didn't know. Names of fancy drinks more often than not eluded her. The rare times she cared to drink, all that really mattered was how fast it would make her forget about work and financial aid applications.

Eli went to get their drinks, leaving her with one last blinding smile in his wake. If he wanted to stun her so she physically couldn't walk away, mission accomplished.

This is going well, she told herself and did *not* mess with her dress again. *It's going very well. I've made a new friend, and I haven't thought about checking my email in a full four minutes. This is progress.*

If you can call awkward small talk and dancing like a zombie progress, said the mean little voice in the back of her head. *He might not come back, you know.*

"Shut up," Stef muttered through gritted teeth.

A flash of blue interrupted her internal argument. It hurled itself at her like a bullet.

"Stef!" Viv smelled strongly of apple juice cocktails and hastily applied perfume. "You're having fun!"

It was a statement, not a question. Had she seen Stef talking to Eli? "Not as much fun as you. Where'd you and Terrance get off to?"

Viv adjusted her mostly intact hairdo, removing some loose hairs which did nothing for her smeared lipstick. "None of your business. We were doing important wedding stuff."

"Right, because practice makes perfect."

"Girl—" Viv play swatted at her. Stef pretended to shield herself from the blow, and the women dissolved into giggles.

A man with colorful dreadlocks and arms covered in silver took the stage to thunderous applause. On his shirt was a globe held by a man on his knees. The music started long before he appeared in a cloud of smoke billowing from a machine off stage. Now the crowd was in his hands, waving their arms in near-perfect synchronicity as Atlas-K spun rhymes faster than Stef could keep up.

"He uh... really puts on a show," she said as the first song came to a drawn-out end.

"I know!" Viv practically bounced with excitement, impressive in heels that high. "And he's even better live than on SoundCloud... okay, what's the deal with you and Eli?"

Stef choked on her own spit. "What deal? There is no deal."

"I saw you two together."

"Yeah dancing. Sort of... mostly just talking. Nothing serious."

Viv rubbed her chin like an old professor. "You know one time, I was at a wrap party for this big movie premiere. Can't remember what it was, I just know it was bad with a capital B. So I'm getting my drink, I'm minding my business, and this guy comes up to me like, 'hey, nice dress.' And I say, 'thanks, nice tux.' And he says 'thanks.'"

Stef nodded. Viv did not continue the story. "Okay, that's... nice?"

"Well, you wanna know what happened to that nice tux guy?" Viv threw her arms in the air, as if presenting her beautiful party and life to the world. "I'm about to marry him. Best man I ever met, all because I was wearing a nice dress that night. You understand what I'm trying to say, right?"

"Of course," Stef said, her resolve fading in an instant. "Actually no, not really."

Viv sighed. "I'm saying you never know when you'll meet that right person. You might never see Eli again after tonight, or you might see him every day for fifty years. Don't you want to find out which it'll be?"

"I can do that by just not talking to him," Stef countered, earning a pout. "Besides, he wouldn't want a relationship with me. Not when he finds out I'm just a cashier."

"What's that got to do with it?"

How about everything? "I just mean he's probably used to dating models and actresses. Women who can afford designer clothes and to jet off to Paris for the weekend. Can't expect a big executive type to want a minimum wage worker, can I?"

Viv's face shifted as Stef rambled, going through several unidentifiable emotions before settling on pure, and inexplicable, confusion. "Uh… we are still talking about Eli Johnson, right?"

*

"Was that Stef you were dancing with? Viv's friend?"

Terrance had ambushed him at the bar, coming out of nowhere and nearly getting a face full of champagne for his troubles. Eli wondered if he should do it anyway. Might get Terrance to stop smiling like that.

"We were just talking. What about it?"

"Nothing, but if I knew you liked white girls, I'd have hooked you up a long time ago."

"Shut up," Eli tried to dodge, but ended up in Terrance's ridiculously powerful grip, unable to escape. "I can talk to a woman without it being a thing."

"Yeah, but what if she wants it to be a thing? You not gonna go for it?"

"No. Yes. I don't know." Terrance was momentarily distracted by someone waving at him across the way. Eli seized the opportunity and slid smoothly out of Terrance's grip, leaving an empty hole where his head had been. "I didn't come here looking for a hookup, and it's not like a model is looking for a guy who lives in a basement."

"Man, you gotta have more confidence in yourself. You got game." Terrance grinned. "You just need to have the attitude. Don't you know today is Be A Millionaire Day?"

Eli raised an eyebrow. "The hell is that?"

"National holiday, E, and you should celebrate." Terrance paused, his smile fading. "Wait, did you say model?"

Eli rolled his shoulders. "Look, I'm not trying to say she's a snob, but you know, gas station workers aren't as appealing as celebrities."

Terrance gave him a weird look. "You know what they say about assumptions right? They make an ass out of you."

"That's 'make an ass out of u and me,'" Eli said. "Get it right before you lecture."

"Yeah, well—"

"Mr. Kirby!" A man in a suit with an earpiece blaring garbled words emerged from the crowd and stepped in between the two men. "I'm sorry to interrupt, but we're having a slight issue with Atlas-K's manager, and he's asking to speak to you right away."

"Can't you and Robbie handle it?" Terrance glanced at Eli. "I'm in the middle of something."

"I'm sorry, sir, he's asking for you and Ms. Walker personally. He won't agree to see anyone else."

"It's fine," Eli stepped in. "Gotta head back. You deal with whatever this guy wants."

"Primadonna bullshit," Terrance muttered. "This is why I wanted Jay-Z. I'll be back, E. Sorry."

"It's cool." The two men bumped fists. After he left, Eli scanned the crowd. Stef was hard to miss, towering over the other women and quite a few men. The sun made her hair shine and there was something utterly mesmerizing about her profile as she chatted with Viv.

Eli took a breath. He could do this.

*

"Look, I get what you're trying to say, but you have Eli all wrong."

Stef chewed on her bottom lip. "I'm not implying that he's shallow, but you know... we're talking about something that only ever works in movies and fairy tales. Not that you *can't* date someone who has more money than you, but in my experience, it rarely works out so well."

Before Viv could tell Stef all the reasons why it could work and give a rousing speech about love (or potentially mutual attraction between strangers) conquering all, her phone rang. She ignored it for a moment, but when her wind chime ringtone failed to cease, she groaned and answered it.

"This is Vivian." She listened in silence for a moment. "What? We negotiated the fee three months ago, we… ugh, *fine*. I'll be right there."

She hung up and muttered to herself before throwing Stef an apologetic look. "Sorry, I'll be right back. Have to go do *business* at my *engagement party* because people *suck*."

"Is everything all right?" Stef asked.

"Just Atlas-K's manager being a greedy dick," Viv folded her arms, as, over her shoulder, a pale-faced man holding a phone waved to get her attention. "He's saying they need to charge extra for travel, even though this was already discussed when we hired him. Now there's some bullshit about the contract we signed. I do not need one percent of this right now, but what can you do?"

Viv had this uncanny ability to go from steaming at the ears to calm in seconds. Someday, maybe, Stef would learn the secret of her best friend's take-no-shit businesswoman ways, but that day was not today.

"It's okay," she said. "I'll be right here when you get back."

"You'd better be. This conversation is not over."

"Sure thing."

"I mean it, Stefania!"

Viv's swishy princess dress vanished into a sea of black and silver. Stef meandered a bit, not sure if she should go get more food or just relax and try to enjoy the music. So far it was a bit too heavy on the dubstep for her taste. She could barely hear a word out of Atlas-K's mouth.

A shadow hovered at her side just in time for the song to end and her bones to stop vibrating.

"Hey," said Eli, holding two glasses of champagne. "Got your drink. Sorry it took so long."

"It's okay," Stef said. "Lot of people here to talk to."

"Yeah," Eli said as they drank quietly for a time. "Did I hear Viv call you Stefania?"

Did you? How he heard anything over those planet-sized speakers, she didn't know. "Yeah, that's my real name. Did you think Stef was short for Stephanie?"

He gave a slight nod, his cheeks darkening. It was actually adorable, but Stef tried not to laugh.

"It's okay, everyone thinks that, but my family is way too Italian."

"That's cool," he said. "It's a pretty name."

"Thanks," Stef said. "Eli's a pretty name, too."

He laughed a little as once more, conversation halted. Everything seemed to be on mute, even the pounding backtrack and partying guests. Stef's head was down as she mentally kicked herself. *Eli's a pretty name??? That's great. As if you haven't been lame enough.*

*

This... could be going better.

Eli was two steps away from dunking his head in the nearest fountain. At this point, it would be far less embarrassing. He turned his now empty glass over in his hands, wanting another but unable to move. Meanwhile, Stef bobbed her head to the music and almost seemed to be enjoying it a little. Eli wished he could relate. This was his biggest exposure to Atlas-K yet, and all it did was make him wish he had his Tupac or De La Soul tapes.

Say something, his inner voice said. It sounded like his mother. Had the same 'I know exactly what you're trying to hide from me so don't bother' tone and everything.

Yeah, like what? he asked it.

Ask her questions about herself. Show interest.

Eli took a deep breath. He thought back to their previous attempts at conversation. What did he know about her so far? Aside from her being beyond out of his league. He knew she lived in New York, he knew she was ambivalent about her job, and he knew her family was Italian.

"You uh..." he coughed. "You ever been to Italy?"

She blinked, like she didn't realize he was talking to her. "Ah—no. I haven't. I want to, but it hasn't happened yet."

"Work keeping you busy?"

"Something like that." She stretched her neck. Her skin was clear and creamy up close. His fingers twitched, and he shoved them into his pockets. "My great-grandparents immigrated here before my grandparents were born, so it's cool to think I might have fourth or fifth cousins over there I've never met before."

"Well, you'd better get over there and introduce yourself," Eli grinned. "Least drop 'em a text. 'Hey guys.' or 'Ciao amigos.' Wait, that's Spanish…"

Stef snickered. "You're close. It's amici or amiche. Amici for male friends, amiche for female."

Eli's eyebrows shot up. "You speak Italian, too? Damn, you're all ready to go."

"Barely," Stef replied. "It's been a long time since my high school language classes. I can give you one useful phrase to never forget. Dov'e' il bagno?"

Eli tried to remember his two years coasting through Spanish with a C average. None of that sounded familiar. "Okay, I give up."

"Where's the bathroom?"

He whistled. "You're right, that is useful."

They shared a laugh which ended when Stef frowned and dropped her half empty glass on the nearest table. "Now that I think about it, I might need to go inside for a minute."

Eli almost asked why then almost physically smacked himself. "Oh, okay. I mean, you want me to come with?"

She blinked. "To the bathroom?"

You moron… "I just meant uh…" he swallowed. "It's a big house. Lot of rooms. Easy to get lost if you don't know your way around. Unless you've been here before, and then I'd just wait here."

"No, I haven't," Stef said, crossing her legs as the call of nature rapped at her door. "So uh, yeah. It'd be nice to have someone to help me navigate."

They moved through the grass, around tables and waiters, careful not to lose track of each other. Next to the stage, Viv and Terrance were in a heated debate with a bearded man surrounded by hulking giants in sunglasses. Viv had her own entourage of bodyguards backing her up. Scary as they were, none of them held a candle to Terrance's pronounced frown and folded arms as he stood behind his ranting fiancée. A good two feet separated Atlas-K's people from the couple, and none of them dared step over the line.

"That looks rough," Stef remarked, wincing sympathetically as Viv yelled so loud it almost overpowered the music. "I'd hate to be that guy right now."

"It'll be worse if he tries something," Eli smirked as Terrance leaned the tiniest bit closer and one of the bodyguards jumped out of his skin. "Super mega punch…"

"What was that?"

"Nothing." Eli led her up the stairs to the patio. "I'll tell you later."

Viv caught sight of them as they entered the house. Her eyes widened, and she flashed a thumbs up which Stef hesitantly returned. Eli copied her, not knowing if he should be playing it cool. Then the manager spoke, and Viv went back to berating him. That was Stef and Eli's cue to get moving.

The house, L-shaped and twenty thousand square feet according to an article Eli had read about the ten most expensive homes in New York (only number five somehow), seemed much bigger on the inside than on the outside. The halls went on forever. The walls were marble white. Mahogany doors led to bedrooms, sitting rooms, more bedrooms, bedrooms inside bedrooms. No bathrooms yet, at least none that weren't already occupied by staff and other guests.

"Down by the kitchen," a man shouted from behind the third door they tried. "Take a right, then a left, then a right. Can't miss it."

"They need a fucking map in here," Eli muttered in Stef's ear as they departed.

The first right became a left thanks to Eli's piss poor sense of direction. Retracing their steps helped until neither of them could remember if it was a left or another right from there. They chose the latter and spent a few minutes wandering through the maze like a pair of mice after a hunk of cheese. Stef managed to walk without trouble, though Eli could tell she was getting more uncomfortable the longer she went without relief.

As they searched, they chatted about whatever happened to be on their minds. From movies ("I don't know, everyone says *Judgment Day* is better than the first *Terminator*, but I just don't see it." "Are you kidding? It's literally one of the greatest sequels ever made." "It's no *Empire Strikes Back*, that's all I'm saying."), to childhood memories ("We used to watch wrestling when Terrance's parents weren't home and practice our moves. Almost broke one of his mom's fancy vases one time." "Did you get in trouble?" "We would've if I hadn't blamed it on the cat. They let that thing get away with everything."), to the delicate and divisive issue of pizza toppings ("Pineapple does not belong on pizza. Period." "You know that's right.").

Eli wasn't sure what time it was when they finally reached an open door with a tiled floor and toilet inside. The muffled pounding of music from outside had stopped a while ago. That or they were so deep inside the house that they'd been completely consumed and would never see the light of day again. Stef did not seem to care either way as she bolted inside and slammed the door.

"Sorry," she said. "Be right out."

"Take your time."

Eli tapped his foot and stared at a light fixture shaped like a lantern until his vision blurred. A maid with a vacuum cleaner nodded at him as she walked by. Nobody else was in sight. He half-expected a pair of twins to appear and ask him to play with them. With any luck, they'd find their way out of here before the party ended.

At least you're finally getting somewhere, said his inner mom voice. *That only took an hour.*

"Thanks for the pep talk," he mumbled.

But it was okay. This might actually work out.

*

"Wow, this might work out."

Stef washed her hands in a sink the size of a bathtub, scrubbing her skin with water so clear, it had to be imported. The mirror wrapped around the wall giving her multiple angles. She didn't have anything in her hair, no wedgie, and no toilet paper trailed on her shoe. As far as discount clothes and makeup went, she looked pretty good.

You know you have to tell him the truth eventually.

Her stomach deflated, though her mood was not yet dead. Whatever happened after tonight, she was going to have a good time. No stress, no worries, just a nice evening with a really sweet, hot guy who would definitely still like her when he found out she wasn't rich.

After months of cram sessions and closing shifts, she deserved this, dammit!

Stef fixed her hair one more time. Everything was clean and presentable. She moved with confidence into the hall where Eli dutifully awaited her.

"Don't look now, but I think that sink is made of gold," she said.

Eli started to answer, but then a snap sent her world sideways. Stef stared at the closet at the end of the hall, partly covered by something black like a coat sleeve. Her feet were no longer under her, a fact which took her far too long to notice. One of her shoes was on the floor, sans heel. A sad, jagged stump was all that remained.

That left her on her ass with her head smashed into the wall. A wall which was strangely warm and expanding like the hard, muscular chest of a guy who boxed for fun. Eli's warm brown eyes stared at her in shock. His hands were on her sides, not too high or too low, and strong as steel.

"Uh," Stef said, meaning it now more than ever before. "I... I'm sorry, I..."

Eli nodded. "'S okay. It happens."

He pulled her to her feet with ease. Skinny as she was, Stef couldn't claim to be the lightest woman around, so no one could blame her for blushing. Again.

"You good?" he asked, looking her over. "Not bruised or anything?"

"Just my ass," Stef said. "You good?"

He straightened his back. He was indeed several inches taller than her now. "Yeah, I'm great. Don't worry about me, I ain't letting a little fall bring me down."

"In a manner of speaking." Stef took off her other shoe—no use in walking in one heel and one bare foot—and picked them up, gazing mournfully at the ruined heel. Painful and annoying as they were, they'd always *looked* nice. "But hey, we got one milestone out of the way. Who knows? Maybe next we'll reach for something at the same time and touch hands."

"Right?" Eli chuckled. "And then we'll have to stay the night and there's only one bed."

"And it's raining so hard we can't leave until morning," Stef supplied. "Just so you know, I'm a blanket hog."

"I can live with that."

The way out was no more fun than the way in. Every corner led to a path that split in two. Though most doors were closed, she spotted a few rooms that made the Plaza look like a backroad motel. Eli didn't look at any of them. Clearly, he'd seen places like this before and was numb to it all.

Hell, maybe his house was even bigger.

She pictured a mansion with a built-in gym and a home office. There'd be an indoor pool, flat screen TVs, and a massive back yard, perfect for practicing new moves without breaking things. Eli would have a closet full of designer clothes and one of those memory foam beds that did away with back pain.

She tried not to delve too deep into the fantasy. In her wildest dreams, he'd invite her over, they'd drink and talk about life while watching the sunset. Whether they did it as friends or something more remained to be seen. Or not. It was getting harder and harder to remember that they'd probably never see each other again.

"I think the concert's over," Eli said.

"Might just be the intermission. Viv has some speeches and a tribute to her grandmother planned. Atlas-K should be ready for an encore by then."

"Oh, that's too bad."

Stef snorted. "Really?"

"I'm sorry, I'm just not feeling it with this guy," Eli said, "he has no flow."

"Hmmm... yeah, you're right." Stef chewed the inside of her mouth. Words sat on the tip of her tongue, clamoring to get out. It would be best for her not to let them, but then... "Would you ever want to hang out?"

Eli looked at her. "You mean, after tonight?"

"Yeah," Stef said. She rubbed her knuckles. It was a good alternative to wearing a hole in her dress. "I've had a nice time talking to you, and I thought if you were having a nice time talking to *me*, then maybe we could, you know..."

Stef stared at the floor. It looked like he was, too. Was that a good sign or a bad sign?

"I mean we don't have to—"

"I'd like to, so—"

Stef stopped.

Eli stopped.

"I was gonna say—"

"I was just thinking—"

They stopped again, sharing a laugh.

"Maybe just one of us should talk," said Stef.

"Sounds good," said Eli. His face fell into a pensive frown. Silence overtook them, and Stef couldn't bring herself to end it.

Now's the time, said the voice in her head. *Just say it.*

"I need to tell you something," Eli said, his arms folded over his chest almost like he was in shame.

Stef steeled herself. "Me too. I..."

She looked him in the eye. There was nothing to be afraid of. If he thought she wasn't good enough for him because she lived paycheck to paycheck, then he wasn't good enough for her. Other opportunities were out there, plenty of fish in the sea and all that junk. Whatever happened, she could handle it.

There was an open room right behind him, different from the rest. The doorway was narrower, the inside small and stark compared to the ornate vastness of the rest of the house. Powder blue carpets, simple wooden shelves under soft yellow light. Designer jackets and silky pashminas lined the walls, neatly arranged and waiting to be returned to their owners.

The coatroom!

"What's wrong?" Eli waved at her. "Are you okay?"

Boy, what her face must look like right now. "I'm sorry, I need a minute. Give me a second."

Stef rushed into the closet. Her shoes fell out of her grasp, landing somewhere she didn't care to see. The interior stretched ten feet in both directions and was crammed full of bags and outerwear. She dove for the nearest coat and worked her way down the line.

Outside, a phone rang. Eli cursed and fumbled with his pockets before the ringing stopped. "Hello, this is Elijah Johnson."

Stef tore through hangers five at a time. The further she got, the more cramped and disorganized the closet became. Countless styles and fabrics assaulted her senses, her fingers dragging along leather and velvet and (hopefully) faux fur. Nothing thin like a purse strap or heavy with the weight of a phone. It might not even be in here. What if Viv knew she'd find the coatroom eventually and had her stuff hidden somewhere else?

"Gotta be here," she muttered, digging deeper. "Stay calm. It's gotta be here. *Come on...*"

There.

There in the corner between a fleece jacket and a denim blazer. Long enough to brush the floor, threads sticking out at the seams and ugly black creases along the flap.

"Yes!" Stef moved at warp speed. Her purse was empty on the floor and her phone in her hand faster than a jump cut.

She had seven new emails. Three coupons, one note from her mom asking her to call her grandma, two ads for upcoming sales, and...

Stef dropped the phone. "Oh my God."

*

Eli's eyes glazed over as the hiring manager thanked him and hung up. He dropped the phone. "Oh my God."

*

Stef didn't know how they found the back door again. One second she was running screaming down the halls (hearing an oddly deep, masculine voice overladen with her own), and then she was on the grass, kicking her bare feet up and screaming.

"I did it!" She must have leapt ten feet in the air. "I got in! I did it!"

"I got the job!" Eli was next to her, his high pitched shriek somehow drowning her out. "I'm getting out of the basement!"

"I'm getting out of McDonald's!"

Stef grabbed him and hugged him as they jumped around like a pair of teenage girls meeting their favorite rockstar. At some point, she didn't quite know when, the screaming stopped. Probably around the time she jumped into Eli's arms and met his lips in a passionate kiss.

It was a random impulse, one she would've instantly regretted were she not in a state of total euphoria. Instead, she savored the taste of his lips, the way he kissed her back, and the feel of his hard body pressed tight against hers.

It was one of those perfect moments that never should've ended.

"Ahem."

But that was the thing about perfection. It came and went in an instant.

Breaking the kiss, Stef looked out at a crowd of at least a hundred partygoers staring back at her. On stage, Viv held the mic in one hand and a candle in the other. In fact, all the tables had candles. Not the colorful kind one would typically find at a party. These were long and white, and would've been more fitting for a funeral home.

"Oh," Stef's stomach dropped, "were you doing the memorial thing?"

Viv pursed her lips, and that knowing spark in her eye had never been more irritating. "We were just about to have a moment of silence for those who can't be with us today."

Stef looked at Eli. He was still dazed from their sloppy near-makeout session and needed a moment to process everything.

"Uh…" he said smartly. "I mean, we knew that. Right?"

"Of course!" Stef nodded so hard her skull ached. "We totally knew that and that's why we're so happy."

"Yeah, we love honoring the dearly departed," Eli announced to the bemused crowd. "It's our favorite thing to do."

"Makes us so happy to remember them!"

"Right. We're happy they're dead."

"Eli." Stef nudged him with her elbow.

"That is to say, we're happy that Terrance and Vivian have taken the time to put together this beautiful tribute. That kind of dedication deserves to be celebrated and so we were celebrating so..."

Someone coughed and another person shook their head at the couple. If Stef could spontaneously sink into the dirt and never come up again, that would be great. She could imagine Eli felt the same way.

On stage, Terrance laughed. "Looks like our friends here are really in the spirit, if you catch my drift."

One or two people politely laughed while Viv winced at his poor attempt at humor. She tapped her ear piece and moved away from the mic to speak into it. Then she came back with a grin. "Well, I hope everyone's ready to eat because I've just received word. Soup's on!"

A line of thirty waiters in identical clothes bearing identical covered trays filed out the back door. Some of them even looked alike. They were so in-sync, Stef wondered how long it would take before they burst into song. The guests all left to find their tables, eager for a world class meal and no longer caring about the two idiots slinking off into the shadows.

The smell of food hit Stef's nose. She'd ordered the chicken parmesan, but she wasn't so hungry anymore. Eli was watching her, and at some point, she'd have to look back.

"So uh..." He coughed into his hand. "Back there... did you say McDonald's?"

Stef nodded, zombie-like. "Yeah... did you say basement?"

Did we just kiss? was the question she probably should've asked first, and when she finally got the nerve to turn her head, she could see it written across his face, too.

"Does this mean you're not a model?" he asked.

Her jaw fell. "A *model*? You thought I was a model."

"I don't know, you look like one," he said defensively. "What'd you think I was?"

"I…" Stef faltered, shoulders sagging as heat rose from her stomach to her face. "I thought you were an executive or something… I mean, you're friends with Terrance."

"You're friends with Viv," he countered.

They were at an impasse. Stef knew it, and Eli clearly knew it, too. As the party went on without them, they traded glances and tried not to be the one to break the silence. More than once, Stef found herself staring at Eli's lips. They were just as nice to look at as they were to kiss. Eventually, they'd have to talk about that kiss…

"Maybe we should start over," Stef said, standing up a little straighter and sticking out her hand. "Hi, I'm Stef. I work at McDonald's, I just got into grad school, and I'm not a model."

Eli hesitated for only a second, then engulfed her small hand in his large one. "I'm Eli. I live in a crappy basement, and I just got an entry level corporate job after getting fired from the gas station."

"Nice to meet you, Eli." Stef didn't let go of his hand, and together they walked back into the party, moving around the many tables in search of their nameplates. "You want to meet up sometime?"

"You mean like friends or like…" Eli gave her a funny sort of look.

"I don't know. Could be as friends, but I was thinking more like…" She gave him the same funny look.

He chuckled. "A date sounds good to me. Any ideas?"

"How about McDonald's?" she asked. "I have a fifty percent employee discount."

"Half off nuggets? Now you're talking."

They found their seats, rather conveniently at the same table right next to each other. Stef eyed Viv at the head table, but she was too busy tearing into a quesadilla to notice. The food did smell amazing, and as the embarrassment waned and joy at her success returned, Stef found she could eat her entire plate and possibly Eli's too. Those hors d'oeuvres felt like a million years ago.

"I swear, this stuff would cost me a full paycheck most days," she said through a mouthful of chicken.

"Just one?" Eli marveled. "Damn. McDonald's pays good."

Stef elbowed him softly. "You think you're funny. Did you know today is Be a Millionaire Day?"

"Yeah, Terrance told me." Eli took a bite of his filet mignon, sighing like he hadn't eaten real food in days. "What's that even mean anyway? Be a Millionaire Day…"

"I don't know, probably one of those weird national holidays nobody knows anything about."

He hummed and nodded. "Well, I don't know about you, but I sure feel like a million bucks."

Stef smiled at him. Her phone hadn't pinged her with any new alerts, and she wouldn't have read them if it had. The sun was just starting its descent over the horizon. Gentle music poured from the speakers, way better than any Atlas-K. They no longer touched, but Eli's free hand was close to hers. She was looking at his lips again. She had a feeling she'd get to taste them again before the night was out. The way he was looking at hers definitely told her that.

"Yeah," she said as she took his hand again, "me too."

About the Author

Ava Bari is a native New Yorker who now makes her home in the American Midwest. She currently attends the University of Iowa working towards a degree in English with a focus on Creative Writing. She is an avid manga collector and a singer who spent nine years in concert choir. A lifelong lover of the tall, dark, and handsome stranger, she firmly believes in the power of true love conquering all.

Tumblr: avabari.tumblr.com
Twitter: @avabari27

Finding Pride
♥
Diana Ferris

Story Information

Holiday: National Pride Day
Holiday Date: June 28 (Last Sunday in June)
Heat Rating: 3
Relationship Type: F/F
Major Trigger Warnings: Internalized homophobia, workplace sexual harassment, minor ableist language, lots of swearing.

Student by day, recluse by night, Louise safeguards her secret. But when she meets Fernanda her life is turned upside down.

Finally, Louise is free to be herself as she never has before.

But will she fight for this love? Or will her demons snuff out her light forever?

Finding Pride

"Hey, baby, what's your name?" slurs some rando as he sloppily attempts to catch my attention with his drunken virility.

This is great, just fucking great. It's two hours 'til the bar closes, and all I can manage is to attempt to ignore the idiot in front of me. The guys at table thirteen have been giving me the stink eye for God knows how long because Lenny can't be bothered to cook up their spicy wings, even though I've asked for them four times already. I turned him down on a date, and now he's taking his revenge. Go figure!

My feet are about to explode inside my shoes as I rush to pour all the drink orders. Meanwhile, this perv staggers his way through what he believes is suave flirtation. I've had a migraine since before I set foot in the bar, and McSloppy here just won't give up. Despite his friends' repeated attempts to call him off, he simply waves his hands dismissively and ignores them. Admittedly, they're not trying very hard. It makes me wonder if they actually don't want to be associated with the drunkest guy at the bar. I can't possibly be sure of what McSloppy is thinking, but I am not about to entertain him any longer than I have to.

"Come on, baby, you wo-on't regret it. We can have fun. I promiiisse to rock your world," hiccups McSloppy as he sways his hips unsteadily in my direction. I'm guessing it's supposed to be an expression of his smoldering attractiveness, but instead it comes off looking like one of the weirdest Jim Carrey expressions I've ever seen.

Honestly, this is really on me for having answered the phone when Victor, my boss, called, but I need the extra hours if I'm going to have enough to pay this month's tuition. Not to mention, I still need to pay the rent.

Marina was not happy when I told her of my plans for the evening, which had, at that moment, included a bonus of overtime at the bar. She wanted to hang out for the rest of the night but, sadly, adulting kind of superseded her wants, which then evolved into her berating me for the fifth time that day about my lack of a healthy and well-defined sleeping schedule.

Throwing her arms in the air, she groaned, "Fine, you don't have to hang out with me, but, for fuck's sake, you barely even slept last night, much less all week for that matter, and now you're volunteering to cover a shift. Are you freaking seriously kidding me right now?!"

She was right, I had barely caught up on any sleep. But how could I? Finals are only a week away, and I need to pass this stupid statistics class to maintain my 3.5 GPA. Not that I ever really gave much attention to my 'academic excellence,' but this is the first time I've ever actually enjoyed school. It's also the first time there's no one around to question my choices or successes. For once, the grades are for me and me alone. I'm proud of what I've accomplished so far, which only makes me more determined to improve. Fertile ground for the perfectionist monster growing within me. It's both a blessing and a curse.

It was so hard to deny that I was tired, but Marina, being my best friend, knew better. She looked at me in that pointed way of hers that always exasperates me. She knows I can't lie to her while she's tapping her toes on that linoleum floor. I had been putting in the last 'finishing touches' to the project I'd been trying to complete since forever ago.

"Uh-huh, sure, 'not tired,'" she said, emphasizing with air quotes while rolling her eyes.

I merely nodded wordlessly before she continued, "Riiight, tell me when was the last time you got laid, or better yet, when was the last time you even went out on a date?"

I gaped at her wordlessly, searching my brain for anything to counteract her accusations, but I couldn't recall a single memory. It was then that I began to question what on Earth I was doing in college, besides anxiously nerding out of course. I blinked several times before closing my mouth.

Marina already knew the answer, though. She simply rolled her eyes once more and shrugged. "That's what I thought." Her deadpan face stated clearly that she was not believing whatever bullshit I was about to come up with. After a moment's silence, she shook her head in defeat and beckoned for me to follow her out of the room.

Perhaps she realized my stubbornness could very well block whatever argument she was about to dish out and thought it better to save her breath. If that truly was her intention then I was all the more thankful for it. I couldn't stand wasting energy or time. Marina always says I am too pragmatic for my own good, and maybe she's right. I do have a knack for planning and carefully observing all situations thoroughly before logically placing everything into my idea of order. It helps me with my day-to-day routines and self-reflection, but it isn't so good for the people who find spontaneity a diversion from the everyday drag.

Marina's the fun one, while I enjoy spending my days cutting out grocery coupons and making lists. She calls them my quirks; I call them everyday necessities.

The high pitch of guitar feedback pierces through my reverie, and McSloppy winces, covering his ears like the rest of the patrons. I smile in spite of my discomfort. Serves him right for being such a douche. Sadly, my little victory doesn't last long. As soon as the noise ceases, he's back to flirting and is still trying against all futile hope to get into my pants. His noisy perseverance is grating deeper on my nerves by the minute. I'm far too busy to care, yet here I am wiping the bar counter, rinsing glasses in the small sink next to me, and setting them to dry on top of a thick towel. While I'm doing all of this and trying to ignore McSloppy, I'm also scanning the room for Frank, our only waiter, but of course, he's busy furiously rushing to clean the small tables spread throughout the room. A local band plays some sort of melancholic, shitty song that is only intensifying my once dull headache, turning it into a pounding pain. I wipe my hand on the towel hanging at my hip, sighing as McSloppy continues to clumsily think of something flirty to say to me. After a moment's deliberation, all he comes out with is, "You have some nice tits."

Oh, how classy. Honestly, he's lucky I really need this job, or I would deck him right here and now. I look around for any sort of help from his friends, but they have all disappeared, and McSloppy is still blearily looking at me, his red, sweaty face hiccuping as he runs his hand through his greasy hair, only messing it up even further. He leers at me and leans in, his forearm barely supporting his unstable stance. He puts his hand slavishly on top of the counter and slides a twenty my way. He's in no shape to be drinking more, and now I'm wondering where in the ever-loving fuck is Michael. But, I guess even security gets a smoke break or a trip to the men's room. Antonio's at the door to card patrons; he's our first line of defense. Too bad he missed this douchenozzle. Guess I can't rely on him. Honestly, there should be more than two bouncers in this shithole, but Victor's cheap. He's always repeating the same old, tired excuse of the bar being small enough and that, 'two men is more than enough. They're big guys. They'll watch everything. You'll be fine.' Fuck me and my sense of security, I guess.

Here I am getting accosted by some gross rando, and I'm pretty damn close to calling the cops. Then again, Victor did say cops were the ultimate solution for emergencies. Well, this fucking constitutes an emergency. McSloppy is looking like he's ready to either pass out or throw up on my precious floor. "He'd better not throw up on my floor, or I'm gonna hurt him," I mutter under my breath.

"Hey, gorgeous, get me another shot of vodka," slurs McSloppy, displaying his large, expensive watch as if, somehow, I would jump into his arms because 'shiny things' impress the female population.

"Don't call me gorgeous," I growl, my nostrils flaring. I've had enough of this weirdo, and if no one is going to help me, then I guess I'll have to piss him off just enough to get him to leave but not so much that he gets all homicidal on me. At least I hope not. After all, I don't even think he could aim his piss into the toilet bowl with the amount of swaying he's doing right now.

"I'm giving you a compliment; the least you could say is thank you," he slurs in between hiccups. His frown gives me some satisfaction. At least for this moment, I've ruined his skewed ideas of me almost as much as he's ruined my night.

Now to get him to leave. "No, I don't like compliments. I'm a frigid bitch, and I can't serve you anymore to drink."

Reeling back, McSloppy is visibly shocked. How dare I, a woman, tell him no! The audacity! It's just too inconceivable. "Why not?!" he demands.

"You are far too drunk to function; I suggest you ask for a taxi and leave," I curtly reply through gritted teeth.

"I'm a paying customer, damn it!" He slams his hand on the counter, catching the attention of a few people nearby.

Hoping someone will come to my defense, I look around, but the audience has gone back to minding their own business. I sigh as I push an errant curl off my forehead. "I can't serve you anymore because it's against the law. Now, you can either leave peacefully, or you can continue to act like a total dildo, and I'll just call the cops."

"You're an uppity bitch, do you know that? Do you even know who I am?" He spits his venom through bared teeth.

I grin tightly, shrugging as I return to wiping the glasses down for the next round of orders. I can feel the man's flushed face searing into my back, and it's all I can do to ignore it. I mean, he wouldn't try to get all closeted-incel-released-into-society-while-raging and kill me, would he? Then again, people who've had too much to drink are not exactly known as shining examples of good decision making.

"Hey, beautiful," he slurs.

Oh God, he's back to flirting. Doesn't he ever just give up! I roll my eyes, sighing deeply before turning around. I expect him to be giving me the gross look he's been giving me all night, but instead I see a petite woman with a short bob sitting in front of me, rummaging in her wallet for something.

She offers me a tight smile and quickly turns away from him. She looks at me and raises her eyebrows. Her dark brown eyes roll, and she gulps down a laugh. "Give me a strawberry martini, please." She passes a twenty across the counter. Her green nails gleam against the dim light of the bar as she takes a seat. It's a weird color; almost like moss, but for some reason, it fits her skin tone. The tips of her short bob seem a bright purplish color, but I can't be quite sure. Sighing, the brunette turns her head to observe the band playing in front, swaying from side to side in time with the music with a dreamy look on her face, completely ignoring McSloppy, who's currently shouting next to her ear.

"Hey, didn't you hear me? I'm offering to buy you a drink if you want," slurs McSloppy. Amazing! Seconds ago I was the one he was accosting before this poor girl stepped into the crossfire.

Looking over her tanned shoulder at him, she blinks slowly as if seeing him for the first time. She shakes her head while wrinkling her nose in distaste. "No thanks, I'm good."

I gotta admit, this girl with terrible taste in music and mossy polished nails has some serious balls of steel. Her serenity is so contagious that I forget about McSloppy for a short time; that is until he starts to tap her on the shoulder.

Fury causes my nostrils to flare. If Michael doesn't show up within two minutes, I'm going to call the cops! To hell with this dude's discomfort; he's gotten more vulgar and is now bothering the customers. Except I don't get much of a chance. The short-bobbed girl is leaning closer, pointing to a table nearby. A large, burly man nods to her, and she shows the drunkard her left hand where a simple, thin band adorns her ring finger. Funny, I don't remember her having it before; maybe I just didn't pay enough attention.

McSloppy, who moments ago boasted a brash machismo, suddenly goes paper white and stammers a quick "sorry" as he visibly shrinks, pretending to be overly preoccupied with his watch. By this time, I'm internally screaming, because the douche still hasn't left even after becoming perfectly aware he's an uncomfortable presence. I hope he doesn't think he can continue to be a pain in my ass after this girl leaves. Where the hell is Michael when you need him, damn it!

By this point, I've finished mixing the martini, and this girl, this wonderful girl, is sitting idly by slowly sipping her concoction as she continues to sway to the music. Turning, she gives me a gentle smile. She turns to look back at something, or maybe someone, because Michael finally shows up in all his muscled virtue. I point to McSloppy as discreetly as I can, and Mike makes his way over to tap the drunk idiot on the shoulder before walking his ass out.

Suddenly, I realize that maybe I should be thanking the perfect stranger before me, so I tap the bar to get her attention. "Thanks."

She shrugs and gestures vaguely with her hand. "I could tell you were ready to explode. Besides, no one else was helping; you must be short-staffed, huh?"

"Is it that obvious?" I ask.

Nodding her head, she clarifies further, "I've been a waitress before. I can tell. So, rough night?"

"Tell me about it." I exhale loudly with a smile on my face and a short nod. My eyelids feel heavy with a mixture of relief and exhaustion. My once pounding headache lowers down to a dull ache as I take out two more glasses and look over at the woman before me. "Let me offer you and your husband a drink, on the house."

She looks toward her companion and back at me while pointing at him with her thumb. "Who, Ben? Oh, he's not my husband."

"But your ring…" I point to her left hand.

Taking off the ring, she slides it onto her index finger instead. "Ben would never marry me in a million years. He's gay; he would never look at women as anything more than friends. We just do this from time to time. It's a good deterrent. I get to keep creeps off my back, and he gets to show off his muscles. But I will take those free drinks you offered."

"Okay, but what does he want to drink?" I ask, truly smiling for the first time that night.

Her forehead crinkles in thought. It's almost too adorable to not notice. "Hm, he'll take a… mango daiquiri, and I'll have another martini like this one. It's so good I might have to come back for thirds or fourths."

"I'm glad you like it," I say before getting to work on the drinks.

Taking them, she turns to me and smiles before winking at me. "By the way, I'm Fernanda, but you can call me Fer." Her tongue rolls softly over the R, giving me goosebumps. It's almost as if she were singing her name to me, and all I can do is grin awkwardly before stuttering my name.

"Louise, huh, that's a pretty name," she replies. I'm used to people complimenting my name for the sake of politeness, but this woman makes the praise sound sincere. She looks back at Ben, who's now calling her name and pointing at the drink. "Whoops, I gotta get back before this daiquiri ends up being mostly water. I'll be back up later. It was nice to meet you." As she turns away, I notice the Aquarius sign tattooed on her upper back.

I want to say something, but it's as though I'm frozen, and all I can muster is a stammered "Y-yeah. See-see you later." Of course, being the awkward dork I've always been, she's out of earshot. *Louise, you nimrod!*

*

The blinding morning sun pierces my eyelids, and I cringe. Reaching for my covers, I try to pull them over me but to no avail. Blearily, I open my eyes and groan, "Marina, let go of the covers!"

"Nope, you have to get up." She grunts as she struggles with me, trying to pull the comforter off me. We play tug-of-war for a few seconds until I give in. Marina stumbles back with a gasp as she taps her foot on the floor.

I grumble and instead opt for curling up on my side, grabbing the pillow in an attempt to cover my face. I can feel Marina crossing her arms, her disapproving glare boring holes through the stuffing. I pretend to ignore her until the smell of coffee wafts through the room. Sighing, I toss off the pillow and flip to my back while sluggishly opening my eyes and sitting up. Irritation is seeping out of my pores. "I hate you; you're a sadist." Marina simply rolls her eyes while I reach for my coffee mug and take a careful sip.

"Sure, whatever," Marina says, grabbing her coffee and sitting on a chair in front of me.

Finally waking up, I look outside and notice the condensation clinging to the window panes. "What time is it?"

"Eight o'clock," Marina states, shrugging as she blows the steam off her coffee.

My eyes widen. "You woke me up at eight in the morning on a Sunday! Have you lost your damn mind?! I thought you said you wanted me to catch up on my sleep during finals!"

"Yeah, during finals. I didn't say you should turn into a hibernating bear during vacation, dorko." Marina looks up at me critically, her hazel eyes judging. I don't know what's worse, not having a friend or having one whose disapproving gaze could make you feel like an errant child. True, she can be a bit overprotective and overbearing, but I know it stems from good intentions. However, I have enough dealing with the mother I already have. I don't need another one in college.

"You could've let me sleep in on the weekend, at least. You rip me a new one for not sleeping, and now you're not letting me do the one thing you kept yapping about all semester long," I moan.

Marina nods. "True, I did do that, but it's been weeks, and all you've done is sleep the days away. I let it go because, as you said, I did complain that you weren't sleeping enough. You gotta get out of your head, though. Get out of this room and have some fun. You know, live? You've spent weeks working, ordering takeout, and sleeping. I know you have bills to pay and things to take care of, but you're young, and you need to do something different with your life."

Considering her words, I put my mug on the bedside table. Perhaps Marina is right. Again. Maybe it's because she's older than me but, God, will there ever be a moment when she's not right? A five-year age difference can't possibly mean that she's had so much more experience in life than I have, right? We both go to the same college, attend the same classes, so why is it that she knows more than me? I'm not completely stupid; I know I'm full of responsibilities, mainly regarding my mother and the downward spiral of her many illnesses. I also know that if I continue to fall into the same old hermit-like routine, I'll start to look like a scrawny troll.

"I hate socializing; it's exhausting, you know that," I grumble, drooping my shoulders in defeat.

Marina nods. "I know."

I've always been more of an introvert, and my shyness tends to relegate me to the role of a lonesome wallflower. Pets are my preferred companions during any party, and, if all else fails, I'll shut myself in the bathroom. It isn't that I hate people, but sometimes it just gets to be too much when they constantly jabber on about some nonsensical shit or another. I especially hate awkwardly standing there answering idle questions about the weather, gossip, or, worse, myself. Specifically when it's about what I'm doing or whom I'm dating. Since the questions normally come from people I don't much care for, I mostly just shrug or make an excuse to leave. It's tiresome having to smile for the sake of appearances, but I deal with it. I drag myself to social events only because I can't very well wallow in my self-pity.

Slumping forward, my muffled voice complains, "I don't wanna go!"

"Not even if I told you Bryan was coming with?" Marina taunts, dragging out every syllable of her secret friend's name.

Swiftly sitting back up, I look at my friend. "Bryan? The guy you're seeing?"

Marina nods, an impish gleam in her eyes.

"I thought you said you guys weren't exclusive though." I frown in confusion.

Marina averts her eyes from my face, staring intently into her mug, and all the while blushing furiously. "Well, things got a bit more serious."

I jump up and clap my hands excitedly. "In that case, I'm definitely coming."

"I'm regretting this already," Marina mumbles while I search through my closet for something to wear.

"I can't wait to meet this guy." An idea occurs to me, and I turn to look at Marina. "He must be really special if you're letting me meet him, hmm?" I wiggle my eyebrows suggestively.

"Oh my God, please promise me you'll be on your best behavior and won't act like the nerd I know you to be." It's Marina's turn to moan.

I gasp, leaning back with a hand to my chest. "Moi? I would never!"

Marina squints and points at me accusingly. "Then why do you have that smile on your face?"

"Smile, what smile is this which thou speaketh of?" I reply with the best British accent I can muster.

"Please, I beg you to be on your best behavior!" Marina wails.

Raising my hand in a Girl Scout's salute, I stand rigidly. "All right, all right, I promise not to be a complete disaster, but only because it's you; otherwise it would be a whole different ball game out there!"

"Thank you for so charitably bestowing your blessings, goddess of dateless nights!" Marina replies with a smirk. Normally I would take offense, but seeing my best friend happy fills me with relief. She had been carrying a torch for some dude who didn't appreciate her for so long that I was beginning to wonder if she would ever move on.

I chuckle. "You bitch." I grab whatever soft thing I can reach and throw it at her.

"You know it." She giggles, blocking the stuffed animal and letting it plop onto the floor with a wink in my direction.

*

Once I'm wrangled into a booth of the diner Marina insisted was 'just the cutest little place,' I glance down at the menu and covertly look at the entrance to see who this Bryan guy is.

Marina taps her fingers on the table as she gnaws the side of her lower lip. "Ugh, I'm so freaking nervous!"

"Um, why? It's not like I'm gonna bombard him with questions," I assure her, glancing back down at the menu.

"God, I hope you don't!" Marina looks as though her worst nightmare is coming true in front of her eyes.

I reach over and cover her hand with mine. Her tapping is driving me crazy. "Relax, you spaz. If he can handle you, Judgy McJudgerson, he can handle me."

"I am not judgy!" Marina gasps.

"Sure you're not," I answer quickly, patting her arm.

Suddenly the door jingles. I quickly glance up but when I realize it's two guys, I return to the menu in my hand. However, Marina is waving both guys over. Putting down my menu, I look back up as Marina rises and gives a tall, dark-haired man a peck on the lips.

I say hi and turn to the stranger who followed Bryan to our booth. He smiles shyly as he digs his hands into his pockets, waiting for Bryan to stop whispering sweet nothings to Marina. After what seems like an age, he clears his throat. "Uh, you gonna introduce me?"

Blushing, Bryan stutters, "O-oh, my bad, bro. Marina, Louise; this is my brother, Aaron. I'm not normally this awkward, I promise."

Bryan finally settles down, resting his forearms on top of the table as he gives me a kind smile.

"I'm sorry my husband couldn't come; he got caught up at work. He promised to meet up at the parade later though," Aaron adds as he pushes his auburn hair back.

I adjust my glasses and blink rapidly. "Your husband?"

"Yes, he wants to meet you all, but his boss asked him to stay longer," Aaron replies, fiddling with his silverware.

How can I have not realized Aaron is gay? He's wearing a white shirt with the word #PRIDE written in rainbow colors. The man is carrying some sort of purse, for God's sake. Not that I mind his sexual preference, especially when I still haven't clarified my own preference to my family. It just shocks me that he is so open and free about it when I've had to resort to practically running away for my own peace of mind. Louisville, although tolerant of most things, has yet to catch up with the rest of the world as far as the LGBTQ+ community is involved. For once in my life, I'm envious of the carefree nature that exudes from Aaron. I want to be like him, to accept myself and be as open and untroubled as he so clearly seems. More than anything, I long for the closeness that he has with Bryan.

I grin tightly at Aaron and nod. "I'm sure we'll meet him soon."

"Well, yeah. As I said, he's supposed to meet up with us later at the parade." Aaron chuckles.

I need to stop looking like I'm somehow ignorant of everything I'm hearing, but I can't help it. I knew California was known for its infamous Pride Parade, but I hadn't the foggiest idea when it was held. "I-is that today?"

"Yeah, it's National Pride Day! Actually, why don't you join us? That way we can all get to know each other better!" Aaron's light brown eyes shine enthusiastically while Bryan nods eagerly, echoing his brother's invitation.

Marina excitedly agrees, but before I know what I'm doing, I blurt out, "I can't go." Suddenly I freeze up. Looking around the stunned table, I feel the heat of my blush rise up my neck and settle onto my cheeks.

"But it'll be so much fun!" Marina insists, breaking the silence.

My eyes widen in terror, and I shake my head desperately.

Marina, noticing my panic, excuses us from the table and drags me to the bathroom. "What the hell is wrong with you!" she says through gritted teeth as the door slams shut behind her.

"I can't go to the Pride Parade, Marina!"

Frowning, Marina blinks. "Why not?"

"Because they're going to be taking pictures and posting them on the internet or in the papers, and my mother is sick. I can't afford to give her a heart attack when she's so fragile." My hands fly everywhere with frenzied terror.

Grabbing my shoulders, my best friend's eyes soften. "Louise, calm down. Nothing is going to happen. You'll be fine."

"But what if it isn't?!" My lips shake as I swallow down a sob.

"I'll make sure nothing happens. We—we'll make sure to tell the people at the entrance of the parade that we don't want any pictures with you printed or anything, okay?" She searches out my eyes as I stare down at the floor.

My shoulders droop. "I won't be able to show my face back home; I'll be an embarrassment to my family."

Marina crosses her arms and frowns. "Louise Dubois, you know that's not true. You are not an embarrassment. You are kind, funny, and a royal pain in the ass, but I love you, and I wouldn't want you any other way."

I blush. "According to them, people like me are destroying families and I can't, or rather I won't, destroy mine."

Marina bumps my shoulder with her own to catch my attention, and when I look at her she simply shakes her head.

Maybe I'm wrong. I want to be wrong about Kentucky and my family. If Marina can love me unconditionally despite having no family connection to me, then maybe I can learn to love and accept myself for who I am. I can't possibly be that bad, can I?

"You're not the problem. The people who made you feel like there is something wrong with you are the ones who are twisted," Marina reassures me. "But, if you're that worried, we'll take precautions and make sure nothing happens unless you're comfortable."

Gulping back a sob, I sniff as I reach out and hug her. "You're such a sap, you know that?"

"I'm your best friend," she whispers, patting my back. It's almost as if her explanation is somehow the most natural response. Leaning back, she points at me. "But you're not allowed to tell anyone I'm a closet teddy bear. I'm trying to maintain my bad bitch image, and I do not need it ruined."

I snort and nod my head. "Okay, fine." Marina leaves me to compose myself before walking out. When I finally do have the nerve to open the bathroom door, I take a deep breath. Having reached my decision, I walk up to the booth. Marina is whispering to her boyfriend and his brother, but when I get close enough to hear, they stop and greet me. Great, now I probably seem like some kind of loner type idiot. I can't fault Marina for explaining even a small part of my problem. Who wouldn't be weirded out if someone walks away so abruptly? I just hope she didn't elaborate too much.

"You coming to the parade?" Aaron asks, looking at me expectantly.

I steel myself as I ball my hands into fists and nod. "Yeah, let's go."

"Are you sure? You don't have to come if you don't want to. We understand, right, guys?" Marina looks at Bryan and Aaron, who both nod earnestly.

I offer the trio a small smile. "I want to go, I promise. I want to see what I've been missing."

*

As I shuffle the flyers, one escapes, flying just out of reach. I look down at the mess of objects that have been so kindly distributed and wonder why I didn't think to get a bag. I awkwardly readjust the flyers once more and scan through the crowds for a nearby vendor. I look down to the small purse slung diagonally across my shoulder, wondering how many of these papers I could stuff into it before I realize it's far too small for me to carry all this precious information. Walking off toward a stand, I look back when I feel a hand pausing my steps.

"Where are you going?" Marina asks.

I point with my chin to the small stall full of souvenirs I found, and she nods before reassuring me that they'll wait for me in the same spot where the parade is jubilantly passing by.

Reaching out for the first tote I can get my hands on, I start to place the handouts on the vendor's small table, rummaging in my purse for my wallet. I'm handing a twenty over when suddenly a small, manicured hand stops me.

"Nah, you don't want that one," someone interrupts.

Surprised, I look up to see the same girl who saved me at the bar a couple of months ago. Her purple tips are still there, but her hair is longer. Her short bob is now a flurry of thick, shoulder-length waves blowing every which way in the rush of a slight breeze.

Now, what was her name again? I remember it being a strong Spanish name; it started with an F. Ugh, curse my amnesiac tendencies.

"Hey," I say with an arch of my eyebrows. *Please don't ask me what your name is, please don't ask me what your name is!*

"Hey, Louise, right?" She points to me with a smile. Great, now she's going to be super offended I forgot her name.

"Yeah, I'm sorry, but I'm not good with names," I reply lamely. Might as well be honest and avoid an even more awkward situation. I've been on the receiving end of too many people who have not quite understood that my lack of memory is not due to a lack of caring.

She laughs and shrugs. "It's okay. I have a hard name to remember. It's Fernanda, by the way, but you can call me Fer or Nanda."

I knew it started with an F!

"Right," I say, smiling shyly. Honestly, I've felt so out of sorts with most people lately, but something about her makes me hyper-aware of everything that could possibly go wrong... or not. Almost as if the capacity for sensitivity is exponentially higher. It's both frightening and exciting, and I don't quite know what to do.

She waves my apology away as she pushes her waves out of her face and reaches for another tote. "This is better, it has more room and side pockets for you to carry your water bottles." She smiles as she shows it to me.

I nod, impressed. "Do you work here?"

"No, I've just been to this parade way too many times, and some of the vendors are constant." She reaches for a packet of hair ties and quickly buys it before tearing into the packaging. Running her fingers through her hair while facing in the direction of the wind, she gathers it into a messy ponytail before securing it with several hair ties. "Honestly, curse this thick hair. I can never get it to behave."

I shrug. "I think it's pretty!"

"Thanks." She blushes. "I thought cutting it would help, but I got bored and decided to grow it out again. Now I just want it out of my face. It's a pain to brush and style because it's so thick, but at least I have enough to do whatever I want with it, right?"

I nod. "I know what you mean." I point to my tight curls.

"Oh right, sorry!" Fer cringes.

I smile and shake my head. "It's fine, promise."

Feeling an awkward silence creeping between us, I look back at my group. "Well, thanks for the help. I gotta go join my friends now."

"Who are you here with?" she asks suddenly.

I point over to Marina and her boyfriend. "I'm kind of third-wheeling, to be honest," I say, as I see Aaron hugging someone I presume is his husband. He's pulling a small cooler along behind him, and around his neck hangs a variety of colorful beads.

"Ah," Fernanda says. "Well, you can always come and join me and my friends. I'm kind of third-wheeling, too."

I turn to give her my attention. I want so badly to ask her and her friends to join us, but the fear of being photographed grips me so I don't say anything.

Fer's eyes light up, "Hey, I've got an even better idea. Why don't you guys all join? I'm sure it'll be way more fun that way, right?"

Crap! The one thing I didn't want to happen, and here I am unable to deny her when her soft brown eyes are shining with hope. A nervous smile spreads across her face.

"I'd love to but..." I look down at the floor, blushing. She's going to think I'm a total loser, but it's better if she doesn't think I hate her or something. "I can't."

"Why?" Her pretty face scrunches with a frown.

I gulp and take a deep breath. "I don't want to be photographed," I mumble as I stare at the ground.

Her soft hand on my arm catches my attention. "You're not exactly out of the closet yet, right?" she asks gently, her brown eyes softening.

I blink rapidly and shake my head. I'm feeling all sorts of confused. I've never considered the possibility that anyone would affect me this much after such a short time. I feel so discombobulated and frazzled; it's almost as if my head and heart aren't agreeing for the first time in a long time. Sure, I've had crushes on my friends, and there were many days where my fantasies took me beyond what was logical, but that was as far as any of my infatuations went. Besides, this is no mere infatuation. It's an entirely different monster, and I don't quite know what to do with it. My crushes usually dissipate faster than a rainstorm; they never hit me with the force of a hurricane. This is definitely a new experience. It's both a shock to the senses as well as to the orderly, logical recesses of my mind.

She shifts her weight from one leg to another and puts her hand on her hip. "It's okay, I get it. It's your first Pride Parade?"

I nod. *Am I that obvious?*

"Maybe you should look at the flyers more closely." She points to my sweaty hands.

I look down as she leans over to reach for the tote while I try to sort through the pile of papers. Fernanda, sensing my confusion, grabs them and quickly helps me, putting the unnecessary ones into the tote until she finds the one she's after. "Here, read this."

Scanning my eyes across the page, I read the simple page of rules. The pink and blue paper had just been another unremarkable scrap in the sea of information that had been handed to me, but now I realize it's my lifeline.

"As you can see here, there's a set of suggestions for everyone. After all, some people here are still in the closet." Fernanda leans over and points to rule number two, which goes on to explain about the parade's expectations concerning photography. For a moment I'm distracted by her hair. It smells like berries, and I want to move closer, but I'm pretty sure she might end up thinking I'm some kind of creep. Fer looks at me and offers a gentle smile, snapping me back in to focus on the paper. "See?" she says. "It's normal around here to expect privacy for the sake of protection. We make it a habit to look out for each other, and if you're still worried, there's a sticker around here somewhere that says you don't want pictures of yourself taken." She rummages through the bag in search of it.

I feel a knot in my throat as my eyes begin to water with unshed tears. I try to control my burning nose as I start to sniffle, but it proves to be difficult. I inhale deeply before I reach out to hold her hand and squeeze it gently. "Thank you."

"Sure, any time. Now, do you want to join us?" she asks earnestly.

A slight wind blows my way, and I push an errant curl behind my ear. "Yeah, just let me ask my friends first."

"Cool," she says nonchalantly.

Fer's friends are waiting close by. She quickly introduces me to Bianca and Sharon, who seem completely besotted with each other. According to Fer, they've been married for the past four years. "We got married as soon as it was legalized," Sharon explains with a smile that lights up her entire face. She looks up at her wife, who's returning the affection with equal fervor. It's infectious and sweet, and I'm all the more reminded of my crushing loneliness. My yearning grows for the type of love they seem to possess for one another.

Fernanda looks at me and earnestly asks about my group. I look behind me and see Marina craning her neck while her eyes search for me. "I think I'm about to give my best friend a heart attack if I don't show up soon."

Looking at her friends, Fernanda tells them of our plan, and they readily agree.

As I rush back to Marina, she looks relieved. "There you are!" she huffs, exhaling deeply.

"Sorry, I met up with someone," I sheepishly reply.

Marina focuses her attention on Fer and her friends as they approach. I turn to introduce them when Fernanda's infectious smile renders me silent. Damn it! I must look like a malfunctioning robot. This disorientation is starting to frustrate me. How am I supposed to look like a capable, grown woman if I can't even handle a slight whatever-this-is?

Fernanda steps forward and takes control as she introduces herself and her companions to my group. Her eyes radiate with joy, and I can't help but be compelled to smile just as much.

Marina, who up to this point has been looking both pleasantly surprised and confused, is now staring at me as though she's trying to unravel a puzzle.

"… and this is Aaron and his husband, Terry," Marina finishes her introductions.

I'm left wondering if things are truly turning out as good as it feels. I see that my wishful thinking has become a reality. I smile to myself for a second as we begin to discuss plans for the day.

*

By late afternoon, the nerves that were clinging to my pores are slowly beginning to disappear. It's been so long since I've laughed with such abandon. My face and ab muscles must've forgotten what true happiness felt like. However, I'm still waiting for the other shoe to drop; it won't be long before someone realizes how out of the loop I am.

"What do you think?" asks Terry, catching my attention.

Blinking rapidly, I'm hoping the June heat conceals my blush. Guess I was too deeply involved in my thoughts. "Huh?"

"I was asking if you're hungry enough to go look for a place to eat?" Terry asks, his eyes begging me to agree to a group lunch.

Honestly, I'm still full from the kabobs we bought from one of the many food trucks lining the streets, but we've been walking for such a long time that sitting in a chair would be appreciated at this point. My jelly legs are becoming less likely to continue for much further without rest. "Uh, yeah, sure." *Fuck it! I'll order something small.*

We exchange ideas of where we'd all like to go and compromise on a quaint mom-and-pop restaurant down the street. Well, not all of us. Terry is hesitant to walk down there.

"Why not? It's a cute place, and they have great food!" chimes in Marina.

Terry looks down the street, a drop of sweat running down his forehead. I suspect it has nothing to do with the heat. His normal, relaxed posture is beginning to stiffen as I see worry clouding his eyes.

"The Westboro Baptist Church people tend to park themselves near there all the time. Terry and Aaron already had a problem with them before," Bryan explains.

Marina, who up to this point has been completely clueless, nods in understanding. Sympathy overtakes her, and she gently puts her hand on Terry's shoulder and squeezes him in comfort.

"Fuck them!" Fernanda says, her voice full of disdain. We all turn to look at her. "Yes, fuck them! They don't get to decide my future. They can continue to live whatever twisted life they have, and I never say anything because it's not my business. But I am done letting people like that decide who I get to hang out with, much less love. I've been done for a long time, and, right now, I'm hungry." Fer begins to walk briskly, her head inching up a notch, her hair flying along behind her. She looks like a soldier about to go into the frontlines of battle.

I feel pride, but there's also something else stirring that I can't even begin to describe. I'm fearful of the church encountering us. I've never had the displeasure, but Fer's confidence reassures me that maybe things won't be so bad. At least I'm not alone, right?

The rest of the crew follow behind her, but as we near the restaurant, Terry pauses. The protesters line the street. Marina takes his hand and squeezes while Aaron takes the other. They smile at one another and push their shoulders back, walking forward as nonchalantly as possible.

I mimic my friends and try to ignore the voices from the side shouting at us to 'repent for our sins,' and that 'God will smite us.' My curiosity gets the better of me, and I look over. They have large signs that they wave viciously, and their chants rise in pitch when they see me watching.

All the signs are similar to their horrible insults, but it's one in particular that catches my eye. It's Leviticus 18:22: 'Thou shalt not lie with mankind, as with womankind; it is an abomination.'

"Are you okay?" Fernanda asks, waving her hand in front of my face, blocking my view of the protesters as she peers into my eyes with a worried frown.

I jump as though coming out of a trance and blink several times. "What?"

Fernanda repeats her question, and I give her a curt nod in reply. I'm not okay, but what else can I do? I can't ruin my friends' plans due to my lack of control. That would just be monumentally selfish.

"Come on, let's go somewhere else," Marina says.

"No, really, I'm fine. See?" I force a smile.

Fer shakes her head. "I can tell when someone's not doing okay, and right now, you're not fine. Something's wrong."

I begin to protest, but Bryan cuts me off. "It's okay, I promise. Besides, Terry isn't comfortable here either. We can't force you guys to eat here. We'll find a different place."

I nod and start to walk away but pause once more to look back. That's when I notice a group of people dressed in brightly colored leotards and sporting massive amounts of rainbow-colored beads around their necks as they whoop and dance around the protesters, who try their damnedest to ignore their taunts.

Fernanda rolls her eyes and chuckles as Terry, Aaron, and Fer's two friends all look like they're going to burst out laughing. "Serves them right," snickers Aaron.

Suddenly, a transgender woman passes by wearing a pink, blue, and white dress while maintaining perfect balance on a hot pink hoverboard. She holds up a sign that says, 'Westboro Baptist Church likes Nickelback.' Finally, none of us can hold it in anymore, and we burst out laughing. The bitter reminder of why I left Kentucky is soon replaced by the sheer ridiculousness of the situation.

Fer pulls on my hand. "Come on, I know another place nearby." We leave the others to their lighthearted shenanigans and the obviously uncomfortable protesters who are now inching as far back as possible from the rowdy strangers.

The afternoon quickly turns into evening. We've all had a good share of cocktails accompanied by a lot of laughter. I'm going to wake up to a wicked hangover, but it's worth it. I look up to the sky as a small breeze caresses my face and smile. The one place I'd thought I would feel uneasy has now become my safe haven. Here, I don't have to hide who I like or who I truly am. For the first time in my life I feel peace, acceptance, and, above all, a sense of belonging. I can't remember the last time I'd ever felt so unabashedly fearless of the consequences. Oh well, I'm sure I'm bound to regret something by tomorrow, but, for now, I don't care.

*

I groan helplessly while blindly reaching for my phone. A pounding headache drums through my skull, and I can feel the filmy residue of my unbrushed teeth. I fumble about for a couple of minutes until someone slaps my hand.

"Not now, Mom, five more minutes," mumbles a voice next to me, and I can feel a body as it begins to shift into a better position. I yank the blanket off my face and immediately regret my decision. The bright sunlight intensifies my headache, and my eyes instantly water. Blearily, I peer at someone next to me; no, not someone, a girl. Nope, not a girl, a woman with tanned, olive skin and short, dark hair. The tips are purple. It's Fernanda. I sit up, pressing my palm to my forehead, hoping to will the pain away.

Looking around, I see Marina is sleeping next to Bryan. Her leg is thrown over his hip while his arm is angled in what I assume is a painful position. Marina's tiny twin bed is not big enough for both of them. Aaron and Terry lie on the floor. Blankets are haphazardly thrown on top of the pair. I don't see Sharon and Bianca anywhere and wonder if they left before we got to the dorm. Gingerly, I ease my way off the bed as quietly as humanly possible so as not to wake anyone else. I look down at myself and realize that I'm wearing the same clothes from last night. Leaning over to smell my armpits, I cringe away. *Oh hell no! This won't do.*

Tiptoeing to my closet, I slowly take out some sweats and a hoodie to change into before I head out for some coffee. *That's safe, right? It's not like I'm running away or anything. I could just pop back in here with a nice surprise for everyone, and no one will know that I'm an awkward fool who fell asleep next to the most beautiful woman in the world knowing full well I snore like a wild hog. Yup, definitely not running,* I reason with myself as I close the bathroom door and proceed to dress as quickly as I can without waking anyone up.

Standing in line at the coffee shop, I pick at my cuticles and try to recall what I might've done the night before, but everything is such a blur that I can't quite remember if I pulled off my 'no pictures pls' sticker or if I did anything to embarrass myself. I muffle my groan as I cover my face.

"Next!" I hear the barista's voice call just as someone taps me impatiently on the shoulder. I'm startled for a second but proceed to order coffee for Marina and me.

"Will that be all?" asks the bored-looking barista. Crap! I don't know what anyone else might like, and I can't just go back to the dorm with only two coffees. I war with myself about whether I should just order the most popular thing on the menu or cancel the order entirely.

Suddenly, I hear a rapid huff to my left. "You're a hard person to catch up to!"

Turning, I see Fer's pretty brown eyes staring back at me. She leans against the counter trying to catch her breath.

The customers behind me complain, but I turn to the barista and cancel the previous request, instead ordering myself a large black coffee, no sugar. As I rummage through my purse for my wallet, Fer places a hand on mine to stop me before she orders herself a coffee as well, handing the cashier the money.

"You didn't have to do that. I could've paid for myself," I say lamely as I close my purse slowly.

She shrugs and waves my appreciation away. "It's no biggie. We can go halfsies on the coffees for the rest of the crew." I thank her, nodding in agreement as we choose seats at a small table outside the coffee shop. We sit in silence for a couple of seconds, Fer facing me, nursing our coffees, before she starts to talk. "I'm sorry about yesterday."

"What are you talking about? I had the best day of my life." My eyes are wide, and I have to blink several times as I try to recollect what could've happened that she feels the need to apologize.

Fer shakes her head. "Not when we went to the mom-and-pop restaurant, though."

"That wasn't your fault," I say, reaching for her.

Fernanda sighs and withdraws her hand. "It was. I knew you and Terry weren't okay with the place, but I guess I just thought that what little confidence I have was enough to help you two out. I guessed wrong and ended up making things worse."

"Actually, I was feeling pretty confident up until I saw the Bible verses on their signs." I take a sip of my coffee.

Fernanda leans closer. "Yeah, what exactly happened, if you don't mind me asking?"

Normally I would mind the question, but not when she is the one asking. In fact, I feel like I could talk to her about almost anything. "To be completely honest, I don't know."

"You kind of spaced out for a bit; it was almost as if you couldn't hear us."

I cringe. "Yeah, it must've been kinda weird to see."

"Not really. I've seen it before. It used to happen a lot to my dad. He's had a rough life," Fernanda explains as she leans back. We both pause, almost as if we are gauging whether we feel comfortable with where the conversation is taking us.

"So, are you a college student like me?" I ask, changing the subject. I almost feel bad about it, but deflection is my one tool for protection. I'm still not used to emotionally exposing myself to any extent. It took damn near forever to even open up to Marina, and when I finally did, it was almost as if the floodgates had opened. I was so scared that I'd frightened her off with all my baggage, but she just acted as though it never bothered her. However, that was Marina. This is Fernanda. Both kind, both sweet, but I'm only interested in one, and I don't want to fuck up any chance to at least be her friend. God knows if Fer would be as easygoing as Marina. I'm not even sure I could express my vulnerability without breaking apart like kinetic sand. *I'm a goddamn mess.*

She looks at me for a minute before giving me a gentle smile. "Yup, I'm a psychology major at UCLA."

"I go to UCLA, too! I'm a music major." I'm so pleasantly surprised that it prompts me to grab my chair and scooch it over to sit closer to her. "I've never seen you around, though."

Fer shrugs. "Eh, we don't exactly have any classes in common, but I'm glad we met."

I blush as I look down at my palms. "Thanks," I whisper.

"Hey, I am sorry for making things worse at the parade. I didn't know it would affect you so much, and I don't need to know why, but I just need you to know that I meant no harm." Fer angles her head as if searching for my gaze. When I finally do look up, she gives me an encouraging smile.

"I'm not sure if you're aware that I'm not out to my family yet?"

"I guessed as much. I wanted to ask more questions, but I didn't feel like it was my place," Fer says, looking at me cautiously.

Sighing deeply, I clench my hands together until my knuckles turn white. I want to focus on something other than whatever reaction Fer might have to my story. I'm not exactly sure why I am compelled to tell her everything, but I am about to anyway. "I come from Kentucky, and usually people are very welcoming, as long as you fit in."

"And you don't?" Fernanda frowns.

I shake my head, but still, I continue, "I'm bisexual. It shouldn't be a big deal, except if you're from a Black family who's barely trying to scrape by. It's just my mom, brother, and me."

"What about your dad?" Fernanda asks.

"He died some time ago. We make do with what we have, but sometimes it's just not enough. I feel a little guilty." Propping up my elbow on the table, I rest my chin on my palm.

There's a long pause before Fernanda asks, "For what?"

"Me being here is putting a strain on our bank account. I mean, I do have a scholarship, but still..." I shake my head and straighten up once again. "I just couldn't stay in Kentucky any longer. It was too much for me."

Fernanda gestures for me to continue while sipping her coffee.

I look down at my cup and mimic her to give myself something to do with my hands. "A guest pastor at my church read the same passage as the one written on the protester's signs. He went on to tell us an anecdote about how he had been a mailman. He would refuse to deliver packages to homes and businesses where he knew gay people resided. According to him, he couldn't compromise his faith. Hell, he even made it a point to mock the men and women who he guessed were gay; he wasn't even sure if they were, but he just made up his mind because of what he had heard or seen. I felt sick hearing about it. No one said anything against it, either. Instead, everyone just nodded and accepted what this man was saying at face value despite not even knowing him on a personal level. I knew I could never be accepted back home, so I finally made up my mind and left."

"So you moved here instead?" Leaning back, Fernanda exhales loudly and shakes her head.

I nod. "Yep. Turns out I'm a coward. I essentially ran away and left my sick mother and my brother, who has a gambling problem, alone. I don't know what it was about that day that made me decide my path. Maybe it was because I was already thinking of going to college and had even filled out some applications. Or maybe it was because I'd heard that same sermon so many times before throughout my life but never in the way that pastor mocked what I could see as a future for myself."

"I get it, trust me, I get it very well." Fernanda gives me a tired smile.

Tilting my head to the left, I regard her thoughtfully. "Do you?"

"I come from a staunchly conservative Latino family with a strong Catholic background."

I nod, realizing she must've gone through many of the same things as I have. "How do you deal with it?"

"Look, not everyone is going to agree with my lesbian 'lifestyle,' as they call it, but I can't compromise myself to make them comfortable. Besides, not all of them are like the people you described. Sure, you get the occasional family member that has shitty, twisted views in life, but it's no sweat off my back. I know it sounds cold, but I'm an adult, and I deserve to live life the way I want. I deserve to be happy; I can't let anyone else choose my life for me because, at the end of the day, that person has no idea what it's like to be me. Besides, if they don't care enough to accept me for who I am, they never really cared about me to begin with, did they?" When I nod in agreement, she looks out to the street and smiles to herself, staring wistfully at the people walking by.

I look at her for a long time and feel as light as a feather. Once again, I long to get closer to her, to touch her and call her mine, but being the awkward bean that I am, I blurt out instead, "You're gorgeous, do you know that?" I freeze, my eyes widening as I realize that I just ended up coming off exactly as weird as I expected I was. *Fuck! Louise, you stupid buffoon! Now she's really gonna think I've gone off the deep end.*

She turns to look at me, her smile deepening. Her eyes are bright as she blushes prettily. "Th-thanks."

I mentally kick myself as my mortification washes over me like magma. "I know that came off weird. I'm sorry; it's just... I don't know. It—it's almost as if I feel this connection to you, you know?"

"Is that why you kissed me last night?" Fer asks me.

My brain goes into total malfunction as I gape like a fish. "I-I'm sorry, I-I d-did what?"

"Yeah, you kissed me. Then again, you were pretty drunk, so I didn't think anything of it." She shrugs it off with a smile.

I can feel my blush intensify as I bury my face in my hands. "Oh my God, I'm so sorry! You must think I'm such a creep."

"I didn't think much to be honest, except that there I was getting kissed by a beautiful woman. It was nice, and you're a good kisser," Fer replies. "Besides, I wanted you to kiss me. I'd been sending you signals all night."

I glance up from my hands. "You were? And… and you think I'm pretty?"

"Actually, I think you're hot, but that's not everything. You're funny, very sweet, and I can tell there's a lot more to you than you give yourself credit for." Fer reaches for my hand, unrolling my fist and drawing little circles on my palm.

I watch her trace the patterns. "So, I know this is gonna sound super lame and all, but I like you, too. Maybe we can hang out sometime?"

"Like a date?" Fer asks.

I nod. "Yes, like a date."

She smiles so brightly I can see her eyes shining. "Okay. Let's go on a date. But first, I want to ask for something." I nod and gesture for her to continue. "I would like another kiss." I look around nervously, but she grips my hand tighter. "Don't worry about anybody else."

"Okay." My voice is huskier than I expect. Slowly, I reach out for her with my free hand, catching her lips with mine. I start off a little hesitantly, but her moan is enough to undo all my worries. I can feel her arms looped around my neck. I lift my newly freed hand and caress her cheek as I hungrily drink my fill from her. She smells like berries, and it feels almost as if I am back home. I pull away just a bit, resting my forehead against hers.

"Whoa," she whispers breathlessly as she raises her eyebrows.

I nod. "Right?"

I can feel my cheeks burning as I lean back to look at Fer's face in wonder. I can't understand how, why, or what she could see in a person like me, but I try to ignore the nagging feeling of doubt, instead forcing myself to focus on the positives.

I can't possibly be that bad, right? Otherwise, Marina wouldn't be my friend.

"Penny for your thoughts?" Fernanda asks.

I shrug. "It's nothing." Sighing, I gently lace my fingers with hers, but upon realizing that I've overstepped the limit of comfort, I glance up at Fer earnestly. "I don't know if this is okay, but… is it?"

Fer nods, brushing her other hand on my cheek and pushing my hair behind my ear. "It's fine."

"I'm not usually like this," I mutter, glancing down as I play with her hand absentmindedly.

Fer frowns. "With what?"

"Dating, being in a relationship... I don't know how far to take anything or what to do. I was never one to make the first move, or any move whatsoever for that matter. I feel a little awkward, to be honest." Feeling deep shame, I blush as I look back up at the woman who simply gazes back at me as if I was her entire world.

Suddenly, she giggles.

Great, now she thinks you're an uneducated potato. Way to fucking go, Louise, you dumbtastic plebe. I internally roll my eyes at myself, feeling like the stupidest dork ever.

"I feel a little awkward, too. All new relationships are like that. Anyone who says otherwise is full of shit." Her nervous smile slowly turns serious as she tightens her hold on my hands. "But listen, it's okay. If you ever feel uncomfortable about anything at all, let me know, and we'll figure out what to do about it. We can try to fix the situation, or if you need to stop whatever it is we have together, we will. Okay?"

I ponder her words for a moment and frown. "Well, I hope you don't end up thinking I'm some idiot, because I have absolutely no idea what I'm doing." I laugh nervously to mask the doubts I just voiced.

"I would never think that you're an idiot. Why would I? Hell, even I don't know what I'm doing, most times I just kind of wing it and hope for the best. Inexperience is a part of life; no one is born knowing anything at all."

I feel as if the weight I'd been carrying is suddenly being lifted off my shoulders. For the first time in a long time, I feel as light as a bird, and for once I want to take flight. "You're incredible, you know. It's no wonder I was so attracted to you from the beginning." Once I realize what I just said, I clap my hands over my mouth. Curse this stupid, loose tongue. Why must it always do whatever it wants at the most inappropriate time?!

Fer's eyes widen, and suddenly her tinkling laugh bubbles out of her red semi-swollen lips.

Well duh, of course she laughs. You're an idiot with the social skills of a blobfish. I keep staring at her lips and feel an unrecognizable surge of pleasure to know that it's because of me that she looks like that.

"You're cute as hell, do you know that?" Fer asks, propping her face on her chin and looking at me as though I were a piece of art to admire.

Cute, sure. I've been pretty comfortable knowing that I was able to achieve a cute level of attractiveness most of the time. I was never thought of as hot or sexy, and it used to bother me. Now, it just feels as though it would be stressful to maintain such a position. However, with Fer I don't want to be referred to as cute. I want so badly for her to see me as a desirable woman. But really, how is she going to find me sexy if I don't even think I am?

I fidget in my chair and try to inconspicuously fix my hair as I give her a hesitant smile. "Thanks."

"Anyway, we gotta get back to the dorm. Everyone will probably be wondering where we are. Not to mention they might be hangry at this point," Fer interrupts my thoughts, looking at her phone and reaching for her coffee cup. She drains it in one gulp and grabs her purse.

I nod, mimicking her moves and returning to the cafe to get some bagels and other assorted breakfast goodies.

Walking back to the dorm, Fer reaches for one of the bags of goodies.

"Oh, you don't have to do that. I'm fine," I say.

"Nope, I want to help," Fernanda replies, holding her hand out. "Please?"

I give in, handing her one of the bags. We walk like that for several minutes before she switches the bag to her other side and reaches for my free hand, lacing it with her own. She glances at me cautiously. "Is this okay?"

I nod. "Yeah, it is."

Before we could open the dorm door, Fernanda suddenly pulls me back. I look at her, eyebrows raised in question.

"How do you want to do this?"

I look at the door in confusion. "Do what?"

"Do you want to be obvious about us dating or do you want to keep it on the down-low?" Fer explains.

Fair point. I hadn't thought of that. "I'm not exactly sure. I guess we can just keep it chill for now? If you don't mind, I mean," I reply hurriedly.

Fer nods. "Yeah, I'm cool with that. But can I get just one kiss before we go in?"

Looking around the empty hallway, I give her a sly smile before I grab her hand and pull her around the corner. Hastily dropping the bags to the floor, I look back at Fer, who's leaning against the wall nonchalantly. I breathe in, drinking up her beauty with my eyes before I pull her to me by the waist. "You're so beautiful," I murmur as I run my hand gently over her cheek and her eyes flutter shut in response. Her nose nuzzles mine as she wets her lips, the edge of her tongue lining the seam. Gulping, I lean in and finally, tentatively, close the gap to give her a soft kiss. My hands are shaking, and I can feel the heat rising within me. Fer coaxes me for more as she wraps her arms around me. When she moans, I feel any resolve I had been holding back melt away. Running my tongue across her bottom lip, I ask for permission. I feel her shudder as she opens her lips to me, granting me access. I can taste the sweet coffee she'd been drinking earlier as my hands play with her thick, soft hair. The smell of her berry perfume is intoxicating and, for an instant, I become brazenly selfish as I deepen our kiss.

Smiling wickedly, Fernanda pulls away, breathing heavily. "Are you okay?" she asks in between breaths as she looks at me with hooded eyes through her long, dark lashes. Her cheeks are flushed, and her lips are swollen.

I realize I can't remember the last time I've been so turned on. All I want to do is undress her with my teeth, but instead, I nod. "Yes, definitely yes."

She leans in for more as I feel my skin blaze with need, but before we can get any further I hear footsteps rushing in our direction.

"Shit," I grumble, reluctantly pulling away.

Fer hangs her head down and giggles silently to herself. The footsteps are getting closer, and I can now hear a guy talking alarmingly to another person who must be practically running considering the urgency of his friend's voice. Something about 'needing to hold it in because bro can't hurl out here or he'll have to pay for it later.'

Fer cringes as the steps finally recede down the hall. We listen for a minute or two before finally relaxing enough to make ourselves as inconspicuous as possible. After all, we did agree on maintaining our relationship as a secret, for now anyway.

We look around the corner before rushing back to the dorm and barging into a room full of barely awake people. Aaron is clutching his head while Terry is gingerly putting his pants on. Bryan is making the bed when Marina walks out of the bathroom with a toothbrush in hand. "Hey, where were you? I was beginning to worry."

Fer and I look at each other and lift the bagel bags in answer.

"Oh thank God, I was just about to go for some breakfast. We're starving!" Bryan exclaims, sitting on the bed.

"Ugh, speak for yourself," Aaron mumbles, looking a little pale.

Terry looks at his husband. "Well, maybe some starch will settle your stomach."

Aaron nods and then winces.

"Sorry, it was a long line," Fer says, placing the bags on the bed. She looks at me with a smirk.

I look back at her and snort.

"What?" Marina asks.

"Nothing," I reply. Marina squints at us before she shrugs and walks back to the bathroom to finish her task.

Soon we're all sitting on the floor with mugs of coffee nestled in our hands and several delicious goodies piled on paper plates, laughing and chatting amongst each other. I feel Fer looking at me, and I smile brightly at her. For now, everything is perfect.

About the Author

Diana Ferris is a Peruvian immigrant who has been residing in Connecticut for the past 21 years. She's currently working toward her associate degree in Liberal Arts. A woman of many passions, Diana's interests range from history to anime; from writing to tarot. She is constantly hounded by incessant plot bunnies who are trying to destroy her sanity, all while surrounded by supportive family and friends who lend a helping hand whenever possible, and she's all the more grateful for it.

Website:
dailyshenanigansbuzz.wordpress.com/author/dianaferris1986
Twitter: @dianaferris86

Dane's Redemption

♥

Susannah Kade

Story Information

Holiday: International Bat Night
Holiday Date: August 27
Heat Rating: 2
Relationship Type: M/F
Major Trigger Warnings: Stalking, domestic violence, involuntary transformation, animal trauma, mention of medical procedures.

Trapped in the body of a bat, Dane has lost hope of being human again. On International Bat Night, he's drawn to Tessa, a descendant of the witch who cursed him. Tessa is wary of bats, but when one's injured, she has to save it.

Dane counts himself lucky that Tessa cares for him, and his attraction to her grows each day, but will either of them survive her attempts to break the spell?

Dane's Redemption

What am I doing here?
In a cave on Rook Island off the coast of Maine.
Unreal.
Almost as unreal as International Bat Night.

Tessa tuned back into the tour leader's excited voice. "Let's go further into the cave and see how many bats are roosting!" The tour leader assisted an elderly lady through the tunnel. "Follow me. Let's take a look at them getting ready for the night. As soon as the sun sets, they'll fly out to catch millions of moths and other insects, and we want to be outside at the cave's entrance to watch the spectacular display."

Tessa hung back, waiting for the last person to go through the tunnel into the cave network. With shaking hands, she flicked on her flashlight, illuminating the craggy walls. According to her late Aunt Evelyn's map, the key should be hidden along this wall ten paces inside this chamber.

Up on this five-foot-high ledge. Behind a flat rock.
Which flat rock?

Breathing fast, snatching a glance back to check no one was coming, she touched her aunt's letter tucked in her jacket pocket.

Arm's length left of the center of the ledge.

Her fingernails scraped on a rock, right at eye height. An awkward position to work at. She pushed the rock aside and uncovered a dark hole. Her heart thumped hard. The map was right.

She shone the flashlight into the recess. Something about the size of a deck of cards was tucked in there. She reached in and pulled it free. Waxed fabric and string protected the contents.

According to the letter there should be a key inside. She rattled the parcel. It sounded like a key in a metal box.

"Is someone still in the other chamber?" The tour leader's shout echoed, and Tessa almost dropped the parcel.

"Yes! Yes, sorry. I... ahh... dropped my... phone and was hunting for it," she called. She shoved the small parcel deep inside her jacket pocket next to the letter. "It's okay, I've found it now." She'd done it. Her heart racing far faster than it needed to, she aimed her flashlight down at the rocky ground and hurried along the short tunnel to rejoin the group.

A disgusting odor assaulted her nose.

Tessa noticed the tour guide's disapproving glance at her, but most of the tour group stared up at the ceiling.

The cave roof was high above them. Breath rushed out of her lungs.

Bats.

Shivers shot down her spine and turned her knees to jelly.

Hundreds, maybe thousands, of bitey little bats, strangely known as Big Brown Bats, hung from the cave roof flapping their mini-Dracula wings, and all her instincts cried "RUN!"

She stumbled back, clutching her pocket, until she hit the cave wall.

She'd followed the instructions, found the small canister. No need to get any closer to a bunch of scratching, rabies-infected bats.

Her science background told her to take a breath and be sensible. But fascinating as they were to the tour leader, she preferred creatures that didn't have flappy leathery wings and beady eyes.

Something warmed her wrist. She wasn't used to this bracelet that her aunt's letter had instructed her to wear all the time. She pulled back her sleeve.

Her eyes widened. The strange bracelet's stones glowed blue.

Someone called, "Oh, look, that one's coming close."

One of the bats moved down the wall toward the bracelet's light. Tessa shuddered and pulled her jacket sleeve over the shiny stones.

People moved nearer to watch the creepy, staring bat.

Tessa was backed up against the wall and surrounded. She pressed a hand to her chest and tried to think about nice, light things. Bounding Golden Retrievers. And kittens, cute playful ones.

The dark furry wave of bat bodies made the cave seem alive like a giant beast that had swallowed her. Her lungs labored under the overpowering guano smell. The familiar ringing in her ears warned her she was close to blacking out. She backed away. "I need fresh air, let me through." She stumbled on loose rubble, turned, and rushed along the tunnel.

*

In the form of a bat, Dane flew after the golden-haired woman wearing the witch's bracelet. He bared his teeth.

That bracelet belonged to the witch who had cursed him.

He'd seen it on the wrists of other women, but never before had it glowed. He'd lost track of time, one decade much the same as the one before it. But he'd never accepted his fate. Never accepted his curse.

Dusk approached, the sun's last rays harsh to his eyes, but nothing would stop his pursuit of the woman. *Who is she?* He smelled her sweat. Where was she going, and what evil had she committed? Fear surrounded her like a cloak. She was so hopeless in the dark, her weak human eyes unused to his familiar environment.

Why was she so frantic? He was the one who was cursed and trapped in this body.

She scrambled up the sloping entrance to the narrow cliff path. Perhaps she could feel Dane's hatred. Her features were different, softer, but he sensed the blood of that vile woman running through her veins.

Memories, like the stings of vicious wasps, stabbed him. If only he'd stayed on the ship, anchored in the harbor, on that day long ago. But he hadn't been able to bear to see his mother in such pain, and he'd sought the local healer, rumored to be a witch.

His chest ached now as it had at the moment of his mother's death.

Devastated and angry that the witch hadn't saved her, he'd neglected to fulfill the promise he'd made to her.

And he'd been cursed to life as a bat for his betrayal.

Tonight, for the first time, he could smell the elusive scent of freedom. The woman's scent attracted him more than streetlights attracted moths.

Perhaps touching the stones in her bracelet would break the spell.

*

Outside the cave, Tessa assured the tour leader she'd be fine walking back down the cliff path to her car on her own.

She put on her most confident voice. Nothing would make her go back to that cave or hang around here any longer. Against her expectations, there had actually been a hidden parcel. She stroked the blue stones of the bracelet. If it hadn't done that weird heat thing the first time she'd touched it, she wouldn't have believed anything in her aunt's letter. But it had warmed and glowed for her and not for her best friend, Sarah.

Tessa's logical brain couldn't explain it. It had intrigued her, and so she'd come to this island to find out about her mother's family. Also, to get away from her ex, but she wasn't thinking about that.

Something flew close to her cheek, its airy wake brushing her skin. Her heart thumped hard against her ribs. "Get away from me!" She swatted at it, but the bat swooped again, raising goosebumps on her arms.

Shoulders hunched, she ran stooped over as wind whipped her hair across her eyes. She tripped and fell, pain shooting through her knee and palm. She sat on the ground and blinked back tears. The sound of waves crashing against the rocks below was a loud warning to take care.

She looked around wildly for the bat. She had to get a grip, or she'd end up slipping right over the cliff's edge.

Why had she told the tour guide not to worry about her? She wasn't cut out for this Indiana Jones stuff. It was a twenty-minute walk down to the parking lot. She couldn't do it if she was being mobbed by bats.

She filled her lungs with salt-tanged air, lifted her shoulders, tied her jacket hood to keep her hair back from her eyes, and searched the purple-streaked sky.

"You're only a tiny bat. I'm a big human."

A prickling between her shoulder blades warned her to go as fast as her feet could safely go over the rocky terrain. A sprained ankle would top off her night.

She snapped a thin branch from a dead shrub and held it aloft. "Go away, bat. Go back to your cave."

The sky above was bat free, but the path was uneven, and purple lichen-covered rocks marking the cliff edge were way too close. A mountain goat she wasn't. Her idea of exercise was cycling along a flat bike path.

She hobbled along the path, trying to search the sky and check the ground at the same time for the safest route. "I really shouldn't have left the city."

What had she been thinking? She didn't belong on this island, the island of her mother's family. She belonged in a nice, organized food testing lab.

She patted her pocket.

She'd gotten what she'd come for.

She had the key to the book of her ancestors.

*

Dane had to stick close to that bracelet.

He couldn't lose this chance to be free even if it meant being near a witch.

Her vehicle was moving. What if she was planning to take the night ferry? He wouldn't be able to follow. He'd tried many times to leave Rook Island. The spell bound him to live and die and live and die here over and over.

This was going to hurt.

*

Thud!

Tessa screamed.

Something black had hit the car window and bounced off.

She hit the brakes. "No. Oh no."

A bat lay in front of the car on the dirt road.

She yanked open her door. Shaking, nauseous, she knelt next to it. She peered at it. No blood. It was so small, but furry. Did she have to touch it? Did its chest move? It was the bat who'd been chasing her, she was sure of it.

"You're going to be okay. I'm so sorry." Should she go for help? The tour leader might know what to do, but she didn't want to further disrupt his special International Bat Night study tour. And if she was honest with herself, she couldn't face going back along that path to the cave, carrying a wounded bat all the way.

The bat twitched.

"I think you're going to be fine, little bat." Her voice hitched. She didn't know anything about caring for injured bats. Maybe it was good she hadn't had pets. She couldn't cope with the worry. With the lightest of touches, she stroked a finger along its furry back, cringing at the feel of soft trembling skin. It didn't leap up and bite her. She took off her jacket, the cold breeze chilling her arms. She wrapped the bat up, holding it close so it wouldn't fall out.

"I'll take you home and call a rescue place." She shuffled onto the driver's seat, making sure not to hit the creature against the steering wheel. "There's got to be someone here who can take care of you. My father never let me have a pet, and my apartment has… had a no pets rule too. So, I may not be your best bet, you see?"

She placed the securely wrapped bat onto the front passenger seat where she could keep an eye on it and unfolded the cloth from its face. The bat stared at her with shiny dark eyes. She hoped it wasn't badly hurt and in great pain. How must it feel with a giant human peering down at it?

The drive across the island back to her family's ancestral cottage took half an hour, and having the bat watching her the whole way was unsettling. She drove cautiously, half-expecting it to burst free of the folds of fabric and fly at her face.

She made soothing clucky noises. The bat stared.

"Why'd you fly at my car, you silly creature? I wonder, are you the same one who was flying around me on the cliff path, or was that a buddy of yours?" Could it really be the same bat that she'd thought was staring at her in the cave? That would be inconceivable. Creepy horror movie feelings made her skin crawl. She tried to keep her eyes on the road while keeping the bat in her peripheral vision. If it'd been behind her on the back seat, she would be sweating ice cubes and too afraid to check the rear-view mirror. After tonight, she was going to stop watching scary movies and switch to feel-good films.

Bright blue light glowed again in the center of her bracelet's stones, and it warmed her wrist. What had set it off now? She was beginning to think it glowed when she made a decision that directed her toward a goal it agreed with, which sounded like a fantasy novel. She wouldn't dare speak about it to anyone other than Sarah who accepted such things as perfectly normal.

The light reflected in the bat's tiny eyes.

"I think you like my bracelet. Maybe it reminds you of glow worms. I guess you get a few of them in your cave." It appeared to be old. The bracelet may have been made on this island. Perhaps the answer was inside the mysterious locked book hidden under the floorboards by Aunt Evelyn. Tessa had figured Aunt Evelyn was a bit eccentric and had gotten some satisfaction from planning a treasure hunt for her niece when writing her last will and testament, but now she was beginning to wonder.

"I was planning to do some reading tonight, Missy Bat, but now I'll be doing bat research instead, won't I?" Learning about this creature might be fun. She used to love learning new things. It was surprising how easily she'd fallen into the going-to-work, same-old routine. When had she last had a new hobby? Years ago. No wonder she'd let herself get so downtrodden in her last relationship. If it wasn't for the occasional meal out and odd bike ride, she'd be a lost cause.

She'd let herself become a very boring thirty-two-year-old.

She drew back her shoulders and glanced at the bat. "I'm not boring anymore, am I? If you'd've told me two months ago that I'd be crawling around caves in the dark and getting up close with bats, well, who'd have thought, huh?"

The bat squirmed and maintained its unflinching gaze on her.

"Well, one person didn't think I was crazy for quitting my job and coming here. My best friend, Sarah, is into crystals and herbs and tarot, and she said I had big change coming, that it was destiny. She'd love to see you!"

*

Dane's head hurt.

He'd known he'd be in for a world of pain when he smacked into that window.

And being called 'Missy Bat' was doing nothing to help his disposition.

This woman had better be good at researching because he needed some healing, and traveling in this vehicle was unnerving. The last vehicle he'd ridden in had been a carriage pulled along by horses.

He focused on the blue stones and the sound of her voice to keep him conscious.

Having someone speak to him as if he was human made him ache to be able to reply. He could only listen to her speak about her life and wonder if she was truly as naive and good-hearted as she seemed.

"I didn't know I had an aunt. My mother left me as a newborn." He heard a tremor in her voice. "I know she died a year later, but my father refused to speak about her, so I didn't either. I never knew about her family or this island."

Odd. Had she not known that she was descended from witches? Did she know now? She must. She'd been in the cave and collected a key. And she must wonder why the bracelet glowed on her wrist.

Fear gripped his heart. If she didn't know witchcraft, she couldn't save him. He was running out of chances. Shivers wracked his body.

"You poor thing." She turned a dial and a current of warm air touched his face. "We're nearly home."

Warmth spread through his body, his skin heated by the air, and his insides warmed by long-forgotten human feelings. This gray-eyed stranger cared for him.

Words heard on that fateful night long ago raced into his mind.

You will remain a bat
Day and night
Until you gain the trust
Of one of mine
Until you gain the love
Of one of mine
Until you sacrifice
For one of mine

Trust, love, and sacrifice.

She showed sympathy. Perhaps he could gain her trust if he didn't frighten her. But love? How could she love a bat? Impossible. And sacrifice? What could a bat sacrifice for this woman that would do her any good at all?

He moved his wings, and hot pain crippled him.

"Wait. We're here. Hold on one more minute, and I'll take you indoors and make you comfortable."

*

"Here we are."

The weather had turned stormy, and Tessa was glad to be off the road.

She nudged the door closed with her hip and flicked the light switch with her elbow. Her little wrapped bat made a lot of noise, but thankfully it didn't wriggle about, or she might have dropped it.

She could manage to be in close proximity to it while it behaved in a nice, calm way, but what if it got loose and flitted around the house out of control? A cold shiver raced along her spine. She ought to put it in a container. "Where shall I put you? I need a box." She remembered the overpowering bat guano smell from the cave. "And something to line it with. Newspaper." Newspaper she had in abundance from the move to this house. She still had unpacking to do but hadn't figured on the place being so full of furniture and knickknacks. A lot of it would have to go in time.

She sighed. Having objects from the past around made her both happy and sad. She adored vintage and hand-made things, but it was her aunt's past. Her mother's childhood home, and yet she'd never known either woman. She pressed her hand to her heart.

The bat wiggled. Its beady eyes shone in its pug-like face.

She sniffed back tears, clearing her throat. "All right, all right, I got distracted there for a minute. Stay on the couch for a minute while I rustle up a bed for you." What could she put it in? She'd seen boxes in the top of Aunt Evelyn's wardrobe.

That odd little expression the bat had could mean anything. Her skin chilled. It might launch toward her face.

It'd been calm in the car; maybe the sound of her voice soothed it. "Good girl. Actually, I have no idea if you're a girl, so forgive me if you're a little boy."

The bat made a couple of clicking noises. She took it for agreement that it was a girl.

Aunt Evelyn's wardrobe smelled of rose petals. Sachets of potpourri were in every drawer and cupboard. Tessa held a pouch to her nose and inhaled the dusky scent, imagining the woman picking the petals on a warm summer's day. An ache of such longing for what might have been filled her chest, and she sat heavily on the edge of the bed.

Framed photos on the dressing table showed her aunt and mother as children with their parents. Aunt Evelyn had meticulously labeled all the photos in several albums, or Tessa wouldn't have known her own mother as a child.

Tessa straightened her spine and lifted a round hat box from the wardrobe. Inside was a green felt hat with a beautiful silver pin that would perfectly match her favorite winter coat. She set it on the dressing table with the photos.

The bat was flopping about on the floor.

"Oh, I'm so sorry! I shouldn't have left you on the couch. I'm not good at this." She threw in some newspaper, keeping watch that the bat didn't move too close to her legs. "Wait while I stab some air holes for you."

She used the jacket to scoop the bat into the box. "Please understand why I have to shut the lid. Sorry, but I won't sleep all night if there's a chance of you landing on me in the dark."

She filled a jar lid with water, lifted the box lid quickly, and fingers trembling she popped the lid in without spilling too much water. "Sorry for splashing you. You'll be safe in there, and I'll talk to you so you know I'm here."

The bat squeaked, and paper rustled in the box.

She squatted down level with the air holes she'd poked through the cardboard. "It's okay. Don't be frightened. I'm sure you're in pain, but I've got the number for a twenty-four hour vet."

Were those little squeaky noises sounds of distress? The pitch of the bat's call pulled at her emotions triggering a great well of empathy. "Poor little girl. Hang in there."

She held her phone to her ear and stroked the lid of the box.

A woman answered.

Tessa let out the breath she'd been holding. "Hi, I'm Tessa Schrale and I have an injured bat in a box. Can I bring her to you?"

The bat squeaked louder, and the box vibrated with her wriggling.

The person on the other end said, "I can hear it. It sounds nice and alert. Is it moving around?"

Tessa touched the outside of the box. "I can feel her shuffling about. I think she has a broken wing but is quite active now."

"Good, that's good. Look, our exotic pet specialist will be in tomorrow and can take a look at your bat at 10:30, if it survives the night."

Tessa's stomach lurched. "Oh." She hoped Missy Bat hadn't heard that comment. "No, of course that's all right. Thanks."

She kept a couple of inches away and peered through an air hole, but it was too dark to see anything in the box. "Well, Missy Bat, it appears that you're having a sleepover at my place." Her place. She hadn't thought of the house as hers before. But it truly was. The walls were decorated with paintings chosen by a woman she had never met. The furniture had been used by family she hadn't known existed. But this evening, for the first time since she'd arrived, the place seemed warm and cozy.

Missy Bat's squeaking and Tessa worrying about her would guarantee a lack of sleep for both of them. Sleep was overrated, according to her workaholic father.

*

In Aunt Evelyn's bedroom, Tessa took the beautiful leather-bound book out of its wooden case. Her mother's family name was stamped into the leather in deep gold lettering and surrounded by etchings of flowers and leaves.

She ran her finger over the indentations, and her eyes filled with moisture at the sense of connection to those who had touched the aged leather. It warmed her inside to think that someone related to her might have decorated the book before filling its pages.

She slid the old-fashioned brass key into the lock.

Blue light danced in the stones on her bracelet. The skin under her wrist tingled. The mysterious bracelet intrigued and challenged her scientific understanding of the world.

Missy Bat let out a string of high-pitched chirps.

"It's okay, Missy Bat, you're okay."

The letter had instructed her to read this book. She sat at the writing desk and turned the key. The lock clicked open. Her fingers fumbled over the catch, and a prickling sensation along her spine made her hesitate. Her father had thought her foolish for coming here, but touching the bracelet and reading Aunt Evelyn's words had, for Tessa, been like emerging from a thick cloud of fog. Her path was clear.

She lifted the cover. Sparks shot from the book like it didn't want her to open it. She scooted back from the table nearly tipping the chair. "Whoa. Whoa." Her facts-and-figures-only upbringing had not prepared her for spooky stuff like this. Science was her forte. Heebie-jeebie thingies were Sarah's domain. Maybe she should have been more open-minded.

Her hands were shaking so much that she was afraid she'd drop the book, and her heart pummeled her ribs like a heavy metal drummer. Wind howled outside and branches rapped the window. The bat squealed louder and louder.

She threw a blanket over the book and backed through the doorway into the living room, closing the door behind her.

She flattened her right palm on the lid of the box. "I'm feeling a bit out of my depth. Maybe things will be less frightening in daylight when the storm passes."

The presence of the bat was oddly comforting in its normality. It didn't challenge her thinking. How could she ever have been frightened of something so small and helpless? It was real and normal. Not spooky at all.

The bat made a squeak that she took for agreement.

She shivered at the thought of the book, seemingly alive, in Aunt Evelyn's bedroom.

"I hope you don't mind if I leave the light on."

*

Dane blinked to adjust his eyes to the daylight streaming in as the box lid was lifted.

"You're alive!" Tessa's smile at his survival warmed him and made him want to smile back despite the pain in his wing and his head—and pretty much all over.

"We've got an appointment with the vet. Come along."

The box tilted, and he rolled like the helpless creature he was. Why was she making him suffer so; couldn't she just cast a spell to make him better? She wasn't much of a witch. Maybe the power had diluted with time. What hope was there for him? He let out a stream of vehement shrieks expressing what he thought about her whole family.

The journey was mercifully short.

The vet's examination wasn't.

The vet prodded and bent his wing until he expressed his opinion in the only way he could. He sank his teeth into her probing finger.

"Ow!"

"Oh, I'm so sorry. She's been good as gold," Tessa said, clearly embarrassed.

She's apologizing for me. Dane shouldn't have bitten the vet. Tessa was his only chance, and he couldn't have her think he was dangerous. He hadn't thought things through. He lay still and tried to look contrite.

Tessa surprised him by touching his back. "It's okay."

The vet said, "By the way, your bat's a fella, and you'd better get the rabies vaccine."

"Oh. You won't bite me, *Mr.* Bat, will you?" Tessa's voice sounded confident, but her eyes were wary.

Never. He couldn't afford to have her leave him here. He tried to look non-threatening.

A frown line formed between Tessa's eyebrows. "I'll make myself an appointment at the doctor's office."

His meek look hadn't been convincing. If only he could communicate. If his wing was better and he recovered enough to move, he would do something. He had to let her know he wasn't a regular bat before she decided to send him to some unknown carer.

He crawled toward her despite the pain.

"Oh, look at him." Tessa's expression softened.

He didn't want to startle her. He rolled onto his back, and when she went to stroke his belly, he touched his tongue to her finger. He would be human again. He wouldn't miss his chance.

"He licked me."

The vet raised an eyebrow. "That's promising. I'll do what I can for his wing."

Dane nuzzled Tessa's finger. *Please don't abandon me.*

"I've grown quite fond of the little guy. And it was my car that damaged him. I feel responsible. Would it be okay for me to look after him?"

Dane held his breath, and his heart pumped hard in his chest.

"I don't see why not. I'll give you some information for his care, and we'll go from there."

Breath whooshed out of Dane's lungs, and he knew hope.

*

Tessa brought the book into the living room.

She'd had lunch, made coffee, and made sure the bat was comfy in his box on the table. She'd procrastinated enough. "Let's do this."

She laid the book on the table next to the box, sat down, and lifted the cover.

Her bracelet glowed. Sparks jumped and sparkles swirled over the book's cover, but this time she was ready. With the sun's rays streaming through the living room window, it didn't seem nearly so frightening.

She inhaled and turned to the first page.

Ornate writing was surrounded by gloriously illustrated margins. The old English text was awkward to read at first, but she'd seen some before. She turned page after page, admiring the sheer beauty of the book's creation.

The front part of the book was a family history over centuries, followed by many pages filled with detailed descriptions of plants for healing and recipes for poultices, potions, and tonics.

Tessa had such a warm sense of belonging, of being connected. "I've always loved making my own face and hand creams." Maybe this was where that instinctive skill and desire had come from.

Further on were charts of seasonal changes, phases of the moon and, "Oh, Mr. Bat. These are spells." Light shot from the pages of the book. Tessa clamped a hand over her mouth and stood up. "I need to talk to Sarah." With the time difference, she might catch Sarah before she boarded her flight to India for her annual yoga retreat.

She grabbed her cell phone. "Sarah. I'm so glad I caught you, I can't believe what I'm about to tell you. Strange things are happening. I think my ancestors dabbled in..." She had to muster the strength to utter the word. "Witchcraft." There, she'd said it. It hadn't been so difficult.

"What? Tessa, oh my gosh! That's the most exciting thing I've ever heard you say. Do you feel safe?"

Tessa looked around. "It's a little unnerving. There's this book. It's got a weird energy, which I'm almost okay with now. There's family history, but you'll love this: there are spells. Pages and pages of them."

"Take photos for me. I can't wait to visit."

There was an echoing voice in the background telling everyone to please turn their electronic devices to airplane mode.

Sarah sighed. "Darn, I want to hear more, but I've got to go now. Keep me posted. Ciao, Bella."

"Okay. I'll send photos. But I need to chat." About the book—and she hadn't even mentioned the bat. There was so much she needed to discuss. But Sarah was already gone.

Tessa took a photo with her phone.

The photo was blank. She frowned.

She tried again. Blank. Turned the page and tried another shot. Nothing.

"What's wrong with the camera?" She took a shot of the room, and there it was, in the photo gallery.

Legs weak, stomach unsettled, she backed away from the table. "I'm scared, Mr. Bat."

Her little wounded bat looked up, all trusting and really quite cute.

"I'm glad you're here, or I'd be freaking out." She touched his soft fur. He was real and alive and natural. His heart was beating, his body warm.

He nudged at her finger and crawled to the wall of the box, as if directing her to look.

She blinked twice. *H E L P* was clearly scratched on the cardboard side wall.

She heard a scream and realized the sound came from her. She shoved the box away, scrambled into the bathroom, and locked the door.

Stars winked in and out in her vision, and she slumped to the floor.

Just breathe and breathe and it will be okay, it will all be gone.

Imagination. Lack of sleep. That's what it had to be.

I'm not going mad. Except she wasn't sure if that might not be preferable to the reality of a sentient bat.

*

Dane regretted scratching the message.

Tessa's face had paled instantly.

What if she'd fainted and banged her head? He needed her. He'd starve to death in this box.

He tried flapping his good wing and jumping, but the box was too deep, and his bad wing ached constantly.

She'd mentioned witchcraft and spells to her friend, and he'd gotten excited. He should have waited a few more days to give her a chance for the strangeness to sink in. It was difficult to be patient with her when he had been waiting for so long to be freed. He'd been familiar with spells and curses and witchcraft for hundreds of years. From what he'd seen and heard over time, it wasn't something familiar to most people.

He'd flown over this house many times and seen the bracelet on other women's wrists, but there had been no light from within the stones. But there was something in Tessa that made the bracelet respond.

He had to read that spell book. There had to be something in there to help him.

The floorboards creaked, and the woman's determined face appeared above him. A surge of hope rose from within him.

"Right. You can spell."

Good. She was a tough one.

His hopes for future freedom rekindled the fire in his gut. He waved his good wing to show he'd heard her.

He scratched, *YES.*

Her eyes widened, but she didn't back away. "I better find something that's easier for you to write on with your little claw."

She disappeared from view for a few minutes.

Tessa lifted him out of the box. A palette of dry paint was on the table and a large sheet of paper. She wet the paint. "Try that."

He dipped his claw in and made a mark on the paper.

It was messy, but easier than scratching the cardboard.

What should he say? There was so much he wanted to know. Where to start? He looked up at her sweet face. Her expression was half-frightened, half in awe.

Thank you, he scrawled.

She made a squealing noise and covered her mouth. Her eyes were wide with astonishment and disbelief. "I honestly didn't think that would work."

Human, he wrote, squishing paint under his feet. She'd had a few shocks these past days, and he needed her to accept the strange and find out how to cure him.

"Yes, I'm a human, and you're a bat. I've got an idea to make this easier. There are charts online to help people communicate. I'll print one out. Your claw doesn't look strong enough to hit a keyboard and probably wouldn't work a touchscreen." She went to the desk and used a machine.

She was right. It was difficult to scrape the letters big and clear enough to be decipherable. And explaining his situation and asking for help would take many whole sentences.

He'd observed humans over the years and had seen the changes in the machines they used. He watched them clicking away as they walked and talked and sat and ate their meals. He hadn't expected to be human in this world again, and the realization that perhaps he would thrilled and, yet, terrified him. He'd have a lot of learning to do and was starting to empathize with Tessa's situation.

She picked up sheets of paper, taped them together into one large square, and put it on the table.

Words and images covered the page. The alphabet and YES and NO.

He walked around and tapped out *Hello,* looking up for her to read it out loud.

She clapped her hands. "Hello to you too. It's nice to finally meet you. Do you have a name? Calling you Mr. Bat is rude, I'm sure."

He spelled out his name.

"Dane. I like it. Can any of your bat friends spell too?"

She thought he was a bat who could spell. What friends? Of course, she thought all the bats in the cave were his friends. He'd lived and died so many times within that cave, and he'd merely survived in the colony. Survival, not friendship.

He had to convince her he was human.

He indicated, *No,* and trotted around the letters.

She wrote them out on a notepad, reading as she got the message. "Oh! 'Cursed by your ancestor.' That's horrible."

The expression of pity on her face seemed genuine, and he began to believe she would want to help make amends.

She reached over, and he let her pick him up even though her fingers pressed on his sore wing. Close to her cheek, he smelled her soft scent. It reminded him of summer days wandering through fields of wildflowers. It reminded him of home.

"I'm so very sorry. I feel like I've fallen into a fairy tale. This is so weird."

Her lips, warm and gentle, touched his wing triggering human feelings of love long forgotten that he didn't want to end. It wrenched when she put him back on the table.

He wanted to tell her more, to make her understand. *I broke a promise.*

"Oh. I see. It's not nice to break a promise, but your punishment seems extremely harsh."

He should have kept his word, but the witch hadn't saved his mother. He'd had many, many years to agonize over his actions.

"I have an idea. I can try to fix this." Her eagerness was clear in her voice.

She brought a thick leather-bound book to the table.

"My aunt bequeathed this to me. The key was hidden in your cave; that's why I was there."

He stepped closer to the book's aged vellum pages, and tingles raced up his spine.

*

"I forgive you for whatever you did hundreds of years ago." Tessa uttered the words, hoping that perhaps something as simple as speaking words of forgiveness would break the spell on Dane.

She counted to sixty seconds, watching him. Nothing happened.

His little black eyes flicked her way before he tapped, *Thank you.*

"I thought forgiving you might do the trick. Sorry. I'm convinced there's an answer in this book, but it's going to take some reading time."

Dane nudged up against her wrist and put his nose to her bracelet.

The stones glowed faintly. Tessa said, "I didn't think of trying that. Pity it didn't work. How about I'll read the left pages and you read the right, and between us we'll search faster."

Agreed. He positioned himself to the right of the book, and she pulled up a chair.

"Nudge me if you find anything interesting."

Hours later she'd learned more than she'd ever wanted to know about wormwood and chamomile, nettles and marshmallow root. While interesting, it frustrated her to have to read a whole book to find the answer she needed. If she opened the book to later pages, the text was blurred, only clearing if she had read up to that point. Nice to know the reason for the missing index and table of contents. Maybe once the whole book had been read, those would appear so that she could flip to a particular section.

Dane nudged her hand.

She flicked a glance his way. "What have you found?"

He edged around the book and tapped halfway down the page.

She read out loud, "'Curses should be rarely used.' Well, that's a relief. It's nice to know this island isn't full of creatures my relatives have cursed."

There were no more gems of wisdom to be found in the following pages.

She rubbed her eyes. "Unlike you, I'm not good at late nights. My bed's calling, and you can't turn the pages by yourself, so let's try again tomorrow. I've ordered some groceries to be delivered so I won't have to go out."

She hesitated over lifting him into the box. He was a bat, but also a person with human rights. Maybe he wanted to putter around in the dark. She didn't shudder at the thought; the feeling was more like having a house guest. A little awkward at first.

At least—unlike her ex—he wouldn't hog the bathroom.

*

Dane watched the night through the window.

He couldn't fly to hunt and had to rely on the mushy mix Tessa made up for him. And to add injury to insult, delicious moths fluttered against the window seemingly mocking him.

Nights would be long without the hunt, but he could explore the rest of the house.

She didn't seem mean so far, but the blood of witches ran in her veins. If she had secrets, he'd find out during the hours of her slumber.

Photographs lined the sideboard. Tessa was easy to spot, and her photo was next to that of a woman who was clearly her mother. Dane barely recognized the other frozen-in-time faces, though a few were familiar. He'd heard people singing sometimes, and he had lingered in the oak tree to listen. And while the sound continued, he would become lost in the melodies and forget he was a bat.

Tessa's companionship had released him from his isolated existence. His humanity, long buried beneath the instincts for survival, now shone bright within his soul, and aromas in this house triggered human memories.

His mother at the fireplace stirring the stew.

His mother in their cabin on the ship, shaking, feverish. His despair at the doctor's pronouncement.

The sick feeling in his belly during the rowboat journey to shore to search for the healer he'd been told about.

His promise to her to deliver the package to her youngest daughter before she'd departed the island.

In his grief, blinded by anger and despair that the witch hadn't saved his mother, he'd thrown the package into the bay.

The ship the daughter had traveled in had hit stormy seas and wrecked. She'd died.

And not long after, he'd been consumed by the pain and agony and disorientation of his body's transformation into that of a bat.

Years of anger, grief, and loneliness. Nights of flying at the windows of the witch's house and seeing her turn her back to him. Watching her funeral and those of her descendants.

Visiting the house on fewer and fewer occasions.

Giving up on redemption.

Until Tessa visited his cave and gave him the greatest gift of all.

Hope.

*

Late the next morning a knock at the door interrupted Tessa's research.

She checked the room before answering the door.

The book was locked away in her bedroom. Dane was having his daytime snooze in the spare room wardrobe. The place looked appropriately magic-free.

She opened the door.

Oh crap. Richard. Her fingers clenched around the doorknob. What was he doing here?

"Hello, Tessa." Her ex's expression matched the exasperation in his voice.

She'd ended their year-long relationship two months ago. She had to swallow to get enough moisture in her throat to speak. "I doubt you were passing by this island, so why are you here?" She straightened her posture and looked up at him, maintaining eye contact. This was her home, and she didn't have to do anything she didn't feel comfortable with.

A clear flash of annoyance crossed his features before he hid it behind a charming smile. "Actually, I'm here on business, and your father asked me to look in on you."

"My father?" What was her father doing speaking with Richard behind her back? He hadn't been too upset when she'd wrestled her way out of the engagement, though he wasn't a man who displayed much emotion. Could he really have liked Richard more than she'd known?

"Yes, he's worried about you being in this isolated cottage on your own. And he's not the only one." His tone reprimanded her. "Resigning from the university, selling your apartment, and breaking off our engagement. All signs that something's very wrong."

What was wrong was being stupid enough to allow him to think she would marry him. She hadn't even said yes, really; he'd bulldozed her by asking her in front of a crowd and embarrassing her. Trapping her like Dorothy in *The Wizard of Oz* in the tornado of arrangements that followed. Until Aunt Evelyn's letter had given her the courage, the ability, to escape the storm by speaking up.

He moved closer and reached for the door, peering over her head. "Aren't you going to ask me in? I'm not leaving until we talk."

Bile rose from her stomach, and for some reason, she thought of vampire films. "We can talk out here on the porch."

She clicked the door shut behind her, not giving him a chance to protest.

*

Dane flinched awake.

He could hear a man's loud voice outside.

He hopped to the front door and listened.

Tessa said, "I came here for me. It had nothing to do with trying to avoid you."

The man's voice was clipped. "We were together for a year, and you never said you were unhappy. I don't get it."

"I let you make the decisions about where we went and how we spent time. Sometimes I wanted to do other things, but we always ended up doing what you wanted," Tessa spoke, her tone clear and steady.

"You didn't protest."

Through the gap under the door, Dane could see Tessa's feet in front and the man's shoes less than two feet away.

"And that was a mistake," Tessa said. "Because I hid my feelings to keep the peace."

"For a whole year! That's crazy. There must be more to it," said the man, agitation clear in his voice.

Tessa hadn't screamed or yelled for help, so Dane assumed she wasn't in trouble. But he had that niggling feeling of unease, the sixth sense that warned him all was not as it should be.

Tessa spoke calmly, sounding like she wanted him to accept her decision and move on with his life. "No. It's my fault. I should have spoken up earlier."

"Yes, you should have. Before I bought that damn ring."

Dane could hear the man pacing back and forward across the porch.

"Which I gave back."

The man's voice got louder. "I didn't want it back. I have it here and want you to come back home."

She spoke firmly. "No. That's not going to happen."

"You're not thinking straight. It's this whole inheritance thing. It's affected your brain."

"On the contrary. My aunt's letter is what clarified things for me. I'm sorry if I caused you embarrassment."

Dane didn't like how the man had closed in on Tessa. His shoes were almost touching her feet.

"Yes, you did. My parents are livid, and my friends can't understand—"

Tessa cut him off. "They would have been more upset if we got married and then broke up afterward. Look," she moved further along the porch. "This is getting us nowhere. It's over. I'm sorry you're unhappy about my decision, but I'm not going to change my mind."

Dane heard a car horn beep twice. The grocery van.

"Goodbye, Richard," Tessa said.

Her voice getting fainter and the sound of gravel crunching under her feet told Dane she was walking to the delivery truck.

He heard the squeal of tires and hoped that was Richard leaving for good. Being a bat left him few options for finding out.

Curse you, witch. Curse you a thousand times for trapping me in this useless body.

*

Tessa sank into the couch, relief warming her like a cashmere blanket.

Dane hopped onto her lap.

"I guess Richard's loud voice woke you. He's an intelligent adult, so I hope he understands not to bother me again."

He touched a claw to her hand.

"Okay, let's go to the chart." She put him on the table and got ready with the pen and paper. "Go ahead."

Dane lost no time in letting her know how he felt. *Feels wrong.*

"I'm not sure I know what you mean. Do you mean you're worried?"

Yes.

"It's not just me then. There is something about him, isn't there? I think I stayed in the relationship because I was scared to break up with him. Don't get me wrong, he was never violent, but there was an undercurrent of something. I had an awareness that being with him wasn't good for me. He was charming to everyone, but I'd catch the odd expression on his face when he didn't realize I could see him. It gave me an uncomfortable feeling, that what he said and how he acted, wasn't a true reflection of his thoughts."

Lock doors.

"Yes, I will." Tessa looked toward the windows. She'd lock them, too. "I'm sure it's an overreaction, but as he said, this cottage is isolated. Even though you strike me as courageous, other than biting him on the ankles you're probably not going to win in a fight."

Read book. Make me human. Can fight.

"You're a brave fellow." Tessa hoped there wouldn't be any fighting, but she desperately wanted to break the spell.

*

The rain eased to drizzle during the night as Dane kept watch.

Headlights stopped up the road. His heart beat faster. He had known that Richard would come back. He had to wake Tessa.

He tapped on her bedroom door but could hear her soft breathing. They hadn't planned well, for the door ought to have been left open tonight. He screeched.

He could hear Richard outside on the path. He wouldn't know the layout of the cottage and would probably check around the outside first for unlocked doors or windows.

Dane hoped Tessa had drawn her curtains. That Richard might stare at her sleeping form through the window made his skin crawl. That he might break the window and attack Tessa made his guts wrench.

What could a bat do? He could make noise. Get her attention.

Music. Her phone. His mind whirled with possibilities then discounted them in split seconds. Knock something over. Break something.

Sorry for your loss, Aunt Evelyn. He leapt and flapped his wings, his good one doing most of the work to get him up to the mantelpiece. He pushed and shoved the glass vase to the edge.

CRASH!

The bedroom door was flung back. Tessa ran out and hit the light switch.

Blinding him.

"What on earth happened? Oh my gosh, that vase was beautiful!"

He hopped to the chart on the table. *R here.*

Her eyes showed confusion. "Richard?" She spun around, crouched in defense, and whispered, "Where?"

CRASH!

Glass shattered in the bedroom.

Tessa ran and grabbed the key from the other side of her door and locked it. She punched numbers on her phone as she yelled out, "Richard, you need to leave this house now! I'm calling the police."

Her hand gripped Dane around the middle and tucked him into her handbag. He was bounced around as the sound of Richard pounding on the bedroom door followed them outside.

Dane peered over the edge of the bag to watch the house. Tessa hadn't wasted time putting on shoes, and the ground must be freezing and painful to her feet, but she got them into the car and had the engine started before Richard slammed a fist into the back window.

"Tessa! Get out of the car!" His words slurred.

Tessa hit the gas, spinning the wheels in her haste to get them away.

Speaking on her phone to the police, she said, "I'm in my car heading to town." She sounded calmer than Dane expected. "His car is parked on the road, so he'll be chasing me any minute. He's been drinking."

Dane heard the person on the other end tell her to keep the line open. She wouldn't be able to speak to him, or they'd wonder who she was talking to.

He scrambled out of the bag and up onto the seat back to see headlights gaining on them.

Tessa spoke faster than normal, not so calm now. "He's close behind me. The road's wet. I don't know if I can control the car around the corners if I speed up."

Dane's chest ached at the tremor in her voice.

They headed for a sharp bend.

An impact from behind jerked the bag, and him, from the seat onto the floor.

He heard horn blasts from behind. Sweat beaded on Tessa's forehead, and her knuckles whitened on the steering wheel.

They hit the bend. Slid off the road edge and onto the narrow shoulder. Dane rolled, bounced, and slammed down.

Shaken, he crawled free of the bag and up between the seats. Tessa's fingers gripped the steering wheel, and though she had to be afraid, her eyes were wide alert and her expression showed her determination to succeed.

Sirens blasted his ears, and blue and red lights lit up her face. Relief relaxed Tessa's features. She slowed the car, brought it to a stop, and smiled down at him.

Dane had never thought anyone more beautiful.

A police officer told her to stay in the car.

Richard was handcuffed and walked to the police vehicle.

"He's really done it. I might not have pressed charges over him breaking my window and scaring me in the night, but this." Tessa's eyes reflected her disgust at Richard's behavior. She rolled down the window and called out, "Please speak to someone, Richard. You need help."

He glanced at her; his head lowered. "I'm really sorry, Tessa. I don't know what came over me."

Dane admired Tessa's compassion. After such horror, she thought not of herself but of Richard. The blood of healers truly ran in her veins. The one who'd cursed him had been a healer first, and he'd wronged her.

He'd impelled her to curse him by breaking his promise. He hadn't had to do much, but to her it had been of vital importance. The parcel he should have delivered to her daughter had contained a talisman for safe travels. In her grief, the witch had blamed him.

In the past, he'd thought that if he could turn back time and deliver the parcel that all would be well. But then he wouldn't have met Tessa. And he couldn't bear to think of a life without her in it. She inspired him. The strength in her face, the skill with which she controlled the car, the bravery she displayed all left him in awe.

Hundreds of years of lonely existence were worth it to be with this woman in this moment.

*

Next morning, inside the wardrobe, Dane couldn't breathe.

He shoved at the door and fell onto the hardwood floor.

A flood of emotion like a surging wave swamped him. Tears of relief pooled in his eyes.

He had legs. And arms. And...a big penis.

"Tessa!" His voice croaked. He swallowed then rubbed his throat. He wanted to holler and jump, but every part of his body ached like he'd woken after a bout of influenza. Instead, he crawled like a baby to the bed and pulled himself up.

Light from the window speared into his eyes making him blink. Bird calls sounded odd to his now human ears. Furniture, ornaments, the window—all appeared smaller than his brain-recently-encased-in-a-bat-body recalled.

"Tessa." He tried to amplify his voice. It sounded harsh and dry. Water. He had to get a drink.

He shuffled his way to the bathroom and leaned heavily on his elbows at the sink. He gulped cool water down his throat. It tasted like he imagined the nectar of the gods would.

He stared at the mirror. His reflection stunned him. His eyes knew so much more than the last time he'd seen them.

*

Tessa woke to the sound of running water coming from the bathroom.

Fear tightened her chest. Had Richard been released? Why hadn't Dane woken her? Was he okay?

She hefted the brass bedside lamp in both hands. She took a breath and kicked the door wide.

Not Richard.

She let out a shriek and brandished the lamp at the naked, dark-haired man who stood in her bathroom. She backed away and slammed the door shut. Looked for her phone.

"Tessa! It's me. Dane. You know, DANE." The door opened.

She had trouble processing the vision, the voice. *Dane.* Tall, athletic, gorgeous olive-toned skin. Realization hit her, and the lamp clattered to the floor. Heat rushed to her cheeks, and she studied the pattern on the floor tiles. Not knowing where else to look when all she wanted to do was stare at his face, his body, and those ripped muscles.

"I woke up." His voice was hoarse, labored. He held out his left hand toward her. "I tried to call out to you, but everything feels odd. It will take a bit of getting used to."

She took his hand in hers and turned it over. "Dane?" His skin was warm and smooth.

"Yes. Really. It's hard to believe." His eyes twinkled with humor. "I'm having trouble myself."

His good-looking face was that of a man in his twenties, but his true age showed in the depths of his eyes. And the way he was looking at her like she was some sort of goddess. *Whew!* A surge of desire tightened her nipples. Her legs wobbled. "I have to sit down."

He reached out a hand but toppled into the door frame. "I'll join you shortly, when my legs work."

Tessa was overwhelmed and could only imagine the huge emotional adjustment he was going through. She liked that he seemed to have a wry sense of humor. "Oh. I'm so sorry. I should help you. Here, lean on me." Awareness of his nakedness made her cheeks hot. "Umm. Maybe wrap a towel around your waist. Here." She handed him a towel and helped him secure it. Her fingers brushed his skin, and she glanced up. His eyes darkened with something she could only call primal, and in response, heat burned her cheeks.

She had to think of him as a patient and her as his carer to get herself under control. Patient. Nothing more. The spell had broken, and that was wonderful. *But how did it happen? How does he feel? What will he do?*

"Umm. Sit on the couch, and I'll make breakfast." Occupying herself in the kitchen would give her time to process her feelings, and hopefully she'd be able to speak to him without ogling his body like a teenager with a crush.

"Thank you for being so kind to me and caring for me." The solemn tone showed how heartfelt the words were.

Tessa smiled. "That's okay. I learned a whole lot about bats."

"You believed in me. Are you okay after last night? I don't want to be a burden. Somehow I'll pay you back for everything."

Tessa would never think of him as a burden. "I'm feeling remarkably well, actually. But what about you? I imagine eating regular food will be strange." Dane was holding his arms out, inspecting them, maybe marveling at their amazing form, Tessa thought.

He said, "I must have been a bat for a couple of hundred years. I craved a hot stew for many years. The smell of food in this cottage brought back many memories of my human life, but I can't remember the taste. I hope the memory of swallowing insects fades in time."

Good, good. Conversation was a great distraction. She tried to focus on his words, not on the image of him naked that had been burned into the back of her brain. "That's going to be weird for you. As is living in this time as a human." She busied herself with breaking eggs into the frying pan, conscious of the tenderness of her nipples and the desire moistening her panties. "You said you'd learned a lot over the years observing humans and the changes in technology, so at least it won't be a total culture shock for you. Not like falling asleep in your time and waking up today would be."

His dark eyes, the way he focused on her, had increased her desire levels so much that she could hardly tear her gaze away. She didn't know him. He hadn't been with a woman for some ridiculous number of years, and she shouldn't confuse his feelings of desire as desire for her in particular. She had to get a grip.

She liked him. The rich tone of his voice, her sixth sense telling her he was trustworthy.

He studied her phone then held it to his ear. "I've seen people using different technology over time, and I've been dying to know how on earth this works."

Where should she start? "You know what. Let's start with basic needs. Here. Eggs. I thought it might be best to try one food at a time to get your stomach used to different foods."

He put the phone aside and smiled. "Good idea. I have a lot to learn. Here goes." He couldn't get the eggs onto the fork.

How would he fit into society?

He had to stay here with her. There was no doubt about that. He didn't exist as a person in this age and couldn't just turn up in town with no clothes and no money. Her mind whirred with working out the logistics of it all.

Tessa gently took the fork from his hand. "Have a spoon. You've got to get used to holding things."

"Like a baby." He grinned; the self-deprecating humor reflected in his eyes.

She turned away and cleaned up the eggshells. He didn't need her watching his struggle to scoop the eggs onto a spoon.

There'd have to be some work done to sort things out. He'd have to be a visiting friend. On the island, everyone knew everyone. She worried for his future. It was going to be difficult for him to adjust.

His eyes closed as he savored the food. "Delicious."

The happiness on his face over such a simple meal made her feel like a Michelin-star chef. "I'm glad you're enjoying it." She fluffed about the kitchen, trying not to stare at his mouth. She wiped the bench for the umpteenth time. She couldn't say he'd arrived by helicopter either, because Mr. Francis kept tabs on all flights and would know something odd was going on. "Eat slowly. Give your digestive system time."

"Thank you for preparing this for me. You're a wonderful cook." Every glance he sent her way, every smile, seemed loaded with a level of affection that should take years to develop.

"You survived on insects, but you did okay. You look strong and healthy."

He laughed, hesitantly at first, then fully, the sound of his laughter urging her to join in. So she did. Laughing with Dane gave her a level of joy she didn't remember feeling before.

They should be celebrating.

Dane was free. The curse was ended, lifted, gone. He was going to be fine, and she'd helped him. She'd stepped outside her comfort zone and done the impossible.

She wiped her eyes.

"You look serious. Are you all right?" Dane pushed back his chair, stood, and swayed.

"I'm okay. I wonder what happened to break the spell."

He frowned as he hovered near. "Maybe it was because we were in danger."

"Yes. Perhaps working together did the trick." To break the spell so quickly was a lucky break. She liked to think her ancestors were cheering her on.

"I'm glad I could help. Although, at this moment, I feel weaker than I did when I was a bat."

She fought a strong urge to throw her arms around him. Though her body ached for him, she didn't know him at all. She'd take a walk in the garden. Alone. "Shall I run a bath for you? It might help you feel better. Take it easy for a few days."

His lips quirked into a half-smile. "Do I smell like a bat?"

No. He smelled yummy. Having a bat in the house was one thing. Having a strange male in the house was going to take some adjustment. She avoided answering. "Relax in the bath, and I'll go find you something to wear. There's a bunch of boxes in the attic full of old clothes."

What a dilemma. She hadn't thought as far as what would happen if they lifted the curse. Perhaps, she hadn't really believed it possible.

Well, it was, and it had happened. She owed it to him on behalf of her family to make things right.

*

"Will you walk outside with me?" Dane asked after lunch. He had to get away from the kitchen before he ate everything.

Tessa nodded. "Let's go."

He took one step through the doorway and *zap!* He was a bat flying above Tessa's head.

What the hell?

He flew back into the house and crashed onto the floor, human again. His clothes were a puddle of fabric on the doorstep.

Tessa ran and brought them to him. Panting, her eyes full of concern, she said, "Oh dear! I'm so very sorry it hasn't worked. But it has half-worked. You didn't stay a bat."

He had been so sure the curse was gone.

"At least my wing's healed." He smiled to reassure her he was okay. "I'll experiment." He went in and out of the door a few times. He tried the windows. Same thing. In the house, he was human. Outside, he was a bat. There must be more he needed to do to redeem himself. He had been so happy to be human. To find the transformation incomplete, possibly only a temporary reprieve, threatened to crush his hopes. But that wouldn't help. He had to fight. He squared his shoulders and ran through the doorway.

"Enough, Dane. You're not going to find out any more by torturing yourself."

Hitting the floor repeatedly was taking a toll on his body. He had grazed his knees and bruised both hips and elbows. Tessa was right. He was being an idiot. He sat with his back to the wall and caught his breath.

She sat in front of him, her beautiful, sympathetic face showing worry for him. "Let's take a look at the book again. Now that you're human, it'll be faster. We can communicate easily. Come on."

He should be grateful for small mercies. He could speak to Tessa and get to know her. What did it matter if he couldn't go outside? He'd survived far worse.

He followed her to the table.

Reading with her, sitting close was nice. She smelled great. He inhaled and relished the banana coconut tang of her body lotion. She'd told him she mixed her own creams and scented oils, and she obviously had a flair for fragrance combinations.

"Are you going to sell the creams you make?"

"I'd like to. I've been a bit side-tracked lately." She graced him with a shy smile, and he liked the playful glint in her eye.

"I like spending the hours with you." He searched her eyes hoping to see a sign that she felt the same way.

"I do too. But I want to free you. You should be able to leave if, and when, you like."

A pang of emotion made his chest ache. He'd read a quotation on the fridge door that seemed apt. *If you love something, set it free.* Did she love him? Surely it was too soon. She cared. She'd shown him that.

He respected her and admired her courage. It was difficult to remember his first impression of her as ungainly, helpless, and possibly evil. She was the polar opposite of those.

"Listen to this." She pointed to the last passage on the page. "A curse will be lifted when the price is paid and the conditions are met."

"The witch said something to me. The words are fuzzy sometimes, but now they're clear in my mind. *You will remain a bat day and night. Until you gain the trust of one of mine. Until you gain the love of one of mine. Until you sacrifice for one of mine.*"

"Look!" Tessa held up her wrist where the stones in her bracelet pulsed with a fierce glow. Her eyes widened.

He met her gaze. "Let's take that as a sign that we're getting close."

"I certainly trust you, and you've sacrificed for me."

He'd sacrifice anything for her. "I don't think I've sacrificed enough. I knocked over a vase and got shoved in a handbag. That's probably not going to cut it."

And he had yet to gain her love. He wanted to kiss her and touch her gorgeous body, but to do so now would seem false after reciting the witch's words. He'd have to be patient and wait for her to make the first move. He surreptitiously widened his legs to give himself more room.

At sunset, he turned into a bat.

No stew tonight. Insects were on the menu for supper.

*

Outside in the morning light, Tessa opened a large umbrella. "Ready."

She held her breath.

Dane stepped outside into the shade of the umbrella and turned into a bat.

Frustration flared up like a firecracker and disappeared just as quickly. She had to stay positive for Dane. "Well, that blows the sunlight idea." He'd have to stay inside.

He flew past her into the house and morphed into his human form mid-air as he always did. She kicked the mattress a little to the left as he plummeted to the ground.

"Did that help any?" She handed him his sweatpants.

He huffed out a breath and got dressed. "I didn't graze myself. Sorry to keep flashing you."

That wasn't a problem. She couldn't help smiling. Looking at his well-toned body was no hardship at all, and she had to keep herself from staring at the planes of his chest. She wanted to run her hands over every inch of him, but he hadn't shown any sign that he thought of her as more than a helpful friend. And that's what she must continue to do. Be helpful. "Leave your sweatshirt off. Onto experiment two. Follow me." The lotion she'd made was ready in the bathroom.

"Are you sure you want to bother?" He leaned against the door frame; his nose wrinkled up.

"Look, I know it smells terrible, but a footnote in the book makes me think it might help."

The note in question had mentioned healing creatures of the night. It was worth a shot.

"It can't do any harm." He sniffed again and raised an eyebrow. "Can it?"

She pointed to the chair. "No. Stop being a baby and sit down." She smeared the foul goo over his back, feeling the warmth of his smooth skin and back muscles. Her body heated, and she wanted to take off her sweater, but her hands were covered in goop. So much for keeping things clinical. The ache between her legs was unbearable.

"That feels good." Dane's voice was pitched deeper than normal.

It sure did. "I'm..." Desire made her voice way too throaty. She coughed. "I'm finished." *Right as I'm getting started.* If she was going to break the spell, she had to ground herself and think like a scientist. "If it doesn't work, the next step is to try slathering it on when you're a bat."

*

The little guy slipped out of her hands. "Oops, I may have been too generous with the lotion."

He blinked up at her, his fur slick with the foul-smelling oily concoction.

"I don't get why all these lotions smell so disgusting. My ancestor clearly didn't know too much about aromatherapy."

She wrapped a hand towel around him and laid him in a box. "Try and settle in for the night. I appreciate that it probably feels revolting, but it may need time to be absorbed into your skin."

The next morning Dane came into her room, hair damp from the shower, a pair of boxers low on his hips. "That stuff was the worst."

"Tonight, we'll see if it worked."

He rubbed a towel through his hair and gave her a heated gaze. He hesitated, as if he wanted to say something, then walked off. "I'll make coffee."

"Thanks."

What had he wanted to say? Did he find her attractive?

After Richard, she'd sworn off men and planned to live in the cottage and take it one day at a time. She rolled over and drifted in a dreamy state thinking about riding in a forest with a dark-haired man. Dane.

"Are you asleep?"

"Mm. Sort of." The sweet smell of pancakes wafted in from the kitchen. "You made breakfast again?"

"Yes, twenty minutes ago. You drifted back to sleep because you've been spending too many hours poring over those pages."

"I'm not stopping until I've read the whole book."

"You're letting this take over your life. How about you take some time off and go visiting?"

"I don't have anyone to visit because I'm new here and haven't made any friends here yet."

"At least give yourself a break from the book and your ancestor's evil-smelling potions and make some of your own products. I've drawn some designs that you might like to use for logos."

"Really? Show me."

"Later." He touched her cheek, his fingers lingering, his gaze on her lips. "Eat first."

All she wanted to taste was him. She reached up and, seeing the answering heat in his eyes, kissed him, a tentative touch to his mouth.

His eyes darkened and he angled his head, deepening the kiss.

"Ow!" She pulled back from the kiss. "My bracelet's burning me." Blinding light flared from the stones.

Dane unfastened the catch and dropped it onto the bed. Tessa let him examine her wrist. "Your skin's red," he said. "I'll get a wet cloth."

"It's not too bad. It's never done that before."

Dane sat on the bed and rested her wrist on his thighs while he wrapped the cool cloth around it. "Better?" He looked worried.

"I'm fine. I'm thinking that bracelet is a bit annoying."

She reached up and touched her lips to his, inhaling his spicy scent.

Dane pulled back and shut his eyes. He nuzzled his nose to her cheek. His voice husky, tinged with regret, he said, "I think we should heed the bracelet's warning and keep our relationship platonic. I don't want you hurt."

Tessa really didn't want to move away, but she could see his muscles trembling from the strain he was under. She dipped her head and sighed against his chest. "My ancestor is a pain in the butt."

*

Dane worried about Tessa. After two weeks of late nights reading and mixing potions, she was pale and gaunt. She'd put the bracelet back on, which worried him.

He held up a hand. "Don't rub any more stuff on me."

Tessa looked distraught. "Please, don't give up."

"I'm not giving up, but I'm worried that you've become obsessed with sorting out my problem, and there may be no solution." Dark circles had become fixtures under her eyes.

"There has to be." She scraped a hand through her golden hair, messing it up further.

He had to convince her to take a day off. Go to town. Spend time in the sunshine. Call her friend Sarah. Tessa hardly spoke with her these days. "You don't know that, and you need to get on with your life." He was confined to the house. It hurt him that she was the one suffering. He hadn't lost weight or condition. He still flew out every night.

If he flew off tonight and didn't come back, Tessa would eventually start living a normal life again. She'd sacrificed her own goals for him, and the toll on her body and mind were obvious. She barely slept or ate anymore. She spent far too many hours indoors instead of tending the garden that she loved.

He couldn't bear to see her becoming ill because of him. His mother's health had deteriorated fast, so very fast, and fear for Tessa filled him with an urgent need to do something, anything to prevent that from happening. But he also couldn't bear to leave her.

"I'm sorry you're upset with me." She eyed the floor; her tone was subdued.

Oh no! Now she'd apologized to him. He ached to see her smile again. The woman was a saint. "Don't be sorry. I'm not upset with you. You've done far too much for me, and I want to see you do something for you. Why don't you take a long hot bath while I cook dinner?"

"You always cook these days. I'm such a slouch."

"I like cooking." He'd always liked living off the land as a boy with his father and brothers. Sleeping under the stars, eating freshly caught game around an open fire.

Camping with Tessa and counting the stars with her would be a dream come true, but he had to leave. He squeezed his eyes shut and clenched his fists. Worrying about him was making her sick. He straightened his back and lifted his chin.

He wouldn't let that happen any longer. He reached for her arm and gently wrapped her in his arms enjoying the feeling of her snuggling into him, her head tucked under his chin. "Take a break. Do something for yourself tomorrow. You love the garden; why not spend the day outside or visit a park in town? I'll spend the day reading up on all the history I've missed and learning how to use the phone you bought for me."

She leaned back and chewed her lip. "If you're sure. You're right, I'm feeling a little frazzled."

"Absolutely sure. Go and have some fun." Dane liked the full smile that brightened her eyes.

*

Tessa had smothered him with creams and with her attention. She'd treated him like a laboratory test subject.

She reluctantly ended the hug and ran her hands over her hair, aware that she hadn't combed it at all today. *I've never been like this.* "Being in this house is affecting my brain. I think I must have soaked up all the witchy vibes. I really thought it would be easy to find the solution, because I hate not being able to solve problems."

Dane filled two glasses with water and handed one to her. "You're a kind person who always tries to do the right thing. Don't be hard on yourself. Take a break, a nice long one, then get back to the book and find a cure. Treat yourself to some time off."

It was so comfortable having him here, and she ought to enjoy what time they did have together. "Okay. I'll do it. I'm going to spend the whole day in town tomorrow." She tapped her glass to his, happy that her decision lifted the line of tension from between his brows.

*

Two nights later, Tessa was having a glass of pinot noir and watching a movie.

Her bracelet warmed for the first time since it had burned her. For a second she panicked and started to reach for the clasp, but it didn't get any hotter. Light beamed through the window, hitting the spell book where it lay on the desk. Sparks flew up and out. The cover whipped open and pages flicked over in a whirl of color like gaseous rainbows escaping through a vent.

I promised to take a break, but that's one big neon sign.

The book settled open. The light show finished, so she read the page.

Purple lichen. Moonlight.

There had been purple lichen on the rocks on the cliff's edge.

She glanced out of the window. The spell called for a handful of lichen gathered under the light of a full moon, and there was the moon now glowing beautifully high in the dark sky. But it was close to midnight. She chewed a fingernail. She'd promised Dane she would stop with the spells, but this magical display couldn't be ignored. The bracelet, the sparks, the moonbeam all urged her to get to it.

Her nerves settled as a sense of certainty filled her.

She hadn't had too much to drink, just enough to convince her that a trip to the rocky cliff path in the middle of the night was a great idea. Her ancestors wouldn't have been scared. No one else could make things right for Dane.

*

A light sea breeze tickled her face and tousled the clumps of grass along the flashlight-lit path. The lichen must be further up the slope. She couldn't remember exactly where it was, only that its color had caught her attention.

There, toward the edge of the cliff, lighter patches clung to two small boulders a little too close to the edge for her liking. A flick of the flashlight beam showed no lichen closer to the path. Her heart raced, but she pushed through the fear and took careful steps.

A handful wouldn't take too long to scrape off those rocks, and she could be home before dawn. One patch should do it. She leaned forward and reached out.

The gravel under her right foot shifted. Rolled. Her heart pumped louder behind her ribcage. Her feet slid down the slope creating an avalanche.

She was going to pitch over the side, crash onto the rocks. *No! I can't die! Who'll save Dane?*

Panic tore through her mind as sharp rocks tore her grappling palms. Desperate, she grasped at a scraggy plant at the cliff's edge and held it for a second. Hope turned to sheer, this-is-it-for-me-I'm-done-for, terror. Its roots ripped free of the soil, sending her tumbling into nothingness.

A scream tore from her lungs.

Her body hit rock. Her chest deflated. Pain ripped through her leg and shoulder.

In her dazed mind, she thought of Dane.

*

Returning from the night's hunt, Dane spotted a strange shape on the rocks.

And before he could properly see what it was, the sense of dread and his racing heart told him Tessa was on that ledge.

Had she come looking for him? God, he deserved to be cursed again for causing this woman to put herself in danger. The horror of seeing her there felt like a hole had been ripped through his chest. She had to be alive. *I don't want to live without her. I can't live without her.*

He landed beside her. The twisted angle of her leg didn't look good. The slow rise of her chest made his own soften with relief.

But that caused another conundrum. If he roused her, she might startle and roll off the ledge.

Gentle brushes of his wing against her face woke her. Joy filled his heart, and he knew he would do anything for this woman: the woman he loved.

She opened her eyes, and his heart swelled when he saw them focus and knew she recognized him.

She moved her right hand. "I'm sorry I broke my promise," she whispered. Her fingers stroked gentle circles on his chest. "I hurt all over."

He rubbed his face on her cheek in sympathy, wishing he could soothe her pain with words and hands.

How could a bat contact rescuers?

Her phone. She wouldn't have driven here without it.

There, the top of her phone was in the right pocket of her jeans. He tapped her hand to get her attention and then the pocket.

"My phone, of course. I'm not thinking clearly."

She managed to make a call to the island's emergency services, and he waited until they turned up before retreating to a crevice in the cliff to watch.

*

Dane flew to the cave, a sick feeling in his stomach. He had to leave Tessa to recover and get on with her life. His presence put her in danger. He would convince her that he *wanted* to be a bat forever. That being a human would be too difficult for him after so many years. With the passing of time, her memories of him would fade and she'd find someone deserving of her love.

At dawn, pain unexpectedly wracked his body. He knew this feeling well, and before his wings disappeared he flew to the cave floor.

His body became human.

He didn't feel weak, nor did he feel like celebrating. How long would the transformation last?

All day he fought the urge to go outside to see what would happen. Better to stay in the cave and remain human.

That afternoon, as the last rays of sunshine faded and the sun dipped below the horizon, his body didn't tingle, his skin didn't shrink, his skeleton didn't morph into that of a bat. He remained human.

Is the spell truly broken this time?

Could he believe he was finally free to live his life as a man?

Hope, like a vine in springtime, wrapped tendrils around his negative thoughts. He wanted to believe, but after that first disappointment of remaining human only under certain conditions, he couldn't be confident. *Could I?* He couldn't give in to hope.

*

At the end of the following day, Dane remained human.

He had to go find Tessa.

Dane ducked behind a tree to avoid a vehicle's headlights.

Luckily, at this time of night. a naked man could walk along the road for a good distance before having to hide. The cave had been no place for a naked human. Starving and chilled to the bone, he'd decided to walk back to Tessa's home.

The soles of his feet screamed in agony, but knowing her cottage was close gave him the will to push through the pain.

He hobbled around the last corner and through her front gate.

The house was in darkness, locked. But she hid a spare key under the garden gnome.

His energy flagged. Tessa wasn't here. *Is she okay?* He had to find out. The accident had happened two days ago.

He grabbed the phone from the desk, glad she'd told him her number and how to work the phone. His hands were filthy. Dirt streaked his body. He glanced back to the front door. Bloody splats marred the floor tiles. He had to hear her voice and make sure she was okay. The throbbing in his feet demanded attention, but he forced the pain to the back of his mind. It didn't matter.

He tapped the keypad and listened to the phone's sounds that told him it was calling her cell phone. Could she get to it? Was it out of charge? Of course the battery might have run down.

There'd be a number for the hospital. He flipped open the laptop and searched for the town's hospital. His next call was answered, and he was relieved to hear a woman's voice confirming he'd reached the hospital.

"I need to know if Tessa is okay?"

"Sir, do you have her last name?"

Dane mentally slapped himself. *Calm down.* "I'm sorry. Tessa Schrale."

The woman asked him to wait while she checked. She asked if he was her husband, and without thinking he said yes. "Could I speak with her?"

"I'm sorry, it's very late and she's sleeping right now, but she's being discharged tomorrow and we've organized transport for her, unless you can pick her up?"

He wished he could. "No, unfortunately I can't drive. Thank you for your assistance. Good night."

The woman reassured him that Tessa was going to be fine, wished him a good night, and ended the call.

Before morning he had to get himself cleaned up, patch his wounds, and then wipe up the mess he'd made.

He grabbed an apple from the fruit bowl and devoured it in three bites. No fruit had ever tasted as sweet and juicy as this apple in this moment.

*

Dane spent the morning cleaning and staring at the clock. Finally, a car pulled into the driveway.

He didn't rush outside. Tessa didn't know he could leave the house, and he wanted to surprise her. After the extreme efforts she'd gone to to help him, she'd be overwhelmed by his news. It could wait until she was sitting comfortably.

The driver helped her get steady on her feet with the aid of crutches. Dane almost ran out to help when she wobbled. He had the door open and one foot outside, which he pulled back over the threshold when Tessa gained her balance and walk/hopped toward him.

"Hello, Tessa." Dane hadn't been this nervous since he'd been a child. Her smile echoed his own. He put his hands on her waist and held her body to his chest soaking up the feel of her soft curves against him and the wonderful sensation of being whole again.

Her smile disappeared, and her expression turned wary. She shuffled to the couch. "Thanks for saving my life. Are you mad at me for going to the cliffs?"

"You're beautiful, Tessa, and I could never be angry with you." He sat next to her and looked into her eyes, which shone with unshed tears. He imagined his own were the same. "Seeing you on that ledge…" A lump formed in his throat. Tessa flung her arms around him and he sank into her warm embrace.

He lifted her chin to look deep into her eyes, studying their flecks of gray and amber. "I couldn't bear to see you hurting yourself over me. And then you went up to the cliff at night. I'm guessing that had to do with me too."

She swiped moisture from her cheek with the back of her hand. "Yes. I thought the purple lichen spell might help."

Dane caught the hand she'd used and touched his lips to the tips of her fingers. "Don't cry, sweet Tessa—you saved me. When I saw you on the ledge, my heart broke. And when you opened your eyes, I knew I wouldn't put you in danger anymore. I vowed to leave you alone and let you make a life for yourself. I honestly preferred to live as a bat rather than cause you harm."

She poked his chest. "It was my choice to help you. You don't get to say who I lo…care about."

His heart skipped a beat. *She was going to say 'love.'* "I think that's why… the spell broke." Dane watched her eyes widen as she comprehended his words.

"You're human all the time?" She shrieked and smiled a you've-given-me-the-best-present-ever smile.

Happy feelings blasted away his doubts; he was certain his own smile was as wide. "Let me show you." He held out his hand for her, and when their fingers touched light blue sparks shot from the bracelet right to the ceiling.

"The spell broke after I found you on the ledge. I imagine I made the ultimate sacrifice by deciding that I would stay a bat forever rather than see you hurt. And I think, I hope, perhaps, you care for me enough that the terms the witch set have been fulfilled."

Tessa tipped her head back, and he could see such joy in her eyes that his every nerve ending thrummed.

"I love you," she said.

"And I love you more than life itself." Holding her close, breathing in her scent, filled the empty space in his middle like sunlight brightening a dark well.

Tessa's bracelet split apart, and a rolled-up piece of paper fell from under the largest stone.

"Are you hurt?" Dane checked Tessa's wrist, running his thumbs over her silky skin.

"No, it didn't burn. Look, the writing on this paper is so tiny. It's another map. Of here. In the garden. Something's buried."

*

Tessa sat on the garden bench while Dane dug holes around the old oak tree.

Metal clanged against metal. Dane looked her way.

Tessa grabbed her crutches and hobbled over, apprehensive one minute, excited the next. "Treasure?"

"A small chest," Dane said. He hauled it out. "Heavy."

Tessa moved close to the tree, her curiosity getting the better of her. Dane opened the chest. Inside something was wrapped in an oiled cloth.

"It's like a scavenger hunt. My family sure likes hiding things."

"I'm glad they did, or you'd never have found me." He stood up and grinned. "You do the honors. It's yours to reveal."

Excitement and fear battled in Tessa's belly. Dane seemed serenely calm, as if by gaining his humanity he was already a winner. She wouldn't rush into revealing the contents. Whatever they may be. It felt like this important discovery needed reverence. "Let's take it inside."

Tessa studied the chest, which sat on a square of newspaper in the middle of the kitchen table.

She looked into Dane's dark eyes for courage. "I'm a bit scared to see what's in here. The women in my family were witches. It might be toad's feet or something else equally odd."

"All right. Do you want me to look first?" Dane asked.

Tessa pushed up from the table. "No. We'll look together. We've come this far. Do it."

Dane unwrapped the metal box and pried off the lid. Tessa met his eyes. They took a synchronized breath.

Gleaming gold coins filled the inside.

Tessa's face ached from smiling. "Well, that's good. That's *really* good." She winked at Dane. "You're going to need some cash to live in this age. Now, how do I get you a fake ID?" Dane's joyous laughter was worth more to her than any amount of gold.

*

On International Bat Night the following year, Tessa listened to the tour guide.

"If we tried to hang onto the roof of the cave, our arms would tire in minutes, but unlike humans, bat ligaments work differently. When the bats' claws are relaxed, they clench tight, so they are holding on, but we're relaxed when our hands hang loose."

Dane would know. He'd found his place in this time as an expert on bats. He studied zoology with a side study in history to formalize his credentials, to add to his hundreds of years of knowledge of bat behavior and the changes that had occurred over time.

"Think and care about our bats not only on this special night, but every night. They eat their body weight in insects each day. They are our friends and an integral part of the ecosystem."

Dane ascended by cable to the cave roof as he spoke, adding theater to the talk, which thrilled the younger members of the audience. His tours were popular because people said his affinity with the bats was awesome, and the bats seemed to like him.

He held a bat and brought it to the cave floor for the group to have an up close and personal view. 'Know the parts of your bat,' he called this session.

He said he didn't miss being a bat, but Tessa thought he had to miss the feeling of flying through the night with thousands of bat buddies.

Dusk descended. "Let's go outside now and watch the best part of the show."

Small dark shapes zipped through the air from the cave entrance. First a few dozen, then hundreds and thousands whirling into a swirling mass of tiny bodies high above their heads. The swirl elongated into a stream of bats weaving their way through the night sky to feast on every insect in their path.

Dane licked his lips.

"Hungry?" Tessa asked.

"Hmmm." He gave her a look. The one that said his hunger wouldn't be satiated by food. "Time to wind this up and go home."

"For some private Bat Night celebrations?"

"Ending the night with you is what I call celebrating."

He touched his lips to hers, and it was as if they soared together through the star-speckled night sky.

About the Author

Susannah Kade spent the first ten years of her life in the English countryside daydreaming, chasing butterflies and reading fantastic tales of magic and mystery.

One day her parents decided Australia would be a nice place to live.

During the long voyage, Susannah learned the value of an active imagination and spent her days making up stories.

She still loves the sea, but prefers to feel the sand between her toes.

A librarian and mum to one human and two fur babies (canine and feline), she loves to write fantasy and sci-fi adventure romance stories set on Earth and other worlds.

Website: susannahkade.com
Twitter: @susannahkade

Dear Dolly

♥

M. T. Kearney

Story Information

Holiday: World Letter Writing Day
Holiday Date: September 1
Heat Rating: 1
Relationship Type: M/F
Major Trigger Warnings: None

Dolly Carter is excited to finally meet her pen pal. But a stranger shows up in her friend's stead making an outrageous request. Bystander Jim Markson, who has been following the stranger for days, insists that Dolly needs protection. Will she accept the help of this smart, handsome, quirky man?

Dear Dolly

The aroma of coffee filled the air as Dolly drummed her pale pink polished nails on the formica tabletop. The only other customers in the small diner were a teenage couple, sitting entwined at the counter. Dolly tuned out their affectionate whispers to ponder the imminent arrival of her elderly pen pal, Sarah Delaney.

Sarah was the childhood friend of Dolly's late Aunt Joan. Sarah's correspondence had been a blessing these past couple of years as Dolly grieved for the loss of her only relative.

She opened her clutch purse to retrieve the envelope that held her pen pal's most recent letter. Curiously it was printed on computer paper instead of handwritten on fancy stationery like the other letters. Dolly read it again for the umpteenth time. 'I'll be in Springfield on September 1st. Let's meet at Dave's Diner at 10 a.m.'

She found it amusing that Sarah had suggested World Letter Writing Day for their meeting—the perfect time for two pen pals to connect in person. Hoping to make a positive impression, Dolly had worn her favorite outfit, a green shirtwaist dress, and made an extra effort to tame her shoulder-length, wavy auburn hair.

As Dolly put the letter away, the door opened, causing a loud bell to chime. Her eyes flew up in anticipation of seeing her friend.

Only to be disappointed.

A slender red-haired man dressed in faded, baggy jeans who looked not much older than her own twenty-one years stood in the doorway. He glanced around the diner before approaching her booth. "Are you Dolly Carter?"

Surprised, she answered, "Yes."

Without an invitation, he slid into the seat across from her, pulled a cell phone from his back pocket, and set it on the table.

What is he doing? "Do I know you?" Dolly asked, her tone polite but unwelcoming. "You see I'm expecting someone and—"

The man interrupted. "You're expecting my grandmother. But she couldn't make it. I'm Patrick Delaney, her grandson."

Dolly frowned. *Grandson? But Sarah never married.* "I don't understand."

Patrick's face crumpled, tears appearing in his bloodshot eyes. "Grandma's sick. She needs a heart operation. But she doesn't have any money."

The chime indicating the opening of the door sounded again, drawing Dolly's attention away from Patrick. The love-struck teenagers were leaving, and the boy was holding the door open for two new customers. The new patrons appeared to be a father and son, both having the same long gait, lean build, and sandy-colored hair. Like the changing of the guard, they took the exact stools at the counter that the teenagers had vacated.

As soon as the new customers sat down, the younger of the pair swiveled round on his stool to glance at Dolly and Patrick. Admiring how the blue plaid of his button-down shirt enhanced his broad shoulders, Dolly's heartbeat sped up when he suddenly winked at her. Flustered, she focused her attention back to Patrick, whose face bore a look of irritation.

"I was hoping you could help," he continued. "The doctor will only operate if he can get two thousand dollars upfront."

Something's not right. His story doesn't make sense. "That's a lot of money."

Patrick was somber. "I know." He bit down on his lower lip and wiggled it between his crooked front teeth. Leaning across the table, his voice grew animated. "Grandma would be furious if she knew I was even here. But I don't know what else to do. I know you two are close. She speaks so highly of you, as if you're part of the family." His voice broke at the end, and tears ran down his face.

He seems so upset, though. Could there be any truth to what he's saying?

Dolly looked to the napkin holder to get Patrick something to wipe away his tears. But it was empty. Sighing, she opened her purse to pull out a handkerchief. She handed it to Patrick who gave her an odd look. She knew it was old-fashioned, but Dolly liked old-fashioned things. After a moment's hesitation, Patrick accepted the white cloth with its delicate embroidered edge. He wiped his face then blew his nose into it, before placing it next to his phone.

A tired-looking waitress bearing an order pad and pen appeared at the table. "Have you folks decided what you want yet?"

The menus still stood upright on the table, wedged between the empty napkin holder and a silver basket that contained salt and pepper shakers.

"We haven't gotten that far," Dolly said. *I'm not sure I even want anything now.*

The server plucked the menus from their perch and set them flat on the table. "I'll give you a few minutes, then."

"I could go with you to the bank," Patrick volunteered after the waitress had left. "You could get a cashier's check for $2,000 made out directly to the doctor. That way Grandma would never know about it."

Dolly's mouth fell open, an alarm going off in her head. She shifted in her seat uncomfortably. *This has to be a scam.* "Sarah was my aunt's childhood friend; I don't have that kind of money lying around." She was prevaricating, and she knew it. But Patrick's pushiness set her on edge.

"Grandma said you inherited your aunt's house after she died. You could take out a loan against it."

Dolly's eyebrows rose, the alarm now blaring. *How does he know all this? What exactly did that sweet old lady I've been writing to tell him?* "I'd like to talk with Sarah. Maybe you could give me her phone number. I never found it in my aunt's things."

In a voice as smooth as honey, Patrick said, "Oh, that's not necessary. You can talk with her doctor yourself. He'll verify everything. I'll call him now." He picked up his phone and swiped at the screen.

Oh my gosh, how am I going to get rid of this guy?

The door chimed yet again, and a police officer entered.

Thank heavens.

Patrick gave the officer a sideways glance and slunk down into his seat. "You know, I think the doctor is in surgery this morning. I'm supposed to meet a friend for lunch in less than an hour. I'll swing by your house afterwards, and we can go to the bank together."

"But I didn't agree to anything." And she wasn't going to. Not until she talked to her pen pal.

"See you later." Patrick put Dolly's soiled hankie into his back pocket along with his phone. He was out the door in less than ten seconds. Before the chime stopped ringing, the older man at the counter stood up and left as well.

Dumbfounded, Dolly sat in a daze staring at the menu in front of her. *What just happened?*

The loud door chime that sounded as the police officer left the diner sipping from a large paper cup startled Dolly from her trance. Suddenly the waitress was at her side again. "Have you decided yet?" The woman's voice radiated annoyance.

And rightfully so. Frantically, Dolly scanned the menu. *I've been here at least twenty minutes. I should order something.*

"I'd recommend the coffee," a baritone voice called out. Dolly raised her head from the menu to find the young man in blue plaid, now the only customer other than herself left in the diner, turned in her direction. "It's good."

"I guess I'll have coffee," she told the waitress.

With a long-suffering sigh, the server padded away to retrieve a mug, sugar, and cream. It wasn't long before a steaming mug of heavenly-scented liquid sat before her.

He's right, Dolly decided after the first sip. *It's good.*

As she set down her cup, he stood up from his stool. But instead of settling his bill, he strode straight to her booth. "Mind if I ask you a few questions?" He didn't wait for a response. Instead he slid into Patrick's seat across from her. "I couldn't help but overhear some of the conversation between you and your friend."

A flash of anger came over her. *Why was he eavesdropping?* "You were spying on me?"

A momentary dark look crossed his face, but he recovered quickly. "How well do you know that guy?"

About as well as I know you. Two strange men in less than twenty minutes was two too many. Dolly pursed her lips. "I'm sorry, but who are you? Why should I tell you anything?"

The stranger smiled broadly, showing off his straight white teeth and a dimple in his left cheek. "James Ryan Markson. But you can call me Jim." He pulled a card from his pocket and set it on the table. "Keep it."

She picked it up, noting its simple layout, classic font, and ivory color. It read 'Markson Private Investigation.' Underneath the business name was an address in Franklin. *That's where Sarah lives.*

"My dad and I are following that man you spoke with. He's a con artist."

"You're following him?" Dolly took in a sharp breath. *I knew something wasn't right about Patrick's story.* Relieved to have her hunch confirmed and eager to talk about the bizarre encounter, her words bubbled forth without thinking. "I've never seen that man before in my life. He introduced himself as Patrick and said he was the grandson of the woman I was supposed to be meeting."

"Who were you supposed to be meeting?" Jim leaned forward.

Dolly cupped her hands around the coffee mug. Its warmth brought comfort to her rattled nerves. "Sarah Delaney. She's my late aunt's childhood friend. We've been pen pals ever since my Aunt Joan died two years ago. Only Sarah never married, so I'm not sure how she could possibly have a grandson." Dolly lifted the mug to her lips.

Jim's eyes lit up. "Now we're getting somewhere."

Dolly swallowed the mellow brew and set down the cup. "What I can't figure out is how Patrick would know about my connection to Sarah. Or how he knew I was supposed to meet her today." She reached for her purse to show Jim the letter.

Jim glanced at the short note, shaking his head all the while. He put it back into the envelope and pushed it across the table toward Dolly. "Were all your previous letters from Sarah typed like this one?"

"No. They were handwritten on fancy stationery, decorated with birds and flowers. It doesn't make any sense." Dolly picked up the envelope.

"It makes perfect sense," Jim countered in a gentle tone. "The man you met with was the one who sent this letter. He used to work for the Sunny View Nursing Home in Franklin. He was fired for stealing from the residents, but it seems he hasn't stopped. Now, with the personal information he gleaned from them, he's going after their friends and family."

"But Sarah doesn't live in a nursing home." Dolly turned the envelope in her hand over to study the return address. Just numbers and a street name. She closed her eyes trying to remember if her friend had mentioned it in one of their early letters.

Jim cleared his throat, and Dolly's eyes flew open to find him examining her face. Embarrassed, she looked down at her mug.

"I live in Franklin," he said. "I can assure you that's the address of the Sunny View Nursing Home. Have you ever visited your friend?"

"No, I've never been to Franklin. After my aunt died, I found Sarah's address among her papers. I wrote to tell her about Aunt Joan's death. Sarah wrote back, and we became pen pals."

The waitress set Dolly's bill at the edge of the table. Dolly's hand reached for it, but Jim got there first.

"Hey, you don't need to do that."

"My treat, Dolly."

"How do you know my name?" she blurted out suddenly wary.

"I could say it's because of my ace investigative skills, but the letter you showed me began with the salutation 'Dear Dolly,'" he reminded her. He paused, giving her a small smile. "It suits you."

She scowled. She'd heard patronizing comments all her life about her name matching her appearance. Still, Jim likely didn't realize how short she was—only five feet tall—because he hadn't seen her standing yet. *At least the wedge heels I'm wearing today make me a couple of inches taller.* "It's a nickname."

"Is your real name Delores?"

She snorted. "No, you're way off." She had no intention of revealing her legal first name to him, though, because she didn't like it.

He raised his index finger to his lips to hold back a smile. "You've got me wondering now." He pulled a leather wallet from his front pants pocket. "Look, I'll pay up, and then I'll go home with you in case Patrick shows up again."

Go home with me? I don't think so.

She slid across the booth seat and stood up, shoving the envelope into her open purse. "Thanks for your concern, but I don't need a bodyguard. I've been living alone for the past two years. I know how to take care of myself. I have no intention of giving Patrick any money." An understanding look appeared on Jim's face while she lectured him, but it turned exasperated when she added, "He can't force me to do anything."

"That's where you're wrong," Jim said looking up at her. "The Sunny View Nursing Home hired us because that guy has threatened people, robbed them, even pulled a gun on someone. You're lucky that police officer stopped by. It obviously scared him off; otherwise he might have been more insistent about getting money from you."

"Wouldn't he…" She was going to argue that by leaving, Patrick had given her time to phone Sarah to check out his story, but then she remembered she'd told Patrick she didn't have Sarah's number. *He knows I have no way of verifying what he told me.*

"My dad's following Patrick now," Jim broke in. "I'd feel better if you let me get you home safely."

"But I don't even know you." She wanted to trust him. Really, she did. He was attractive. He was paying for her coffee. But she had no way of verifying Jim's story either. He could be just as much a liar as Patrick.

Jim flushed. "You already have my dad's business card. But I can prove I am who I am. Sit back down, and I'll show you."

This is getting annoying. Still Dolly returned to her seat across from Jim, drumming her nails impatiently on the table while she awaited his evidence. He opened his wallet and pulled out a few cards, turning them toward her. His driver's license was on top. A surreptitious glance at his birth date informed Dolly he'd just turned 26.

"Not such a great picture, but this is me, James Ryan Markson." As he lifted the license up so she could see it, another photo identification card showed from beneath it.

"What's that?" She tilted her head to see it better.

He slid it into view. "My student I.D. I'm a doctoral candidate in American History at Franklin State."

Dolly's eyes narrowed. "I thought you said you were a private investigator."

"I work with my dad during the summer. But this is my last job for him. I'm starting my final year in the doctoral program tomorrow. I'm even teaching a class this semester." He returned the cards to his wallet. "I can show you more." He pulled his phone from his back pocket. "Here's a picture of my dad and me."

That does look like the man who came in with Jim and followed Patrick out. But then Jim continued through a slew of family photos that included his mother, father, and high-school-aged sister. Dolly suppressed a chuckle at the over-the-top display. At the end though, she couldn't help but envy the close relationship he had with his family.

"So will you allow me to escort you home?" he asked.

I'm not sure I have much choice. "I suppose so, after all that overwhelming proof. Although, I did notice you left out the photos of you and your girlfriend."

Jim stood up abruptly. "I don't have one. I don't even have any spare time to take a woman out for coffee."

You expect me to believe that? She followed him to the cash register. "Good, then. Just wanted to be sure you didn't think this was some kind of date."

After Jim gave the tired waitress who was operating the till payment for both their checks, he turned to Dolly. "I never mix business and pleasure, Della."

Della? Am I being guarded by the absent-minded history professor? Has he forgotten my name already? "It's Dolly, remember?"

The waitress held out a few bills in change, but Jim motioned her hand away. "Keep it for your tip." He turned back to Dolly. "Just guessing at your real name. Della Street is the secretary to fictional attorney Perry Mason," he explained.

Why does he care about knowing my real name? "I know all about Della Street," Dolly said. "My aunt loved to watch *Perry Mason* reruns on TV."

As they exited the diner, Jim glanced at the curb. "My dad took the car. We'll have to take yours."

"My car? I don't even have a driver's license." Aunt Joan had given up driving years earlier, and without access to a vehicle Dolly had never learned. Besides, it didn't seem necessary because she was able to get around Springfield just fine using public transportation.

Jim's eyebrows rose. "Isn't that inconvenient?"

"No, I take the bus. Anyway, I'm not going straight home today. I have errands."

"Okay then. I'll text my dad and let him know what I'm doing." He pulled out his phone and fiddled with it for a moment while she waited growing slightly impatient. Afterward, Jim held his arm out to Dolly.

She didn't take it. "Not a date," she reminded him. Instead, she set off walking with Jim close at her side.

"What's the first stop?"

"Fabric store. I need three yards to make a dress."

"You know how to sew?" He seemed surprised.

It was a reaction Dolly was long used to. "I made the dress I'm wearing."

Jim's eyes looked her over from top to bottom. "That's some impressive sewing."

Dolly blushed at his compliment. She was pleased he'd praised her skill and not her figure. It made her trust him just a little more. "I make almost all my clothes," she offered to keep the conversation flowing. "My Aunt Joan taught me how."

As they reached the street corner, the signal light changed from green to red, causing them to stop, although their conversation didn't. "I didn't think anyone did that sort of thing anymore," Jim said.

"Well, I do. I'm studying clothing design at The Fashion Institute here in Springfield." She smoothed her hands down her bodice.

"This dress is from a pattern from the mid-1940s. I made it when I took a historic costuming class."

"World War II era." He smiled, taking a step closer so that their arms almost touched. "That must be why I like it so much."

She cocked her head. "Are you an expert on that time period?"

"You could say I'm a big fan of it, but it's not my main course of study."

The light changed to green and they set off again. "What is your main course?" Dolly asked.

"The American Revolution."

"Ugh, that sounds exhausting. Too many dates and battles to remember."

Jim burst into a hearty chuckle.

I like the way his eyes crinkle when he laughs. "I was never very good at history," Dolly explained, trying to distract herself from thinking about his eyes crinkling. "My teachers were boring."

"That's too bad. I hope none of my students would ever say that about me. I want to make history come alive for them. I want them to understand that these events happened to ordinary people just like us."

He'll be a good professor if he can figure out a way to do that. With regret she pointed to a building across the street. "We can cross at the corner." She'd enjoyed her walk with Jim and was a little sad for the interruption. She always loved visiting the fabric store, but Dolly wasn't sure that Jim would share her passion. "I won't be too long," she warned him, as he held the door open for her.

"Take your time. There's no hurry." He was scanning the store with an interested eye.

Looking for a flowered print, she set off for the section where the cotton fabrics were housed to see if there were any that caught her attention. After careful deliberation, she decided on a print with small blue flowers against a yellow background.

This is so pretty. It would make a perfect dress with a sweetheart neckline.

Removing the bolt of material from the shelf, she turned to look for Jim. He was on the other side of the store standing in an aisle of luxury fabrics. She walked over, and found him stroking a piece of red velvet. "You look like you're enjoying yourself."

He turned to smile at her. "It's so soft. Reminds me of a rabbit's foot I used to have as a kid."

The thought of young Jim and his rabbit's foot made her giggle. "Did your rabbit's foot bring you any luck?"

"Not at the time, but I'm thinking maybe all the luck was saved for today." He locked eyes with her, and Dolly suddenly got nervous.

Is he flirting with me?

Looking away, she shifted the bolt in her arms and reached out to brush her hand across the fabric Jim had caressed. "Velvet has been around since early Egyptian times," she said. "The technique used to create it was so time-consuming that it was only used by royalty and the very rich."

Jim pointed at some shiny fabric further down the aisle. "What is that slippery stuff over there? It feels as smooth as butter."

"That's satin. It was first made in China. People mix it up with silk, but actually it's a kind of woven silk."

Jim grinned at her. "And you said you weren't good at history."

"This isn't history," Dolly exclaimed. "This is working knowledge of the tools of my trade."

His eyes twinkled. "I disagree." He reached for the bolt in her arms. "Let me help you with that." She handed it over to him and pointed him to the cutting table. Once the material was measured, paid for, and bagged, Jim carried it out of the store for her.

I could get used to having someone tote my purchases around for me.

Standing in front of the shop, he gave Dolly an expectant look. "Where to now, Donna?"

Confused, Dolly asked, "Who's Donna?"

"Donna Karan, women's clothing designer. Is your real name Donna?"

Ah, he's back to that again. "No, and we're going to the library next. I have a book on hold."

They ambled down the sidewalk for two blocks, stopping to look in the occasional store window before turning left on Oak Street where the brick library building stood. Dolly retrieved her mystery novel, only to have Jim call her Dorothy as they exited the library.

Not again. "How did you come up with Dorothy?"

"Dolly is a nickname for Dorothy; but I also see you're a fan of mysteries. Dorothy L. Sayers was a renowned British crime and mystery writer."

Dolly knew that. She'd even read some of Sayers's work when she was younger. Smiling, she shook her head at his silly diversion. "You don't let up, do you?"

"I'm up for a challenge."

"Oh really?" *I just might give you one.* She met his gaze for the first time and even held it for a short moment, tamping down the blush that threatened to form. "Knowing I like mysteries isn't going to help you. I like all kinds of books, even romance."

"Did you say romance, Danielle?"

"Danielle Steele?"

"Ah, you're catching on. So am I right?"

"Nope."

"Game on then. How about we get some lunch?"

"This isn't a date, remember?"

"Of course, but I'm hungry, and I imagine you are as well."

"A little," Dolly admitted. She'd only had the coffee at the diner.

"I'm not from around these parts. Can you recommend someplace? Or we could return to Dave's Diner."

I don't think I can handle more of that door chime. "There's a tea shop that has sandwiches. Aunt Joan and I occasionally ate there."

The tea shop was down a side street a few blocks from the library. It was filled to capacity when they arrived, but a table opened up next to the front window after only a few minutes. Jim got ahead of Dolly to pull out her chair.

"This isn't a date," she murmured.

"Mom taught me to be a gentleman." He sat down, pulled his phone from his pocket, and swiped at the screen.

"It isn't very gentlemanly to be checking your phone," Dolly pointed out.

He gave her an apologetic look. "You're right; it's rude. I hate people who do it, too. I've noticed you're far more polite. You haven't pulled yours out once."

"That's because I don't have a cell phone," she explained. "I can manage fine with the landline at home. I guess I'd rather write letters than texts."

A bemused look appeared in his eyes. "You're like someone from a simpler time. It's refreshing." He set his phone, screen down, onto the table. "I'm sorry. I was looking for a response from my dad, but he hasn't sent one."

Sensing his unease, Dolly tried to reassure him. "He's been doing this job for a while, hasn't he?"

"Ever since I was little. He got his license when I was three and set up shop when I was six."

That was twenty years ago. His dad had to be an old hat at this, and she reminded him, "Then, I'm sure he'll be okay."

The waitress brought the menu and after a few minutes they made their selections: grilled cheese for Dolly, and turkey and avocado for Jim. They agreed to share a pot of peppermint tea. The tea arrived before the sandwiches. Dolly poured for the both of them. Jim picked up the delicate flowered cup. "Is it Diana?"

She didn't even have to ask for clarification. "For the Princess of Wales? No."

While they waited, Dolly took the opportunity to find out more about Jim. *All I've done is talk about myself.* "What made you decide to become an expert on the American Revolution?"

"I fell in love with the Founding Fathers." His voice grew animated as he told her about his favorite: Thomas Jefferson. "Did you know he wrote almost 20,000 letters over the course of his lifetime? He wrote not only to family and friends, but to political leaders, scientists around the world, and leading horticulturists. He had so many interests."

His soliloquy stopped when the waitress arrived with the food. Before he took a bite of his sandwich, he threw out a question for Dolly. "Do you have any other pen pals besides your friend in Franklin?"

Dolly smoothed out the cloth napkin she'd placed on her lap. "Not as many as Thomas Jefferson; I only have three. There's Bridgette in Ireland, Mary in England, and Sally in Australia."

"Have you met any of them?"

"No." Dolly picked up a half of her sandwich, appreciating the way the melted cheese oozed out the sides. *I forgot how delicious this is.*

They ate in silence for several minutes, each enjoying their selections, before Jim spoke again. "Do you mind if I ask how you connected with your pen pals?"

Dolly set down the last bit of her sandwich onto the plate. "I found their names listed in the pen pal column of a magazine I used to read as a child. I've been corresponding with all of them for more than ten years."

"I'm amazed that you continued to keep in touch. Most people would have moved on from their childhood pastimes by now."

"I'm not most people," she said primly, taking a sip of tea. "Besides, they're like family to me. Knowing they're out there, thinking about me, caring for me… it's comforting, even if I never meet them in person."

"Is family important to you?" he asked softly.

Thinking about the photos Jim had shared with her earlier, Dolly realized he could never understand how important it was for her unless she said something. She took a deep breath. "My parents died when I was little. I was placed in foster care and bounced from home to home until Aunt Joan, who was my mother's great-aunt, retired from her overseas job and took me in when I was fourteen."

"That must have been tough."

Dolly could hear the compassion in Jim's voice and see the tenderness in his eyes. Momentarily panicked, she wondered, *Why did I tell him all that?* "It was. But it's in the past now." She picked up the last bit of her sandwich and stuffed it into her mouth so she couldn't answer him if he wanted to know more.

"I don't know that the past ever really goes away, but then again I'm a student of history." Jim wiped his napkin across his lips and pushed his empty plate forward.

"You must have been hungry," Dolly exclaimed, desperate to get away from the deeply personal direction the conversation had taken.

Thankfully, he took up the thread. "I got up early this morning and didn't eat breakfast. We've been following that conman around Franklin for a couple of days. We had no idea he'd drive two hours down the road to Springfield this morning." Jim picked up the bill the waitress had left on the table.

A sinking feeling came over Dolly as Jim's words reminded her that he wasn't from around here. *Don't get attached.* "This isn't a date," she said. "I can pay my own share."

"But I asked you to join me," he insisted, pulling out a credit card and lifting his arm to wave down their server.

"Thank you, then," Dolly said, deciding not to argue any further.

After they left the tea shop, Dolly walked with Jim to the bus stop. They sat down on the bench.

"Will we have to wait long?" Jim asked.

"I would think you'd be good at waiting by now. Don't you have to kill a lot of time on stake outs?"

"My dad does that stuff. I'm more into the research end of the detective business—looking up the facts and getting everything documented. It's what I do as a student of history, too."

"I didn't realize there were any similarities." She wanted to ask more, but something caught her eye. Dolly stood up. "The bus is coming."

Jim picked up her shopping bag and stood up as well. Dolly got on the bus first, dropping enough money in the box for both their fares.

"You didn't have to do that."

"You paid for lunch." Dolly led the way down the narrow aisle to an empty seat on the right and slid across the bench to the window. Jim sat next to her.

His close physical proximity made her suddenly self-conscious. *It isn't like me to react so strongly to someone I just met.*

"How far, Dora?"

His dopey question brought her back to herself. "Dora the Explorer?" She didn't know whether to laugh at him or swat him. *What a funny guy.* "You know, you're like a little child. You just won't give up, will you?"

"Nope! Not when something intrigues me."

Feeling her cheeks grow warm, she shifted in her seat to look out the window. "Just sit tight. It's a ten minute ride."

Her prediction held true, and they soon arrived at the stop nearest to Dolly's house. She set off with Jim at her side along a narrow lane lined with cars. The thought occurred to her that she'd never brought any guy to her house before. She'd only been on a few dates in her life, but she'd met them elsewhere. But after spending only a few hours with Jim, she felt comfortable enough to welcome him into her house. *There's something about his presence that seems reassuring.*

"I can understand now why you don't drive," he said. "You'd never find a place to park."

She hummed but didn't answer him either way.

They walked on the dirt path that sufficed for a sidewalk until Dolly stopped. "I live here." She pointed to a colonial-style residence. It had a small, grassy yard with nary a dandelion in sight. The flowerbed at the front of the house was filled with daisies. Dolly opened the mailbox that stood atop a wooden post next to the sidewalk and pulled out a letter and a bill.

"It's good you don't have any bushes up against the front siding," Jim said. "It would be easy to hide behind them. Why don't you stay here, and I'll walk around the house to make sure Patrick isn't lurking nearby."

This whole day felt like something out of one of her mystery novels. It was a little absurd. Dolly smirked. "Isn't that a bit overly dramatic? It all looks exactly like I left it."

A furrow appeared on Jim's brow. Ignoring him, she set off for the front door. She unlocked it, pushed it open, and called out, "Are you coming inside?"

Wearing a look of resignation, he followed her in.

The front door opened into a hallway. On the left wall were lined hooks to hang coats, scarves, and bags. A narrow table stood against the right wall. Straight ahead were the stairs to the second floor. Dolly set her mail and her purse on the entry table then bent down to take off her wedge shoes. *That feels good.*

Jim set her shopping bag down onto the table. "Lead the way," he said.

Dolly turned to give him a smug grin. Of course, there was nothing to be concerned about. There was no evidence of a forced entry at the front door. Nothing. Patrick had her address, but he didn't have her keys. *I'll be surprised if he even shows up.*

As they continued down the hallway, Dolly assumed the banter of a real estate saleswoman. "You'll notice the hardwood floors in the entry extend into the dining room to your right and the living room on your left."

Her eyes took in the polished dining table and straight back chairs. Beyond them was a large china cabinet with fancy plates and stemware.

I don't think I've used any of that since Aunt Joan died. She hoped Jim didn't look too closely, though. She hadn't dusted the room in some time. She hadn't been expecting company.

Jim only glanced at the dining area. Instead his eyes turned toward the living room. It was filled with a lumpy couch and two big armchairs. All the furniture was turned to face the fireplace.

"Nice room," he said. "No place for anyone to hide."

"See, I told you." Dolly said. "The kitchen is next." She walked up to the swinging door to push it open, but Jim reached for her wrist to stop her. It was the first time he'd touched her, and an electric tingle went up her bare arm. The surprising sensation caused her to let out a small gasp. *This isn't a date.*

"I'll go in first," he said, his voice strangely husky.

He must have felt it, too.

Dolly stepped back as Jim started to push the door open. Suddenly he stopped. "Your back door is busted in."

She ducked under his arm, gaping at the sight. The door was twisted in the frame and there was a hole at the bottom. Frightened, she forced herself forward to inspect it further.

"I assume it wasn't like this when you left this morning." The timbre of his voice was a blend of light humor and carefully modulated concern.

She knew Jim was trying to keep her calm, but her emotions were swirling. Her fear dissolved into anger. "I swear, I could run a sword through whoever did this."

"It will be alright, d'Artagnan."

She threw Jim an indignant look. "This isn't the time to joke."

"You're right. I'm sorry."

They took a few moments to survey the room. Other than the broken door, the kitchen looked the same.

"Where do you keep your valuables?" Jim asked.

Dolly rolled her eyes. "What valuables?"

"Jewelry, cash, credit cards, your checkbook."

"I'm a student," she said as if it explained everything. "Other than the house, Aunt Joan didn't leave me much."

"But if someone were to get ahold of your personal information, they could cause a lot of trouble for you. Haven't you heard of identity theft?"

She'd forgotten all about that. Dolly gulped. "I keep that stuff upstairs."

"In a safe?" he sounded hopeful.

A hope she had to dash. "In my top dresser drawer." Without thinking she turned back to the swinging door to go upstairs, but once again Jim's hand stopped her. And it was a good thing too, because not five seconds later a crash sounded overhead.

"Someone's up there now," Jim said, his voice a harsh whisper. "We need to get out of here." His large hand enveloped Dolly's small one as footsteps pounded on the stairs. "Outside," he hissed, his head nodding toward the broken door.

But Dolly had another idea. She pointed to a door that was slightly ajar next to the stove. "The pantry," she mouthed. Seeing the hesitation in his eyes, Dolly pushed Jim toward the tiny room. They weren't even able to close the door behind them in the small, dark enclosure when the swinging door burst open and the intruder entered the kitchen.

Through the narrow opening, Dolly watched as Patrick turned his head wildly in every direction. He carried a flowered pillowcase from her bed. It looked as if it was partially filled.

He must have heard us talking.

In the dark, closed-in space, she became strongly aware of Jim's presence. She was still holding his hand and found it to be a comfort in the midst of this frightening situation. *I guess Patrick got tired of waiting for me and decided to rob me instead. Thank goodness Jim insisted on seeing me home.*

Patrick rushed out the broken back door his footsteps fading into the distance.

When she couldn't hear any sound of the conman, Dolly tugged her hand free from Jim's and pushed forward to leave the pantry, but Jim placed his hands on her shoulders to hold her back.

"Let him go." Dolly felt Jim's warm breath on the side of her face as he spoke.

"But he's got my pillowcase and probably all my things," she argued.

"We have his vehicle description and license plate; the police will get him. Besides, I'm sure my dad's around here somewhere and will follow him. We'll call the police first, and then I'll text my dad." He dropped his hands from her shoulders and found his way to her hand again to give it an encouraging squeeze.

But when he let go of her, Dolly pressed past him and into the kitchen. She hurried to the twisted back door and looked out. "He's long gone," she fumed. *How am I going to get my things back? The police won't be here for ages.*

"Let's go outside through the front," Jim suggested. "We don't want to mess with a crime scene."

Despite wanting to go upstairs immediately to determine what Patrick had taken, Dolly could see Jim's point. This time he led the way through the front hallway, although Dolly made a point of putting on her shoes and grabbing her purse.

They sat on the front stoop waiting for the police to arrive. Dolly took a deep breath to try to calm her overwhelming emotions. Anger had faded into despair. She wanted to cry. She wanted to feel safe. *Why did this have to happen to me?* "I feel so helpless."

Jim's arm went around her shoulder. "It's normal to feel that way when someone has broken into your home and taken your things."

A police officer arrived shortly. "Wait here with your boyfriend so I can be sure no one's hiding inside," he told Dolly. She didn't have the energy to correct him about her relationship with Jim, and oddly enough, Jim didn't correct the officer either. Instead, she leaned against him while the police officer went inside. She closed her eyes and concentrated on the weight of his arm around her. It was nice. Safe. Like he was an anchor in a turbulent storm.

Jim's arm dropped from around her when the officer returned, and she felt its loss keenly.

"The house is clear," the officer said. "Why don't you come inside, look around, and tell me what's missing."

Dolly went upstairs immediately. The first door on the right was her sewing room. Patrick had ransacked it. All of her notions, which had been so neatly organized, were strewn around. Rhinestones and buttons and zippers lay across her worktable. Her cutting mat and rotary cutter were on the floor, alongside the dress form she pinned her designs on. The big tub she stored her fabric in was tipped over. It was obvious the thief had pawed through her stash.

"Oh, no," she gasped.

"Is anything missing?" the officer asked.

How can I tell? The only items still in their regular spot were Aunt Joan's old Singer and the serger sewing machine Dolly had purchased when she'd started school at the Fashion Institute. "It's hard to know with all this mess."

She followed the officer to the next room along the hall—her bedroom. The drawers of the high top dresser were pulled out and the contents were flung across the floor and even over her bed. Normally she would have been embarrassed to have the male officer and Jim view her undergarments, but it was the sight of her empty, open top drawer that caused her throat to tighten. That space was home to her only credit card, a couple of hundred dollars in cash she kept for emergencies, and the few items of real jewelry that Aunt Joan had left to her.

"He took my credit card, cash, and jewelry."

"Let's keep looking," the officer said.

The next room along the hallway was the bathroom. The door of the mirrored medicine cabinet was open, but at a quick glance nothing appeared to be missing.

"What would he want in here?" she questioned.

"Prescription drugs," the officer said.

"I don't have any."

The room at the end of the hallway was Aunt Joan's old bedroom. "There's nothing of monetary value in this room," Dolly announced as she stepped inside.

Even though it hadn't been used for a couple of years, the room still housed her aunt's bedroom set with its maple bed frame, two night stands, and a matching dresser. Patrick had left her aunt's bureau drawers open, but they had already been empty. Dolly had donated the clothing they had contained to charity long ago.

Still, it angered her that Patrick had even entered the room. Early in her grief, Dolly would sit on Aunt Joan's bed and talk to her sometimes. It had been a great solace. She hadn't done it much lately and doubted she'd ever do it again. Knowing that a trespasser had been inside ruined the safety the room had once provided.

They went downstairs, and the officer led her through the other rooms. But Dolly had already seen them. She knew they hadn't been touched.

Sitting in the dining room with the policeman, she made an official list of the stolen items for him. Somewhere along the way, Jim disappeared. When the officer was finishing up, Jim reappeared with his father. The pair joined them at the table.

Mr. Markson pulled out his identification and PI license and told the officer about being hired to investigate Patrick. Dolly hadn't been his only target in Springfield that day. Jim's dad had lost track of the con artist after stopping to question one of his other victims. "We've been following him around Franklin for a couple of days," Mr. Markson said. "My son and I followed his vehicle to Springfield this morning. Here's his plate number."

That detail seemed to excite the officer, and he rose to his feet after copying down the number and vehicle description. "I'll be in touch," he told Dolly before leaving her alone at the dining table with the two Markson men.

"I should have used my phone to take a video of him before he ran out the door with Dolly's things," Jim said to his father. He threw Dolly an apologetic glance.

You couldn't. You were busy holding my hand and making me feel protected.

"It's all right, son. But next time walk around the entire property to check things out before you go inside."

Jim sighed. "Yeah, I know. I wasn't thinking."

That was my fault, not Jim's. I could have gotten us injured or worse if Patrick had caught us in the house. "But I insisted..." Dolly began.

"No, that's on me," Jim interrupted. Changing the subject, he added, "We need to fix Dolly's back door before we go. She lives here alone." He got up and led his father to the kitchen, with Dolly trailing behind.

After a quick survey of the damage, Mr. Markson asked, "Do you have any tools we can use?"

Dolly reached into the junk drawer, pushing aside some wooden spoons and a box of Band-Aids, to pull out a key. "Everything is in the shed behind the house."

After a quick trip outside, the men returned with a hammer, a hand drill, and some wood epoxy. They removed the door completely off the hinges. "Hold this upright," Mr. Markson ordered his son, "while I fix the bent hinge."

Jim's arms went around the heavy door, leaning it against his chest like an oversized shield.

"You're strong," Dolly blurted out.

"Just like Samson, huh," Jim joked. His head tilted when she didn't say anything, only crossed her arms in front of her chest.

Once the door was set back into the frame, Jim turned to Dolly. "It's Delilah, isn't it?"

Dolly winced. *I hate that name.* She refused to acknowledge his guess.

"I'll be right back," Mr. Markson said, unaware of the tension that had risen in the room. "I think I saw a small piece of wood in the shed I can use to cover up this hole."

When his father left, Jim turned to her. "You didn't answer me. Did I guess right?"

She could lie, but she wasn't a liar, and he had guessed correctly. *Besides, what does it matter? I'll never see him after today.* "You got it."

Jim shook his head. "I don't understand why you don't like that name. It's lovely."

"Not when you're a kid teased in Sunday School because you're named after the woman who seduced and tricked the hero of the story. Being 'Dolly' is just easier."

"And Dolly sounds sweet, and cute, and safe. But it's intriguing to know there might be a temptress underneath all that adorableness."

Me, a temptress? Dolly rolled the idea over in her mind, before it dawned on her that he'd called her adorable. *He's hitting on me, and I like it.*

His father suddenly appeared with a small piece of plywood. "I'll use this to hold the door jamb in place for now, but you'll need to get someone to come over and replace this door, young lady. Might want to look at getting some more secure locks while you're at it." When he was done, Mr. Markson turned to Jim. "It's about time we headed home. We have…"

The telephone on the kitchen wall interrupted him. Dolly answered it. It was the officer who had taken her report. "We've just arrested your burglar. He has a couple of warrants against him, too. He'll be locked up for a good long while."

"That was fast." She smiled and gave a thumbs up sign to Jim and his dad.

"Well, that license plate helped greatly. Wouldn't have been able to catch him without it."

"What about my things?"

"Cancel your credit card and order a new one. We'll call you in a few days regarding the jewelry and cash. He's accumulated a lot of stolen items. We need to catalog everything for the court before we can return it. It might take a few months, and if this goes to trial you might need to come in and testify, but that'll be up to the district attorney. You should also probably call your insurance about the damage."

Dolly hung up and told Jim and his father everything. "Thanks to you both for all your help today. If you hadn't been here…" Her voice dropped off as she watched their faces. Mr. Markson bore a pleased expression, but Jim had gone pale as if he were imagining something horrible happening to her.

"If you're nervous after this break-in you might consider getting a dog, security system, or maybe a roommate," Mr. Markson suggested. "Just be sure to get references if you go the roommate route."

"I'll think about it." Dolly knew she didn't want a dog—she was a student and couldn't give a pet much attention. But she did have Aunt Joan's bedroom available. And extra cash would come in handy to pay for house repairs or maybe even a security system. A roommate was something to consider.

Feeling exhausted now after all the excitement, she walked father and son out through the front. *How am I going to say goodbye to Jim?*

"I'll be a few minutes, Dad."

I wonder if he feels heartsick like I do?

"Okay, I'm parked up the street," his father responded after a glance between them, leaving so the two had some privacy.

Jim reached for Dolly's hand. "Are you going to be all right in the house tonight? If you're scared, I could stay here with you—on the couch, of course—until you feel better. I could get a bus back to Franklin tomorrow or the next day."

"But what about school?"

"I could probably get someone to cover my class for me."

It was silly to drag out their farewell. If Jim stayed, it would only make it worse for Dolly when he left. After all, what future could they possibly have? And why was she feeling this way? They'd only just met! "No, you should go. I'll be fine. I had a nice time today with you, right up until my house got robbed."

He gave her a sad smile and let go of her hand. "Goodbye, Dolly." He left her on the stoop and set off for the sidewalk. He got to the mailbox, rested his hand on it for a moment, and then jogged back. "Look, this may sound crazy. But I don't want to say goodbye, and I know how you feel about dates."

How I feel about dates? You're the one who said you're too busy to date.

"How would you like another pen pal?" Jim asked.

A feeling of lightness came over her. "That would be great." *For now.*

"Your boyfriend won't mind?"

"I don't have one. Hey, let me get something to write with." Dolly went back into the house and grabbed the notepad and pen she kept on the entry table. She came outside and shoved them into Jim's waiting hands.

He wrote down his information then handed the pad back to her. She wrote her name and address at the bottom of the page and tore off the strip of paper for him.

In the distance, a car horn blared. "That's my dad. I'm guessing he's ready to hit the road. I'll write you tonight, I promise." He smiled and held out his arms. Taking a step forward she walked into them, reveling in his embrace. For a moment, his chin rested on the top of her head.

Dolly sighed, liking the way their bodies fit so neatly together.

"Your hair smells like lavender," he murmured. "Such a comforting scent." But he let go of her all too soon for Dolly's liking and set off down the street.

Is it strange to miss him already? Her heart told her no.

*

His first letter showed up in the mailbox a couple of days later. It was a welcome respite after dealing with the aftereffects of the burglary. Dolly had arranged for a carpenter to replace the door, called her insurance, had the adjuster come by, and gone to the police station to fill out yet more reports. She'd also put a notice on the bulletin board at The Fashion Institute advertising for a roommate.

She made herself a cup of tea and settled on the sofa to read Jim's letter. Before opening the envelope, she took a moment to admire his large, loopy scrawl and picture him sitting at a desk writing to her.

Tearing open the envelope, she pulled out a single sheet written in cursive on thin, white paper. The writing was straight across the page, each line evenly spaced—as if he'd followed an invisible template that only he could see. *Is it weird to admire his penmanship?*

She smiled to herself and began to read. The letter began with a series of questions about what precautions she'd taken to be sure she was safe in her home. *He cares about me. He'll be glad to hear about what I've done.*

At the end of the letter, he made a curious request. 'You mentioned you took a class in historic costuming. Do you think you'd be able to design and sew an outfit typical of what the founding fathers wore during the American Revolution? I already have a powdered wig, tricorn hat, and black boots. I can easily get some white stockings. I was thinking it might be fun to wear the costume when I teach. I'll reimburse you for the cost of the fabric and for your time, of course.'

He ended the letter abruptly, signing 'Jim' in a large scrawl.

Teach in costume? That's one way to make history come alive for your students. A more practical thought followed. *What does a Revolutionary War outfit even look like?* Dolly ran upstairs to find the textbook she still had from her historic costuming class. She spent the evening studying it. Men had worn white linen shirts, a waistcoat, a frock coat that was sometimes cut short in front and long in the back, and breeches that ended just below the kneecap. They'd also worn a lacy jabot at their throat and lacy cuffs at their wrists.

Closing her eyes, she pictured Jim in the outfit. Was she weird to think it would suit his tall, lean frame? After careful thought, she decided to do it. *But I'll need his measurements—chest, shoulder width, arm length, waist, inseam, and rise.*

The idea of taking those measurements in person thrilled Dolly—she'd not only get to see Jim again, but also have her hands all over him. She stopped herself. *Professional seamstresses shouldn't think this way! Besides, it isn't... practical.* He was too far away and probably so busy with school and teaching that he wouldn't be able to come back to

Springfield for even a day. The thought filled her with disappointment.

It was late when she finished planning, too late to write Jim back. *I'll do it tomorrow.*

The next day brought even more news to add to her letter. Sophie Tyler, a fellow student at The Fashion Institute, phoned about renting the spare bedroom. However, it wasn't for herself, but for her boyfriend Kyle Kohama. "Kyle's a part-time student at Springfield Community College," Sophie said. "He can't stay where he is because his roommates only want to party and he can't get any studying done, or even get much sleep for that matter."

Dolly had some reservations about having a male roommate—she'd imagined the sister-like relationship she might have with a woman—but agreed to meet Kyle. The couple showed up at her house within the hour.

Kyle had a muscular build, but his appearance belied his demeanor. He was soft-spoken and gentle with his girlfriend, treating Sophie so sweetly that it made Dolly ache for Jim.

He's your pen pal not your boyfriend, she reminded herself and forced her attention back to Sophie and Kyle. Dolly recognized Sophie from a class they'd taken together the prior year. *She's got a knack for creating patterns. If this works out, maybe she can help me with Jim's outfit.*

After showing the pair the room, Kyle expressed his interest. "Do you have any references?" Dolly asked, grateful to Mr. Markson for suggesting she get some and even telling her how to look up someone on the internet.

"My boss could provide one, and I could probably get another from one of my professors."

"And I'll need to run a credit check, too," Dolly added. She'd noticed that it was a requirement on most of the rental units posted on the board at The Fashion Institute. *It seems like a good idea.*

"No problem," Kyle said.

"Great." *I have so much news to write Jim about!*

The day Kyle moved into her aunt's old bedroom, Dolly received another letter from Jim. *He wrote back so quickly after receiving my letter. He must be eager to get his outfit.* Or eager to write to her, but she tried to put that out of her mind.

She didn't open it until she retired to her room that evening. She sat on her bed in her pajamas, tearing open the thick missive. The letter opened with a funny story about Jim's embarrassment over his grandmother taking his measurements for his historic garb. 'I trust she'll get them right because she used to sew when she was young.'

Dolly chuckled at the mental image of Jim, *my Jim* as she often found herself thinking of him, letting his granny measure the rise of his pants. *That must have been awkward.*

'Let me know the cost of the material, and I'll send you a check,' he wrote. He then transitioned to talking about his class and the thesis he was writing. But his closing advice suggesting she reconsider her male roommate irked her. *Why would that bother him? His father was the one who suggested I look for someone. And Kyle's muscles would intimidate most people.*

It dawned on Dolly that Jim might be jealous. *Could he be feeling the same way I feel for him?* The thought made her giddy.

She waited a week to respond to his letter. She had classes and homework, and she needed time to price the fabric. But Dolly had also taken on another project, a more personal one—entering the twenty-first century.

When Jim said I was like a person from a simpler time, he had no idea how right he was. Spending her teen years with an elderly woman whose health was in decline had limited Dolly's opportunities to interact with her peers—or even develop some basic life skills.

Spending time with Kyle and Sophie had only made that more obvious to her. *It's okay to prefer handkerchiefs over tissues, or favor dresses instead of blue jeans, but there's so much I don't know how to do.* But her new friends were enthusiastic teachers. Sophie was giving her driving lessons, and Kyle was teaching her the finer points of operating her new cell phone.

One evening in early November, Dolly decided to take a break from her sewing and do some investigating of her own. She had no photos of Jim, and his face was beginning to blur in her mind. She wondered if any existed online. It didn't take her long to find one. A headshot was posted on Franklin State's website under the History Department. *He's even more handsome than I remembered.*

But as Dolly explored the school's site and noticed all the attractive women who were enrolled there, insecurity came over her. *I'm only his pen pal.*

Part of her wanted to go upstairs and throw away the outfit she'd been working on for him. But she knew that was childish. Anyway, he'd already paid her for the fabric and made partial payment for labor.

Maybe I should use fancier stationary and scent it with lavender. Instead of being Dolly, I'll give Delilah a chance to win him over. The problem is I've been Dolly for so long. I have no idea what Delilah would write.

*

 The costume was completed in mid-November. Dolly hung it up in her sewing room to admire. She could wrap it in tissue and mail it to Jim, but she'd come up with a better idea. She'd rent a car, drive to Franklin, and deliver it to him in person. She'd passed the driving test a week ago. The plan both thrilled her and scared her. *What if I've misinterpreted everything? What if he was only interested in me for my sewing?* She didn't like to think about being rejected.
 Still, a visit to Franklin would also give her a chance to finally meet Sarah. Her pen pal had been quite alarmed when Dolly had written about Patrick pretending to be her grandson. Of course, she'd minimized the danger of the event. But Sarah had still been concerned and had invited Dolly to come up and visit anytime.
 Deciding to chance it, she wrote Sarah of her plan to visit over the Thanksgiving holiday but decided to surprise Jim. He'd already mentioned he'd be spending the holiday in Franklin with his family so she knew he'd be around.

*

 Just look at how far I've come in the last few months, Dolly thought as she punched Sarah's address into the car's GPS.
 She arrived at the Sunny View Nursing Home in the early afternoon. She was directed to a bright room with floor-to-ceiling windows and watched as schoolchildren performed a play about the first Thanksgiving for a couple dozen elderly residents. Dolly scanned the group trying to guess at which woman was Sarah—her friend had told her to look for a little old lady with white hair, but that description fit most of the women there. Baffled, Dolly took a seat in the back.
 The kids wore traditional black and white pilgrim outfits, although Dolly knew that the pilgrims had also worn colorful clothes most of the week. The stereotypical black and white dress had been their Sunday attire. Dolly wondered how the seniors could even hear the actors as they spoke so softly, but the audience seemed engaged

and laughed loudly when one child carried out a rubber turkey on a tray, tripped, and dropped it onto the floor.

When the show ended, a woman announced that apple cider and cookies would be served in the dining room. The audience stood up and left. Dolly introduced herself to the announcer and asked her to point Sarah out.

"Sarah will be so pleased to have a visitor." The announcer indicated a woman using a walker.

Dolly followed Sarah out of the room and waited until she sat down at a table in the dining room to introduce herself. It was strange to finally be able to put a face to the person she'd been corresponding with for so long, but Sarah seemed over the moon to finally meet her. She introduced Dolly to her friends who were already seated, Doris, Betty, and Ed.

"Is this your daughter?" Ed asked.

"No, she's my pen pal."

Ed grinned. "I wouldn't mind writing to a cutie like you. Are you single?"

Doris and Betty laughed. "Watch out, Dolly," Doris said. "He's in the market for another wife."

Dolly's face grew warm.

"She's got a beau already," Sarah told him with some cheek.

Dolly eyed her pen pal sharply. Sarah knew all about Jim, but Dolly had never referred to him as her boyfriend. *Why would she say that?*

Small talk at the table continued for fifteen minutes more, then Sarah pulled her walker close and stood up. "Let's go back to my room and visit." They were soon seated in a sunny room with a bed, a dresser, and two armchairs that faced each other.

"I'm lucky to have a private room," Sarah said as Dolly took in the surroundings. "Now tell me about your young man."

"I wouldn't call Jim my young man." She could already feel her cheeks starting to heat.

"Well, you obviously feel something for him to take on such a big sewing project while you're in school."

"He and his dad helped me."

"And I'm sorry about that terrible business," Sarah said, apologizing yet again for the problems Patrick had brought to her. "The administrators here say that he'll be in jail for a long time. But maybe some good came of the bad if it led you to meeting Jim. What do you like about him?"

Dolly leaned forward, eager to talk to someone about her Jim. "He's got a good sense of humor, he's easy to talk with, and he's very passionate about his interests. Even though he's busy with school, he still finds time to write me often."

Sarah's lips quirked into a little smirk. "So, I'm guessing you didn't come all the way to Franklin to see only me?"

"I finished Jim's costume and I decided to deliver it in person to be sure it fit properly."

"Of course," Sarah said, her expression solemn. "The fit is of the utmost importance."

They both burst into laughter. When they regained their composure, Dolly spoke, "You're right that I like Jim a lot, but I have no idea how he feels about me."

"Men can be a lot shyer than they let on," Sarah said. "Especially well-educated men who hide themselves in their books or in historic costumes."

Jim, shy? He seems confident to me.

"I'm so glad you'll be joining me for Thanksgiving dinner," Sarah changed the subject, clearly noticing Dolly's wish to stop talking about Jim. "It will be nice to sit with a friend who I consider family."

I guess that con artist, Patrick, wasn't lying about Sarah's feelings for me. It warmed Dolly's heart to know how much Sarah cared.

Their conversation continued. Dolly described her drive to Franklin, and Sarah told her about a squirrel that lived in the tree outside her window. When Sarah began to yawn, Dolly stood up. "I should go. I want to check into my lodgings before it gets dark." She promised to meet Sarah at noon on Thanksgiving for dinner.

Dolly had booked herself three nights at a bed and breakfast. A middle-aged woman met her at the door and showed her to the bedroom she'd been assigned. "There's hot water and tea in the dining area, and I put out cookies around 4:30 p.m. every day," the proprietress said. "Breakfast is served at 8 a.m."

She left Dolly to explore the room more thoroughly. It was all blues and florals with two twin beds, a small white dresser, and an upholstered armchair. The lone window overlooked the grassy backyard. A small table and chairs were just outside the back door. After unpacking, Dolly sat in the armchair, staring out the window, and nervously readied herself to call Jim to announce her arrival in Franklin. *Maybe I should have written him that I was coming.*

She retrieved her phone from her purse and dialed the number on Mr. Markson's business card because she didn't have Jim's direct number.

His father picked it up after two rings. "Markson Private Investigation," he answered.

"Hello, Mr. Markson. This is Dolly Carter. You helped me when my house in Springfield was robbed a few months back."

"I remember." He sounded jovial, and Dolly couldn't help but wonder if Jim had shared anything or everything she'd written with his father. *This is a little weird.*

"I'm in Franklin visiting my pen pal—the one who resides at the Sunny View Nursing Home. I was hoping I could meet up with Jim while I'm here."

"I don't know his schedule, so how about I take your number and have him call you?"

"All right," Dolly said and gave him her number. She hung up disappointed that his father hadn't given her Jim's number outright. Would Jim even call back when he got the message? *At least I have his address. I can leave the costume at his door before I go.*

Dolly changed out of her traveling clothes replacing them with yoga pants and a blue t-shirt. It was 4 p.m. when she went downstairs carrying her phone in her hand. *I'll get some tea and sit at the table in the backyard. There's still some light left.*

She carried her cup of peppermint tea outside and shivered. *I should have put my coat on.*

As soon as she sat down at the table, her phone rang. She answered to hear Jim's warm voice. "You're in Franklin? Why didn't you tell me you were coming? Where are you now?"

"I'm staying at the Almost Heaven Bed and Breakfast."

"That's on State Street, right?"

"Yes."

"I'm coming right over." He hung up.

Dolly jumped to her feet. *I should change my clothes.* She carried her cup back into the house but was waylaid by the proprietress, who asked about how she was finding her room. Before Dolly could even get to the stairs, the doorbell rang. The owner opened it to reveal Jim.

He looked so different from when Dolly had met him before. Instead of appearing neatly dressed and clean-cut, now his hair was tousled, his face scruffy from a couple of days of beard growth, and he was wearing a leather jacket and jeans.

I can't decide which version of him I like better.

He looked beyond the proprietress, caught Dolly's eye, and winked. Her heart melted. *Still my Jim.*

"You got here so fast," she said. He came closer and threw his arms out. Dolly set her cup down on a side table, anticipating his embrace. She closed her eyes as his chin came to rest on her hair.

"Good old lavender," he murmured.

Dolly wanted to tell him that because of that single comment, she'd thought of him every time she'd washed her hair. *If he doesn't want me, I'll have to change my shampoo.*

She inhaled deeply as her face rested against his jacket, struggling to identify the scent that clung to it. *Old books?*

"I'll leave you to your visitor," the owner said, disappearing down the hall.

Jim was the first to let go. He stepped back and gave her a careful look over. "You're in the twenty-first century today."

Dolly blinked for a moment, not understanding at first. But then it dawned on her that he was describing her clothing. *Is he disappointed that I'm dressed so casually?* "I didn't have time to change."

"Don't you know, you're perfect exactly as you are."

She blushed. "Would you like some tea?"

"Of course."

Dolly reached for her cup. Jim followed her to the dining room where shortbread cookies now sat next to the tea supplies. She sat down at the dining table and watched Jim make a cup of tea.

"I can't believe you're here," he said as he sat down across from her. "I just wrote to you. Did you get my letter? It was about Christmas." He picked up his cup to take a sip.

She shook her head. "Why were you writing about Christmas?"

Jim set down his cup. "I had this idea that I could drive down to Springfield and pick you up and bring you here to celebrate the holiday with me and my family. My grandmother has an extra room at her place, and she said you could stay with her. We could spend some time together, she could help you finish the outfit I commissioned, and you could meet the rest of my family. Writing letters is nice, but I'd like to be more than your pen pal."

His words were rushed at the end, and Dolly remembered Sarah's suggestion that Jim might be shy. A wave of confidence came over her as she realized that he was as nervous as she was with sharing his feelings. "I'd like to visit you at Christmas and do all those things. But your outfit is finished. I brought it with me."

His eyes grew big. "It's done?"

"Yes. It's in the trunk of my rental car."

His eyes locked onto hers. "You drove up here, yourself? You are full of surprises."

She met his gaze headlong and managed to give him what she hoped was a Delilah-type smile. "I'm very mysterious."

"You sure are." He paused for a moment as if debating with himself. "Do you have any plans for this evening?"

"No." Her tone was light, flirtatious. She didn't want him to think she wasn't interested.

He reached his hand across the table for hers. "Let me take you out for dinner. There's so much I want to tell you, and so many questions I want to ask. Writing letters is okay, but it can't beat being together in the same room."

"Why, Mr. Markson, are you asking me out on a date?"

Jim swallowed once. Twice. "Yes, I am."

Putting on her best Delilah-smile, she whispered. "Okay, I accept."

Jim let go of her hand and rose to his feet. He walked around the table to tug her up to him. "When we first met I told you that I didn't have a girlfriend because I was too busy, but really it's because I hadn't wanted one until I met you. Would you be willing to give me a chance to be your boyfriend?"

In the soft lamplight of the dining room, Jim's expression was so adorable that Dolly couldn't help but lean forward and press her lips to his. "Does that answer your question?" she breathed. In response, he wrapped his arms around her and slanted his lips over hers. As she parted her lips to allow him to deepen the kiss, she thought, *Maybe there is a little Delilah in me.*

About the Author

M. T. Kearney's stories, both fiction and nonfiction, have been published in more than twenty print magazines and various online sources. She's written a young adult sports fiction book, See Andie Run.

A native of California, she's a graduate of California State University, Northridge, with degrees in American History and Journalism. She currently resides in the Pacific Northwest with her family. In her spare time she sings in a contemporary worship band, knits hats for the homeless, and surfs the internet for story ideas.

Facebook: www.facebook.com/mttkearney
Tumblr: mtk4fun.tumblr.com

The Seadog's Wife

♥

Katherine Moore

Story Information

Holiday: Talk Like a Pirate Day
Holiday Date: September 19
Heat Rating: 1
Relationship Type: M/F
Major Trigger Warnings: Depression, minor racism.

Thrown together when cast as the leads in a pirate movie, a pair of formerly married actors realize that their divorce was a mistake.

The Seadog's Wife

Olivia was not looking forward to meeting Laura for lunch. She didn't really want to admit it to herself, but she was afraid the lunch at her favorite restaurant was going to be a three-course goodbye as she fired her as a client.

She wouldn't blame Laura if she did let her go. She and her wife were putting their twin daughters through college and even though Lucia was a high-profile production executive at Mar Vista Studios, money was still tight for them.

Except for a small part in an episode of *The Rookie*, Olivia hadn't worked in two years.

Notoriously picky about her roles even before her divorce, afterward Olivia had retreated into her shell. She read books but not scripts. She swam in her landlady's pool. She'd walked away from her social media accounts after the split but developed a mania for Pinterest, often staying up until the wee hours to curate the perfect boards she created. She had several hundred followers and took satisfaction in that since she didn't use her real name on the account.

She found herself drawn to pictures of abandoned places and had been surprised to find how many other people shared her fondness for the wrecked beauty of empty buildings and lost cities. She was fascinated by pictures from Chernobyl although the idea of disaster tourism horrified her.

It was all too easy to think of Chernobyl as a metaphor for her life.

She knew she was depressed. Her doctor had prescribed Celexa, which had helped some, but not enough to rekindle her interest in working at her craft. She'd proudly refused her ex-husband's offers of alimony, even when he'd struck it lucky a month after the papers were filed—landing the lead in a television series and a box-office smash of a movie. She'd refused to reopen negotiations of what he called "their deal."

Money was starting to get tight. Olivia knew she couldn't stay wrapped in her warm cocoon of solitude much longer if she wanted to keep the lights on.

Laura insisted that work was what she needed. That immersing herself in a make-believe experience would be just the thing to take her mind off her everyday cares as well as put some money in both their pockets.

She'd employed every tactic in her arsenal to convince Olivia to come back to work from playing the nurturing mother to pressuring her in the name of tough love. "It's a great part," she always said, and then went on to describe a role that sounded like half a dozen characters Olivia had already played. Some were *literally* characters she'd already played, and much to Laura's distress, Olivia had turned down sequel opportunities several times. The annoyed filmmakers had then gone on to recast her parts and, in at least one case, the sequel had earned more than twice what the original movie had, so the filmmakers had had the last laugh and her reputation for being "difficult" had become more entrenched.

She'd just missed out on being cast in *Big Little Lies*, and that had been a disappointment. She'd turned down a part in a horror movie—Laura had referred to it as a "Gothic drama" and "an intense exploration of the psychological nature of fear"—and then watched the Canadian actress who had accepted the role win an award at the Sitges Film Festival and then get signed to star in a trilogy of films that was already getting buzz before the first one was released. She'd passed on the story of a serial killer Laura had pitched as a story of "female empowerment," telling her agent she felt it had been done in *Monster*. And then saw the movie blow up big when Kim Kardashian West took up the real-life killer's cause and got her released from prison.

Laura hadn't exactly said, "I told you so," but she had not been pleased. When Olivia had had to bow out of a part in a popular superhero franchise to take care of her ailing mother, Laura had nearly wept in despair. "Can't your brother handle things for a couple of months?"

The answer to that had been "no." Benedict and his husband had adopted a special needs child and already had their hands full trying to make ends meet in London. Plus, their mother had been simply hideous to her brother when he'd come out, and the two had been estranged for years.

Olivia had had a complicated relationship with her mother while she'd been alive, but since she had lived in Los Angeles, it wasn't like Olivia could have ignored her and simply left her to rot in an assisted living facility.

When money had gotten tight, Olivia had sold her car to economize, using Uber and taxis and public transportation to get around. She wasn't a snob about riding the bus or the Metro—it gave her an opportunity to observe people and study their mannerisms—but it took so long to get from anywhere to anywhere that sometimes it just wasn't practical.

She lived frugally, but in Los Angeles, it was absurd how much money got swallowed up on rent, even when that rent was on a studio apartment carved out of an old Victorian house in Echo Park. She got along well enough with her landlady—the widow of a diplomat who preferred sunny Southern California weather to her native London—and she had the run of an overgrown garden in the back of the house, sharing it with her landlady's cats who seemed content to lounge about in the sun without being overly curious about what was beyond the borders of their fenced-in domain.

Some days, the cats were the only living creatures she interacted with.

Olivia knew that wasn't healthy.

She also knew her reputation for "being difficult" was morphing into something more negative the longer she was out of the public eye. She knew very soon people would stop asking if she was available for this movie or that. And then where would she be?

Laura wondered the very same thing, and of late, her conversations with Olivia had been pointed and sharp. "You are one step away from being the subject of one of those *WatchMojo dot Com* documentaries on 'Why Hollywood won't cast Olivia Buchanan anymore,'" Laura warned. But Olivia couldn't bring herself to care. Some days, it was all she could do to drag herself out of bed and get dressed.

If you call yoga pants and a T-shirt dressed, Olivia thought.

When Laura had called and told her she wanted to meet for lunch, Olivia had made an effort to put herself together. She knew there were always paparazzi stationed outside the restaurant, and she knew that at least one would recognize her, take pictures, and sell one to the *National Enquirer* or *TMZ*. They'd choose the most unflattering shot, she knew, in order to make her seem more pathetic.

She didn't want to give their readers the satisfaction.

She chose her clothing as carefully as putting together a costume—a vintage burnt-orange shift straight out of *Mad Men*—and accessorized it with a string of amber beads and silver and amber earrings. She'd bought the dress on Poshmark and the jewelry on Etsy but knew no one would be able to tell her outfit hadn't come from a trendy little boutique on Melrose. She pulled out a pair of brown leather mules she'd had so long they'd been re-soled twice and finished off the outfit with an envelope bag she'd bought at a yard sale. Her mother, who'd rarely praised her for anything, often had admitted she'd admired Olivia's flair for finding gems among other people's discards.

Rather than pay someone thirty dollars for a manicure, Olivia had done it herself, although she had splurged to get her hair trimmed and styled.

If her career was on the chopping block, she wanted to go out in style.

*

Laura was waiting for her at the restaurant when she arrived, sitting on the little outdoor patio that was adjacent to the restaurant's front door. "Is your car in the shop?" she asked after the ritual air kissing was over.

"Yes," she said and hoped Laura would leave it at that. In Los Angeles, people's cars were always in the shop; Olivia didn't think she'd be curious enough to ask for details.

At least there's the mezzelune di zucca barucca to look forward to, she thought, already savoring the taste of the plump pasta pockets stuffed with pumpkin puree and sage butter.

She ordered a mineral water and waited for Laura to tell her why she'd wanted to meet.

"I have a movie for you," she said.

"Mmmm," Olivia said noncommittally, sipping from her glass of mineral water.

"It's a historical drama," Laura said, "just your sort of thing."

"What era?" she asked, thinking of how much she liked Victorian costumes.

"The seventeenth," she said. "The story takes place in Jamaica. Your character is a woman from an aristocratic island family."

Island family, Olivia thought. *Which is code for...*

"The part of Justine is perfect for you. With your… exotic… looks."

Exotic.

"I'm biracial," Olivia said flatly, "not part alien."

Laura blushed. She always got flustered when talking about race or politics or any number of topics that a grown woman should be comfortable discussing.

"What's it about?" she asked, putting Laura out of her misery.

"I have the script right here," she said, which Olivia took to mean that the one-liner on the project was something she thought Olivia might turn down reflexively. That was not a good sign.

She reached for the script and then became aware of a rising tide of chatter as a tall, golden-haired man walked into the restaurant. She heard a pair of Japanese tourists whispering "Chris Hemsworth" to each other and wanted to lean over and tell them they had the wrong golden-haired actor. But then, if it made them happy to think they'd seen Hemsworth, who was she to kill their tourist buzz?

The man towered over the restaurant's hostess, who looked like it was all she could do not to take him by one muscled forearm and direct him to his location, but she merely nodded in the direction of Olivia and Laura's table.

The man strode toward them, a broad smile on his face.

Laura stood up to greet him with his hand outstretched.

"Church," Laura said as they shook hands, and then the newcomer looked over at Olivia.

"Nice to see you, Livvy," he said and bent to kiss her on the cheek, knowing that she hated being called Livvy. Thomas "Church" Churchill knew her so well.

They'd been married for five tempestuous years.

*

Part of Olivia wanted to scrub Thomas' kiss away with her starched white napkin and another part wanted to grab him by the lapels of his beautifully tailored sports jacket, pull his head down, and kiss him again properly. Olivia often lied to herself about unimportant things—she considered it a necessary strategy for dealing with life—but on the matter of Thomas Churchill, she was ruthlessly honest.

She was still in love with him. It was no secret their marriage had been complicated. Due to movie commitments, they'd spent hardly any time together in their first two years of marriage, and it didn't help that gossip mongers had been eager to repeat rumors of infidelity and supposed cheating almost from the day pictures from their private wedding had leaked to TMZ. They'd tried to ignore the gossips but every time one of them went on a publicity tour, the same questions came up.

Then, on the set of the movie that proved to be his breakout role, Thomas had been photographed having dinner with his much-younger and very pretty co-star. Olivia might have laughed that off, but then there had been a follow-up photo of the young woman apparently leaving Thomas' hotel room the next morning, still dressed in the clothes she'd worn the night before. The film had been shot in Croatia, and with the time difference, the story had broken overnight while Olivia had still been asleep. When she'd turned on her phone the next day, her voicemail had been full and she'd had texts from Thomas, her mother, Laura, and her best friend Rina.

Thomas had sworn up and down that the story was a setup between his costar and her friend, celebrity-watcher Jacklyn Eastman, who'd been battling to find her own space in the already crowded entertainment ecosystem. The meal, he'd said, had been a working dinner and they'd spent most of their time talking about the antics of the power hungry lead actor who'd been making both of their lives miserable. He'd insisted she hadn't been in his hotel room; that photo had been staged. His relationship with the young woman was, he'd assured Olivia, purely professional, an on-set friendship that would fade as soon as the movie wrapped.

"Friendship," Olivia's mother Amanda had said scornfully. "A friendship with benefits, most likely." Olivia's mother had not believed men and women can be friends. Thomas had never given Olivia any reason to believe he was the sort to be unfaithful, but the allegations had widened fissures that had already existed between them. She no longer even remembered which of them had been the first to use the "D word." But like a lot of things lovers say to each other in anger, once said it could not be unsaid.

Olivia had not wanted the divorce, had wanted to go to couples counseling to see if things could be worked out.

Thomas had wanted that too. And then Olivia's mother had put in her two cents' worth.

"If he cheated once, he'll do it again," her mother had said. "You caught him this time, but how many times didn't you catch him?" Everything her mother had said had chipped away at the hard-won self-worth Olivia had accumulated, and in the end, she'd collapsed under the weight of her own insecurities and filed the papers. Someone at the courthouse had leaked the documents to TMZ, and for Olivia, that had put the cherry on the sundae of her misery. It had also made the decision feel irrevocable.

And yet, here she was, sitting across from Thomas, and thinking about how much she still loved him.

He looked so good. And he looked like he didn't have a care in the world. And while he was cordial, it was clear this meeting was totally professional. Not personal at all.

Damn him, Olivia thought.

She looked at Laura as Thomas sat down across from her and picked up the menu as if he didn't know it by heart. "You ambushed me," she said to Laura.

"Don't blame Laura," Thomas said. "I swore her to secrecy."

She wasn't going to give Thomas the satisfaction of asking him "Why?" but when she started to gather her things and stand up, he quickly said, "I didn't want you to pass up an opportunity because you're still mad at me."

"Get over yourself," she said. "I haven't given you an hour's thought in years."

He gave her a look and she felt it all the way to her groin. "You're a great actor," he said, "but a piss-poor liar."

The waiter materialized then, blocking Olivia's escape, and she seethed as Thomas ordered penne arrabiata with a salad on the side.

"Please hear him out," Laura said, and Olivia settled back into her seat with a sigh.

"Tell me about this opportunity," she said.

"The script is called *Seadog*," Laura answered, sounding somewhat anxious. "You would play Justine, the female lead."

"*Seadog* takes place in the seventeenth century," Olivia said.

"Correct."

"In Jamaica," Olivia said, "just to clarify."

"Yes," Laura said.

"*Seadog*?"

"Yes, Olivia," Thomas finally said impatiently. "It's a pirate movie."

Olivia knew Thomas had always wanted to make a pirate movie. He loved all of them, from *Swashbuckler* to *Nate and Hayes* to the various incarnations of *Treasure Island*.

"Who wrote it?" Olivia asked.

"Kid who just graduated from UCLA."

"So, her first film?" Olivia guessed.

"His," Thomas said. "It's actually his second sale, but the first never got made." He forked up some of his pasta. "It's a good script."

"And you're playing the title role?"

"I'm also an executive producer."

"They must have wanted you badly."

"They do seem to think I'll provide added value," Thomas said mildly. "Plus, they're paying me about half my usual money and thought that might sweeten the deal." He didn't seem bothered by that.

"How hands-on are you going to be?" she asked.

"I have co-star approval," he said. "Hence this meeting."

"And if I say no?"

"I'm talking to a few other actors for the part," he said. "Nathalie Emmanuel, Carmen Jojo, Tana Benjamin, Claire-Hope Ashity, Pippa Bennett-Warner." He smiled at Olivia. "It's a great part. And there are lots of women who could play Justine."

That stung, and unexpectedly, Olivia felt tears prick at the back of her eyes. She suddenly wondered if Thomas had set her up just so he could knock her down again. He'd never been into playing such petty games, but she hadn't seen him in a few years and had no idea if he'd changed that much.

"I'm sure any one of those actors would be marvelous in the part," she said and stood up again, leaving her mezzelune untouched. "Good luck with the project."

Thomas stood too. "Olivia—"

She ignored him. "I'll speak to you later, Laura," she said, knowing that it would probably be the last conversation they ever had. Then she sailed out of the restaurant with her head held high and a fake smile plastered on her face.

I'm a three-time BAFTA nominee, bitches, she thought, *I can sell this*. She walked almost half a mile before she stopped to order an Uber to take her home.

*

Back in her apartment she changed into yoga pants and a tank top and went outside to vent her frustration by pulling the weeds that threatened to choke her little pocket garden. Oscar, her landlady's golden-eyed black cat, materialized next to her meowing for treats.

"You're a greedy little kitty," Olivia told it fondly, "but I'm fresh out of treats."

The cat didn't seem to mind. He rolled around in the dirt Olivia had scratched up and then settled down for a nap on the sun-browned grass.

"Don't tell me you've turned into a cat lady," Thomas said, startling her.

He'd come in through the side gate of the garden, a gate her landlady normally kept locked.

"Mrs. Halbeck let me in," he said.

"Really?" That surprised Olivia. Her landlady had been quite undiplomatic when she'd first started renting the studio apartment, making no secret of her disdain for Olivia's ex-husband and the reason she needed to find a new place to live. "You're well rid of him, dear," she'd said with enough vehemence to make Olivia suspect that the late Mr. Halbeck might have cheated on her.

"I think she thinks I'm Chris Hemsworth," he said. "She told me she really liked me in *Avengers*."

"You really don't look that much like Chris Hemsworth."

"I'm taller," he said.

"What are you doing here?"

"I come in peace," he said. "And also, I brought pastries."

He held out a little box with her favorite restaurant's logo on it. Without even looking inside she knew it would contain three tiny cannoli, one filled with vanilla pastry cream, the others with chocolate and caramel cream. Her favorite dessert. As he well knew.

"Thank you," she said and rose to take the box. "Come in," she said. "I need to put this in the fridge."

Thomas followed her obediently, making no effort to disguise his curiosity as he looked around at the studio while she put the pastries away. The cat followed them both.

"Where are all your books?" he asked.

"I've gone digital," she said, rather than admitting that most of her books were in a San Fernando storage unit along with the furnishings she couldn't bear to part with but didn't have room to display. She took longer than was necessary to put the cannolis away, but she didn't want to turn around. He looked so good, and she could feel the pull of attraction between them.

Don't let him charm you, a voice said in her head, and she knew it wasn't her own voice but her mother's. Finally, she took a deep breath and turned. Thomas was watching her.

"I appreciate you thinking of me for—"

"Just read the script," he said.

"It doesn't sound like my kind of thing," she countered.

"Because it's not Shakespeare?" he asked. "Because it's not Oscar bait? When did you get to be such a snob?"

"That's not fair," she protested, knowing that she did indeed sound like the world's biggest snob.

"Olivia," he said gently. "Your mother is dead. Don't you think it's time you stopped hearing her voice in your head?"

Olivia stiffened. "This has nothing to do with my mother."

"No?" He gave her a skeptical look, then launched into a pitch-perfect imitation of her mother. "'Olivia, dear, you simply cannot entertain the idea of playing that role. The girl is so common, and the subject matter is distasteful.'" Thomas gave a little shoulder shimmy and wrinkled his nose, gestures her mother had used so often that Olivia almost laughed.

"Laura is worried about you, you know," Thomas said, his voice returning to his normal deep tones. He gave her another of those penetrating looks.

And again, Olivia felt a tug of desire.

"She says you haven't been eating."

"I've been eating."

"What's in your refrigerator besides the cannoli?"

"A variety of nutritious groceries," Olivia said, hoping Thomas wouldn't call her bluff and investigate for himself.

"And by variety, you mean the six-pack assortment of Chobani yogurt," Thomas said, and Olivia had to stop herself from reacting. He knew her *so* well.

"You look thin," he said, his voice full of concern.

"I have small bones," she said.

He didn't answer, just looked at her with those blue eyes. "I know you need money," he said finally.

Olivia stiffened. "I'm fine with money."

"We both know that's not true."

Olivia had the sensation she was slipping down an angled pane of glass, sliding into some sort of abyss with no way to climb back out. Thomas and his blue eyes were seeing much too much.

"I need to think. I need to have time to think, Thomas."

"You've had time."

"Not enough. Please. I need more."

"Okay, but at least consider doing this movie with me," he said. "It's going to be a romp, a *Romancing the Stone* for this century. You'd be perfect for it."

"I'm not good with comedy," she protested.

"You're great with comedy," he said. "You were a terrific Beatrice in *Much Ado About Nothing*."

"Well, Shakespeare—"

"You're such a snob," he said again, but not in a mean way. "Don't worry, your part is written as the straight man anyway. Sort of like Evie's character in *The Mummy*." Olivia had once confessed to a teenage crush on Brendan Fraser and admitted *The Mummy* was one of her favorite movies, so Thomas was bringing the big guns to bear when he used the reference.

"I can't agree when I haven't even read the script yet."

"No problem," Thomas said, pulling a script from his man bag.

Oscar came over and pawed at Thomas' leg. Without missing a beat, he picked the cat up and put it in his lap.

The cat nuzzled at him, and Olivia found herself staring at her ex-husband's hands, at the fine blond hairs on his wrist. He was wearing the watch his father had given him as a high school graduation present. He never took it off except at night or when in costume. It was an old school kind of watch on a leather strap. It was a watch meant to tell time and not an object meant to convey his net worth.

When Thomas had proposed to her, he hadn't had the money for a ring, so he'd given her the watch as a pledge of his love, punching extra holes in the strap so it would fit on her wrist.

She knew how much the gesture meant and had been prouder of that watch than she would have been with a diamond the size of an almond.

When they'd married, by mutual consent they'd exchanged simple gold bands rather than something more elaborate and expensive. Her mother had been contemptuous. "That ring looks like a prize from a Cracker Jack box," Amanda had said scathingly. "He could have found something nicer at a pawn shop."

"What are Cracker Jacks?" Olivia had said to distract her mother, who'd hated to be reminded that she was an aging Baby Boomer.

"Fade in," Thomas said, turning to the first page of the script and beginning to read. Olivia had always loved the sound of his voice, a growling baritone that oozed sex. As he read, he acted out all the parts with the agility of Jim Dale narrating the *Harry Potter* audiobooks. She found herself getting lost in the story, forcing herself to ignore the sight of his strong hands absently petting the old cat.

She had to admit to herself that he'd been right about the script. It was smart and funny. The chemistry between the pirate and the woman who was his co-conspirator and then his lover was clear on the page and would be a dream to act. It was as close to a Spencer Tracy/Katharine Hepburn movie as a movie in the twenty-first century could get. Nobody got raped; only one bad guy got killed, and he deserved it. Love and justice conquered all.

"So, what do you think?" he asked when he'd read the last page.

"It's kind of like *Captain Blood*, isn't it?"

"Yeah," Thomas said, "but with more structure. Have you seen *Captain Blood* lately? The story's all over the map."

She thought about that. "Do you think anyone wants to see a pirate movie after all the *Pirates of the Caribbean* movies?"

"It's been a decade since the last one," Thomas said. "And *Seadog* is more of a classic adventure romance."

She hadn't ever made a movie like *Seadog*. It sounded like it could be fun. A nightmare to shoot on the water, but fun, nevertheless. "Will you promise me one thing?"

"Anything," he said promptly, which was what he had always said when they were married, right before he'd gone out and broken whatever promise he had just made.

"The studio is going to make a big deal of us being together again on screen."

"Yes," he said. "I know how you feel about actors working with their spouses. But we're already divorced, so it's not like it's going to wreck our marriage."

He said that so lightly that again Olivia felt a pang.

"True," she said, hoping her response matched his nonchalant tone. "Just promise me if you're going to have a fling with the property mistress or the continuity person or the first AD that you'll keep it discreet."

She held her breath waiting for his answer. The intense media coverage of their marriage and its breakup had almost killed her. The public had sided with Thomas, who'd widely proclaimed his innocence. When she had refused to forgive him and filed for divorce anyway, the public's reaction had only deepened her misery.

"Promise me," she repeated.

Thomas looked chagrined. "I know I hurt you—" he began.

Olivia cut him off. "Under the bridge."

Thomas looked a little taken aback, as if he wanted to argue the point, but then he simply nodded. "I won't embarrass you," he said, which was not exactly what Olivia was hoping for, but good enough.

"I'll do your pirate movie," she said.

"Historical romantic adventure," he corrected her. "Thank you."

He gently put the cat on the floor and stood up. "What are you doing September Nineteenth?" he asked.

"Nothing," she said warily.

"Great. It's International Talk Like a Pirate Day. We're going to kick off the start of principal photography with a party. You can bring a guest."

"Brilliant," she said, feeling anything but as she watched him disappear.

*

The first person she called was her friend Rina, one of the few people she'd kept in contact with while wallowing in her one-woman pity party. She and Rina had been roommates when they'd first arrived in Los Angeles, Olivia fresh from RADA and Rina with her newly minted degree from Oxford and a near-native speaker fluency in Russian thanks to her Muscovite mum.

Rina had professed to find almost every aspect of American culture inferior to the English, but she'd been mad about movies and so bored by her job as a security analyst that she'd jumped at the chance to go to parties and screenings and events Olivia had tickets to.

Rina was thrilled to hear that Olivia had a job, and she was even more excited when she heard the job offer had come from Thomas himself. Rina had been Olivia's maid of honor and she'd approved of the match. She and Thomas' father had spent most of the wedding reception quaffing champagne and chatting about fly fishing which had turned out to be a mutual interest. They'd gotten along so well that Olivia had wondered if they'd made a love connection, but though they'd friended each other on Facebook, nothing else had ever come of their meeting.

Rina had known Olivia's mother almost as well as Thomas had, and she had been horrified when Amanda had bullied Olivia into leaving Thomas.

"Your mother is a bitter old hag. Don't let her mess up your life over this," she had said at the time. Olivia knew there was more she wanted to say but because she was a good friend, she'd kept it to herself.

The truth was, Olivia didn't know what "this" was. She still couldn't quite wrap her head around the idea that someone would wreck a marriage just to get a scoop for an online blog. And it troubled her that the problems in their marriage had suddenly seemed unsolvable. Both of them had retreated into work in the horrible time between the first pictures being published and the final death throes of their relationship. She had often wondered what would have happened if they'd gone off together to talk things out instead of just avoiding the subject... and each other.

"How did he look?" Rina asked, breaking into Olivia's reverie.

"Good," Olivia said. "He's grown his hair out for the movie."

"I love long hair on a man."

"Yes," Olivia said, "I know." The only men Rina dated were musicians who dressed like extras from *Sons of Anarchy*. She even appreciated man-buns. "Two words," she would croon when Olivia mocked that particular preference. "Jason Momoa."

"You realize objectifying a man is just as bad as men objectifying a woman, right?" Olivia always chided her.

Rina eagerly agreed to be Olivia's plus one at the pirate party. "Do you think there will be swag bags?"

"No doubt," Olivia replied.

"Excellent," Rina said. She sold all her swag bags on Etsy and gave the proceeds to a charity that rescued wild horses. Rina ended the call after a few more minutes. Afterward, Olivia wandered into her tiny kitchen and retrieved the pastry box Thomas had brought.

Olivia ate the cannolis and then called in a full order of crispy sweet and sour chicken and fried dry green beans from the nearest City Wok, devouring everything, including the rice and fortune cookie.

While she was eating, she opened her laptop and Googled "Thomas Churchill" to see what he'd been up to. She'd consciously avoided doing that for years, afraid that if she started stalking him online it would end badly.

She went to TMZ first, and the site did not disappoint. There was a story about Thomas donating a chunk of money to a literacy project in the town where he'd shot his last movie. There was a shot of him coming out of the Popeye's Chicken on Laurel Canyon with a snarky comment about what he'd ordered and the suggestion he should lay off the biscuits if he wanted to keep his six-pack abs. Just a little lower in the feed was a picture that showed off those abs to perfection as Thomas walked along the beach in front of his condo. Olivia knew Thomas hated being objectified like that, but she had to admit, it was a great picture.

I really need to read TMZ more often, she thought to herself, clicking past the ten thousand articles dedicated to musicians behaving badly. Then she saw it: an obituary for Thomas' father.

Oh, Tommy.

She had adored her ex-father-in-law. Robert Churchill had worked the assembly line at an auto parts factory in Janesville until it had shut down when the car manufacturer took the plant overseas. He'd been in his late fifties then and hadn't known what he was going to do for a living. Refusing to succumb to despair, he'd taught himself electrical engineering by watching YouTube videos, a skill that had brought him a second career and job security. A widower, he'd even started dating again and, the last she had heard, was getting pretty serious with a woman he'd met in church.

Olivia scanned the article for the names of survivors, but only Thomas was listed.

Robert had died in a car accident, the victim of a drunk driver who'd also died.

Olivia felt a pang that Thomas hadn't even thought to call her and give her the news. He'd known how much she loved his father.

She was about to get angry with him all over again when she noticed the date on Robert's obit. Checking her phone, she saw there had been three calls from Thomas the day he'd died. Calls she'd ignored because he hadn't left a message. Calls she hadn't wanted to return because talking to him was torture.

Grief threatened to overwhelm her, along with pity and sorrow for the man she knew she still loved, no matter how much she wanted to deny it. It made her sad that she hadn't responded to him when his father had died. Thomas hadn't come to her mother's funeral, but he had sent Olivia flowers and a note reminding her he was there if she needed him. She'd been so overwhelmed at the time, she hadn't acted on the invitation. And then pride had kept her from following up.

Olivia sighed. She'd worked so hard to be a strong and independent woman, and yet there was still so much baggage she needed to lose. She was about to power off the computer when a new posting popped up on the TMZ site.

It was the picture of Thomas kissing her at the restaurant. From the angle of the shot, it wasn't obvious he was only kissing her on her cheek. Her face was obscured, but Laura's smiling face was front and center.

She clicked away to avoid reading the comments on the story.

She had learned the hard way that no good ever came from reading the comments on a news story.

*

Invitations to the launch party for *Seadog* were hand delivered rolled up in old bottles and made to look like treasure maps with X marking the spot at the Warner Bros. sound stage where the event would be held. Olivia felt a stab of nostalgia at the sight of the iconic water tower as she and Rina pulled in and were directed to the parking lot to their left.

When she'd first moved to Los Angeles, she and Rina had lived in an apartment building a block away and across the street from the Warner Ranch. Despite the fence around it, they'd been able to watch filming from the makeshift deck on the roof of their building. It had all seemed very exciting to get a "behind-the-scenes" look.

Everyone they knew had been broke, and they'd often made meals from the samples given out at grocery stores and at See's candies. The company where Rina had worked paid for lunches as a perk, and she'd bring leftovers home. It was an existence only a twenty-something could love, and they had loved it.

Olivia had found a young agent who was broke too—driving his brother-in-law's Mercedes in return for detailing it every weekend and living in his sister's spare room so he could buy nice suits and play at being a player. Edgar had badgered casting agents to give Olivia a chance, and she'd built up a reel by stringing twenty short snippets together, the kinds of parts that often didn't have names. Three whole years of her career had been spent playing "feminist party guest" and "convenience store clerk" and "kidnap victim."

"Perhaps it's time you took a course in dental hygiene," her mother had suggested numerous times during those years. "I understand there's a demand for people doing medical billing." For once in her life, Olivia had ignored her mother, defiantly asserting that she was sure her big break was just around the corner.

Amanda, whose belief in luck had run out about the same time as Olivia's father had died, had scoffed at her daughter's bravado, but eventually dropped the subject as the no-name roles gradually gave way to more substantive parts, and then to second leads and co-starring roles. By the time Olivia snagged her breakthrough role in an artsy film called *Incandescent*, Amanda's bitterness had found another target—Olivia's husband Thomas. The two had met on a blind date arranged by his agent, who'd thought they might like each other. They'd married three months later, much to Amanda's chagrin.

Thomas and Amanda had hated each other, and Olivia had been caught between them.

"I can't choose between my husband and my mother," she'd said to Rina at the time. To Rina's credit, she hadn't chimed in on the matter, but had simply let Olivia vent. She knew enough of Olivia's backstory to know that the situation was complicated. Olivia was the youngest, and when her older brother had left for London, leaving his mother angry and ashamed over his sexual orientation, Olivia had tried her best to fill the void by becoming the perfect child.

When her agent had decided he wanted to make movies himself, Olivia had ended up with Laura, and under her care her career had flourished. She owed her a lot. And she had negotiated a handsome deal for her on *Seadog*, bluffing with her "no quote" status to get her twice the money she'd been paid for her last movie.

She was glad she was getting a hefty ten percent out of it after some of the piddly paychecks she'd seen from her one-day appearances in low-budget movies.

She deserved it. *And damn it*, Olivia thought, *I deserve it too*.

The one thing that worried her was the director who'd been hired. His name—and he claimed it was his real name—was Ransom Hawkins. Of course, he wanted to be called "The Hawk," and of course, people obliged him with a straight face, even when he referred to himself in the third person. The one meeting Olivia had had with him so far did not convince her that The Hawk was up to the logistical difficulties of filming on the ocean. "He's only budgeted thirty days shooting for the water scenes," she'd said to Thomas.

"I'm aware," he'd responded, and she could tell from his clipped response that he was worried too. She got the distinct impression that he was stuck with the guy and none too happy about it. He was probably related to one of the producers. The Hawk had a reputation as a diva, but his behavior was tolerated because he was a critic's darling. Indeed, his taste in projects was so anti-commercial, Olivia had been somewhat surprised that he'd signed on to direct a pirate movie.

Perhaps, it will all turn out all right, Olivia thought as she and Rina approached the door to the soundstage where perky young women dressed as sexy pirates were taking names and handing out little keychains with fake gold doubloons attached to them. "Ahoy," Perky Pirate Number One said to Olivia. "Welcome aboard."

Rina was delighted by the cheesiness of it all. The invitation had insisted guests wear "pirate attire," and while Olivia had compromised by donning a pair of black silk trousers and a low-cut frilly white shirt, set off by a purple sash she'd made from a shawl, Rina had embraced the concept and decked herself out in an outfit clearly inspired by Keith Richards playing Johnny Depp's father in *Pirates of the Caribbean*. Many earrings were involved.

Inside, the stage had been dressed to look like a pirate lagoon, complete with a half-submerged ship in the background.

"This reminds me of something," Rina said.

"They've replicated the pirate lair from *The Goonies*," Olivia said. She'd seen the movie dozens of times on cable when she was a teenager. Josh Brolin had been her first celebrity crush.

"Ooh, look at the centerpieces," Rina said as they found seats at a small two-top.

Each table was draped with black Jolly Roger flags held down by small treasure chests filled with gold-wrapped chocolates and jellybean "jewels."

Rina was impressed. "They spent some money on this," she said. "I wonder who sponsored it."

"Some artisanal brand of rum, I think," Olivia said, distracted because she'd just seen Thomas walk in.

By himself.

God, he looks fantastic, Olivia thought, *even with the man-bun and that beard*. She watched him circulate with an ease she envied, charming everyone he spoke to. He caught her looking at him and nodded but gave her nothing else.

"Da-yum," Rina said as she spotted Thomas, "Emphasis on the 'yum.'"

Rina sounds more and more like an American every year, Olivia thought.

"Are those highlights in his hair?"

"It does that naturally," Olivia said. "All he has to do is walk around outside for a couple of hours."

She had never thought it was fair. To get that kind of golden, sun-kissed look had cost her a fortune in time and money.

"You're thinking about him," Rina observed.

"Of course, I'm thinking about him," Olivia snapped. "I'm about to make a movie with my ex-husband."

"Let's go have our fortunes told," Rina said to change the subject.

"Maybe later," Olivia said. "I'm famished." She had not been happy to see a "gypsy" fortune teller's booth set up in a corner of the stage. *Cultural appropriation*, she thought sourly, mostly because she'd straddled the color line all her life, much like the Duchess of Sussex. She'd played parts on both sides, but "colorism" had been an issue a couple of times, and she was sensitive on the subject.

Her attention was diverted by a handsome waiter in pirate costume serving drinks. "Would you beauties care for a cup of grog?"

"God, yes," Rina said, taking a cup and handing it to Olivia before snagging one for herself.

The "grog" turned out to be a sweet and fruity rum punch that went down way too smoothly. The room began to get more animated. Olivia could hear people saying "avast" and calling each other "bilge rat," clearly taking the holiday to heart and talking like pirates. Most of the guests had been creative with their costumes as well. Olivia counted four stuffed parrots and one very real cockatiel. Olivia hoped there wouldn't be birds involved in the production. Her grandmother had kept a budgie that had hated her, puffing up whenever Olivia was around and trying to peck her. She'd be in trouble if a parrot tried to bite her.

Legendary producer Michael Eliades, who had lost a leg in Vietnam, stomped by on a peg-leg he'd swapped for his usual prosthetic. His wife wore a vaguely period-accurate gown and looked radiant. She paused to kiss Olivia's cheek and say how happy she was to see Olivia working again.

Olivia had another cup of grog.

Wait staff circulated with plates of small bites.

"These shrimp mango skewers are sinfully delicious," Rina said, polishing off her fourth or fifth.

"You need to pace yourself," a tall Black woman dressed as a pirate queen commented. "They've got something like ten more courses coming out."

"Your costume is fantastic," Olivia said. "Did you design it yourself?"

"No, I'm a production accountant. My brother's the designer. I'm kind of his muse."

"It's absolutely gorgeous," Rina said. "I love watered silk."

"Hand-dyed," the Pirate Queen said. "Using authentic period color made from beets." The woman looked at Rina. "What are you, about a size eighteen?"

Rina looked a little taken aback by the personal question, but said, "Yes, why?"

"Because my brother designs for full-figured women such as you and me, and he needs more customers. Do you have an Instagram account?"

"Yes."

"Excellent. Let's go meet Jimi."

Rina didn't have to be asked twice. "You'll be all right?" she asked Olivia.

"I'll be fine," Olivia assured her.

"Sorry, sweetie," the Pirate Queen said to Olivia, not sounding apologetic at all. "You're not at all his type."

"Have fun," she said to Rina and settled back in her seat, wondering what the next course would be.

She knew she'd have to get some food into her.

"Livvy," said a passing woman Olivia didn't recognize. A publicist, maybe? "Darling," the woman said and kissed Olivia's cheek. "I just saw Thomas. Is it true you two are back together?"

Now Olivia recognized the woman. Jacklyn Eastman. She'd parlayed her scoop and subsequent coverage of Olivia and Thomas' divorce into a semi-regular position on one of the all-celebrity, all-the-time cable shows. She'd brightened her hair, which was now cut in a curly lob, and it looked like she might have had some plastic surgery.

"No," Olivia said, with what she hoped was a breezy tone. "Just for the movie, I'm afraid."

"Do you think it'll be hard filming a romantic adventure with your ex-husband?" the woman asked, her eyes glinting, eager for a bit of gossip.

Before Olivia could say something she might regret, Rina was back at her elbow in rescue mode. "Jacklyn," she said in a very fake tone. "Do you mind if I borrow Olivia? There's a pirate captain who wants to say hello." Without waiting for the woman's reply, Rina drew her away.

"Thank you," Olivia said gratefully. "So, what did the designer have to say?"

"He wants me to come into his atelier next week," Rina said happy to turn the conversation away from Jacklyn. "He's going to make me some clothes for the price of the materials if I pimp him out on Instagram."

"That sounds like a good deal," Olivia said.

"I need to find a bathroom," Rina said. "Those punches are going right through me."

"I'll see if I can find us another seat," Olivia said, but Rina had already been swallowed up by the pirate-talking crowd.

"Olivia," a young man wearing an eyepatch called out as she passed his table. It took her a moment to recognize Conor Tarr, the screenwriter. He was with a forty-something couple she assumed were his parents. His dad was dressed in a "dad" version of a pirate outfit while his mother rocked an elegant black dress. Conor introduced his parents. His mother knew Olivia's work and said nice things; his father was cordial but much more interested in the crab cakes on his plate than making small talk.

Conor steered Olivia over to a quietish corner so they could talk. "I'm so glad you agreed to be in *Seadog*," he said. "I wrote the part of Justine for you."

"Really?" she said, not certain if he was sincere.

"I saw you play Lady Macbeth last year in San Diego. You were stunning."

"Thank you," she said, stunned and a little humbled. "How did you come to write a pirate movie?" she asked. "Most UCLA graduates I've met want to write terribly important movies that put people to sleep."

"Like Gore Verbinski and Francis Ford Coppola," he said, making fun of her for being presumptuous but not in a mean way. "Why do you prefer making important, boring movies to genre film?" he asked her, turning the tables.

"It's not that I don't—" she began, but he waved her denial away.

"I know you were offered the part of Hannah in *The Chilling Place*," he said. "That was a good script."

"I don't believe in ghosts," she said. "I'm not a good enough actress to make it real."

He was about to say something when they were distracted by a huge splash.

"Someone just walked the plank," Conor said as a guest climbed out of the fake lagoon.

"Seriously?"

"First rule of screenwriting," he said. "If there are people around a pool, someone has to get wet before the third act. It's a Chekhov's Gun."

Olivia decided she liked Conor a lot.

"Seriously, why'd you take this job?" he asked.

"I needed the money," she said and then realized that she'd probably had at least one too many of the rum punches. "And it was a good script," she added belatedly.

He laughed. "You're a better actress than you give yourself credit for, Olivia. I almost believed that."

"I didn't mean to insult you, Conor. I thought it was well-researched, and the character isn't a ninny."

"My girlfriend would have given me hell if I'd made her a ninny," he said.

"Is she here?" Olivia asked, wanting to meet the woman who'd refused to let her boyfriend fall into the old sexist tropes.

"No, she's on call tonight."

"Doctor?"

"Trauma surgeon," he said. "Her younger brother was my roommate at UCLA." He looked around. "She'd enjoy this, I think."

"What's not to like about rum drinks and crab cakes?"

"No, she works hard to keep her inner child alive. The ER is a real gun and knife club, and she likes retreating into fantasy to get that out of her head."

"What's her name?"

"Katy," he said.

"You named Justine's mother after her."

"I did."

"You're a romantic," Olivia said. "I approve." As a teenager she'd thought that women were all about the romance and that men simply indulged them. Later, she'd come to realize that the men she knew were much more romantic than many of the women. That had certainly been true of Thomas, who had been inventive in dreaming up low-cost romantic escapades for the two of them—such as her favorite midnight picnics. Trips to Mount Pinos to watch the meteor showers, wrapped up in blankets and drinking hot chocolate out of thermoses. Later, when they'd both started to achieve some traction, there had been surprise trips to Ojai for the day to catch a

Shakespeare play or visits to obscure museums followed by feasts of street food. Life with Thomas had been fun.

She missed that. Missed it more than she'd let herself acknowledge.

*

It took Olivia a while to find a vacant table. She'd no sooner sat down than Thomas appeared beside her. "Is this seat taken?" Thomas asked, removing the purse she'd set on the empty chair to reserve it for Rina, and sliding into the seat as if she'd been saving it for him all along.

Maybe I was, she thought. She looked over at his plate, which was full of things that smelled good but that she couldn't immediately identify.

"Hello, me proud beauty," he said.

"If you say, 'Want to see my jolly roger?' I will strangle you with that ridiculous headscarf you're wearing."

"Fair enough," he said. "But I was going to go with, 'Could I drop anchor in your lagoon?'"

"Eeuw."

He shrugged. "There's a whole bunch of suggested pirate pick-up lines online."

"Do I even want to know?"

He grinned. "I'd like to shoot me cannon through your porthole."

"Again, I say, eeuw."

"Want to see me cannonballs?"

"Stop," Olivia said, laughing.

"Blow me down?"

She gave him a look.

He put up his hands defensively. "Don't blame me. You can Google it under Talk Like a Pirate Day."

"I wonder if any of those cheesy lines work."

"Not with proud beauties, I'd say," Thomas said. "But let me know."

Olivia ignored that and stared at Thomas' plate. "What are you eating?"

"I think this is fried plantains," he said. "It was the only thing I could find that was vegan, although I think they fried them in butter."

"No cow has to die to produce butter," Olivia said, wondering when Thomas had gone vegan. When they'd lived together, he'd rarely eaten any vegetables other than potatoes.

As if he'd heard her question, Thomas looked up. "I went dairy free last year and decided to try the vegan thing." He looked at the plantains on his plate and up at her. "Want a bite?"

As if it were the most natural thing in the world, Thomas offered her a taste from his fork. And as if it was the most natural thing in the world, she tasted the bite.

"Good," she said, which was an understatement. She wondered who'd catered the event, because the fried plantains were better than those at Versailles, the Cuban restaurant that served them as a side dish to their addictively garlicky roast chicken.

She watched him eat for a while, simply enjoying the nearness. She wanted so much to reach out and touch him but was afraid to. His manner toward her was warm but superficial, no more than he showed to the other people in the room. That hurt so much.

"Tell me who's who," she said as a middle-aged couple dressed like Jack Sparrow's grandparents passed by with plates piled high with seafood salad.

"That's Jennifer Gold," Thomas said. "She got custody of her husband Jason's production company, Gold Standard, when they divorced. This'll be the first movie she's produced by herself."

Olivia wanted to ask why they'd gotten divorced, but instead asked, "Who's the guy?"

"That's Shaheen Zad. He owns a distribution company. Be nice to him."

"How nice?"

"On a scale of one to ten, about an eight. You don't have to overdo it. He's heard you don't like schmoozing."

Olivia gave Thomas a sour look. "You didn't used to like schmoozing either," she observed.

He shrugged. "Shaheen's a good guy. Loves movies and genuinely roots for every single one he buys."

Someone took their picture, and then so did someone else.

"You know we're going to be all over TMZ come tomorrow," Thomas said.

"Maybe we should give them something to talk about," Olivia suggested, thinking, *Take that Jacklyn.*

For the first time, something that looked like uncertainty flickered on his face.

"Sure," he said. And making a show of it, he put down his fork, gathered her in his arms, and kissed her.

This was such a bad idea, Olivia thought, but her body responded to him like it always had, and when their lips parted, it felt like part of her was being ripped away.

Thomas' eyes were serious as he searched her face for her reaction, then, heartened by what he saw there, he stood up and bowed to the applauding crowd.

As if it was a joke, Olivia thought.

"I'll see you on the set," Thomas said, clearly unaffected by the kiss.

"Yes," Olivia said faintly. "I expect you shall."

No sooner had Thomas sauntered—no, swaggered—off, than Rina finally appeared. "That was quite a spectacle," she said.

"Are you ready to go?" Olivia asked.

"*Vamonos*," Rina said, and that was all she said until they were in her car, headed for Olivia's apartment. "You know, he couldn't take his eyes off you all night."

"I didn't notice," Olivia said.

"Whose idea was the kiss?"

"Mine," Olivia said miserably.

"Your instincts are good."

"He kissed me and then he walked away, Rina."

"Who walked away from him first?"

"What?"

"Don't hate me, Livvy. But I've watched you torture yourself for the last couple of years. You're still in love with Thomas, and I'm pretty sure he's still in love with you. And what both of you need to do is get stranded on a deserted island somewhere to figure that out." Rina looked at Olivia sideways. "Or stuck together on a film set."

*

By the third day of filming, everyone heartily detested The Hawk. He'd managed to alienate everyone from the local production caterer to legendary French actor Jean-Jacques Lapin, who'd been coaxed out of retirement to play a small but pivotal role.

The Hawk's brother—the crew called him "Little Hawk" behind his back—was the first AD on the shoot, and nobody got close to the director without going through him first. Olivia had gotten very tired of having to relay everything through a third party.

All of the things that could go wrong on a difficult shoot went wrong. Seasickness was an ongoing problem. Within a week, the production was behind schedule and over budget. Someone on the set was leaking info to the press, and the advance buzz was starting to get horrible.

Conor, who'd paid his own way to be on set, was relentlessly optimistic. "Everyone thought *Avatar* was going to be a bomb," he said, "and then it made half a bazillion dollars."

The Hawk had arranged for Conor to be cast as one of the pirate extras, and the screenwriter was over the moon, not realizing it was the director's way of keeping him out from underfoot so he could rewrite chunks of dialogue himself.

And it wasn't just dialogue he wanted to change.

The day Olivia and Thomas shot their first love scene was incredibly awkward. "You'd think we'd never done this before," Thomas whispered in Olivia's ear as they maneuvered around each other in pretend passion.

"Cut," The Hawk yelled. "Livvy, I really need to see your tit."

"Not in my contract," she said. In truth, she might have considered it—it was a love scene after all, and she'd done tasteful nudity a couple of times—but yelling it out in front of everyone annoyed her.

"Livvy," he whined.

"We're behind schedule," Thomas said to end the discussion and shut down the Hawk. "Let's do this."

"Thank you," she whispered to him.

"Anytime."

It was The Hawk's custom to screen dailies for everyone back at the little hotel they'd commandeered. The purpose of the exercise was less to keep people in the loop as it was to provide an audience to mirror The Hawk's self-aggrandizement and tell him what a genius he was. Attendance had fallen off sharply by the middle of the shoot, but the day the love scene was shot, there was a larger than usual crowd back at the hotel for the screening.

"Wow," Conor said after watching the scene. "You guys are hot." Olivia gave him a disapproving look, and he backpedaled. "I mean, your acting is really—"

"It is a hot scene," one of the grips said, and this time it was Thomas who gave him a dirty look.

"Grow up," he said, and then he left the room.

The longer the shoot went on, the more morale deteriorated. Thomas set up soccer games and other diversions to build team spirit, but The Hawk never participated, preferring to stay in his room with Little Hawk. Pressure from the studio was mounting. It was becoming clear that there was no way they'd be able to finish principal photography on schedule, and Jennifer Gold had sent her production accountant Tina Langford—the woman Olivia had met at the party dressed as the Pirate Queen—to see what she could do to salvage things.

Rather than treat her as an ally, The Hawk freaked out, and paranoia kicked in. He was certain she was there to personally ruin his life.

Everything came to a head the day The Hawk was supposed to shoot a tricky scene that involved Olivia's character falling off the ship. Her stunt double was ready to go when The Hawk approached Olivia and said, "I need you to do the stunt yourself, Livvy."

Olivia had looked over at her stunt double in a panic.

"Shari?" she said.

"It's too dangerous," Shari said.

"I need her to do it, Shari."

"I can't," Olivia said. "I'm not a strong swimmer, and the sea's choppy."

"You'll be fine," The Hawk said and looked at his watch, a showy timepiece she knew had cost more than most economy cars.

Out of the corner of her eye, Olivia could see the Stunt Coordinator walking toward them.

"Hawk, I'm in sixty percent of the shots. If I drown, you don't have a movie."

"They managed to finish *Fast and Furious Seven*," he replied smugly, "even after Paul Walker died."

You are a horrible person, Olivia thought. And while she was thinking that, she missed the look The Hawk gave Little Hawk.

"Rolling," Little Hawk shouted.

And The Hawk pushed Olivia overboard.

She hit the water so hard it felt solid, and it pushed all the air out of her lungs. Unable to breathe, she fell and fell and fell. Her costume clung to her like a shroud. Though made of light fabric, its sodden weight pulled her down. Frantic, she tried to breathe and ended up swallowing water.

Her vision was starting to dim when she felt strong arms close around her, pulling her up. Desperate to reach the surface, she practically climbed up Thomas' body and nearly pulled him back under.

She was nearly unconscious by the time he pulled her out of the water and onto the sandy beach. He turned her over and pounded on her back.

She coughed out water and gasped for air.

"Livvy," Thomas said, and there was something in his voice she hadn't heard for a long time.

She clung to him like a kitten, gulping more air until she could finally talk. "I'm all right, Tommy. I'm all right."

Suddenly a shadow blocked out the sun. The Hawk was standing over them.

"Livvy, I need you to get dried off. We didn't get the shot."

No sooner had the words left his mouth than Thomas stood up and punched him in the face.

"What the—"

The Hawk went down, and Thomas put his foot on his throat so he couldn't get back up. "You nearly drowned my wife," he said, his voice deadly calm.

Wife? Olivia thought, and his use of the word gave her a thrill.

Thomas looked at Olivia. "You want to kick him?"

"No, I'm good," she said, though she really, really did want to kick The Hawk, preferably in his balls.

"You're fired," Little Hawk yelled.

Thomas laughed.

"I got it all, Church," Shari said, holding out her cell phone. She looked down at The Hawk. "Assault. Attempted murder. And the insurance company is not going to be too happy with you either." Shari looked over at the Stunt Coordinator for confirmation.

He nodded grimly. "I could shut you down right now," he told The Hawk.

Tina, who'd been on the beach watching the filming, came over with her cell phone. She looked at Thomas. "Jennifer wants to talk to Big Bird."

Thomas nodded and backed off as The Hawk took the phone.

Thomas came to kneel beside Olivia on the sand. His hand reached out as if to clasp hers, then stopped short, as if he wasn't sure how welcome his touch would be.

"You love me," she said, wonderingly. "Rina said you did, but I didn't believe it."

"Not sure what Rina has to do with it," he said.

"But you do, don't you?" Olivia asked.

"Never stopped."

"Then why have you been so mean to me? Acting like you didn't care when I kissed you? Acting like it was all business between us when I clearly… wanted things to be the way they were?"

Thomas sighed and ran his hand through his wet hair, raking it back from his face. Finally, he said, "I guess, it's because I wanted to punish you," he said. "Plain and simple, I wanted you to feel what I've felt these last few years." He looked away, toward The Hawk, who was now shouting into the phone. "I know you were hurt. I know I destroyed your trust. But I hoped we could work past that. But then your mother—" He stopped himself.

"My mother," Olivia said. "I know. I know now." She took his hand. "I'm so sorry."

"Don't cry," he said, but it was too late.

She could feel tears falling. "Do you think we can fix this?" Olivia asked. "This stupid, stupid thing I've done."

"We've done," he said. "I should have fought harder for you."

"Why her?" Olivia asked, realizing she'd never asked him that before, only reacted to his protests that nothing had happened.

"There was no 'her,' Olivia. There was only ever you." His eyes sought hers. "Miranda and her publicist thought it would be great publicity if it looked like we were having an affair. Kind of a *Mr. & Mrs. Smith* kind of thing. Are they or aren't they? And the idea was people would be intrigued enough to see the movie, to see if they could detect the chemistry."

"It was all about selling tickets?"

"More like making Miranda a household name." Thomas' expression darkened. "She found out the hard way that fame and notoriety aren't the same thing. I'm not the only one who'll never work with her again."

"And you tried to tell me," Olivia said, "but I was too angry to listen."

"You weren't the only angry one," he said. "I took some anger management classes. Did some exercises. Realized I needed to be a better guy, even if I wasn't cheating. When my father died, it put things in a whole new perspective."

"I'm sorry I didn't pick up your calls," Olivia said. "I didn't realize—"

"I don't blame you," Thomas said.

"So," she said. "What happens now?"

"Reboot?" he asked, hopefully.

Before Olivia could answer, Tina called out to Thomas, "Jennifer wants to talk to you, Thomas."

Thomas gave Olivia a look and squeezed her hand before standing and walking over to take the phone. Hawk and Little Hawk were already halfway down the beach.

Tina came over to where Olivia was sitting. "Are you really all right? Do you need to see a doctor?"

"I'm fine," Olivia said. "What's going on?"

"Jennifer wants Thomas to direct the rest of the movie. There isn't time to bring someone else up to speed. The guild might squawk some, but Thomas has his DGA card. And with that video Shari shot, I don't think there's going to be too much sympathy for Mr. Hawkins."

*

Two hours later, filming resumed. Thomas made a speech to the cast and crew, asking for their help and rallying them to the cause. Then with the Second AD filling in for Little Hawk, and Conor madly pulling scenes apart and rewriting as he and Thomas consulted between takes, a plan for finishing the film began to take shape.

As the days ticked down and the pressure on everyone increased—Tina was under orders to stop the filming if it went even one second over the projected days—Thomas was confident and secure, and everyone followed his lead. Conor was a wizard. He stayed cool too and seemed to thrive on the pressure.

"How do you stay so calm?" Olivia asked him one morning as they waited for the fog to clear.

"One of the things Carrie Fisher used to say," he said. "Bad life, good anecdote. This is going to make such a cool story."

You are so adorable, Olivia thought.

*

The last shot of the film took place at the magic hour on the very last scheduled day. It was a simple enough setup—with Olivia and Thomas looking out to sea. "Does this shot say 'sequel' or what?" Thomas asked as they held their pose for a ten-count.

"Don't jinx it," Olivia said.

The words "that's a wrap" had never sounded sweeter, and when all the equipment was packed up, the remaining cast and crew headed back to the little hotel they'd taken over as headquarters during the shoot. There were three people waiting for them—Jennifer Gold, who was there to thank everyone for hanging in; Thomas' assistant Shavonne, who had a rough cut of the first trailer on her laptop; and a small, serious-looking woman with enormous glasses and an asymmetrical haircut. Conor's face lit up when he saw her, and the two hugged so tightly it looked like they were trying to merge into one organism.

Olivia watched the two affectionately and glanced over at Thomas. "The girlfriend?"

"Katy Nguyen," he said.

"You had something to do with this, didn't you?"

"I had some extra air miles."

"They're adorable," Olivia said.

Thomas smiled. "They are."

After drinks and snacks, everyone gathered around Shavonne's computer to watch the trailer. When it was over, everyone cheered.

"We made us a movie," Jennifer said, pumping her fist like a teenager.

"I think we might have," Thomas said, smiling, and then everyone watched the trailer again.

About an hour later, Thomas leaned over to yell in Olivia's ear, "Do you want to get out of here?"

"Yes," she said and took his hand as he led her out the nearest door and down to the beach. The moon was so bright, they had no trouble making their way to the edge of the water. Despite the lateness of the hour, the air was mild. Since his rescue of her, Olivia and Thomas had not found a minute to be together. They'd brushed up against each other as they passed and exchanged a few stolen kisses, but when they were on the clock there was no time to indulge themselves, and they'd been on the clock since The Hawk had been fired.

Neither Olivia nor Thomas seemed inclined to say anything, so for a while, they simply walked along the beach in companionable silence, kicking off their shoes to squish barefoot through the wet sand. When they came to the rock formation they'd dubbed "the Mermaid's Chair," Olivia sat down and patted the smooth rock beside her.

To her surprise, Thomas remained standing.

"Will you marry me, Livvy?" he asked. "Again?"

"Ask me on your knees, bilge rat," she said.

He obligingly dropped to his knees and reached for her hands. "Will you?"

Olivia found she couldn't speak, so she threw her arms around his neck and buried her face in his chest. It felt so good.

It feels like home.

"The beard has to go," she said.

"So that's a yes, then?" Thomas asked.

"Yes."

"I don't have a ring."

"I'll take your watch," she said.

"Deal," he said, and he unbuckled the strap.

About the Author

Born in Washington, D.C., Katherine Moore now lives in a small Pacific Northwest town very much like Silver Birch. She has worked as a food writer, a caterer, and a movie extra as well as a freelance lifestyle reporter and staff writer for magazines in Honolulu, Los Angeles, and Richmond, Virginia.

Website: kattomic-energy.blogspot.com
Twitter: @eyeofthekat

Feral Heart
♥
Regina Griffiths

Story Information

Holiday: Feral Cat Day
Holiday Date: October 16
Heat Rating: 2
Relationship Type: M/F
Major Trigger Warnings: Secondary character death, depression, smoking, animal trauma, discussion of death, discussion of suicide, discussion of miscarriage, descriptions of blood, MFC and cat are both injured, though not badly, mention of medical procedures.

Candice hopes her childhood home will offer her comfort and a place to hide from a life that's not turning out the way she wanted. She doesn't expect a cat and an old friend to complicate things and send life spinning out of her control.

Feral Heart

Candice's favorite spot on the wraparound porch of her childhood home had many advantages. Sure, the white peeling paint got all over her dark clothes. The railing occasionally offered a gentle protesting creak at her weight. Those minor flaws didn't outweigh the draw of a place where, on a muggy August afternoon, no one *else* was inclined to linger on the west side of the house. She could spend hours sitting on the railing, her back against a column with sunlight beating against her eyelids as she listened to the world and let her mind float, unthinking. Spending time out here meant not having to talk to her mother, not having to answer questions or deflect well-meaning comments.

They were always, always, always well-*meant*. As if that helped.

I should go in, she thought for the fourth time in an hour, fingers twitching toward the pocket of her skirt. Kitchen sounds floated through the open screen door, slightly muted by their passage through the laundry room. Her mother was baking, probably. Or preparing to bake, or cleaning up from baking. *It's practically compulsive*, she thought. There were enough paths through the house that Candice could easily avoid passing through her mother's domain, so the sounds that came from it always had a faintly mysterious air to her. As a kid, she'd preferred the outdoors and the workshop—

Candice's thoughts, breath, and motion stuttered to an infinitesimal halt, eyes flicking open and across the garden. Not even the foundation was left, but a large rectangle of dirt remained like a ghost among the living green grass.

An unexpected danger of coming home, she'd found. *Memories*. She'd run from one set smack into the arms of another.

She drew a deep steadying breath and pulled an old, engraved cigarette case from her pocket. She wasn't allowed to smoke in the house. She wasn't allowed to come in right after she smoked, either.

That was at least another half an hour's worth of reasons to stay outside, much as she'd always hated the habit. It had been hell picking it up. Somewhere in the half-unpacked boxes littering her room were three or four bright containers of cigarettes that smelled too much like memory. These, at least, mostly smelled like cloves.

The crunch of tires on gravel coincided with the flick of her lighter, and Candice cocked her head, curious in spite of herself, and blew a futile breath at the dark curls tumbling into her eyes. Sweat glued the summer frizz to her forehead, defying the half-hearted puffs of air.

In the twelve days she'd been home, this was the first unexpected visitor. It was almost intriguing enough to tempt her from her perch.

On second thought, an unexpected visitor probably meant she'd have to be polite to some old condescending crony of her grandmother's. If there were any left, after all these years, who could still make the social rounds. *Nana sure never goes anywhere.* Candice pulled her pale feet closer to the shelter of her body, as if the new arrival could see her through a house weighed down by a century of haphazard additions. As if curling into herself would hide her away.

The sound of tires on gravel was followed by footsteps moving from driveway to lawn to creaking porch. A knock at the front door followed, and Candice coughed out a harsh breath of smoke in her surprise. Her mom's voice, high in cheerful greeting, was entirely normal. The response was a low rumble, unmistakably masculine. *Does Mom have a boyfriend? Ugh, I don't want to think about that.*

The offhand thought fluttered away in surprise at the vibration of her porch rail. She straightened and shook her head, refocusing on the here, the now, the new arrival in her territory. This one was also unmistakably masculine. A fluffy orange cat, half again as big as her ex's idiot terrier, was seated on the far end of the rail, watching her.

"Shit, buddy," she heard herself say, still half-focused on the voices in the house. She couldn't hear what was being said, but the footsteps winding up the back set of stairs and across Nana's sun-porch, directly above her, were clear enough. "You've been through the wars, huh?"

From one tattered ear to a tail like right-angle pipes, she'd never seen a more ragged cat. As if he could sense the path of her thoughts, the cat shook himself and stood up, arching and giving her a yellow-eyed glance. *Yeah,* those eyes seemed to say, *but you should see the other guys.*

Her lips quirked unwillingly even as she flicked her cigarette at him. "Yeah, yeah. Shoo. Nobody wants you here, buddy. This is a dog house." Though she wasn't sure if Nana's geriatric pug, Pogo, *really* counted. He definitely didn't have the presence of the big dogs they'd had when she was a kid. Though, to be fair to Pogo, it was hard to have the same impact as a trio of hyperactive Labradors when you were fifteen and weighed less than a Thanksgiving turkey.

That low voice sounded again, this time drifting down from the room above. Her Nana's voice responded in a familiar cadence and tone. Those querulous notes were etched into her bones and her soul.

"Ah!" The jolt of pain at her fingertips startled her into a gasp. The cigarette, barely smoked but still merrily burning, now sat on the porch instead of in her grasp. The ember glowed sullenly, and she slid down to stamp it out in the same mood, holding her singed finger in her mouth for lack of any better solution. Butter would have been her mother's suggestion, but damned if she was going into that kitchen to get it.

Getting back onto the railing was an awkward job. It had definitely been designed for leaning, not climbing or being sat upon, especially when the climber barely topped 5'1" and featured curves that would have qualified as zaftig if she'd been a foot taller. At her height, she was just round.

At the apex of the inelegant maneuver, the screen door creaked open and clanged shut, providing someone—*dear God let it be Mom*—a view of her beskirted ass sticking in the air as she balanced on her knees, one hand braced on the column. A distinctly masculine throat-clearing followed on the heels of that thought, and Candice had to stifle a bark of laughter as she wondered if she could just stay very still and hope the roses on her skirt would blend into the scenery. *I'm not here. Would you believe I'm not here?*

"Fuck," she hissed instead, forgoing safety concerns and finishing her scramble as quickly as possible. Giving up the high ground now was simply unacceptable.

When she was settled and let herself look up, she shivered despite the heat. The tall man leaning against the door frame definitely wasn't her mom's boyfriend. The last time she'd seen that face, it had been sun-darkened from tawny topaz to almost copper—still childishly round at sixteen—and under a cloud of dark curls even more voluminous than her own. His hair was clipped close to his scalp now. The baby fat had melted away, revealing sharp cheekbones, but the same freckles still danced across his broad nose. The wide-set hazel eyes still carried a glint of humor. It was a less awkward face than it had been in adolescence—not *quite* handsome, but… interesting. Bright. Alive, as if he were always looking outward and liking what he saw.

One of her mother's prize-winning lemon bars rested in his elegantly long-fingered hand. Isaac Shaw raised it in salute to the cat before transferring his gaze to her, his expression shifting from sardonically acknowledging to cautiously polite.

"Oh my God, Isaac," Candice finally blurted.

His face brightened. "And here I thought you'd forgotten me, Candy!"

She shivered and half-snarled her low response, "Don't call me that."

The brightness in his eyes shuttered immediately. Something twinged in her chest. Chagrin, maybe. Regret. She pushed on anyway, annoyed at the sudden lurch of clumsy eagerness that surged in her at the sheer familiarity radiating from him. *Hush*, she told herself. *We're not here to make friends, new ones or old.* It didn't matter what she'd felt at sixteen when they'd been thick as thieves and swirling with hormones. It didn't matter that she'd spent time in his kitchen, his mother's pale face flushed as she carefully tried to make the Haitian recipes passed down from her husband's mother. It didn't matter what they might have had, before… She shook the flare of memory away like her discarded cigarette. "Don't tell me you're still creeping around this dump."

Whatever remained of friendliness—and possibly hope—leaked away from his smile, leaving behind only polite fiction. "Every other Sunday," he agreed quietly. "For Pogo's arthritis shots." A twitch of the shoulders like an aborted shrug. "He'd do fine with an oral anti-inflammatory, but your gran seems to like the company, so…"

She pulled out the cigarette case and took another, ignoring his raised eyebrow and dubious *hmm* as he watched. *Yes, it's a filthy habit*, Candice thought at him. *Like you don't have any vices.* She'd known all of his, once, but everyone changed. "So you're the vet. Good for you. Take that mangy thing when you leave." She gestured with the unlit cigarette at the cat, still sitting calmly at the end of the railing. He seemed, with his patiently attentive expression, to be a part of the conversation. He blinked bright yellow eyes at her gesture and after a moment seemed to take it as an invitation, standing again and sauntering toward her with a noise like a smoker's cough.

Attention caught by this violation of her personal space, Candice was startled by the suddenness of Isaac's low chuckle.

"You don't recognize him, do you?"

She frowned, curious in spite of herself, attention swinging back and briefly caught on the width of his shoulders. The battered ball of fluff didn't seem familiar. "Should I?"

"Huh." He seemed nonplussed. "That litter of kittens we rescued out of the old barn at my aunt's place, remember? The year before you left."

Not a summer she wanted to remember. She'd rolled that stretch of months up a long time ago, wrapped it around her grief and carefully tucked it away. She considered telling him so. *My dad died that year, asshole, do you remember?* It took all her effort to clench her teeth against it and think of something else. Anything else.

A thread came loose unbidden, dangling invitingly in her mind. An early summer carefree wandering in the woods, laughing and chasing and tickling each other, turned into a quest for the source of plaintive cries. It had been pleasantly warm, the kind of day when cool breezes and hot sunlight strike a perfect equilibrium, nothing like this sticky lingering August heat. They'd felt like brave heroes, hadn't they, daring to climb through a decaying and probably spider-filled barn. She was vaguely ill at the thought of the fragile wood they'd clambered over to reach the noises, vaguely amazed that they'd managed it without some perilous injury. There'd been five kittens in that web-strewn barn: three gray, one pale cream, and… yeah. One a fluff of pure marigold. Her gaze refocused on the cat.

"He certainly smells like he's that old." *Go away*, she thought at both of them.

Psychically unaware of her mental demand, Isaac popped the last of the lemon bar into his mouth. "The grays disappeared a long time back." His face remained passive, but his eyes darkened. "Fox, maybe. Coyotes. It's hard to tell, when they just up and vanish. Used to see them lurking around the feed store by the post office a lot before that."

"The other one?" The question was pulled out of her almost unwilling by her curiosity. "There was a girl, right? Sort of pale, like coffee with way too much cream."

"You do remember." His lips twitched into a smile that even in irritation never seemed far from his face. "My cousin kept that one, actually. Even took her to college with him."

Yes. She remembered that, Candice realized, and shied away from the thought. She hadn't wanted to remember that summer, and damn this walking fragment of her history for bringing it up. She let her face go stony, settled into it like a second skin. "So, does he creep around here too—" she flicked the still-unlit cigarette at the cat again "—or is that just you?"

A flush bronzed Isaac's cheeks. She felt almost guilty—almost—at the hurt that flickered across his features. After a moment, he rocked back a half-step. Barely a few inches, but the added distance fell heavily between them, thick with silence. "Your mom said you were in a bad mood," he finally muttered, voice flat. "I'll let you be."

"*Thank* you." It was meant as a snarl, but her voice cracked in a far-too-plaintive way. He didn't respond, turning and striding away—around the porch, not through the kitchen—stung pride in the set of his departing shoulders.

The cat chirped again, and Candice half-turned, hissing through her teeth as loud as she could. It stared back with equanimity. She inhaled to do it again, and the cat took that opportunity to leave, dropping to the porch with a heavy thud and trotting away in the opposite direction from Isaac without a care in the world. Candice released the breath in a long, stuttering sigh.

Candice remained on the railing long minutes after the gravel crunched beneath Isaac's departing tires, even as the late afternoon sun dropped drowsily beyond the distant horizon and painted the world pink and gold. Somehow, with her uninvited company gone, the porch felt different. Empty instead of quiet. Pleasant solitude transmuted to uneasy isolation.

Fuck this. I'll be all over mosquito bites if I'm out here any longer. She slid down from her high perch one last time, into the laundry room and up the back stairs to her room and whatever whiskey was left from last night.

*

"Candy—"

"Cand*ice*," Candice muttered. Her mom didn't seem to hear it over the general susurrus of the fall fair.

The old fairgrounds withstood the crowd admirably. The area's agricultural heyday had fled the scene well before Candice had been born, and the population now seemed much like the house: cheerful enough, but falling to pieces from age.

I'm not afraid of crowds. The mantra had started five minutes into the ticket line. *I have lived in a city. I cannot possibly be afraid of crowds.* She wondered when it would start helping.

"*Candy!*" Her mother stopped in her tracks, knocking the spiral of thoughts sideways. "Did you hear a single thing I just said to you?"

"Candi—" Candice began, then sighed. "No."

"I swear to—" It was her mother's turn to sigh, one pale and garnet-nailed hand raising to cover her eyes in a familiar gesture. After a moment she went on, voice painstakingly even and scrupulously kind in way that made Candice want to shrink in on herself. "Would you like to go home, Candy?"

The softness of it cut deeper than any sharp note of irritation would have. It made Candice want to invent a time machine and go back to the moment she'd called her mom, sobbing, and wailed, *I want to come home.* Or to the moment last month when she'd finally spilled the whole story, two beers in, to her mother's stony face. *Stop feeling sorry for me,* she demanded, but the words that left her lips were, "Yes, please."

Instead of walking back through the crowd to the entrance as Candice expected, her mom dug into the massive turquoise bag at her hip and came up after a few moments with a set of keys dangling from a crayon-bright lanyard Candice had made in kindergarten. "I filled it up yesterday, so you can just go straight home if you want."

"Uh—"

"I'll catch a ride, honey. Go." Candice was left staring as her mother pivoted and strode into a building hosting floral displays and quilts.

After a moment, she dropped her gaze to the keys in her hand. Her mother's truck was a prized possession. That story had been told over more than one holiday dinner in Candice's childhood: how her city born-and-bred mom, perfectly happy to use public transit for every and all occasions, had found herself stuck on the farm one summer with a small child, a broken-down car, and the behemoth of an ancient truck she didn't know how to drive. *Oh yes,* her mother would admit with a laugh, *I could have just called out a mechanic, but you know, I thought if I fixed the situation myself... I don't know. It just seemed like something I had to do!*

Candice turned against the flow of the crowd and made her way to the entrance. She actually remembered that week, or maybe remembered remembering it. That had been the first year her father had had to leave the farm to bring in money. Nana hadn't even moved back from town back then, and it had been just the two of them, driving up and down the long dirt road to the farm as her mother taught herself to drive a stick shift. The old beast didn't have air conditioning, so they'd opened the windows and driven through clouds of warm golden dust kicked up by the tires.

Candice had only just learned to drive the summer she'd turned seventeen. She'd *never* driven the old truck.

"Oh my God." She stopped dead in her tracks just like her mother had a few minutes ago. "She just treated me like an adult."

It was a novel sensation. Mildly terrifying, in fact. Part of her exulted—*yes, yes, thank you! Notice me! I can Do Things!*—while another cowered, as convinced as ever that of everything she was, *adult* wasn't on the list.

"I can fix that," a voice called from her left. Blinking away her momentary confusion, Candice looked across the broad fairground avenue to where Isaac stood in the middle of the petting zoo, momentarily unassailed by eager children. In fact, it was assailed by absolutely no one at all, the crowd briefly dispersed to other attractions. And Isaac, in black jeans and a plaid shirt in fall colors that suited his sunlit copper skin, was definitely an attraction.

Candice's breath hitched. *No.* Shove that thought down, down, down; into the box with everything else. She didn't do attraction anymore. Attraction meant contact, meant connection, meant at some point she was going to hurt. Again. *If I walk away now, it will be awkward. Do not be awkward. You are a normal human who can human with other humans, just... go.*

She strode over on the close of that thought, hoping it looked confident. She didn't slow until she was close enough to see his freckles and smell the pungent aroma of baby goats. "Fix what?"

"Whatever made you look like somebody slapped you with a fish."

"I do not!"

He laughed. It was richer and deeper now, but still the same cackling cadence of utter glee. At her embarrassment, as usual. The heat that prickled up from her chest to her cheeks just made him laugh harder.

"Shut *up*, oh my *God*," she said, sliding the key-laden lanyard over her neck and hiking up her bright red skirt, trying not to think about the fact that her face was probably the same color. At least the way her heart tripped over itself at that laugh wasn't visible. There was no way for him to see how far down her flush went, or the brief surge of want that coiled along her skin, diffuse and undefined. She couldn't have named *what* it was she wanted. Maybe for him to reach out, grab her elbow, steady her. Maybe to feel the heat of skin on hers, the simple warmth of human contact. She hopped the low fence quickly, shoving the sensation to the back of her mind, booted feet finding clean straw with a knack learned in childhood and never quite forgotten. "You're such an asshole."

"Ah," Isaac, bent double by this point and weakly fending off a curious lamb, gasped. "I know, I know. Sorry. Just—your face, Candice. You look like a kettle about to go off. Thank you. I needed that. But seriously, whatever's bugging you, trust me that a kid'll fix it right up." He scooped the smallest of the goats up, offering it up to her as he stood straight. His broad smile fell as he took in her expression. "Shit. What did I say?" He seemed to be replaying the words over in his head, trying and failing to figure out what had hurt her. That was Isaac: always trying to help, but not always succeeding.

She couldn't stay; not when his innocent comment set off an avalanche of hurt. He couldn't know. Only her mother knew. She had to escape. "Nothing," Candice gasped. She flung herself back over the fence and took off for the parking lot at something just short of a run.

*

She made it to the truck on autopilot, Isaac's voice still ringing in her ears. A dull pain crawled down from her temples and up from her heart, meeting in a throbbing knot at her throat that she couldn't swallow past. The effort squeezed tears past her eyes as she narrowed them against the too-bright sky and pulled slowly out of the dirt lot.

The farmhouse, when she rounded the last curve of the long dirt drive, was less comforting than usual. August's muggy heat had trailed lazily into September and pressed the air into a thick haze that did strange things to her vision. Inside would be cooler—cool was what she wanted, and dark, and silence. Candice's mental chant of *go, go, go* thudded in time to her pain and her footsteps. Forward momentum pushed her up the stairs, until she nearly tripped over Pogo halfway.

"Hey, dummy, you okay?" The fat and ancient pug looked sad, but since that was the only expression Candice had ever seen on his face, it didn't seem like a useful indication of anything. "You hate the stairs, you decrepit old thing." She sighed. "And you're going to make me take you back up, aren't you?"

She scooped him up as she spoke. He smelled worse than the cat, although maybe that was because she was carrying him. After their first meeting, the old cat hadn't deigned to come nearer than the opposite end of her rail. *Suits me.*

"Nana, I'm home," she called, childhood habit prompting her to the almost dance-like steps it took to make it down the upstairs hallway without an accompanying chorus of creaks. Some of the old quiet boards were just as noisy as the rest now, another reminder of how old and falling-apart the place really was. Reaching the only door on the right, she poked her head into the broad sunroom. "Pogo was on the stairs, Nana. I can take him out if you think… he should… go…"

Her grandmother's room was quiet and still. Realization hit between one breath and another, but she caught it deftly, tucking it away with all the other pain. "Nana?"

No answer. Pogo whined, and she put him down, biting her lip until she tasted blood. The fresh stinging pain was something to focus on as she moved, inelegant, robotic, to check the old woman's pulse.

The paper-thin wrinkled skin beneath her finger was cool, but it was always cool. It was pale, but it was always pale. The fingers were curled tight, but they were always curled and gnarled.

Pogo whined again. Candice pulled her fingers away and stumbled out of the room.

I should have stayed home. It was a thought without heat, as cool as the corpse that had been her grandmother. *I should have been there,* some part of her insisted. As if it would have helped.

She waited on the front steps with the pug in her lap until unfamiliar cars brought her mother and the coroner.

*

Hordes of distant family descended on them within the next few days. Most didn't seem to care about Candice, her mother, or even the dead relative they'd supposedly come to honor; instead they wandered the house as if it were theirs and asked pointed questions about the antiques. A few exceptions kept her faith in humanity from shredding completely, but from the acquisitive gleam in their eyes, she didn't think this latest batch would be among them.

Her mom, ducking into the parlor to share her view out the window, looked as happy to see them as Candice felt.

"Vultures," was all the unkindness that passed her lips. "Candy, go let them in, honey. I need to clean up." A vague gesture indicated the kitchen, currently in a state of wanton disarray the likes of which Candice had never seen. She was almost tempted to offer some help; that untidiness, from her achingly precise mother, was alarming.

A sea of nearly indistinguishable faces greeted her when she opened the door. The pack of blonde vultures seemed mostly befuddled, but the blue eyes of the old woman in the lead were sharp and determined.

"Where's your mother, girl," she muttered. It didn't really sound like a question, and Candice was barely aware of the polite welcome that fell from own her lips as she stepped back. Worse than the old woman sweeping imperiously into the entryway were the cooing women her mother's age following behind her, their syrupy sympathy descending on her in a wave.

Her salvation was sudden, unexpected, and badly needed an oil change. Isaac's beater truck—the one they'd both learned to drive in—rolled up the long drive, and she dove for her chance, spotting a certain fluffy orange acquaintance sitting calmly on the porch steps and eyeing a blonde toddler with disdain. "I've got to, ah," she waved a hand in almost the same gesture her mother had used, then darted out the door with a forced smile the moment her mother's tread made the board in the kitchen doorway creak. *Sorry, Mom.*

She scooped up the cat and strode purposefully toward Isaac's truck as he got out.

His smile was unsure as he gave her a nod, glancing at her burden. For a moment, she thought he would bring up their last encounter, but all he said was, "How'd you know?"

Candice blinked, losing the confidence her Bavarian Fire Drill tactic required. Perplexed, she looked at the cat too. "Know?"

"That I'm here to—uh." He must have seen the confusion in her eyes, for his own drifted over to the other visiting vehicle and then to the house behind her where voices drifted out an open window. Her mother's carried the best, tight and sharply enunciated. "I'm on my... um, my personal rounds. Bring him to the bed, please." As he spoke, he reached back into the truck and pulled out a well-worn leather bag.

"Personal rounds." Candice forced her voice to be flat and uninviting. Isaac might be her rescuer at the moment, but that was no reason to encourage renewing their friendship. Or anything else.

He seemed to understand the question in her words and shrugged, cheeks going surprisingly pink under his copper skin. "There's a lot of cats around that don't belong to anybody, but they're not really feral." He eyed the cat. "Well, most of them aren't. Strays and barn cats—dogs, too. Just because nobody takes care of them doesn't mean they deserve to die from something I can prevent," he continued defensively, making a minute gesture with the hypodermic he'd expertly prepped as he spoke. In one fluid motion, Isaac grabbed the loose skin at the cat's scruff and gave him the shot, pulling the needle out again before Candice or cat could react. The cat glared at vet, flexing his claws against Candice's skin.

I know how you feel, she thought, rubbing a finger between furry shoulder blades. *He gets under my skin too.* Wait. No. Where had that thought come from? *Ignore. Ignore, ignore, ignore.* Was there some button she could press to close off that train of thought entirely? With a small shake of her head, Candice refocused. "That's really sweet of you, actually." And unexpected. It was as if he'd reached out and wiped a layer of grime from her vision, echoes of the past peeling off. She remembered with a lurch of pain how close they'd been. Best friends. *More than that*, she had to acknowledge, if only to herself. Barely there, yes, but some tentative seed of romance had begun to unfurl in their hearts that summer. Had she been that close to anyone since? Had she been that close to Cas before it all went to hell?

She'd lost Isaac somewhere in those long weeks between death and funeral, the weeks she wouldn't remember.

Stop, she told herself, over and over again, an insect whine in the back of her mind. *New topic.* She glanced down at the cat, choosing him as her shield against the growing pressure in her chest and throat. "He's not feral though, is he?"

"He's…" Isaac prepped another needle. Another quick shot, another grumble and flex. "Special. I think you moved before we released the litter, right?"

How the hell should I know? She nodded anyway, assuming he was right.

"Those grays pretty much went wild immediately… well, the smallest would come around for food now and again. This guy… I don't know."

He gestured to take the cat from her. She released him, grudgingly and not sure what to do with her arms. She crossed them, uncrossed them to wipe some fine and annoying fur from her cheek, and crossed them again, flicking her fingers in a *go on* gesture.

"He went off with the others, and he never came back around for food like the gray runt, but he would show up, sometimes." A shrug as long-fingered hands probed for wounds or lumps. The cat looked grumpy but put up with it. "Just show up and sit for a while. Move one inch toward him and he'd take off—not running, just sauntering, always keeping ahead. He probably thinks he's the king of the county." Examination finished, he handed the cat back. "When I came back after school—"

A frisson of shock stuttered through Candice. Of course, she'd never heard of any veterinary schools nearby, but somehow she'd pictured him never leaving. He'd been a constant, a part of home, a dream she'd hidden from the world—and herself—because it wasn't possible, couldn't be possible. Not after she'd left. Had her leaving broken him loose, sent him spiraling unmoored? Or would he have left anyway? But he'd returned, and now she had too. The unmet dream flickered, brightened, came closer.

"—that was a few years back, and not much had changed, honestly. Except he started coming over here instead of my dad's place. I think he doesn't like the new dogs."

The cat, as if agreeing, almost sighed his meow.

"Then one day he comes right up to the door. The dogs went so nuts we thought there must be a fox outside or something, but when I opened the door to chase it off, there's *this* old fellow, bleeding like a stuck pig and staring up at me. Don't ask me how he knew. I dared to pick him up—carefully—took him down to my practice, and stitched him up. Calm as you please, the whole time, barely even complained when I gave him shots. I kept him for a few days, got him all cleaned up and snipped—wish we'd had it done when they were kittens, but I never thought about it back then. By that point his ear was pretty well healed, and that's when I decided to start doing my rounds. He's still not a fan of being picked up, usually. By me, anyway. But he lets me do my work without much of a fight. He's… just special." He glanced at her burden of orange fluff—now rumbling something almost like a purr—with a soft smile before he turned to repack his kit.

"Unique, certainly." The cat had taken to sitting with her on the porch most evenings. Some nights she'd even swear they were having a conversation, although to onlookers it probably sounded like intermittent grumbling meows and equally grumbling curses. It worked for them.

"So…" Isaac slung his kit back into the truck without looking at her, the only item left a pen in his right hand that he clicked arhythmically. "About the other day."

"…Shit. I'm sorry—"

"—You don't have to tell me anything about it," he interrupted, raising his hands in a warding gesture. "You can if you want to, but I'm not going to dig, okay? I just wanted you to know that."

"Um." *Not where I thought that was going.* "Okay. I *am* sorry, though. I kind of… don't do well with a lot of things, lately. Apparently crowds are now included in that."

"Your mom mentioned you've been having a rough time. Split up with your husband or something?"

"Fiancé." She paused, tilting her head and letting a wry smile settle on her lips. "Thought you weren't going to dig."

"Hey, hey. Asking," Isaac responded primly, "isn't digging. I'll have you know I'm perfectly willing to accept 'fuck off, you nosy asshole' as a response."

Candice couldn't help it. She laughed, absently tucking a strand of hair behind one ear. The cat grumbled, startled by the bark of noise over his head, and flexed his claws until she set him down. She was still giggling when she leaned up. "Fuck off, then? Sorry, sorry. Fuck off, you nosy asshole."

Isaac's answering grin came dangerously close to breaching the layers of protection she had wrapped around her like a winter cloak. Her heart fluttered traitorously. "Have to, in fact. My shift starts in thirty."

"Candy!" Her mother's voice rang out before she could respond. She stood in the doorway winding a kitchen towel over and around her hands, face set.

Candice couldn't help but twitch at the name, but she kept her lips clamped on the tart response that begged for release. The visiting relations flooded past her mom and descended the steps en masse like a herd of cows. *Greedy cows*, she amended, noting darting and speculative glances from the adults.

"Family duty calls?" Isaac's voice was low and warm.

"Yeah." Her voice managed to remain steady. It didn't betray shock at the responding wriggle of warmth his voice dragged from her belly to throat, where it transmuted on a wave of something bleak and blinding that threatened to overwhelm her. "Talk to you later, okay?"

She didn't wait for his response, turning back to the porch and managing to force polite goodbyes past an only slightly frozen smile, while dodging hugs from all but the sharp-eyed great-aunt who, from her scent, bathed in baby powder. Her mother smelled like raw dough and cinnamon—far better. Almost comforting. Strangely, so was the rage that hardened the older woman's eyes and whitened her knuckles. Candice admired the way the fury never touched her smile. *Do I do that? Can I?*

"Come on," her mother muttered. "Kitchen."

It wasn't a request, and Candice couldn't find the words to decline. She followed through parlor and hall to her mother's kingdom.

*

The thunk of glass on wood broke Candice from her nervous reverie. Afraid to touch anything, she'd sat herself at the kitchen table and watched her mom dart from surface to surface, keeping up a constant barely-audible mutter as she'd tidied. It was almost hypnotic, and after a few minutes Candice had slid into a kind of anxious fugue.

The noise that broke it was also courtesy of her mother. Two heavy tumblers sat in front of her now, each receiving a generous dose of something dark and smelling fruit-sweet. Candice tried, and failed, to remember the last time she'd seen her mother *drink*. Unlike her nana, who'd more than once taken her various medications with a glass of wine when no one was around to see her, her mother had been a pinnacle of straight-laced perfection all of Candice's life.

Her mother sat down across the table and remained silent for a long moment, gaze absently tracking the dust motes that danced on a lance of light between them. Candice hooked a finger on the rim of one glass and pulled it slowly to herself.

"I want to talk to you about selling the house," her mother announced.

"No." The response was as much a reflex as the sullen tone it came out in. Candice cleared her throat and sat up straight. "Why should we sell the house? I like the house." It was home. Nearly all her ghosts lived here—her father, her grandmother. Even Isaac as he'd been, that teenage version with gangling limbs and a cherubic face, launching himself up the stairs two at a time.

"With what your grandmother left you—"

"I don't want to talk about that. Please."

"Candice Rene!" It wasn't so much words as a frustrated keen in the shape of her name. "You're going to have to talk about it. You're going to have to talk about something, at some point! Your grandmother," she went on, voice going tight and icy, "is *dead*, and we need to figure out what to do next."

A startling thought glanced across the outer perimeter of Candice's mind. Her mother looked tired. Dark brown hair, gone almost amber as it grayed, curled limply from a patterned headband, the dusky bruises of missed sleep turning the skin beneath her eyes sallow. *When's the last time you smiled?*

Her mom had visited the apartment only once, maybe six years before. The polite fiction pasted to her lips hadn't been a smile, not with the way it had left her eyes totally out of the equation. There'd been a painful longing in those eyes that Candice had glanced away from the same way she glanced away from a mirror. 'You look just like your mother' had been flattering until it became inescapable.

"I needed you," her mother went on in a voice that was calmer on the surface. Candice wasn't fooled by those still waters. "I can't do this alone again."

It stung. It cut. It slithered under her skin and wound like a chill up her shoulders. Candice muffled a flinch, biting her tongue against a protest. *I was there, I was there the whole time. I didn't leave you, you left me.* All she forced out was a quiet, "I'm here now."

"Hmmh." The unspoken *but why* landed between them, as sticky and treacherous as the liquor.

It was a bad idea to drink. It was impolite not to. She took a sip.

When Candice didn't offer her motivations up for dissection, her mother sighed and picked up her own glass, leaning back. "I can't afford the house on my own. Even if you got a job, probably. With what your grandmother left you," she repeated, "we could probably manage taxes a few years running, but really, Candy—"

"—*ice,*" Candice hissed.

"—Candice," her mother went on smoothly. Another sip. Her voice was changing as she spoke, dropping slightly in pitch and growing flatter, more nasal. Probably indetectable to anyone else, but Candice couldn't help recognizing it as a mirror of her own shift, her city-flattened tones beginning to flake away and reveal the rural girl beneath. "Are you planning to resurrect the glory days? Do you have any idea how much work your father put in?"

"This is my *home*," Candice all but whimpered. It felt like she'd just gotten back. The handful of boxes she'd packed still sat, half-sorted, in the corner of her room. There were possibilities she had to prepare for, unexpected—okay, sure, she'd come home to heal, but she hadn't finished yet. She'd barely started. She wasn't ready to leave, possibly forever.

Her mother snatched the ever-present dish towel from the back of her chair and flung it to the table. "Candice, I've lived in this house since I was younger than you are now. I took care of your grandfather when he was dying, and I've taken care of your grandmother nearly every damned day since! I—"

"You want to leave," Candice supplied, wrapping her fingers around the cool sides of her glass and hunching her shoulders unconsciously.

"*I want to stay!*" Her mother's sharp words startled them both into momentary silence. The too-familiar hazel eyes across from her drifted closed, and her mother's sigh carried the faintest note of tears. "You took your first steps across this table," she went on, tapping one hard nail on the weathered wood.

The turn caught Candice unaware, like a blow. She pulled her knees up and wrapped her arms around them. "I'm tired."

"Talk to me, Candice."

"I'm *tired*," she repeated, dropping her feet to the floor again and pushing her chair back. "I'm going to take a nap. Can we talk about it later?"

Up came the towel, wound twice around her mother's hand and twisted into a tight loop before being dropped again. To Candice, it was as eloquent a comment on that lie as any other she could possibly make. For a moment, the expression crossing her mother's tired face grew raw. Her eyes, catching Candice's, burned.

Talk, Candice willed her. *You want inside my thoughts, but you never show yours. It's not fair.* It looked as though she might. Her mouth, chewed free of the lipstick that usually graced it, worked as if trying to gnaw through bone. *Talk to me.*

"I just don't see how we can stay, Candy, honey," was what she finally said. The words fell, leaden, between them. "I wish it was different, too. I wish your father hadn't left—"

"No. No, stop—" *I take it back.* Her own festering grief recoiled from the raw heat of her mother's.

"*Left*, Candice. That," her voice dropped to a husky whisper, almost flat, a voice merely relaying facts, "was a *choice*. He couldn't bear the weight of it on his shoulders, year after year of debt. All those successful ancestors buried him in their expectations. He'd get drunk and weep about it."

Six months ago, Candice had woken in bloody sheets and been instantly shocked by the copper reek of her pregnancy's end. Sixteen years ago it had been the sight of blood rather than the scent that had shattered her summer and her heart. The smell of her father's blood, where he'd slumped over his workshop table with a pistol in his hand, had been buried in sawdust and old metal tools. Those were smells she'd loved, once. *Honest smells, Candy-cane. Honest work.* The scion of a farming family faded into nothing but wisps, he'd still believed that. She'd thought he'd believed it. He'd stayed, after all, come back with a city bride and bright ideas after college. She'd always thought she would stay too.

"We can't change it now." It was like waking up. Her mother stood abruptly, tone utterly matter-of-fact. The kitchen was as well-lit as ever, and the tears on both of their cheeks glittered. "I had to learn how to accept that, Candice. I can't change the choices your father made, or mine, or yours. All I can do is keep going on."

Candice stood too, searching for a response. *I know*, she could say, sullen or accepting. *I'm tired. I don't want to remember. I understand.*

I understand. "Forward momentum," she breathed, a sliver of childhood resentment quivering for attention but filtered by the strange sensation of *seeing* her mother, properly, for the first time. "I'll help you with dinner."

*

Candice included a beer with her evening cigarette the following night, and the ones after that. It didn't do much to help her stay asleep, but given a choice between tipsy half-doze and staring sleeplessly at the ceiling for hours, she decided to take the beer, nasty hoppy taste and all. *I don't know how Mom can stand this stuff*, she thought with every evening's first sip, but by the bottom of the can she always found herself pleasantly foggy.

Waking up every night to piss and rinse her dried-out mouth became part of the ritual, but a week after Isaac's round—*Why am I dating everything by Isaac's visits?*—it was something besides her bladder that woke her. The first cool breath of rainy night air felt like a dream after months of oppressive heat, and she wasn't sure at first what she'd heard. The border between sleep and wakefulness tangled her thoughts in a sticky morass, sights and sounds and smells blending in unreality.

Maybe I was dreaming? Thin starlight gave the stacks of packing boxes littering Candice's room an ominous air, like silent gray-shadowed watchers. *Yeah.* She had been. An old dream, tangled with a fresher one, both full of blood. For a long drifting moment, she thought it must have been her own scream that woke her, and wondered if her mom would come to see what was wrong.

Then the wailing came again, almost human and razor-edged with agony. Candice shot to her feet, stumbling in the tangle of her blankets as she scrambled for yesterday's clothes. Some brief flash of logical thought stuttered through her mind, long enough that she thought *grab phone* and *shit no jacket, robe will do* before thudding down the stairs and out the back door.

The night was quiet except for the wind and the patter of light rain. She stood frozen on the porch for a long moment, staring at the monochrome nightscape. Her heart slowed.

"Candy, honey." The screen door creaked as her mom nudged it open, wrapped in a thin black robe patterned with roses, her wild sleep-tangled curls falling into her eyes. She was holding the old behemoth of a flashlight she kept in the kitchen. Its light was dim; probably it needed new batteries. "What's wrong?"

"Did you hear that?" Maybe she'd imagined it after all. Candice strained, trying to listen past the whistling wind.

"Hear wh—"

The third scream cut across her mother's words, and Candice launched herself from the porch, racing toward the stand of trees that hid most of their drive from view of the house. She ignored her mother's shouts, but survival instinct managed to kick in at the tree line. The flashlight on her phone wasn't exactly high-powered, but it was better than stumbling around blind.

Her first pass with the light revealed nothing. The second glinted off stunningly reflective eyes. Candice froze. So did the fox. *Thank God.* She swallowed, terrified. *Is it rabid? Shit, what do I do?* Thinking back to her childhood didn't help. Back then she probably would have tried to make friends with the damned thing.

It stared back at her, silent and still. Red marks scored the creature along its neck and side. None of the slashes were deep, but a rich trickle of blood dripped from the one slice across its snout.

"Candy!" With a wild roar, her mother bowled past her. She waved a steel bat in one hand. The other held a stock pot lid like a shield, glinting in the weak light from Candice's phone. The stunned moment shattered. The fox bolted.

Probably twice as terrified as I am, she thought and stifled a hysterical bubble of laughter. Sound drew her attention to the right and up. In the light of her phone, the blood trailing up pale bark was a stark, sticky, shining red.

"Oh, *honey*." Fear and concern twined in her mother's voice. Next would be *please don't get yourself hurt*. "Please don't—"

"Yeah, no, I'm not leaving him up there." Candice dodged her mother's reaching hand. She shucked her robe and tossed her phone onto it, refusing to think about what she was doing. *Forward momentum*. Never mind that it was a slender tree. She wasn't sure she'd have dared climb it even sixteen years and fifty pounds ago.

"Oh my God. Candy, no! You'll fall!" A note of hysteria overlaid the concern now.

"I won't!" *Don't stop. Don't look down. Don't stop, don't stop, don't think*. She let her feet and hands choose branches. *Don't think about ten years at a desk job and all those times you should have gone to the gym. All the times you thought about taking up mountain climbing. Hah*. Hand, foot, hand. Some of the branches were slick and sticky. *Don't think*.

Her orange cat hunkered in a fork halfway up the trunk. The wind seemed to blow harder and sharper up here, as if she really had climbed a mountain instead of three-fifths of a tree.

"Hey, buddy," she whispered. The wind whipped leaves into her face and made her eyes water. "You've been through the wars, huh?"

He trembled. His low crouch and raised fur betrayed his terror too, but the golden eyes flashed at her with clear pride and ferocity. Candice felt a lurch of joy in her chest, unbidden. *Yeah*, those eyes seemed to say, *but you saw the other guy, right?*

*

"Where is he?" Isaac's voice, usually soft and polite, cut hard through Candice's fugue.

She blinked, sitting straighter in her chair at the kitchen table. "There, you see?" The lump in her lap didn't stir, but a steady faint beat thudded against the fingers she'd kept pressed behind his left leg for—a bleary-eyed glance at the stove proved it to be eleven past three—twenty-odd minutes. "I told you he'd be here. You're going to be fine."

Isaac entered the kitchen with wide, rapid strides. Her mother hovered in the door, twisting a towel. Their expressions were almost identical. Her mother had been wearing it all of those twenty minutes, but shock was a new expression on Isaac's face. It made his eyebrows rise like bunched up caterpillars. *They're kind of cute. I kind of want to kiss them.* Candice snorted in tired amusement at the thought. "Don't worry. It's not as much as it looks like. Or all his." That broke loose a giggle. Her mother made an irritated noise halfway between sigh and groan and turned away. *Maybe she doesn't want to see her kitchen get all bloody*, Candice thought inanely. She giggled again. *Too late.*

She couldn't help but watch him cross the kitchen, kneel, open his old leather bag. The world felt like a dream. She was going to blink awake any moment. Open her eyes to another day of dull sunlight and oppressive heat and sitting in wailing silence locked in the fortress of her head.

"Hi," she said, lips curling into an unfamiliar smile. A shard of anger snagged in her mind, a brief flicker of resentment that he'd torn a real smile from her again. Then it was gone, so quickly that it seemed to leave a hollow space behind, and a faint longing to bury her head in his chest. *Christ, but I'm tired.*

"Hi," he murmured back. His long-fingered hands tugged her prize away. "Lord, old man, what kind of scrape…"

There was a long pause. Her thoughts felt like mud. *Maybe it's the rain.* "Was a fox," Candice said at last. It might have been seconds or minutes or even hours later. She didn't know. Another glance at the clock showed—*what? No.* She sat straighter, spine cracking as she rolled her shoulders back. A glance at the dim dawn light dripping through the windows confirmed the clock's ridiculous assertion that it was now nearly five in the morning. Isaac was washing his hands. She'd been talking. *Right. Fox.* She gestured at the long-abandoned doorway. "My mom yelled at it with a bat."

"The hell, Candy?" Isaac turned from the sink, wiping his hands on a clean towel before his eyebrows shot up once more. He grabbed her wrist, holding her arm still, staring at the marks with worried eyes. The shallow red tracks that had caught his eye traced all the way up to her shoulder, beneath the old hoodie that was failing to warm her up in the least. Stinging, but not bleeding. Anymore. Mostly.

"Oh." She nodded. "The old man and I had some disagreements about how to get out of a tree." His hands were very warm against her skin as he rolled the sleeve up. Maybe she was catching a chill.

"I'll say," Isaac breathed. "Who won?"

"The ground." She failed to tug her wrist from his grip. "Fix the cat, please."

"You—"

"My mom took care of it," Candice lied. *I can wait, idiot.* "Veterinarian fixes cat now."

"Veterinarian fixed cat," he retorted, pointing to the bandaged animal. "Veterinarian is lucky that cat didn't go into shock like you're trying to do."

"Am not." The indignant reply slipped out in reflex. It hadn't required thought. "I'm cold."

"I'm sure you are," he agreed to the second while looking her over and feeling her pulse, "and no, you're not really in shock." She followed when he tugged. "But you *are* going to wash the living hell out of your arms, and then I'm going to fix *you*. Dumbass." His tone was fond. Familiar. Warm. She wanted to lean into it. Her ears ached to hear more; her heart ached to tease apart his tone, discover if that rich promise was really there.

Her body, though, ached for simple heat. Candice shivered and followed him to the sink, pulling the hoodie over her head. He made coffee while she washed and returned to the table. Halfway through her second cup, as he finished winding paw-patterned medical tape around her bandages, the world started to come back into focus. "Ow," she sighed.

Isaac snorted and rocked back on his heels, a grin teasing at the corners of his mouth. "Ow? *Now* you're complaining? Not a word at the iodine, not a whimper at the stitches. The bandage is what gets you."

"A testament to your bedside manner." *Stop*, she commanded herself. *Abort. Bad plan. Withdraw.* Maybe it was it something about the early morning hour that left her feeling defenseless. Maybe it would fade as the sun rose. *I can hope.*

It was too easy, falling into rhythm with him.

"I'm surprised your mom didn't actually take care of these," he said.

"Oh. Yeah. She was doing great—did I tell you she ran at a fox with a bat?" She thought she had.

His grave nod warred with the twinkle in his dark eyes. "You mentioned, sort of."

"Yeah." She waved her hands in a loose motion, momentarily distracted by the adorable pattern on her bandage wraps. "She was doing great until I fell out of the tree. Then she kind of… fell apart."

"Oh, shit," he breathed. "Right. She got weird about climbing after your dad fell."

"Mm-mm." The noise might have been noncommittal if not for the way it broke on the tightness of her throat. Her mind's eye snagged on an early memory: her father, joking with his brothers, painting a new addition to the house—the last. Had she been five? Six? Something like that. Playing with the chickens, oblivious in that childishly fixated way. There'd been no reason to look up, but she had. She'd looked and watched as her father stepped back an inch too far and slipped from the second-story roof, as he hit the porch roof and bounced then fell out of her sight beyond the garden. Not fatal, but he'd been different after. And her mother had been terrified of heights ever since.

Was that why I was always climbing trees? Oh, God. Let's not do this. "He's going to be okay, right?"

He's an old cat, she chided herself before Isaac could respond. *He's not even yours. He just comes and hangs out with you sometimes.* She tried to coil the anticipatory grief tight and tuck it away with the rest.

"He's strong." Isaac sighed. Shaking his head, he rose to his feet and poured a cup for himself. "He's old, too. None of it was too bad—well," he corrected with a grimace, "I don't like that bite on his back leg, but yeah. If we keep him warm, well-fed, and up to the gills with antibiotics, he should make it. Thank God he's up on his shots," he added with just a hint of smugness.

"Oh, *God*," Candice echoed. "*I'm* not. Do I have to get—"

"Yes."

"But—"

"Yes."

"What about the fox?" She leaned forward, chasing the flicker of surprise on his face. The upper hand felt good, however briefly.

"What about it?"

"The old man got it pretty good. Is it going to be okay?"

Isaac's cup barely made a noise as it touched the table. His silent stare out the kitchen windows was unreadable.

"'*Red in tooth and claw*,'" he finally said. His voice was low. A little sad. "If she wanted to take on an old fighter like him, she earned a few scratches. I'll keep an eye out, though," he insisted, voice rising slightly as he glanced at her. What he saw on her face she couldn't imagine, the glint of alarm in his eyes unfathomable until he reached one tentative hand to her cheek, rubbing his thumb over wet skin.

The world was still, for a moment. It was a long moment. The last bit of grief had been too much. Everything was too much. Her breath stuttered and everything coiled in, heart and mind and soul and body. Candice slid from her chair with a stifled wail that shattered, on the broad wall of his chest, into aching sobs. She didn't know why she sought comfort in the cradle of Isaac's arms, only that she craved the safety he offered simply by existing. He felt right in a way that no one else ever had. Isaac rocked her gently, not interrupting the flood of words that spilled between hiccuping breaths.

At sixteen, Candice had seen the world as a challenge. Trees were meant for climbing, flat stretches for running, and every possibility at her fingertips. Isaac had been waiting, solid and steady, keeping her grounded so she could fly. Another sixteen years since hadn't dulled the moments those possibilities died and peeled away, one by one. The struggle was in not remembering sunlight peeking through the workshop doors and glinting off tools and chunks of her father's brain.

The so-climbable trees stood on property so deeply in hock that his life insurance had barely made the dent he'd surely intended—her mother's theory, an overheard whisper that had wound Candice in layer after layer of guilt. After all, she'd heard all her life about the expenses of raising a child from those same lips; it wasn't hard to put the two ideas together.

"Jesus," Isaac breathed when her litany stumbled to a stop, her heart tripping over that suddenly remembered tidbit. It was a comment she still hadn't forgiven her mother for, the moment she'd understood that *she* was part of the expenses. The guilt of the thought was a dull pain now, the grooves of *your fault, your fault, your fault* worn smooth in her heart. It had hurt so much more, the first time.

With firm hands, Isaac tugged Candice out of the kitchen, directing her, unresisting, to the back living room and the ancient couch in front of a doubly ancient wood stove. She sat at his prompting, still struggling to breathe evenly, squeezing her eyes shut until his footsteps returned. The warmth he settled in her lap before dropping to the couch himself was welcome, if worryingly limp.

Candice slitted her eyes open, watching the shallow rise of the cat's chest.

"I had no idea it was you that found him."

"It's always me," she responded in a flat whisper. *Maybe Nana was it, though*, she thought. *Maybe it's done.* Something about three deaths. Didn't everything come in threes?

"Shit, right. And your gran—sorry, nana."

Candice bit her lip, opening her eyes all the way and tilting her head up to inspect him. An open face in warm autumn shades, waiting, less awkward than it had been in adolescence but still giving the sense of being made of spare parts, each perfectly reasonable in their own right but combining into a slightly unflattering but good-humored whole. She'd spilled her heart and thoughts to that face, once upon a time, in blissful innocent expectation of being heard and not judged.

"I'm sorry I ran away from you back then." The words startled both of them. Candice considered for a moment, examining the words. Yes, it was true. "I should have talked to you. Trusted you. I don't know why I—" She shook her head, cutting herself off with a growl of frustration. She rubbed her palms over her eyes, willing herself not to cry again.

"It hurt." Isaac's voice was soft when it came at last. "I'd never lost anyone before... I didn't know what you needed. But you didn't run away from *me*, Candice. I always knew you were going to leave, find something awesome to kick ass at. I honestly didn't expect you to come back."

The wistful look in his eyes almost took her breath away, stars shining in his gaze the same way they had when they'd been sixteen. How had she not recognized that look?

"The last I heard, you were just about on your way to the moon, or at least to married and handing your mom some grandkids to fixate on."

It startled a bark of pained laughter from her. "I'm so tired. I thought, if I came home, I wouldn't be so tired all the time." No tears sprang to her eyes. Dried up, maybe. Candice shivered and lowered her gaze to the cat. "Does he have a name?"

"Nah. Didn't really seem like it was my place. You want to give him one?"

What are we going to name our ship, Candy? Where do you want to go for summer vacation, Candy? He'd always handed her the lead, even when no one else thought she could handle a damned thing.

She opened her mouth to suggest something suitably rakish, but what came out was, "I lost my baby."

Silence filled the room. Distantly, in the hall to the front stairs, the grandfather clock ticked.

"Is..." Isaac drew the word out in a doubtful lilt. He stopped, inhaled, and gestured vaguely with his hand. "Not really any good way to ask, I guess. That's why you came back?"

"No. Maybe." Candice stared at her lump of cat, awash in unwelcome recollection. Mouth dry, she went on with only a slight tremble in her voice, the memory of blood beating in time with her racing heart. "I got engaged a couple of years ago. Cas. Casper, actually, but he hates it. We met—you probably don't care about that."

"I've always cared about what you had to say."

The words were so achingly sincere, so utterly without ulterior motive. Candice almost wanted to throttle Isaac. *Stop listening*, she wanted to shout. *Stop hearing me. Let me hurt in peace.*

His honesty hypnotized her, compelled honesty in return. Maybe it was the hour of the morning or the exhaustion of an adrenaline hangover, but even omission felt like a lie right now. She was petting the cat, she realized, hands stroking rhythmically over his unbandaged side. He was beginning to come around, a faint rumble responding to her touch. "After I left, my mom's cousin Danny gave me a job at his construction company. God, I was so bad. The alphabet is harder than you'd think."

Isaac laughed, rich and warm. It dragged a brief flicker of a smile from her.

"Cas was working there while he got his degree. Talked me into going to school..." She shrugged and rubbed the back of her neck. "I don't know why. God knows what I thought I was going to get out of it. I think I took every class that place offered, and when he graduated a few years later I was still wondering what I wanted to be when I grew up. Started working through a temp agency while Cas looked for work. We got engaged, and then it never seemed like the right time to get married. It was... fine." She inhaled, bracing for what came next. "I didn't mean to get pregnant. I don't even know if I want kids. I don't even know if I wanted that one. I was... a little scared, a lot worried."

One of Isaac's long-finger hands covered hers, pressing it against the cat's fur. He was about to say something kind. *You don't have to tell me this,* maybe. The thought jerked a croaking laugh from her, stung her eyes with heat. *Too late.* The walls were down, the box was open, the wound was lanced. She couldn't stop if he begged her.

"Almost three months along. We'd talked about it constantly for all three. Yes, no, maybe. His career. Our future. I think he wanted it more than I did. He had this vision, this plan…" Another laugh, softer. Wistful. "I never had a plan. I just went. Forward momentum. But I liked his plan. It would have been really good. And then one morning I woke up cramping. I thought it was just something normal, maybe, but when I got up there was blood all down the sheets."

Breathe, that's right. Need to keep breathing. "Cas had already gone to work. I didn't have any classes that day. Should have gone to the hospital, but I just… went to the bathroom. I sat in the tub and cried and watched her slide out of me." The cat made a muffled noise when she snatched her hands up, cupping them together. "Not even that big. She looked like a shrimp." Tears were flowing again. She couldn't stop crying. She couldn't stop talking. She couldn't breathe. "I just want everything to stop."

Isaac's embrace was warm and unyielding. No wracking sobs now, she cried in choked noises between stuttering breaths that verged on hyperventilation. He let her cry again, the way he let her talk. She loved and hated him in equal parts for it.

"I wish I could help you," he murmured into her hair. His warm breath raised goosebumps along her neck. "Your gran talked to me when I came for Pogo's shots. Well…" He tilted his head, cheek bumping gently against the crown of hers. "I think she was talking *at* me, really. All kinds of stories. Her kids. Thirteen pregnancies."

Something in Candice's mind caught that number and did the math. Her dad had had two brothers; a sister who had died young. "Nine times?" Her voice broke. It was almost a wail. The purring in her lap stuttered to a halt. "I'd have died."

"I don't think you would. You're tough the way she was. Like whipcord. I could tell when she talked that it still hurt. I don't know if those big heartbreaks ever go away… they just get a little easier to carry."

"Somebody took a smart pill." An old joke, one she hadn't remembered until it slipped out.

"If you say so. I'm just hoping, if I keep talking, you'll stop crying."

With his arms wrapped around her, there was no leverage to punch him in the chest. She made a rude noise instead, made even damper by residual tears. She could feel his responding chuckle in her chest, surprisingly pleasant. It seemed to fill the suddenly empty spaces. She ached with the pain of pressure released.

"I ran back here," she finally finished. "Cas was… he was good. It wasn't the only thing that came between us, but I didn't leave because of him. I just… left. Left the ring on the kitchen table and came back here. It's all I ever do. Run away. Try not to think or remember or feel. Real healthy, I know," she added with a snort.

Isaac hummed agreement. "And now?"

"I'm feeling. I guess it's a good thing."

He nodded, pulling away.

Golden light pooled through the windows. The back room didn't have a clock, and the distant *tick tick tick* of the grandfather clock in the front parlor was uninformative. *Christ, How long have we been sitting here?*

"It's useful data." Isaac scooped the cat gently from her lap, fingers probing and earning a lazy, half-sedated grumble in response. "If you didn't feel heat, you'd never know you were burning. Stands to reason your heart works the same way. At least you know you're alive. If you—"

Barely aware of her own intention, Candice raised a finger to his lips. He silenced immediately. "I think you're tired, too."

Isaac blinked thoughtfully, followed by a slow nod that dragged his lips against her finger. Her heart might have skipped a bit if it weren't as exhausted as the rest of her. By the time she built the cat—*I really have to think of a name*—a bed out of an old blanket and one of her packing boxes hastily emptied onto her bedroom floor, true morning sunlight spilled through the windows, and Isaac had slumped, snoring, against the arm of the couch. She considered going back to her room to sleep, but the sunlight seemed to fill the emptiness left behind where her pain had been. She left him sleeping and went to the kitchen to start breakfast.

*

Her grandmother's funeral took place another two weeks into October. Four weeks from death to ceremony seemed like far too long and not nearly long enough at the same time. A crowd of people milled gently at the top of the graveyard's softly sloping hill. Prime real estate, that; she wondered when it had been bought.

She turned at the sound of footsteps behind her and spotted Isaac, looking remarkably polished in a sleek charcoal suit.

Catching her glance, he flushed. "It's the darkest thing I own."

"She wouldn't have minded," Candice responded with quiet approval of her own, reaching out to pluck a stray marigold hair from his elbow. "How's the old man?"

"Irritated that I've kept him so long."

"Why did you?"

The corner of Isaac's mouth twitched. His eyes were bright. "Official reason or the real one?"

"...Both?" Absently, she noted how well his suit went with her own dress, a purple so dark it looked black unless she stood in direct sunlight. It made her look a little like a vampire, Casper had once said. *To stop me wearing it,* she thought, *but maybe I like looking like a vampire. So nyah.* Her mental middle finger made her feel a little better, even if the recipient would never know.

"The official reason is to make sure the cat without the rabies certificate didn't get rabies."

"But you—"

"That is the reason on the paperwork." This time he did smirk. "The actual reason is that I'm a sucker and I got to see him every day, which for some inexplicable reason makes me happy. Don't ask me what I see in that grumpy asshole. You can spring him tomorrow, if you want—didn't mean to hoard him."

They walked slowly to the top of the hill as they spoke, hands bumping gently. Candice thought about grabbing his, then she stopped thinking and did it, twining their fingers together. "I was researching feral cats—well, cats." She shrugged. "I've never owned one."

"I don't think you own one now. Pretty sure what *his* opinion is on the matter."

Candice wiggled the fingers of her free hand at him, shushing. "Did you know today is Feral Cat Day?"

He laughed. "You're kidding. Should we throw the old man a party?"

The crowd of funeral-goers were shifting into a kind of order now. Candice wound through them, trailing Isaac behind her—he seemed as unwilling to let go of her as she was of him—until she reached her mother's side. The glares that met her small smile, she ignored. The distant family members surrounding her hadn't really known her grandmother, not the way she had, growing up on the old farm. The handful of friends and acquaintances from town she felt more charitable toward.

The ceremony was thankfully brief. *Just like Nana*, Candice thought wryly. Every practical consideration had been taken care of long ago: burial plot purchased, will written. *Everything else*, the old woman had directed in a note tucked into the same envelope as the will and addressed to Candice's mother, *is up to you, Margaret. No frippery. You know what I like.*

So it was a small, plain ceremony. A small, plain coffin lowered into this plot. The view was stunning from the top of the low hill. To the south and west the land dipped away, opening into a broad valley farmed in neat quilted rows. North and most of east trailed into open woods that blocked the town from view. It seemed strange to offer that view to the dead, but remembering all the time her grandmother had spent in that upstairs sunroom with its view of farm and field and forest, she couldn't begrudge it in the least. *Enjoy the view, Nana. Take care of my girl. Say hi to Dad.*

It felt like scratching all around a healing wound. Pain, but good pain. Satisfying.

"Wait here," she muttered to Isaac as it ended and the crowd, released from social strictures, milled again.

Instead of letting her slip away, Isaac squeezed her hand. "You wait," he said, stepping out of the flow of foot traffic. "You're planning to sell the house, right?"

"Um. Yes?" She glanced across the way at the herd of familiar and frowning faces that she wanted to talk to for that very reason

He followed her gaze, brows furrowing gently before he turned back with a shrug. "I want to buy it."

Candice pinched herself. "Oh, *ow*," she breathed, to Isaac's general amusement. "Okay, not dreaming. You want to—how? Why? Why and how?"

"Well, *how* is this really complex situation involving this thing where I go to a place, and I do stuff, and they pay me money, and then when I get that money I put some in the bank and *ow, hey!*" He clutched his shoulder as she withdrew her finger, pushing out his lower lip.

She waved her pointed finger at him. "I can poke you again, mister. Don't tempt me."

"All *right*," he relented with a sigh. "I do have a lot saved, though, and Dad offered to loan me more. As for why… the local animal rescue scene is pretty abysmal, and the house has all that space, and…" He sighed again. "And I practically grew up there, and the idea of someone buying it and changing it makes me want to take a shower."

"I…" Her hand slowly dropped. "I didn't realize you were so invested in it."

"And if you and your mom helped run the rescue," he went on quickly, as if he hadn't heard her, "You could just keep living there. And we could see each other lots, because I'd need to come check on the cats."

She laughed, catching his hand. "Or you could just come see me for no reason at all."

He inhaled, eyes sparkling bright as they locked on hers. The world seemed to slow a little.

"We should celebrate," Isaac murmured. Candice raised her eyebrows in inquiry. "Feral Cat Day, remember?"

"Oh! Right." She brightened. "I was thinking a picnic. Do you think he'd like tuna?"

"Too much, yes. Let's stick to cat food." He nodded to the dwindling collection of cars at the base of the hill. "Make you a deal? Sell me your house, and I'll buy you a shake."

"Hmm." She hid her smile. "Agree to sell my large tracts of land—" she paused, and Isaac obligingly snickered "—in exchange for a frozen dairy beverage. Very even exchange."

They crunched onward over gravel to the wide dirt parking lot. She managed to ignore the maternal matchmaking glint that lit her mother's eyes, visible from thirty feet away, at their clasped hands and pointed to Isaac's truck. "I still don't know what to name him, you know."

"You know," Isaac retorted as they tumbled into his beater truck, "somehow, I think he'll be fine with that."

Candice laughed. "Yeah. Me too." She rolled down the window, an action that required pushing down on the glass. "I can't believe you haven't gotten this thing fixed yet."

"Pfft, it's a classic. I'm not going to mess with perfection."

"Hmm." She laughed again, then faltered to a surprised stop. That was… a lot of laughing. A lot of smiles. She couldn't remember the last time she'd felt this light.

I thought it was what I lost that hurt so much. Her gaze turned to Isaac, considering. *Maybe it's what I left.*

"You all right?" He glanced at her from the corner of his eye, trying to watch her and the road before giving up and focusing on driving. "No freakouts, Candice, use your words."

"I'm good, actually." The breeze of acceleration tugged at her hair. She waited until they reached a four-way stop to make her move, popping the seatbelt open and leaning over the small gap between them. The truck shook a little as she leaned up and pressed a warm, dry kiss to Isaac's mouth, and she made a mental note to make him get that fixed before the fingers of his right hand slid into her hair and he started to deepen the kiss. Then she didn't think of anything at all until he broke away, his entire face dancing with laughter.

"I really hate to stop you, but traffic safety compels me."

"Understood." She saluted him, which only made him laugh harder as she scrambled back into place and clicked her seatbelt shut.

"You going to run again?" His question was calm. He wasn't pressing her. He'd kept to his promise not to dig, and for that as much as anything Candice wanted to kiss him again.

"No." She kicked her heels into the floorboard and wiggled her toes. "No. I don't think I will."

About the Author

An Earth-origin carbon-based lifeform currently residing in the Sacramento Valley, Regina Griffiths is possessed of an unusually high caffeine to blood ratio and as a result has more sass than sense. A female of the species, her family unit consists of one husband, one viking, one child, three cats, five dogs, and a snake. When not falling down Wikipedia rabbit holes she can be found smashing words together until they cooperate and turn into stories.

Facebook: www.facebook.com/regina.griffiths.5
Twitter: @r_v_griffiths

Crewel Intentions
♥
Joy Demorra

Story Information

Holiday: Pins and Needles Day
Holiday Date: November 27
Heat Rating: 4
Relationship Type: M/M/F
Major Trigger Warnings: BDSM, dom/sub dynamic, consensual polyamory, bondage, consensual humiliation, consensual name calling.

Vlad, Nathan, and Ursula are enjoying a brief romantic sojourn in the dazzling city of Ingleton. While the whole city is on pins and needles in anticipation of the upcoming winter festivities, the trio only have time for each other. Until an unavoidable social event arises, along with some worrying concerns about Nathan's formal attire. Between the two of them, however, Vlad and Ursula are certain they can find a way to get the shirt off his back.

Crewel Intentions

November 27th 1881

It was a truth universally acknowledged throughout the Nevrondian Empire that, when it came to matters of style, vampires were considered to be the height of refined elegance and fashionable attire. This was owed largely in part to a dramatic predisposition toward wearing black evening attire, and an inherently svelte outline that could only be realistically achieved through several hundred years of liquid dieting. There was, Vlad felt, a great deal more to be appreciated about the robust and rugged nature of the Northern werewolf.

If not, however, their wardrobe choices.

"What, and I cannot stress this enough, the *hell* are you wearing?" he asked, running a critical eye over the broad expanse of Nathan's back and shoulders.

Nathan, who was fussing with his necktie in the reflection of the mirror, flicked bright blue eyes toward him. "Clothes?" he said, his voice pitched low to avoid waking the other occupant of the bed. "You do remember what those are, don't you?"

Vlad shook his head in amusement. He hadn't seen his reflection yet, but he could take a wild guess at how disheveled he looked. "Vaguely," he said, glancing down to where Ursula's head lay pillowed in his lap, her coppery-blonde curls twined loosely between his fingers.

Without her fairy glamors in place, the Sìdhe looked deceptively small and vulnerable as she slept. But even at rest, she maintained an iron grip around his waist, her fingers digging firmly into Vlad's hips as though afraid he might vanish while she slept.

She wasn't normally this clingy, but after six weeks apart, Ursula had all but jumped Vlad's bones the moment he'd stepped off the ferry. Nathan, ever the soul of restraint, had managed to wait until they made it to their hotel room before pouncing on him. But it had been a close thing.

Vlad was only just now beginning to regain the feeling in his legs.

Normally they met in the city at least once a month but matters at home had kept Vlad unavoidably detained. He'd felt their absence keenly, like a part of him was missing. The better parts. It had been a relief to finally return to them, even if they did have to carry on the charade of merely being friends in public. It was a role they played well, though a more observant onlooker may well have noted the way they leaned toward each other over the dinner table, or the lingering little glances and touches stolen under the soft glow of candlelight. But if anyone did notice they were far too polite to say anything. And besides, this was Ingleton, where the rich, eccentric, and the undead could all do whatever the hell they liked. Provided of course, they did it with *style*.

Something which Nathan was severely lacking at this precise moment.

"No but really, darling, what are you wearing?" Vlad persisted, motioning for Nathan to turn around and let him see. The werewolf complied, turning a slow circle and holding his arms out.

As quality went, the clothing wasn't half bad. It was plain but well-made, the kind of thing a country lord such as Nathan might wear while out surveying his lands or tramping over misty moorland. But it was entirely unsuitable for Ingleton high society. The colors were dull and muted. While Vlad conceded to the necessity of function over form when it came to the loose fitting cut when it came to werewolves, there was absolutely no excusing the drab, shapeless disaster of a waistcoat currently hanging off of him.

"Satisfied?" Nathan asked, completing the circle and letting his hands drop to his sides, waiting for Vlad's verdict.

"With you? Always." Vlad tilted his head to the side and gave Nathan another considerate once over. "Just not with the clothes. In fact, I think you should take them off right this minute and come back to bed."

"I agree," Ursula said muzzily, untangling herself from Vlad and rolling over onto her back. As she opened her eyes, Vlad noted that both he and Nathan were enraptured by her awakening, their gazes lingering appreciatively on her exposed curves. She smirked, stretching out catlike against the white linen sheets, basking in their admiration. The fae were vain creatures, but as far as Vlad was concerned, she'd more than earned his reverence. "What were we talking about?" she asked.

"His Lordship's clothes," Vlad supplied helpfully, watching as she rummaged around the mess of rumpled bedding for something to wear, and eventually settled on one of Nathan's baggy shirts. "And how he ought to remove them. Preferably out the window."

"Ah," Ursula gave a short little laugh, tugging the shirt down over her head as she came to lean against the headboard beside him, her golden-curled head listing against his shoulder. "Yes, I rather thought you'd have some opinions on the matter."

"What?" Nathan demanded. "You never said anything to me."

"I did, dear," Ursula said, examining her nails carefully. "Back home when we were packing and I asked if those were the clothes you were bringing to Ingleton."

"And I said yes!"

"Yes," Ursula said, continuing to examine her nails, "and then I tactfully suggested we ought to go shopping, and you said, 'yes, dear,' like you do when you're not listening and walked away."

"I—" Nathan began, then trailed off, his blue eyes narrowing as he recalled the moment. "Ah. That was tact, was it?"

"Yes, dear."

"See, that's where you went wrong," Vlad said jokingly, leaning into Ursula's warmth and resting his head atop hers. "I just tell him when something looks hideous."

Nathan folded his arms over his chest and glowered at them. It was a very good glower; he'd obviously put a lot of practice into it. The effect was somewhat ruined, however, by the fact that he never seemed able to keep a straight face when looking at the two of them together.

Vlad hadn't meant to fall for Ursula. Truthfully, he hadn't meant to fall in love with *either* of them. He'd spent the last two hundred years of his unlife guarding his heart against such things; nursing the shards of his broken heart and burying his loneliness beneath a façade of cheerful recklessness.

And then Nathan had walked into his life. Or more precisely, hobbled.

At the time, Vlad hadn't any idea what he'd been letting himself in for when he'd agreed to take on an injured werewolf as Captain of the Eyrie Guard, but whatever he'd expected, it hadn't been Captain Nathaniel J. Northland. He could still remember the first time he'd laid eyes on the other man. He'd looked so dashing in his red

Imperial uniform; even with the dark shadows under his eyes, a shoulder brace to keep him upright, and freshly healed scars marring the side of his handsome face. But it had been his mannerisms that had drawn Vlad to him; the soft-spoken confidence of his smile and the kindness in his eyes, his entire being radiating a quiet and easy sort of authority that had pinged something deep within Vlad's soul and left him weak at the knees with longing.

He'd never *dreamed* his affections might be returned.

Vampires and werewolves did not make for likely bedfellows in any given sense of the word. But Nathan had surprised him, and as the weeks turned into months and the month into a year, Vlad had slowly unbarred his heart and allowed himself to hope that perhaps this time things would be different... And then tragedy had struck, first when Nathan's father had died, soon followed by the unexpected death of his eldest brother, leaving behind a void in the line of succession that only Nathan could fill.

Vlad had been brokenhearted for Nathan at the time, but also selfishly for himself as well. He'd known then that this would be the end of their relationship, even if Nathan seemingly hadn't. He could still remember the harrowing ache that had opened up in his chest when Nathan had returned to tell him he was to be married. And the even greater pain when he'd refused to give Vlad up, and Vlad had been forced to do it for him.

And then there had been Ursula, bright fiery Ursula with her voluminous copper curls, golden-tawny eyes, and a heart so big it could swallow the ocean and still have room for all the stars. It had been quite by accident that she and Vlad had met. The look on Nathan's face upon seeing them talking together had been priceless, though not nearly as priceless as when she'd suggested the two men keep seeing each other.

"I don't mind the idea of sharing if you don't," she'd said, a beguiling smile tugging at her lips.

And Vlad had found himself surprised to find that he didn't mind the idea at all. If sharing Nathan was what it took to be able to love him, then Vlad was willing do so. What they had not accounted for, however, was that they'd end up falling for each other as well. It had been a happy surprise, and no one had been happier than Nathan to watch his two loves fall head over heels in love for each other.

Even if they were currently ganging up on him.

"So, what do you suggest I do instead then, hmm?" He arched an eyebrow at the pair on the bed, gesturing down at himself. "I can hardly go out in my drawers."

"Well, you could," Ursula countered, giggling softly, "but I think you'd find it a trifle cold."

They glanced collectively at the windows where the late November wind drove the snow up against the foggy glass pane in drifts. Ingleton was not as damp as Eyrie, but Vlad still felt the cold keenly, the chill working its way into his centuries-old bones with a dull familiar ache. He shivered reflexively, and Ursula snuggled closer to him, hooking her bronze-skinned legs over his deathly pale ones. A creature of light and fire, she was always a source of comfort and warmth, even more so than Nathan who ran hot with the blood of the wolf.

Suddenly, the idea of spending the rest of the winter in bed was vastly appealing.

"Wait," Vlad said, a horrifying thought occurring to him, "the first winter ball at court is this Saturday. We're all invited."

"Yeah, so?" Nathan asked.

"Tell me you've got something to wear…"

"I have clothes," Nathan said evasively after a pause.

Vlad groaned into his hands. "Nathan, love, this is your first social debut at court as a member of Parliament, *and* as the Wolf Lord. You're representing both your home and all the werewolf clans this side of the Empire. You need to make a good first impression."

"That's what I tried to tell him," Ursula said, blowing her ornery werewolf husband a kiss when his glower landed on her again. "Well, I did."

"Stuff and nonsense," Nathan muttered, reaching up to rub distractedly at the back of his neck, rolling his injured shoulder uncomfortably. His old war wounds always ached when he was stressed, and this instance was no exception as Vlad watched him reach up to tug at his left ear, fussing with the fit of the metal bracket that kept his hearing aid in place. "I really don't see what all the fuss is about… my father never bothered with any of this."

Vlad felt Ursula stiffen. Her lips were pursed together in a thin line—no doubt to keep from saying something unkind. He'd only met the late Lord Northland once, but once had been enough. Cantankerous and stubborn to a fault, the man's refusal to move with the times had very nearly cost his family everything. Nathan had managed to salvage the situation, though only just.

Vlad could only imagine the things Ursula might have to say about the old wolf.

"Yes, but you're not your father," she reasoned instead, "you don't have to keep trying to be."

"I'm not..." Nathan began, then trailed off visibly uncomfortable. "Look, we all know I'm not good with... with this." He gestured around the opulence of the hotel room and out the window towards the city beyond. "I'm a solider. I was a solider," he amended quietly. "I don't know how to fit in here."

"A decent tailor would be a start," Vlad tried, teasingly.

Nathan gave him a skeptical look.

"I'm serious! Look, you're a handsome man Nathan. You are in fact, stunningly handsome. You deserve nice things and to look your best. With the right attire, you wouldn't just fit in, you'd be head and shoulders above everyone around you. And let's be honest here, you have a lot of height and shoulder to work with."

The werewolf laughed softly through his nose, shaking his head. "I dunno..."

"And it's not like we're telling you to change *everything*," Ursula wheedled, holding up her thumb and forefinger and pinching them together. "Just a few small tweaks here and there..."

"Small things," Vlad agreed, sliding Ursula's legs out of his lap, moving up onto his knees and crawling over to the end of the bed to where Nathan was stood.

He gave only the merest token effort of resistance when Vlad pulled him forward, allowing himself to be encircled by Vlad's arms as the vampire peered adoringly up at him. It was only somewhat exaggerated for the other man's benefit. Partly because he knew how much Nathan liked it, but also because Vlad was truly that much in love with him. He could admit that to himself now.

"And we can start by getting rid of this gods-awful waistcoat."

Nathan laughed again, snorting gently through his nose as his hands came to rest reflexively on the dip of Vlad's hips, fully aware that he was being mollified through his baser instincts, but seeming not to object. "And just what do you propose we do about it?" Nathan asked, the shaggy chestnut curls of his hair falling boyishly into his piercing blue eyes in a way that never failed to make Vlad's heart stutter. "In case you hadn't noticed, my tailor is four hundred miles north of here."

"Well," Vlad said thoughtfully, tipping his head to the side, "we could always go see mine. I'm sure Angelo could fit you in..."

Not to mention be positively thrilled at the chance to work with such a strong, broad canvas, he thought, keeping that particular comment to himself.

"I think that's a *splendid* idea," Ursula agreed, leaning back against the cushioned headboard in a languid stretch, causing her borrowed shirt to ride up over her hips in a tantalizing display of immodesty. Vlad felt his mouth turn dry. "It certainly wouldn't hurt to try."

Tearing his gaze away from her, Nathan seemed to think about it and then shook his head dismissively. "Ach, it's all just pomp and circumstance. They can either take me as I am or lump it."

Vlad and Ursula shared a meaningful look, and then Ursula's expression grew sly, the corners of her mouth ticking up a notch.

"We could always take a trip down the West End while we're at it," she said.

Vlad felt Nathan's posture stiffen, his grip on Vlad's hips tightening. It wasn't painful, but it was enough to elicit an uncomfortable squirm. He gasped a moment later when Nathan's fingers tightened again, holding him in place as a pulse of desire twitched through Vlad's cock.

"Vlad's never been there," Ursula carried on, her tone light and innocent on the surface but laden with a heavy undercurrent of temptation underneath.

Vlad watched as Nathan's gaze swiveled down toward him again. There was a telltale bloom of warmth beginning to color his cheeks, and it sent an answering jolt of heat down Vlad's spine. He was aware of Ursula prowling up behind him, the heat of her body pressing up against his back as her arms snaked around his front, her chin coming to rest on his shoulder, and Vlad knew the picture they must paint. He could see it in the inferno of Nathan's darkening gaze, the grip on his hips now tight enough to leave a bruise. At least, he certainly hoped so.

"It could be our little… *treat*," Ursula said, and Vlad shivered as much from her nearness as the lasciviousness of her tone. He had no idea what the West End entailed, but he was more than willing to find out.

Nathan let out a low rumbling growl of a sigh, the werewolf evidently torn between letting himself be led down the garden path by the end of his nose and wanting what was on offer on the other side.

"But I suppose, if you're really that set against it—"

"Fine," Nathan ground out, a smile tugging at the mulish line of his mouth that made Vlad want to kiss him. It was clear as much as

Nathan hated shopping that he wanted to please the pair who held his heart more.

And Nathan was right, nothing would please Vlad more than to paint Nathan's beautiful form in the colors and fabrics it so very much deserved. Without prompting, Vlad began envisioning just what fashions would suit his werewolf lord best. Velvet, of course. And perhaps satin with a watered-silk waistcoat. Nathan's voice cut off Vlad's imaginings. "But just to look, mind, and none of your frippery," he warned, raising a cautionary finger under their noses and giving them both a meaningful stare. "Either of you. I'm not going to let you truss me up like some…" he trailed off, seeming to realize what he'd been about to say.

Vlad clucked his tongue against the roof of his mouth reproachfully. "I thought you *liked* dandies," he said, nipping at the offending finger in front of him and licking it better just because he could. "I distinctly remember a conversation about that."

"I said I liked bending them over my knee," Nathan countered gruffly, sounding decisively more strained than he had done a moment before. "I mean it, though, no nonsense…"

"All right, fine, fine," Ursula placated him, her hands starting to wander distractingly over the front of Vlad's chest, gliding tantalizingly close to the waist of his silk undergarments. "No fripperies. Just some new shirts. And a couple of waistcoats. And a new coat."

"Maybe some neckties…" Vlad added thoughtfully, wishing he had a pen and paper handy.

"What about my trousers?" Nathan asked wryly. "I can't help but notice you haven't mentioned those yet."

"Oh, I think we can think of some fairly pressing reasons to get rid of them," Ursula grinned, her laughter vibrating pleasantly through the hollow of Vlad's chest. It was enough to make his toes curl, almost as much as the feeling of Nathan's hardening erection pressing up against his front. It was suddenly entirely too warm in here.

"Off," he commanded, working to divest Nathan of the offensive waistcoat as quickly as possible. He let it drop to the floor where it belonged, his hands fumbling to undo the buttons of Nathan's shirt, palming hungrily over the firm expanse of his chest and abdomen.

"You'd almost think you've been starved for touch these last few days," Nathan said lightly, his voice rich and thick with amusement as he adjusted the straps of his shoulder brace to better maneuver out of his undershirt, the muscles in his abdomen and chest rippling in a mouthwatering display of strength and power as they moved. "Have we not been taking care of you?"

"Looks like we'll have to try harder," Ursula added before Vlad could reply, burying her face against the side of his neck and peeking out to watch the rest of the show as Nathan stripped out of the remainder of his clothing, shucking his trousers to the floor, followed closely by his drawers.

Vlad was always fascinated by the way Nathan moved when naked. He was surer of himself, more confident, like his clothing was a hindrance that merely got in the way of his natural prowess. And Vlad supposed it would be when his other form was that of a giant reddish-brown wolf with a jaw that could snap bone like a toothpick.

"Move over," Nathan commanded, the mattress dipping under his added weight as he climbed up beside them. His hands were warm and hot against Vlad's flanks as he claimed Vlad's mouth in a searing open-mouthed kiss, guiding him gently backward to a more central spot on the mattress. Ursula remained close at his back, her mouth hot and wet against the side of his neck as she sucked and nipped at the skin, adding to the marks of her affection that already adorned his body.

He jolted at a particularly hard bite, tipping his head back against her shoulder with an audible moan. He was keenly aware of their weight pressing in on him, the sound of their shared kiss obscenely wet and loud so close to his ear. But it was nowhere near as debauched as the ragged moan that escaped his lips as his hips began to move of their own volition, rubbing up against Nathan's front in shivery, fitful little thrusts.

The werewolf drew back, unable to keep the grin from his handsome face as he reached down to grip Vlad's hips again, stopping them from moving. "Needy," he chided fondly.

Once upon a time Vlad knew his soul would have shriveled up at the use of such a word, but the last year and a half had turned it into an endearment. Nathan didn't mind that Vlad was needy and clingy in this way; if anything he *adored* it. And while Ursula might feign indifference or annoyance, she too enjoyed this side of him for entirely different reasons.

"What's your word?" Ursula prompted from behind him, her hands splayed out flat against his abdomen and chest as she held him securely upright.

"Red," he breathed out, his eyes fluttering closed as he let the sensation of being pressed between them wash over him, solid and reassuring.

"Good boy," she purred close to his ear, the endearment tinged with an edge of patronization that made Vlad *squirm,* burying his face against the crook of Nathan's neck as a hot flush began to crawl over his skin.

It was embarrassing just how hard and needy those two words could render him. He'd balked at their use at first, torn by the shamefaced flood of arousal that had washed over him, and the desperate need to hear it over and over again. But while Nathan was quick and sincere to praise, there was just something about the way Ursula said it that got under his skin and *prickled* in all the right ways. It wasn't cruel, not exactly, but it wasn't kind either, which was precisely what Vlad liked about it. He liked being roughed about and talked down to, he *liked* being made to feel small and helpless, and Ursula could be downright ruthless.

When he wanted her to be.

"And what do we feel like today, hmm?" Ursula crooned, deceptively sweet as she pressed a hot, sucking kiss to the side of his throat again. "Do we want to be naughty?" She bit down sharply against the tender juncture between Vlad's neck and shoulder, laughing throatily at the hitched sob of desire that caught in his throat before pressing her lips to the injured spot, kissing it better. "Or nice?"

Naughty, even the word sent a guilty little thrill through him. But they couldn't play that particular game right now, not if they actually wanted to make it out of the bedroom any time soon.

"Nice," he rasped out, sounding breathless even to his own ears.

Ursula made a thoughtful, little humming sound. "Well, I suppose we have been a *little* demanding these past few days," she said, feigning disappointment but reassuring him with another quick kiss, her hands rubbing soothingly over his biceps. "I suppose we can let you have a break."

Vlad laughed, the sound muffled by Nathan's chest as the werewolf, ever the coddler, soothed and petted him fondly, his blunt fingernails scratching at the sensitive spot at the nape of Vlad's neck. They all knew there was no "let" about anything they did—it was all negotiated, in a hundred thousand tiny little ways. But it was still nice to be reassured.

"Thank you," he said, lifting his head and turning his face to the side to look at her, catching the sly little wink she gave him, understanding his choice. "You're too kind."

"Lies and slander," she hissed back, maneuvering up the bed to claim the bottle of oil from the nightstand, stripping unceremoniously out of her borrowed shirt as she went.

Nathan chuckled, a low deep rumbling sound that shuddered through Vlad's bones. His heart leapt into his throat a moment later when Nathan hauled him up off his knees, flipping Vlad onto his back with dizzying ease. "All right, come here, you," he said, pinning Vlad in place with a wolfish grin as Ursula slotted herself beside him, pressing close to his side. "Let's get *nice*."

And it didn't matter how many times they did this, Vlad still always found himself shockingly overwhelmed by how good it felt. How *right* it felt. How easily they slipped into the rhythm of each other's movements, kissing and sighing into each other until it was impossible to tell where one breath began and another one ended. And even now, after all this time, Vlad still found there was always something new to learn, something that provoked a gasp or a squeal, and this time it was something about himself.

"Oh dear," Ursula laughed, leaning in again to tease her tongue over the shell of his ear, making Vlad twitch and squirm under Nathan's weight holding him in place. "Did I find something?"

"I think you did," Nathan agreed, the burr of his Northern accent thickened by arousal and amusement.

"Try the other side," Ursula said, sounding as though they were discussing the weather, and not like she had Vlad's thigh pressed between her legs and was grinding up against him for her own relief. "See if it works there too."

Nathan obligingly did as he was told, leaning over to kiss and mouth at the tender flesh. It felt good, but it was nowhere near the same level of shockingly intensive pleasure that had spiked through him before.

"So just this side then," Ursula hummed thoughtfully, and Vlad near jumped out of his skin when she gave his left earlobe an experimental nibble. "Interesting. I'll have to keep that in mind."

"Fuck me," Vlad muttered.

Ursula treated him to another one of her blazingly bright smiles. "If you'd like. Though not right now, I don't have the right tools with me."

"We don't have *any* tools with us at all," Nathan commented lightly, his mouth still attacking the side of Vlad's neck, and Vlad felt his cheeks start to burn at the thought of all the toys locked away in the trunk at the foot of his bed back home.

It had started out as small things from Nathan at first: a bottle of scented oil here, a risqué book to add to his collection there, the items gradually progressing to a more intimate nature as their relationship grew. From simple silk ties to blindfold him with, to the leather bindings that made him quake and shudder just remembering the pull of them around his wrists—the helpless thrill of being bound in place as sharp and delicate as standing on a knife edge. And then there had been the… *other* toys.

Vlad swallowed, sucking in air as he tried to keep his brain in his skull where it belonged. It was a losing battle.

Ursula had been teasing him for quite some time about pegging him ever since an inadvertent slip of the tongue had revealed it was something he had more than just a passing interest in trying. Thus far it had remained purely in the realms of fantasy, the wily Sìdhe weaponizing it against him at opportune moments. Usually when it would be entirely inconvenient for him to have a throbbing erection, or when he was already half-gone with lust—dripping salacious honeyed words into his ear about all the things she'd do to him if given half the chance. The first time she'd done it, Vlad had come so hard and unexpectedly it had punched the air from his lungs, and he'd seen stars. After that, it had been fair game as part of their play to wind him up, tormenting him and tying him into verbal knots so effective they might as well have been physical from how well they paralyzed him with want.

It was a skill both Ursula and Nathan had in common, knowing exactly what to say and how best to say it for maximum effect. Together they made for a formidable pair, and Vlad found himself helpless to resist.

He gasped harshly when a warm hand closed around the length of his shaft, palming him through the slippery smooth silk of his underwear. He'd been so far inside his own head he hadn't even noticed Nathan's shift in position, the other man leaning up on one arm to watch as Vlad bucked and writhed up into the simple touch.

"So needy," Nathan admonished again, his voice little more than a low rumble of indulgent fondness. "You'd think after four days you'd have had enough."

Vlad bit his lip, feeling the blush burn even hotter over his face and neck, spreading down to his chest. He knew it wasn't a real rebuke, but he felt it just as keenly as one, the shame of being made to feel so wanton making his stomach twist pleasantly. He choked on a moan when Nathan gave him another squeeze, aware that Ursula had shifted her position to slot a hand between her legs, watching his expression intently as she touched herself.

He tried to reach for her, to do some of the work himself, but Ursula merely swatted his hand away. "Who said you could touch?"

"Sorry," Vlad murmured, working moisture into his mouth and trying to remember how words worked. "Can I—"

"No, you can lie there and keep your hands to yourself," Ursula informed him sternly, though not as severely as she might have done otherwise. After all, they were supposed to be playing *nice*. "Hands flat, on the bed," she instructed, and Vlad let out a pitiful whine of protest.

It was sheer torture not to be allowed to touch them. He gasped harshly a moment later when Nathan roughly shucked his drawers down, freeing Vlad's painfully hard erection and letting it curve up toward his abdomen.

"Beautiful," Ursula commented, her breath leaving her in a sigh as Nathan trailed light fingertips over the head of Vlad's cock, coming away slick with his arousal.

"So wet already," the other man commented.

Vlad couldn't help the half moan half laugh that escaped his chest, arching up into the fleeting touch. "Can't help it with you pawing at me."

The look Nathan gave him told him that if they weren't currently playing *nice*, Vlad would already have been flipped over onto his front and counting out the number of smacks it would take him to break and say sorry. But because they *were* playing nice, he merely prolonged the moment for longer, his touches maddeningly soft and gentle, stimulating, but not enough to give him any real friction. When Vlad tried to thrust up into the loose circle of the other man's fist, Nathan promptly shoved him back down, using his weight to pin Vlad's legs in place. "Behave," he warned.

The words *'make me'* were on the tip of Vlad's tongue when the mattress dipped under Nathan's weight, and Vlad found himself arching up with a cry into the enveloping wet heat of Nathan's mouth. It was sheer willpower that kept his hands where they were, his fingers splaying out reflexively before tangling in the mess of sheets beneath him.

"Oh, good boy, keep your hands where they are. That's it," Ursula crooned close to his ear, her voice low and indulgent, a playful facsimile of the praise Nathan showered so freely and earnestly over him.

"Beautiful," Ursula continued, carrying on her litany of praise as she watched him writhe. Vlad pried his eyes open to look at her. Her tawny eyes were dark and glittering with arousal. "Just beautiful."

Nathan, his mouth otherwise preoccupied, added his own hum of approval, rocketing Vlad closer to the edge with a strangled groan, his hands opening and closing futilely against the sheets, searching for something to hold onto.

"P-lease—"

"Oh gosh, we're begging already are we?" Ursula teased, reaching over to trail the fingers of her free hand over his chest, the ticklish touch entirely at odds with the fire Nathan was stoking under his skin stroking Vlad off with his mouth and hands.

She glanced down, and Vlad followed her gaze, a visceral shudder running through him at the sight of Nathan's bowed head. It made Vlad's head swim, a senseless tumble of thoughts and conflicting desires crashing together as his desire to come warred with his need to be the one on his knees.

"Open," Ursula said, and Vlad opened his eyes again when she tapped her finger against his mouth, realizing belatedly he'd been biting his lip to keep quiet. "None of that; we want to hear you, don't we, love?"

Nathan made another sound of approval that caused Vlad's hips to buck up wildly. Nathan promptly shoved him back down again, holding his hips firmly in place against the mattress as he laved his tongue over the hot length of Vlad's cock, kissing and sucking until all Vlad could do was lie back and whine.

"Please," he tried again, not entirely sure what he was asking for, but knowing that he needed it.

"That's it," Ursula encouraged him, and Vlad could feel the urgency with which she was working herself, the heel of her palm grinding against the apex of her thighs, a shudder rippling through her hard enough for him to feel it. "Louder."

"*Please.*"

Above him, Ursula gave a stifled gasp of her own, a hot pink flush rising over her cheeks as she squirmed against him. Pulling her hand away, she raised her index and middle fingers expectantly to Vlad's lips, and the vampire obediently opened his mouth. He moaned at the taste of her on his tongue, sucking greedily on her fingertips. He all but whined when she withdrew them, but the sound Ursula made when she pressed the slick digits into herself was very nearly close to a squeal, and Vlad felt the first warning signs of his own imminent release ripple through him.

"Close," he gasped out, the sound pitching up embarrassingly high when Nathan took that as incentive and redoubled his efforts, swallowing Vlad down to the root. It was all Vlad could do not to spend himself there and then, his lips peeled back in a silent keen.

"Close, close, I'm so close," he warned again. The words turned into a pleading mantra as his body wound tighter and tighter, his back arching uncontrollably as the coil of heat at the base of his spine clawed its way upward and outward, shattering over him like a tidal wave as he came.

He was barely sensate when he felt Nathan crawling up the length of him, his own erection hot and hard against Vlad's abdomen as he pressed an open mouth kiss to his lips, licking into his mouth and sucking the air from his lungs.

"Good boy," he all but growled when they parted, his normally blue-eyed gaze tinged yellow with the hungry animal gleam of the wolf lurking within. "And all mine too."

"Yours." Vlad managed a breathy laugh, reaching up to card shaky fingers through Nathan's reddish-brown curls. His limbs however were too heavy, and he missed, managing instead to bop his lover squarely on the nose. He laughed again, and Nathan pressed a tender kiss to the inside of his wrist before letting it drop, turning his attention to Ursula, who was still watching them, panting slightly at her own exertions.

"Also mine," Nathan declared, shifting his weight off of Vlad to pull Ursula down the mattress by her ankle, the Sidhe squealing in protest at being manhandled so.

"Brute!" she admonished, working her way up onto her elbows.

Nathan snorted, tilting his head to the side as he looked down at her. "Only because you like it."

"That is neither here nor there."

"What's your word?" Nathan asked, and Ursula rolled her eyes dramatically.

"Red. What's yours?" she countered back, and Nathan gave another little huff of patient laughter.

"Silver. Now come here you." He yanked her down once more, likely just to hear her squeal again.

Vlad rolled over onto his side to watch as Nathan pushed into her, the two of them groaning in unison as they slotted together and began to move as one. He was content to watch, but Ursula reached out blindly for him, threading her fingers through his hair and tugging gently. Taking the hint, Vlad leaned up on his elbow and claimed her mouth with his, swallowing her panted moans hungrily.

He drew back just in time to watch her tip over the edge, her expression utterly rapturous as she came. Nathan thrust into her once, twice, and then a final third time before stilling over the top of her, his head dropping down between his shoulders as his orgasm shivered out of him in a low drawn out breath of laughter. He shook his head dazedly as he slipped free to fall languidly at her side, the three of them sprawled together in a messy, panting tangle of limbs as they recovered.

After too short a time, Ursula sat up, looking expectantly between the vampire and werewolf on either side of her. "So, shall we get ready to go shopping?" she asked, ignoring their groans as she scrambled up onto her knees with far too much exuberance for someone who had just been so thoroughly fucked.

"I call dibs on the first bath," she said, causing the bed to bounce alarmingly as she jumped off the end, heading into the adjacent room. The sound of running water filled the air a moment later.

Nathan and Vlad shared an exhausted look.

"I blame you," Nathan informed him.

"You married her," Vlad countered.

Nathan chuckled into the pillow he was currently trying to bury his face into. "This is true."

"Come on, slow-pokes," Ursula called, her golden-haired head appearing around the side of the door as she threw a pair of damp towels at them. "Last one up buys lunch."

*

It was roughly just after noon when they finally made their way out into the world. The snow had stopped by then, at least, but the wind was enough to make them reconsider, and it was only by sheer force of will that they didn't retreat to their little love nest on the thirteenth floor. But needs must—and it was an absolute necessity that Nathan find some new clothes. Not least of all because Ursula, mischief maker that she was (and no doubt in collusion with Vlad), had absconded with the worst of them while he'd been in the bath and was now refusing to tell him where she'd hidden them.

"I really don't know about this," he said for the umpteenth time since they'd started walking, his feet dragging as Vlad led them toward a modest sandstone building on the corner of Oath Street. The window display was artfully arranged in a tasteful array of top hats, gloves, and the occasional sparkle of jewelry to catch the light—as well as the fancy of any passersby. It was entirely too sparkly for Nathan.

Oath Street was well renowned as being the epicenter of culture and fashion throughout the Empire. Indeed, it was said a person could walk no less than four paces before tripping over a tailor with their measuring tape outstretched. The streets were lined with tall sandstone buildings that looked more like elegant townhouses than places of commerce, the shop fronts bright and dazzling and inviting… for those with the coin to spend in them. And Nathan was beginning to feel increasingly out of place amidst the sea of bobbing top hats and winter bonnets. He glanced sideways at Vlad and Ursula, their heads bowed together as they admired something in the window.

They looked like they belonged here, at least Vlad certainly did, in his trim black winter coat and gray woolen top hat tipped at a jaunty angle to protect his eyes from the worst of the daylight. Ursula, on the other hand, tended to disregard all current modes of fashion with the cheerfulness of someone who knew they would outlive all of it and wore whatever the hell she felt like. But she always looked good doing it. Today was a purple day, and the thick velvet of her cloak fell around her shoulders, giving her a soft, almost romantic look that seemed to belong to another era. Primarily because it did.

"I said, I really don't know about this," he repeated, just in case they hadn't heard him and weren't just ignoring him. He eyed a jeweled and lace encrusted tailcoat in the window, and suppressed another shudder of distaste. "This doesn't exactly look like my sort of scene…"

"Oh nonsense," Vlad soothed, reaching up to stop his hat from being swept away by a cold gust of wind that sent Ursula skittering to Nathan's side for warmth. "It's only Angelo, and he's everyone's scene."

"Easy for you to say," Nathan grumbled, "you're built for this sort of thing."

"What, wearing clothes?"

"Fashion," Nathan replied darkly. "You've got the height for it."

"Oh, don't be ridiculous, we're the same bloody height," Vlad protested, not for the first time.

"Yes, but you're," Nathan gestured vaguely toward Vlad's lithe, whip-lean silhouette, "mostly leg."

"He's right you know," Ursula agreed, her teeth beginning to chatter loudly as she stood huddled against Nathan, her hood drawn up to protect her hair from the worst of the elements. The addition of a hat would have kept her both warmer and dryer, but she claimed there was no point in wearing one, not when her hair had a willful energy of its own and liked to devour combs with vengeful alacrity. "You are very leggy."

"Thanks awfully," the vampire said drolly.

Ursula gave him her most winsome smile. "You're welcome."

"Right, come on you two, before we freeze to the pavement," Vlad said, holding the door open and motioning them inside. "After you."

Nathan grumbled some more, moving reluctantly toward the door and frowning at the cheerful sign in the window he hadn't noticed until now. "Pins and Needles Day Sale," he read aloud.

"I wonder what that's about," Ursula said, giving his hand a gentle tug, and then another more insistent one when he still didn't move. "Must be some sort of holiday for tailors."

"I think it means I'm about to get stuck with a lot of pins," Nathan muttered dourly as he followed after her, bowing his head to get through the door without knocking his top hat off. He missed his tricorn, it was comfortable and worn from years of use, and much less inclined to accidental mishaps in doorways.

A bell above the door chimed as they entered, welcoming them into a pleasant interior that had been made over to look more like a fashionable salon than a tailor's shop. Behind the counters, bolts upon bolts of fabric lined the walls: deep rich velvets to thick musty wool, luminescent silks, and gauze so sheer it might as well have been spun from gossamer.

Glancing around, Nathan couldn't decide which immediate sensation was worse: sticking out like a sore thumb or feeling like a bull in a fine-china shop. He turned, ready to leave, only to find Vlad standing firmly behind him, barring the way.

"Nice try," his lover said, giving him a smile that was all teeth.

Nathan sighed, resigning himself to the inevitable. After all, there were worse things in life than being fitted for new clothes.

Vlad led them toward the counter where several store clerks were standing around, seemingly arguing over something. A short, squat little man was at the center of it, his arms waving animatedly. His slicked black hair was near comically shiny in the glaring light of the lamps. His age was indiscernible at a glance, and for a moment, Nathan would have perhaps mistaken him for another vampire, had his scent not been so decisively human. If somewhat pomade-y. When he looked up and saw Vlad coming, his round face broke into a friendly grin, his arms held out wide in exuberant welcoming.

"Ah! Master Blutstein! What a pleasure, I wasn't expecting to see you!" His Imperial accent was refined but tinged with a note of warmth that belonged to somewhere else, somewhere with bluer skies and warm sands.

"Settle a debate, my friend: carmine or burgundy?" he said, holding up two swatches of fabric that looked absolutely identical to Nathan.

Vlad pulled off his leather gloves, dropping them into his top hat as he took both swatches in hand and considered them thoughtfully, while Nathan took the opportunity to admire him out the corner of his eye.

There was no denying he cut a striking figure, even bundled up in his thick black winter coat. Turned early on in his life, the vampire had been blessed with his high cheekbones, a clever mouth, and dark, almost black eyes that glittered and gleamed like onyx. There was a pink tinge in his face from the cold, and his black hair was somewhat more ruffled than usual too, though not from the winter wind. As well as hiding some of Nathan's clothes, Ursula had also taken the opportunity to hide the vampire's pomade, declaring firmly that she liked him best when he was just a little bit undone.

Nathan was inclined to agree with her.

"What's it for?" the vampire asked, rubbing the cloth between his fingertips, evidently trying to decide if he liked one better than the other based on how they felt. He was delightfully tactile when it came to such things, and Nathan had gotten a lot of mileage out of that particular quirk.

"The winter solstice display," the little man said, wringing his hands together. "We are already so far behind this year, I don't know how we will ever manage."

Vlad gave them another moment of thoughtful consideration, then leaned over the counter to pluck a silk handkerchief from one of the displays.

"This one," he glanced at the tag, "raspberry wine. Far more cheerful."

"Ah! Perfection!" the little man cried, and a collective shudder of relief rippled around the assembled staff. "You are correct as ever, my friend. I don't know what I'd do without you. Now, tell me, what can old Angelo do for you today?"

"Well, it's not precisely for me," Vlad began, "though I would consider it a rather personal favor. You see this rather tall gentleman behind me? Of course you do; this is Cap—sorry," he laughed, cutting himself off, "force of habit. *Lord* Nathaniel Northland of Castle Tuath, our most recently appointed member of Parliament, he's also the current Wolf Lord to the collective wereclans. And this divine creature of loveliness is his wife, Lady Ursula. Nathan, Ursula, this is Angelo Mortoletti, an absolute cad about town, but a genius with a needle and thread."

Nathan watched as Angelo did the double take most people did when confronted with a Northern werewolf for the first time, even one in human form. Although, perhaps, his eyes went wide merely from hearing the titles alone; it was hard to tell sometimes. Nathan personally detested them. They sounded like they belonged to someone far grander, and more importantly, someone who knew what they were doing. He envied Ursula's easy confidence in that regard, watching as the tailor took her proffered hand and bowed floridly over it.

She'd been Lady this or Lady that for most of her life, flitting from title to title down through the centuries as easily as the change of the seasons. At least, she made it seem easy, and Nathan could only applaud the way in which the Sìdhe wore her titles and lineage like a mantle—something to be drawn up around her when necessary and pulled back when it was not. He supposed it came with age, but Nathan could never imagine a time when he'd be comfortable hearing himself addressed as *Lord Northland*. It would always make him think of his father.

He smiled at Angelo, though, reaching up to doff his hat to him. Uncomfortable as he was, that wasn't any excuse to be impolite. "Master Mortoletti, you have quite the establishment here."

"You honor me, sir," the little man said, touching his hand to his forelock and bowing formally. "And my lady too, what exquisite beauty. Good heavens, Vlad, however did you find yourself in such respectable company?"

"Sometimes I wonder," Vlad laughed. "Anyway, it was brought to my attention this morning over breakfast that Nathan's winter wardrobe, while utterly splendid for up North, is a touch…" he made an ambiguous gesture with his hand, "*out of season* for Ingleton society. I was rather hoping you might be able to fit him in."

"Oh, why yes, yes of course!" Angelo said, pushing aside the swatches of fabric on the counter and retrieving a book from somewhere under the pile. He flipped it open with hurried anticipation, pulling a pencil down from behind his ear. "When would be most convenient for you?"

"Today," Ursula said, offering him an impish smile when Angelo's eyes rolled up slowly to see if she was joking. "The winter ball debut is this weekend, so today would be convenient."

The little man glanced between them, then blankly out to his shop, then back again. "You want an entire new outfit, for this weekend? In less than three days?"

"It really is quite urgent," Vlad said apologetically, "and I know you're not a miracle worker, Angelo, but if anyone could do it…"

He left the sentence hanging hopefully in the air, and Nathan watched as Angelo's face worked slowly into a grin.

"And who am I to say no to such a glorious challenge?" He beamed, clapping his hands together and sending his staff into a flurry of motion. "Molly, turn the sign over on the door. Oliver, bring out the measuring stool and tell Madame Ellie to make some refreshments."

His grin took on a manic gleam as he slid the measuring tape from around his shoulders and snapped it taut between both hands. "I've got *the* Wolf Lord to dress."

*

Nathan had never considered shopping for clothes to be a spectator sport before, but Vlad and Ursula were certainly a participating audience.

"No, too green," Ursula said, dismissing the bolt of fabric the sales assistant held up to Nathan for her inspection.

"Far too bland," Vlad agreed, motioning it away, along with the next few. "Too plain. Too *silver*, good gods get that out of here. No silver thread, gold only. Nickel if you absolutely have to."

"What did I say about no fripperies?" Nathan called from his spot in the center of the room, where Angelo was in the process of pinning a shirt to him. His protests fell on deaf ears, the pair giving him a joint mischievous little wave from where they sat on one of the plush velvet couches that lined the walls, drinking tea and enjoying the delicate array of pastries and sweet fruits that had been procured for them. "Ugh, never mind."

Behind him, Angelo chortled good naturedly. "I would not worry too much, Master Northland; I have never known the Viscount to ever willingly tolerate ugly clothing. He will not allow you to be dressed poorly."

"That's what I'm afraid of," Nathan said weakly, trying in vain to keep his left arm steady, and cringing when the muscle cramped and gave out. "Sorry, old war wound."

"Not to worry, I am done with the sides. You may lower your arms," Angelo said, giving Nathan a thoughtful once over as he came around to his front and continued to fuss with the line of the shirt. "Though not so old a wound, I think, not when sir is so very handsome and young."

"I'm sixty-five," Nathan said wryly, relaxing his other arm more carefully, acutely aware of all the pins so close to his skin. They were gold-coated rather than silver, but it still set his nerves on edge.

Werewolves aged slower than humans, and while Nathan looked to be in his early thirties, there was every chance he was older than Angelo himself. Rather than shocked, however, by this information, the tailor merely flashed him a dazzling smile, giving him a companionable tap on the shoulder. "Ah see, still a boy yet," he said, and Nathan couldn't help but snort.

"You know, I've never dressed a werewolf before," the little man carried on conversationally, pulling out his measuring tape and looping it around Nathan's neck again. Even with the aid of a stool he still had to stand on tiptoe to read the measurement. "Vampires, of course, humans in their abundance, but never a werewolf."

"Fashion isn't really a priority when clothes are optional," Nathan replied, tipping his head back and trying not to imagine how restrictive the shirt collar would feel once it was in place.

"Yes, I imagine there must be some difficulties to that," Angelo said thoughtfully, drawing back and running a critical eye over Nathan again, tapping a finger to his lips. "I wonder, I wonder... I suppose you could always set a daring new trend, a more open collar with a less elaborate tie. Perhaps a frock coat with a more modern cut, some crewel work around the cuffs and lapels… Yes… I do think that would suit you rather well…"

He leaned closer to Nathan, lowering his voice to a conspiratorial whisper. "Truthfully, I think the high collars are starting to look dated, but if the Viscount ever asks, you didn't hear that from me."

Nathan laughed low in his chest, glancing up toward the vampire in question. Feeling Nathan's gaze on him, Vlad looked up, dark eyes questioning, and Nathan merely smiled and shook his head. After a pause, he said, "I'm sure you'll hear it from him later, but thank you for dropping everything at such short notice… you really didn't need to close your store like that. I do hope we're not costing you more clientele…"

"Ah, think nothing of it," Angelo said, waving his thanks away. "When it comes to Master Vlad no favor is too great to ask. For him I will do anything. For friends of his," he gave Nathan a conspiratorial little wink and a friendly nudge on the arm, "almost anything."

Nathan laughed again. "Mortoletti, Mortoletti…" he said thoughtfully, "where have I heard that name before."

"Hopefully somewhere disreputable," the little man quipped back, and Nathan couldn't help but find himself starting to like the fellow. Whatever his expectations about this experience had been, the sharp, quick-witted little man had far surpassed them.

"Wait, I know," Nathan said, snapping his fingers together as the memory clicked into place. "The tailor shop in Eyrie, the one down Euripides Lane…"

Angelo blinked up at him in surprise, his face breaking into a happy grin. "Ah yes, then sir is already familiar with my work. That was my first shop, my apprentice runs it now. They designed the waistcoat Master Vlad is currently sporting, a very popular fit with the vampires… though between you and me, there's not much room to breathe."

Nathan looked around the shop front again, taking in the glittering gilt frames and the expensive quartz lights. "You must have done quite well for yourself."

"Well enough to get by," the little man said, jogging his head modestly from side to side, "not so well as some of the other shops here on Oath Street, but well enough. None of this would have been possible without Master Vlad; he helped set me up in the early days, insisted on it in fact. I think he was just pleased to finally find someone who knew the difference between gray and taupe." He chuckled warmly. "He professed it was a betrayal when I told him I wished to set up shop here in Ingleton, but he still insisted on helping. That's just how he is."

"Yes," Nathan said, glancing up through his lashes to where Ursula was attempting to coax the vampire into trying a morsel of something on the end of her fork. "I know."

"Your lady wife and the Viscount seem to be very good friends," the other man remarked lightly, working carefully to adjust the line of a pin in the shirt, and Nathan felt his gut clench. "Very close."

He glanced down and sideways at Angelo, trying to gauge his unreadable expression. He looked back up to where Vlad had acquiesced and was pulling a face from the sweetness of whatever he'd consumed while Ursula laughed, her nose wrinkled up in that adorable way that it did when she thought no one was looking.

He might well be hard of hearing, but he knew what people were already saying. He could practically *smell* the curiosity roiling out of people when they saw the three of them together... and their judgment. It was an acrid human base smell, like love but turned inside out.

As a werewolf, he was used to people judging him; he'd been dealing with it his entire life and disregarding it for almost just as long. But this wasn't just about him, there were two other people involved, and where Vlad was concerned, a whole mess of ancestral history and familial contention to deal with. And while he wasn't ashamed of loving either of them, it hurt his heart to know that there would be people who disapproved. Who would try to make their lives difficult and paint their love into something perverse. And the fact that it could be used against him, against *them*, made his blood run cold in a way he'd only ever experienced on the battlefield.

He would do anything to protect them, even if that meant keeping their love a secret. While Nathan wasn't so naïve to believe they could carry on like this forever, he did want to prolong the calm before the storm for as long as was inhumanly possible. Eventually they would have to face the world, and their secluded little bubble of intimacy would pop. But it didn't have to be today.

"Yes," he said neutrally, glancing down at his pinned shirt sleeve and watching the needles glint under the surface, "they are. We all are. Very good friends."

There was another tactful pause, and then Angelo, quite to Nathan's consternation, tipped his chin up with a guiding touch under his jaw, his dark eyes brimming over with compassionate sincerity as he looked Nathan squarely in the eye. "*Good*," he said firmly. "He deserves such good friends. And should you ever find yourself in need of a friend, Master Northland, know that you and your lovely lady wife are always welcome here."

He held Nathan's gaze for a moment longer, and then his smile broke through the surface of his seriousness like the sun breaking through rain clouds as he held up an excited finger. "And now, we find you a waistcoat!"

*

The sun had set by the time they left Angelo's shop, the little man waving them off from the front step with a promise to deliver their purchased items to the hotel as quickly as possible. Somehow Nathan believed him.

"So, what shall we do now?" Ursula asked, skipping on ahead of her boys and turning a twirl under the open starry sky, her cloak billowing dramatically as she spun. After several hours of sitting she had an over-abundance of energy to burn and nowhere for it to go but out.

"How about the West End?" Nathan said.

Ursula rounded on him, her eyes wide and wild with barely contained excitement. "Yes! I'd forgotten about that entirely!"

"I haven't. And after being turned into a pincushion and twirling around for you two to play dress up with, you'd better believe we're doing something *I* want."

"You know, you still haven't told me exactly what this entails," Vlad said, sounding faintly apprehensive as he fussed with the fit of his gloves. "I'm not sure I like not knowing."

"Oh, don't worry, it's a fun surprise," Ursula soothed, swinging back around again to loop her arm through his, patting his hand. "Probably. And besides, when have we ever led you astray?"

"Oh dear, was I supposed to be keeping count?"

*

It would have been a lie to say that Vlad had *never* been to the West End before, merely that it had been quite some time—about a century, in fact. And while the façade and shopfronts of the bohemian district had changed with time, the essence of the place remained largely the same, the streets bright and colorful and sprawling with bawdy music halls and public houses.

But rather than turn into one of these venues, Vlad found himself being led down a side street toward a dimly lit shopfront. The window was elegantly dressed in thick black drapes, hiding the interior from view. There were also no wares on display, simply a series of illuminated signs that conveyed the store was open, and welcoming of all customers.

It was the sign above the door that drew Vlad's attention, though, and he made a strange noise in the back of his throat when he realized why it felt so familiar: he already owned several items from this particular establishment, which were all safely locked away in the trunk at the foot of his bed. His stomach swooped pleasantly in a twist of apprehensive anticipation.

"Oh," he said, sounding breathless and light, even to his own ears. "So, this is where… huh." He coughed awkwardly, aware that quite absurdly, his face was starting to flush.

To say that Vlad's sexual exploits before Nathan had been somewhat tame in nature was, to put it mildly, an understatement. He had spent a lot of time frustrated and wanting until Nathan and Ursula had come into his life. And while he'd come a long way in accepting several things about himself, he was still, deep down, ridiculously shy about sex.

"Oh dear," Ursula murmured fondly, detaching from his side but keeping hold of his hand until she was all but dangling from his fingertips. "I think we broke him."

Nathan, who had been walking along unhindered by Vlad's stall in pace, turned back to look at him. His open expression shifted into a frown when he saw the tense line of the vampire's shoulders, his gaze softening with concern as he came closer. "Hey, you okay?"

It was said with such sincerity Vlad couldn't help but laugh, the sound coming out as a harsh explosive sigh that deflated some of his rising anxiety. "I'm fine, I just…" he gestured to the shopfront with a gray-gloved hand, "didn't realize we'd be coming to a sex emporium."

"I told you it would be our little treat," Ursula said and then added, "that is, if you want it to be…"

And there was his out. He knew from experience he could take that opening and run with it all the way back to the hotel and hide under the covers until his face stopped being red. And neither of them would say anything against it. They'd make a fuss of him and reassure him it was all right, and maybe somewhere down the line, they'd talk about it again, and perhaps then he'd reconsider it...

But he was here now, and as intimidated as he felt, he'd have been lying if he denied the fact that deep down, he was somewhat curious about what lay in store.

"Yes, right. Fine." He nodded, feeling the weight lift from his shoulders as the decision was made. Ursula gave a delighted little squeal, pulling him on by his fingertips.

"You're sure?" Nathan pressed, reaching out to place a warm hand on Vlad's side, preventing him from being dragged any further. "Because we can turn back now, go get dinner or see a show..."

"Nathan," Vlad interjected firmly, offering up what he hoped was a reassuring smile even as butterflies turned over in his stomach. "It's fine, really. I'm fine. I want to go in."

Nathan gave him a searching look, then nodded. "All right, but you'll tell us if you want to leave?"

"Yes."

"Promise?"

Vlad gave him a patient look, and the werewolf finally relented, letting him go and bringing up the rear as Ursula all but pulled Vlad bodily toward the door. He had just enough time to read one of the other signs in the window as he passed. "Wait... why does *this* shop celebrate Pins and Needles Day too?"

The inside was tastefully decorated in hues of black and purple, the quartz lamps that hung from the ceiling dimmed to a more intimate glow, creating pools of light in strategic places and deepening the shadow in others. Vlad looked around in fascination at the displays. He was acutely aware that he was using Ursula as a shield.

"See, it's not so bad," she said, reaching back to give him an affectionate pat on the cheek, her hand warm and soft against his wind-chapped skin. "Mostly books and oils and... oh my."

She tilted her head to the side, and Vlad found himself tilting his own in the opposite direction.

"What is that?" he asked.

Ursula gave a little shrug. "No idea, but it's certainly... protruding."

"The Lord Tugginton 5000," a voice said behind them, and Vlad near jumped out of his skin, turning to be met with the thin smile and sharp gaze of sales associates everywhere who worked on commission. "From his latest furniture line of intimate marital aids.

Or non-marital. We don't judge here. Is there anything I can help you with?" they asked, their gaze flicking interestedly between the three of them.

"Uh," Vlad said, glancing around the shop again and swallowing nervously. "Just... uh, looking?"

"Well, if you need anything, give me a shout."

"Will do," Ursula replied cheerfully, grasping Vlad by the hand and leading him away from the intimidating item of sex furniture, Nathan trailing behind them.

"I can't believe you used to come in here every other month," Vlad muttered to him as they came to a halt in front of a display of vaguely familiar looking potion bottles, his gaze flickering around the shop and skittering away from a particularly suggestive display of phallic shaped objects, cast in an array of obscenely bright colors.

Beside him, Nathan made a humming sound of amusement, tilting his head close to Vlad's ear as he spoke in a low, dulcet murmur, "But you were always so glad when I did..."

And Vlad couldn't really refute him there, not when his cheeks turned what he was sure was a brilliant shade of scarlet. He recalled all the times Nathan had surprised him with a new item or toy and had subsequently proceeded to wreck him with it.

"Why don't you go look around?" Ursula suggested, holding up a bottle of scented oil to the light as she read the properties ascribed on the back.

"What, on my *own?*"

"Yes, dear," Ursula said, her tone patient, "and if you find something you think you might like, come get us and we'll have a look."

Vlad opened and shut his mouth, looking to Nathan for support and finding none was to be had. He had a vague suspicion he was being *handled*. It was all there in the light tone of command in her voice. She was giving him a task, something he could *accomplish* and feel proud over later. Even if it terrified him in the interim.

He glanced around the shop again. Apart from themselves and the shop assistant, the place was deserted.

"Fine," he said, tipping his top hat further back out of his eyes, "I can do that."

"Good boy," Ursula said, and Vlad would have perhaps balked at that particular epithet being used out in public, if she hadn't sounded quite so ridiculously proud.

He wandered down some of the aisles, eyeing the merchandise. Most of it was easily recognizable in terms of function, and he soon found the self-conscious swell of anxiety that had been stoppered in his chest beginning to ease. He was even starting to enjoy himself, poking and prodding at things that piqued his interest, and sidestepping away from the things which did not.

Eventually, after staring at the hypnotic display of plasma globes on the far back wall for entirely too long (and several minor shocks later), he found his way over to a glass counter, where expensive looking items glittered under the display lamps.

"I think these might be a little more your type," a familiar voice said, and Vlad looked around to find the shop assistant watching him from behind another counter, leaning back into a corner as they worked on something intricate involving needlework.

Drawn over, he looked down into the display case. It was filled with beautifully refined leatherwear, from cuffs and collars to some more elaborate pieces that somewhat reminded him of Nathan's shoulder brace. When he looked up again, it was to find the assistant watching him expectantly.

"How did you know?"

"I have a knack for reading people," they said mysteriously, and then shrugged, their smile taking on a more impish gleam. "And I remember your partner coming in to buy the custom cuffs last year."

"Yes, I rather suppose he's hard to forget," Vlad said. He glanced over his shoulder to where he could see Nathan and Ursula talking quietly as they browsed. At some point they'd picked up a basket which Nathan was carrying, the delicate wicker reticule looking ridiculously small in his large hands.

And worryingly full.

"Plus, they had bats embossed on the inside of them," the shop assistant said, giving him a cheeky little smile. "Seems more up your alley than hers. I had a lot of fun making those."

Vlad's head whipped back around at that, his curiosity piqued. "You make all of these?"

"Some of them," they said with a modest shrug, "the more personalized items usually."

"You make beautiful work," Vlad said earnestly, leaning over to admire a slender collar crafted from exquisitely supple looking brown leather, the stitching immaculately neat.

"If you're looking for a collar to match, I still have some more strips of that material left…"

Vlad's hand went reflexively to the knot of his cravat before he could abort the gesture. He was suddenly very aware of how bare and exposed his throat felt without Nathan's old military leather collar fitted snugly around his throat. It was meant to be worn as part of the military uniform to keep the wearer from being garroted on the battlefield. But when Nathan had looped the strip of leather around his neck, Vlad had never felt safer. He'd also never been harder and had come kneeling at Nathan's feet. And as sentimental as it was, he couldn't imagine himself wearing anything other than that old, worn down collar with Nathan's initials stamped on the inside.

"No, thank you," he smiled faintly, hoping the heat he could feel prickling under his skin wasn't visible on his face. "Not at the moment."

He looked around the shop, wondering what else there was to discover, when his gaze caught on the sign again that proclaimed the day as a holiday.

"It's about change and better things to come," the other said, following his line of sight and nodding toward the sign. "Everyone always thinks it's about sewing, but that's in July."

"Of course it is," Vlad said, not bothering to question why there were so many obscure holidays. There was likely a day celebrating dry toast. "What sort of change?"

"Any, I suppose. It used to be about labor reform laws," they said, and Vlad's memory threw up a hazy recollection of a workers strike some several decades before. "But now it's about anticipation and all things yet to come..." they trailed off, their grin taking on a wicked glint, "or not, depending on the inclination."

Vlad coughed awkwardly, feeling his ears turn red. He looked down at the display case again, biting his lip thoughtfully as an idea came to him. "Did you say you had pieces left over from the cuffs?"

*

They made it back to their hotel room just before midnight. Ursula was the first through the door, shedding her cloak and making a beeline for the bed where she collapsed face down against the pillows. It took all of her willpower not to burrow under the blankets there and then while still wearing her boots.

"Is it spring yet?" she asked the room at large, rolling over onto her back to stare up at the ceiling.

"Not yet," Vlad said, shucking out of his winter coat and down to his waistcoat, rolling up his shirtsleeves to reveal pale, slender arms.

He wasn't quite so powerfully built as Nathan, but there was a lithe wiriness to him that made him look deadly and sleek when he moved. It was only somewhat mitigated by his tendency to trip over his own feet when flustered, a trait Ursula found as entertaining as it was endearing.

What she was not currently a fan of, however, was the thought of having to sit up and unlace her boots.

"Pet?" she called hopefully, using the endearment most likely to garner a favorable result. She kicked her feet gently against the side of the bed for emphasis. "Come help."

"Why is it that you're only ever sweet when you want something?" Vlad asked, sounding more amused than cross as he traversed the room toward her.

Ursula leaned up on her elbows to watch as he knelt at the foot of the bed, taking her booted foot in hand. "Because you like it," she countered, a warm flutter of arousal turning over in her stomach when Vlad's cheeks turned a healthy pink.

She still remembered fondly the first time he'd done this. He'd been so haltingly shy and reverent, despite being the one to ask if he could do it. There was none of that shyness there now, but some of the reverence remained in the way he cupped the smooth leather of her heel, bracing the sole of her boot against his shoulder as he worked the laces loose with nimble fingers, quick and efficient. Even if he was currently trying to hide it behind a faux mask of irritability.

"I also can't help but notice you never ask *him* to do it."

"That's because you're so much better at it," Nathan replied glibly, moving around the room, unpacking their purchases and carding his fingers harshly through the vampire's thick dark hair in passing as he went.

Vlad shivered noticeably in response to the rough touch, and Ursula smirked, giving him a delicate nudge on the arm with the toe of her other boot just to watch it happen again.

"And besides," she said, affecting a more dulcet and sultry tone, "you always look so pretty down there on your knees." She nudged him again, this time a little harder. "Right where you belong."

Vlad let out a harsh exhale of breath, the pink in his cheeks rising even further as he finished working her foot gently free from one boot, and then the other, his fingers fumbling slightly more than they had before. When he was done, he placed both boots side by side at the foot of the bed and turned expectant, wide eyes up to her, looking for his next directive.

And then, because Ursula was not entirely against being a little cruel, she turned her attention to Nathan instead. "Did you finish unpacking yet?"

"Almost," the other man replied, and only then did Vlad seem to realize the tools being laid out on the bed. There weren't many—not as many as there could have been—but enough to make an impact. Some more than others.

She made a grab for the nearest, a simple pair of silk ties, and sat up just enough to dangle them under Vlad's nose. "Seeing as how *someone* was too indecisive to choose their own toy," she said, and watched the warm red glow rise to Vlad's cheeks, "we made sure to pick up some of our own. What's it to be, sweetheart, tied up and used 'til you can't walk straight, or bent over and paddled 'til you can't sit for a week, hmm?"

There was of course the third option, which was neither. Vlad could use his watchword or even just say "no," and that would be the end of it. But she didn't think he would, not if the ragged hitch in his breathing was anything to go by. But she needed to hear it, so she asked again. "Come on, pet, tell us what you want."

"Tied up and used, please…" Vlad said in a small voice, and Ursula let her smile widen, reaching out to caress him fondly.

"There now, see? That wasn't so hard, was it?" she asked, letting her stockinged foot slide along his inner thigh and smirking at the gasp it elicited when she brushed up against the hardening length of his cock filling out against his thigh. "Or was it?"

"All right, stop tormenting him," Nathan said, grinning wolfishly as he hauled Vlad up off his knees and starting the process of divesting him of his clothes with practiced ease. "That's my job too, you know."

"You'd hardly know it from the way you spoil him," Ursula quipped back, sitting up and making quick work of the fastenings up the back of her dress. She regretted not leaving her boots on when she let it pool to the floor, stepping out of it to reveal nothing more than her stays and stockings underneath, but she was fairly certain the aesthetic was still a pleasing one. Especially if the weak little moan Vlad made was anything to go by.

Not immune to the thrill of being admired, Ursula gave him a salacious little wink as she unlaced the front of her stays, the swell of her breasts spilling over the top of the fabric as she let it slide to the floor, joining the rest of their discarded clothing.

"Hurry up, slowpokes," she admonished, climbing back onto the bed and crawling toward the headboard to tie the silk restraints in place, still wearing her stockings. "I'm not getting any younger here."

"Speak for yourself," Vlad muttered, then yelped when Nathan shoved him back onto the bed, the werewolf crawling up the length of him as they maneuvered awkwardly up the mattress toward her.

"I am going to make you feel so good," he promised between hungry, biting kisses, the low guttural growl of his voice going straight to Ursula's core and making her press her thighs together in sympathy at Vlad's soft whimper of helpless desire. "I'm going to fuck you open, and then I'm going to make you come on my cock."

"Yes, gods, yes please," Vlad breathed out shakily, arching up into him. The next sound came out in a harsh gasp when Nathan pinned his hands above his head, allowing Ursula to tie the silk ties in place.

"Not too tight?" she asked, and Vlad obediently tested his bonds, shaking his head. "Good," Ursula said, moving to straddle his abdomen and running loving fingers up and down the flat of his chest. Her pulse quickened at the sight of him stretched out prone beneath her, and she bit her lip, suppressing the needy little shudder that rippled down her spine. She couldn't decide what she wanted more—to ride him until he begged, or to slide her fingers into his hair and hold him in place while she fucked his mouth. "Doesn't he look lovely like this?"

"Always," Nathan said, leaning up behind her to place a kiss to her bare shoulder. Ursula twisted around to steal a kiss of her own, pulling him up to her and licking hungrily into his mouth. She sighed when he began to palm and knead her breasts, teasing her nipples into stiff peaks as his other hand wandered down between her slick folds, working her open.

The sound Vlad made beneath them was positively tortured, and Ursula couldn't help the giggle that welled up in her chest, turning her gaze down to him even as she continued to kiss Nathan. "What's the matter, sweetheart?" she asked between kisses, shifting higher up so he could get a good look at what Nathan was doing. "Feeling left out?"

The sound he made in response was particularly gratifying, and Ursula couldn't suppress the shudder that tore through her this time as Nathan continued to stroke over the bundle of nerves at the top of her cleft, the throb between her thighs growing to a steady pulse as the swell of her orgasm began to crest, startling a cry out of her in it's sudden intensity.

When she opened her eyes and looked down, it was to find Vlad staring up at her with a glazed, glassy-eyed look that caused another twist of pleasure to shudder out of her.

"He cheated," she said, lowering herself down until she was close enough to steal a kiss from his eager lips. "That was supposed to be your job."

"Still can be," he replied breathlessly, tensing beneath her with a high, reedy keen, and Ursula turned to look over her shoulder, enjoying the spectacle of watching Nathan, now kneeling between Vlad's splayed legs, a bottle of oil in one hand while the other methodically worked him open.

"Oh-my-gods, there," the vampire whimpered, biting his lip between his fangs as he began to writhe, "Right there!"

"Here?" Nathan teased, twisting his wrist and causing Vlad to buck up so hard he nearly managed to lift Ursula off the bed, his hands pulling futilely at the silk ropes.

"Yes! Oh gods why does this feel so good…"

"Maybe because you're a needy little slut who needs to be filled," Ursula crooned sweetly, nibbling and licking at the exposed side of his neck, feeling her arousal beginning to pulse between her thighs again—though she was hardly one to talk.

Her release had been gratifyingly quick, but it had left a hungry ache deep in her core that demanded more. She kept talking though, knowing how the words drove Vlad wild, every hitched breath and stuttered out plea fueling the fire burning within her own veins.

She glanced at Nathan, who looked up from his own labors of love, and arched a questioning eyebrow at him. She could have gone ahead without him, but there was something so much more satisfying about working in unison.

"Now?" he asked, and Ursula nodded.

Sitting up on her knees, she reached behind herself, smirking when Nathan obligingly supplied the lubricant, and pumped Vlad's throbbing cock with her fist, making him swear loudly.

"Ready?" she asked.

Vlad nodded, his face transforming into a look of tortured bliss when Ursula lowered herself onto him. She groaned, unable to help herself at the feel of his hot length filling her up. They both gasped a moment later when Nathan altered their angle, easing himself into

Vlad with a slow roll of his hips that left the vampire swearing and tugging at his bonds. If it was possible, he somehow felt harder inside of her, and Ursula reveled in the low sob that escaped the back of his throat when she began to move, rocking in time with the rhythm Nathan was setting.

"What's the matter pet?" she asked, trying and failing to keep her own voice steady as she fucked herself back down onto him. "Is it too much? Do you want us to stop?"

"No! Gods no, please don't stop, please don't ever stop," he begged, the words breaking off into a high wordless yelp as Ursula picked up the tempo again, leaning forward to kiss and nip and suck at his exposed chest, leaving a trail of red love marks in her wake.

He was so close; she could feel him throbbing inside of her, his body tensing tighter and tighter as he strove to hold back the inevitable. Behind her, she could hear Nathan's labored breathing, his own drawn out groans of pleasure adding to the litany of praise and filth starting to fall out of her own mouth as three moved together as one.

To her own surprise, it was Ursula who came first, clawing stripes down Vlad's front as she shuddered and pulsed around him with a silent cry, her walls spasming and fluttering around Vlad's cock until he too tipped over the edge with a strangled groan, dragging Nathan down with him as he went.

They lay panting in a tangled heap for several moments, the world turned soft and hazy in the afterglow of their carnal satiation. And then Vlad stirred under her, and Ursula remembered the silk ties.

"That was very well done," she said, patting him on the chest as she undid the knots and helped him to lower his arms back down to his sides.

Moving somewhat stiffly, Vlad gave a derisive little snort. "Thank you," he said, sounding decisively wrung out. "You weren't so bad yourself."

"Excuse you, I was *stunning*," Ursula corrected, giving him a half-hearted poke as she rolled off him to land gracelessly on her side. The marks on his chest weren't too terrible, but she healed them anyway, smiling softly when he hummed happily. "Wasn't I, love?"

"Yeah, you were all right," Nathan said, coming up on her other side, his arm heavy and warm as he reached over to cuddle both of them at once.

"All I heard was the words 'you were right,' so that's what I'm going with," Ursula informed him, her mouth curling up into a smile as she felt both men laugh on either side of her.

"We should get cleaned up," she said to no one in particular, aware that if she didn't move soon she was in very real danger of falling asleep like this.

"Yep," Vlad agreed, already sounding half asleep. Nathan, the contented pack animal that he was, didn't even bother to reply, simply snuggling closer and burying his nose against her hair.

"We're going to be disgusting in the morning," she murmured, but still made no effort to move, the space between them too inviting and warm to leave.

And that was her biggest problem, in more ways than just one.

Her last thought before sleep rolled over and claimed her was a hazy but heartfelt sincere wish to the universe from the depths of her fragile soul—*Please, just this once… let me have this…*

*

At some point during the night, someone got up and set things to rights. It might even have been himself for all Nathan knew. But all he *really* knew for sure was that he was wearing drawers when the insistent knock at the door woke him.

Leaving Vlad and Ursula curled around each other, he stumbled blearily to the door, opening it just as the next round of knocking was about to start.

"What?" he asked gruffly, his voice thick and rough with sleep.

The bellhop on the other side did a brief double take, dragging his eyes away from Nathan's bare chest and up to his face. "Uh… mail delivery, sir? It's marked as urgent," he said weakly, gesturing to the luggage cart laden down with packages.

Nathan blinked at it. "At this time in the morning?"

"It's 3:00 p.m., sir," the bellhop said politely, and Nathan shook his head, gesturing him inside. "Would you like me to unpack them, sir?"

"No, thank you," Nathan said, "just leave them by the door, here." He grabbed one of the bank notes from the table by the threshold—*one of Vlad's*—and shoved it into the boy's breast pocket. "Now," he jerked curtly toward the open door with his thumb, "hop it."

"What's all the noise?" Ursula asked as the door clicked shut, sitting up in bed. Her hair was a glorious halo of disaster around her head.

"Packages," Nathan said, gesturing toward them and scrubbing his fingers down his face, squinting down at them. "From… Angelo Mortoletti. That can't be right, can it?"

He opened the first box in the pile, pulling out an exquisite blue velvet coat with gold thread embroidery around the lapels, a swirling note written in Angelo's florid handwriting pinned to the front—*to match Sir's eyes.*

"Good gods," Vlad said, prying himself upright to peer at the rest of the packages, "Angelo must have worked through the night like a man possessed… And I could have sworn he'd given that up."

Ursula opened her mouth then shook her head. "I'm not even sure I want you to clarify that sentence," she said, pulling another box toward her, unfurling the contents to reveal several splendid neckties.

Vlad appeared to think about it. "That's probably for the best."

"What's this?" Nathan said, picking up a smaller package nestled amidst the pile. "It's addressed to you," he said, tossing it to Vlad, who caught it clumsily, then paused to read the note attached.

"Aren't you going to open it?" Ursula asked curiously, and Vlad gave her a mysterious little smile.

"No, but maybe later," he said, setting it down on the nightstand and selecting another box from Nathan's pile. "It's for things yet to come."

About the Author

Joy Demorra is a Scottish born author currently hopping between continents.

When not off gallivanting through time and space you may find her taking a leisurely evening stroll through the floating city of New Paris, or leading a revolutionary revolt by space pirates against ninja librarians. If neither circumstance is currently applicable try under her desk. It's a well known fact that deadlines can't reach you there.

Website: joydemorra.com
Twitter: @joydemorra

Unlawfully Ugly
♥
Caitlyn Lynch

Story Information

Holiday: Ugly Christmas Sweater Day
Holiday Date: December 18 (Third Friday in December)
Heat Rating: 4
Relationship Type: M/F
Major Trigger Warnings: Boss/subordinate relationship, power imbalance.

Forced into planning her office's Christmas party, Jodie strikes gold—ugly sweaters. Unfortunately things don't go as planned. Can hot associate Joseph turn this ugly party into a night to remember?

Unlawfully Ugly

Jodie

"We could have a Santa's Workshop theme?" I suggested, hoping this idea might meet with approval unlike the last five, which had already been shot down in flames.

"We did that five years ago. I never want to see the managing partner dressed in an elf costume again." Tanya shuddered exaggeratedly.

It was a mental image I didn't need either, so I moved on hastily, looking down at the yellow legal pad on my desk. All the ideas I'd come up with had been written down and then crossed out. *Damn my boss for having her baby three weeks earlier than expected and leaving me to organize the office Christmas party, anyway!* "What about *Nightmare Before Christmas*?"

"Seriously? The partners aren't that cool. None of them will have heard of Jack Skellington." Leaning back in her chair and smoothing her glossy black locs, Tanya smirked at me. "*Such* a shame I'm going to be lying on a beach in Antigua and won't be able to help you out."

"Screw you," I muttered half-heartedly, doodling on the legal pad. I did like Tanya despite her being impossibly glamorous and effortlessly beautiful; she always looked like she'd just stepped off the set of *Suits* instead of being, like me, a legal secretary in our very plebeian Denver law office. She was probably the nicest person in the office as well as the most beautiful too, and I didn't really begrudge her engagement to a hot music producer who also happened to come from one of Colorado's wealthiest families. Well... Not often. Only at times like this, when I was reminded that she was going to Antigua with him for two weeks over Christmas and New Year's, and I was going to stay here miserable, cold, and manning the phone lines for the criminal law side of the practice for most of the holidays.

"Bad Santa?" I suggested after a few moments of silence.

"Really? You want to give every partner in the firm a license to grope you? I mean, I know you've got it bad for Mr. Diaz, but…"

"Shut up!" I freaked out, panicking someone might hear her. "Shut up, shut up, shut up!" I threw my legal pad at her to emphasize the point.

She fended it off, laughing. "Jodie, you've practically got hearts in your eyes every time he walks through the office. It's adorable."

"I do not!" She gave me a knowing look, and I groaned. "Can we please just get back on topic? Mara's depending on me to make this happen, and I can't let her down. She's done the hard parts: entertainment, catering, venue. She got the freaking Brown Palace! That place is like beyond swanky. All I have to do is come up with a theme and send out the invitations. I'll look like a complete incompetent if I fail."

Obviously taking pity on me, Tanya reached for her computer, neatly manicured nails rattling on the keyboard as she typed. Probably doing a Google search for Christmas party themes, which I would totally have thought of by now if I wasn't so rattled.

"Ugly Christmas Sweater Party," she said after a few seconds. "We haven't done one of those, and it's boringly conventional enough that the partners will go along with it. Plus," she said, clicking on a link, "Ugly Christmas Sweater Day is the third Friday in December."

"The date we're holding the party," I realized with a sigh. "Why do you get to be beautiful *and* smart *and* nice?" I grumbled, retrieving my fallen legal pad. "It's making it very hard to resent you."

She just laughed, unruffled. "You're welcome, sweetie. And here's hoping Mr. Diaz has a few glasses of Christmas cheer and notices what's right under his nose!"

It was sweet of her to say so, but it was never going to happen. Joseph Diaz was the firm's newest partner, a hotshot defense attorney who'd made a name for himself embarrassing the DA's office over several cases of police officers planting evidence. He'd only been with the firm for three months, but I'd had a crush on him a lot longer. Ever since I saw him in court one day last year. I'd just been there delivering some papers to one of our associates, who'd been co-counsel with Diaz for a second defendant in the case.

Frankly, all our associate had had to do was sit on his ass and get paid. Diaz had been electric, brilliant in his cross-examination. The witness on the stand had started contradicting their own sworn statements, and the DA had actually put his head in his hands. I'd wanted to applaud.

"Earth to Jodie," Tanya said. "Just sent you an email."

I jerked out of my reverie and glanced at her. "What about? I'm sitting right here."

"Links to some sites with cute ugly Christmas sweaters." She winked at me. "You don't have to look hideous even if you're wearing an ugly sweater. Knock 'em dead."

*

Joseph

"Good lord, Diaz, what are you wearing? Is that Santa riding on a shark?"

"It's a sea sleigher," I said, surveying the managing partner's suit with some dismay. "Couldn't find an ugly sweater to wear to the party, Mr. Hadley?"

Mr. Hadley snorted. "Nobody takes that nonsense seriously. Maybe a few of the first-year associates, but certainly *partners* don't have to dress up."

"Wish someone had told me," I muttered to Hadley's departing back. Heading for the bar with a sigh, I looked in vain for someone else who'd adhered to the party's theme. All the men were wearing their usual dark suits, the women mostly in shimmery cocktail dresses. Not an ugly Christmas sweater in sight.

The bartender gave me a raised eyebrow and an amused grin. "Nice sweater. What can I get you?"

"A dark rum on the rocks," I said, deciding I was going to need a whole lot of alcohol to deal with the evening. *What possessed me to go home and change? I don't even have my suit in my car—I could have grabbed it and changed!*

I already knew the answer, though. The office was staying open throughout the Christmas period, and I, as one of the few partners without kids or grandkids, had volunteered to be in the office over the holidays so the other partners didn't have to be. Which meant I had been taking it easy these last few days before the silly season kicked off in earnest and had called it a day at three that afternoon, instead of after eight as was my usual habit.

The rum burned in the best way going down, heating my insides and making me feel just a tiny bit less of a dumbass about the sweater. Taking a deep breath, I turned to face the room and immediately spotted someone else in a terrible sweater.

It was white with tiny silver snowflakes all over it, which wouldn't have been so bad if the design had stopped there. The huge shiny red bow over the wearer's breasts really made it, though.

Especially since they were incredibly attractive breasts. The sweater was closely fitted, showing off not just those sumptuous breasts, but a tiny waist.

I'd been staring for a good minute before I realized I was acting like the worst kind of lecher. I hadn't even looked at the woman's face!

It took a moment to recognize her since she was wearing a tinsel wreath on her piled-up brown hair and Christmas tree earrings with tiny flashing lights on them, but that was definitely Jodie Masters, currently acting as secretary to Mr. Hadley while his usual assistant was on maternity leave. I didn't really know her, not enough to speak to, but I'd definitely noticed her around the office. She always seemed to have a ready smile for everyone, a smile which had brightened more than a few gray winter days for me when she'd turned it in my direction.

That ever-present smile was absent right now; Jodie looked thoroughly despondent, her body language closed off, shoulders hunched forward and head down. Without even thinking about it, I headed in her direction, suddenly wanting to make her feel better.

"Hey," I said as I arrived at her side and she glanced up at me, "that's an incredibly ugly sweater. Is that... *pleather?*"

A hint of a smile teased at full lips painted the same color as the sweater bow. "Yes, it is. *Shiny* pleather," she emphasized.

"Like I said, incredibly ugly. And yet somehow, you're still managing to look absolutely stunning in it. Unlike me, who's just coming off as a complete dork."

She laughed at that, and the room suddenly seemed a whole lot lighter. I smiled back at her, pleased to have brightened her mood a little.

*

Jodie

Joseph Diaz was the furthest thing imaginable from dorky, even wearing a navy blue sweater with Santa riding on a shark on the front of it. Broad shoulders strained at the sweater's seams, speaking to the early-morning gym sessions I knew he put in before starting work. I'd heard him mention it in a meeting once; he used it as time to think and put his brain in gear before getting to his desk or going to court.

"I don't think you look dorky," I said, wracking my brain to try and find something clever to say. "That navy suits you."

"Same color as most of my suits," he commented with a wry little twist of his mouth.

"Well, it looks good on you." Suddenly feeling awkward about blatantly admiring him, I dropped my gaze to study my feet. At least I was wearing cute shoes, black ankle boots with a kitten heel, along with my favorite black skinny jeans.

It was only above the waist I looked like a total dweeb. What had I been thinking? Oh right, that it was Ugly Christmas Sweater Day and that we had an ugly Christmas sweater themed party. If only more people had shown up wearing them, maybe then I wouldn't feel so out of place!

"Would you like a drink?"

"Excuse me?" I looked back up at Mr. Diaz, startled.

He gestured at my empty hands. "Can't help noticing you don't have a drink. Would you like one? Or is somebody getting you one already?"

"No," I said, still surprised that he would think to offer. "I mean—no, nobody's getting me one, but yes, I would like one."

"What are you drinking?"

"Champagne, please." I'd had a glass already when I arrived, but I'd downed it quickly. I wasn't planning on getting hammered, but another glass would be welcome.

"Be right back. Don't go anywhere." He flashed me an unexpectedly warm smile. "I need someone else to be dorky with."

Joseph Diaz wants to spend time with me? It was such an unlikely thought I had to bite back a laugh. He'd probably get waylaid on his way to the bar and forget about me entirely. I'd give him five minutes and then go get my own drink.

He was back in three, holding out a full champagne flute and flashing that smile again, teeth white in his brown face. He had a slightly crooked front tooth, I noticed, but it didn't detract from his handsomeness in the slightest. Quite the opposite: the imperfection only emphasized his exceptional good looks. Honestly, he was the archetypal tall, dark, and handsome, and with his brains too, the guy was the complete package.

"Do I have something in my teeth?" His smile faded, and he lifted a hand to his mouth. "I ate a couple olives off the bar…"

"Oh no, no!" Abashed at having been caught staring, I blushed. "No, I was just noticing that you've got a slightly crooked tooth."

"Ha." His hand dropped. "Yeah. Cuban family from the poorest part of Hialeah, Florida; couldn't really afford orthodontics."

"White trailer trash from right here in Denver; same." I grinned wryly. "It's why I'm so grateful for the firm's awesome health insurance. I finished with my last set of Invisaligns a month ago."

"Yeah? That's great. Maybe I should look into it."

"I dunno. That crooked tooth adds character. Mine were… well, they weren't that pretty. Buck teeth," I explained when he arched a brow quizzically.

"You'd never know. You have a beautiful smile now."

I was still getting used to that fact. That I was, for the first time in my life, something approaching conventionally pretty. Resisting the urge to duck my head, I smiled back at Joseph. "Thank you."

His expression as he looked at me was decidedly appreciative. With a vague feeling of unreality, I sipped my champagne, tried to ignore one of the paralegals who looked from me to Joseph and gave me a not-very-discreet 'hit that' gesture, and tried to think of something clever to say.

"Would you like to dance?" Joseph asked unexpectedly.

"What?" Once again, I gaped at him.

"I'm asking you for a dance, Jodie. You can say no, it's fine, promise I won't be offended. You were just tapping your foot along with the music, and I thought you might like to dance."

I was doubly astounded; first that he actually knew my name, and second that he'd noticed me tapping my foot. One benefit of handling the party organization was that although the DJ had already been booked by the ever-efficient Mara before she'd gone on maternity leave, I got to choose his playlist, and I'd stuffed it with a selection of floor-fillers from different decades. Right now *Love Shack* was playing, and even some of the senior partners were dancing.

"Y'know, I'd really like that," I decided, set my half-drunk champagne down, and accepted Joseph's offered hand. The song was ending as he drew me onto the dance floor, and I hoped fervently the next one up wouldn't be anything too upbeat, as I had visions of me bopping about and smacking Joseph in the face or something equally embarrassing.

I shouldn't have worried; the strains of Santana's *Smooth* reached my ears, and Joseph smiled, not relinquishing my hand but instead pulling me closer to set a hand on my waist. "I like this song. This okay?" he checked with me.

"Sure." I put my free hand on his shoulder and let myself move with him, relaxing into the Latin beat, hips swaying.

I love dancing, always have, and Joseph could really move. He stayed right with me through *Crazy In Love, Shut Up and Dance, Uptown Funk, Dancing In The Dark,* and *Despacito.*

It wasn't until Mick Jagger started crooning about *Satisfaction* that I felt ready to take a break. I tugged at Joseph's hand, nodding toward the edge of the dance floor, and he came with me readily, though he didn't let go of my hand.

"That was fun!" he said loudly into my ear as we moved away from the noise of the speakers.

I grinned up at him. "Been a while since you let your hair down and got your dancing shoes on?"

"Too long. My brother's wedding a couple years ago was the last time I danced, I think. Loving the music tonight."

"Thank you," I said. "I set the playlist."

Joseph gave me a curious look. "You were involved in organizing tonight?"

"Mara did most of it," I admitted, "but when she had her baby early, I had to step in. The ugly Christmas sweater theme was my fault, I'm afraid."

He chuckled, leading me back to the bar and gesturing to the bartender. "You're forgiven. More champagne, or would you like something else?"

"I'll have a club soda first, please. Need to cool off a bit."

"Good plan." He ordered two, then once they were set in front of us, nodded toward the buffet tables set up at the side of the room. "Want to get something to eat? I'm starving."

"Me too." I'd checked out the buffet tables when I'd arrived, wanting to make sure everything was as ordered, but hadn't been hungry then. The exertion of an energetic half an hour of dancing had changed that.

A couple of people tried to stop Joseph to talk, but he just nodded politely at them and kept moving forward with me to the tables. I glanced sideways at him, wondering what he was still doing with me. Surely there were more important and interesting people he could be, or rather should be, socializing with?

"I feel like I'm monopolizing your attention," I said as he fended off a determined second-year associate and picked up an empty plate, handing it to me.

"Why?" He grinned when I sputtered, unable to come up with an immediate response. "I'm enjoying my evening immensely, thank you. Unless there's someone *you'd* rather be spending time with?"

"No!" I denied immediately, then wondered dismally if I'd just managed to sound way too eager.

Joseph's smile was warm, though. "Good to hear. Want some?" He held up a roll with a pair of tongs.

"Sure," I said with a shrug. With all that dancing, I needed some calories.

Plates filled, Joseph nudged my arm and nodded at a vacant table for two. It wasn't until we were settled down with our food in front of us, knees touching under the tiny table, that I wondered if he'd chosen the small table deliberately so nobody else could join us.

Truth was, I didn't care. I was living in a fantastical dreamland where Joseph Diaz was interested in spending time with me—me! Boring Jodie Masters!—and I didn't care why. That he could be romantically interested seemed like some kind of dream, so maybe it was just that he wanted something he thought I could get him, like priority access to the firm's investigative team or something. Which I totally could. Assigning tasks to the team was actually my usual job, but I was also standing in for Mara as Mr. Hadley's executive secretary for the time being.

That must be it, I concluded as I ate. Joseph might be a partner, but he was the *newest* partner. He was buttering me up. Well, he wasn't the first man to try, and he wouldn't be the first to fail, either.

"So," Joseph said, leaning his elbows on the table and grinning at me.

Here it comes, I thought cynically.

"Are you gonna dance with me again, or have I worn you out?"

I already had my mouth open to deliver a polite explanation of why I couldn't possibly do what he was about to ask, and it took my brain a moment to switch gears. "Dance?"

"Sure. C'mon, who doesn't love Bruno Mars?"

Uptown Funk's pretty irresistible, all right. With a shrug, I accepted his offered hand. *Why not?* Dancing with Joseph was the most fun I'd had in ages.

Of course, the moment we got to the dance floor the song ended, and there was a very brief pause before the next song started. About three seconds later, I wanted to kick myself; what possessed me to put *Don't Stop Believin'* on the playlist? It was too slow, and… people were flooding onto the dance floor.

"Popular choice," Joseph said in my ear, his low voice amused.

Behind me, someone crowded a bit too close, and I stumbled forward. A strong arm curled around my waist, his warm hand pressing lightly in the small of my back as Joseph drew me close.

"You okay?" he asked.

"I just tripped." I'd brought my hands up instinctively, and they'd landed on Joseph's upper arms, holding on firmly to steady myself. He felt solidly muscled and very warm through his sweater. "Sorry." I tried to pull back, but he tightened his arm, just a little.

"Don't let go on my account."

For a moment we stared at each other. Joseph wasn't holding on tight, and I could easily have pulled away if I'd really wanted to. Except, I didn't want to.

When I didn't move away, he brought his other hand up to rest lightly on my hip, encouraging me to sway to the music with him. I let my hands, still braced on his arms, slide down a little, holding on rather than supporting me.

"I'm glad you wore that sweater," Joseph said as the song drew to a close.

I glanced down, wrinkling my nose slightly. I kept forgetting about the ghastliness of the giant, shiny, red pleather bow. "Why?"

"It gave me a good excuse to talk to you. I've been trying to come up with one since I joined the firm." He shrugged, looking bashful.

I refrained from asking *Why?* again. "I've had a really nice evening," I said instead.

"Me too! And I was wondering if maybe you'd come out to dinner with me sometime."

I blinked, startled. "Like a date?"

"Not just *like* a date, an actual date. If that's something you'd be interested in."

"Don't take this wrong," I said after a moment of stunned silence, "but why me? You could have your pick of any single girl, I'm sure."

"I think you flatter me, but I'm not interested in any other girl. I told you, I've been trying to come up with a good excuse to talk to you since I joined the firm, Jodie. You have a reputation in the firm as someone way too smart for the job you're currently doing, you know."

"I did *not* know that."

"Why do you think Mara asked you to manage Mr. Hadley while she's on leave? She didn't trust anyone else to do the job right. You're smart, Jodie, and pretty, and you don't seem aware of either of those things. I think that's a damned shame, and I'd like to get to know you better. A lot better."

"I think you should pinch me," I said after a moment.

Joseph grinned. "You're not dreaming, Jodie. And you are completely free to turn me down, for whatever reason, and I promise there'd be no repercussions. I confess I asked your friend Tanya if you were single, and she said you were, but she might not know everything. Or you might not be interested, which is totally your prerogative…"

I reached up and touched a finger to his lips lightly. "You're babbling."

"Sorry," he said against my finger.

"Don't be, it's completely adorable. Especially since I think you're way out of my league, so you being kinda nervous about asking me out is making me feel way better about that." I let my finger drop and put my hand back on his arm.

"So?" Joseph asked. "Is that a yes?"

"It's a yes, but you might have to wait until the holiday season is over. I agreed to work the evening shift straight through until New Year's, because someone needs to be on the phones. And, well, I *am* single and childless."

"So am I, which is why I'm the on-call lawyer through New Year's as well. I'll take that raincheck on taking you out, but there's nothing to stop us eating in if we get a quiet night. There's quite a few good takeout joints near the office."

"You're funny, thinking we're going to get a quiet night." I smiled ruefully up at him. "It's the silly season, and the drunk tank is always full."

"True." His arms tightened, pulling me closer against him. "I'll be lucky to get a glimpse of you in passing."

"So I guess we should make the most of tonight, then?" Emboldened by his clearly expressed interest, I blurted out the not-so-thinly veiled invitation.

For just a second, Joseph looked startled. But he didn't get to be a hotshot defense lawyer by not being quick on the uptake. "I'm down with that," he said immediately. "What did you have in mind?"

"An Uber back to my place?" I sent up silent thanks that the roommate I shared a cute little bungalow with out in Wheat Ridge was up in Keystone for the weekend.

"We could do that." He nodded. "Or… my place is only a few blocks away. No waiting for a car."

The party was winding down, lots of folks leaving, many of them fairly messy drunks. Nobody would notice if we slipped away quietly. Well, not more than they'd noticed us dancing the night away and sitting down together to eat, anyway. The office gossip mill would be running hot for a while, but I couldn't bring myself to care. I was leaving the party with Joseph Diaz, his strong, warm hand wrapped firmly around mine.

We didn't make it a full block up Seventeenth before we started kissing. I'd just managed to trip over a crack in the pavement and he caught me, hauling me up against his chest.

"Tell me you're just a bit clumsy, not intoxicated," he said, tone almost pleading.

"Chronically clumsy, I'm afraid. No excuses."

"That's good, because otherwise I'd have to be a gentleman and send you home." He was very close, his eyes boring into mine as he held onto me.

"I don't want you to be a gentleman," I said, and I reached up to put a hand on the back of his neck, pulling him down for a kiss.

He took me at my word, crowding me back against the wall of the building we were passing and kissing me back thoroughly, one big hand slipping down to cup my ass and lift me against him. I moaned into his mouth, clutching at him greedily, grinding against the thigh he thrust between mine.

"God, Jodie!" Joseph gasped against my lips, lifting his head to look down at me. "We're gonna get arrested for public indecency in a minute."

"Good thing I know this hotshot defense attorney." I grinned up at him cheekily.

He laughed, letting go of me with obvious reluctance, although he promptly put his arm back around my waist. "Or we might freeze. I mean, I'm feeling pretty warm right now," the heated look he shot me was unmistakable, "but in case you hadn't noticed, it's started snowing."

I hadn't noticed at all, but now that he mentioned it, I saw fat white flakes spiraling down from the dark sky in a steadily thickening mass. "Oh yeah. Channel 9 said there was a blizzard coming," I remembered. It was one of the reasons I'd left my old Prius at home.

"So let's get inside. C'mon. I make a mean hot chocolate." Joseph pulled on me gently, urging me to walk faster—not that I needed any encouragement.

His apartment was in a recently renovated building, lots of glass and polished concrete and soft lighting in the lobby. Joseph used a swipe card to let us in and again in the elevator before punching in his floor, the sixth. Which was good, the ride wouldn't take long. Anything more than a minute and I didn't think I'd have been able to resist jumping Joseph again. He was staring at me as though he was thinking the exact same things I was, his hands flexing lightly at his sides.

The soft ping as the elevator doors slid open made us both jump, we'd been so focused on each other. I followed Joseph out and along a short hallway to his apartment, where he fumbled with his keys to let us in.

In my experience, bachelors tend to live in one of two ways: terminally messy or barely-decorated. So when I walked into Joseph's apartment and found bright, cozy furnishings, wooden shelves stacked with well-thumbed books, and framed comic strips and cels from old cartoons on the walls, I nearly fell over my feet with surprise.

"Is that Road Runner?" I stared at the bright bird sprinting on a purple background in disbelief.

"Meep, meep." Joseph grinned.

"And a *Far Side* cartoon—wait. Is that an original?"

"I collect them," he admitted.

I whistled softly, impressed. *Far Side* originals run in the four figure range; he'd picked an expensive hobby, but one that would certainly hold value.

"I could show you the others, if you like? They aren't all framed, yet," Joseph offered.

"Interested though I am," I turned to smile at him, "I didn't come up here to see your etchings," I said, referring to the archaic euphemism for what would now be 'Netflix and chill.'

He chuckled appreciatively at the joke. "Maybe not, but it'd be okay if you changed your mind."

"You're a really nice guy, aren't you?" I realized. He'd been careful all night to make sure I was good with anything we did.

"Shh, don't tell the DA. He'll think I'm losing my edge."

*

Joseph

Jodie made me laugh more than I had in months. Eyes alight with humor, she caught my hand. "Your bedroom."

I'd brought her up here for this and yet somehow, I wanted to delay the moment. Spend more time with her before we hit the sheets. "You're in a rush. You don't want coffee or anything?"

"You can make me coffee afterwards." She pulled on my hand. "Joseph. Let's be clear here. I'm *wildly* turned on right now, and I want to do lots of wildly sexy things to and with you. Right now. Later… well, later, maybe you'll remember I'm just a lowly secretary, and I'll get that Uber home, or maybe you'll make me coffee, and we'll talk, but right now, let's *fuck*."

Well, when she put it like that, I was feeling pretty damn turned on myself. She looked like the most unbearably tempting Christmas gift ever with that big scarlet bow over her beautiful breasts, and the desire to give in and unwrap her was just way too much.

Afterward, though, I was going to do my best to tempt her not to get that Uber.

"This way." I led her to my bedroom, wondering what she was thinking as she looked around the space. It's plainer than the rest of my apartment, the walls and the bedcovers white, the carpet a neutral beige. On the wall is my one piece of 'proper' art, a Tomás Sánchez landscape of a waterfall pouring into a still pool behind a canopy of green jungle foliage. It's a soothing, restful, meditative image, and Jodie's eyes rested on it for a long moment.

"I could fall asleep gazing at that," she murmured, before turning to me with that wicked little grin again. "But not right now."

"Not right now," I agreed, filling my eyes with her as she reached up and pulled out the clip holding her hair on top of her head. It fell loose, a tumble of rich bronze-gold satin reaching halfway to her waist, and I gave in to the urge to reach for her, to sink my fingers into that glorious hair and kiss her again.

Her lips were plush and soft under mine, opening pliantly, her wet tongue sweeping cheekily across my lower lip before retreating, tempting me to taste her more.

Deft fingers pulled at the hem of my sweater, slid underneath, and freed the T-shirt I was wearing beneath from the waistband of my jeans. I twitched as her fingers danced over my abs, and she pulled back from the kiss, her soft hazel eyes questioning.

"Your hands are cold," I admitted sheepishly.

Jodie laughed, low and husky, before reaching one of those cool hands up to the back of my neck and pulling me down again. "The rest of me's plenty warm," she whispered invitingly against my mouth, and I accepted the blatant invitation, folding my arms around her and bringing her in close, her softly curvaceous body pressed against the hard planes of mine.

I was feeling pretty hot under the collar myself and getting warmer all the time as Jodie kissed me back with enthusiasm. She broke the kiss briefly to tug on my sweater in a clear demand for me to get rid of it, and I tore it off unhesitatingly, throwing the ugly thing across the room without care for where it landed.

"This too," Jodie requested with a pull on the hem of my T-shirt, so I yanked that off over my head too. She tilted her head to one side and considered me, a smile curving her plush lips upward as though she liked what she saw.

"I go to the gym," I said inanely.

"I know, and clearly it's time well spent."

"In more ways than one; I do a lot of thinking on the treadmill. Working out the tricky details on cases."

She reached up and tapped her fingertip right between my eyes, making my eyes nearly cross as I tried to follow the movement. "Stop thinking right now, Joseph. You need to switch that brilliant brain off and just *feel*."

I was feeling, all right. Jodie was so soft against me, yielding, yet demanding too as she embraced me back. She gave as much as she took, pulling off her own sweater once I'd removed mine. I nearly swallowed my tongue at the sight of her breasts, full and plump in a lacy bra the same red as the bow on her sweater.

Jodie was watching me, her gaze sharp and assessing.

"You are goddamn beautiful," I said, hearing my voice come out low and needy.

"I'm not anything special."

"I beg to differ." She was; she was *gorgeous*. I like girls with curves, juicy butts and full breasts and something to really hang on to. But even more than her fabulous figure, she struck something in me. Something I didn't want to let go of. Lowering my hands to that gorgeously rounded ass, I squeezed firmly. "If I wanted another girl, I'd have asked them to dance at the party tonight. Truth is I've been trying to come up with a good pretext to ask you out for a while now."

A frown creased her brow. "But you're hot and super successful. You could have anyone."

"I want you." Apparently, I wasn't making myself clear. I squeezed and lifted, pulling her groin up against me, demonstrating wordlessly just how turned on I was.

The frown disappeared, and she went up on tiptoe before hooking one leg up over my hip, grinding against me harder. "That's good. Because I want you too."

Her black jeans were well-worn, soft, like a second skin molded tightly to her ass. I wanted to peel them off, taste every inch of her skin, and I told her that even as I lifted her off her feet completely and lowered her back to the mattress.

"Sounds good to me." Her eyes sparkled up at me, that wicked grin dancing on her lips again. "But only if I get to lick you all over too."

"Beautiful, you can lick any part of me you want to." I put a knee on the bed in between her thighs and leaned down over her. Those glorious breasts were singing an irresistible siren song, summoning me to worship at the altar of their perfection, and I gave in to temptation and buried my face in between them.

Her laugh was soft and husky, her hand firm as it slid into my hair to hold me close, and then she shifted oddly under me. It took me a moment to realize she'd twisted her other arm behind her back to unhook her bra.

"Oh, my." I nearly choked as she tossed the bra aside, her generous breasts tumbling free into my eager hands. "You are *magnificent*." My voice was pretty muffled as I buried my face again, but I was pretty sure Jodie got the message; I heard her pleased little hum.

*

Jodie

Joseph's expression when I took my bra off was priceless; he looked as though he'd just won the jackpot, a huge grin spreading from ear to ear before he literally dived back into my cleavage with a moan and a mumbled compliment.

Definitely a boob man, I thought with amusement, lying back and closing my eyes to savor the sensations of his warm clever hands as they cupped my breasts. Thumbs circled my nipples, teasing them up to aching points.

"Your mouth," I begged, not caring how needy I sounded. Joseph was kissing and sucking gently on the inner slopes of my breasts, but I wanted—*needed*—that hot mouth on my nipples, soothing the aching throb he'd caused with his teasing hands.

"Yes, please," he agreed, making me laugh again with his obvious enthusiasm. I opened my eyes to look at him as he shifted his weight off my lower body, pushing himself up on strong arms before ducking his head, his tongue flickering out to lash lightly over one swollen nipple. I shuddered with the pleasurable shock of it, and he paused, glancing up at my face.

"Okay?"

"A lot better than okay, don't you dare stop there!"

He was obviously more than happy to take my word for it, diving back in with gusto this time, sucking my left nipple fully into his mouth and tonguing it with such skill I was quickly reduced to a near-delirious wreck of pleasure. Throaty cries echoed off the walls, barely recognizable as coming from my own mouth.

Joseph really knew what he was doing, and he evidently enjoyed doing it, too, as he switched from my left breast to my right. His hand came up to soothe the abandoned nipple even as his tongue began that expert torment again.

What he was doing felt amazing, but I wanted so much more, wanted us both naked and rolling around in the sheets. I still had my boots on with their sharp little kitten heels, and as I hooked my legs around his waist they must have dug into his hips.

He winced and pulled back, letting my nipple pop out of his mouth. "Ouch, those are sharp, sweetheart!"

"Take them off then," I begged. "Take everything off."

He nodded, accepting the request, and leaned back to grasp one foot in his hand. Too late, I remembered I was wearing nerdy socks;

he already had one boot off and was admiring the black sock with the red Iron Man logo on my ankle.

"Uh, take that off really quickly?" I suggested, flushing scarlet.

"Funny, I'd have picked you for a Captain America fangirl," Joseph said teasingly, peeling the sock off and reaching for my other foot.

"Dark and intensely clever is more my style," I quipped back.

He pointed at me. "I see what you did there."

"For real, though. Intelligence is super sexy."

"So is competence. I'm no Steve Rogers, but I totally see what he saw in Peggy Carter." Joseph's eyes slid back to my chest, and he grinned. "Apart from the magnificent cleavage, obviously."

"Oh, obviously," I said, heavy on the sarcasm.

He shook his head at me even as he worked my other boot off. "I'm serious! Peggy was sexy as all get out because she was competent and confident." He peeled off my other sock and waved it at me. "Bossy, too. Huge turn-on."

"I'll bear that in mind," I teased, and he laughed.

"You do that." Discarding the sock off the side of the bed, he leaned forward over me again, the muscles in his shoulders and chest rippling pleasingly as he did. "Seriously? If I do anything you don't like, tell me—and you want me *to* do anything, tell me that too."

"You're definitely on the *consent is sexy* train, and I gotta tell you, it's really doing it for me." Smiling up at him, I poked bare toes gently into his defined abs. "Gimme a hand with these jeans."

Joseph obligingly hooked his fingers into the hems at my ankles and tugged, once I'd undone the button and zipper at the waist, and a moment later my jeans were slithering down my legs, leaving me in only the scarlet satin and lace panties that matched my discarded bra.

"Hell's bells," Joseph muttered. The naked admiration I saw on his face as he looked me up and down was a huge boost to my ego.

"You too," I requested, nudging my toes at his belt. He sat back on his heels to undo it, pushing up off the bed to strip off his pants and boxers together.

The light from a wall fitting behind the bed was soft and diffuse, casting Joseph in a soft golden light which did wonderful things for his brown skin, making him shine like polished bronze, towering over me like some ancient Arawak warrior. I could only stare in amazed awe, wondering again why on earth he'd chosen *me*, ordinary Jodie Masters.

"Just gonna get some protection," Joseph said, jolting me from my reverie.

I rolled on my side to watch as he went into the bathroom, delighted to discover the back view was just as good as the front. "Hate to see you go, love watching you leave," I quipped.

He glanced back at me over his shoulder, laughed, and patted one pert butt cheek.

Hot damn. You could bounce quarters off that ass.

"You could try, but would you mind waiting until afterward? Might be uncomfortable trying to lie on my front at the moment."

"Whoops, I said that out loud!" Laughing with embarrassment, I covered my face with my hands, until the bed shifted with Joseph's weight lying down on it. Peeking at him between my fingers, I discovered he was grinning.

"You're so funny. Come here." Gently, he tugged at my fingers, urging me to lower my hands, before leaning in to kiss me again.

Perhaps it was the confidence that we were going to do this, we were actually going to have sex, that helped slow things down a little with this kiss. Whatever it was, there was less urgency—less desperation—this time around. This kiss was something to savor, a slow exploration, our bodies pressed chest to chest, hip to hip.

Which is not to say, I couldn't tell just how eager Joseph was. His erection was rock-hard, pressing into the soft flesh of my tummy. When I worked a hand in between us to touch him lightly, tracing around the tip, he groaned into my mouth and trembled slightly. It was a heady feeling to know I could make him react that way.

Of course, I was having some pretty extreme reactions myself. My nipples were doing really great impressions of bullets, and I was pretty sure the thin fabric of my panties would show an embarrassing damp spot if I let Joseph look at them. Which I had no intention of doing. It didn't take all that much wiggling to dispose of them, though the wiggles elicited some more interesting noises out of Joseph.

"God, you're driving me wild," he mumbled, pulling back to kiss down my throat. "I'm trying to take this slow."

"I'd much rather you didn't," I panted in return, finally kicking the unwanted panties off my ankle before hooking it over his hip. "We could do slow later, maybe, but right now I'm very into fast."

The move left my pussy pressed against the root of his cock; deliberately I ground against him.

He actually yelped before his hands closed over my shoulders, and he pressed me down to my back, leaning over me to look in my eyes. "Jodie..."

"*Please*," I begged, almost mindless with how much I wanted him.

"I was planning to do all sorts of arousing things to you with my mouth." His smile was a little rueful.

"Maybe later." I reached for the condom packet he'd put on the nightstand. "Right now, I want you inside me."

He took the condom when I couldn't get the stupid packet to rip, tore it open easily and rolled the thin latex sheath on with hands which weren't quite steady. And then he surprised me by lying back and making a beckoning motion. "I don't trust myself not to be too rough. It's probably better if you control the pace."

I could do that. Considering how little foreplay we'd indulged in, I could see how he might be concerned I wasn't ready for anything hard and fast, but boy, I was going to prove him wrong. Sitting up, I threw a leg over him and mounted up, grasping his cock to position him just right.

Joseph groaned as I eased down the first little way but didn't close his eyes as I expected. He kept them wide open, staring at me greedily, lifting his hands to cup my breasts and tease my nipples with his thumbs. "God, you're so beautiful," he breathed, his expression almost reverent.

Being looked at that way was a huge turn on all by itself, and I had no problem sliding down onto him, taking most of his cock with one long thrust which had us both gasping.

*

Joseph

She was magnificent, Aphrodite rising above me, taking what she wanted to get her pleasure. I didn't even want to blink; I wanted to see every instant of her passion, every fleeting emotion crossing her expressive face.

Coming before she did was a very real possibility and one I didn't want to entertain, but she'd all but demanded we skip the foreplay, and I just had to hope she could actually come from what we were doing because, damn, I was about ready to burst. I helped her along with slow, grinding thrusts of my hips, lifting up against her as she rode me at a steady canter, her body swaying and jiggling with the rhythm she set.

"Joseph," Jodie gasped, her eyelashes fluttering, and I reached a hand between us to circle my thumb around her button, wet and slippery with her juices. She keened, a soft, wordless sound in her throat, and her body stilled even as her internal muscles quivered and tightened around my aching cock.

"Easy," I whispered, stroking gently, stilling my own movements to let her ride the orgasm out in her own time.

"Ahhh." She sighed softly, her body going limp, and I eased her to lie down on me, putting my arms around her and just holding her, enjoying the soft weight of her on my torso. Her hair was a tumble of soft waves against my neck, a rich scent rising from it: coconut and vanilla.

"Okay?" I asked quietly after a few moments where she just lay still, letting me trace gentle patterns up and down her spine with the tips of my fingers.

"So much better than just okay." She pushed up a little, taking her weight on her arms, and looked down at me, her hair tumbling around her face.

I reached up to tuck some behind her ear, wanting to see her expressions.

"That wasn't that much fun for you."

I laughed, unable to help myself. "Are you kidding? That was fantastic."

Jodie's so pretty when she blushes. She slapped lightly at my chest, shaking her head at me. "You know what I mean—you didn't come!"

"The night's still young. If you're willing." With any luck, I could give her another orgasm too. Seeing her come had somehow taken the worst edge of need off for me; I felt more able to hold on now, take my time bringing her to pleasure again.

"If you're able, I'm willing." She grinned at me, that bright, flashing smile which had caught my attention the very first time I saw her, lighting up her whole face.

"Very much able." I rocked my hips up to demonstrate the point, enjoying the way she gasped, her eyes widening.

"Oh. Hnngh, yeah, that's... okay."

"Just okay?"

"Fuck, yeah, all right, a lot better than just okay, ahh, do that again!"

I laughed, a little breathless myself. "Lay down?" I requested, and she was quick to climb off me, flopping down on her back with a pleasured sigh. She opened her arms—and legs—to me when I pushed up to my hands and knees. I was more than eager to accept the invitation. Sliding back into her felt like coming home, a warm wet clasp of muscles around my shaft I was unable to resist. "Damn, you feel good."

Jodie stroked her hands over my shoulders, reaching up to kiss me. "I was just thinking the exact same thing," she murmured against my mouth.

"Yeah?" Curving my hands under her hips to get a double handful of her deliciously juicy ass, I lifted her toward me, pressing in deep, right to the root. "How's this?"

"Uh-huh." She let herself fall back against the pillows. "Oh, that's, yeah. That's the spot."

She was flushed, a soft rosy color spreading all over her face and throat and those beautiful, bountiful breasts. I couldn't help staring at her as I set up a rhythm, slow at first, pulling almost all the way back before driving deep again.

"Oh God, Joseph, don't stop," Jodie almost whimpered when I paused briefly to shift my knees and adjust the angle. "Don't you *dare* stop now!"

"Not stopping," I assured, my own breath coming in rapid, hungry pants. "Got more for you."

"Yes." Her hands scrabbled at the sheet under her, her fingers clawing at the smooth fabric. "More, yes, oh God, give me more!"

I lost myself in her demands, the impatient buck of her body under mine, the heated slide of skin on skin. Hips snapping rapidly back and forth, I gave her what we both wanted with deep, lunging thrusts, a guttural roar of triumph building in my chest. Until I lost it completely, the climax tearing through me like a lightning strike, shocks of pleasure rippling along every nerve.

Barely aware of Jodie gasping and shuddering out another orgasm of her own underneath me, I managed to drop onto my elbows, taking my weight on them rather than crushing her with it. Sucking in huge gulps of air, I felt as though I'd just run a marathon rather than engaged in a few minutes of passionate lovemaking. Every muscle quivered with the aftershocks.

With a shaking hand, I stroked a long, curling strand of hair off Jodie's sweat-dampened cheek and back behind her ear. She opened her eyes with languorous slowness, gave me a breathtakingly sensual smile, and lifted her hands above her head to stretch.

Still buried deep inside her, my softening cock twitched with interest at her movement, and I stifled a chuckle. After a fuck like that, anyone would think I'd be more than satisfied, but apparently my cock had other ideas.

"What's funny?" Jodie obviously picked up on the stifled laugh, and *oh no*, there was a little worried frown appearing on her face, her brows twitching together.

She thinks I'm laughing at her. "It's me," I said quickly. "You're so sexy, you could bring a dead man back to life. Or in my case, make a thoroughly-fucked one feel like a horny teenager ready to go again two minutes after the last time."

That made her laugh along with me as I eased back, putting a hand down to make sure the condom stayed in place. My knees felt like rubber, but I pushed myself off the bed and staggered to the bathroom to clean up.

*

Jodie

Feeling immediately awkward, I pulled at the bedding as Joseph headed to the bathroom, managed to get the top sheet untucked from the tightly made bed, and scrambled underneath it. This was always the worst part, the *now what?* part, when I had to try and figure out what to do next. Should I just get up and get dressed and call myself a ride home? Would Joseph want me to stay? Did I even want to? Did he have to work tomorrow? I had the day off, my last full day off before the holiday shifts started, but he might need to go into the office or be called to a client at the police station... at least he couldn't have court, it was Saturday...

"Penny for your thoughts." Joseph's voice interrupted the slightly panicky internal monologue I had going on.

I looked up at him standing over me. "Wondering if I should be already dressed and on my way out the door," I admitted.

"Not unless you want to be." He'd shrugged into a bathrobe, tightened the belt, and fiddled awkwardly with the ends as he stood beside the bed. "I was gonna offer to make coffee. Or tea, maybe, if you don't like to drink coffee late at night. Cocoa?"

"Cocoa sounds nice."

"Cool, I'll put some on." He hesitated a moment. "I think I've got another robe here someplace, if you'd like, or I can bring the cocoa to you in bed?"

In bed actually sounded pretty good. It had been a long week, what with making sure everything was ready for the party on top of work, and his bed was almost sinfully comfortable. Post-coital lethargy washed over me, making me reluctant to move, and maybe he sensed my lassitude because he smiled and bent down to brush a warm kiss over my lips. "Why don't you stay there? I'll bring it in. Are you working tomorrow?"

"Nuh uh." I shook my head.

"Me neither, so why don't you stay? It's late. I don't like the thought of you heading home alone at this time of night in this weather."

"If you're sure you don't mind." Basking in the afterglow, I still waited until he left the room to scrabble at the bedcovers and climb into bed properly. At least the bedroom was deliciously warm and I didn't need the yoga pants, Henley, and thick socks I routinely wore to sleep in my icebox of a house. Joseph's bed was way more comfortable than mine too, with soft, high thread-count sheets and plush, springy pillows. It was so all-around relaxing I was already three-quarters asleep when he came back a few minutes later.

"Hey. You still want this?"

"Mm hm?" I had to fight my eyelids open, blinking at him blearily.

He smiled down at me, setting a mug on the nightstand beside me. "You're nearly asleep. Still want the cocoa?"

Since he'd gone to the effort to make it, I didn't want to be rude. I shoved myself half-upright, managing a smile of thanks as I picked up the mug. "Smells great."

Joseph left me alone to drink, going out and clattering around in the other room, probably drinking his own cocoa and washing the utensils he'd used to make it if the noises were any guide. They were curiously comforting, homely sounds, and I found myself relaxing even further, almost spilling my cocoa on the bed until I gave up and put the mug down, still half-full. I'd have to apologize in the morning for not finishing it off.

Sleep was drifting over me like a dark curtain when I heard Joseph come back in. He made a quietly amused sound, and then I felt warm hands pulling the comforter up around me. A weight dipped the bed at my back, the lamp clicked off, and the next thing I knew, the soft gray light of morning was flooding the room.

Joseph was fast asleep beside me still. He slept with his arms flung up over his head, hands not quite touching each other, his head rolled slightly to the side toward me. His stubble was growing in thick and dark already; I'd noticed in the office that he always had a heavy five o'clock shadow by the end of the day. He'd probably shaved before the party last night as well as in the morning before work.

He looked pretty soundly asleep and didn't stir as I tentatively shifted toward the edge of the bed. Spying the robe he'd worn last night laid over a chair just a couple steps away, I made a quick dive for it. Yes, he'd seen all of me naked last night, but in the cold light of morning I really wasn't up for a naked run to the bathroom. The door slid closed soundlessly, and I sank onto the toilet with a sigh of relief.

Business concluded, I washed my hands and dithered about what to do next as I finger-combed my hair into some semblance of order. Should I just wander back out there and get back into bed? Or maybe he'd prefer me to get dressed and leave? *Why are morning afters so damn awkward?*

A light knock on the bathroom door almost made me jump out of my skin.

"I'm gonna make coffee, you want some?" Joseph's voice said through the door.

"Uh, sure!" Hand pressed to my pounding heart, I tried to make my voice sound normal. "Black, two sugars, please."

"You got it." There was a brief pause before he said, "I'll bring it to you in bed, okay?"

Well, that answered the question of whether or not he wanted me to leave. Gathering my courage, I hurried back to bed, wondering suddenly what he was wearing, since I'd stolen his robe. After a moment to think, I slipped out of the robe and put it back on the chair. The sheet covered me, and if I wrapped up in the robe, maybe Joseph would think I wasn't up for a repeat performance of last night, which I most definitely was... if *he* was still interested, anyway.

I was trying hard not to overthink things and failing pretty miserably when Joseph came back in, wearing sweatpants and a tight T-shirt which did all sorts of nice things for his chest and shoulders. He smiled down at me, offering a steaming mug.

"Thanks. I'm pretty unbearable before I've had my first cup of coffee." I inhaled the fragrant steam gratefully.

"Ditto." He settled onto the bed beside me, though he didn't try to get under the covers, and sipped his own coffee.

It should have been awkward, but he'd put music on in the other room, something soft and instrumental which broke the silence just enough for it not to be awkward. I was feeling good, a few muscles let me know their opinion of last night's activities when I moved, but otherwise relaxed and well-rested.

"So." Joseph spoke first, putting his coffee down at last and turning toward me. He chuckled at the apprehensive look I gave him. "God, Jodie, don't look at me like that. I'm not the big bad wolf."

I attempted to excuse myself. "I'm not good at morning after conversations."

His eyes crinkled up charmingly at the corners. "I promise I won't make this too heavy. I just wanted to say—I had a hell of a good time last night, and I'd be ecstatic at the idea of a repeat. Regular repeats. If that's something you're interested in."

"Do you mean just…" I waved my free hand vaguely over the bedcovers. "Or…?"

"As a defense lawyer, I'd like to protest that those are very witness-leading questions."

"Joseph!" I laughed, as he'd meant me to.

He chuckled along, leaning in closer and gently removing the cup I was holding in a death grip, setting it down on the nightstand. "Look, if *this* is all that's on offer," he waved at the bedcovers too, "I'd settle for that, but I'm hoping for more of *everything* we shared last night. Dinner. Dancing. Spending time together."

"Sounds good," I admitted. Last night had been a great time all-around.

"And in the interests of full transparency, I'm not planning on seeing anyone else while we explore where this might go."

Shyly, I reached out to touch his cheek, feeling the roughness of his stubble against the sensitive pads of my fingers. "That sounds good too. If you were mine, I don't think I'd be very good at sharing."

"I could definitely be yours." He turned his face against my hand, seeking more of the caress like a cat who wanted to be stroked, before giving me a mischievous glance and tugging at the comforter over me.

I resisted instinctively, clutching it to my chest. "Don't, I'm… daylight isn't really my friend."

"You're a vampire?" Letting go of the comforter, he clutched at his throat, making panicked faces. "That explains everything; I'm in thrall to you!"

He was so funny and so sweet, I had to laugh.

"But seriously." Lowering his hands, he reached for where mine clutched the edge of the comforter, coving my fingers with his own. "You're beautiful, Jodie. I don't know who made you think you're not, but you're wrong. I got a wonderful eyeful last night, and I think you're gorgeous, inside and out."

Several waste-of-oxygen exes, I thought but didn't say out loud, not wanting to spoil the moment. Joseph looked adorably earnest as he gazed into my eyes, and I found myself starting to believe him.

This time, when he tugged at the comforter, I let him take it.

About the Author

A USA Today bestselling author, Caitlyn Lynch started writing when she was four years old, extending stories she felt ended too soon (usually before the romance bit started in earnest).

It took a lot of years (and a lot of practice writing fanfiction) but she eventually plucked up the courage to share some of her original stories with the world, and remains constantly amazed that people actually enjoy reading them. She hopes to continue sharing love stories with you for many years to come.

Website: www.caitlynlynch.com
Twitter: @caitlynlynch6

CPSIA information can be obtained
at www.ICGtesting.com
Printed in the USA
LVHW010023131119
636966LV00013B/39/P